Mario Vargas Llosa was born in Arequipa, Peru. He attended the University of San Marcos in Lima, and later obtained his doctorate from the University of Madrid. His novels include *Conversation in the Cathedral, The Green House, Aunt Julia and the Scriptwriter, In Praise of the Stepmother, The Notebooks of Don Rigoberto,* and more recently, *The Feast of the Goat* and *The Way to Paradise.* He lives in London.

a novel

CONVERSATION in the CATHEDRAL

Mario Vargas Llosa

Translated by Gregory Rabassa

rayo

An Imprint of HarperCollins*Publishers*

CONVERSATION IN THE CATHEDRAL. English translation © 1974, 1975 by Harper & Row, Publishers, Inc. All rights reserved. Printed in the United States of America. No part of this book may be used or reproduced in any manner whatsoever without written permission except in the case of brief quotations embodied in critical articles and reviews. For information, address HarperCollins Publishers Inc., 10 East 53rd Street, New York, NY 10022.

HarperCollins books may be purchased for educational, business, or sales promotional use. For information, please write: Special Markets Department, HarperCollins Publishers Inc., 10 East 53rd Street, New York, NY 10022.

This book was originally published in Spain under the title *Conversación en la Cathedral*. Copyright © 1969 by Editorial Seix Barral, S.A., Barcelona, Spain.

Published by Harper & Row in 1975.

FIRST RAYO EDITION PUBLISHED 2005.

Library of Congress Cataloging-in-Publication Data is available upon request.

ISBN 0-06-073280-6

05 06 07 08 09 ❖/RRD 10 9 8 7 6 5 4 3 2 1

To Luis Loayza and Abelardo Oquendo

Il faut avoir fouillé toute la vie
sociale pour être un vrai romancier,
vu que le roman est l'histoire privée
des nations.

> BALZAC, *Petites misères de
la vie conjugale*

ONE

1

FROM THE DOORWAY of *La Crónica* Santiago looks at the Avenida Tacna without love: cars, uneven and faded buildings, the gaudy skeletons of posters floating in the mist, the gray midday. At what precise moment had Peru fucked itself up? The newsboys weave in and out among the vehicles halted by the red light on Wilson, hawking the afternoon papers, and he starts to walk slowly toward Colmena. His hands in his pockets, head down, he goes along escorted by people who are also going in the direction of the Plaza San Martín. He was like Peru, Zavalita was, he'd fucked himself up somewhere along the line. He thinks: when? Across from the Hotel Crillón a dog comes over to lick his feet: don't get your rabies on me, get away. Peru all fucked up, Carlitos all fucked up, everybody all fucked up. He thinks: there's no solution. He sees a long line at the taxi stop for Miraflores, he crosses the square, and there's Norwin, hello, at a table in the Zela Bar, have a seat, Zavalita, fondling a *chilcano* and having his shoes shined, he invites him to have a drink. He doesn't look drunk yet and Santiago sits down, tells the bootblack to shine his shoes too. Yes, sir, boss, right away, boss, they'll look like a mirror, boss.

"No one's seen you for ages, Mr. Editorial Writer," Norwin says. "Are you happier on the editorial page than with the local news?"

"There's less work." He shrugs his shoulders, it was probably that day when the editor called him in, he orders a cold Cristal, did he want to take Orgambide's place, Zavalita? He thinks: that's when I fucked myself up. "I get in early, they give me my topic, I hold my nose, and in two or three hours all set, I unbuckle my chains and that's it."

"I wouldn't write editorials for all the money in the world," Norwin says. "It's too far removed from the news, and journalism is news, Zavalita, believe me. I'll end my days on the police beat, that's all. By the way, did Carlitos die yet?"

"He's still in the hospital, but they're going to let him out soon," Santiago says. "He swears he's off the bottle this time."

"Is it true that one night he saw cockroaches and spiders when he went to bed?" Norwin asks.

"He lifted up the sheet and thousands of tarantulas and mice came at him," Santiago says. "He ran out into the street bare-ass and hollering."

Norwin laughs and Santiago closes his eyes: the houses in Chorrillos are cubes with gratings on them, caves cracked by earthquakes, inside there's a traffic of utensils and reeking little old women with slippers and varicose legs. A small figure runs among the cubes, his shrieks make the oily predawn shudder and infuriate the ants and scorpions that pursue him. Consolation through alcohol, he thinks, against the slow death of the blue devils of hallucination. He was all right, Carlitos was, you had to defend yourself against Peru as best you could.

"One of these days I'm going to come across the creatures too." Norwin contemplates his *chilcano* with curiosity, half smiles. "But there's no such thing as a teetotaling newspaperman, Zavalita. Drinking gives you inspiration, believe me."

The bootblack is through with Norwin and now he's putting polish on Santiago's shoes, whistling. How were things at *Última Hora,* what were the scoundrels there saying? They were complaining about your ingratitude, Zavalita, that you should stop by and see them sometime, the way you used to. But since you have lots of free time now, Zavalita, did you take a second job?

"I read, I take naps," Santiago says. "Maybe I'll go back to law school."

"You get away from the news and now you want a degree." Norwin looks at him sadly. "The editorial page is the end of the road, Zavalita.

4

You'll get a job as a lawyer, you'll leave the newspaper business. I can already see you as a proper bourgeois."

"I've just turned thirty," Santiago says. "That's kind of late for me to start being a bourgeois."

"Thirty, is that all?" Norwin is thoughtful. "I'm thirty-six and I could pass for your father. The police page puts you through the grinder, believe me."

Male faces, dull and defeated eyes at the tables of the Zela Bar, hands that reach for ashtrays and glasses of beer. How ugly people are here, Carlitos is right. He thinks: what's come over me today? The bootblack cuffs away two dogs that are panting among the tables.

"How long is the campaign against rabies in *La Crónica* going to last?" Norwin asks. "It's getting boring, another whole page on it this morning."

"I wrote all the editorials against rabies," Santiago says. "Hell, that doesn't bother me as much as writing on Cuba or Vietnam. Well, the line's gone now. I'm going to catch a taxi."

"Let's have lunch, I'm inviting," Norwin says. "Forget about your wife, Zavalita. Let's bring back the good old days."

Hot coney and cold beer, the Rinconcito Cajamarquino in the Bajo el Puente district and a view of the vague waters of the Rímac River slipping along over snot-colored rocks, the muddy Haitian coffee, gambling at Milton's place, *chilcanos* and a shower at Norwin's, the midnight apotheosis at the whorehouse with Becerrita, which brought on deflation, the acid sleep, the nausea and the doubts of dawn. The good old days, maybe it had been then.

"Ana's made some shrimp soup and I wouldn't want to miss that," Santiago says. "Some other time."

"You're afraid of your wife," Norwin says. "Boy, you really are fucked up, Zavalita."

Not because of what you thought, brother. Norwin insists on paying for the beer, the shine, and they shake hands. Santiago goes back to the taxi stop, the car he takes is a Chevrolet and the radio is on, Inca Cola refreshed the best, then a waltz, rivers, canyons, the veteran voice of Jesús Vásquez, it was my Peru. There were still some jams downtown,

5

but República and Arequipa were empty and the car was able to move along, another waltz, Lima women had traditional souls. Why are all Peruvian waltzes so goddamned stupid? He thinks: what's come over me today? He has his chin on his chest and his eyes are half closed, as if he's spying on his belly: God, Zavalita, every time you sit down you get that bulge in your jacket. Was it the first time he'd drunk beer? Fifteen, twenty years ago? Four weeks without seeing his mother, Teté. Who would have thought that Popeye would become an architect, Zavalita, who would have thought that you'd end up writing editorials against the dogs of Lima? He thinks: I'll be potbellied in a little while. He'd go to the Turkish baths, play tennis at the Terrazas, in six months the fat would burn away and he'd have a flat belly again the way he did when he was fifteen years old. Get moving, break the inertia, shake himself up. He thinks: sports, that's the answer. Miraflores Park already, Quebrada, the Malecón, the corner of Benavides, driver. He gets out, walks toward Porta, his hands in his pockets, his head down, what's come over me today? The sky is still cloudy, the atmosphere is even grayer and the light drizzle has begun: mosquito legs on his skin, the caress of a cobweb. Not even that, a more furtive and disagreeable feeling. Even the rain is fucked up in this country. He thinks: if at least there were a heavy rain. What were they showing at the Colina, the Montecarlo, the Marsano? He'd have lunch, a chapter of *Point Counter Point*, which would drag and carry him in its arms to the sticky sleep of siesta time, maybe they were showing a crime movie, like *Rififi*, a cowboy picture like *Rio Grande*. But Ana would have her tear-jerker all checked off in the newspaper, what's come over me today? He thinks: if the censors would only ban all Mexican films he'd fight less with Ana. And after the movies, what then? They'd take a walk along the Malecón, smoke under the cement shelters in Necochea Park listening to the sea roaring in the darkness, they would return to the elf houses, we fight a lot, love, we argue a lot, love, and between yawns, Huxley. The two rooms would fill up with smoke and the smell of oil, was he very hungry, love? The morning alarm clock, the cold water in the shower, the taxi, walking among office workers along Colmena, the voice of the editor, would he rather have the bank strike, the fishing crisis, or Israel? Maybe it would be worth putting out a little effort and getting a degree. He thinks: going backward. He sees the harsh orange walls, the red tiles, the small barred windows of the elf houses. The apartment door is open but Rowdy doesn't appear, mongrel, leaping, noisy and effusive. Why do you leave the door open when you go to the Chinaman's, dear? But no, there's Ana, what's the matter, her eyes are puffy and weepy, her hair disheveled: they took Rowdy away, love.

"They pulled him out of my hands," Ana sobs. "Some dirty niggers, love. They put him in the truck. They stole him, they stole him."

The kiss on the temple, calm down, love, he caresses her face, how did it happen, he leads her to the house by the shoulder, don't cry, silly.

"I called you at *La Crónica* and you weren't there." Ana pouts. "Bandits, Negroes with the faces of criminals. I had him on the leash and everything. They grabbed him, put him in the truck, they stole him."

"I'll have lunch and go to the pound and get him out." Santiago kisses her again. "Nothing will happen to him, don't be silly."

"He started to kick his legs, wag his tail." She wipes her eyes with the apron, sighs. "He seemed to understand, love. Poor thing, poor little thing."

"Did they grab him out of your arms?" Santiago asks. "What a bunch. I'm going to raise hell."

He picks up the jacket he threw onto a chair and takes a step toward the door, but Ana holds him back: he should eat first, quickly, love. Her voice is soft, dimples on her cheeks, her eyes sad, she's pale.

"The soup must be cold by now." She smiles, her lips trembling. "I forgot about everything with what happened, sweet. Poor little Rowdy."

They eat lunch without talking, at the small table against the window that looks out on the courtyard of the houses: earth the color of brick, like the tennis courts at the Terrazas, a twisting gravel path with geranium pots on the side. The soup has grown cold, a film of grease tints the edges of the plate, the shrimp look like tin. She was on her way to the Chinaman's on San Martín to buy a bottle of vinegar, love, and all of a sudden a truck put on its brakes beside her and two Negroes with criminal faces got out, the worst kind of bandits, one of them gave her a shove and the other one grabbed the leash and before she knew what was happening they'd put him in the cage and had gone. Poor thing, poor little creature. Santiago gets up: they'd hear from him about an abuse like

7

that. Did he see, did he see? Ana is sobbing again; he too was afraid they were going to kill him, love.

"They won't do anything to him, sweet." He kisses Ana on the cheek, a momentary taste of raw meat and salt. "I'll bring him right back, you'll see."

He jogs to the pharmacy on Porta and San Martín, asks to use the telephone and calls *La Crónica*. Solórzano the court reporter answers: how in hell would he know where the dog pound was, Zavalita.

"Did they take your dog away?" The druggist puts his solicitous head forward. "The pound's by the Puente del Ejército. You'd better hurry, they killed my brother-in-law's Chihuahua, a very expensive animal."

He jogs to Larco, takes a group taxi, how much would the trip from the Paseo Colón to the Puente del Ejército cost? he counts a hundred eighty soles in his wallet. On Sunday they wouldn't have a cent left, too bad Ana had left the hospital, they'd better not go to the movies that night, poor Rowdy, no more editorials against rabies. He gets out on the Paseo Colón, on the Plaza Bolognesi he finds a taxi, the driver doesn't know where the pound is, sir. An ice cream vendor on the Plaza Dos de Mayo gives them directions: farther on a small sign near the river, Municipal Dog Pound, there it was. A broad yard surrounded by a run-down, shit-colored adobe wall—the color of Lima, he thinks, the color of Peru—flanked by shacks that mix and thicken in the distance until they turn into a labyrinth of straw mats, poles, tiles, zinc plates. Muffled, remote whining. A squalid structure stands beside the entrance, a plaque says Office. In shirtsleeves, wearing glasses, a bald man is dozing by a desk covered with papers and Santiago raps on the table: they'd stolen his dog, they'd snatched it out of his wife's hands, the man sits up, startled, by God, he wasn't going to leave it at that.

"What do you mean coming into this office spouting goddamns?" The bald man rubs his stupefied eyes and makes a face. "Show some respect."

"If anything's happened to my dog I'm not going to leave it at that." He takes out his press card, pounds the table again. "And the characters who attacked my wife are going to be sorry, I can assure you."

"Calm down." He looks the card over, yawns, the displeasure on his face dissolves into beatific weariness. "Did they pick up your dog a couple of hours ago? Then he must be with the ones the truck brought in just now."

He shouldn't get that way, my newspaper friend, it wasn't anyone's fault. His voice is bland, dreamy, like his eyes, bitter, like the folds of his mouth: fucked up too. The dogcatchers were paid by the number of animals, sometimes they committed abuses, what could you do, it was all part of the struggle to buy a little something to eat. Some muffled blows in the yard, whines that seemed filtered through cork walls. The bald man half smiles and, gracelessly, lazily, gets to his feet, goes out of the office muttering. They cross an open stretch, go into a shed that smells of urine. Parallel cages, crammed with animals who push against each other and jump in place, sniff the wire, growl. Santiago leans over each cage, not there, he explores the promiscuous surface of snouts, rumps, tails stiff and quivering, not there either. The bald man walks beside him, his look far away, dragging his feet.

"Take a look, there's no more room to keep them," he protests suddenly. "Then your newspaper attacks us, it's not fair. The city gives us almost nothing, we have to perform miracles."

"God damn it," Santiago says, "not here either."

"Be patient," the bald man sighs. "We've got four more sheds."

They go outside again. Earth that had been dug up, weeds, excrement, stinking puddles. In the second shed one cage moves more than the others, the wires shake and something white and woolly bounces, comes up and sinks back into the wave: that's more like it, that's more like it. Take a snout, a piece of tail, two red and weepy eyes: Rowdy. He still has his leash on, they had no right, a hell of a thing, but the bald man calm down, calm down, he'd have them get him out. He goes off with sluggish steps and a moment later comes back followed by a Negro-Indian half-breed in blue overalls: let's see, he was to get that little whitish one out, Pancras. The half-breed opens the cage, pushes the animals apart, grabs Rowdy by the scruff of the neck, hands him to Santiago. Poor thing, he was trembling, but he turns him loose and he takes a step back, shaking himself.

"They always shit." The half-breed laughs. "It's their way of saying we're glad to be out of jail."

9

Santiago kneels down beside Rowdy, scratches his head, lets him lick his hands. He trembles, dribbles urine, staggers drunkenly, and only outside does he start to leap and scratch the ground, to run.

"Come with me, take a look at the conditions we work under." He takes Santiago by the arm, smiles at him acidly. "Write something for your paper, ask the city to increase our budget."

Sheds that were foul-smelling and falling apart, a gray steel roof, gusts of damp air. Fifteen feet from them a dark silhouette stands next to a sack and is struggling with a dachshund who protests in a voice too fierce for his minimal body as he twists hysterically: help him, Pancras. The short half-breed runs, opens the sack, the other slips the dachshund inside. They close the sack with a cord, put it on the ground, and Rowdy starts to growl, pulling on his leash, whining, what's the matter, he watches, frightened, barks hoarsely. The men already have the clubs in their hands, are already beginning, one-two, to beat and grunt, and the sack dances, leaps, howls madly, one-two, the men grunt and beat. Santiago closes his eyes, upset.

"In Peru we're still living in the stone age, friend." A bittersweet smile awakens the bald man's face. "Look at the conditions we work under, tell me if it's right."

The sack is quiet, the men beat it a little more, throw their clubs onto the ground, wipe their faces, rub their hands.

"We used to kill them the way God wanted, now there isn't enough money," the bald man complains. "You tell him, the gentleman's a reporter, he can make a protest in his paper."

He's taller, younger than Pancras. He takes a few steps toward them and Santiago finally sees his face: oh my God! He releases the chain and Rowdy starts to run and bark and he opens and closes his mouth: oh my God!

"One sol for each animal, mister," the half-breed says. "And besides, we have to take them to the dump to be burned. Only one sol, mister."

It wasn't him, all Negroes look alike, it couldn't be him. He thinks: why can't it be him? The half-breed bends down, picks up the sack, yes, it was him, carries it to a corner of the yard, throws it among other bloody sacks, comes back swaying on his long legs and drying his forehead. It was him, it was him. Hey, buddy, Pancras nudges him, go get yourself some lunch.

"You complain here, but when you go out in the truck to make pickups you have a great time," the bald man grumbles. "This morning you picked up this gentleman's dog, which was on a leash and with its mistress, you nitwits."

The half-breed shrugs his shoulders, it was him: they hadn't gone out on the truck that morning, boss, they'd spent it with their clubs. He thinks: him. The voice, the body are his, but he looks thirty years older. The same thin lips, the same flat nose, the same kinky hair. But now, in addition, there are purple bags on his eyelids, wrinkles on his neck, a greenish-yellow crust on his horse teeth. He thinks: they used to be so white. What a change, what a ruin of a man. He's thinner, dirtier, so much older, but that's his big, slow walk, those are his spider legs. His big hands have a knotty bark on them now and there's a rim of saliva around his mouth. They've come in from the yard, they're in the office, Rowdy rubs against Santiago's feet. He thinks: he doesn't know who I am. He wasn't going to tell him, he wasn't going to talk to him. Who would ever recognize you, Zavalita, were you sixteen? eighteen? and now you're an old man of thirty. The bald man puts a piece of carbon paper between two sheets, scrawls a few lines in a cramped and stingy hand. Leaning against the doorjamb, the half-breed licks his lips.

"Just a little signature here, friend; and seriously, do us a small favor, write something in *La Crónica* asking them to raise our budget." The bald man looks at the half-breed. "Weren't you going to lunch?"

"Could I have an advance?" He takes a step forward and explains in a natural way: "I'm low in funds, boss."

"Half a pound." The bald man yawns. "That's all I've got."

He accepts the banknote without looking at it and goes out with Santiago. A stream of trucks, buses and cars is crossing the Puente del Ejército, what kind of a face would he put on it? in the mist the earthen-colored hulks of the shacks of Fray Martín de Porres, would he start to run? seem to be part of a dream. He looks the half-breed in the eyes and the other one looks at him.

11

"If you'd killed my dog I think I would have killed all of you," and he tries to smile.

No, Zavalita, he doesn't recognize you. He listens attentively and his look is muddled, distant and respectful. Besides getting old, he's most likely turned into a dumb animal too. He thinks: fucked up too.

"Did they pick this woolly one up this morning?" An unexpected glow breaks out in his eyes for an instant. "It must have been black Céspedes, that guy doesn't care about anything. He goes into backyards, breaks locks, anything just so he can earn his sol."

They're at the bottom of the stairs that lead up to Alfonso Ugarte; Rowdy rolls on the ground and barks at the ash-gray sky.

"Ambrosio?" He smiles, hesitates, smiles. "Aren't you Ambrosio?"

He doesn't start to run, he doesn't say anything. He looks with a dumbfounded and stupid expression and suddenly there's a kind of vertigo in his eyes.

"Don't you remember me?" He hesitates, smiles, hesitates. "I'm Santiago, Don Fermín's boy."

The big hands go up into the air, young Santiago, mister? they hang in the air as if trying to decide whether to strangle or embrace him, Don Fermín's boy? His voice cracks with surprise or emotion and he blinks, blinded. Of course, man, didn't he recognize him? Santiago, on the other hand, had recognized him the minute he saw him in the yard: what did he have to say? The big hands become active, I'll be goddamned, they travel through the air again, how he'd grown, good Lord, they pat Santiago on the shoulders and back, and his eyes are laughing at last: I'm so happy, son.

"I can't believe you've grown into a man." He feels him, looks at him, smiles at him. "I look at you and I can't believe it, child. Of course I recognize you now. You look like your papa; a little bit of Señora Zoila too."

What about little Teté? and the big hands come and go, with feeling? with surprise? and Mr. Sparky? from Santiago's arms to his shoulders to his back, and the eyes look tender and reminiscent as the voice tries hard to be natural. Weren't coincidences strange? Who would have thought they'd ever meet again! And after such a long time, I'll be goddamned.

12

"This whole business has made me thirsty," Santiago says. "Come on, let's go have a drink. Do you know someplace around here?"

"I know the place where I eat," Ambrosio says. "La Catedral, a place for poor people, I don't know if you'll like it."

"As long as they have cold beer I'll like it," Santiago says. "Let's go, Ambrosio."

It seemed impossible that little Santiago was drinking beer now, and Ambrosio smiles, his strong greenish-yellow teeth exposed to the air: time did fly, by golly. They go up the stairs, between the vacant lots on the first block of Alfonso Ugarte there's a white Ford garage, and at the corner on the left, faded by the inexorable grayness, the warehouses of the Central Railroad appear. A truck loaded with crates hides the door of La Catedral. Inside, under the zinc roof, crowded on rough benches and around crude tables, a noisy voracious crowd. Two Chinese in shirtsleeves behind the bar watch the copper faces, the angular features that are chewing and drinking, and a frantic little man from the Andes in a shabby apron serves steaming bowls of soup, bottles, platters of rice. Plenty of feeling, plenty of kisses, plenty of love boom from a multicolored jukebox and in the back, behind the smoke, the noise, the solid smell of food and liquor, the dancing swarms of flies, there is a punctured wall —stones, shacks, a strip of river, the leaden sky—and an ample woman bathed in sweat manipulates pots and pans surrounded by the sputter of a grill. There's an empty table beside the jukebox and among the scars on the wood one can make out a heart pierced by an arrow, a woman's name: Saturnina.

"I had lunch already, but you have something to eat," Santiago says.

"Two bottles of Cristal, good and cold," Ambrosio shouts, cupping his hands to his mouth. "A bowl of fish soup, bread and stewed vegetables with rice."

You shouldn't have come, you shouldn't have spoken to him, Zavalita, you're not fucked up, you're crazy. He thinks: the nightmare will come back. It'll be your fault, Zavalita, poor papa, poor old man.

"Taxi drivers, workers from the small factories in the neighborhood." Ambrosio points around them as if excusing himself. "They come all the way from the Avenida Argentina because the food is passable and, most important, cheap."

13

The Andean brings the beers, Santiago fills the glasses and they drink to your health, boy, to yours, Ambrosio, and there's a compact, undecipherable smell that weakens, nauseates and wipes the head clean of memories.

"What a stinking job you've got for yourself, Ambrosio. Have you been at the dog pound a long time?"

"A month, son, and I got the job thanks to the rabies, because there hadn't been any openings. It certainly is stinking, it squeezes you dry. The only relief is when you go out on the truck to make pickups."

It smells of sweat, chili and onions, urine and accumulated garbage and the music from the jukebox mingles with the collective voice, the growl of motors and horns, and it comes to one's ears deformed and thick. Singed faces, prominent cheekbones, eyes made drowsy by routine or indolence wander among the tables, form clusters at the bar, block the entrance. Ambrosio accepts the cigarette that Santiago offers him, smokes, throws the butt on the floor and buries it under his foot. He slurps the soup noisily, nibbles on the pieces of fish, picks up the bones and sucks them, leaves them all shiny, listening or answering or asking a question, and he swallows pieces of bread, takes long swigs of beer and wipes the sweat off with his hand: time swallows a person up before he realizes it, child. He thinks: why don't I leave? He thinks: I have to go and he orders more beer. He fills the glasses, clutches his and, while he talks, remembers, dreams, or thinks he watches the circle of foam sprinkled with craters, mouths that silently open up, vomiting golden bubbles and disappearing into the yellow liquid that his hand warms. He drinks without closing his eyes, belches, takes out cigarettes and lights them, leans over to pet Rowdy: the things that have happened, Jesus. He talks and Ambrosio talks, the pouches on his eyelids are bluish, the openings in his nose vibrate as if he'd been running, as if he were drowning, and after each sip he spits, looks nostalgically at the flies, listens, smiles, or grows sad or confused, and his eyes seem to grow furious sometimes or frightened or go away; sometimes he has a coughing spell. There are gray hairs in his kinky mat, on top of his overalls he wears a jacket that must have been blue once too and had buttons, and a shirt with a high collar that is wrapped around his neck like a rope. Santiago looks at his enormous shoes: muddy, twisted, fucked up by the weather. His voice comes

14

to him in a stammer, fearful, is lost, cautious, imploring, returns, respectful or anxious or constrained, always defeated: not thirty, forty, a hundred, more. Not only had he fallen apart, grown old, become brutalized; he probably was tubercular as well. A thousand times more fucked up than Carlitos or you, Zavalita. He was leaving, he had to go and he orders more beer. You're drunk, Zavalita, you were about to cry. Life doesn't treat people well in this country, son, since he'd left their house he'd gone through a thousand movie adventures. Life hadn't treated him well either, Ambrosio, and he orders more beer. Was he going to throw up? The smell of frying, feet and armpits swirls about, biting and enveloping, over the straight-haired or bushy heads, over the gummy crests and the flat necks with mange and brilliantine, the music on the jukebox grows quiet and revives, grows quiet and revives, and now, more intense and irrevocable than the sated faces and square mouths and dark beardless cheeks, the abject images of memory are also there: more beer. Wasn't this country a can of worms, boy, wasn't Peru a brain-twister? Could you believe it, Odríists and Apristas, who used to hate each other so much, all buddy-buddy now? What would his father have said about all this, boy? They talk and sometimes he listens timidly, respectfully to Ambrosio, who dares protest: he had to go, boy. He's small and inoffensive there in the distance, behind the long table that's a raft of bottles and his eyes are drunken and afraid. Rowdy barks once, barks a hundred times. An inner whirlwind, an effervescence in the heart of his heart, a feeling of suspended time and bad breath. Are they talking? The jukebox stops blasting, blasts again. The thick river of smells seems to break up into tributaries of tobacco, beer, human skin and the remains of meals that circulate warmly through the heavy air of La Catedral, and suddenly they're absorbed by an invincible higher stench: neither you nor I was right, papa, it's the smell of defeat, papa. People who come in, eat, laugh, roar, people who leave and the eternal pale profile of the Chinese at the bar. They speak, they grow silent, they drink, they smoke, and when the Andean appears, bending over the tabletop bristling with bottles, the other tables are empty and the jukebox and the crackling of the grill can no longer be heard, only Rowdy barking, Saturnina. The Andean counts on his darkened fingers and he sees Ambrosio's urgent face coming toward him: did he feel bad, boy? A little headache, it would go

15

away. You're acting ridiculous, he thinks, I've had a lot to drink, Huxley, here's Rowdy, safe and sound, I took so long because I ran into a friend. He thinks: love. He thinks: stop it, Zavalita, that's enough. Ambrosio puts his hand into his pocket and Santiago puts out his arms: don't be foolish, man, he was paying. He staggers and Ambrosio and the Andean support him: let me go, he could walk by himself, he felt all right. By God, boy, it was to be expected, he'd had a lot to drink. He goes forward step by step through the empty tables and the crippled chairs of La Catedral, staring at the chancrous floor: O.K., it's all gone. His brain is clearing, the weakness in his legs is going away, his eyes are clearing up. But the images are still there. Getting tangled in his feet, Rowdy barks impatiently.

"It's good you had enough money, boy. Are you really feeling better?"

"My stomach's a little queasy, but I'm not drunk, the drinks didn't do anything to me. My head's spinning from thinking so much."

"It's four o'clock, I don't know what kind of story I can make up. I could lose my job, you don't realize that. But thanks in any case. For the beer, for the lunch, for the conversation. I hope I can make it up to you someday, son."

They're on the sidewalk. The Andean has just closed the big wooden door, the truck that hid the entrance has left, the mist wipes out the building fronts and in the steel-colored light of the afternoon, oppressive and identical, the stream of cars, trucks and buses flows over the Puente del Ejército. There's no one nearby, the distant pedestrians are faceless silhouettes that slip along through smoky veils. We say good-bye and that's it, he thinks, you'll never see him again. He thinks: I never saw him, I never spoke to him, a shower, a nap and that's it.

"Do you really feel all right, son? Do you want me to go with you?"

"The one who doesn't feel well is you," he says without moving his lips. "All afternoon, four hours of this, it's made you feel bad."

"Don't you believe it, I've got a good head for drinking," Ambrosio says, and, for an instant, he laughs. He stands there with his mouth ajar, his hand petrified on his chin. He's motionless, three feet from Santiago, his lapels turned up, and Rowdy, his ears stiff, his teeth showing, looks at Santiago, looks at Ambrosio, and scratches the ground, startled or

16

restless or frightened. Inside La Catedral they're dragging chairs and seem to be mopping the floor.

"You know damned well what I'm talking about," Santiago says. "Please don't play dumb with me."

He doesn't want to or he can't understand, Zavalita: he hasn't moved and in his eyes there's still the same blind challenge, that terrible dark tenacity.

"If you don't want me to go with you, son," he stammers and lowers his eyes, his voice, "do you want me to get you a taxi then?"

"They need a janitor at *La Crónica,*" and he lowers his voice too. "It's not as nasty a job as the one at the pound. I'll see that they hire you without any papers. You'd be a lot better off. But please, stop playing dumb for a little while."

"All right, all right." There's a growing uneasiness in his eyes, it's as if his voice were going to break up into shreds. "What's the matter, boy, why do you act like this?"

"I'll give you my whole month's pay," and his voice suddenly becomes thick, but he doesn't weep; he's rigid, his eyes opened very wide. "Three thousand five hundred soles. Couldn't you get along with that money?"

He's silent, he lowers his head and automatically, as if the silence had loosened an inflexible mechanism, Ambrosio's body takes a step backward and he shrugs his shoulders and his hands come forward at the level of his stomach as if to defend himself or attack. Rowdy growls.

"Have the drinks gone to your head?" he snorts, his voice upset. "What's the matter, what is it you want?"

"For you to stop playing dumb." He closes his eyes and breathes in some air. "For us to talk frankly about the Muse, about my father. Did he order you? It doesn't matter anymore, I just want to know. Was it my father?"

His voice is cut off and Ambrosio takes another step backward and Santiago sees him crouched and tense, his eyes open wide with fear or rage: don't leave, come here. He hasn't become brutalized, you're not a boob, he thinks, come on, come on. Ambrosio wavers with his body, waves a fist, as if threatening or saying good-bye.

"I'm leaving so that you won't be sorry for what you've said," he

17

growls, his voice painful. "I don't need work, I want you to know that I won't take any favors from you, least of all your money. I want you to know that you don't deserve the father you had, I want you to know that. You can go straight to shit hell, boy."

"All right, all right, I don't care," Santiago says. "Come on, don't leave, come back."

There is a short growl by his feet, Rowdy is looking too: the small dark figure is going off clinging to the fences of the vacant lots, standing out against the gleaming windows of the Ford garage, sinking into the stairway by the bridge.

"All right," Santiago sobs, leaning over, petting the stiff little tail, the anxious snout. "We're going now, Rowdy."

He straightens up, sobs again, takes out a handkerchief and wipes his eyes. For a few seconds he doesn't move, his back against the door of La Catedral, getting the drizzle in his face full of tears once more. Rowdy rubs against his ankles, licks his shoes, whimpers softly, looking at him. He starts walking slowly, his hands in his pockets, toward the Plaza Dos de Mayo and Rowdy trots alongside. People are collapsed at the base of the monument and around them a dung heap of cigarette butts, peels and paper; on the corner people are storming the run-down buses that become lost in dust clouds as they head to the shantytowns; a policeman is arguing with a street vendor and the faces of both are hateful and discouraged and their voices seem to be curled by a hollow exasperation. He walks around the square, going into Colmena he hails a taxi: wouldn't his dog dirty the seat? No, driver, he wouldn't dirty it: Miraflores, the Calle Porta. He gets in, puts Rowdy on his lap, that bulge in his jacket. Play tennis, swim, lift weights, get mixed up, become alcoholic like Carlitos. He closes his eyes, leans his head against the back of the seat, his hand strokes the back, the ears, the cold nose, the trembling belly. You were saved from the pound, Rowdy, but no one's ever going to get you out of the pound you're in, Zavalita, tomorrow he'd visit Carlitos in the hospital and bring him a book, not Huxley. The taxi goes along through blind noisy streets, in the darkness he hears engines, whistles, fleeting voices. Too bad you didn't take Norwin up on lunch, Zavalita. He thinks: he kills them with a club and you with editorials. He was better off than you, Zavalita. He'd paid more, he'd fucked himself up

18

more. He thinks: poor papa. The taxi slows down and he opens his eyes: the Diagonal is there, caught in the headlights of the cab, oblique, silvery, boiling with cars, its lighted ads quivering already. The mist whitens the trees in the park, the church steeples drift off in the grayness, the tops of the ficus trees waver: stop here. He pays the fare and Rowdy starts to bark. He turns him loose, sees him go into the entrance to the elf houses like a rocket. Inside he hears the barking, straightens his jacket, his tie, hears Ana's shout, imagines her face. He goes into the courtyard, the elf houses have their windows lighted, Ana's silhouette as she hugs Rowdy and comes toward him, what took you so long, love, I was nervous, so frightened, love.

"Let's get this animal inside, he'll drive the whole street crazy," and he barely kisses her. "Quiet, Rowdy."

He goes to the bathroom and while he urinates and washes his face he listens to Ana, what happened, sweet, what took you so long, playing with Rowdy, at least you found him, love, and he hears the happy barking. He comes out and Ana is sitting in the small living room, Rowdy in her arms. He sits down beside her, kisses her on the temple.

"You've been drinking." She holds him by the jacket, looks at him, half merry, half annoyed. "You smell of beer, love. Don't tell me you haven't been drinking, right?"

"I met a fellow I haven't seen in a hundred years. We went to have a drink. I couldn't get away, sweet."

"And me here half crazy with worry." He hears her plaintive, caressing, loving voice. "And you drinking beer with the boys. Why didn't you at least call me at the German woman's?"

"There wasn't any phone, we went to a dive." Yawning, stretching, smiling. "Besides, I don't like to keep bothering that crazy German all the time. I feel lousy, I've got an awful headache."

You deserved it, having kept her nerves on edge all afternoon, and she runs her hand over his forehead and looks at him and smiles at him and speaks to him softly and pinches one ear: you deserve to have a headache, love, and he kisses her. Would he like to sleep a little, should she draw the curtains, love? Yes, he gets up, just for a bit, falls onto the bed, and the shadows of Ana and Rowdy busying themselves about him, looking for himself.

19

"The worst is that I spent all my money, love. I don't know how we'll get by till Monday."

"Oh, that's all right. It's good that the Chinaman on San Martín always trusts me, it's good that he's the nicest Chinaman in the world."

"The worst is that we'll miss our movies. Was there anything good showing today?"

"One with Marlon Brando at the Colina," and Ana's voice, far, far away, arrives as if through water. "One of those detective movies you like, sweet. If you want I can borrow some money from the German woman."

She's happy, Zavalita, she forgives you for everything because you brought Rowdy back to her. He thinks: at this moment she's happy.

"I'll borrow some and we'll go to the movies, but promise me that you won't ever have a few beers with your buddies without telling me." Ana laughs, farther and farther away.

He thinks: I promise. The curtain has one corner folded over and Santiago can see a chunk of almost dark sky, and imagine, outside, up above, falling down onto the houses and their elves, Miraflores, Lima, the same miserable drizzle as always.

2

POPEYE ARÉVALO HAD SPENT the morning on the beach at Miraflores.
You look toward the stairs in vain, the neighborhood girls tell him, Teté's
not coming. And, as a matter of fact, Teté didn't go swimming that
morning. Defrauded, he went home before noon, but while he was going
up the hill on Quebrada he could see Teté's little nose, her curls, her
small eyes, and he grew emotional: when are you going to notice me,
when, Teté? He reached home with his reddish hair still damp, his
freckled face burning from the sun. He found the senator waiting for him:
come here, Freckle Face, they would have a little chat. They shut themselves up in the study and the senator, did he still want to study architecture? Yes, papa, of course he wanted to. Except that the entrance exam
was so hard, a whole bunch took it and only a small few got in. But he'd
grind and he'd probably get in. The senator was happy that he'd finished
high school without failing any courses and since the end of the year he'd
been like a mother to him, in January he'd increased his allowance from
twenty to forty soles. But even then Popeye didn't expect so much: well,
Freckle Face, since it was hard to get into Architecture it would be better
not to take a chance this year, he could enroll in the prep course and
study hard, and that way you'll get in next year for sure: what did he
think, Freckle Face? Wild, papa, Popeye's face lighted up even more, his
eyes glowed. He'd grind, he'd kill himself studying and the next year he'd
get in for sure. Popeye had been afraid of a deadly summer, no swim-

21

ming, no matinees, no parties, days and nights all soaked up in math, physics and chemistry, and, in spite of so much sacrifice, I won't get in and my vacation will be completely wasted. There it was, recovered now, the beach of Miraflores, the waves of Herradura, the bay of Ancón, and the images were as real, the orchestra seats in the Leuro, the Montecarlo and the Colina, as wild, the dance halls where he and Teté danced boleros, as those of a technicolor movie. Are you happy? the senator asked, and he quite happy. What a nice person he is, he thought as they went into the dining room, and the senator that's right, Freckle Face, just as soon as summer's over he'll break his hump, did he promise? and Popeye swore he would, papa. During lunch the senator teased him, Zavala's daughter still hadn't given you a tumble, Freckle Face? and he blushed: a little bit now, papa. You're too much of a child to have a girl friend, his old lady said, he should still keep away from foolishness. What an idea, he's already grown up, the senator said, and besides, Teté was a pretty girl. Don't let your arm be twisted, Freckle Face, women like to be begged, it had been awful rough on him courting the old lady, and the old lady dying with laughter. The telephone rang and the butler came running: your friend Santiago, child. He had to see him urgently, Freckle Face. At three o'clock at the Cream Rica on Larco, Skinny? At three on the dot, Freckle Face. Was your brother-in-law going to beat the tar out of you if you didn't leave Teté alone, Freckle Face? the senator smiled, and Popeye thought what a good mood he's in today. Nothing like that, he and Santiago were buddies, but the old lady frowned: that boy's got a screw loose, don't you think? Popeye raised a spoonful of ice cream to his mouth, who said that? another of meringue, maybe he could convince Santiago for them to go to his house and listen to records and call Teté just to talk a little, Skinny. Zoila herself had said so at canasta last Friday, the old lady insisted. Santiago was giving her and Fermín a lot of headaches lately, he spent all day fighting with Teté and Sparky, he'd become disobedient and he talked back. Skinny had come out first in the final exams, Popeye protested, what more did his old man and old lady want?

"He doesn't want to go to the Catholic University but to San Marcos," Señora Zoila said. "That upset Fermín very much."

"I'll bring him to his senses, Zoila, don't you get involved," Don

Fermín said. "He's at the foolish age, you have to know how to lead him. If you fight with him, he'll get all the more stubborn."

"If instead of advice you'd give him a couple of whacks, he'd pay more attention to you," Señora Zoila said. "The one who doesn't know how to raise him is you."

"She married that boy who used to come to the house," Santiago says. "Popeye Arévalo, Freckle Face Arévalo."

"Skinny doesn't get along with his old man because they don't have the same ideas," Popeye said.

"And what ideas does that snotnose still wet behind the ears have?" The senator laughed.

"Study hard, get your law degree and you can dip your spoon into politics," Don Fermín said. "Right, Skinny?"

"Skinny gets mad because his old man backed Odría in his revolt against Bustamante," Popeye said. "He's against the military."

"Is he a Bustamantist?" the senator asked. "And Fermín thinks he's the genius of the family. He can't be much of that if he admires that weak sister Bustamante."

"He might have been a weak sister, but he was a decent person and he'd been a diplomat," Popeye's old lady said. "Odría, on the other hand, is a coarse soldier and a half-breed."

"Don't forget that I'm an Odriíst senator," the senator laughed, "so stop half-breeding Odría, silly."

"He's got the notion of going to San Marcos because he doesn't like priests and because he wants to go where the people go," Popeye said. "He's really doing it because he's an againster. If his folks told him to go to San Marcos, he'd say no, Catholic University."

"Zoila's right, at San Marcos he'd lose his contacts," Popeye's old lady said. "Boys from good families go to the Catholic University."

"There are enough Indians at the Catholic University to give you a good scare too, mama," Popeye said.

"With all the money Fermín's bringing in now that he's buddy-buddy with Cayo Bermúdez, the squirt won't need any contacts," the senator said. "O.K., Freckle Face, on your way."

Popeye left the table, brushed his teeth, combed his hair and went out. It was only two-fifteen, it was better to go along marking time. Aren't we pals, Santiago? come on, give me a little push with Teté. He went up Larco blinking in the sunlight and stopped to look in the windows of the Casa Nelson: those deerskin moccasins with brown shorts and that yellow shirt, wild. He got to the Cream Rica before Santiago, settled down at a table from where he could see the avenue, and ordered a vanilla milk shake. If he couldn't convince Santiago to go listen to records at his house they would go to the matinee or to gamble at Coco Becerra's, what was it that Skinny wanted to talk to him about. And at that moment Santiago came in, long face, feverish eyes: his folks had fired Amalia, Freckle Face. The doors of the branch of the Banco de Crédito had just opened and through the windows of the Cream Rica Popeye watched the revolving doors swallow up the people who had been waiting on the sidewalk. The sun was shining, the express buses went by loaded, men and women fought for taxis on the corner of Shell. Why had they waited until now to throw her out, Skinny? Santiago shrugged his shoulders, his folks didn't want him to think that they were firing her because of the business of the other night, as if he was so stupid. He seemed even thinner with that mournful face, his jet black hair raining over his forehead. The waiter came over and Santiago pointed to Popeye's glass, vanilla too? yes. After all, it's not so bad, Popeye cheered him up, she'll get another job soon, they need maids all over. Santiago looked at his nails: Amalia was a nice person, when Sparky, Teté, or I were in a bad mood they let off steam abusing her and she never told the folks on us, Freckle Face. Popeye stirred his milk shake with the straw, how can I convince you to go listen to records at your place, brother-in-law? he sucked in the froth.

"Your old lady made her complaints to the senator's wife about the San Marcos business," he said.

"She can take her complaints to the King of Rome," Santiago said.

"If San Marcos upsets them so much, enroll at the Catholic University, what difference does it make to you?" Popeye said. "Or are they tougher at the Catholic University?"

"My folks don't give a damn about that," Santiago said. "They don't like San Marcos because there are half-breeds there and because there's a lot of politics, only for that reason."

"You've got yourself into a bind," Popeye said. "You're always against everything, you put everything down and you take things too much to heart. Don't give your life a bitter taste just for the hell of it, Skinny."

"Put your advice back in your pocket," Santiago said.

"Don't act as if you were so smart, Skinny," Popeye said. "It's all right for you to be a grind, but there's no reason for thinking that everyone else is a half-wit. Last night you treated Coco in a way that made me wonder why he didn't kill you."

"If I don't feel like going to mass I don't have to make excuses to that sexton," Santiago said.

"You're playing the atheist too now," Popeye said.

"I'm not playing the atheist," Santiago said. "The fact that I don't like priests doesn't mean that I don't believe in God."

"What do they say at home about your not going to church?" Popeye asked. "What does Teté say, for example?"

"That business about the Indian girl has got me all bitter, Freckle Face," Santiago said.

"Forget about it, don't be a fool," Popeye said. "Speaking of Teté, why didn't she come to the beach this morning?"

"She went to the Regatas Club with some girl friends," Santiago said. "I don't know why you haven't learned your lesson."

"The redhead, the one with freckles," Ambrosio says. "Senator Emilio Arévalo's boy, sure. Did she marry him?"

"I don't like people with red hair or people with freckles." Teté made a face. "And he's both. Ugh, it makes me sick."

"What upsets me most is that they fired her because of me," Santiago said.

"You should have said because of Sparky," Popeye consoled him. "You didn't know what yohimbine was."

Santiago's brother was only called Sparky now, but before, during the time he decided to show off at the Terrazas Club lifting weights, they called him Sparky Tarzan. He'd been a cadet at the Naval School for a few months and when they expelled him (he said for having struck an ensign), he drifted around for quite a while, given over to gambling and drinking and playing the tough. He would show up at San Fernando Square and go over menacingly to Santiago, pointing to Popeye, Toño,

25

Coco, or Lalo: come on, Superbrain, with which one of them did he want to match his strength. But since he went to work in Don Fermín's office he'd become very proper.

"I knew what it was but I'd never seen it," Santiago said. "Do you think it drives women crazy?"

"One of Sparky's stories," Popeye whispered. "Did he tell you it drives them crazy?"

"It does, but if you lay a hand on them you could turn them into a corpse, Sparky boy," Ambrosio said. "Don't get me into any trouble. Remember that if your papa catches on to it, I've had it."

"And did he tell you that with one spoonful any female would throw herself at you?" Popeye whispered. "Stories, Skinny."

"It would have to be tested," Santiago said. "Even if only to see if it's true, Freckle Face."

He was silent, with an attack of nervous laughter, and Popeye laughed too. They nudged each other, the hard thing was to find the one to do it with, excited, worn out, that was it, and the table and the milk shakes trembled with the quivering: they were crazy, Skinny. What had Sparky told him when he gave it to him? Sparky and Santiago got on like cat and dog and whenever he could Sparky played dirty tricks on Skinny and Skinny on Sparky whenever he could: it was probably one of your brother's dirty tricks, Skinny. No, Freckle Face, Sparky had come home like an Easter angel, I won a lot of money at the track, and what was unheard of, before going to bed he went into Santiago's room to give him some advice: it's time for you to shake yourself up, aren't you ashamed of still being a virgin, a big man like you? and he offered him a cigarette. Don't be scared, Sparky said, have you got a girl friend? Santiago lied that he did and Sparky, worried: it's time to devirginize you, Skinny, it really is.

"Haven't I been asking you all the time to take me to a whorehouse?" Santiago said.

"You might catch something and the old man would kill me," Sparky said. "Besides, real men earn what they get, they don't pay for it. You play the know-it-all and you're up on the moon when it comes to females, Superbrain."

"I don't play the know-it-all," Santiago said. "I attack when I'm attacked. Come on, Sparky, take me to a whorehouse."

"Then why do you argue with the old man so much? You get him all upset opposing everything he says."

"I only oppose him when he starts defending Odría and the militarists," Santiago said. "Come on, Sparky."

"And why are you against the military?" Sparky asked. "What the fuck has Odría ever done to you?"

"They came to power by force," Santiago said. "Odría's put a lot of people in jail."

"Only Apristas and Communists," Sparky said. "He's really been gentle with them. I would have shot them all. The country was a mess under Bustamante, decent people couldn't work in peace."

"Then you're not a decent person," Santiago said, "because in Bustamante's time you were bumming around."

"You're asking for a whack, Superbrain," Sparky said.

"I've got my ideas and you've got yours," Santiago said. "Come on, take me to a whorehouse."

"The whorehouse is out," Sparky said, "but I will help you work it out with a woman."

"And do they sell yohimbine in drugstores?" Popeye asked.

"Under the counter," Santiago said. "It's kind of illegal."

"A little bit in a Coca-Cola, on a hot dog," Sparky said, "and you wait for it to take effect. When she starts to get a little restless then it's up to you."

"How old do they have to be for you to give it to them, just for example, Sparky?" Santiago asked.

"You wouldn't be dumb enough to give it to a ten-year-old." Sparky laughed. "You can to one who's fourteen, but just a little. Except that at that age it won't make it easier for you, you'll get into a crazy mess."

"Is it real?" Popeye asked. "Couldn't he have given you a little salt or sugar?"

"I tested it with the tip of my tongue," Santiago said. "It hasn't got any smell, it's a powder with a little bite to it."

On the street there was an increase in the number of people who were trying to get into the crowded taxis and express buses. They didn't stand in line, they were a small mob waving their hands at the buses with blue and white grilles that passed without stopping. Suddenly, among the bodies, two tiny identical silhouettes, two heads of dark hair: the Vallerriestra twins. Popeye pushed the curtain aside and waved to them, but they didn't see him or didn't recognize him. They were tapping their heels impatiently, their fresh and tanned little faces kept looking at the clock on the Banco de Crédito, they must have been going to some matinee downtown, Skinny. Every time a taxi approached they went out onto the street with a determined air, but they always lost their place.

"They're probably going by themselves," Popeye said. "Let's go to the matinee with them, Skinny."

"Are you dying for Teté, yes or no, turncoat?" Santiago asked.

"I'm dying only for Teté," Popeye said. "Of course, if instead of the matinee you want to go to your house and listen to records, I'm all for it."

Santiago shook his head without enthusiasm: he'd got hold of some money, he was going to take it to the Indian girl, she lived around there, in Surquillo. Popeye opened his eyes, to Amalia? and began to laugh, are you going to give her your allowance because your folks threw her out? Not my allowance, Santiago snapped the straw in two, he'd taken a hundred soles from the piggy bank. And Popeye put a finger to his temple: heading right for the booby hatch, Skinny. It was my fault they fired her, Santiago said, what was so bad about giving her a little money? Even if you'd fallen in love with the Indian, Skinny, a hundred soles was a lot of money, with that we can invite the twins to the movies. But at that moment the twins were getting into a green Morris and Popeye too late, brother. Santiago had started to smoke.

"I don't think that Sparky gave any yohimbine to his girl friend, he made that up to look like a devil," Popeye said. "Would you give yohimbine to a decent girl?"

"Not to my sweetheart," Santiago said. "But why not to a half-breed girl?"

"So what are you going to do?" Popeye whispered. "Are you going to give it to someone or are you going to throw it away?"

He'd thought about throwing it away, Freckle Face, and Santiago lowered his voice and blushed, then he was thinking and he stammered, that's when he got an idea. Just to see what it was like, Freckle Face, what did he think.

"So stupid there's no name for it, you can do a thousand things with a hundred soles," Popeye said. "But it's up to you, it's your money."

"Come with me, Freckle Face," Santiago said. "It's right here, in Surquillo."

"But then we'll go to your house to hear records," Popeye said. "And you'll call Teté."

"You really are a shithead suitor, Freckle Face," Santiago said.

"And what if your folks find out?" Popeye asked. "What about Sparky?"

"My folks are going to Ancón and won't be back until Monday," Santiago said. "And Sparky's gone to a friend's ranch."

"Be prepared in case it doesn't agree with her, in case she faints on us," Popeye said.

"We'll only give her a little bit," Santiago said. "Don't be chicken, Freckle Face."

A small light went on in Popeye's eyes, do you remember when we spied on Amalia in Ancón, Skinny? From the roof you could see the servants' bathroom, two faces side by side in the skylight and below a hazy outline, a black bathrobe, delicious, the half-breed, Skinny. The couple at the next table got up and Ambrosio pointed to the woman: that one was a hooker, son, she spent the day in La Catedral looking for customers. They saw the couple go out onto Larco, saw them cross the Calle Shell. The bus stop was deserted now. Express buses and taxis passed half empty now. They called the waiter, split the check, and how did he know that she was a hooker? Because besides being a restaurant and bar La Catedral was also a pickup place, son, behind the kitchen there was a little room and they rented it for two soles an hour. They went along Larco, looking at the girls who were coming out of the shops, the women pushing carriages with crying babies. In the park Popeye bought *Última Hora* and read the gossip aloud, thumbed through the sports pages, and as they passed in front of La Tiendecita Blanca hi, Lalo. On the Alameda Ricardo Palma they crumpled the newspaper and took a few steps until it fell apart and was abandoned on a corner in Surquillo.

"All we need is for Amalia to get mad and tell me to go to hell," Santiago said.

"A hundred soles is a fortune," Popeye said. "She'll receive you like a king."

They were near the Cine Miraflores, across from the market with booths of wood, matting and awnings where flowers, ceramics and fruit were sold, and into the street there came shots, galloping, Indian war cries, children's voices: *Death in Arizona.* They stopped to look at the posters: a cowboy picture, Skinny.

"I'm a little jumpy," Santiago said. "I couldn't get to sleep last night, that must be why."

"You're jumpy because you've lost your nerve," Popeye said. "You put on for me, nothing's going to happen, don't be chicken, and at the zero hour you're the one who loses his nerve. Let's go to the movies, then."

"I haven't lost my nerve, it's passed," Santiago said. "Wait, I'm going to see if my folks have left."

The car wasn't there, they'd gone. They went in through the garden, passed by the tiled fountain, and what if she'd gone to bed, Skinny? They'd wake her up, Freckle Face. Santiago opened the door, the click of the switch and the shadows turned into rugs, pictures, mirrors, tables with ashtrays, lamps. Popeye was going to sit down but, Santiago, let's go up to my room first. A courtyard, a study, a stairway with an iron railing. Santiago left Popeye on the landing, go in and put some music on, he was going to call her. School pennants, a picture of Sparky, another one of Teté in her first-communion dress, beautiful Popeye thought, a big-eared, snouty pig on the bureau, he picked it up, how much money could there be. He sat down on the bed, turned on the clock radio, a waltz by Felipe Pinglo, steps, Skinny: everything O.K., Freckle Face. He'd found her awake, bring me up some Coca-Colas, and they laughed: shh, she was coming, could it be her? Yes, there she was at the door, surprised, examining them with suspicion. She'd folded up against the door, a pink jumper and a blouse without buttons, she didn't say anything. It was Amalia and it wasn't, Popeye thought, how could it be the one in a blue apron who went through Skinny's house with trays or a duster in her hands. Her hair was tangled now, good afternoon, child, a pair of men's shoes and you could see she was frightened: hello, Amalia.

"My mother said you'd left the house," Santiago said. "What a shame that you're leaving."

Amalia left the door, looked at Popeye, how was he, young master, who smiled at her in a friendly way from the sidewalk, and turned to Santiago: she hadn't left because she wanted to, Señora Zoila had thrown her out. But why, ma'am, and Señora Zoila because she felt like it, pack your bags this instant. She spoke and was making her hair peaceful with her hands, adjusting her blouse. Santiago listened to her with an uncomfortable face. She didn't want to leave the house, child, she'd begged the mistress.

"Put the tray on the table," Santiago said. "Stay awhile, we're listening to music."

Amalia put the tray with the glasses and the Coca-Cola in front of the picture of Sparky and remained standing by the bureau, her face puzzled. She was wearing the white dress and low-heeled shoes of her uniform but not the apron or the cap. Why was she standing there? come here, sit down, there's room. How could she sit down, and she gave a little laugh, the mistress didn't like her to go into the boys' rooms, didn't he know? Silly, my mother's not home, Santiago's voice suddenly became tense, neither he nor Popeye would tell on her, sit down, silly. Amalia laughed again, he said that now but as soon as he got annoyed he'd tell on her and the mistress would take it out on her. I swear that Skinny won't tell on you, Popeye said, don't make us beg you and sit down. Amalia looked at Santiago, looked at Popeye, sat down on a corner of the bed and now her face was serious. Santiago got up, went to the tray, don't let your hand slip, Popeye thought and looked at Amalia: did she like the way that group sang? He pointed to the radio, the real thing, right? She liked it, they sang pretty. She had her hands on her knees, she kept herself stiff, she was squinting as if to hear better: they were the Trovadores del Norte, Amalia. Santiago was still pouring the Coca-Colas and Popeye was spying on him, uneasy. Did Amalia know how to dance? Waltzes, boleros, guarachas? Amalia smiled, turned serious, smiled again: no, she didn't know how. She moved a little closer to the edge of the bed, crossed her arms. Her movements were forced, as if her clothes were too tight

31

or her back itched: her shadow was motionless on the floor.

"I brought you this for you to buy something," Santiago said.

"Me?" Amalia looked at the banknotes, without taking them. "But Señora Zoila paid me for the whole month, child."

"My mother didn't send it to you," Santiago said. "I'm giving it to you."

"But why should you be giving me your money, child?" Her cheeks were red, she looked confusedly at Skinny. "How can I accept it?"

"Don't be foolish," Santiago insisted. "Go ahead, Amalia."

He set the example for her: he lifted up his glass and drank. Now they were playing "Siboney," and Popeye had opened the window: the garden, the small trees on the street lighted by the lamppost on the corner, the trembling surface of the fountain, the tile base glimmering, I hope nothing happens, Skinny. Well, child, to your health, and Amalia took a long drink, sighed and took the glass away from her lips half empty: delicious, nice and cold. Popeye went over to the bed.

"If you want, we can teach you how to dance," Santiago said. "That way, when you get a boyfriend you'll be able to go to parties with him without being a wallflower."

"She probably has a boyfriend already," Popeye said. "Tell the truth, Amalia, have you got one?"

"Look how she's laughing, Freckle Face." Santiago took her by the arm. "Of course you have, we've found out your secret, Amalia."

"You have, you have." Popeye dropped down beside her, took her other arm. "Look at the way you're laughing, you devil."

Amalia was twisting with laughter and shook her arms but they didn't let her go, how could she have one, child, she didn't, she elbowed them to keep them away. Santiago put his arm around her waist, Popeye put a hand on her knee, and Amalia a slap: none of that, child, no touching her. But Popeye returned to the attack: devil, devil. She probably even knew how to dance and was lying that she couldn't, come on, confess: all right, child, she accepted. She took the bills that wrinkled in her fingers, just to prove to Santiago that she didn't want to beg, that's all, and she put them in the pocket of her jumper. But she was sorry to take his money, now he wouldn't have any even for the Sunday matinee.

"Don't worry," Popeye said. "If he hasn't got any, we'll take up a collection in the neighborhood and invite him."

"Friends that you are," and Amalia opened her eyes as if remembering. "But come in, even if just for a minute. Excuse my poor place."

She didn't give them time to refuse, she went running into the house and they followed her. Grease spots and soot, a few chairs, religious pictures, two unmade beds. They couldn't stay very long, Amalia, they had an appointment. She nodded, dusted the table in the center of the room with her skirt, just a few minutes. A malicious spark broke out in her eyes, would they wait for her and talk a little while? she was going to buy something to serve them, she'd be right back. Santiago and Popeye looked at each other surprised, delighted, she's a different person, Skinny, she's gone batty. Her laughter echoed through the whole room, her face was sweaty and there were tears in her eyes, her bravado had infected the bed with a squeaking shudder. Now she too was accompanying the music with clapping: yes, yes she knew how. Once they had taken her to Agua Dulce and she'd danced at a place where an orchestra was playing, she's completely mad Popeye thought. He stood up, turned off the radio, turned on the phonograph, went back to the bed. Now he wanted to see her dance, how happy you are, you devil, come on let's go, but Santiago got up: he was going to dance with her, Freckle Face. You bastard, Popeye thought, you take advantage because she's your servant, and what if Teté appeared? and he felt his knees weaken and a desire to leave, bastard. Amalia had stood up and was doing steps by herself across the room, bumping into the furniture, clumsy and heavy, humming, spinning blindly, until Santiago embraced her. Popeye leaned his head on the pillow, reached out his hand and turned out the lamp, darkness, then the glow of the street light sketchily illuminated the two silhouettes. Popeye watched them floating in a circle, heard Amalia's shrill voice, and put his hand in his pocket, did he see that she did know how to dance, child? When the record was over and Santiago came back to sit on the bed Amalia kept leaning against the window, her back to them, laughing: Sparky was right, look what's happened to her, shut up you bastard. She was talking, singing and laughing as if she were drunk, she didn't even see them, her eyes were rolling, Freckle Face, Santiago was a little frightened, what if she faints? Stop talking nonsense, Popeye said in his ear, bring her to the bed. His voice was determined, urgent, he had a hard on, Skinny, didn't you? anguished, thick: he too, Freckle Face. They would undress her, they would fondle her: they would jump her, Skinny. Leaning halfway out over the garden, Amalia was slowly swaying, murmuring something, and Popeye made out her silhouette outlined against the dark sky: another record, another record. Santiago stood up, a background of violins and the voice of Leo Marini, pure velvet Popeye thought, and he saw Santiago go to the balcony. The two shadows came together, he'd given him the idea for all this and now he had him twiddling his thumbs in great shape, you'll pay me for this trick, you bastard. They weren't even moving now, the breed girl was short and seemed to be hanging from Skinny, he must have been petting her beautifully, it was too much, and he imagined Santiago's voice, aren't you tired? clogged up and weak and as if she were strangled, did she want to lie down? bring her over, he thought. They were beside him, Amalia was dancing like a sleepwalker, her eyes were closed, Skinny's hands ran up and down, disappeared behind her back and Popeye couldn't make out their faces, he was kissing her and he an innocent bystander, it was too much, help yourselves, boys.

"I brought these straws too," Amalia said. "That's how you drink it, right?"

"Why did you bother," Santiago said. "We were just leaving."

She handed them the Coca-Colas and the straws, dragged over a chair and sat down opposite them; she had combed her hair, had put on a hairband and buttoned her jumper and was watching them drink. She didn't have any.

"You shouldn't have spent your money like that, silly," Popeye said.

"It's not mine, it's what young Santiago gave me." Amalia laughed. "Just to do a little something for you."

The street door was open, outside it was beginning to grow dark and sometimes and in the distance the sound of streetcars was heard. A lot of people were passing along the sidewalk, voices, laughter, some faces paused to look for a moment.

"They're getting out of the factories now," Amalia said. "It's too bad your father's laboratory isn't near here, child. I'll have to take the streetcar to the Avenida Argentina and then the bus."

"Are you going to work at the lab?" Santiago asked.

34

"Didn't your papa tell you?" Amalia said. "Yes, starting Monday."

She was leaving the house with her suitcase and she met Don Fermín, would you like me to get you a job in the lab? and she of course, Don Fermín, anywhere, and then he called young Sparky and told him to telephone Carrillo to give her a job: what a show-off, Popeye thought.

"Oh, that's good," Santiago said. "You'll be much better off in the lab."

Popeye took out his pack of Chesterfields, offered a cigarette to Santiago, doubted a moment, and another to Amalia, but she didn't smoke, child.

"You probably do smoke and you're fooling us the way you did the other day," Popeye said. "You told us I can't dance and you knew how."

He saw her grow pale, no, child, no, he heard her stammer, he sensed that Santiago was moving in his chair and he thought I put my foot in it. Amalia had lowered her head.

"I was kidding," he said, and his cheeks were burning. "What have you got to be ashamed of, did anything happen, silly?"

She was getting her color back, her voice: she didn't even want to remember, child. How bad she felt, the next day everything was still all mixed up in her head and things danced in her hands. She raised her face, looked at them timidly, enviously, with amazement: didn't Coca-Cola do anything to them? Popeye looked at Santiago, Santiago looked at Popeye and they both looked at Amalia: she'd vomited all night long, she'd never drink Coca-Cola again in her life. And still, she'd drunk beer and nothing happened, and Pasteurina, nothing, and Pepsi-Cola, nothing, could that Coca-Cola have gone bad, child? Popeye bit his tongue, took out his handkerchief and blew his nose furiously. He squeezed his nose and felt that his stomach was going to explode: the record was over, now was the time, and he quickly took his hand out of his pants pocket. They were still sunk in half darkness, come on come on, sit down for a while and he heard Amalia: the music had finished, child. A difficult voice, why had the other child turned out the light, barely fluttering, that they should turn it back on or she was leaving, complaining without strength, as if some overpowering dream or languor were extinguishing her, she didn't like the dark, she didn't like it that way. It was a shapeless silhouette, one more shadow among the other shadows of the room and they seemed

35

to be struggling in a sham way between the night table and the bureau. He got up and went over to them, go out into the garden, Freckle Face, and he it's too much, he bumped into something, his ankle hurt, he wasn't going, bring her to the bed, let me go, child. Amalia's voice rose up, what's the matter, child, she was getting furious, and now Popeye had found her shoulders, let me go, he should let her go, and he dragged her, what a nerve, how dare the young master, eyes closed, breathing heavy and he rolled onto the bed with them: there it was, Skinny. She laughed, don't tickle me, but her arms and legs kept on struggling and Popeye laughed anxiously: get out of here, Freckle Face, leave me alone. He wasn't leaving, why should he leave, and now Santiago was pushing Popeye and Popeye was pushing him, I'm not leaving and there was a confusion of clothing and wet skins in the shadows, a whirl of legs, hands, arms and blankets. They were smothering her, child, she couldn't breathe: the way you laugh, you devil. Get away, they should let her go, a drowned voice, a regular, slow animal panting, and suddenly shh, shoves and little shouts, and Santiago shh, and Popeye shh: the street door, shh. Teté, he thought, and he felt his body dissolve. Santiago had run to the window and he couldn't move: Teté, Teté.

"Now we do have to go, Amalia." Santiago stood up, left the bottle on the table. "Thanks for inviting us in."

"Thank *you*, child," Amalia said. "For having come and for what you brought me."

"Come by the house and see us," Santiago said.

"Of course, child," Amalia said. "And give my best to little Teté."

"Get out of here, get up, what are you waiting for," Santiago said. "And you, fix your shirt and comb your hair a little, you fool."

He had just lighted the lamp, he was smoothing his hair, Popeye tucked his shirt in his pants and looked at him, terrified: beat it, get out of the room. But Amalia kept sitting on the bed and they had to lift up her dead weight, she stumbled with an idiotic expression, supported herself on the night table. Quick, quick, Santiago smoothed the bed cover and Popeye ran to turn off the phonograph, get out of the room, you fool. She was unable to move, she was listening to them with eyes full of surprise and she slipped out of their hands and at that moment the door opened and they let go of her: hi, mama. Popeye saw Señora Zoila and

36

tried to smile, in slacks and wearing a garnet turban, good evening, ma'am, and the lady's eyes smiled and looked at Santiago, at Amalia, and her smile diminished and died: hi, papa. Behind Señora Zoila he saw the full face, the gray mustache and sideburns, Don Fermín's laughing eyes, hello, Skinny, your mother decided not to, hello, Popeye, I didn't know you were here. Don Fermín entered the room, collarless shirt, summer jacket, loafers, and he shook hands with Popeye, how are you, sir.

"You, why aren't you in bed?" Señora Zoila asked. "It's already after twelve."

"We were famished and I woke her up to make us some sandwiches," Santiago said. "Weren't you going to sleep over in Ancón?"

"Your mother had forgotten that she'd invited people to lunch tomorrow," Don Fermín said. "Your mother's outbursts, otherwise . . ."

Out of the corner of his eye, Popeye saw Amalia go out with the tray in her hands, she was looking at the floor and walking straight, they were in luck.

"Your sister stayed at the Vallarinos'," Don Fermín said. "All in all, my plans for a rest this weekend didn't work out."

"Is it twelve o'clock already, ma'am?" Popeye asked. "I've got to run. We didn't pay any attention to the time, I thought it must have been ten."

"How are things with the senator?" Don Fermín asked. "We haven't seen him at the club in ages."

She went to the street with them and there Santiago patted her on the shoulder and Popeye said good-bye: *ciao,* Amalia. They went off in the direction of the streetcar line. They went into El Triunfo to buy some cigarettes; it was already boiling over with drinkers and pool players.

"A hundred soles for nothing, a wild bit of showing off," Popeye said. "It turned out that we did the girl a favor, now your old man has got her a better job."

"Even so, we got her in a jam," Santiago said. "I'm not sorry about those hundred soles."

"I don't want to keep harping on it, but you're broke," Popeye said. "What did we do to her? Now that you've given her five pounds, forget about your remorse."

Following the streetcar line, they went down to Ricardo Palma and they walked along smoking under the trees on the boulevard between rows of cars.

"Didn't it make you laugh when she talked about Coca-Cola that way?" Popeye laughed. "Do you think she's that dumb or was she putting on? I don't know how I held back, I was pissing inside wanting to laugh."

"I'm going to ask you something," Santiago says. "Do I have the face of a son of a bitch?"

"And I'm going to tell you something," Popeye said. "Don't you think her going out to buy the Coca-Cola for us was strictly hypocritical? As if she was letting herself go to see if we'd repeat what happened the other night."

"You've got a rotten mind, Freckle Face," Santiago said.

"What a question," Ambrosio says. "Of course not, boy."

"O.K., so the breed girl is a saint and I've got a rotten mind," Popeye said. "Let's go to your house and listen to records, then."

"You did it for me?" Don Fermín asked. "For me, you poor black crazy son of a bitch?"

"I swear you don't, son." Ambrosio laughs. "Are you making fun of me?"

"Teté isn't home," Santiago said. "She went to an early show with some girl friends."

"Listen, don't be a son of a bitch, Skinny," Popeye said. "You're lying, aren't you? You promised, Skinny."

"You mean that sons of bitches don't have the faces of sons of bitches, Ambrosio," Santiago says.

3

THE LIEUTENANT DIDN'T YAWN once during the trip; he was talking
about the revolution the whole time, explaining to the sergeant driving
the jeep how now that Odría had taken power the Apristas would toe
the mark, and smoking cigarettes that smelled like guano. They had left
Lima at dawn and had only stopped once, in Surco, to show their pass
to a patrol that was manning a roadblock on the highway. They entered
Chincha at seven in the morning. There were no signs of the revolution
there: the streets were alive with schoolchildren, there wasn't a soldier
to be seen on the corners. The Lieutenant leaped to the sidewalk, went
into the café-restaurant called Mi Patria, heard on the radio the same
communiqué with a military march in the background that he had been
hearing for two days. Leaning on the counter, he asked for coffee and
milk and a cream cheese sandwich. He asked the man who waited on
him, wearing an undershirt and with a sour face, if he knew Cayo
Bermúdez, a businessman in town. Was he going, the man rolled his eyes,
to arrest him? Was that Bermúdez an Aprista? How could he be, he
wasn't involved in politics. That's good, politics was for bums, not hard-
working people, the Lieutenant was looking for him on a personal matter. He wouldn't find him here, he never came here. He lived in a little
yellow house behind the church. It was the only one that color, the other
ones around were white or gray and there was also a brown one. The

Lieutenant knocked on the door and waited and heard footsteps and a voice who is it.

"Is Mr. Bermúdez in?" the Lieutenant asked.

The door opened with a creak and a woman came forward: a fat Indian woman with a blackish face that was full of moles, yessir. The people in Chincha said if you could only see her now. Because she wasn't bad-looking as a girl. Night and day, I tell you, what a change, yessir. Her hair was all messy, the woolen shawl that covered her shoulders looked like a burlap bag.

"He's not home." She looked sideways with suspicious greedy little eyes. "What's it about? I'm his wife."

"Will he be back soon?" The Lieutenant examined the woman with surprise, mistrust. "Can I wait for him?"

She drew away from the door. Inside, the Lieutenant felt nauseous in the midst of the heavy furniture, the pots without flowers, the sewing machine and the walls with constellations of shadows or holes or flies. The woman opened a window, a tongue of sun came in. Everything was worn, there were too many things in the room. Boxes stacked up in the corners, piles of newspapers. The woman murmured an excuse and vanished into the dark mouth of a hallway. The Lieutenant heard a canary trilling somewhere. Was she really his wife? Yessir, his wife before God, of course she was, a story that shook up Chincha. How did it begin? A whole string of years ago, when the Bermúdez family left the De la Flor ranch. The family, that is the Vulture, Doña Catalina the church biddy, and the son, Don Cayo, who was probably still crawling in those days. The Vulture had been foreman on the ranch and when he came to Chincha people said that the De la Flors had fired him for stealing. In Chincha he became a loan shark. Anybody needed money, he went to the Vulture, I need so much, what'll you give me for security, this ring, this watch, and if you didn't pay he kept the item and the Vulture's interest was so high that people owed him so much they might as well have been dead. That's why they called him the Vulture, yessir: he lived off corpses. He was loaded with money in a few years and he put the gold clasp around it when the government of General Benavides began to put Apristas in jail and deport them; Subprefect Núñez gave the orders, Captain Rascachucha put the Apristas in the lockup and chased their families away, the Vulture auctioned off their belongings, and they split the pie among the three of them. And with money the Vulture became important, yessir, he was even mayor of Chincha and you'd see him wearing a derby on the Plaza de Armas during parades on national holidays. And he got all puffed up. He saw to it that his son always wore shoes and didn't mix with black people. When they were kids they played soccer, stole fruit in the orchards, Ambrosio visited his house and the Vulture didn't care. When they got money-rich, on the other hand, they kicked him out and they scolded Don Cayo if they caught him with him. His servant? Oh, no sir, his friend, but only when he was this size. The black woman had her stand on the corner where Don Cayo lived then and he and Ambrosio gave her a hard time. Then they were split up by the Vulture, yessir, that's life. Don Cayo was put into the José Pardo School and the black woman, ashamed because of Trifulcio, took Ambrosio and Perpetuo to Mala, and when they came back to Chincha, Don Cayo was always with someone from José Pardo, the Uplander. Ambrosio would meet him on the street and he didn't use the intimate form anymore, only the formal. In the activities at José Pardo Don Cayo recited, read his little speeches, carried the school flag in parades. The child prodigy of Chincha, they said, a future brain, and the Vulture drooled when he talked about his son and said he'd go a long way, they said. And he really did, yessir, right?

"Do you think he'll be very long?" The Lieutenant crushed out his cigarette in the ashtray. "Do you know where he is?"

"And I got married too," Santiago says. "Didn't you get married?"

"Sometimes he comes home very late for lunch," the woman muttered. "Would you like to leave a message?"

"You too, son, and so young?" Ambrosio says.

"I'll wait for him," the Lieutenant said. "I hope he doesn't take too long."

He was already in his last year at school, the Vulture was going to send him to Lima to study to be a shyster and Don Cayo was made to order for that, they said. Ambrosio was living in the group of shacks that used to be outside Chincha then, yessir, on the road to what was Grocio Prado later on. And he'd run into him there once, and right away caught on that he was playing hooky and right away wondered who the female was.

41

Mounting her? No sir, looking at her with the eyes of a lunatic. He was pretending not to notice, somebody watching hogs, somebody waiting. He'd left his books on the ground, he was kneeling, his eyes were turned toward the huts and Ambrosio said which one is it, I wonder which one it is. It was Rosa, yessir, the daughter of Túmula the milk woman. A skinny girl with nothing particular about her, at that time she looked more like a little white girl than an Indian. There are some kids who are born ugly and get better later on, Rosa started off passable and ended up a dog. Passable, not good, not bad, one of those that a white man does a favor for once and if I saw you I've forgotten. Her little teats half formed, a young body and nothing else, but so dirty she couldn't even be fixed up to go to mass. She used to be seen in Chincha driving the donkey with the jugs, yessir, selling it by the gourd from house to house. Túmula's daughter, the Vulture's son, you can imagine the scandal, yessir. The Vulture already had a hardware store and a warehouse and they say he said that when the boy comes back from Lima with his law degree he'll make a pile of money. Doña Catalina spent all her time in church, a close friend of the priest, raffles for the poor, Catholic Action. And the son prowling around the milk woman's daughter, who would have thought it. But that's the way it was, yessir. He was attracted by the way she walked or something, some people would rather have a mongrel than a thoroughbred, they say. He must have been thinking, I'll work her over, wet her and leave her, and she realized that the white boy was drooling over her and must have thought I'll let him work me over, wet me and I'll grab him. The fact is that Don Cayo went ki-yi, yessir: what can I do for you? The Lieutenant opened his eyes, leaped to his feet.

"I'm sorry, I fell asleep." He ran his hand over his face, coughed. "Mr. Bermúdez?"

Next to the horrible woman was a man with a dry and acidy face, in his forties, in shirtsleeves, a briefcase under his arm. The wide cuffs of his pants covered his shoes. Sailor pants, the Lieutenant managed to think, a clown's pants.

"At your service," the man said, as if bored or displeased. "Have you been waiting for me long?"

"Please pack your bags," the Lieutenant said jovially. "I'm taking you to Lima."

But the man didn't change his expression. His face didn't smile, his eyes weren't surprised or alarmed or happy. They watched him with the same indifferent monotony as before.

"To Lima?" he asked slowly, his eyes dull. "Who wants to see me in Lima?"

"Colonel Espina, no less," the Lieutenant said with a triumphal little voice. "The Minister of Public Order, no less."

The woman opened her mouth, Bermúdez didn't blink. He remained expressionless, then the hint of a smile altered the dreamy annoyance of his face, a second later his eyes became uninterested and bored again. His liver's kicking up, the Lieutenant thought, bitter over life, with the wife he's saddled with it's easy to understand. Bermúdez tossed the briefcase onto the sofa.

"Yes, indeed. Yesterday I heard that Espina was one of the ministers of the Junta." He took out a pack of Incas, offered an unappetizing cigarette to the Lieutenant. "Didn't the Uplander tell you why he wanted to see me?"

"Only that he needs you urgently." The Uplander, the Lieutenant thought. "And for me to bring you back to Lima even if I have to stick a pistol in your chest."

Bermúdez dropped into an easy chair, crossed his legs, blew out a mouthful of smoke that clouded his face and when the smoke disappeared, the Lieutenant saw that he was smiling at him as if he was doing me a favor, he thought, as if he was making fun of me.

"It's hard for me to leave Chincha today," he said with a growing laxness. "There's a business deal I have to close on a ranch near here."

"If a person is summoned by the Minister of Public Order, he has no recourse but to go," the Lieutenant said. "Please be reasonable, Mr. Bermúdez."

"Two new tractors, a good commission," Bermúdez explained to the flies or holes or shadows. "This is no time for outings to Lima."

"Tractors?" The Lieutenant put on an irritated face. "Use your head a little, please, and let's not waste any more time."

Bermúdez took a puff, half closing his cold little eyes, and he exhaled the smoke unhurriedly.

"When you're up to here with bills, you have to think about tractors," he said, as if he couldn't hear or see him. "Tell the Uplander I'll come by in a few days."

The Lieutenant looked at him with consternation, amused, confused: if things were that way he would have to draw his pistol and stick it in his chest, Mr. Bermúdez, if things were that way they were going to laugh at him. But Don Cayo as if nothing happened, yessir, played hooky and went into the settlement and the women pointed at him, Rosa, they whispered to each other and laughed at him, Rosita, look who's coming. Túmula's daughter was very bold, yessir. Just imagine, the Vulture's son had come there to see her, who'd have thought it. She didn't come out to talk to him, she curled up, she ran to where her girl friends were, all laughs, all flirty. It didn't matter to him that the girl gave him the cold shoulder, that seemed to get him all the hotter. She knew how to put on, Túmula's daughter did, yessir, and no need to talk about her mother, anyone would have realized it, but not him. He took it all, he waited, he went back to the settlement, the little half-breed would fall someday, black boy, he was the one that fell, yessir. Can't you see that she gets stuck-up instead of thanking you, Don Cayo? Tell her to go to hell, Don Cayo. But he as if he'd been given a love potion, chasing right after her, and people were beginning to gossip. They're talking all over the place, Don Cayo. And he what the fuck, he did what his belly told him and his belly told him to get the girl, naturally. Fine, who was going to call him down, any white boy can get sweet with a little half-breed, do this little thing, and who cares, yessir, right? But Don Cayo chased after her as if the thing was serious, wasn't that crazy? And crazier still was the fact that Rosa gave herself the luxury of treating him like dirt. She seemed to be giving herself the luxury, yessir.

"We've already gassed up, I told Lima we'll be there around three-thirty," the Lieutenant said. "Whenever you're ready, Mr. Bermúdez."

Bermúdez had changed his shirt and was wearing a gray suit. He was carrying a small valise, a crumpled hat, sunglasses.

"Is that all your luggage?" the Lieutenant asked.

"I've got forty bags more," Bermúdez grunted. "Let's go, I want to get back to Chincha today."

The woman watched the sergeant who was checking the oil in the jeep. She had taken off her apron, the tight dress outlined her bulging stomach, her overflowing hips. You'll have to excuse me, the Lieutenant gave her his hand, for stealing your husband, but she didn't laugh. Bermúdez had got into the rear seat of the jeep and she was looking at him as if she hated him, the Lieutenant thought, or wouldn't ever see him again. He got into the jeep, saw Bermúdez vaguely wave good-bye, and they left. The sun was burning, the streets were deserted, a nauseating vapor arose from the pavement, the windows of the houses sparkled.

"Has it been long since you were in Lima?" The Lieutenant was trying to be pleasant.

"I go two or three times a year on business," he said without warmth, without grace, the slack, mechanical, discontented little voice of the world. "I represent a few agricultural concerns here."

"We didn't get to marry, but I had my woman too," Ambrosio says.

"But how come your business isn't going well?" the Lieutenant asked. "Aren't the landowners here pretty rich? There's a lot of cotton, isn't there?"

"You had?" Santiago asks. "Did you have a fight with her?"

"It went well in other days," Bermúdez said; he isn't the most unpleasant man in Peru because Colonel Espina is still around, the Lieutenant thought, but after the Colonel who except this one. "With the controls on exchange, the cotton growers have stopped making what they used to, and you have to sweat blood just to sell them a hoe."

"She died on me there in Pucallpa, child," Ambrosio says. "She left me a little girl."

"Well, that's why we started the revolution," the Lieutenant said good-humoredly. "The chaos is all over now. With the army in charge everybody will toe the mark. You'll see how things are going to get better under Odría."

"Really?" Bermúdez yawned. "People change here, Lieutenant, never things."

"Don't you read the papers? Don't you listen to the radio?" the Lieutenant insisted with a smile. "The cleanup has already started. Apristas, crooks, Communists, all in the lockup. There won't be a single one of the vermin loose on the streets."

"What did you go to Pucallpa for?" Santiago asks.

"Others will appear," Bermúdez said harshly. "In order to clean the

45

vermin up in Peru you'd have to drop a few bombs and wipe us off the map."

"To work, son," Ambrosio says. "I mean, to look for work."

"Are you serious or joking?" the Lieutenant asked.

"Did my old man know you were there?" Santiago asks.

"I don't like to joke," Bermúdez said. "I always speak seriously."

The jeep was going through a valley, the air smelled of shellfish and in the distance bare, sandy hills could be seen. The sergeant was chewing on a cigar as he drove and the Lieutenant had his cap pulled down to his ears: come on, they'd have a couple of beers, black boy. They'd had a friendly conversation, yessir, he needs me, Ambrosio had thought, and, naturally, it had to do with Rosa. He'd got hold of a pickup truck, a farmhouse, and he'd convinced his friend the Uplander. And he wanted Ambrosio to help him too, in case there was trouble. What trouble could there be, tell me? Did the girl have a father and brothers maybe? No, just Túmula, trash. He enchanted to help him, except that. He wasn't afraid of Túmula, Don Cayo, or of the people in the settlement, but what about your papa, Don Cayo? Because if the Vulture found out Don Cayo would only get his whipping, but what about him? He wasn't going to find out, boy, he was going to Lima for three days and when he returned Rosa would be back at the settlement. Ambrosio had swallowed the story, yessir, he was tricked into helping him. Because it was one thing to kidnap a girl for one night, do your thing and turn her loose, and something else, yessir, to marry her, right? That devil of a Don Cayo had made fools out of him and the Uplander, yessir. All of them, except Rosa and except Túmula. In Chincha they said that the one who came off best was the milk woman's daughter, who went from delivering milk on a donkey to being a lady and the Vulture's daughter-in-law. Everybody else lost: Don Cayo, his parents, even Túmula, because she lost her daughter. Or maybe Rosa was a sharp chippy. Who would have said so, yessir, worth so little, and the little toad won the lottery and more. What did Ambrosio have to do, sir? Go to the square at nine o'clock, and he'd gone and waited and they picked him up, they drove around and when the people went to bed, they parked the truck by the house of Don Mauro Cruz, the deaf man. Don Cayo was to meet the girl there at ten o'clock. Of course she came, why shouldn't she come. She appeared, Don Cayo went ahead and they stayed behind in the truck. He must have told her something or she must have guessed something, the fact is that all of a sudden Túmula's daughter started to run and Don Cayo hollered catch her. So Ambrosio ran, caught her and threw her over his shoulder and brought her and sat her in the truck. That's when he caught Rosa's tricks, yessir, that's when you could see her bringing them out. Not a shout, not a moan, just running around, little scratches, little punches. The easiest would have been to start hollering, people would have come out, half the settlement would have been on top of them, yessir, right? Who says she was scared to death, who says she'd lost her voice? She kicked and scratched while he carried her and in the truck she pretended to be crying because her face was covered, but Ambrosio didn't hear her crying. The Uplander pushed the gas to the floor, the truck flew out of the side street. They got to the farm and Don Cayo got out and Rosa, with no need to carry her, she went right into the house, yessir, you see? Ambrosio went to sleep thinking about what Rosa would look like the next day, and whether she'd tell Túmula and Túmula would tell his black mama and his black mama would give it to him. Nobody had any notion of what was going to happen, nosiree. Because Rosa didn't come back the next day, Don Cayo either, or the day after, or the one after that. In the settlement Túmula was all tears, and in Chincha Doña Catalina was all tears, and Ambrosio didn't know which way to turn. On the third day the Vulture came back and notified the police and Túmula had notified them too. You can imagine the gossip, yessir. If the Uplander and Ambrosio ran into each other on the street they didn't say anything, he must have been jumpy too. They only showed up the following week, yessir. He didn't have to do it, nobody had stuck a pistol in his chest saying the church or the grave. He'd looked up the priest of his own free will. They say they were seen getting off a bus on the Plaza de Armas, that he was holding Rosa by the arm, that they were seen going into the Vulture's house as if they were coming back from a walk. They must have appeared there all of a sudden, together, just imagine, Don Cayo must have taken out the certificate and said we got married, can you imagine the face the Vulture must have put on, yessir, what the devil is this all about?

"Are they hunting down vermin over there, Lieutenant?" Bermúdez

47

pointed to the university campus with an insipid smile. "What's going on at San Marcos?"

Military barriers closed off the four corners of the square and there were patrols of helmeted soldiers, assault guards and mounted police. Down with Dictatorship, said some placards stuck to the walls of San Marcos, Only Aprismo Will Save Peru. The main door of the university was closed and mourning drapes fluttered on the balconies, and on the rooftops small heads watched the movements of the soldiers and police. The walls of the university courtyard breathed with a sound that grew and shrank between bursts of applause.

"A few Apristas have been holed up inside there since October twenty-seventh." The Lieutenant waved to the officer in charge of the roadblock on the Avenida Abancay. "The 'buffalo squad' hoodlums won't learn their lesson."

"Why don't they shoot them?" Bermúdez asked. "Is this how the army has started its cleanup?"

A police lieutenant came over to the jeep, saluted, examined the pass the Lieutenant handed him.

"How are those subversives getting along?" the Lieutenant asked, pointing to San Marcos.

"Over there raising hob," the police lieutenant said. "Sometimes they throw their little stones. Go ahead, Lieutenant."

The policemen moved the sawhorses out of the way and the jeep went through the University Square. On the waving drapes there were white pieces of cardboard, In Mourning for Freedom, and skulls and cross-bones drawn in black paint.

"I'd shoot them, but Colonel Espina wants to starve them out," the Lieutenant said.

"How are things going in the provinces?" Bermúdez asked. "I imagine there's trouble in the North. The Apristas are strong there."

"All peaceful, that business about the APRA controlling Peru is a myth," the Lieutenant said. "You saw how their leaders ran for asylum in foreign embassies. You've never seen a more peaceful revolution, Mr. Bermúdez. And the San Marcos affair could be settled in one minute if the higher-ups wanted to."

There was no military movement on the downtown streets. Only on

48

the Plaza Italia did helmeted soldiers appear again. Bermúdez got out of the jeep, stretched, waited for the Lieutenant, looking at everything with ennui.

"Have you ever been in the Ministry?" the Lieutenant tried to cheer him up. "It's an old building, but the offices are quite elegant. The Colonel's has paintings and everything."

They went in and two minutes hadn't passed when the door opened as if there had been an earthquake inside and Don Cayo and Rosa came tumbling out with the Vulture behind, cursing a stream and charging like a bull, a sight to see, they say, yessir. He wasn't mad at Túmula's daughter, he didn't seem to have hit her, just his son. He knocked him down with a punch, lifted him up with a kick, and just like that all the way to the Plaza de Armas. There they held him back because otherwise he would have killed him. He wouldn't accept his getting married that way, snotnose that he was, and especially to the one he did. He never did accept it, of course, and he never saw Don Cayo again or gave him a penny. Don Cayo had to earn his own keep for himself and for Rosa. The one the Vulture said was going to be a future big brain didn't even finish high school. If instead of a priest they'd only been married by a justice of the peace, the Vulture would have fixed it up overnight, but how can you make a deal with God, sir? Doña Catalina being the church biddy she was too. They probably had a consultation, the priest must have told them there's nothing you can do, religion is religion and till death do them part. So there was nothing left for the Vulture except despair. They say he gave a beating to the priest who married them, that afterward he was refused absolution and as a penance they made him pay for one of the steeples of the new church in Chincha. So even religion got its slice of meat from the whole business, yessir. The Vulture never saw the couple again. It seems that when he sensed he was dying he asked have I got any grandchildren? Maybe if he'd had any he would have forgiven Don Cayo, but Rosa hadn't only turned into a horror, yessir, to top it off she never grew full. They say that just so his son wouldn't inherit anything, the Vulture began to get rid of what he had in drinking bouts and charity and that if death hadn't caught him all of a sudden he would have given away the house he had behind the church too. He didn't have time, nosiree. Why did he stay with the Indian for so many

49

years? That was what everyone said to the Vulture: the love will wear off and he'll send her back to Túmula and you'll have your son again. But he didn't do it, I wonder why. Not because of religion, I don't think so, Don Cayo never went to church. To make his father mad? Because he hated the Vulture, you say? To cheat him so that he could see all the hopes he'd put in him go up in smoke? Fucking himself up to kill his father with disappointment? You think that's why? Making him suffer no matter what it cost, even becoming trash himself? Well, I don't know, no sir, if you think so it must be because of that. Don't look that way, we were having a good talk. Don't you feel good? You're not talking about the Vulture and Don Cayo but about yourself and young Santiago, yessir, right? All right, I'll keep quiet, yes, I can see that you're not talking to me. I didn't say anything, no sir, don't act like that, no sir.

"What's Pucallpa like?" Santiago asks.

"A small town that's not worth anything," Ambrosio says. "Haven't you ever been there, son?"

"I've spent my whole life dreaming about traveling and I only got fifty miles away, just once," Santiago says. "At least you've traveled a little."

"It brought me bad luck, son," Ambrosio says. "Pucallpa only brought me trouble."

"It means things have gone bad for you," Colonel Espina said. "Worse than for the rest of our class. You haven't got a penny and you're still a country boy."

"I didn't have time to follow in the footsteps of the rest of the class," Bermúdez said calmly, looking at Espina without arrogance, without modesty. "But you, of course, you've done better than all the rest of us put together."

"The best student, the most intelligent, the one who studied the hardest," Espina said. "Bermúdez will be President and Espina his Minister, old Dapple Gray used to say. Remember?"

"Even then you wanted to be a minister, really," Bermúdez said with a sour little smile. "There you are, now you are one. You must be happy, right?"

"I didn't ask for it and I didn't look for it." Colonel Espina opened his arms in resignation. "They laid it on me and I accepted it as a duty."

"In Chincha they said you were an Aprista officer, that you'd gone to a cocktail party given by Haya de la Torre," Bermúdez went on, smiling without conviction. "And now, just think, hunting down Apristas like vermin. That's what the little lieutenant you sent to get me said. And, by the way, it's time you told me why so much honor for me."

The office door opened, a man with a circumspect face came in bowing, with some papers in his hand, could he come in, Mr. Secretary? but then the Colonel Dr. Alcibíades stopped him with a gesture, no one was to disturb them. The man bowed again, very well, Mr. Secretary, and he left.

"Mr. Secretary." Bermúdez cleared his throat, without nostalgia, looking around lethargically. "I can't believe it. Like sitting here. Like the fact that we're already in our forties."

Colonel Espina smiled at him affectionately, he'd lost a lot of hair but the tufts he still had showed no gray and his copper-colored face was still vigorous; he ran his eyes slowly over the tanned and indolent face of Bermúdez, the old-before-its-time, ascetic body sunken in the broad red velvet chair.

"You fucked yourself up with that crazy marriage," he said with a sweetish and paternal voice. "It was the great mistake of your life, Cayo. I warned you, remember."

"Did you send for me to talk about my marriage?" he asked without anger, without drive, the same mediocre little voice as always. "One more word and I'm leaving."

"You're still the same. Still grumpy." Espina laughed. "How's Rosa? I know you haven't had any children."

"If you don't mind, let's get to the point," Bermúdez said; a shadow of fatigue clouded his eyes, his mouth was tight with impatience. Roofs, cornices, aerial trash piles were outlined against fat clouds through the windows behind Espina.

"Even though we haven't seen much of each other, you've always been my best friend." The Colonel was almost sad. "When we were kids I thought a lot of you, Cayo. More than you did of me. I admired you, I was even jealous of you."

Bermúdez was imperturbably scrutinizing the Colonel. The cigarette he had in his hand had burned down, the ash fell on the rug, the curls of smoke broke against his face like waves against brown rocks.

"When I was a minister under Bustamante, the whole class looked me up, all except you," Espina said. "Why? You were in bad shape, we'd been like brothers. I could have helped you."

"Did they come like dogs to lick your hands, to ask you for recommendations, to propose business deals to you?" Bermúdez asked. "Since I didn't come, you must have said that fellow must be rich or maybe he's dead."

"I knew that you were alive but half dead from hunger," Espina said. "Don't interrupt, let me speak."

"It's just that you're still so slow," Bermúdez said. "A person has to use a corkscrew to get the words out of you, just the way you were at José Pardo."

"I want to help you," Espina murmured. "Tell me what I can do for you."

"Just give me transportation back to Chincha," Bermúdez whispered. "The jeep, a bus ticket, anything. Because of this trip to Lima I may have lost out on an interesting piece of business."

"You're happy with your lot, you don't mind growing old as a penniless country boy," Espina said. "You're not ambitious anymore, Cayo."

"But I'm still proud," Bermúdez said dryly. "I don't like to take favors. Is that all you wanted to tell me?"

The Colonel was watching him, as if measuring him or guessing what he was thinking, and the cordial little smile that had been floating on his lips vanished. He clasped his hands with their polished nails and leaned forward.

"Do you want to get down to cases, Cayo?" he asked with sudden energy.

"It's about time." Bermúdez put out his cigarette in the ashtray. "You were getting me tired with that great show of affection."

"Odría needs people he can trust." The Colonel spaced his syllables, as if his safety and confidence were suddenly threatened. "Everybody here is with us and nobody is with us. *La Prensa* and the Agrarian Society only want us to abolish controls on exchange and to protect free enterprise."

"Since you're going to do what they want, there's no problem," Bermúdez said. "Right?"

"*El Comercio* calls Odría the Savior of the Nation just because it hates APRA," Colonel Espina said. "They only want us to keep the Apristas in the clink."

"That's an accomplished fact," Bermúdez said. "There's no problem there either, right?"

"And International, Cerro and the other companies only want a strong government that will keep the unions quiet for them," Espina went on without listening to him. "Each one pulling in his own direction, see?"

"The exporters, the anti-Apristas, the gringos and the army too," Bermúdez said. "Money and power. I don't see that Odría has any reason to complain. What more could he ask for?"

"The President knows the mentality of those sons of bitches," Colonel Espina said. "Today they support you, tomorrow they stick a knife in your back."

"The way you people stuck it in Bustamante's back." Bermúdez smiled, but the Colonel didn't laugh. "Well, as long as you keep them happy, they'll support the regime. Then they'll get another general and throw you people out. Hasn't it always been that way in Peru?"

"This time it's not going to be that way," Colonel Espina said. "We're going to keep our backs covered."

"That sounds fine to me," Bermúdez said, stifling a yawn, "but what the hell have I got to do with all this?"

"I talked to the President about you." Colonel Espina studied the effect of his words, but Bermúdez hadn't changed his expression; his elbow on the arm of the chair, his face resting on his open palm, he listened motionless. "We were going over names for Director of Security and yours came to mind and I let it out. Did I do something stupid?"

He was silent, a look of annoyance or fatigue or doubt or regret, he twisted his mouth and narrowed his eyes. He remained for a few seconds with an absent look and then he sought Bermúdez' face: there it was, just as before, absolutely quiet, waiting.

"An obscure position but important for the security of the regime," the Colonel added. "Did I do something stupid? You need someone there who's like your other self, they warned me, your right arm. And your name came to mind and I let it out. Without thinking. You can see, I'm talking frankly to you. Did I do something stupid?"

Bermúdez had taken out another cigarette, lighted it. He took a drag, tightening his mouth a little, biting the lower lip. He looked at the end of it, the smoke, the window, the piles of garbage on the Lima rooftops.

"I know that if you want it, you're my man," Colonel Espina said.

"I can see that you have confidence in your old classmate," Bermúdez finally said, in such a low voice that the Colonel leaned forward. "Having chosen this frustrated and inexperienced hick to be your right arm, it's a great honor, Uplander."

"Cut your sarcasm." Espina rapped on the desk. "Tell me whether you accept or not."

"Something like that can't be decided so fast," Bermúdez said. "Give me a few days to mull it over."

"I won't even give you a half hour, you're going to answer me right now," Espina said. "The President expects me at the Palace at six. If you accept you're coming with me so I can introduce you. If not, you can go back to Chincha."

"The functions of Director of Security I can imagine," Bermúdez said. "On the other hand, I have no idea what it pays."

"A base salary and some living expenses," Colonel Espina said. "Around five or six thousand soles, I would calculate. I know it isn't very much."

"It's enough to live modestly." Bermúdez barely smiled. "Since I'm a modest man, it'll do me."

"Not another word, then," Colonel Espina said. "But you still haven't answered me. Did I do something stupid?"

"Only time will tell, Uplander." Bermúdez gave a half-smile again.

Whether the Uplander ever recognized Ambrosio? When Ambrosio was Don Cayo's chauffeur he got into the car a thousand times, yessir, he'd taken him to his house a thousand times. Maybe he recognized him, but the fact is that he never showed it, no sir. Since he was a minister then, he was probably ashamed that he'd known Ambrosio when he was a nobody, he wouldn't have found it amusing that Ambrosio knew he'd been mixed up in the kidnapping of Túmula's daughter. He'd probably erased him from his head so that black face wouldn't bring back bad memories, no sir. The times they saw each other he treated Ambrosio

54

like a chauffeur seen for the first time. Good morning, good afternoon, and the Uplander just the same. Now he was going to say something, yessir. It's true that Rosa turned into a fat Indian covered with moles, but underneath it all her story made you feel sorry for her, yessir, right? After all, she was his wife, right? And he left her in Chincha and she couldn't enjoy anything when Don Cayo became important. What became of her during all those years? When Don Cayo came to Lima she stayed there in the little yellow house, she's probably still there turning to bone. But he didn't abandon her the way he did Señora Hortensia, without a penny. He sent her her pension, many times he told Ambrosio, remind me that I have to send Rosa some money, black man. What did she do all those years? Who can say. Probably the same life she always had, a life without friends or relatives. Because from the day she was married she never saw anyone from the settlement again, not even Túmula. Don Cayo must have forbidden it, he must have. And Túmula went on cursing her daughter because she wouldn't receive her in her house. But that wasn't why, no sir; she didn't get into Chincha society, never, who wanted to mix with the milk woman's daughter, even if she was Don Cayo's wife and wore shoes and washed her face every day. They'd all seen her driving the donkey and pouring out gourds of milk. And besides, knowing that the Vulture didn't recognize her as his daughter-in-law. There was nothing left for her to do but shut herself up in a little room that Don Cayo took behind the San José Hospital and live the life of a nun. She almost never went out, from shame, because they pointed at her in the street, or from fear of the Vulture, maybe. Then it must have become a habit. Ambrosio had seen her sometimes, in the market or taking out a washbasin and scrubbing clothes, kneeling on the sidewalk. So what good was all her spark, yessir, all the tricks to catch the white boy. She might have got a better name and joined a better class, but she was left without any friends and even without a mother. Don Cayo, you say? Yes, he had friends. On Saturdays he could be seen having his little old beers in the Cielito Lindo or tossing coins at the toad in the Jardín el Paraíso, and in the whorehouse and they said he always had two of them in the room. He almost never went out with Rosa, no sir, he even went to the movies by himself. What kind of work did Don Cayo do? At the Cruz warehouse, in a bank, in a notary's office, then

55

he sold tractors to the ranchers. He spent about a year in the little room there, when he was better off he moved to the southern part of town, in those days Ambrosio was already an interprovince driver and didn't get to Chincha very often, and one of those times he got to town they told him that the Vulture had died and that Don Cayo and Rosa had gone to live with the church biddy. Doña Catalina died during Bustamante's government, yessir. When Don Cayo's luck changed, with Odría, in Chincha they said now Rosa will get a new house and have servants. None of that, no sir. Visitors rained down on Rosa then. In *La Voz de Chincha* they printed pictures of Don Cayo, calling him a Distinguished Son of Chincha, and who didn't rush to Rosa to ask her for some little job for my husband, a little scholarship for my son, and my brother to be named schoolteacher here, subprefect there. And the families of Apristas and Aprista-lovers to cry in front of her for her to get Don Cayo to let my nephew out or let my uncle come back into the country. That was where Túmula's daughter got her revenge, yessir, that was where the ones who had snubbed her got what was coming to them. They say that she would receive them at the door and give them all the same idiot face. Her little boy was in jail? Oh, that's too bad. A position for her stepson? He should go to Lima and talk to her husband and so long. But Ambrosio only knew all that from hearsay, yessir, can't you see he too was already in Lima then? Who had convinced him to go look up Don Cayo? His black mama, Ambrosio didn't want to, he said they say everyone from Chincha who goes to ask him for something gets turned away. But he didn't turn him away, no sir, he helped him and Ambrosio was grateful to him for it. Yes, he hated the people in Chincha, who knows why, you can see that he didn't do anything for Chincha, he didn't even have a single school built in his town. When time passed and people began to say bad things about Odría and the exiled Apristas came back to Chincha, they say that the subprefect put a policeman at the yellow house to protect Rosa, can't you see how much Don Cayo was hated? Yessir. Pure foolishness, ever since he was in the government they didn't live together and they didn't see each other, everybody knew that if they killed Rosa that wouldn't have hurt Don Cayo, it would have been more like doing him a favor. Because he not only didn't love her, no sir, he even must have hated her, for having got so ugly, don't you think?

"You saw how well he received you," Colonel Espina said. "You've seen what kind of a man the General is."

"I've got to get my head in order," Bermúdez muttered. "It's like a potful of crickets."

"Go get some rest," Espina said. "Tomorrow I'll introduce you to the people in the Ministry and they will bring you up to date on things. But tell me if you're happy at least."

"I don't know if I'm happy," Bermúdez said. "It's more like being drunk."

"All right, I know that's your way of thanking me." Espina laughed.

"I came to Lima with just this satchel," Bermúdez said. "I thought it was a matter of a few hours."

"Do you need some money?" Espina asked. "Yes, sure, I'll lend you some now and tomorrow we'll get them to give you an advance in the payroll department."

"What bad luck happened to you in Pucallpa?" Santiago asks.

"I'll find a small hotel in the neighborhood," Bermúdez said. "I'll come by early tomorrow."

"For me, for me?" Don Fermín asked. "Or did you do it for yourself, in order to have me in your hands, you poor devil?"

"Someone who thought he was my friend sent me there," Ambrosio says. "Get yourself over there, boy. All a story, son, the streets are paved with gold. The biggest roasting of the century. Oh, if I only told you."

Espina took him to the office door and shook his hand. Bermúdez left with the satchel in one hand, his hat in the other. He had a distracted and serious look, as if he were looking inside. He didn't answer the bow or the salute of the officer at the door of the Ministry. Was it quitting time in all the offices? The streets were full of people and noise. He mingled with the crowd, followed the current, he came, went, returned along narrow and jammed sidewalks, dragged along by a kind of whirlwind or spell, stopping at times at a corner or a doorway or a lamppost to light a cigarette. In a café on the Jirón Azángaro he ordered tea with lemon, which he slowly savored, and when he got up he left a tip that was twice the bill. In a bookstore hiding in an alley off the Jirón de la Unión, he thumbed through some novels with flashy covers and cramped and tiny letters, looking without seeing, until *The Mysteries of Lesbos* caught his eyes for a second. He bought it and left. He wandered awhile longer through the downtown streets, the satchel under his arm, his hat crumpled in his hand, smoking ceaselessly. It was already getting dark and the streets were deserted when he went into the Hotel Maury and asked for a room. They gave him a card and he paused with the pen for a few seconds at where it said profession, he finally wrote civil servant. The room was on the third floor, the window opened onto an inner courtyard. He got into the bathtub and went to bed in his underwear. He thumbed through *The Mysteries of Lesbos,* letting his eyes run blindly over the tight little black figures. Then he turned out the light. But he couldn't fall asleep until many hours later. Awake, he lay on his back, his body motionless, the cigarette burning between his fingers, breathing with anxiety, his eyes staring at the dark shadows above him.

4

"So in Pucallpa and that Hilario Morales' fault, so you know when and why you fucked yourself up," Santiago says. "I'd give anything to know at just what moment I fucked myself up."

Would she remember, would she bring the book? Summer was ending, it seemed like five o'clock and it wasn't even two yet, and Santiago thinks: she brought the book, she remembered. He felt euphoric going into the dusty entranceway with flagstones and chipped columns, impatient, he should get in, she should get in, optimistic, and you got in, he thinks, and she got in: ah, Zavalita, how happy you felt.

"You've got your health, you're young, you've got a wife," Ambrosio says. "How could you have fucked yourself up, son?"

Alone or in groups, their faces buried in their notes, how many of these would go in? where was Aída? the candidates walked around the court-yard with the steps of a processional, they reviewed their notes sitting on the splintery benches, leaning against the dirty walls they asked each other questions in low voices. Half-breed boys and girls, proper people didn't come here. He thinks: you were right, mama.

"Before I left home, before I got into San Marcos, I was pure," Santiago says.

He recognized a few faces from the written exam, he exchanged smiles and hellos, but Aída didn't appear, and he went to stand by the entrance. He listened to a group reviewing geography, he listened to a boy, motion-

59

less, his eyes lowered, reciting the names of the viceroys of Peru as if he were praying.

"The kind of pure tobacco cigars that the moneybags smoke at bullfights?" Ambrosio laughs.

He saw her come in: the same straight, brick-colored dress, the same low-heeled shoes from the written exam. She came along with her look of a studious schoolgirl in uniform through the crowded entranceway, she turned her overgrown child's face from one side to the other, no glow, no grace, no makeup, looking for something, someone with her hard adult eyes. Her lips were tight, her masculine mouth open, and he saw her smile: the hard face grew softer, lighted up. He saw her come toward him: hello, Aída.

"I said to hell with money and I thought I was capable of great things," Santiago says. "Pure in that sense."

"Melchorita the holy woman lived on Grocio Prado, she gave away everything she had and spent her time praying," Ambrosio says. "Did you want to be a saint like her when you were a boy?"

"I brought you *Out of the Night*," Santiago said. "I hope you like it."

"You've told me so much about it that I'm dying to read it," Aída said. "Here's that Frenchman's novel about the Chinese Revolution."

"Jirón Puno, Calle de Padre Jerónimo?" Ambrosio asks. "Do they give away money in that place to broken-down black men like yours truly?"

"That's where we took the entrance exams the year I entered San Marcos," Santiago says. "I'd been in love with girls from Miraflores, but on Padre Jerónimo I really fell in love for the first time."

"It isn't much like a novel, it reads more like a history book," Aída said.

"Oho," Ambrosio says. "And did she fall in love with you?"

"Even though this one is an autobiography, it reads like a novel," Santiago said. "Wait till you get to the chapter called 'The Night of the Long Knives,' about a revolution in Germany. Fantastic, you'll see."

"About a revolution?" Aída thumbed through the book, her eyes and voice full of mistrust now. "But is this Valtin a Communist or an antiCommunist?"

"I don't know whether she fell in love with me or not, I don't even

60

know whether she knew I was in love with her," Santiago says. "Sometimes I think she was, sometimes I think she wasn't."

"You didn't know, she didn't know, what a mess, do you think that things like that can be ignored, son?" Ambrosio asks. "Who was the girl?"

"I warn you that if he's anti, I'll give it back to you," and Aída's soft, timid voice grew challenging. "Because I'm a Communist."

"You're a Communist?" Santiago looked at her in astonishment. "Are you really a Communist?"

You still weren't, he thinks, you wanted to be a Communist. He felt his heart beating strongly and he was amazed: in San Marcos you didn't study anything, Skinny, they just played politics, it was a nest of Apristas and Communists, all the grumblers in Peru gather together there. He thinks: poor papa. You hadn't even entered San Marcos, Zavalita, and look what you'd found.

"Actually I am and I'm not," Aída confessed. "Because where can you find any Communists around here?"

How could she be a Communist without even knowing whether a Communist Party existed in Peru? Odría had probably put them all in jail, had probably deported or murdered them. But if she passed her orals and got into San Marcos, Aída would find out in the university, she would get in contact with those who were left and study Marxism and join the Party. She looked at me with a challenge, he thinks, come on, argue with me, her voice was quite soft and her eyes insolent, tell me that they're atheists, burning, come on, deny what I say, intelligent, and you, he thinks, listened to her, startled and surprised: all that existed, Zavalita. He thinks: did I fall in love then and there?

"A girl in my class at San Marcos," Santiago says. "She talked politics, she believed in the revolution."

"Oh, Lord, you didn't fall in love with an Aprista, did you, son?" Ambrosio asks.

"The Apristas didn't believe in the revolution anymore," Santiago says. "She was a Communist."

"The devil you say," Ambrosio says. "The hell you say."

New candidates were arriving on Padre Jerónimo, coming in the entranceway, the courtyard, running to the lists tacked up on a bulletin

61

board, eagerly checking their grades. A busy murmur floated about the place.

"You've been looking at me as if I were some kind of ogre," Aída said.

"What a thing to think, I respect all ideas, and besides, you can believe it or not, I've got . . ." Santiago fell silent, searched for words, stammered, "advanced ideas too."

"Well, I'm happy for you," Aída said. "Are we going to have the orals today? With so much waiting I'm terribly confused, I can't remember anything I've studied."

"We can review a little, if you want," Santiago said. "What are you most scared of ?"

"World history," Aída said. "Yes, let's ask each other questions. But while we're walking. I can study better that way than sitting down, what about you?"

They went through the entranceway with wine-colored floor tiles and classrooms along the sides, where did she live? he wondered, there was a small courtyard with fewer people in back. He closed his eyes, he could see the narrow little house, clean, with austere furniture, and he could see the streets around it, and the faces—strong, dignified, serious, sober? —of the men who came along the sidewalks in overalls and gray jackets, and he could hear their conversations—all for one and one for all, spare, clandestine?—and he thought workers, and he thought Communists and he decided I'm not a Bustamantist, I'm not an Aprista, I'm a Communist. But what was the difference? He couldn't ask her, she'll think I'm an idiot, he'd have to worm it out of her. She must have spent the whole summer like that, her fierce little eyes fastened on the questions, pacing back and forth in a tiny little room. There probably wasn't much light, in order to take notes she probably sat at a little table lighted by a lamp with no shade or by candles, she probably moved her lips slowly, closing her eyes, she would get up and, as she walked, repeat names, dates, nocturnal and dedicated, was her father a worker, her mother a maid? He thinks: poor Zavalita. They walked very slowly, the dynasties of the pharaohs, asking each other questions in a low voice, Babylonia and Nineveh, could she have heard Communism talked about in her home? the causes of World War I, what would she think when she found out that his old man was an Odríist? the Battle of the Marne, she probably

62

wouldn't want to meet you anymore, Zavalita: I hate you, papa. We asked each other questions but we didn't ask each other anything, he thinks. He thinks: we were getting to be friends. Could she have studied at a national high school? Yes, in a central school, what about him? at Santa María, ah, a school for rich boys. There were all kinds, it was an awful school, it wasn't his fault if his folks had sent him there, he'd rather have gone to Guadalupe and Aída began to laugh: don't blush, she wasn't prejudiced, what happened at Verdun. He thinks: we expected great things at the university. They were in the Party, they went to the press together, they hid in a union hall together, they put them in jail together and they exiled them together: it was a battle, not a treaty, silly boy, and he of course, how foolish, and now she who was Cromwell. We expected great things of ourselves he thinks.

"When you got into San Marcos and they shaved your head, Missy Teté and young Sparky hollered pumpkin head at you," Ambrosio says. "Your papa was so happy that you'd passed the exams, son."

She talked about books and she wore skirts, she knew about politics and she wasn't a man, the Mascot, the Chick, the Squirrel all faded away, Zavalita, the pretty little idiots from Miraflores melted away, disappeared. Discovering that one of them at least was good for something else, he thinks. Not just to be climbed on top of, not just to make him masturbate thinking about them, not just to fall in love with. He thinks: for something else. She was going into Law and Education too, you were going into Law and Letters.

"Are you supposed to be a vamp, a clown, or what?" Santiago asked. "Where are you going all prettied up and with all that makeup on?"

"What's your major in Letters going to be?" Aída asked. "Philosophy?"

"Wherever I feel like and what business is it of yours?" Teté asked. "Who said anything to you and what right have you got to talk to me?"

"Literature, I think," Santiago said. "But I'm still not sure."

"Everybody who goes into Literature wants to be a poet," Aída said. "You too?"

"Stop your fighting," Señora Zoila said. "You're like a cat and a dog, that's enough."

"I had a notebook of poems hidden away," Santiago says. "No one was

63

to see it, no one was to know about it. You see? I was a pure boy."

"Don't blush because I asked you if you wanted to be a poet." Aída laughed. "Don't be so bourgeois."

"They drove you crazy too by calling you Superbrain," Ambrosio says. "All the fights you people had, child."

"You can go change that dress and wash your face," Santiago said. "You're not going out, Teté."

"And what's wrong with Teté's going to the movies?" Señora Zoila asked. "Since when have you been so strict with your sister here, you, the liberal, the priest-eater?"

"She's not going to the movies, she's going dancing at the Sunset with that damned Pepe Yáñez," Santiago said. "I caught her making her plans by phone this morning."

"To the Sunset with Pepe Yáñez?" Sparky asked. "With that half-breed?"

"It's not that I want to be a poet, just that I like literature," Santiago said.

"Are you out of your mind, Teté?" Don Fermín asked. "Is all this true, Teté?"

"All lies, lies." Teté trembled and singed Santiago with her eyes. "Damn you, you imbecile, I hate you, go drop dead."

"So do I," Aída said. "In Education I'm going to take Literature and Spanish."

"Do you think you can fool your parents like that, you little devil?" Señora Zoila said. "And what do you mean by telling your brother to drop dead? Have you gone crazy?"

"You're not old enough for nightclubs, child," Don Fermín said. "You won't be going out tonight, tomorrow, or Sunday."

"I'm going to take Pepe Yáñez apart," Sparky said. "I'll kill him, papa."

Teté was shouting and weeping now, she'd spilled her cup of tea, why don't you drop dead, and Señora Zoila you're acting crazy, crazy, such a great big man and such a great big coward, and Señora Zoila you're staining the tablecloth, instead of gossiping like a woman go write your fairy poetry. She got up from the table and left the dining room still shouting your fairy gossip poetry and go drop dead, damn you. They heard her go up the stairs, slam her door. Santiago stirred the spoon in the empty cup as if he had just put some sugar in it.

"Is it true what Teté says?" Don Fermín smiled. "Do you write poetry, Skinny?"

"He keeps it hidden in a little notebook behind the encyclopedia, Teté and I have read it all," Sparky said. "Love poetry, and about the Incas too. Don't be ashamed, Superbrain. Look at his expression, papa."

"You're barely literate, so it must have been hard for you to have read anything," Santiago said.

"You're not the only person in the world who knows how to read," Señora Zoila said. "Don't be so stuck-up."

"Go write your fairy poetry, Superbrain," Sparky said.

"What have the pair of you learned, why did we send you to the best school in Lima?" Señora Zoila sighed. "You insult each other like truck-drivers right in front of us."

"Why didn't you tell me you were writing poetry?" Don Fermín asked. "You have to show me some, Skinny."

"Sparky and Teté's lies," Santiago babbled. "Don't pay any attention to them, papa."

There was the examining board, there were three of them, a fearful silence had come over the place. Boys and girls watched the three men cross through the entranceway led by a beadle, watched them disappear into a classroom. Let me get in, let her get in. The buzzing started up again, thicker and louder than before. Aída and Santiago went back to the rear courtyard.

"You're going to pass with high marks," Santiago said. "You know all the answers right down to the last comma."

"Don't you believe it, there's a lot I just barely know," Aída said. "You're the one who's going to get in."

"I spent all summer cramming," Santiago said. "If they flunk me, I'll blow my brains out."

"And I'm against suicide," Aída said. "Killing yourself is a sign of cowardice."

"Priests' tales," Santiago said. "It takes a lot of courage to kill your-self."

"I don't care about priests," Aída said, and her little eyes think: come

65

on, come on, I dare you. "I don't believe in God, I'm an atheist."

"I'm an atheist too," Santiago said immediately. "Naturally."

They started walking again, the questions, sometimes they became distracted, they forgot about the questions and they began to chat, to argue: they agreed, disagreed, joked, time was flying and suddenly Zavala, Santiago! Hurry up, Aída smiled at him, and hoped he got an easy question. He passed between two rows of candidates, went into the examination room, and you can't remember anything else, Zavalita, what question you got or the examiners' faces or what you answered: just that you were happy when you came out.

"You remember the girl you liked and the rest is all erased," Ambrosio says. "That's natural, son."

You liked everything about the day, he thinks. The place that was falling apart from old age, the shoe-polish, earthen, or malarial faces of the candidates, the atmosphere that bubbled with apprehension, the things that Aída was saying. How did you feel, Zavalita? He thinks: like on the day I had my first communion.

"You came because it was Santiago making it," Teté pouted. "You didn't come to mine, I don't love you anymore."

"Come here, give me a kiss," Don Fermín said. "I came because Skinny took first place, if you'd have gotten good marks I would have come to your first communion too. I love all three of you the same."

"You say that, but it's not true," Sparky complained. "You didn't come to my first communion either."

"With all this jealousy, Skinny's day will be ruined, stop the nonsense," Don Fermín said. "Come on, get in the car."

"To Herradura beach to have milk shakes and hot dogs, papa," Santiago said.

"To the Ferris wheel they've set up in the Campo de Marte, papa," Sparky said.

"We're going to Herradura," Don Fermín said. "Skinny's the one who made his first communion, we have to give him what he wants."

He ran out of the classroom, but before he got to Aída, did you get your grade right there, were the questions long or short? he had to hold off the candidates' attack, and Aída received him with a smile: from his face you could see he'd passed, wonderful, now he wouldn't have to blow his brains out.

"Before I picked the ball with the question, I thought, I'll sell my soul for an easy one," Santiago said. "So if the devil does exist, I'm going to go to hell. But the end justifies the means."

"Neither the soul nor the devil exists"—I challenge you, I dare you. "And if you think that the end justifies the means, then you're a Nazi."

"She had a negative answer for everything, she had an opinion about everything, she argued as if she wanted to start a fight," Santiago says.

"A pushy girl, the ones you say white to and they say black, black and they say white," Ambrosio says. "Tricks to get a man all heated up, but which have their effect."

"Of course I'll wait for you," Santiago said. "Do you want me to go over some questions with you for a little while?"

Persian history, Charlemagne, the Aztecs, Charlotte Corday, the external factors of the disappearance of the Austro-Hungarian Empire, the birth and death of Danton: hoping she would have an easy question, hoping she would pass. They went back to the first courtyard, sat down on a bench. A newsboy came in hawking the evening papers, the boy who was next to them bought *El Comercio* and a moment later said bastards, that was too much. They turned to look at him and he showed them a headline and the picture of a man with a mustache. Had they put him in jail, exiled him, or killed him, and who was the man? There was Jacobo, Zavalita: blond, thin, his blue eyes furious, his finger pointing to the picture in the newspaper, his drawling voice protesting, Peru was going from bad to worse, a strange Andean trace in that milky face, where you stuck your finger, pus came out, as González Prada had said, seen on occasion and from a distance on the streets of Miraflores.

"Another one of those?" Ambrosio asks. "Lord, San Marcos was a nest of subversives, boy."

Another exact model of one of those, he thinks, in revolt against his skin, against his class, against himself, against Peru. He thinks: is he still pure, is he happy?

"There weren't so many, Ambrosio. It was only by chance that the three of us came together that first day."

67

"You never brought those friends from San Marcos home," Ambrosio says. "On the other hand, young Popeye and his schoolmates were always having tea at your place."

Were you ashamed, Zavalita? he thinks: that Jacobo, Héctor, Solórzano didn't visit your home and the people you lived with, didn't meet your old lady and listen to your old man, that Aída didn't hear Teté's delightful idiocies? He thinks: or that your old man and old lady shouldn't know who you hung around with, that Sparky and Teté shouldn't see Martínez' toothless half-breed face? That first day you began to kill off the old folks, Popeye, Miraflores, he thinks. You were breaking away, Zavalita, entering another world: was it then, was it then that you shut it off? He thinks: breaking with what, entering what world?

"They heard me talking about Odría and they left." Jacobo pointed to a group of candidates going off and he looked at them with a curiosity that had no irony. "Are you people afraid too?"

"Afraid?" Aída straightened up immediately on the bench. "I say that Odría is a dictator and a murderer and I'll say it here, in the street, anywhere."

Pure, like the girls in *Quo Vadis,* he thinks, impatient to go down into the catacombs and come out into the arena and throw herself into the lions' claws and fangs. Jacobo was listening to her disconcertedly, she'd forgotten about the exam, a dictator who'd risen to power at bayonet point, she was raising her voice and waving her arms and Jacobo was nodding and looking at her sympathetically and he'd suppressed parties and the freedom of the press and now all worked up and had ordered the army to massacre the people of Arequipa and now bewitched and had jailed, deported and tortured so many people that no one even knew how many, and Santiago was looking at Aída and Jacobo and suddenly, he thinks, you felt tortured, exiled, betrayed, Zavalita, and he interrupted her: Odría was the worst tyrant in the history of Peru.

"Well, I don't know if he's the worst or not," Aída said, pausing for breath. "But he's one of the worst, that's for sure."

"Give him time and you'll see," Santiago insisted, with drive. "He'll be the worst."

"Except for that of the proletariat, all dictatorships are the same," Jacobo said. "Historically."

"Do you know the difference between Aprismo and Communism?" Santiago asks.

"We can't give him time to become the worst," Aída said. "We have to overthrow him before that."

"Well, there are a lot of Apristas and only a few Communists," Ambrosio says. "What other difference is there?"

"I don't think those people there went off because you were going after Odría, but because they're studying," Santiago said. "Everybody has to be a radical at San Marcos."

He looked at you as if he'd spotted a small pair of wings on your back, he thinks, San Marcos wasn't what it used to be anymore, like a good but backward child, Zavalita. You didn't know, you didn't even understand the vocabulary, you had to learn what Aprismo, what Fascism, what Communism were, and why San Marcos wasn't what it used to be: because since Odría's coup the student leaders had been persecuted and the federated centers disbanded and because the classes were full of informers enrolled as students and Santiago frivolously interrupted him: did Jacobo live in Miraflores? He seemed to have seen him around there at some time, and Jacobo blushed and unwillingly said yes and Aída started to laugh: so the two of them were from Miraflores, so the two of them were nice little boys. But Jacobo, he thinks, didn't like kidding. His blue eyes pedagogically fastened on her, his voice patient, Andean, smooth, he explained that it didn't matter where one lived, but what one thought and did, Aída that was right, but she hadn't been serious, she was joking about that nice boys business, and Santiago would read, study, learn Marxism the way he had: oh, Zavalita. The beadle shouted a last name and Jacobo stood up: they were calling him. He went slowly toward the classroom, as confident and calm as he had spoken, intelligent, right? and Santiago looked at Aída, very intelligent, and besides, he knew so much about politics and Santiago decided I'm going to know even more.

"Can it be true that there are plainclothesmen among the students?" Aída asked.

69

"If we find one in our class we'll beat him up," Santiago said.

"You're already talking like a student, what chance have you got?" Aída said. "Let's review some more."

But they'd barely started the questions and their circular walk again when Jacobo came out of the classroom, slow and thin in his frayed blue suit, and he came over to them, smiling and disappointed, the exams were a farce, Aída had nothing to worry about, the chairman of the board, a chemist, knew less about letters than you or I. You had to answer with assurance, he only flunked those who seemed unsure. He'd made a bad impression on me, he thinks, but when they called Aída and they went with her to the classroom and returned to the bench and talked alone, you liked him, Zavalita. You lost your jealousy, he thinks, I began to admire him. He'd finished high school two years ago, he didn't enter San Marcos the year before because of an attack of typhoid, he gave opinions like a person chopping with an ax. You felt dizzy, imperialism, idealism, like a cannibal seeing skyscrapers, materialism, social consciousness, confused, immoral. When he got better he used to come in the afternoon to walk around the Faculty of Letters, he went to read at the National Library, and he knew everything and had answers for everything and talked about everything, he thinks, except about himself. What school had he gone to, was his family Jewish, did he have any brothers and sisters, what street did he live on? He didn't grow impatient with the questions, he was abundant and impersonal with his explanations, Aprismo meant reform and Communism revolution. Did he ever come to esteem you and hate you, he thinks, to envy you the way you did him? He was going to study Law and History and you listened to him dazzled, Zavalita: you studied together, went to the underground press together, you conspired, worked, prepared the revolution together. What did he think of you, he thinks, what could he be thinking of you now? Aída came back to the bench with her eyes sparkling: an A, she was tired of talking to them. They congratulated her, smoked, went out onto the street. The cars were passing along Padre Jerónimo with their headlights on, and a glorious breeze cooled their faces as they went along Azángaro, talkative, excited, toward the Parque Universitario. Aída was thirsty, Jacobo hungry, why didn't they stop and have something? Santiago proposed, they good idea, he it was on him and Aída agh what a bour-

70

geois. We didn't go to that dive on Colmena to have pork rind and biscuits but to tell each other about our plans, he thinks, to become friends arguing until our voices gave out. Never again such exaltation, such generosity. He thinks: such friendship.

"At noon and at night this place is packed," Jacobo said. "The students come here after class."

"I've got to tell you something right off." Santiago clenched his fists under the table and swallowed. "My father's in the government."

There was a silence, the exchange of looks between Jacobo and Aída seemed eternal, Santiago could hear the seconds pass and bit his tongue: I hate you, papa.

"It occurred to me that you might be a relative of that Zavala," Aída said, finally, with an afflicted smile of condolence. "But what difference does that make, your father's one thing and you're another."

"The best revolutionaries come out of the bourgeoisie," Jacobo raised their morale, soberly. "They broke with their class and were converted to the ideology of the working class."

He gave some examples and, emotional, he thinks, thankful, Santiago told them about his fights over religion with the priests at school, the political arguments with his father and his friends in the neighborhood, and Jacobo started to look through the books that were on the table: *Man's Fate* was interesting but a little romantic and *Out of the Night* wasn't worth reading, the author was an antiCommunist.

"Only at the end of the book," Santiago protested, "only because the Party refused to help him rescue his wife from the Nazis."

"Worse yet," Jacobo explained. "He was a renegade and a sentimentalist."

"If a person is sentimental, can't she be a revolutionary?" Aída asked, saddened.

Jacobo reflected a few seconds and shrugged his shoulders: maybe it's possible in some cases.

"But renegades are the worst there is, look at APRA," he added. "A person is a revolutionary right down the line or he isn't at all."

"Are you a Communist?" Aída asked, as if she were asking what time is it, and Jacobo lost his calm for an instant: his cheeks flushed, he looked around, he gained time by coughing.

71

"A sympathizer," he said, cautiously. "The Party is outlawed and it's not easy to get in contact. Besides, in order to be a Communist you've got to do a lot of studying."

"I'm a sympathizer too," Aída said, enchanted. "What luck that we met."

"So am I," Santiago said. "I don't know much about Marxism, but I'd like to know more. But where, how?"

Jacobo looked at them one by one, into their eyes, slowly and deeply, as if calculating their sincerity or discretion, and he took another look around and leaned toward them: there was a secondhand bookstore, here downtown. He'd discovered it the other day, he went in to look around and he was thumbing through some books when he came across some numbers, very old, very interesting, of a magazine that he thinks was called *Cultura Soviética*. Forbidden books, forbidden magazines and Santiago could see shelves overflowing with pamphlets that weren't sold in bookstores, volumes that the police had taken out of libraries. In the shadow of walls gnawed by dampness, through cobwebs and mildew, they consulted the explosive books, argued and took notes, on nights which were as dark as the mouth of a wolf, in the light of improvised candelabras they made résumés, exchanged ideas, read, taught each other, broke with the bourgeoisie, armed themselves with the ideology of the working class.

"Aren't there any more magazines in that bookstore?" Santiago asked.

"There probably are," Jacobo said. "If you want, we can go together and see. What about tomorrow?"

"We could go to an art gallery and a museum too," Aída said.

"Yes, indeed, I haven't been to any museum in Lima so far," Jacobo said.

"Me either," said Santiago. "Let's take advantage of these days before classes start and visit them all."

"We can go to the museums in the morning and in the afternoon go through secondhand bookstores," Jacobo said. "I know a lot of them and sometimes you find some good things."

"Revolution, books, museums," Santiago says. "Do you see what it is to be pure?"

"I thought that being pure was living without fucking, son," Ambrosio says.

"And the movies too one of these afternoons to see a good picture," Aída said. "And if Santiago the bourgeois wants to treat us, let him treat us."

"I'm never going to treat you again, not even to a glass of water," Santiago said. "Where shall we go tomorrow, and at what time?"

"Well, Skinny," Don Fermín said. "Was the oral very hard, do you think you passed, Skinny?"

"Ten o'clock on the Plaza San Martín," Jacobo said. "At the express bus stop."

"I think so, papa," Santiago said. "Now you can give up your hopes that someday I'll go to the Catholic University."

"I ought to box your ears for being sassy," Don Fermín said. "So you passed, so you're a full-fledged university man. Come here, Skinny, let me give you a hug."

You didn't sleep, he thinks, I'm sure that Aída didn't sleep either, that Jacobo didn't sleep either. All the doors open, he thinks, at what moment and why did they begin to close?

"You've had your own way, you got into San Marcos," Señora Zoila said. "You must be happy, I imagine."

"Very happy, mama," Santiago said. "Especially because I won't have to associate with proper people ever again. You can't imagine how happy I am."

"If you want to become a peasant half-breed, why don't you get a job as a servant instead?" Sparky said. "Go around barefoot, don't bathe, breed lice, Superbrain."

"The important thing is that Skinny has gotten into the university," Don Fermín said. "The Catholic University would have been better, but a person who wants to study can study anywhere."

"The Catholic University isn't any better than San Marcos, papa," Santiago said. "It's a priests' school. And I don't want to learn anything from priests. I hate priests."

"And you'll go straight to hell, imbecile," Teté said. "And you let him raise his voice to you like that, papa."

73

"I'm sorry you've got those prejudices, papa," Santiago said.

"They're not prejudices, I don't care whether your classmates are white, black, or yellow," Don Fermín said. "I want you to study, not waste your time and be left without a career like Sparky."

"Superbrain raises his voice to you and you give it to me," Sparky said. "That's just fine, papa."

"Politics isn't a waste of time," Santiago said. "Or are the military the only ones who have the right to be in politics here?"

"First the priests and now the army, the two same little tunes," Sparky said. "Change the subject, Superbrain, you're like a broken record."

"How prompt you are," Aída said. "You were talking to yourself, that's amusing."

"Nobody can get along with you," Don Fermín said. "Even if we treat you with love, you always give us a kick in the pants."

"The fact is I am a little crazy," Santiago said. "Aren't you afraid to be with me?"

"All right, don't cry, get off your knees, I believe you, you did it for me," Don Fermín said. "Didn't you think that instead of helping me you could have sunk me forever? Why did God give you a head, you poor devil?"

"Don't you believe it, I love lunatics," Aída said. "I was undecided between Law and Psychiatry."

"The fact is that I let you have your own way too much and you take advantage," Don Fermín said. "Go to your room, right now, Skinny."

"When you punish me, you take away my allowance, when it's Santiago, you only send him to bed," Teté said. "What kind of a way is that, papa?"

"The fact is that nobody is happy with what he's got," Ambrosio says. "Not even you, and you've got everything. Look at my situation."

"Take his allowance away too, papa," Sparky said. "Why these preferences?"

"I'm glad you chose Law," Santiago said. "Look, there's Jacobo."

"Don't butt in when I'm talking to Skinny," Don Fermín said. "If you do, you two won't get any allowance."

74

5

THEY GAVE HER A PAIR of rubber gloves, a smock, they told her she was
a bottler. The pills began to fall and they had to put them into the bottles
and put in pieces of cotton on top. The ones who put the caps on were
called cappers, labelers the ones who put on the labels, and at the end
of the table four women gathered the bottles and arranged them in
cardboard boxes: they were called packers. The woman next to her was
named Gertrudis Lama and she was very quick with her fingers. Amalia
began at eight, stopped at twelve, came back at two and quit work at six.
Two weeks after she went to work at the laboratory her aunt moved from
Surquillo to Limoncillo, and at first Amalia went to have lunch at her
house, but so long a bus ride cost a lot and the time was very tight. One
day she got back at two-fifteen and the woman in charge are you taking
advantage because you were recommended by the owner? Bring your
lunch the way we do, Gertrudis Lama advised her, you'll save time and
money. From then on she brought a sandwich and a piece of fruit and
went to have lunch with Gertrudis by a drainage canal on the Avenida
Argentina where vendors came to offer them lemonade and ices and
fellows who worked in the area to tease them. I'm making more than
before, she thought, I don't work as much and I have a girl friend. She
missed her room a little and young Teté, but I've already forgotten about
that other devil, she was telling Gertrudis Lama, and Santiago Amalia?
and Ambrosio yes do you remember her, son?

She hadn't been at the laboratory a month when she met Trinidad. He made coarse remarks with more humor than the others, Amalia would remember his nonsense when she was alone and burst out laughing. Nice, but a little crazy, don't you think? Gertrudis told her one day, and another day the way you laugh at him, and another time it's easy to see that you're beginning to like the nut. You more likely, Amalia said, and thought am I beginning to like him? and Santiago Amalia your wife, Amalia the one who died in Pucallpa? One night she saw him waiting for her at the trolley stop. As fresh as you like he got on the streetcar, sat down beside her, sang a snatch of *"Negra Consentida"* and started with his jokes, spoiled Half-breed, she was serious on the outside and dying with laughter inside. He paid her fare and when Amalia got out he bye-bye lovey. He was quite thin, dark, crazy, straight black hair, a good lad. His eyes were shifty and when they got to know each other Amalia told him he had Chinese blood, and he you're a white half-breed, we'll make a good combination, and Ambrosio yes, boy, the very same. Another time he took the downtown bus with her and got on the bus to Limoncillo with her and also paid her fare and she all the money I'm saving. Trinidad wanted to invite her to have something to eat but Amalia no, she couldn't accept. Let's get off, love, you get off, I haven't even been introduced to you. I'll leave if we're introduced, he said and shook her hand, Trinidad López pleased to meet, and she shook his, pleased to meet you Amalia Cerda. On the following day Trinidad sat down beside her at the canal and began to tell Gertrudis what a spoiled little friend you've got, Amalia makes me lose sleep. Gertrudis picked up the thread and they became friends and later Gertrudis to Amalia pay some attention to the nut and you'll forget about Ambrosio, and Amalia I've already forgotten that one, and Gertrudis really? and Santiago were you involved with Amalia ever since she started working at the house? Amalia was shocked by the foolish things Trinidad said, but she liked his mouth and he shouldn't try anything. The first time he tried was on the bus to Limoncillo. It was packed, people were pressed up against each other, and there she noticed that he was beginning to rub. She couldn't retreat, she had to play the innocent. Trinidad looked at her seriously, brought his face close, and suddenly I love you and he kissed her. She felt hot, that someone was laughing. You're abusive, when they

76

got off she was furious, he'd shamed her in front of everybody, taking advantage. She was the woman he was looking for, Trinidad told her, I've got you in my heart. I'm not crazy enough to believe what men say, Amalia said, all you want to do is take advantage. They went toward the house, before getting there come on over to this corner for a while, and there he kissed her again, you're nice, he hugged her and his voice weakened, I love you, feel, feel the way you've got me. She held his hands back, she wouldn't let him open her blouse, lift her skirt: they'd already made love at that time, son, but things got serious later on.

Trinidad worked in a textile factory near the laboratory, and he told Amalia I was born in Pacasmayo and worked in a garage in Trujillo. But that he'd been jailed as an Aprista he only told her later, one day when they were going along the Avenida Arequipa. There was a house with gardens and trees, trenches all around, patrol cars, police, and Trinidad raised his left hand and said into Amalia's ear Víctor Raúl the Aprista people salute you, and she have you gone crazy? That's the Colombian Embassy, Trinidad told her, and that Haya de la Torre had taken asylum inside, and that Odría didn't want to let him leave the country and that's why there were so many cops. He laughed and told her: one night a friend and I went by here making the Aprista toot on the horn, and the patrol cars chased them and they were arrested. Was Trinidad an Aprista? and he to the death, and had he been in jail? and he yes, to show the confidence I have in you. He'd become an Aprista ten years ago, he told her, because in that garage in Trujillo they were all in the party, and he explained to her that Víctor Raúl Haya de la Torre was a wise man and APRA the party of the poor people and peasants of Peru. He'd been put in jail for the first time in Trujillo because the police caught him painting LONG LIVE APRA on the walls of the street. When he got out of jail they wouldn't take him back at the garage and that's why he came to Lima, and here the party found work for me at a factory in Vitarte, he told her, and that during the Bustamante government he'd been a street fighter; he went with his comrades to break up rallies of the oligarchs or the redtails and he also came out beaten up. Not because he was a coward, his physique was of no help, and she of course, you're so thin, and he but a man, the second time he was put in jail the informers had knocked out two teeth and I didn't turn anyone in even because of that. When the October third uprising in Callao came off and Bustamante outlawed APRA, the comrades in Vitarte told him to hide, but he I'm not afraid, he hadn't done anything. He kept on going to work and later, on October twenty-seventh, there was Odría's revolution and they asked him aren't you going to hide now either? and he not now either. The first week in November, coming out of the factory one afternoon, a guy came up to him, are you Trinidad López? your cousin's waiting for you in that car. He started to run because he didn't have any cousins, but they caught him. At the station house they wanted him to tell them the group's plans for terrorism, and he what plans, what group? and to tell them who put out the clandestine paper *La Tribuna* and where. That was when they knocked out the two teeth, and Amalia which ones? and he what do you mean which ones? and she but you've got all your teeth, and he they're false and you can't tell the difference. He was in jail for eight months, the station house, the penitentiary, Frontón, and when they let him out he'd lost twenty pounds. He was bumming around for three months until he got into the textile place on the Avenida Argentina. Now it was going well for him, he was already specialized. The night they took him in because of that business at the Colombian Embassy he thought I've screwed myself again, but they believed him when he said it was a drunken escapade and they turned him loose the next day. Now he had to watch out for two things, Amalia: politics, because they had him on file, and women, rattlesnakes with a fatal bite, and he had them on file. Really? Amalia asked him, and he but you appeared and I fell again, at home nobody knew that you were making it with Amalia, Santiago says, not even my brother and sister or my folks, and Trinidad trying to kiss her, and she let me go, roving hands, and Ambrosio they didn't know because we kept it quiet, son, and Trinidad I love you, come close, I want to feel you, and Santiago why quiet?

Amalia was so frightened to learn that Trinidad had been in jail and that they might arrest him again that she didn't even tell Gertrudis. But she soon discovered that Trinidad was more interested in sports than in politics, and in sports soccer and in soccer the Municipal team. He would drag her to the stadium very early in order to get a good seat, during the game he would get hoarse from shouting so much, he would make coarse remarks if they scored a goal on Skinny Suárez. Trinidad had played for the Municipal scrubs when he was working in Vitarte, and now he had got together a little team at the textile factory on the Avenida Argentina, and there was a game every Saturday afternoon. You and sports are my vice, he would tell Amalia, and she it must be true, you don't drink much and you don't seem to be a woman-chaser. In addition to soccer he liked boxing, wrestling. He would take her to Luna Park and explain to her that the good-looking fellow getting into the ring with a bullfighter's cape is the Spaniard Vicente García, and that he rooted for El Yanqui not because he was good but because at least he was a Peruvian. Amalia liked Peta, so elegant, he was wrestling and suddenly he told the referee to stop it and he combed his jungle of hair, and she hated the Bull, who won by sticking his fingers in eyes and throwing flying tackles. But hardly any women were to be seen at Luna Park, there were loud drunks and there were worse fights in the seats than in the ring. I went along with you on soccer, but that's enough of sports, she told Trinidad, take me to the movies instead. He whatever you say, love, but he always had his tricks to get back to Luna Park. He showed her the wrestling ad in *La Crónica*, started talking about locks and pinning, tonight they'll take off the Doctor's mask if the Mongol wins wouldn't that be something? I don't think so, Amalia told him, it'll be the same as it always is. But she was already sweet on him and sometimes all right, Luna Park tonight, and he happy.

One Sunday they were eating a minute steak after the wrestling matches and Amalia saw that Trinidad was looking at her in a strange way: what's wrong? Leave your aunt by herself, she was to come live with him. She pretended to be annoyed, they argued, he swore so much that he finally convinced me, Amalia told Gertrudis Lama afterward. They went to Trinidad's place, in Mirones, and that night they had the big fight. He was very loving at first, kissing and hugging her, calling her love in a dying voice, but at dawn she saw he was pale, bags under his eyes, his mouth trembling: now tell me how many have gone through here before. Amalia only one (fool, you little fool, Gertrudis Lama told her), only the chauffeur at the house where I worked, no one else had touched her, and Ambrosio: so that his mama and papa wouldn't catch them, son, do you think they would have liked it? Trinidad began to insult her and to insult himself for having respected her, and with a slap he knocked her to the floor. Someone knocked and opened the door, Amalia saw an old man who was saying Trinidad what's going on, and Trinidad insulted him too and she got dressed and ran out. That morning at the laboratory the pills fell out of her fingers and she could barely talk because of the sorrow she felt. Men have their pride, Gertrudis told her, who told you to tell him, you should have denied it, silly, denied it. But he'll forgive you, she consoled her, he'll come looking for you, and she I hate him, I wouldn't make up with him even if I were dead, and Ambrosio but later they had a fight, son, Amalia went her way and even had her love affairs there, and Santiago of course with an Aprista, and Ambrosio only much later and just by chance they'd run into each other again. That afternoon, when she went back to Limoncillo, her aunt called her bad and inconsiderate, she didn't believe she'd slept over at a girl friend's, you'll be a fallen woman and the next time you don't come home to sleep I'll throw you out. She spent a few days without any appetite and was depressed, nights awake when it never dawned, and one night when she left the laboratory she saw Trinidad at the streetcar stop. He got on with her, and Amalia didn't look at him but she felt hot listening to him speak. Stupid, she thought, you love him. He asked her to forgive him and she I'll never forgive you, especially since she had pleased him by going to his place, and he let's forget the past, love, don't be proud. In Limoncillo he tried to hug her and she pushed him away, threatening him with the police. They talked, they struggled, Amalia gave in and on the usual corner he, sighing, I got drunk every day since that night, Amalia, love had been stronger than pride, Amalia. She sneaked her things out of her aunt's, they got to Mirones at nightfall, holding hands. In the alley Amalia saw the old man who had come into the room and Trinidad introduced him to Amalia: my girl friend, Don Atanasio. That same night he wanted Amalia to quit work: was he a cripple, couldn't he earn enough for the two of them? She would cook for him, wash his clothes, and later on take care of the children. Congratulations, Engineer Carrillo said to Amalia, I'll tell Don Fermín that you're going to get married. Gertrudis embraced her with wet eyes, I'm sorry to see you go but I'm happy for you. And how did you know that the fellow Amalia was living with was an Aprista, son? He'll take good care of you, Gertrudis predicted, he won't cheat on you. Because Amalia had come to the house twice to ask the old man to get the Aprista out of jail, Ambrosio.

Trinidad was jolly, loving, Amalia thought what Gertrudis told me is coming true. With just what he earned the two of them couldn't go to the stadium so Trinidad went by himself, but on Sunday nights they went to the movies together. Amalia became friends with Señora Rosario, a washerwoman with a lot of children who lived on the alley and was very nice. She helped her wrap packages and sometimes Don Atanasio came to talk to them, he sold lottery tickets, was a drinker and knew all about the life and miracles of the section. Trinidad would get back to Mirones around seven o'clock, she would have dinner ready, one day I think I'm pregnant, love. You threw the noose around my neck and now you're pulling it tight, Trinidad said, I hope it's a boy, they'll think he's your brother, he'll have such a young little mother. Those months, Amalia would think later, were the best of my life. She would always remember the movies they saw and the walks they took downtown and along the beach, the times they ate fried pork rinds beside the Rímac, and the Amancaes Festival they went to with Señora Rosario. Soon there would be a raise, Trinidad said, it'll be good for us, and Ambrosio that textile worker died too: died, oh yes? Yes, half crazy, Amalia thought from some beatings he'd been given during the Odría days. But there was no raise, they said there was a recession, Trinidad got home in a bad mood because those bastards were talking about a strike now. Those union bastards, he cursed, those scabs who get paid by the government. They got elected with the help of informers and now they're talking strike. Nothing would happen to them, but he was on file and they'd say the Aprista is the agitator. And indeed there was a strike and the next day Don Atanasio came running into the house: a patrol car stopped at the door and they took Trinidad away. Amalia went to the police station with Señora Rosario. Ask here, ask there, they didn't know any Trinidad López. She borrowed bus fare from Señora Rosario and went to Miraflores. When she got to the house she didn't dare ring, he'll probably answer the door. She was walking back and forth in front of the door and suddenly she saw him. A face of surprise, of happiness, and when he saw her pregnant of fury. Aha, aha, he pointed at her belly, aha, aha. I haven't come to see you, Amalia began to cry, let me in. Is it true that

81

you hooked up with somebody at the textile factory, Ambrosio said, that the child you're expecting is his? She went into the house and left him talking alone. She waited in the garden, looking at the row of geraniums, the tiled fountain, her room in back, she felt sad, her knees were shaking. With her eyes foggy she saw someone come out, how are you young Santiago, hello Amalia. He was taller, more of a man, still so thin. I came to visit you people here, but, child, what happened to your head? He took off his beret, he had short fuzz and was very ugly. They'd shaved his head, that's how they baptize people who have just got into the university, except that in his case it was taking a long time to grow back. And then Amalia began to weep, that Don Fermín who was so good should help me again, her husband, who hadn't done anything, had been put in jail for no reason, God will repay him, child. Don Fermín came out in his dressing gown, calm down, girl, what's the matter. Young Santiago told him and she didn't do anything, Don Fermín, he wasn't an Aprista, he likes soccer, until Don Fermín laughed: wait, wait, let's see. He went to make a phone call, it took a while, Amalia felt all worked up at being back in the house, at having seen Ambrosio, at what was happening to Trinidad. It's all set, Don Fermín said, tell him not to get mixed up in any more trouble. She tried to kiss his hand and Don Fermín said easy, girl, everything can be fixed up except death. Amalia spent the afternoon with Señora Zoila and young Teté. How beautiful she was, such big eyes, and the Señora made her stay for lunch and when she left, for you to buy something for your child, she gave her forty soles.

The next day Trinidad appeared in Mirones. Furious, those scabs had thrown the ball to him, cursing as Amalia had never heard him before, they'd accused him of a thousand things, because of those mother buckets they'd beaten him up again. Fists, rubber hoses so he'd tell them he didn't know what or who. He was more angry with the union scabs than with the informers: when APRA comes to power those bastards will see, the ones who sold out to Odría will see. You're not on the roster anymore they told him at the textile mill, they fired you for leaving your work. If I complain to the union I already know where they'll send me, Trinidad said, and if I go to the Ministry I know where they'll send me. You're wasting your time cursing the scabs, Amalia said, it would be better if you looked for a job. When he began to make the rounds of factories,

82

the recession was still on they said, and they were living off loans, and suddenly Amalia realized that Trinidad was telling more lies than ever: and what did Amalia die of, Ambrosio? He would leave at eight o'clock in the morning and come back a half hour later and fall onto the bed, he'd walked all over Lima looking for work, he was dead. And Amalia: but you just left and here you are back again. And Ambrosio: from an operation, son, And he: they had him on file, the scabs had passed on the information, they looked at him as if he had the plague, he'd never find work. And Amalia: forget about scabs and go look for work, they were going to starve to death. I can't, he said, I'm sick, and she what are you sick with? Trinidad stuck his finger down his throat until he gagged and vomited: how could he look for work if he was sick? Amalia went back to Miraflores, wept to Señora Zoila, the mistress spoke to Don Fermín and the master to young Sparky tell Carrillo to take her back. When she told him that they had taken her back at the lab, Trinidad began to look at the ceiling. You're proud, what's wrong with my working until you get well, aren't you sick? How much had they paid you to humiliate me now that I'm down? Trinidad asked.

Gertrudis Lama was happy to see her back at the laboratory, and the woman in charge you've got it pretty good, you can put a job on and take it off like a skirt. During the first few days she dropped the pills and the bottles rolled away on her, but within a week she had her skills back. You have to take him to the doctor, Señora Rosario told her, can't you see that all he does is rave all day long? Not true, he only goes off at mealtime or when the subject of work comes up, afterward he's just the way he used to be. When he finished eating he would stick his finger down his throat until he vomited, and then I'm sick, love. But if Amalia paid no attention to him and cleaned up the vomit as if nothing had happened, in a little while he would forget about his illness and how were things at the lab and he even teased and petted her. It'll pass, Amalia thought, prayed, wept secretly, it's going to be the way it was before. But it didn't pass and instead he took to going out the door into the alley and shouting scab at passers-by. He tried to tackle them, put wrestling locks on them, and he's so thin that they bring him back to me all bloody, Amalia told Gertrudis. One night he vomited without sticking his finger down his throat. He turned pale and the next day Amalia took him to the Workers'

83

Hospital. Neuralgia, the doctor told her, he should take a couple of spoonfuls every time he has a headache and from then on Trinidad spent the day saying my head is splitting. He took the medicine and nausea. Playing at getting sick so much has made you sick, Amalia scolded him. He became haughty, grouchy, mocked everything and they could barely hold a conversation anymore. When he saw her return from work, what, you haven't left me yet? and what about the little girl? Santiago asks. He ended up lying on the bed, if I move I don't feel well, or chatting with Don Atanasio, and he hadn't asked about his child again. If Amalia said to him I'm getting fatter or it's moving now, he looked at her as if he didn't know what she was talking about. He scarcely ate, because of the vomiting. Amalia would steal paper bags from the laboratory and ask him vomit in here, not on the floor, and he, on the contrary, would open his mouth over the table or the bed, and with a sticky voice, if it disgusts you so much go ahead and leave: she'd stayed in Pucallpa, son. But afterward he repented, I'm sorry, love, I've got a bad case, bear with me a little while because I'm going to die. They went to the movies on occasion. Amalia tried to get him into good spirits by getting him to go to the stadium, but he clutched his head: no, he was sick. He got as thin as a stray dog, his pants with the fly he didn't close drooped down his legs, he no longer asked Amalia cut my hair the way he used to, and why had he left her in Pucallpa? aren't you disappointed in a man who gives up without a fight after the first fall and acts crazy and lets his wife support him? Gertrudis asked her. Just the opposite, when she saw him turned into a rag she loved him all the more. She thought about him all the time, she felt that the world was coming to an end when she heard him spout nonsense, when he stripped her, pulling off her clothes in the darkness, she felt dizzy. A lady who had become friendly with Amalia volunteered to bring her up, son. Trinidad's headaches disappeared and came back, came and went again, and she never knew whether they were real or inventions or exaggerations. And besides, Ambrosio had got into some trouble and had to beat it out of Pucallpa. Only the vomiting never went away. It's your fault, Amalia said to him, and he the scabs' fault, love, he wasn't going to lie to her.

One day Amalia found Señora Rosario at the entrance to the alley, her hands on her hips, her eyes like hot coals: he'd shut himself up with

Celeste, he'd tried to take advantage of her, he only opened the door when I threatened to call a patrol car. Amalia found Trinidad feeling sorry for himself, Señora Rosario had a dirty mind, calling the police when she knew they had his name on file, perverse, what did he care about dumpy Celeste, he'd only wanted to play a trick on her. Shameless, ingrate, Amalia insulted him, kept man, crazy, and finally she threw a shoe at him. He let her shout and wave her hands without protesting. That night he threw himself to the floor clutching his head and Amalia and Don Atanasio dragged him to the street and got him into a taxi. At the emergency ward they gave him an injection. They slowly returned to Mirones, Trinidad in the middle, stopping to rest at every block. They put him to bed and before he fell asleep Trinidad made her cry: leave me, she shouldn't waste her life on him, he was finished, find someone who suits you better. The little girl's name was Amalita Hortensia and she must be five or six by now, son.

One day when she got back from the laboratory, she found Trinidad jumping up and down: our troubles are over, he'd found a job. He hugged her, pinched her, he looked happy. But what about your sickness, Amalia said astounded, and he it's gone, I'm cured. He had met his comrade Pedro Flores on the street, he told her, an Aprista with whom he'd been in jail on Frontón, and when Trinidad told him what was going on Pedro come with me, and he took him to Callao, introduced him to some comrades, and that very afternoon he had a job in a furniture store. You see, Amalia, that's what comrades were like, he felt like an Aprista right down to his bones, long live Víctor Raúl. He wouldn't make very much, but what difference did that make since it was good for his morale. Trinidad left very early but he got back before Amalia did. His mood was better, my head doesn't ache as much, his comrades had taken him to a doctor who didn't charge anything and gave him some injections and you see, Amalia, he told her, the party takes care of me, it's my family. Pedro Flores never came to Mirones, but Trinidad went out many nights to meet him and Amalia was jealous, do you think I could cheat on you after you've helped me so much? Trinidad laughed, I swear that I'm going to underground meetings with my comrades. Don't get mixed up in politics, Amalia told him, the next time they'll kill you. He stopped talking about the scabs, but the vomiting continued. On many afternoons she found him lying on the bed, his eyes sunken and with no desire to eat. One night when he'd gone out to a meeting, Don Atanasio came and told Amalia come and took her to the corner. There was Trinidad, all alone, sitting on the curb, smoking. Amalia watched him and when Trinidad came back to the alley how did it go? and he fine, he argued a lot. She thought: another woman. But why was he so loving, then? After the first week of work he waited for Amalia before opening his pay envelope, let's buy something for Señora Rosario so she'll get over her annoyance, they picked out some perfume for her, and then what should I buy you, love? It would be better to pay the rent, Amalia told him, but he wanted to spend that money on her, love. Amalita for her mother, and Hortensia for a lady where Amalia had worked, son, one she liked a lot and who died too: of course after what you did you have to leave here, you poor devil, Don Fermín said. You were my salvation, Trinidad told her, tell me what you want. And then Amalia let's go to the movies. They saw a picture with Libertad Lamarque, sad, a story like theirs. Amalia came out sighing and Trinidad you're very sentimental, love, you're a good woman. They were joking and once more he remembered the child and touched her belly, nice and fat. Señora Rosario started to weep over the perfume and told Trinidad you didn't know what you were doing, hug me. The next Sunday Trinidad let's go see your aunt, she'd make up with Amalia when she found out about the child. They went to Limoncillo and Trinidad went in first and then the aunt came out with open arms to call Amalia. They stayed to eat with her and Amalia thought the bad's all gone, everything's patched up. She felt very heavy now, Gertrudis Lama and other friends at the laboratory were sewing clothes for the baby.

The day that Trinidad disappeared, Amalia had gone to the doctor's with Gertrudis. She got back to Mirones late and Trinidad wasn't there, dawn came and he hadn't come, and around ten in the morning a taxi stopped in the alley and a fellow got out asking for Amalia: I want to talk to you alone, it was Pedro Flores. He had her get into the taxi and she what's happened to my husband, and he he's in jail. It's your fault, Amalia shouted, and he looked at her as if she were mad, you fixed things for him to get into politics, and Pedro Flores me, in politics? He hadn't got mixed up and he never would get mixed up in politics because he hated politics, ma'am, and instead that big nut of a Trinidad could have got him involved in a big mess last night. And he told her: they were coming back from a little party in Barranco and when they went by the Colombian Embassy Trinidad stop for a minute, I've got to get out, Pedro Flores thought he was going to urinate, but he got out of the taxi and started shouting scabs, long live APRA, Víctor Raúl, and when he started up in fright he saw that the cops were all over Trinidad. It's your fault, Amalia was weeping, APRA is to blame, they're going to beat him up. What was the matter with her, what are you talking about: Pedro Flores wasn't an Aprista and Trinidad had never been an Aprista either, I know only too well because we're cousins, they'd been raised together in Victoria, we were born in the same house, ma'am. That's a lie, he was born in Pacasmayo, Amalia whimpered, and Pedro Flores who made you believe that story. And he swore to her: he was born in Lima and he's never left it and he was never mixed up in politics, except that once they arrested him by mistake or for some reason during Odría's revolution, and when he got out of jail he got the crazy idea of passing himself off as a northerner and an Aprista. She should go to the police station, tell them that he was drunk and half out of his mind, they'll turn him loose. He left her in the alley and Señora Rosario went with her to Miraflores to weep to Don Fermín. He wasn't at the station house, Don Fermín said after telephoning, she should come back tomorrow, he'd find out. But the following morning a boy came into the alley: Trinidad López was in San Juan de Dios, ma'am. At the hospital they sent Amalia and Señora Rosario from one ward to another, until an old nun with the stubble of a man's beard ah yes, and began to counsel Amalia. She had to resign herself. God has taken your husband away, and while Amalia was weeping to Señora Rosario they told her that they'd found him early that morning by the hospital door, that he'd died of a stroke.

She almost didn't mourn for Trinidad because on the day after the burial her aunt and Señora Rosario had to take her to the Maternity Hospital, the pains quite close together now, and early that morning Trinidad's son was born dead. She was in the Maternity Hospital for five days, sharing a bed with a Negro woman who had given birth to twins and who tried to talk to her all the time. She answered her yes, fine, no. Señora Rosario and her aunt came to see her every day and brought her something to eat. She didn't feel pain or grief, only fatigue, she ate listlessly, it was an effort for her to talk. On the fourth day Gertrudis came, why didn't you let us know, Engineer Carrillo might think she'd quit work, it's good you've got pull with Don Fermín. Let the engineer think whatever he wanted to, Amalia thought. When she left the Maternity Hospital she went to the cemetery to bring some gladioli to Trinidad. The holy picture that Señora Rosario had put there was still by the grave and the letters that his cousin Pedro Flores had scratched on the plaster with a stick. She felt weak, empty, listless, if ever she got any money she would buy a stone and I'll have them carve Trinidad López in gold letters. She began to talk to him slowly, why did you go now that everything was all set, to scold him, why did you make me believe so many lies, to tell him things, they took me to the Maternity Hospital, his son had died, maybe you've met him up there. She went back to Mirones remembering the blue coat that Trinidad said is my mark of elegance and how badly she sewed the buttons for him as they fell off again. The small room was padlocked, the landlord had come with a dealer and sold everything he found, leave her something to remember her husband by Señora Rosario had begged, but they refused and Amalia what do I care. Her aunt had taken in boarders in the little house in Limoncillo and didn't have any room, but Señora Rosario made space for her in one of her two rooms, and Santiago what trouble did you get mixed up in, why did you have to hightail it out of Pucallpa? A week later Gertrudis Lama appeared in Mirones, why hadn't she come back to the lab, how long do you think they'll wait for you? But Amalia wouldn't ever go back to the lab. And what was she going to do, then? Nothing, stay here until I'm kicked out, and Señora Rosario silly, I'm never going to kick you out. And why didn't she want to go back to the lab? She didn't know, but she wasn't going back, and she said it with such anger that Gertrudis Lama didn't ask anymore. A terrible mix-up, he had to hide because of something to do with the truck, son, he didn't even want to remember. Señora Rosario made her eat, counseled her, tried to make her forget. Amalia slept between the girls Celeste and Jesús, and the youngest of Señora Rosario's daughters complained that she talked about Trinidad and her child in the darkness. She helped Señora Rosario wash the clothes in a trough, hang them on the line, heat up the charcoal irons. She did it almost without paying attention, her mind blank, her hands weak. Night came, dawn came, evening came, Gertrudis came to visit her, her aunt came, she listened to them and said yes to everything and thanked them for the gifts they brought. Are you still thinking about Trinidad? Señora Rosario asked her every day, and she yes, about her little son, too. You're like Trinidad, Señora Rosario told her, you lower your head, you don't fight, she should forget about her troubles, you're young, she could remake her life. Amalia never left Mirones, she was nothing but an old rag, she rarely washed or combed her hair, once when she looked at herself in a mirror she thought if Trinidad saw you he wouldn't love you anymore. At night when Don Atanasio came home, she would shut herself up in his room to talk to him. He lived in a room with such a low ceiling that Amalia couldn't stand, and on the floor were a mattress with the stuffing coming out and a thousand odds and ends. While they were chatting, Don Atanasio would take out his bottle and have a drink. Did he think that the informers had beaten Trinidad, Don Atanasio, that when they saw he was dying they dropped him by the door of San Juan de Dios? Sometimes Don Atanasio yes, that was probably what happened, and others no, they probably let him go and he didn't feel well and went to the hospital on his own, and other times what does it matter to you now, he's dead, think about yourself, forget about him.

6

HAD IT BEEN THAT FIRST YEAR, Zavalita, when you saw that San Marcos was a brothel and not the paradise you'd thought? What hadn't you liked, son? Not that the classes began in June instead of April, not that the professors were as decrepit as the desks, he thinks, but his schoolmates' lack of interest when the subject of books came up, the indolence in their eyes when it was politics. The peasants were a lot like our well-bred little boys, Ambrosio. The professors were probably paid miserable salaries, Aída said, they probably worked in ministries, gave classes in private schools, who could ask anything better from them. You had to understand the students' apathy, Jacobo said, the system made them that way: they needed to be stirred up, indoctrinated, organized. But where were the communists, where in the world were the Apristas? All in jail, all in exile? Those were backward-looking criticisms, Ambrosio, he didn't realize it at the time and he liked San Marcos. What had become of the professor who in a whole year got through two chapters of the *Synthesis of Logical Investigation* published by the *Revista de Occidente?* Phenomenologically suspending the problem of rabies, putting in parentheses, as Husserl would have said, the grave situation created by the dogs of Lima: what sort of face would the supervisor have put on? What about the one who only gave spelling tests, the one who asked for Freud's mistakes on his exam?

"You're wrong, you have to read the obscurantists too," Santiago said.

"It would be nice to read them in their own language," Aída said. "I'd like to know French, English, even German."

"Read everything, but with a critical sense," Jacobo said. "The progressives always seem bad to you and the decadents always good. That's what I criticize in you."

"I'm only saying that *The Making of a Hero* bored me and that I liked *The Castle,*" Santiago protested. "I'm not generalizing."

"The Ostrovsky translation is probably bad and the Kafka one good, don't argue anymore," Aída said.

What about the little old man with a fat belly, blue eyes and long white hair who lectured on historical sources? He was so good that he made me want to go into History and not Psychology, Aída said, and Jacobo yes, too bad he was a Hispanist and not an Indigenist. The classrooms, packed during the first days, were thinning out, by September only half the students attended and it wasn't hard to find a seat in class anymore. They didn't feel defrauded, it wasn't that the professors didn't know anything or didn't want to teach, he thinks, they weren't interested in learning either. Because they were poor and had to work, Aída said, because they were contaminated with bourgeois formalism and only wanted to get their degrees, Jacobo said; because in order to get them you didn't have to go to class or be interested or study: you only had to wait. Was he happy at San Marcos Skinny, did the great minds of Peru really teach there Skinny, why had he become so withdrawn Skinny? Yes he was papa, they really do papa, he wasn't withdrawn papa. You came in and went out of the house like a ghost, Zavalita, you shut yourself up in your room and didn't show your face to the family, you were like a bear, Señora Zoila said, and Sparky you were going to go cross-eyed from so much reading, and Teté why didn't you ever go out with Popeye anymore, Superbrain. Because Jacobo and Aída were enough, he thinks, because they were friendship which excluded, enriched and compensated for everything. There, he thinks, did I fuck myself up there?

They had registered for the same courses, they sat in the same row, they went together to the San Marcos or National libraries, it was hard for them to go their separate ways and home to sleep. They read the same books, saw the same movies, got all worked up over the same newspapers. When they left the university, at noon and in the afternoon, they would talk for hours in El Palermo on Colmena, argue for hours in the Huérfanos pastry shop on Azángaro, talk for hours about the political news in a café and billiard parlor behind the Palace of Justice. Sometimes they would slip into a movie, sometimes go through bookstores, sometimes take long walks through the city as an adventure. Asexual, fraternal, the friendship also seemed eternal.

"The same things were important to us, we hated the same things, and we never agreed on anything," Santiago says. "That was great too."

"Why were you so bitter, then?" Ambrosio asks. "Was it because of the girl?"

"I never saw her alone," Santiago says. "I wasn't bitter; a little worm in my stomach sometimes, nothing else."

"You wanted to make love to her and you couldn't with the other one there," Ambrosio says. "I know what it's like to be close to the woman you love and not be able to do anything."

"Did that happen to you with Amalia?" Santiago asks.

"I saw a movie about it once," Ambrosio says.

The university reflected the country, Jacobo said, twenty years ago those professors were probably progressives and readers, then because they had to work at other things and because of the environment they became mediocre and bourgeois, and there, sticky and tiny at the mouth of his stomach: the little worm. It was the students' fault too, Aída said, they liked the system; and if everybody was to blame, was conforming the only thing left for us to do? Santiago asked, and Jacobo: the solution was university reform. A diminutive and acidy body in the underbrush of conversations, all of a sudden in the heat of the arguments, interfering, leading astray, distracting with flashes of melancholy or nostalgia. Parallel teaching chairs, cogovernment, popular universities, Jacobo said: everyone who was capable should come to teach, the students could get rid of bad professors, and since the people didn't come to the university, the university should go to the people. Melancholy from those impossible dialogues alone with her that he yearned for, nostalgia for those strolls alone with her that he invented? But if the university was a reflection of the country San Marcos would never be in good shape as long as Peru was so badly off, Santiago said, and Aída if what was wanted was to cure the disease at its roots there shouldn't be any talk of university reform but of revolution. But they were students and their field of action was the university, Jacobo said, by working for reform they would be working for the revolution: you had to go through stages and not be pessimistic.

"You were jealous of your friend," Ambrosio says. "And jealousy is the worst kind of poison."

"Jacobo was probably going through the same thing I was," Santiago says. "But we both kept it hidden."

"He probably felt like getting rid of you with a magic look too so he could be alone with the girl." Ambrosio laughs.

"He was my best friend," Santiago says. "I hated him, but at the same time I loved and admired him."

"You shouldn't be such a skeptic," Jacobo said. "That business of all or nothing is typically bourgeois."

"I'm not a skeptic," Santiago said. "But we talk and talk and here we are in the same place."

"That's right, up till now we haven't gone beyond theory," Aída said. "We ought to do something else besides talk."

"We can't do it alone," Jacobo said. "First we have to make contact with the progressives at the university."

"We've been there two months and we haven't found a single one," Santiago said. "I'm beginning to believe they don't exist."

"They have to be careful and it's logical," Jacobo said. "They'll turn up sooner or later."

And in fact, stealthily, suspiciously, mysteriously, little by little, they had been turning up, like furtive shadows: they were in the first year of Letters, right? Between classes they would usually sit on a bench in the courtyard of the Faculty, it seemed they were taking up a collection, or walking around the fountain in Law, to buy mattresses for the students in jail, and sometimes there they exchanged words with students from other faculties or other classes, who were being held in the cells of the penitentiary sleeping on the floor, and in those quick fleeting dialogues, behind the mistrust, opening a path through the suspicion, hadn't anyone told them about the collection before? they noticed or seemed to notice a subtle exploration of their way of thinking, it wasn't a matter of anything political, a discreet sounding, just a humanitarian act, vague indications that they were getting ready for something that would come, and even simple Christian charity, or a secret call so that they could show in the same coded way that they could be trusted: could they maybe give just one sol? They would appear alone and slippery in the courtyards of San Marcos, they would come over to chat with them for a few moments about ambiguous things, they would disappear for several days and suddenly reappear, cordial and evasive, the same cautious smiling expression on the same Indian, half-breed, Chinese, black faces, and the same ambivalent words in their provincial accents, with the same threadbare and faded suits and the same old shoes and sometimes a magazine or newspaper or book under their arm. What were they studying, where did they come from, what were their names, where did they live? Like a bald bolt of lightning in the cloudy sky, that boy in Law had been one of those who had shut themselves up in San Marcos during Odría's revolution, a quick confidence suddenly tore through the gray conversations, and he had been imprisoned and had gone on a hunger strike in jail, and lighted them up and made them feverish, and he had only been let out a month ago, and those revelations and discoveries, and that one had been a delegate from Economics when the Federated Centers and the University Federation still functioned, awoke in them an anxious excitation, before the police had destroyed the student organizations by putting their leaders in jail, a fierce curiosity.

"You come home late so you won't have to eat with us and when you do us the honor you don't open your mouth," Señora Zoila said. "Did they cut off your tongue in San Marcos?"

"He spoke against Odría and against the Communists," Jacobo said. "An Aprista, wouldn't you say?"

"He plays silent in order to make himself more interesting," Sparky said. "Geniuses don't waste their time talking to ignoramuses, isn't that right, Superbrain?"

"How many children does young Teté have?" Ambrosio asks. "And how many have you got, son?"

"A Trotskyite more likely, because he had good things to say about Lechín," Aída said. "Don't they say that Lechín is a Trotskyite?"

"Teté two and me none," Santiago says. "I didn't want to be a father,

94

but maybe I'll decide to one of these days. The way we're going, what difference does it make?"

"And besides, you go around like a sleepwalker with the eyes of a slaughtered lamb," Teté said. "Have you fallen in love with some girl at San Marcos?"

"When I get home I see the lamp on your night table still on," Don Fermín said. "It's fine for you to read, but you ought to be a little sociable, Skinny."

"Yes, with a girl in braids who goes barefoot and speaks only Quechua," Santiago said. "Are you interested?"

"The old black woman used to say that every child comes with his loaf of bread under his arm," Ambrosio says. "If it was up to me, I'd have a lot of them, I'll say that. The old black woman, my mama, may she rest in peace."

"I'm a little tired when I get home. That's why I go to my room, papa," Santiago said. "Why don't I stay and talk to you all? Don't you think I'm crazy?"

"That's what happens to me for having spoken to you, you're a stubborn mule," Teté said.

"Not crazy, just a little strange," Don Fermín said. "Now that we're alone, Skinny, you can talk frankly to me. Is something bothering you?"

"That one just might belong to the Party," Jacobo said. "His interpretation of what's going on in Bolivia was very Marxist."

"Nothing, papa," Santiago said. "Nothing's wrong with me, I give you my word."

"Pancras had a son in Huacho years and years ago and his woman ran off on him one day and he never saw her again," Ambrosio says. "Ever since then he's been trying to find that son. He doesn't want to die without knowing if he turned out as ugly as he is."

"That one doesn't come over to sound us out but to be with you," Santiago said. "He only talks to you, and all those little smiles. You've made a conquest, Aída."

"What a dirty mind you've got, you're such a bourgeois," Aída said.

"I can understand it because I've spent days too thinking about

95

Amalita Hortensia," Ambrosio says. "Wondering what she's like, who she looks like."

"Do you think that only happens to the bourgeoisie?" Santiago asked. "That revolutionaries don't ever think about women?"

"There you are, now you're mad because I called you a bourgeois," Aída said. "Don't be so sensitive, don't be so bourgeois. Agh, I let it slip again."

"Let's go have some coffee," Jacobo said. "Come on, Moscow gold is paying for it."

Were they solitary rebels, were they active in some underground organization, could one of them be an informer? They didn't go around together, they rarely appeared at the same time, they didn't know each other or they made people think they didn't know each other. Sometimes it was as if they were going to reveal something important, but they would stop on the threshold of revelation, and their hints and allusions, their threadbare suits and their calculated manners aroused restlessness in them, doubts, an admiration held back by mistrust or fear. Their casual faces began to appear in the cafés where they went after class, was he a messenger, was he exploring the terrain? their humble silhouettes as they sat down at the tables where they were, then let's show them that there was no reason to pretend with them, and there, outside San Marcos, there are two informers in our class Aída said, instead of waiting for a trap, we found them out and they couldn't deny it Jacobo said, the dialogues began to be less ethereal, they excused themselves alleging that as lawyers they would go up the ladder, Santiago said, sometimes taking on a boldly political tone, the fools didn't even know how to lie Aída said. The chats would begin with some anecdote, the dangerous ones were not the ones who let themselves be found out said Washington, or joke or story or inquiry, but the small-fry informers who don't appear on police lists, and then, timid, accidental, the questions came, what was the atmosphere like in the first year? was there restlessness, were the kids concerned about problems? was there a majority interested in setting up the Federated Centers again? more and more sibylline, serpentine, what did they think of the Bolivian revolution? the conversation would slip, and Guatemala, what did they think about that? toward the international

96

situation. Animated, excited, they gave their opinions without lowering their voices, let the informers hear them, let them arrest them, and Aída became stimulated, she was the most enthusiastic he thinks, she let herself be won over by her own emotions, the most daring he thinks, the first boldly to shift the conversation from Bolivia and Guatemala to Peru: we were living under a military dictatorship, and her nighttime eyes glowed, even if the Bolivian revolution was only liberal, and her nose grew thinner, even if Guatemala hadn't even gotten as far as a democratic-bourgeois revolution, and her temples throbbed more rapidly, they were better off than Peru, and a lock of her hair danced, governed by a stinking general, and it bounced on her forehead as she spoke, and by a pack of thieves, and her small fists pounded on the table. Uncomfortable, restless, alarmed, the furtive shadows interrupted Aída, changed the subject, or got up and left.

"Your papa said that San Marcos was bad for you," Ambrosio says. "That you stopped loving him because of the university."

"You gave Washington a hard time," Jacobo said. "If he belongs to the Party he has to be careful. Don't talk so strongly about Odría in front of him, you could get him in trouble."

"Did my father tell you that I'd stopped loving him?" Santiago asks.

"Do you think Washington left because of that?" Aída asked.

"It was the thing he was most worried about in life," Ambrosio says. "Finding out why you'd stopped loving him, son."

He was in the third year of Law, he was a white and jovial little Andean who spoke without taking on the solemn, esoteric, archepiscopal air of the others, he was the first one whose name they learned: Washington. Always dressed in light gray, always with his merry canine teeth showing, with his jokes he imposed on the conversation in El Palermo, in the café-poolroom, or in the courtyard of Economics a personal climate which didn't come out in the hermetic or stereotyped dialogues they had with the others. But in spite of his communicative appearance, he also knew how to be impenetrable. He'd been the first to change from a furtive shadow into a being of flesh and blood. Into an acquaintance, he thinks, almost into a friend.

"Why did he think that?" Santiago asks. "What else did my father tell you?"

"Why don't we organize a study group?" Washington asked casually. They stopped thinking, breathing, their eyes fastened on him.

"A study group?" Aída asked very slowly. "To study what?"

"Not me, son," Ambrosio says. "He'd be talking to your mama, your brother and sister, friends, and I'd listen to them while I was driving the car."

"Marxism," Washington said in a natural way. "They don't teach it at the university and it might be useful to us as a part of our general culture, don't you think?"

"You knew my father better than I," Santiago says. "Tell me what other things he used to say about me."

"It would be most interesting," Jacobo said. "Let's organize the group."

"How could I know him better than you," Ambrosio says. "What a thing to say, child."

"The problem is getting hold of books," Aída said. "In secondhand bookstores the only thing you can find is some back number of *Cultura Soviética*."

"I know he talked to you about me," Santiago says. "But never mind, don't tell me anything if you don't want to."

"You can get them, but we have to be careful," Washington said. "Studying Marxism is enough to make yourself liable to be put on file as a Communist. Well, you people know that better than I."

That was how the Marxist study groups had been born, that was how they'd begun, without noticing it, to become active, to sink into the prestigious, yearned-for underground status. That was how they had discovered the tumble-down bookstore on the Jirón Chota and the old Spaniard with dark glasses and a snowy goatee who had copies of *Siglo XX* and *Lautaro* in his back room, that was how they had bought, thumbed through avidly that book which brought the discussions of the group to a fever pitch for many weeks, that book with answers for everything: *Elements of Philosophy*, he thinks. He thinks: Georges Politzer. That was how they had met Héctor, another furtive shadow until then, and had found out that the skinny, laconic giraffe was studying Economics and earned his living as a radio announcer. They'd decided to meet twice a week, they'd discussed the place for a long time, they'd finally chosen Héctor's boardinghouse on Jesús María where they would go from then on and for months, every Thursday and Saturday afternoon, feeling themselves followed and spied on, looking suspiciously about the neighborhood before going in. They would get there around three, Héctor's room was old and large, with two wide windows that faced the street, on the third floor of the boardinghouse run by a deaf woman who would come up sometimes to roar at them do you want some tea? Aída installed herself on the bed, the negation of negation he thinks, Héctor on the floor, the qualitative leaps he thinks, Santiago in the only chair, the unity of opposites he thinks, Jacobo on a windowsill, Marx put the dialectics that Hegel had standing on its head back on its feet he thinks, and Washington always standing. He thinks: in order to grow and he laughed. Every time a different person would review a chapter from Politzer's book, the reviews were followed by discussions, they met for two, three, or even four hours, they left by twos, leaving the room full of smoke and ardor. Later on the three of them would meet again and in some park, some street, some café, could Washington belong to the Party? Aída asked, they kept on talking, could Héctor be in the Party? Jacobo asked, supposing so, could the Party exist? Santiago asked, how was self-criticism done? and fervently arguing. That was how they had used the first year, that was how he'd spent the summer, not going to the beach a single time he thinks, that was how he'd begun the second year.

Had it been that second year, Zavalita, when you saw that it wasn't enough to learn about Marxism, that you had to believe? What had probably fucked you up was that lack of faith, Zavalita. A lack of faith in God, child? In order to believe in anything, Ambrosio. The idea of God, the idea of a "pure spirit" who created the universe didn't make sense, Politzer said, a God outside space and time was something that could not *exist*. You were going around with a face that wasn't your usual face, Santiago. You had to take part in idealistic mysticism and consequently not admit any scientific control, Politzer said, in order to believe in a God who existed outside time, that is, who didn't exist in any given moment, and who existed outside space, that is, who didn't exist in any given place. The worst thing was to have doubts, Ambrosio, and the wonderful thing was to close your eyes and say God exists or God

99

doesn't exist and believe it. He'd realized that sometimes he was playing tricks in the group, Aída: he said I believe or I agree and deep down he had doubts. Materialists, supported by the conclusions of science, Politzer said, affirmed that matter existed in space and in a given moment (in time). Clenching your fists, grinding your teeth, Ambrosio, APRA is the solution, religion is the solution, Communism is the solution, and believing it. Then life would become organized all by itself and you wouldn't feel empty anymore, Ambrosio. He didn't believe in priests, son, and he hadn't gone to mass since he was a child, but he did believe in religion and in God, didn't everybody have to believe in something? Consequently the universe could not have been created, Politzer concluded, since it had been necessary for God to be able to create the world in a moment which had never been a moment (since time did not exist for God) and it would have been necessary too for the world to have come *out of nothingness:* and did that worry you so much, Zavalita? Aída would ask. And Jacobo: if it was necessary in any case to start believing in something, it was better to believe that God doesn't exist than that he does. Santiago also preferred that, Aída, he wanted to be convinced that what Politzer said was right, Jacobo. What got him all upset was having doubts, Aída, not being able to be sure, Jacobo. Petit-bourgeois agnosticism, Zavalita, disguised idealism, Zavalita. Didn't Aída have any doubts, did Jacobo believe right down to the last letter what Politzer was saying? Doubts were fatal, Aída said, they paralyze you and you can't do anything, and Jacobo spending your life digging around, would that be right? torturing yourself, would that be a lie? instead of acting? The world would never change, Zavalita. In order to act you have to believe in something, Aída said, and believing in God hasn't helped change anything, and Jacobo: better to believe in Marxism, which can change things, Zavalita. Inculcate the workers with methodical doubt? Washington said, peasants with the quadruple root of the principle of sufficient reason? Héctor said. He thinks: you thought not, Zavalita. Closing your eyes, Marxism rests on science, clenching your fists, religion on ignorance, sinking your feet into the earth, God doesn't exist, grinding your teeth, the motive force of history was the class struggle, hardening your muscles, when it freed itself of bourgeois exploitation, breathing deeply, the proletariat would free humanity, and attacking: and set up a world without classes. You couldn't, Zavalita, he thinks. He thinks: you were, you are, you always will be, you'll die a petit bourgeois. Were nursing bottles, private school, family, neighborhood stronger? he thinks. You used to go to mass, to confession and communion on first Fridays, you prayed and even then a lie, I don't believe. You went to the deaf woman's boardinghouse, quantitative changes, as they accumulated, produced a qualitative change, and you yes yes, the greatest materialist thinker before Marx was Diderot, yes yes, and suddenly the little worm: a lie, I don't believe.

"No one should notice, that was the main thing," Santiago says. "I don't write poetry, I believe in God, I don't believe in God. Always lying, always faking."

"Maybe you'd better not have any more to drink, son," Ambrosio says.

"In prep school, at home, in the neighborhood, in the study group, in the Party, at *La Crónica*," Santiago says. "My whole life spent doing things without believing, my whole life spent pretending."

"I'm glad papa threw your Communist book into the garbage, ha-ha," Teté said.

"And my whole life spent wanting to believe in something," Santiago says. "And my whole life a lie, I don't believe in anything."

Had it been a lack of faith, Zavalita, couldn't it have been timidity? In the box of old newspapers in the garage behind the new copy of Politzer piling up were *The Chief Task of Our Times,* he thinks, books read and discussed in the group, *The Origins of Family, Society and State,* he thinks, poorly bound books with small print, *The Class Struggle in France,* he thinks, that came off on your fingers. Previously observed, studied, investigated, and brought into the group were Martínez the Indian, who was studying Ethnology, and later on Solórzano from Medicine, and then an almost albino girl whom they nicknamed The Bird. Héctor's room became too small, the eyes of the deaf woman becoming alarmed at the chronic invasion, so they decided to rotate. Aída offered her place, The Bird hers, and then they met alternately on Jesús María, in a small red-brick house on Rímac, in an apartment on Petit Thouars with fleur-de-lis wallpaper. An effusive and gray-haired giant received them the first time they met at Aída's house, I'd like to introduce you

101

to my father, and while he shook their hands he looked at them with melancholy. He'd been a printer and a union leader, he'd been imprisoned during the days of Sánchez Cerro, he'd almost died of a heart attack. Now he worked by day at a press, and at night he was a proofreader at *El Comercio*, and was no longer involved in politics. And did he know that they were coming here to study Marxism? yes he knew, and didn't it bother him? of course not, he thought it was fine.

"It must be great to have a relationship like a friend with your old man," Santiago said.

"The poor man has been my father, my friend and my mother too," Aída said. "Ever since my real mother died."

"In order for me to get along with my old man I have to hide what I think," Santiago said. "He never agrees with me."

"How could he, being a bourgeois gentleman," Aída said.

As the group grew, from the quantitative accumulation to the qualitative leap he thinks, it changed from a center of study into a political discussion group. Going from analyzing Mariátegui's essays to refuting the editorials in *La Prensa*, from historical materialism to the atrocities committed by Cayo Bermúdez, from the bourgeois shift of APRA to poisonous gossip against the subtle enemy: the Trotskyites. They had identified three of them, had spent hours, weeks, months guessing who they were, checking them out, spying on them and abominating them: intellectual, disturbing, they strolled through the courtyards of San Marcos, their mouths full of quotations and provocations, cataclysmic, heterodox. Were there many of them? Not many but quite dangerous Washington said, did they work with the police? Solórzano asked, probably and in any case it was the same thing Héctor said, because dividing, confusing, deviating and intoxicating was worse than informing Jacobo said. In order to fool the Trotskyites, to avoid informers, they had agreed not to hang around together at the university, not to stop and chat when they met in the hallways. There was unity in the group, complicity, even solidarity, he thinks. He thinks: friendship only among the three of us. Were the others bothered by that little island they constituted, that tenacious triumvirate? They continued going to class together, to libraries and cafés, strolling through the courtyards, seeing each other alone

102

after meetings of the group. They chatted, discussed, walked, they went to the movies and *Miracle in Milan* had excited them, the white dove at the end was the dove of peace, the music was the Internationale, Vittorio de Sica must have been a Communist, and when a Russian film was announced at some neighborhood theater, with great hopes they fervently rushed over, even though they knew that they would probably be watching some old movie with interminable ballet scenes.

"A shudder?" Ambrosio asks. "A cramp in the belly?"

"The same as when I was a kid, at night," Santiago says. "I used to wake up in the dark, I'm going to die. I couldn't move, not even light the lamp or cry out. I stayed there all huddled up, sweating, shaking."

"There's someone in Economics who might want to join," Washington said. "The problem is that there are so many of us in the group already."

"But where does it come from, son?" Ambrosio asks.

It appeared, there it was, tiny and glacial, gelatinous. It would twist delicately at the mouth of his stomach, secrete that liquid that wet the palms of his hands, make his heart beat faster, and go away with a shudder.

"Yes, it's not wise for so many of us to meet," Héctor said. "The best thing would be to divide up into two groups."

"Yes, let's split up, I was the one most convinced, it hadn't even occurred to me," Santiago says. "Weeks later I woke up repeating like an idiot, it can't be, it can't be."

"What basis shall we use for the split?" Indian Martínez asked. "It has to be done right now, we can't waste time."

"He's in a hurry because he's got his concept of unpaid work all sharpened up like a razor." Washington laughed.

"We could draw lots," Héctor said.

"Luck is a bit irrational," Jacobo said. "I propose that we split up alphabetically."

"Of course, that's more rational and much easier," said The Bird. "The first four in one group, the rest in the other."

There hadn't been any catch in his heart, the little worm hadn't popped out. Only surprise and confusion, he thinks, only that sudden ill feeling. And that set idea: a mistake. And that set idea, he thinks: a mistake?

"Those who agree with Jacobo's proposal raise your hands," Washington said.

A growing ill feeling, his brain dulled, a dizzy timidity silencing his tongue, raising his hand a few seconds after the others.

"All set, then, agreed," Washington said. "Jacobo, Aída, Héctor and Martínez one group and the other four of us the second."

He hadn't turned his head to look at Aída or Jacobo, he'd taken a long time to light a cigarette, thumbed through Engels, exchanged a smile with Solórzano.

"Now, Martínez, now you can show off," Washington said. "What's the story on the unpaid work?"

Not just the revolution, he thinks. Lukewarm, hidden, a heart too, and a small brain, alert, quick, calculating. Had he planned it, he thinks, had he made a sudden decision? The revolution, friendship, jealousy, envy, all together, all mixed in, he too, Zavalita, made from the same dirty clay, Jacobo too, Zavalita.

"There weren't any pure people in the world," Santiago says. "Yes, that was when it was."

"Wouldn't you see the girl anymore?" Ambrosio asks.

"I was going to see her less, he was going to see her alone twice a week," Santiago says. "And besides, I was hurt by the low blow. Not for moral reasons, because of envy. I was timid and I never would have dared."

"He was sharper." Ambrosio laughs. "And you still haven't forgiven him for that piece of bitchery."

Martínez the Indian had the gestures and the voice of a schoolteacher, in brief, it was unpaid work, and was repetitious and monotonous, a proportion of the product tricked away from the worker which would increase the capital, and Santiago stared eternally at his round copper-colored face and listened endlessly to his didactic teacher's voice, and looked around at the glow of cigarettes every time hands went up to lips and in spite of so many bodies crowded into such a miserly space there was that feeling of loneliness, that emptiness. The little worm was there now, making soft monotonous turns in his guts.

"Because I'm like those little animals that curl up in the face of danger and remain still, waiting to be stepped on or to have their heads cut off," Santiago says. "Being without faith and timid besides is like having syphilis and leprosy at the same time."

"All you do is say bad things about yourself," Ambrosio says. "If someone else said the things you're saying about yourself, you wouldn't stand for it."

Had something that seemed eternal been broken, he thinks, did it hurt me so much because of her, because of me, because of him? But you'd pretended as always, Zavalita, more than always, and you'd left the meeting with Jacobo and Aída, and you'd talked too much while you walked down, Engels and unpaid work, without giving them a chance to answer, Politzer and The Bird and Marx, incessant and loquacious, interrupting them if they opened their mouths, killing topics and bringing them back to life, stumbling, profuse, confused, so that the monologue would never end, fabricating, exaggerating, lying, suffering, so that Jacobo's proposal wouldn't be mentioned, so that it wouldn't be said that starting Saturday they would be on Petit Thouars and he on Rímac, feeling too now and for the first time that they were together and were not, that the respiratory communication of past times was missing, the corporal intelligence of past times, while they crossed the Plaza de Armas, which horribly here and now was also something artificial and lying and isolated them, like the conversations with my old man, he thinks, and made them be wrong and began to turn them against one another. They had gone down the Jirón de la Unión without looking at one another, he talking and they listening. Was Aída sorry about it, had Aída worked it out in advance with him? and when they got to the Plaza San Martín it was quite late, Santiago had looked at his watch, had hurried to catch the express bus, had put out his hand to them and left on the run, without setting up where and what time we'd meet tomorrow, he thinks. He thinks: for the first time.

Had it been during those last weeks of the second year, Zavalita, those last hollow days before final exams? He had set himself to reading furiously, working furiously in the study group, believing furiously in Marxism, growing thin. Boiled eggs were useless, Señora Zoila said, orangeade useless and corn flakes useless, you'd turned into a skeleton and one of those days you were going to fly away. Is it also against your ideas to eat, Superbrain? Sparky said, and you you didn't eat because your face takes my appetite away and Sparky was going to whack you, Superbrain, he was going to hand you one. They still saw each other and the little head inevitably appeared when Santiago went into class and sat down with them, it opened its way through tangles of tissues and tendons and appeared, or when they went to have some coffee together at El Palermo, amidst bloody veins and white bones it appeared, or a glass of dark chicha at the Huérfanos pastry shop, or a hero sandwich at the café-poolroom, and behind the little head the small acidy body appeared. They talked about classes and the upcoming exams, about the preparations for the election of Federated Centers, and about the discussions in their respective study groups and prisoners and Odría's dictatorship and Bolivia and Guatemala. But they only saw each other because San Marcos and politics sometimes brought them together, he thinks, sometimes only by chance, sometimes only through obligation. Did they see each other alone after the meetings of their group? did they take walks, did they go to museums and bookstores or movies the way they did with him before? did they miss him, think about him, talk about him?

"A girl wants you on the phone," Teté told him. "My, how secret you keep it all. Who is she?"

"If you listen in on the extension I'll give you a rap, Teté," Santiago said.

"Can you come to my house for a minute?" Aída asked. "You're not doing anything, are you, I'm not interrupting anything?"

"What a thing to think, I'm on my way," Santiago said. "It'll take me a half hour, maybe a little more."

"My, I'm on my way, my, what a thing to think," Teté said. "Can you come to my house for a minute? My, what a nice little voice."

It had appeared while he was waiting for a taxi on the corner of Larco and José Gonzales, grew as the car went up the Avenida Arequipa, and there it was, enormous and sticky, as he rode along huddled in the corner of the automobile, his back getting soaked in an icy substance, while he felt colder and colder, fear and hope, on that afternoon which was turning into night. Had something happened, was something going to happen? He thought that it had been a month now that we only saw each other at San Marcos, he thinks, she'd never called me on the phone, he thought probably, he thinks, he thought maybe. He'd seen her from the corner of Petit Thouars, a small figure that was fading into the dying light, waiting for him at the door of her house, she'd said hello with her hand and he'd seen her pale face, that blue dress, her serious eyes, that blue jumper, her serious mouth, those horrible black schoolgirl shoes, and he'd felt her hand trembling.

"Excuse me for calling you, I had to talk to you about something," that crisp voice seemed impossible, he thinks, that intimidated voice incredible. "Let's walk a little, shall we?"

"Aren't you with Jacobo?" Santiago asked. "Has something happened?"

"Are you going to have enough money to pay for so many beers?" Ambrosio asks.

"What had to happen had happened," Santiago says. "I thought that it had already happened and it had only just happened that morning."

They'd been together all morning, a little worm like a cobra, they hadn't gone to class because Jacobo had told her I want to talk to you alone, a cobra as sharp as a knife, they'd walked along the Paseo de la República, a knife like ten knives, they'd sat down on a bench by the pool in the Parque de la Exposición. Along the parallel lanes of Arequipa cars passed and one knife entered softly and another one came out and went back in slowly, and they went along between the trees where it was dark and empty, and another one, as into a loaf of bread with a thin crust and lots of body, into his heart, and suddenly the little voice became silent.

"And what did he want to talk to you about all alone?" without looking at her, he thinks, without separating his teeth. "Something about me, something against me?"

"No, nothing about you, something about me," a voice like the whimper of a kitten, he thinks. "He took me by surprise, he left me not knowing what to say."

"But what was it he told you?" Santiago murmured.

"That he's in love with me," like Rowdy's whines when he was a puppy, he thinks.

"Block ten on Arequipa, December, seven o'clock at night," Santiago says. "Now I know, Ambrosio, it was there."

107

He'd taken his hands out of his pockets, had put them to his mouth and whistled and tried to smile. He'd seen Aída uncross her arms, stop, hesitate, look for the nearest bench, he'd seen her sit down.

"Hadn't you realized until now?" Santiago asked. "Why do you think he proposed that the group be divided up that way?"

"Because we were setting a bad example, because we were almost a faction and the others might have resented it and I believed him," an insecure little voice, he thinks. "And that it wouldn't change anything and that even though we were in different groups it would all go on the same with the three of us. And I believed him."

"He wanted to be alone with you," Santiago said. "Anybody would have done the same thing in his place."

"But you got angry and didn't look us up," alarmed and above all sorrowful, he thinks. "And we didn't get together again, and nothing's been the way it was before."

"I didn't get angry, everything's still the way it was before," Santiago said. "Except that I realized that Jacobo wanted to be alone with you and that I was in the way. But we're still the same friends we were before."

It was someone else talking, he thinks, not you. The voice a little stronger now, more natural, Zavalita: it wasn't he, it couldn't be. He understood, he explained, he advised from neutral heights and thought it's not me. He was something small and mistreated, something that huddled under that voice, something that slipped away and ran and fled. It wasn't pride, or spite, or humiliation, he thinks, it wasn't even jealousy. He thinks: it was timidity. She listened to him motionless, she was watching him with an expression that he couldn't decipher and didn't want to, and suddenly she'd got up and they'd walked half a block in silence, while, tenacious, silent, the knives went on with their butchery.

"I don't know what to do, I feel confused, I have doubts," Aída finally said. "That's why I called you, I thought all of a sudden that you could help me."

"And I began to talk about politics," Santiago says. "See what I mean?"

"Of course," Don Fermín said. "Getting away from the house and

Lima, disappearing. I'm not thinking about myself, you poor devil, I'm thinking about you."

"But what do you mean when you say that," as if startled, he thinks, scared.

"In the sense that love can make a person very much an individualist," Santiago said. "And then he gives it more importance than anything, the revolution included."

"But you were the one who said that the two things weren't incompatible," hissing, he thinks, whispering. "Do you think they are now? How can you be sure that you're never going to fall in love?"

"I didn't believe anything, I didn't know anything," Santiago says. "Just wanting to leave, escape, disappear."

"But where, sir?" Ambrosio said. "You don't believe me, you're kicking me out, sir."

"Then it's not true that you have doubts, you're in love with him too," Santiago said. "Maybe in your case and Jacobo's they're not incompatible. And besides, he's a good boy."

"I know that he's a good boy," Aída said. "But I don't know whether or not I'm in love with him."

"Of course you are, I've noticed it too," Santiago said. "And not just me, everybody in the group. You should accept him, Aída."

You insisted Zavalita, he was a great boy, you were dogged Zavalita, Aída was in love with him, you demanded, they'd get along very well and you repeated and you went back to it and she listening silently at the door of her house, her arms folded, calculating Santiago's stupidity? her head down, taking measure of Santiago's cowardice? her feet together. Did she really want that advice, he thinks, did she know that you were in love with her and wanted to find out if you dared say so? What would she have said if I, he thinks, what would I have said if she. He thinks: oh, Zavalita.

Or had it been when one day or week or month after seeing Aída and Jacobo walking hand in hand on Colmena, they discovered that Washington was, in fact, the contact they'd been yearning for? There'd hardly been any comments in the group, only a joke by Washington, two of them had feathered their little love nest in the other group, such a quiet

109

little love, only a passing comment from The Bird: and what a perfect little couple. There wasn't time for anything else: the university elections were on top of them and they met every day, they discussed the candidates they would present for the Federated Centers, and the alliances they would accept and the slates they would support and the fliers and wall posters they would make, and one day Washington summoned the two groups to meet at The Bird's place and he went into the small living room on Rímac: he had something that was pure dynamite. Cahuide, he thinks. He thinks: Organization of the Communist Party of Peru. They were crowded in together, the smoke from the cigarettes fogged the mimeographed sheets that passed from hand to hand, irritated their eyes, Cahuide, which they avidly read, Organization, now and then, of the Communist Party of Peru, and they looked at the strong face of the Indian with wool cap, poncho, sandals and his belligerent fist raised, and once more the hammer and sickle crossed under the title. They'd read it aloud, commented, discussed, had riddled Washington with questions, had taken it home. He'd forgotten his resentment, his lack of faith, his frustration, his timidity, his jealousy. He wasn't a legend, he hadn't disappeared with the dictatorship: he existed. In spite of Odría, here too men and women, in spite of Cayo Bermúdez, secretly gathered and formed cells, informers and banishment, they printed Cahuide, jail and torture, and they were preparing the revolution. Washington knew who they were, how they operated, where they were, and he'll sign me up he thought, he thinks, he'll sign me up, that night, while he turned out the light on the night table and something risky, yet generous, anxious, burned in the darkness and kept on burning in his dreams, had it been there?

7

"HE WAS ARRESTED FOR STEALING or for killing somebody or because they grabbed him for something someone else did," Ambrosio said. "I hope he dies in jail, the black woman said. But they let him out and then I met him. I only saw him once in my life, sir."

"Were they interrogated?" Cayo Bermúdez asked. "All Apristas? How many have records?"

"Heads up, here he comes," Trifulcio said. "Heads up, he's coming down now."

It was noontime, the sun fell straight down onto the sand, and a buzzard with bloody eyes and black plumage was flying over the motionless dunes, descending in tight circles, his wings folded back, his beak ready, a slight glimmering tremor on the desert.

"Fifteen were on file," the Prefect said. "Nine Apristas, three Communists, three doubtful. The other eleven had no record. No, Don Cayo, they haven't been interrogated yet."

An iguana? Two maddened little feet, a tiny, straight-lined dust storm, a thread of gunpowder lighting up, a rampant invisible arrow. Softly the bird of prey flapped his wings at ground level, caught it with his beak, picked it up, executed it as he climbed back up into the air, methodically devouring it while still ascending through the clean, warm summer sky, his eyes closed by the yellow darts the sun was sending out to meet him.

"Have them interrogated right away," Cayo Bermúdez said. "Are the ones who were injured any better?"

"We talked like two strangers who don't trust each other," Ambrosio says. "One night in Chincha, years ago. Since then I never heard anything about him, son."

"Two students had to be sent to the Police Hospital, Don Cayo," the Prefect said. "The police came out all right, just a few bruises."

It kept on climbing, digesting, obstinate and in the shadows, and when it was about to dissolve in the light it extended its wings, drew a large, majestic curve, a shadow without shape, a small splotch moving across motionless white and wavy sands, motionless yellow sands: a circumference of stone, walls, barred windows, half-naked creatures who were barely moving or lay in the shade of a pulsating zinc overhang, a jeep, stakes, palm trees, a strip of water, a broad avenue of water, shacks, houses, automobiles, squares with trees in them.

"We left a company at San Marcos and we're repairing the door that the tank knocked down," the Prefect said. "We also left a detachment at the Medical School. But there hasn't been any attempt at a demonstration or anything, Don Cayo."

"Leave me those files to show to the Minister," Cayo Bermúdez said.

He unfolded his jet black, harmonious wings, tilted his body, turned solemnly and flew over the trees again, the avenue of water, the motionless sand, he circled slowly over the gleaming zinc, still watching it, he came down a little lower, indifferent to the murmuring, the greedy talk, the strategic silence that followed in that order in the rectangle enclosed by walls and bars, intent only on the corrugated overhang as the reflections from it reached him, and he continued his descent—fascinated with that orgy of lights, intoxicated by the brilliance?

"You gave the order to take San Marcos?" Colonel Espina asked. "You, without consulting me?"

"A great big black man with gray hair who walked like an ape," Ambrosio said. "He wanted to know if there were any women in Chincha, got some money out of me. I don't remember him very well, sir."

"Before we talk about San Marcos, tell me about your trip," Bermúdez said. "How are things up North?"

He cautiously stretched out his gray feet—testing the resistance, the

112

temperature, the existence of the zinc? he folded his wings, alighted, looked and guessed and it was too late: the stones sank into his feathers, broke his bones, cracked his beak, and metallic sounds burst forth as the stones returned to the courtyard, rolling along the zinc.

"They're all right, but I want to know if you've gone crazy or something," Colonel Espina said. " 'Colonel, they've taken the university, Colonel, the assault guards in San Marcos,' and me, Minister of Public Order, out of touch with it all. Have you gone crazy, Cayo?"

The bird of prey slid down in rapid death throes along the lead-gray roof that it was staining garnet, reached the edge, fell, and hungry hands received it, fought over it, plucked it, and there were laughs, insults, and a cook fire was already crackling beside the adobe wall.

"Has the headman got an eye or not?" Trifulcio asked. "A person who knows knows, and let's see if anyone wants to doubt me and how he plans to do it."

"That boil at San Marcos was lanced in a couple of hours and nobody was killed," Bermúdez said. "And instead of thanking me, you ask me if I've gone crazy. That's not fair, Uplander."

"The old black woman never saw him again after that night either," Ambrosio says. "She thought he was born bad, son."

"There'll be protests abroad, just what the government doesn't need," Colonel Espina said. "Didn't you know that the President wants to avoid incidents?"

"What the government didn't need was a subversive cell right in the heart of Lima," Bermúdez said. "In a few days the police can be pulled out, San Marcos will open up and everything will be quiet."

He was diligently chewing the piece of meat he had won with his fists and his arms and hands were burning and he had purple scratches on his dark skin and the fire where he had roasted his booty was still smoking. He was squatting down in the corner shaded by the zinc, his eyes half closed because of the bright sun or better to enjoy the pleasure that was growing in his jaws and was reaching the hollow of his palate and his tongue and his throat where the remains of feathers clinging to the singed meat scratched delightfully as they passed.

"When it comes right down to it, you had no authorization, and the decision should have been up to the Minister and not you," Colonel

113

Espina said. "A lot of countries haven't recognized the government. The President must be furious."

"Heads up, company's coming," Trifulcio said. "Heads up, they're here."

"The United States has recognized us and that's the important thing," Bermúdez said. "Don't worry about the President, Uplander. I talked to him last night before I made my move."

The others were walking in the homicidal sun, reconciled, without rancor, forgetting how they had insulted each other, pushed and punched to get the crumpled prey, or, stretched out beside the walls, they were sleeping, dirty, barefoot, open-mouthed, brutalized by boredom, hunger, or heat, their bare arms over their eyes.

"Who've they come to call on?" Trifulcio asked. "Who are they going to beat up?"

"I don't think he'd ever done anything to me," Ambrosio said. "Until that night. I wasn't mad at him, sir, even though I didn't like him very much. And that night I was sorry for him more than anything else."

"I gave the President my word that nobody would be killed, and I kept it," Bermúdez said. "Here are the police records of fifteen of the ones arrested. We'll clean up San Marcos and classes can start again. Aren't you satisfied, Uplander?"

"Not sorry because he'd been in jail, you understand, son," Ambrosio says. "But because he looked like a beggar. No shoes, toenails this long, scabs on his arms and his face which weren't scabs but filth. I'm telling you the truth."

"You acted as if I didn't exist," Colonel Espina said. "Why didn't you consult me?"

Don Melquíades was coming along the corridor escorted by two guards and followed by a tall man who was carrying a straw hat which fluttered in the white-hot wind, the brim and the crown wavering as if they were made of tissue paper, and wearing a white suit and a blue tie and a shirt that was even whiter. They had stopped and Don Melquíades was talking to the stranger and pointing out something in the courtyard to him.

"Because there was risk," Bermúdez said. "They might have been

114

armed, they might have started shooting. I didn't want the blood to be on your head, Uplander."

He wasn't a lawyer, no shyster would ever have been so well-dressed, and he wasn't from the authorities either, because did they give them noodle soup today, did they have them sweep out the cells and latrines the way they always did when there was an inspection? But if he wasn't a lawyer or an official, who was he?

"It could have hurt your political future and I explained that to the President," Bermúdez said. "I'll make the decision, I'll assume the responsibility. If there are any consequences, I'll resign and the Uplander will come out clean."

He stopped gnawing on the small polished bone that he held in his big hands, remained stiff, lowered his head a bit, his startled eyes looking at the veranda: Don Melquíades was still signaling, still pointing at him.

"But things turned out all right and now the credit is yours," Colonel Espina said. "The President's going to think that the man I recommended has more balls than I do."

"Hey, you, Trifulcio!" Don Melquíades shouted. "Can't you see I'm calling you? What are you waiting for?"

"The President knows I owe this job to you," Bermúdez said. "He knows that all you have to do is frown and I'll say thanks for everything and go back to selling tractors again."

"Hey, you!" the guards shouted, waving their arms. "Hey, you!"

"Three switchblades and a few Molotov cocktails, there wasn't any reason to get upset," Bermúdez said. "I've added some revolvers and a few more knives and brass knuckles for the newspapers."

He got up, ran, crossed the courtyard, raising a cloud of dust, stopped a few feet from Don Melquíades. The others had put their heads forward and looked and remained silent. The ones walking had stopped moving, those who were sleeping were squatting and observing and the sun was like liquid.

"Did you call in the press too?" Colonel Espina asked. "Don't you know that the Minister signs communiqués, that the Minister holds press conferences?"

"Come on, Trifulcio, lift up that barrel, Don Emilio Arévalo wants to see you do it," Don Melquíades said. "Don't make me look bad, I said that you could."

"I called them so you could talk to them," Bermúdez said. "Here's the report in detail, the files, the weapons for the photographers. I called them with you in mind, Uplander."

"I haven't done nothing, sir." Trifulcio blinked and shouted and waited and shouted again. "Nothing. My word of honor, Don Melquíades."

"All right, let's drop it," Colonel Espina said. "But remember that I wanted to clean up the San Marcos business after the problem of the unions had been settled."

Black, cylindrical, the barrel was at the foot of the veranda, beneath Don Melquíades, the guards and the stranger in white. Indifferent or interested or relieved, the others looked at the barrel and Trifulcio or exchanged mocking glances.

"The San Marcos business hasn't been cleaned up and it's time now to clean it up," Bermúdez said. "The twenty-six we have are shock troops, but most of the leaders are still on the loose and we have to grab them now."

"Stop playing the fool and pick up that barrel," Don Melquíades said. "I know you haven't done anything. Go ahead, pick it up so that Mr. Arévalo can see you."

"The unions are more important than San Marcos, they're the ones we have to clean up," Colonel Espina said. "They haven't said a word yet, but APRA is strong among the workers and one little spark could set off an explosion."

"If I shat in my cell it's because I was sick," Trifulcio said. "I couldn't hold it in, Don Melquíades. My word of honor."

"We'll do it," Bermúdez said. "We'll clean up everything that needs cleaning up, Uplander."

The stranger began to laugh, Don Melquíades began to laugh, laughter broke out in the yard. The stranger leaned over the railing, put his hand in his pocket and took out something shiny that he showed to Trifulcio.

"Have you read *La Tribuna,* the underground paper?" Colonel Espina asked. "Terrible things against the army, against me. We have to stop that dirty little sheet from circulating."

116

"A sol, just to lift that barrel, sir?" Trifulcio blinked and started to laugh. "Of course, why not, yes sir!"

"Of course they talked about him in Chincha, sir," Ambrosio said. "That he'd raped an underage girl, stolen, killed a guy in a fight. He couldn't have done all of those terrible things. But he must have done some of them, because why else would he have been in jail for so long?"

"You military men are still thinking about the APRA of twenty years ago," Bermúdez said. "Their leaders are old and corrupt, they don't want to get themselves killed anymore. There won't be any explosion, there won't be any revolution. And that little sheet will disappear, I promise you that."

He raised his hands to his face (wrinkled now on the eyelids and around the neck and alongside his kinky gray sideburns) and he spat on them a couple of times and rubbed them and took a step toward the barrel. He touched it, felt it, put his long legs and his domed belly and his broad chest against the hard body of the barrel and hugged it hard, lovingly, with his long arms.

"I never saw him again, but I heard him mentioned once," Ambrosio says. "They'd seen him in the towns of the district during the 1950 elections, campaigning for Senator Arévalo. Putting up posters, giving out handbills. For the candidacy of Don Emilio Arévalo, your papa's friend, son."

"I've got the little list for you, Don Cayo, only three prefects and eight subprefects among those appointed by Bustamante have resigned," Dr. Alcibíades said. "Twelve prefects and fifteen subprefects sent telegrams congratulating the General for having taken power. The rest silent; they probably want to be reappointed but don't dare ask for it."

He closed his eyes and, as he was lifting the barrel, the veins on his neck and temples puffed up, the worn skin of his face became moist and his fat lips turned purple. Arching, he supported the weight with his whole body, and a big hand descended roughly along the side of the barrel and it was raised a little more. He took two drunken steps with his burden, looked proudly at the railing, and with a shove returned the barrel to the ground.

"The Uplander thought that they were going to resign en masse and he wanted to begin naming prefects and subprefects like crazy," Cayo

Bermúdez said. "You can see, doctor, that the Colonel doesn't know his Peruvians."

"A regular bull, Melquíades, you were right, it's incredible at his age." The stranger in white tossed the coin into the air and Trifulcio caught it on the fly. "Say, how old are you?"

"He thinks they're all like him, men of honor," Dr. Alcibíades said. "But tell me, Don Cayo, why would those prefects and subprefects remain loyal to poor old Bustamante? He's never going to raise his head up again."

"I don't know for sure." Trifulcio laughed, panted, dried his face. "I've got lots and lots of years behind me. More than you, sir."

"Reappoint the ones who sent telegrams of support and the silent ones too, we'll calmly go about replacing all of them," Bermúdez said. "Thank the ones who resigned for services rendered and have Lozano put them on file."

"Here's one of the kind you like, Hipólito," Ludovico said. "He comes with a special recommendation from Mr. Lozano."

"Lima's still flooded with underground fliers," Colonel Espina said. "What's going on, Cayo?"

"Where the underground *Tribuna* is printed and who's printing it, one, two, three," Hipólito said. "Remember, you're one of the kind I like."

"These subversive sheets have got to disappear right away," Bermúdez said. "Do you understand, Lozano?"

"Are you all set, black man?" Don Melquíades asked. "Your feet must be burning up, right, Trifulcio?"

"You don't know who or where?" Ludovico asked. "Then how come you had a *Tribuna* in your pocket when you were picked up in Vitarte, pappy?"

"Am I all set?" Trifulcio laughed with anguish. "All set, Don Melquíades?"

"Right after I came to Lima I sent money to the old woman and would go visit her from time to time," Ambrosio said. "Then nothing. She died without knowing what I was doing. It's one of the things that bother me, sir."

"Did they put it in your pocket without your knowing?" Hipólito

118

asked. "But that was awful silly of you, pappy. And just look at the skin-tight pants you're wearing and all that grease on your hair. You're not even an Aprista, you don't even know where *La Tribuna* is printed and who prints it?"

"Have you forgotten that you're getting out today?" Don Melquíades asked. "Or are you so used to it here now that you don't want to leave?"

"I found out that the old woman had died, from a person from Chincha, son," Ambrosio says. "When I was still working for your papa."

"No, sir, I didn't forget, sir." Trifulcio shuffled his feet, rubbed his hands. "Absolutely not, Don Melquíades."

"See? Hipólito got mad and look what happened to you. You'd better get your memory back pretty quick," Ludovico said. "Remember, you're the kind he likes."

"They don't answer, they lie, they point their finger at each other," Lozano said. "But we're not asleep, Don Cayo. Whole nights without shutting our eyes. We'll get rid of those handbills, I promise you."

"Give me your finger. That's it, now make an X," Don Melquíades said. "All set, Trifulcio, free again. You can't believe it, can you?"

"This isn't a civilized country, it's barbarian and ignorant," Bermúdez said. "Stop sitting around and find out what I need to know right away."

"But look how skinny you are, pappy," Hipólito said. "With your coat and shirt on, you wouldn't think it, I can even count your ribs, pappy."

"Do you remember Mr. Arévalo, the one who gave you a sol to pick up the barrel?" Don Melquíades asked. "He's an important rancher. Do you want to work for him?"

"Who and where? One, two, three," Ludovico said. "Do you want us to go on like this all night? What if Hipólito gets mad again?"

"Of course I do, Don Melquíades," Trifulcio answered with his head and his hands and his eyes. "Right now or whenever you say, sir."

"You're going to get your body hurt and it kills me," Hipólito said, "because I'm getting fonder and fonder of you, pappy."

"He needs people for his election campaign, because he's a friend of Odría's and he's going to be a senator," Don Melquíades said. "He'll pay you well. Take advantage of this opportunity, Trifulcio."

"You haven't even told us what your name is, pappy," Ludovico said.

119

"Or maybe you don't know that either, maybe you've forgotten it too."

"Go get drunk, visit your family, whore around a little," Don Melquíades said. "And on Monday report to his ranch, on the way out of Ica. Just ask anybody and they'll tell you."

"Have your nuts always been so small or is it because you're scared?" Hipólito asked. "And I can barely see your little deal, pappy. Is that because you're scared too?"

"Of course I'll remember, sir, what more could I want?" Trifulcio said. "I can't thank you enough for recommending me to the gentleman, sir."

"Leave him alone, Hipólito, he can't hear you," Ludovico said. "Let's go to Mr. Lozano's office. Leave him alone, Hipólito."

The guard gave him a pat on the back, fine, Trifulcio, and closed the gate behind him, until never again or until the next time, Trifulcio. He walked rapidly ahead, through the dust that he knew so well, that he could see from the block of better cells, and soon he reached the trees that he also knew from memory, and then he went forward along a new stretch until he reached the shacks on the outskirts, where instead of stopping he quickened his pace. He went through the huts and human figures almost on the run, while they looked at him with surprise or indifference or fear.

"And it's not that I was a bad son or didn't love her, the old black woman deserved heaven, just like you, sir," Ambrosio said. "She broke her back raising and feeding me. What happens is that life doesn't give a body any time, not even to think about his mother."

"We left him because Hipólito got carried away and the guy began to say crazy things and then he fainted, Mr. Lozano," Ludovico said. "I don't think that Trinidad López there is an Aprista or even has any idea what he is. But if you want, we'll wake him and keep on with it, sir."

He continued forward, more and more in a hurry and wilder, unable to get his bearings on those first paved streets that his bare feet were treading furiously, going deeper and deeper into the city that was so much longer, so much wider, so different from the one his eyes remembered. He walked without direction, without haste, finally he dropped down onto a bench shaded by the palm trees of a square. There was a store on the corner, women and children were going in, some boys were throwing stones at a street light and some dogs were barking. Slowly silently, without realizing it, he began to weep.

"Your uncle suggested I call you, Captain, and I wanted to meet you too," Cayo Bermúdez said. "We're colleagues of sorts, right? And we'll certainly have to work together someday."

"She was good, she worked hard, she never missed mass," Ambrosio says. "But she had her ways, son. For example, she never hit me with her hand, only with a stick. 'So you don't turn out like your father,' she'd tell me."

"I already knew you by name, Mr. Bermúdez," Captain Paredes said. "My uncle and Colonel Espina appreciate you very much, they say that this whole setup is functioning only because of you."

He got up, washed his face in the fountain on the square, asked two men where he could catch the bus to Chincha and how much it cost. Stopping from time to time to look at the women and the things that had changed so much, he walked toward another square, covered with vehicles. He asked, bargained, begged and got into a truck that waited two hours before leaving.

"Let's not talk about merits because you'll leave me way behind," Cayo Bermúdez said. "I know that you got deeply involved in the revolution by lining up officers, that you got military security rolling along. I learned from your uncle. You can't deny it."

All through the trip he was standing, holding onto the side of the truck, smelling and looking at the sand, the sky, the sea that appeared and disappeared behind the dunes. When the truck got to Chincha, he opened his eyes wide and turned his head from side to side, startled by the changes. There was a cool breeze, no more sun, the tops of the palm trees on the square danced and whispered as he walked under them, agitated, nauseous, still in a hurry.

"The part about the revolution is all true and there's no need to be modest," Captain Paredes said. "But as far as military security is concerned, I only work for Colonel Molina, Mr. Bermúdez."

But the way to the slum settlement was long and tortuous because his memory went back on him and he had to keep asking people how to get to the road to Grocio Prado. He got there when it was already the time of lamps and shadows, and the settlement was no longer a collection of shacks but a group of well-built houses, and instead of the cotton fields

121

that began where the edge used to be, the houses of another settlement started. But the hut was the same and the door was open and he recognized Tomasa at once: fat, black, sitting on the floor, eating, to the right of the other woman.

"Colonel Molina's the one who heads it up, but you're the one who keeps the wheels rolling," Bermúdez said. "I know that too from your uncle, Captain."

"Her dream was to win in the lottery, sir," Ambrosio said. "Once an ice cream man in Chincha won, and she maybe God will send it here again and she bought her pieces of a ticket with the money she didn't have. She'd take them to the Virgin, light candles for them. She didn't even get a rebate prize, sir."

"I can imagine what this Ministry was like under Bustamante, Apristas everywhere and sabotage the order of the day," Captain Paredes said. "But it didn't do the devils much good."

He went in with a leap, pounding his chest and grunting, and stood between the two and the stranger gave a cry and crossed herself. Tomasa, huddling on the ground, looked at him and suddenly fear left her face. Without speaking, without standing up, she showed him the door of the shack with her fist and finger. But Trifulcio didn't leave, he began to laugh, he dropped down merrily to the ground and began to scratch his armpits.

"It did them enough good not to leave any traces, at least, the security records are useless," Bermúdez said. "The Apristas got rid of the files. We're reorganizing everything, and that's what I wanted to talk to you about, Captain. Military security could help us a lot."

"So you're Mr. Bermúdez' chauffeur," Ludovico said. "Pleased to meet you, Ambrosio. So you're going to help us out a little in that matter of the slums."

"There's no problem, of course we have to work together," Captain Paredes said. "Any time you need some piece of information, I'll supply it, Mr. Bermúdez."

"What have you come for, who sent you, who invited you?" Tomasa roared. "You look like an outlaw, you look like what you are. Didn't you see how my friend took one look at you and ran away? When did you get out?"

122

"I'd like something else, Captain," Bermúdez said. "I'd like to have access to the whole political file at military security. Have a copy of it."

"His name is Hipólito and he's the dumbest of all the dumbbells on the staff," Ludovico said. "He'll be back soon, I'll introduce you. He's not on the civil service list and he probably never will be. I hope to be someday with a little bit of luck. Say, Ambrosio, you must be on it, right?"

"Our files are untouchable, they're classified secret," Captain Paredes said. "I'll tell Colonel Molina about your plan, but he can't make a decision either. The best thing would be a request from the Minister of Public Order to the Minister of War."

"Your friend ran off like I was the devil himself." Trifulcio laughed. "Listen, Tomasa, let me have some of that food. I could eat a horse."

"That's precisely what we have to avoid, Captain," Bermúdez said. "The copy of that file should reach the Director of Public Order without either Colonel Molina or the Minister of War himself knowing anything about it. Do I make myself understood?"

"Killing work, Ambrosio," Ludovico said. "Hours on end losing your voice, your strength, and then along comes someone on the list and he insults you, and Mr. Lozano threatens to cut your pay. Killing for everybody except that horse of an Hipólito. Do you want me to tell you why?"

"I can't give you a copy of top-secret files without my superiors' knowing about it," Captain Paredes said. "They hold the life and future of every officer and thousands of civilians. It's like gold in the Central Bank, Mr. Bermúdez."

"Yes, you'll have to go away, but calm down now and have a drink, you poor devil," Don Fermín said. "Tell me now just what happened. Stop crying."

"Precisely, Captain, of course those files are worth their weight in gold," Bermúdez said. "And your uncle knows that too. The matter has to stay just among those responsible for security. No, it's not a matter of offending Colonel Molina. . . ."

"Because after working a guy over for half an hour, that horse of an Hipólito, all of a sudden, boom, he gets all excited," Ludovico said.

123

"Your morale gets low, you get bored. Not him, boom, he gets all excited. You'll meet him, you'll see."

"It's a matter of promoting him," Bermúdez said. "Giving him the command of a unit, a detachment. And no one will dispute the fact that you're the person most indicated to take Colonel Molina's place in charge of security. Then we can merge the services discreetly, Captain."

"Not for one night and not for one minute," Tomasa said. "You're not going to stay here for one minute. You're leaving right now, Trifulcio."

"You've got my uncle in your pocket, friend Bermúdez," Captain Paredes said. "You've only known him for six months and now he trusts you more than he does me. I'm joking, of course, Cayo. It's time we got on a first-name basis, don't you think?"

"They don't lie because they're brave, Ambrosio, but because they're afraid," Ludovico said. "Just try to see if you can get something out of one of them sometime. Who's your leader? So-and-so, what's-his-name. How long have you been an Aprista? I'm not. Then how can you say that so-and-so and what's-his-name are your leaders? They're not. Killing, believe me."

"Your uncle knows that the survival of the government depends on security," Bermúdez said. "Everybody's all applause right now, but pretty soon the tug of war and the battle of interests will start, and because of that everything will depend on what security has done to neutralize ambitious and resentful people."

"I don't plan on staying, I'm just passing through," Trifulcio said. "I'm going to work for a rich fellow from Ica named Arévalo. That's the truth, Tomasa."

"I know that quite well," Captain Paredes said. "When there aren't any Apristas left, the President will have enemies in the government itself."

"Are you a Communist, are you an Aprista? I'm not an Aprista, I'm not a Communist," Ludovico said. "You're a sissy, friend, we haven't touched you and you're lying already. Like that for hours, whole nights like that, Ambrosio. And that gets Hipólito excited, can you see what kind of a guy he is?"

"That's why we have to take the long view," Bermúdez said. "The most dangerous element today is the civilian sector, tomorrow it'll be the military. Can you see why there's so much secrecy about the files?"

"You didn't even ask where Perpetuo is buried or whether Ambrosio is still alive," Tomasa said. "Have you forgotten that you had children?"

"She was a happy woman who loved life, sir," Ambrosio said. "The poor woman, hitching up with a guy capable of doing that to his own son. But naturally, if the old woman hadn't fallen in love with him, I wouldn't be here today. So it was good for me."

"You have to get a house, Cayo, you can't keep staying at the hotel," Colonel Espina said. "Besides, it's absurd for you not to use the car that goes with your being Director of Public Order."

"I don't care about the dead," Trifulcio said. "But I would like to see Ambrosio. Does he live with you?"

"The fact is, I've never owned a car and, besides, taxis are convenient," Bermúdez said. "But you're right, Uplander, I'll use it. It must be rusting away."

"Ambrosio is leaving to look for work in Lima tomorrow," Tomasa said. "What do you want to see him for?"

"I didn't believe that about Hipólito, but it's true, Ambrosio," Ludovico said. "I saw it, nobody told me."

"You shouldn't be so modest, make use of your prerogatives," Colonel Espina said. "You're shut up in here fifteen hours a day and work isn't everything in life either. Let your hair down once in a while, Cayo."

"Just out of curiosity to see what he's like," Trifulcio said. "I'll see Ambrosio and I promise to leave, Tomasa."

"For the first time they gave a guy from Vitarte to the two of us alone," Ludovico said. "Nobody on the list there to bawl us out, there weren't enough people. And that's when I saw it, Ambrosio."

"Of course I will, Uplander, but first I've got to get a lot of work cleared up," Bermúdez said. "And I'll get a house and set myself up in more comfort."

"Ambrosio was working here as a long-distance driver," Tomasa said. "But it's going to be better for him in Lima and that's why I've pushed him to go."

"The President is very pleased with you, Cayo," Colonel Espina said. "He thanks me more for having recommended you than for all the help I gave him in the revolution, imagine that."

"He was hitting him and he began to sweat, hitting him more and sweating more and he hit him so much that the guy began to say crazy things," Ludovico said. "And all of a sudden I saw his fly puffed up like a balloon. I swear, Ambrosio."

"The one coming this way, that big fellow," Trifulcio said. "Is that Ambrosio?"

" 'What are you hitting for, you've left him half loony, you've already sent him off to dreamland,' " Ludovico said. "He wasn't even listening, Ambrosio. All excited, just like a balloon. Just the way I'm telling you, I swear. You'll meet him soon enough, I'll introduce you to him."

"Our hopes are with you people now so we can get out of this danger," Don Fermín said.

"I recognized you right away," Trifulcio said. "Come here, Ambrosio, give me a hug, let me take a little look at you."

"The government in danger?" Colonel Espina asked. "Are you joking, Don Fermín? If the revolution isn't sailing along with a good tail wind, how can anybody . . . ?"

"I would have gone to wait for you," Ambrosio said. "But I didn't even know you were getting out."

"Fermín is right, Colonel," Emilio Arévalo said. "Nothing will sail along with a good wind if elections aren't held and General Odría isn't returned to power anointed and consecrated by the votes of all Peruvians."

"At least you're not throwing me out like Tomasa," Trifulcio said. "I thought you were a boy and you're almost as old as this black father of yours."

"Elections are a formality, if you want, Colonel," Don Fermín said. "But a necessary formality."

"You've seen him, now be on your way," Tomasa said. "Ambrosio's going away tomorrow, he has to pack his things."

"And in order to have elections the country has to be pacified, that is, the Apristas all cleaned up," Dr. Ferro said. "If not, the elections could blow up in our faces like a bomb."

"Let's go have a drink somewhere, Ambrosio," Trifulcio said. "We'll talk a little and you can come back and pack your bags."

126

"You haven't said a word, Mr. Bermúdez," Emilio Arévalo said. "It would seem that politics bore you."

"Do you want to give your son a bad reputation?" Tomasa asked. "Is that why you want people to see him with you on the street?"

"Not seems, the fact is I am bored by them," Bermúdez said. "Besides, I don't understand anything about politics. Don't laugh, it's true. That's why I'd rather just listen."

They went along in the dark, through streets that wavered and made sudden turns, among reed huts and a brick house here and there, looking through windows and seeing by the light of candles and lamps hazy silhouettes that chatted as they ate. There was a smell of earth, excrement and grapes.

"Well, for someone who knows nothing about politics, you're doing quite well as Director of Security," Don Fermín said. "Another drink, Don Cayo?"

They came across a donkey lying in the street, invisible dogs barked at them. They were almost the same height, they went along in silence, the sky had cleared, it was hot, no breeze was blowing. The man resting in his rocking chair got up when he saw them come into the deserted bar, served them beer and sat down again. They clinked glasses in the half-light, still without having spoken to each other.

"Fundamentally, two things," Dr. Ferro said. "First, maintaining the team that has taken power. Second, continuing the cleanup with a strong hand. University, unions, administration. Then elections and working for the good of the country."

"What would I have liked to have been in life, son?" Ambrosio asks. "A rich guy, naturally."

"So you're going to Lima tomorrow," Trifulcio said. "What are you going to do there?"

"For you it's being happy, son?" Ambrosio asks. "Me too, naturally, but for me being rich and being happy is the same thing."

"It's all a matter of loans and credit," Don Fermín said. "The United States is ready to help a government that maintains order, that's why they backed the revolution. Now they want elections and we have to give them what they want."

"To look for work there," Ambrosio said. "You can make more money in the capital."

"The gringos believe in formalities, we have to understand them," Emilio Arévalo said. "They're happy with the General and all they ask is that democratic forms be preserved. With Odría as an elected president, they'll open their arms to us and give us all the credit we need."

"And how long have you been working as a driver?" Trifulcio asked.

"But above all we have to bring forward the National Patriotic Front or the Restoration Movement or whatever it's to be called," Dr. Ferro said. "That's why the program is basic and that's why I insist on it so much."

"Two years as a professional," Ambrosio said. "I started out as a helper, filling in with the driving. Then I was a regular truckdriver and up till now I've been driving buses around here, from one district to another."

"A patriotic and nationalist program that would bring together all sound forces," Emilio Arévalo said. "Industry, commerce, workers, farmers. Based on simple but efficient ideas."

"So you're a serious man, a hard worker," Trifulcio said. "Tomasa was right in not wanting people to see you with me. Do you think you'll find work in Lima?"

"We need something that will remind people of Marshal Benavides' excellent formula," Dr. Ferro said. "Order, Peace and Work. I've thought of Health, Education, Work. What do you gentlemen think of it?"

"Do you remember Túmula the milk woman, the daughter she had?" Ambrosio asked. "She married the Vulture's son. Do you remember the Vulture? I helped his son run away with her."

"Of course, the General's candidacy has to be launched at the highest level," Emilio Arévalo said. "All sectors would have to proclaim it in a spontaneous way."

"The Vulture, the loan shark, the one who was mayor?" Trifulcio asked. "Yes, I remember him."

"It'll be proclaimed, Don Emilio," Colonel Espina said. "The General's getting more popular every day. In just a few months people will have seen the tranquillity we have now as opposed to the chaos the country was in with Apristas and Communists loose on the streets."

"The Vulture's son is in the government, he's important now," Ambrosio said. "Maybe he'll help me find work in Lima."

"Why don't just the two of us go have a drink, Don Cayo?" Don Fermín asked. "Haven't you got a headache from friend Ferro's speeches? He always leaves me seasick."

"If he's important, he probably won't want to have anything to do with you," Trifulcio said. "He'll look right past you."

"With great pleasure, Mr. Zavala," Bermúdez said. "Yes, Dr. Ferro does talk a lot. But you can see that he's had experience."

"In order to win him over, take him a little present," Trifulcio said. "Something that'll remind him of his home town and touch his heart."

"Enormous experience, he's been in every government over the past twenty years," Don Fermín said. "This way, my car's over here."

"I'm going to bring him a couple of bottles of wine," Ambrosio said. "And what are you going to do now? Are you going back to the house?"

"Whatever you're having," Bermúdez said. "Yes, Mr. Zavala, whiskey, fine."

"I don't think so, you saw how your mother received me," Trifulcio said. "But that doesn't mean that Tomasa's a bad woman."

"I've never liked politics because I've never understood what it was all about," Bermúdez said. "Circumstances got me involved in politics in my old age."

"She says you abandoned her a whole lot of times," Ambrosio said. "That you only came back home to get the money she made working like a mule."

"I hate politics too, but what can we do," Don Fermín said. "When hard-working people stay out and leave politics to the politicians, the country goes to the devil."

"Women exaggerate and, after all, Tomasa is a woman," Trifulcio said. "I'm going to work in Ica, but I'll come back and see her now and then."

"Is it true that you've never been here?" Don Fermín asked. "Espina's been exploiting you, Don Cayo. The show is pretty good, you'll see. Don't think I'm a big night-lifer. Very rarely."

"And how are things here?" Trifulcio asked. "You should know, you

129

should know a lot at your age. Women, whorehouses. How are the whorehouses here?"

She was wearing a skin-tight white evening gown that had a slight sparkle about it and outlined the lines of her body so neatly and vividly that she seemed to be naked. A dress, the same color as her skin, which touched the floor and made her take short little steps, cricket hops.

"There are two of them, one expensive and one cheap," Ambrosio said. "By expensive I mean twenty soles, at the cheap one you can go as low as three. But they're terrible."

Her shoulders were white, round, soft, and the whiteness of her complexion contrasted with the darkness of her hair, which flowed down her back. She tightened her mouth with slow avidity, as if she were going to bite the small, silver-plated microphone, and her large eyes gleamed and kept looking over the tables.

"A pretty-looking Muse, eh?" Don Fermín said. "At least compared to the skeletons that came out to dance before. But her voice doesn't help her very much."

"I don't want to take you or for you to go with me, and besides, I know it's best if you're not seen with me," Trifulcio said. "But I'd like to take a walk over there, just to see. Where's the cheap one?"

"Very pretty, yes, a beautiful body, beautiful face," Bermúdez said. "And I don't think her voice is so bad."

"Close by here," Ambrosio said. "But the police are always hanging around because they're always having fights."

"Let me tell you that that woman who's so much of a woman there isn't really that at all," Don Fermín said. "She likes other women."

"That's the least of my worries, because I'm used to cops and fights." Trifulcio laughed. "Come on, pay for the beers and let's go."

"Is that so?" Bermúdez said. "A woman as pretty as that. Is that so?"

"I'd go with you but the bus to Lima leaves at six o'clock," Ambrosio said. "And my things are still all scattered around."

"So you don't have any children, Don Cayo," Don Fermín said. "Well, you've saved yourself a lot of problems. I've got three and right now they're beginning to give Zoila and me headaches."

"You can leave me at the door and take off," Trifulcio said. "Take me along a way where nobody will see us, if you want."

"Two young gentlemen and a little lady?" Bermúdez asked. "Already grown up?"

They went out onto the street again and the night was brighter. The moon showed them the potholes, the ruts, the stones. They went through deserted alleys, Trifulcio turning his head from right to left, observing everything, taking an interest in everything; Ambrosio with his hands in his pockets, kicking stones.

"What future could the navy hold for a boy?" Don Fermín asked. "None. But Sparky insisted and I used my influence to get him in. And now you see, they threw him out. Lazy in his studies, undisciplined. He's going to end up without a career, that's the worst of it. Of course, I could make some moves and get him reinstated. But no, I don't want a son who's in the navy. I'd rather put him to work for me."

"Is that all you've got, Ambrosio?" Trifulcio asked. "Only twenty soles? Only twenty soles, a driver and everything?"

"Why don't you send him abroad to study?" Bermúdez asked. "Maybe with a change in surroundings the boy will straighten out."

"If I had any more I'd give it to you too," Ambrosio said. "All you'd have to do is ask and I'd give it to you. Why did you pull that knife? You didn't have to. Look, come to the house and I'll give you more. But put that away, I'll give you another fifty soles. But don't threaten me. I'm glad to help you, give you more. Come on, let's go to the house."

"Impossible, my wife would die," Don Fermín said. "Sparky all alone in a foreign country? Zoila wouldn't hear of it. He's the one she spoils."

"No, I won't go," Trifulcio said. "This is enough. And it's a loan, I'll pay you back your twenty soles because I've got a job in Ica. Were you scared because I took out the knife? I wasn't going to do anything to you, you're my son. And I'll pay you back, I give you my word."

"And has your younger son turned out difficult to handle too?" Bermúdez asked.

"I don't want you to pay me back, I'm giving it to you," Ambrosio said. "I wasn't scared. You didn't have to take out the knife, I swear. You're my father, I would have given it to you if you'd asked. Come to the house, I swear I'll give you fifty soles more."

"No, Skinny is just the opposite of Sparky," Don Fermín said. "First in his class, winning all the prizes at the end of the year. You have to rein him in to stop him from studying too hard. A beauty of a boy, Don Cayo."

"You must be thinking that I'm worse than what Tomasa's told you," Trifulcio said. "But I took it out for no reason, really, I wasn't going to do anything to you, even if you didn't give me a single sol. And I'll pay you back, word of honor, I'll pay you back your twenty soles, Ambrosio."

"I can see that the younger one is your favorite," Bermúdez said. "What career is he going into?"

"All right, you can pay me back if you want to," Ambrosio said. "Forget about all this, I've already forgotten. Don't you want to come to the house? I'll give you fifty soles more, I promise."

"He's still in the last part of high school and doesn't know," Don Fermín said. "It isn't that he's my favorite, I love all three of them the same. It's just that Santiago makes me feel proud. Well, you understand."

"You must think that I'm a dog who'd even steal from his own son, who'd pull a knife on his own son," Trifulcio said. "I swear to you that this is a loan."

"You make me a little jealous listening to you, Mr. Zavala," Bermúdez said. "In spite of all the headaches, being a father must have its compensations."

"But it's all right, I do think it just happened like that and that you will pay me back," Ambrosio said. "Now forget about it, please."

"You're living at the Maury, right?" Don Fermín said. "Come on, I'll drop you there."

"You're not ashamed of me?" Trifulcio asked. "Tell me frankly."

"No, thanks a lot, I'd rather walk, the Maury is close by," Bermúdez said. "I'm very pleased to have met you, Mr. Zavala."

"But what a thing to think, what have I got to be ashamed of?" Ambrosio asked. "Come on, we'll go into the whorehouse together if you want."

"What are you doing here?" Bermúdez asked. "What brings you here?"

"No, go pack your bag, you shouldn't be seen with me," Trifulcio said.

"You're a good son, I hope everything works out for you in Lima. Believe me, I'll pay you back, Ambrosio."

"They sent me from one place to the other, they made me wait here for hours, Don Cayo," Ambrosio said. "I was ready to go back to Chincha, I tell you."

"Generally the Director of Public Order's chauffeur is someone from the Police Department, Don Cayo," Dr. Alcibíades said. "For reasons of security. But if you prefer."

"I've come to look for work, Don Cayo," Ambrosio said. "I'm sick of driving that broken-down old bus. I thought that maybe you could help me get a job."

"Yes, I prefer it this way, doctor," Bermúdez said. "I've known this black fellow for years and I have more confidence in him than in some X from the police. He's outside by the door, would you take care of it, please?"

"I know all about driving, and I'll get used to the Lima traffic right away, Don Cayo," Ambrosio said. "You need a chauffeur? That would be great, Don Cayo."

"Yes, I'll take care of it," Dr. Alcibíades said. "I'll have them put him on the rolls of the Prefecture or sign him up or whatever is necessary. And I'll have them get the car for you today."

"All right, you're hired, then," Bermúdez said. "You're in luck, Ambrosio, you arrived at just the right moment."

"To your health," Santiago says.

8

THE BOOKSTORE WAS INSIDE A BUILDING with balconies, you went in through a vague entranceway and from there you could see it huddled in back, barred and deserted. Santiago arrived before nine o'clock, scanned the bookcases in the entrance, thumbed through the time-worn books, the faded magazines. The old man with a beret and gray sideburns looked at him indifferently, good old Matías he thinks, then he began to look at him out of the corner of his eye, and finally he went over to him: was he looking for something? A book on the French Revolution. Ah, the old man smiled, over here. Sometimes it was does Mr. Henri Barbusse live here or is Don Bruno Bauer in? sometimes touching the door in a certain way, and sometimes there were comical confusions, Zavalita. He led him to a room that had been invaded by piles of newspapers, silvery cobwebs and books stacked up against black walls. He pointed to a rocking chair, he should sit down, he had a slight Spanish accent, eloquent little eyes, a very white goatee: he hadn't been followed? You had to be very careful, everything depends on the young people.

"Seventy years old and he was pure, Carlitos," Santiago said. "The only one I've ever known at that age."

The old man gave an affectionate wink and went back into the courtyard. Santiago browsed through old Lima magazines, *Variedades* and *Mundial,* he thinks he set aside those that had articles by Mariátegui or Vallejo.

"Of course, in those days Peruvians could read Vallejo and Mariátegui in the press," Carlitos said. "Now they read us, Zavalita, that's a backward step."

Moments later he saw Jacobo and Aída come in. Not yet a little worm or a snake or a knife, it was a pin that sank in and disappeared. He saw them whispering beside the aged shelves and saw the carefree look and the joy on Jacobo's face and saw them separate when Matías went over to them and saw Jacobo's smile disappear and a frown of concentration appear, abstract seriousness, the face he had been showing the world for some months. He was wearing the brown suit that he rarely changed now, the wrinkled shirt, the tie with the loosened knot. He's taken to disguising himself as a proletarian Washington joked, he thinks he only shaved once a week and didn't shine his shoes, one of these days Aída's going to leave him Solórzano laughed.

"All that mystery because that was the day we were going to quit playing games," Santiago said. "Things were about to start for real, Carlitos."

Had it been at the start of that third year at San Marcos, Zavalita, between his discovery of Cahuide and that day? From readings and discussions to the distribution of mimeographed sheets at the university, from the deaf woman's boardinghouse to the small house in Rímac to Matías' bookstore, from dangerous games to the real danger: that day. The two groups hadn't merged again, he only saw Jacobo and Aída at San Marcos, other groups were active, but if they asked Washington he would answer that a fly can't get into a closed mouth and would smile. One morning he called them: at such and such a time, at such and such a place, just the three of them. They were going to meet someone from Cahuide, they could ask him any questions they wanted to, air any doubts they might have, he thinks I didn't sleep that night either. Sometimes Matías would raise his eyes from the courtyard and smile at them, in the room in back they smoked, thumbed through magazines, kept looking at the entranceway and the street.

"He said nine o'clock and it's nine-thirty," Jacobo said. "He probably won't come."

"Aída changed a lot when she started going with Jacobo," Santiago said. "She joked, she looked happy. On the other hand, he became

135

serious and stopped combing his hair and changing his clothes. He wouldn't laugh with Aída if anyone was looking, he almost never said a word to her in front of us. He was ashamed to be happy, Carlitos."

"Just because he's a Communist doesn't mean he's stopped being Peruvian." Aída laughed. "He'll come at ten, you wait and see."

It was a quarter to ten: a bird face in the entranceway, a hopping little walk, skin like yellow paper, a suit that danced on him, a little garnet tie. They saw him talking to Matías, looking around, coming over. He went into the room, smiled at them, sorry I'm late, a thin little hand, the bus he was on had broken down, and they stood looking at each other, embarrassed.

"Thanks for waiting." His voice was very thin too, he thinks. "A fraternal greeting from Cahuide, comrades."

"The first time I'd heard the word comrades, Carlitos, you can imagine Zavalita and his sentimental heart," Santiago said. "I only knew his *nom de guerre,* Llaque; I only saw him a few times. He was in the Workers' Section of Cahuide, I never got beyond the University Section. You can imagine, one of those pure ones."

That morning we didn't know that Llaque had been a law student during the time of Odría's revolution, he thinks, that he'd been a victim of the police attack on San Marcos, that he'd been tortured and exiled to Bolivia, and that in La Paz he'd been in jail for six months, that he'd returned clandestinely to Peru: only that he looked like a little bird, that morning as his frail voice summarized the history of the Party for them and they watched him as he moved his thin yellow hand in a repeated rotary movement, as if he had a cramp in it, and kept watching the courtyard and the street out of the corner of his eye. It had been founded by José Carlos Mariátegui and as soon as it came into being, it grew and organized teams and won over segments of the working class, he wanted to show us that we could be trusted, he thinks, and he didn't hide from us the fact that it had always been tiny or its weakness as compared to APRA, and that had been the golden age of the Party, the period of the magazine *Amauta* and the newspaper *Labor* and the organization of labor unions and students sent into Indian communities. When Mariátegui died in 1930, the Party had fallen into the hands of adventurers and opportunists, old Matías died and they tore down the building on Chota and built a cube with windows in it he thinks, who had given it a bungling line that separated it from the masses who therefore came under the influence of APRA, whatever became of Comrade Llaque, Zavalita? Adventurers like Ravines, who became an agent of imperialism and helped Odría overthrow Bustamante, could he have become a renegade, tired of the difficult and stifling militancy, could he have a wife and family and a job in a ministry? and opportunists like Terreros who became a religious fanatic and every year dressed up in a purple habit and hauled a cross in the Procession of Our Lord of Miracles, or was he still carrying on and speaking in that little bird voice of his to student groups when he wasn't in jail? Betrayals and repression had almost wiped out the Party, and if he was still carrying on was he pro-Soviet or pro-Chinese or one of those Castroites who had died in guerrilla actions or had he turned Trotskyite? and when Bustamante took office in 1945 the Party had won legal status again and began to rebuild and fight among the working classes against APRA reformism, could he have gone to Moscow or Peking or Havana? but with Odría's military coup the Party had been broken up again, could he have been accused of being a Stalinist or revisionist or adventurer? the whole Central Committee and dozens of leaders and militants and sympathizers jailed and exiled and some murdered, would he remember you, Zavalita, that morning at Matías's place, that night at the Hotel Mogollón? and the surviving cells of that great shipwreck had slowly, laboriously come together as the Cahuide Organization, which published that pamphlet and was made up of the University Section and the Workers' Section, comrades.

"You mean that Cahuide has only a few students, only a few workers?" Aída said.

"We operate under difficult conditions, sometimes because a comrade falls months of effort are lost." He was holding his cigarette between the nails of his forefinger and his thumb, he thinks, smiling in a timid way. "But in spite of the repression, we've been growing."

"And naturally, he convinced you, Zavalita," Carlitos said.

"He convinced me that he believed in what he was telling us," Santiago said. "And besides that, you could see that he liked what he was doing."

"How does the Party stand on unity of action with other outlawed organizations?" Jacobo asked. "APRA, the Trotskyites?"

"He didn't hesitate, he had faith," Santiago said. "At that time I still

137

envied people who had a blind faith in something, Carlitos."

"We would be ready to work with APRA against the dictatorship," Llaque said. "But the Apristas don't want to give anyone the reason to call them extremists and they do everything they can to prove their anti-Communism. And there can't be more than ten Trotskyites in all and they're most likely police agents."

"It's the best thing that can happen to someone, Ambrosio," Santiago says. "Believing in what he says, liking what he does."

"Why does APRA, which has become pro-imperialist, still get support from the people?" Aída asked.

"By force of habit and by their demagoguery and because of the Aprista martyrs," Llaque said. "Especially because of the right wing in Peru. They don't understand that APRA isn't their enemy anymore but their ally, and they keep on persecuting it and that's why all the prestige with the people."

"It's true, the stupidity of the right has made APRA a big party," Carlitos said. "But if the left has never gone beyond being a kind of freemasonry, it hasn't been because of APRA but because there haven't been any capable people."

"Capable people like you and me don't get involved," Santiago said. "We're content to criticize the incapable people who do. Do you think that's right, Carlitos?"

"I don't, and that's why I never discuss politics," Carlitos said. "You force me to with your disgusting nightly show of masochism, Zavalita."

"Now it's my turn to ask a question, comrades." Llaque smiled, as if ashamed. "Do you want to join Cahuide? You can work as sympathizers, you don't have to join the Party yet."

"I want to join the Party right now," Aída said.

"There's no rush, you can take your time and think it over," Llaque said.

"We've had more than enough time for that in the group," Jacobo said. "I want to join too."

"I'd rather keep on as a sympathizer," the little worm, the knife, the snake. "I've got some doubts, I'd like to study a little more before I join up."

"Fine, comrade, don't join up until you've got rid of all your doubts," Llaque said. "As a sympathizer you can play a very useful role too."

"That's when it was shown that Zavalita wasn't pure anymore, Ambrosio," Santiago says. "That Jacobo and Aída were purer than Zavalita."

And what if you had joined up that day, Zavalita? he thinks. Would militancy have pulled you along, getting more and more involved, would you have become a man of faith, an optimist, another pure person, dark and heroic? You would have had a hard life, Zavalita, the way Jacobo and Aída must have, he thinks, in and out of jail a few times, hired and fired from dirty jobs, and instead of editorials against mad dogs in *La Crónica*, you would have been writing for the poorly printed pages of *Unidad*, when there was enough money and the police didn't stop you, he thinks, about the scientific advances in the socialist fatherland and the victory in the bakers' union of Lurín's revolutionary slate over that of the defeatist, pro-management Apristas, or in the even worse printed pages of *Bandera Roja*, against Soviet revisionism and the traitors of *Unidad*, he thinks, or maybe you would have been more generous and would have joined a rebel group and dreamed and acted and failed in guerrilla operations and you'd be in jail, like Héctor, he thinks, or dead and rotting in the jungle, like Half-breed Martínez, he thinks, and made semiclandestine trips to youth congresses, he thinks, Moscow, bearing fraternal greetings to journalistic meetings, he thinks, Budapest, or received military training, he thinks, Havana or Peking. Graduated as a lawyer, a married man, counselor to a union, a deputy, would you have been worse off or the same or happier? He thinks: oh, Zavalita.

"It wasn't horror over the dogma, it was the reflex of a two-bit anarchist child who doesn't like to take orders," Carlitos said. "Underneath it all you were afraid of breaking with people who eat and dress and smell well."

"But I hated those people, I still hate them," Santiago said. "That's the only thing I am sure of, Carlitos."

"Then it was the spirit of contradiction, the chip on your shoulder," Carlitos said. "You should have stuck to literature and forgotten about revolution, Zavalita."

"I knew that if everybody set himself to being intelligent and having his doubts, Peru would go on being fucked up forever," Santiago said. "I knew there was a need for dogmatic people, Carlitos."

"Dogmatic people or intelligent people, Peru will always be fucked

139

up," Carlitos said. "This country got off to a bad start and it's going to end up bad. Just like us, Zavalita."

"Capitalists like us?" Santiago asked.

"Scatographers like us," Carlitos said. "We're all going to explode and foam at the mouth, like Becerrita. To your health, Zavalita."

"Months, years dreaming about joining the Party, and when I get the chance, I draw back," Santiago said. "I'll never understand it, Carlitos."

"Doctor, doctor, I've got something that keeps on going up and down in me and I don't know what it is," Carlitos said. "It's a crazy little fart, madam, you've got a face like an ass and the poor little fart doesn't know which way to get out. The thing that's upsetting your life is a crazy little fart, Zavalita."

Do you swear to dedicate your lives to the cause of socialism and the working class? Llaque had asked, and Aída and Jacobo I swear, while Santiago looked on; then they picked their pseudonyms.

"Don't feel left out," Llaque said to Santiago. "Sympathizers and militants are on an equal footing in the University Section."

He shook hands with them, good-bye comrades, they should leave ten minutes after him. The morning was cloudy and damp when they left Matías' bookstore behind and went into the Bransa on Colmena to have some coffee.

"Can I ask you a question?" Aída said. "Why didn't you join up? What doubts have you got?"

"I talked to you about it once," Santiago said. "I'm still not convinced about some things. I'd like . . ."

"Are you still not convinced that God doesn't exist?" Aída laughed.

"Nobody has any right to argue about his decision," Jacobo said. "Let him take his own time."

"I'm not arguing about it, but I'm going to tell you one thing," Aída said, laughing. "You're never going to join up, and when you finish at San Marcos you're going to forget all about the revolution, and you'll be a lawyer for International Petroleum and a member of the Club Nacional."

"You've got one consolation, the prophecy wasn't fulfilled," Carlitos said. "You're not a lawyer and not a member of the Club Nacional, you're not a proletarian and not a bourgeois, Zavalita. Just a poor little turd somewhere in between."

"What ever became of that Jacobo, that Aída?" Ambrosio asks.

"They got married, I suppose they have children, I haven't seen them for years," Santiago said. "I learn about Jacobo's existence when I read in the papers that he's been arrested or just let out."

"You're still jealous of him," Carlitos said. "I'm going to forbid you to bring the matter up with me again, it does you more harm than drinking does to me. Because that's your addiction, Zavalita: that Jacobo, that Aída."

"That thing in *La Prensa* this morning was horrible," Señora Zoila said. "They shouldn't print stories about atrocities like that."

Jealous because of Aída? Not anymore, he thinks. Because of that other business, Zavalita? He would have to see him, talk with him, find out if that sacrificed life had made him better or worse. He thinks: find out if his conscience is at rest.

"You spend all your time complaining about crime and that's the first page you read," Teté said. "You're awfully funny, mama."

He probably didn't feel alone, at least, he thinks, but surrounded, accompanied, protected by people. That thing that was a little warm and viscous that he felt during discussions in the group and the cell and the section, he thinks.

"Another child kidnapped and raped by a monster?" Don Fermín asked.

"Ever since that day we saw even less of each other than before," Santiago said. "Our groups became cells, so we kept on being separated. At the meetings of the section we were surrounded by people."

"You're worse than the newspapers," Señora Zoila said. "You shouldn't talk that way in front of Teté."

"But how many were there and what the devil were they doing?" Carlitos asked. "I never heard of Cahuide during Odría's times."

"Do you think I'm still ten years old, mama?" Teté asked.

"I never knew how many there were," Santiago said. "But we did some things against Odría, at the university, at least."

"Isn't anyone going to tell me what the piece of news that's so horrible is?" Don Fermín asked.

141

"Did they know at home what you were mixed up in?" Carlitos asked.

"Selling his children!" Señora Zoila said. "Did you ever hear of anything as horrible?"

"I tried to avoid seeing them and talking to them," Santiago said. "Relations with my folks kept getting worse and worse."

Days, weeks without rain in Puno, the drought had destroyed crops, decimated livestock, emptied villages, and there were Indians painted against a backdrop of parched landscapes, Indian women walking across cracked furrows with their children on their backs, dying animals with open eyes, and the titles and subtitles appeared followed by a question mark.

"They have feelings, but most of all they're hungry, mama," Santiago said. "If they sell them it must be so they won't starve to death."

Slave trade between Puno and Juliaca under the effects of the drought?

"What else did you do besides discussing newspaper editorials and reading Marxist books?" Carlitos asked.

Indian women selling their children to tourists?

"They don't know what a child is, what a family is, poor simple animals," Señora Zoila said. "If you don't have enough to eat, you shouldn't have children."

"We revived the Federated Centers, the University Federation," Santiago said. "Jacobo and I were elected delegates from our classes."

"I don't suppose you're going to blame the government because it hasn't rained in Puno," Don Fermín said. "Odría is trying to help those poor people. The United States has made an important donation. They're sending them food, clothing."

"The elections were a success for the section," Santiago said. "Eight Cahuide delegates from Letters, Law and Economics. The Apristas had more, but if we voted together we could control the centers. The nonpolitical people weren't organized and it was easy for us to split them up."

"Don't tell me again that the gift from the gringos will only line the pockets of the Odriists," Don Fermín said. "Odría has asked me to head up the commission in charge of distributing the aid."

"But every agreement between us and the Apristas came at the price of endless arguments and fights," Santiago said. "For a whole year my

142

life was nothing but meetings, at the center, at the section, and secret meetings with the Apristas."

"He'll probably say that you're stealing too, papa," Sparky said. "Superbrain thinks that everyone who's respectable in Peru is an exploiter and a thief."

"Here's another news item in *La Prensa* made to order for you, mama," Teté said. "Two people died in the Cuzco jail and when they performed an autopsy they found shoelaces and the soles of shoes in their bellies."

"Why did you get so bitter over losing the friendship of that pair?" Carlitos asked. "Didn't you have any other friends in Cahuide?"

"Do you think they ate the soles of their shoes because they didn't know any better, mama?" Santiago asked.

"The only thing this sassy little boy hasn't done is call me an imbecile and give me a slap, Fermín," Señora Zoila said.

"I was friends with all of them, but it was a functional friendship," Santiago said. "We never talked about personal things. With Jacobo and Aída friendship had become kind of deep."

"Don't you keep saying that the newspapers lie?" Don Fermín said. "Why does it have to be a lie every time they talk about government projects and the truth when they publish a horror story like that?"

"You ruin lunch and dinner for us every time," Teté said. "Do you always have to be looking for a fight, Superbrain?"

"But I'll tell you one thing," Santiago says. "I never regretted going to San Marcos instead of the Catholic University."

"Here's the clipping from *La Prensa,*" Aída said. "Read it so you can vomit."

"Because, thanks to San Marcos, I didn't become a model student, a model son, or a model lawyer, Ambrosio," Santiago says.

"The drought has created an explosive situation in the South," Aída said, "an excellent stew for agitators. Keep on reading, you haven't seen anything yet."

"Because you're closer to reality in a whorehouse than in a convent, Ambrosio," Santiago says.

"Garrisons should be alerted, the farmers who suffered damages should be watched closely," Aída said. "They're worried about the

143

drought because there might be an uprising, not because Indians are dying of hunger. Have you ever seen anything like it?"

"Because, thanks to San Marcos, I fucked myself up," Santiago says. "And in this country a person who doesn't fuck himself up fucks up other people. I don't regret it, Ambrosio."

"It's precisely because they're filthy trash that these newspapers are a great stimulant," Jacobo said. "If you feel demoralized, all you have to do is open up any one of them to bring back your hatred for the Peruvian bourgeoisie."

"So you might say that with our scatography we're stimulating eighteen-year-old rebels," Carlitos said. "So don't let your conscience bother you so much, Zavalita. Look, even though it's indirect, you're still helping your ex-buddies."

"You're making fun, but it just might be true," Santiago said. "Every time I write something that's repugnant to me, I make the article as disgusting as I can. Suddenly, on the following day a boy reads it and feels like throwing up and, well, something's happened."

On the door was the sign Washington had spoken about. Dust completely covered the crude letters of "Parlor," but the picture of the table, the cue, the three billiard balls stood out very clearly and there was also the sound of balls coming from inside: that was it.

"Now it turns out that Odría is noble." Don Fermín laughed. "Did you read *El Comercio?* He's the descendant of barons, and so forth, and if he wants to, he can claim his title."

Santiago pushed open the door and went in: a half-dozen pool tables and, between the green velvet and the naked beams of the ceiling, faces dissolved in waves of smoke; a wire network hung over the table, the players kept count of their points with their cues.

"What did that streetcar workers' strike have to do with your leaving home?" Carlitos asked.

He crossed the playing area, then another room with only one table being used, then a courtyard overflowing with garbage cans. In the back, beside a fig tree, there was a small closed door. Two knocks, he waited, then two more, and it opened at once.

"Odría doesn't realize that by allowing that kind of fawning he's becoming the laughingstock of Lima," Señora Zoila said. "If he's noble, what can we be, then?"

"The Apristas haven't got here yet," Héctor said. "Come in, the comrades are here already."

"Up till then our work had been on the student level," Santiago said. "Collections for students in jail, discussions at the centers, the distribution of fliers, and Cahuide leaflets. That streetcar strike let us go on to greater things."

He went in and Héctor closed the door. The room was older and dirtier than the ones used for billiards. Four pool tables had been pushed up against the wall to make more space. The delegates from Cahuide were spread about the room.

"What fault is it of Odría's if someone writes an article saying that he's noble?" Don Fermín asked. "Sharp people will think of anything to make a little money. Even invent family trees!"

Washington and Half-breed Martínez were standing and talking near the door, Solórzano was sitting on a table looking through a magazine, Aída and Jacobo had almost disappeared into the shadows of a corner, The Bird had made herself comfortable on the floor, and Héctor was peeping into the courtyard through the cracks in the door.

"The streetcar workers' strike wasn't political, but for a pay raise," Santiago said. "The union sent a letter to the San Marcos Federation asking for the students' support. In the section we thought it was our great opportunity."

"The Apristas were told to come one at a time, but they don't give a damn about security," Washington said. "They'll come in a gang the way they always do."

"Then call that fellow up and have him check our titles too," Señora Zoila said. "Odría noble, that's all we needed."

They arrived a few minutes later, in a group, just as Washington had feared, five of the twenty-odd Aprista delegates: Santos Vivero, Arévalo, Ochoa, Huamán and Saldívar. They mixed in with the Cahuide people, without taking a vote it was decided that Saldívar would run the meeting. His thin face, his bony hands, his graying hair gave him a responsible look. As always, before starting, they swapped jokes, sarcastic remarks.

"In the section we agreed to try to have a strike at San Marcos in support of the streetcar workers," Santiago said.

"I can see now why you're so worried about security," Santos Vivero told Washington. "Because you're all the redtails left in the country and

145

if the cops come and arrest us, Communism will disappear in Peru. The five of us, on the other hand, are just one drop in the broad sea of Peruvian Aprismo."

"Anyone who falls into it won't drown in water but in a sea of bourgeois snobs," Washington said.

Héctor had remained at his observation post by the door; they were all speaking in low voices, there was a continuous murmur, a fluffy sound, and suddenly a laugh would arise, an exclamation.

"The delegates from the section couldn't decide a strike, we only had eight votes in the Federation," Santiago said. "But with the Apristas we could. We had a meeting with them in a pool parlor. It started there, Carlitos."

"I doubt that these guys will support the strike," Aída whispered to Santiago. "They're divided. Everything depends on Santos Vivero, if he agrees the rest will follow him. Like sheep, you know, whatever the boss says is fine."

"It was the first big argument in Cahuide," Santiago said. "I was against the sympathy strike; the one who headed those in favor was Jacobo."

"All right, companions." Saldívar clapped his hands twice. "Come closer, we're going to begin."

"It wasn't just to go against Jacobo," Santiago said. "I didn't think we would get the support of the students, I thought it would be a failure. But I was in the minority and the idea carried."

"Companions must apply to you people." Washington laughed. "We're all in the same place, but don't get us mixed up, Saldívar."

"Those meetings with the Apristas were like friendly soccer matches," Santiago said. "They began with embraces and sometimes ended up with punches."

"All right, companions and comrades, then," Saldívar said. "Come closer or I'm going to the movies."

A circle was formed around him, the laughs and murmurs died out. Adopting a sudden funereal gravity, Saldívar summed up the reasons for the meeting: tonight at the Federation they would discuss the petition for support of the streetcar workers, companions, to decide if we could bring off a motion together, comrades. Jacobo raised his hand.

146

"In the section we would rehearse those meetings like a ballet," Santiago said. "Taking turns, each one developing a different argument, always knocking any contrary opinion down."

His tie was hanging loose, his hair was uncombed, he was speaking in a low voice: the strike was a magnificent occasion to take over the students' awareness. His hands hanging beside his body: to develop the student-worker alliance. Looking at Saldívar very seriously: to initiate a movement that could be extended to demands like the freeing of imprisoned students and political amnesty. He stopped speaking and Huamán raised his hand.

"I'd been against the idea of a strike for the same reasons as those expressed by Huamán, an Aprista," Santiago said. "But since the section had agreed on a strike, it was up to me to defend it against Huamán. That's called democratic centralism, Carlitos."

Huamán was small and mannered, it had taken us three years to rebuild the centers and the Federation of San Marcos after the repression, his gestures were elegant, how could we start a strike for reasons that lay outside the university which might be rejected by our power base? and he spoke with one hand on his lapel and the other fluttering about like a butterfly, if the base rejected the strike we would lose the confidence of the students, and his voice was artificial, florid, shrill at times, and furthermore, repression would come and the centers and the Federation would be dismantled before they'd been able to operate.

"I know Party discipline has to be like that," Santiago said. "I know that if it wasn't there'd be chaos. I'm not defending myself, Carlitos."

"Don't get bogged down in details, Ochoa," Saldívar said. "Stick to the point under discussion."

"Exactly, precisely," Ochoa said. "I ask: is the Federation of San Marcos strong enough to make a frontal action against the dictatorship?"

"Say what you've got to say, we haven't got much time," Héctor said.

"And if it isn't strong enough and goes on strike," Ochoa said, "what will the attitude of the Federation be? That's my question."

"Why don't you get a job running the Kolynos program, 'The Twenty Thousand Soles Question'?" Washington asked.

"Would it or wouldn't it be an act of provocation?" Ochoa said imperturbably. "I ask a question and I give a constructive answer: yes, it would be. What? A provocation."

"It was in the middle of those meetings that all of a sudden I felt I'd never be a revolutionary, a real militant," Santiago said. "All of a sudden, anguish, nausea, a feeling of a horrible waste of time."

"The young romantic didn't want discussions," Carlitos said. "He wanted epic actions, bombs, shooting, attacks on a military post. All stuff out of novels, Zavalita."

"I know it bothers you having to speak in defense of the strike," Aída said. "But you've got one consolation, all the Apristas are against it. And without them the Federation will reject our motion."

"They should have invented a pill, a suppository to work against doubts, Ambrosio," Santiago says. "Just think how beautiful, you stick it in and there you are: I believe."

He raised his hand and he began to speak before Saldívar recognized him: the strike would consolidate the centers, it would fire up the delegates, the student base would give their support because hadn't they shown their support for them by electing them? He kept his hands in his pockets and dug in his nails.

"Just the same as when I made the examination of my conscience on Thursdays before confession," Santiago said. "Had I dreamed about nude women because I'd wanted to dream about them or because the devil had wanted it and I couldn't stop him? Were they there in the dark as intruders or as invited guests?"

"You're wrong, you did have the making of a militant," Carlitos said. "If I had to defend ideas that were contrary to my own, all that would come out would be brays, grunts or peeps."

"What are you doing on *La Crónica*?" Santiago asked. "What are we doing each one of these days, Carlitos?"

Santos Vivero raised his hand, he'd listened to the speeches with an expression of soft uneasiness, and before he spoke, he closed his eyes and coughed as if he still had his doubts.

"The omelet was flipped at the last minute," Santiago said. "It looked as if the Apristas were against it, that there wouldn't be any strike. Maybe everything would have been different, then, I wouldn't have gone to work at *La Crónica*, Carlitos."

He thought, companions and comrades, that the fundamental thing at this time was not the struggle for university reform, but the struggle against the dictatorship. And an effective way of fighting for civil liberties, the release of prisoners, the return of exiles, the legalization of parties was, companions and comrades, by forging the worker-student alliance, or, as a great philosopher had said, the one between manual and mental workers.

"If you quote Haya de la Torre again, I'll read you the Communist Manifesto," Washington said. "I've got it right here."

"You're like an old whore thinking back about her youth, Zavalita," Carlitos said. "We're different that way too. What happened to me as a boy has been erased for me and I'm sure that the most important thing is going to happen to me tomorrow. You seem to have stopped living when you were eighteen years old."

"Don't interrupt him, he might change his mind," Héctor whispered. "Can't you see he's in favor of the strike?"

Yes, it could be a good opportunity because the companions on the streetcars were showing courage and fight, and their union wasn't full of yellow dogs. The delegates shouldn't follow their electorate blindly, they should show them the direction: wake them up, companions and comrades, push them into action.

"After Santos Vivero, the Apristas began to talk again and we talked again," Santiago said. "We left the pool parlor in agreement and that night the Federation approved an indefinite strike of sympathy with the streetcar workers. I was arrested exactly ten days later, Carlitos."

"Your baptism of fire," Carlitos said. "Or rather, your death certificate, Zavalita."

9

"MAYBE IT WOULD HAVE BEEN BETTER if you'd stayed at the house, not gone to Pucallpa," Santiago says.

"Yes, a lot better," Ambrosio says. "But who could have known, son."

See how pretty he talks, Trifulcio shouted. There was scattered applause in the square, horn-blowing, a few hurrahs. From the steps of the platform Trifulcio saw the crowd curling like the surface of the sea in a rainstorm. His hands were smarting, but he kept on clapping.

"First, who sent you to shout Long live APRA by the Colombian Embassy?" Ludovico asked. "Second, who are your buddies? And third, where are your buddies? Out with it, Trinidad López."

"And, while we're on it," Santiago says, "why did you leave the house?"

"Take a seat, Landa, we stood long enough during the Te Deum," Don Fermín said. "Take a seat, Don Emilio."

"I was getting tired of working for other people," Ambrosio says. "I wanted to try it on my own, son."

Sometimes he shouted Long live Don Emilio Arévalo, sometimes Long live General Odría, sometimes Arévalo-Odría. From the platform they made signs to him saying don't interrupt while he's speaking, cursing under their breath, but Trifulcio didn't obey: he was the first to start clapping, the last to stop.

"I feel like a hanged man in this stiff shirt," Senator Landa said. "I wasn't meant to wear full dress. I'm just a country boy, what the hell."

"Come on, Trinidad López," Hipólito said. "Who sent you, who are they, and where are they. Out with it."

"I thought my old man had fired you," Santiago says.

"Now I know why you didn't accept Odría's offer of the senate seat from Lima, Fermín," Senator Arévalo said. "So you wouldn't have to wear a full dress suit and a high hat."

"What an idea, just the opposite," Ambrosio says. "He asked me to stay on with him and I refused. See how wrong you've been, son?"

Sometimes he would go to the railing of the platform, face the crowd with his hands in the air, three cheers for Emilio Arévalo! and he himself would roar hurrah! three cheers for General Odría! and in a stentorian voice, hip, hip, hurrah!

"Parliament is fine for people who have nothing to do," Don Fermín said. "For you people, landowners."

"I'm all excited now, Trinidad López," Hipólito said. "Now I really am excited, Trinidad."

"I only got into this mess because the President insisted that I head up the ticket in Chiclayo," Senator Landa said. "But I'm sorry already. I won't be able to look after Olave. This goddamned stiff shirt."

"How did you find out that the old man died?" Santiago asks.

"Stop your fooling, the senate seat has made you ten years younger," Don Fermín said. "And you've got no reason to complain, in elections like these a person is glad to be a candidate."

"In the newspapers, son," Ambrosio says. "You can't imagine how sorry I was. Because your papa was a great man."

The square was boiling with songs, murmuring and shouts now. But when the voice of Don Emilio Arévalo came out through the microphone, it turned off the noise: it fell onto the square from the roof of the City Hall, the belfry, the palm trees, the park in the middle. Trifulcio had even set up a loudspeaker on the Hermitage of the Holy Woman.

"Hold it right there, the election may have been easy for Landa, who ran unopposed," Senator Arévalo said, "but in my district there were two slates and it cost me half a million soles to win, which is no joke."

"You see, Hipólito got excited and he whacked you," Ludovico said. "Who was it, who are they, where. Before Hipólito gets excited again, Trinidad."

"It's not my fault that the other slate in Chiclayo had Aprista signatures on its petitions." Senator Landa laughed. "The Electoral Court turned it down, I didn't."

What happened to the banners? Trifulcio said suddenly, his eyes full of surprise. He had his pinned to his shirt like a flower. He pulled it off with one hand, showed it to the crowd with a challenging gesture. A few banners here and there rose up over the straw hats and the paper hats many had made to protect themselves from the sun. Where were the others, what did they think they were for, why didn't they bring them out? Quiet, boy, the man who gave the orders said, everything's working out fine. And Trifulcio: they took their drinks, but they forgot about the banners, sir. And the man who gave the orders: leave them alone, everything's fine. And Trifulcio: it's just that the ungrateful bastards make me mad, sir.

"What did your papa die of, son?" Ambrosio asks.

"This election hurly-burly may have made Landa younger, but it's turned my hair gray," Senator Arévalo said. "I've had enough elections for a while. I'm going to get laid five times tonight."

"A heart attack," Santiago says. "Or from the rages I made him have."

"Five?" Senator Landa laughed. "You won't have any ass left, Emilio."

"And now Hipólito's got all aroused," Ludovico said. "Oh, mama, now you're really going to get it, Trinidad."

"Don't say that, child," Ambrosio says. "Don Fermín loved you so much. He always said Skinny's the one I love the best."

Solemn, martial, Don Emilio Arévalo's voice floated over the square, went down the unpaved streets, was lost in the planted fields. He was in shirtsleeves, waving his arms, and his ring flashed beside Trifulcio's face. He raised his voice, had he become angry? He looked at the crowd: quiet faces, eyes reddened with alcohol, boredom, or heat, mouths smoking or yawning. Had he become angry because they weren't listening?

"You've become infected from rubbing elbows with the rabble so much during the campaign," Senator Arévalo said. "I hope you won't make jokes like that when you speak in the senate, Landa."

"So much that he went through hell when you ran away from home, son," Ambrosio says.

"Well, the gringo gave me his complaints, this is what they were all about," Don Fermín said. "The elections are over, it makes a bad impression on his government to have the opposition candidate still in jail. Those gringos believe in formalities, you understand."

"Every day he went to your Uncle Clodomiro's and asked about you," Ambrosio says. "What do you hear from Skinny, how's Skinny?"

But suddenly Don Emilio stopped shouting and smiled and spoke as if he was happy. He smiled, his voice was soft, he was moving his hand, he looked as if he were holding a *muleta* and the bull had passed by, brushing his body. The people on the platform were smiling, and Trifulcio, relieved, smiled too.

"There's no longer any reason to keep him in jail, they're going to release him any day now," Senator Arévalo said. "Didn't you tell that to the Ambassador, Fermín?"

"What do you know, you've started talking," Ludovico said. "Or maybe you'd rather have Hipólito petting you than hitting you. What do you say, Trinidad?"

"And to the boardinghouse in Barranco where you were living," Ambrosio says. "And asking the landlady what's my son doing, how's my son."

"I don't understand those shitty gringos," Senator Landa said. "It seemed fine to them for Montagne to be put in jail before the elections, but now it doesn't. They send us circus people for ambassadors, those people."

"He used to go to the boardinghouse and ask about me?" Santiago asks.

"I told him that, of course, but last night I spoke to Espina and he has his doubts," Don Fermín said. "We have to wait, if Montagne is let out now people might think he was put in jail so that Odría could win the elections without any opposition, that the business of the plot was all a lie."

153

"That you're Haya de la Torre's right-hand man?" Ludovico asked. "That you're the real headman of APRA and Haya de la Torre is your flunky, Trinidad?"

"Of course, son, all the time," Ambrosio says. "He'd give the landlady a tip so she wouldn't tell you."

"Espina's a hopeless dumbbell," Senator Landa said. "He evidently thinks there's someone who swallowed the tale of a plot. Even my maid knows that Montagne was put in jail to leave the field to Odría."

"Don't kid us like that, pappy," Hipólito said. "Do you want me to stick my prick in your mouth, or what, Trinidad?"

"The boss thought you'd get mad if you found out," Ambrosio says.

"The truth is that arresting Montagne was a bad step," Senator Arévalo said. "I don't know why they allowed an opposition candidate if they were going to take a step backward at the last minute and put him in jail. The political advisers are to blame. Arbeláez, that idiot Ferro, and even you, Fermín."

"You can see how much your papa loved you, son," Ambrosio says.

"Things didn't turn out the way they were expected to, Don Emilio," Don Fermín said. "We could have had a scare with Montagne. Besides, I wasn't in favor of putting him in jail. In any case, now we have to try to patch things up."

He was shouting now and his arms were like those of a windmill, and his voice rose and thundered like a great wave that suddenly broke Long live Peru! A volley of applause on the platform, a volley on the square. Trifulcio was waving his banner, Long Live Don Emilio Arévalo, now a lot of banners did appear among the heads, Long Live General Odría, now they did. The loudspeakers scratched for a second, then they flooded the square with the National Anthem.

"I told Espina what I thought when he announced to me that he was going to arrest Montagne on the pretext of a plot," Don Fermín said. "Nobody's going to swallow it, it's going to hurt the General, don't we have people we can trust on the Electoral Court, at the polling places? But Espina's an imbecile, no political tact."

"So, the headman, so, a thousand Apristas are going to attack Headquarters and rescue you," Ludovico said. "You think that by acting crazy you're going to make fools out of us, Trinidad."

"I'm not being nosy, but why did you run away from home that time, son?" Ambrosio asks. "Weren't you well off at home with your folks?"

Don Emilio Arévalo was sweating; he was shaking the hands that converged on him from all sides, he wiped his forehead, smiled, waved, embraced the people on the platform, and the wooden frame swayed as Don Emilio approached the steps. Now it was your turn, Trifulcio.

"Too well off, that's why I left," Santiago says. "I was so pure and thick-headed that it bothered me having such an easy life and being a nice young boy."

"The funny thing is that the idea of putting him in jail didn't come from the Uplander," Don Fermín said. "Or from Arbeláez or Ferro. The one who convinced them, the one who insisted was Bermúdez."

"So pure and so thick-headed that I thought that by fucking myself up a little I would make myself a real little man, Ambrosio," Santiago says.

"That all of it was the work of an insignificant Director of Public Order, an underling, I can't swallow either," Senator Landa said. "Uplander Espina invented it so he could toss the ball to someone else if things turned out badly."

Trifulcio was there, at the foot of the stairs, defending his place with his elbows, spitting on his hands, his gaze fanatically fastened on Don Emilio's feet, which were approaching, mixed in with others, his body tense, his feet firmly planted on the ground: his turn, it was his turn.

"You have to believe it because it's the truth," Don Fermín said. "And don't tar him so much. Whether you like it or not, that underling is becoming the man the General trusts the most."

"There he is, Hipólito, I'm making a present of him to you," Ludovico said. "Get those ideas of being headman out of his brain once and for all."

"Then it wasn't because you had different political ideas from your papa?" Ambrosio asks.

"He believes him implicitly, he thinks he's infallible," Don Fermín said. "When Bermúdez has an opinion, Ferro, Arbeláez, Espina and even

155

I can go to the devil, we don't exist. That was evident in the Montagne affair."

"My poor old man didn't have any political ideas," Santiago says. "Only political interests, Ambrosio."

Trifulcio took a leap, his feet were already on the last step, he gave a shove, another, and he crouched down and was going to lift him up. No, no, friend, a smiling, modest and surprised Don Emilio said, thank you very much but, and Trifulcio let go of him, drew back confused, his eyes blinking, but, but? and Don Emilio seemed confused too, and in the group tight around him there were nudges, whispering.

"The fact is that even though he may not be infallible, he does have balls," Senator Arévalo said. "In a year and a half he's wiped the map clean of Apristas and Communists and we were able to hold elections."

"Are you still the headman of APRA, pappy?" Ludovico asked. "Fine, very good. Go right ahead, Hipólito."

"The Montagne affair was this way," Don Fermín said. "One fine day Bermúdez disappeared from Lima and came back two weeks later. I've covered half the country, General, if Montagne runs in the election, you'll lose."

What are you waiting for, you imbecile, said the man who gave the orders, and Trifulcio shot an anguished glance at Don Emilio, who made him a signal of quick or hurry up. Trifulcio's head lowered rapidly, crossed the fork made by his legs, and he lifted Don Emilio up like a feather.

"That was nonsense," Senator Landa said. "Montagne never had a chance of winning. He didn't have the money for a good campaign, we controlled the whole electoral apparatus."

"And why did you think my old man was such a great person?" Santiago asks.

"But the Apristas would have voted for him, all the enemies of the government would have voted for him," Don Fermín said. "Bermúdez convinced him. If I run under these conditions, I'll lose. That's how it ended up, that's why they arrested him."

"Because he was, son," Ambrosio says. "So intelligent and such a gentleman and so everything else."

156

He heard applause and cheers as he went along with his load on his back, surrounded by Téllez, Urondo, the foreman and the man who gave the orders, he also shouting Arévalo-Odría, secure, tranquil, holding the legs tight, feeling Don Emilio's fingers in his hair, seeing the other hand that was giving thanks and shaking the hands that reached out to him.

"Leave him alone now, Hipólito," Ludovico said. "Can't you see that you've already sent him off to dreamland?"

"I didn't think he was a great man, I thought he was a swine," Santiago says. "And I hated him."

"He's faking," Hipólito said. "Let me show you."

The National Anthem had finished when they were through walking around the square. There was a roll of drums, silence, and a *marinera* started up. Among the heads and the food and drink stands Trifulcio saw a couple dancing: O.K., take him to the black truck, boy. To the truck, sir.

"The best thing would be for us to talk to him," Senator Arévalo said. "You tell him about your talk with the Ambassador, Fermín, and we'll tell him that the elections are over, poor Montagne is no danger to anybody, let him go and that gesture will win him support. That's the way you have to work with Odría."

"Child, child," Ambrosio says. "How can you say that about him, son?"

"You really do know peasant psychology, senator," Senator Landa said.

"You can see he's not faking," Ludovico said. "Leave him alone now."

"But I don't hate him anymore, not anymore now that he's dead," Santiago says. "He was one, but he didn't know it, it was unconscious. Anyway, there's a surplus of swine in this country, and I think he paid for it, Ambrosio."

Put him down now, said the man who gave the orders, and Trifulcio squatted down: he watched Don Emilio's feet touch the ground, watched his hands brush off his pant legs. He got into the van and behind him Téllez, Urondo and the foreman. Trifulcio sat in front. A group of men and women were looking, open-mouthed. Laughing, putting his head out the window, Trifulcio shouted at them: Long live Don Emilio Arévalo!

"I didn't know that Bermúdez had so much influence in the Palace," Senator Landa said. "Is it true that he's got a mistress who's a ballerina or something like that?"

"All right, Ludovico, don't carry on so much," Hipólito said. "I've already left him alone."

"He's just set her up in a house in San Miguel," Don Fermín said. "The one who used to be Muelle's mistress."

"Did you also think the one you worked for before you were my old man's chauffeur was a great man?" Santiago asks.

"The Muse?" Senator Landa said. "I'll be damned, she's quite a woman. Is she Bermúdez' mistress? She's a high-flying bird and if you want to keep her caged up you've got to have your pockets well lined."

"I think he's already got away from you. Shit," Ludovico said. "Throw some water on him, do something, don't just stand there."

"So high-flying that she put Muelle in his grave." Don Fermín laughed. "And a dyke and she takes drugs."

"Don Cayo?" Ambrosio asks. "Never, son, he couldn't come close to your papa."

"He didn't get away, he's still alive," Hipólito said. "What are you afraid of, I didn't leave a scratch or a bruise on him. He passed out from fright, Ludovico."

"Who isn't queer these days, who doesn't take drugs in Lima?" Senator Landa said. "We're really getting civilized, aren't we?"

"Weren't you ashamed to work for that son of a bitch?" Santiago asks.

"It's all set, then, we'll see Odría tomorrow," Senator Arévalo said. "Today they've put the presidential sash on him and we have to let him spend his day looking at himself in the mirror and enjoying it."

"I had no reason to be," Ambrosio says. "I didn't know that Don Cayo was going to treat your papa so bad. Because they were such good friends at the time, son."

When they reached the ranch house and he got out of the van, Trifulcio didn't go to get something to eat, but went to the creek to wet his head, his face and his arms. Then he stretched out in the backyard under the eaves by the cotton gin. His hands and throat were burning, he was tired and content. He fell right off to sleep.

"That fellow, Mr. Lozano, that Trinidad López," Ludovico said. "Yes, all of a sudden he went crazy on us."

"You ran into her in the street?" Queta asked. "The one who'd been Gold Ball's maid, the one who went to bed with you? Was that the one you fell in love with?"

"I'm glad you got Montagne released, Don Cayo," Don Fermín said. "The enemies of the government were using that as a pretext to say the elections were a farce."

"What do you mean, went crazy?" Mr. Lozano asked. "Did he talk or didn't he?"

"They were, as a matter of fact, and just between you and me, we can see that," Cayo Bermúdez said. "Jailing the only opposition candidate wasn't the best solution, but there was nothing else we could do. The General had to be elected, didn't he?"

"Did she tell you that her husband had died, that her son had died?" Queta asked. "That she was looking for work?"

He was awakened by the voices of the foreman, Urondo and Téllez. They sat down beside him, offered him a cigarette, chatted. The rally in Grocio Prado had turned out pretty good, hadn't it? Yes, it had turned out pretty good. There'd been more people at the one in Chincha, hadn't there? Yes, more people. Would Don Emilio win the election? Of course he'd win. And Trifulcio: if Don Emilio went to Lima as a senator, would they let him go? No, man, they'd keep him on, the foreman said. And Urondo: you'll stay with us, you'll see. It was still hot, the late-afternoon sun was tinting the cotton fields, the ranch house, the stones.

"He talked, but he said crazy things, Mr. Lozano," Ludovico said. "That he was the second in command, that he was the headman. That the Apristas were coming to rescue him with cannons. He went crazy, I swear."

"And you told her there's a house in San Miguel where they're looking for a maid?" Queta asked. "And you took her to Hortensia's?"

"Do you really think Odría would have been defeated by Montagne?" Don Fermín asked.

"I'd say, rather, that he made fools of you," Mr. Lozano said. "Oh, what a useless pair. And on top of it, stupid."

159

"So it's Amalia, the girl who started work last Monday," Queta said. "Maybe you're dumber than you look. Do you think nobody's going to find out about it?"

"Montagne or any other opposition candidate would have won," Cayo Bermúdez said. "Don't you know Peruvians, Don Fermín? We're a complex bunch, we like to support the underdog, the one who's out of power."

"Nothing of the sort, Mr. Lozano," Hipólito said. "We're not useless and we're not stupid. Come take a look at how we left him and you'll see."

"That you made her swear she wouldn't tell Hortensia you were the one who told her about it?" Queta said. "That you made her think Cayo Shithead would kick her out if he found out she knew you?"

At that moment the door of the ranch house opened and out came the man who gave the orders. He crossed the courtyard, stopped in front of them, pointed his finger at Trifulcio: Don Emilio's wallet, you son of a bitch.

"It's too bad you didn't accept the senate seat," Cayo Bermúdez said. "The President had hoped you'd be the majority leader in parliament, Don Fermín."

"The wallet, that I took it?" Trifulcio stood up, pounded his chest. "Me, sir, me?"

"You pair of fools," Mr. Lozano said. "Why didn't you take him to the infirmary, you pair of fools?"

"Do you steal from the one who feeds you?" said the man who gave the orders. "From the one who gives you work and you a known thief?"

"You don't know women," Queta said. "One of these days she'll tell Hortensia that she knows you, that you brought her to San Miguel. One of these days Hortensia will tell Cayo Shithead, one of these days he'll tell Gold Ball. And that's the day they'll kill you, Ambrosio."

Trifulcio had knelt down, had begun to swear and whimper. But the man who gave the orders wasn't moved: he was ordering him arrested again, a criminal, a known hoodlum, the wallet, right now. And at that moment the door of the ranch house opened and Don Emilio came out: what was going on there.

"We took him but they wouldn't take him in, Mr. Lozano," Ludovico said. "They wouldn't accept the responsibility, only if you gave the order in writing."

"We've already talked about that, Don Cayo," Don Fermín said. "I'd be more than pleased to serve the President. But a senate seat is getting into politics full time and I can't do it."

"I'm not going to say anything, I never say anything," Queta said. "Nothing in the world is any business of mine. You're going to fuck yourself up, but not because of me."

"Wouldn't you accept an ambassadorship either?" Cayo Bermúdez asked. "The General is very thankful for all the help you've given him and he wants to show it. Wouldn't you be interested in that, Don Fermín?"

"Look how he's insulting me, Don Emilio," Trifulcio said. "Look at the terrible thing he's accusing me of. He even made me cry, Don Emilio."

"I wouldn't even think of it," Don Fermín said, laughing. "I'm not cut out for a legislator or a diplomat either, Don Cayo."

"I didn't do it, sir," Hipólito said. "He went crazy all by himself, he fell on his face all by himself, sir. We barely touched him, believe me, Mr. Lozano."

"It wasn't him, man," Don Emilio said to the man who gave the orders. "It must have been some peasant at the rally. You'd never stoop so low as to rob me, would you now, Trifulcio?"

"The General is going to be hurt by your being so stand-offish, Don Fermín," Cayo Bermúdez said.

"I'd let them cut off my hand first, Don Emilio," Trifulcio said.

"You people complicated this whole thing," Mr. Lozano said, "and you're going to uncomplicate it all by yourselves, you bastards."

"Not stand-offish, you're wrong," Don Fermín said. "The time will come when Odría can pay me back for my services. You see, since you're so frank with me, I can be the same with you, Don Cayo."

"You're going to take him out nice and quiet, you're going to take him nice and carefully," Mr. Lozano said, "you're going to leave him somewhere. And if anyone sees you, fuck you, and I'll fuck you besides. Understood?"

Oh, you black scoundrel, Don Emilio said. And he went into the ranch house with the man who gave the orders, and Urondo and the foreman also left after a while. You let them insult you all they wanted, Trifulcio, Téllez laughed.

"You're always inviting me out and I'd like to return it," Cayo Bermúdez said. "I'd like to invite you to have dinner at my house one of these nights, Don Fermín."

"The man who insulted me didn't know what he was leaving himself open to," Trifulcio said.

"It's all set, sir," Ludovico said. "We took him out, carried him away, left him, and nobody saw us."

"Did you lift the wallet?" Téllez asked. "You can't fool me, Trifulcio."

"Whenever you say," Don Fermín said. "It would be my pleasure, Don Cayo."

"I lifted it but he didn't know it," Trifulcio said. "Do you want to go to town tonight?"

"At the door of San Juan de Dios Hospital, Mr. Lozano," Hipólito said. "Nobody saw us."

"I've taken a house in San Miguel, near the Bertoloto Hotel," Cayo Bermúdez said. "And besides, well, I don't know whether you heard, Don Fermín."

"Who, what are you talking about?" Mr. Lozano said. "Haven't you forgotten about it yet, you bastards?"

"How much money was there in the wallet, Trifulcio?" Téllez asked.

"Well, I'd heard something, yes," Don Fermín said. "You know what parrots people in Lima are, Don Cayo."

"Don't be so nosy," Trifulcio said. "Be happy that I'll be buying the drinks tonight."

"Oh, yes, oh, of course," Ludovico said. "Nobody, nothing, we've forgotten all about it, sir."

"I'm a country boy, in spite of a year and a half in Lima, I'm still not sure of the customs here," Cayo Bermúdez said. "Frankly, I felt a little hesitant. I was afraid you'd refuse to come to my house, Don Fermín."

"Me too, Mr. Lozano, word of honor, I forgot," Hipólito said. "Who was Trinidad López? I never saw him, he never existed. You see, sir? I've forgotten already."

Téllez and Urondo, drunk now, were nodding on the wooden bench

162

in the cheap bar, but in spite of all the beers and the heat, Trifulcio was still awake. Through the holes in the wall the sandy little square turned white by the sun could be seen, the shack where the voters were going in. Trifulcio was looking at the policemen standing in front of the shack. During the course of the morning they had come over a couple of times to have a beer and now there they were in their green uniforms. Over the heads of Téllez and Urondo a strip of beach could be seen, a sea with splotches of shining algae. They'd seen the boats leave, they'd seen them dissolve into the horizon. They'd eaten marinated fish and fried fish and potatoes and had drunk beer, lots of beer.

"Do you take me for a monk, a boob?" Don Fermín said. "Come on, Don Cayo. I think it's wonderful that you've made a conquest like that. I'd be delighted to dine with you two, as many times as you want."

Trifulcio saw the cloud of dust, the red van. It crossed the small square through the barking dogs, stopped in front of the bar, the man who gave the orders got out. Had a lot of people voted already? An awful lot, they'd been going in and coming out all morning. He was wearing boots, riding breeches, a pullover shirt: he didn't want to see them drunk, they shouldn't have any more. And Trifulcio: but there were a couple of cops there, sir. Don't worry about it, said the man who gave the orders. He got into the van and it disappeared in the midst of barking and a cloud of dust.

"After all, you're partly to blame," Cayo Bermúdez said. "Remember that night at the Embassy Club?"

The ones who were coming out after voting approached the bar, the woman who owned it barred their entry: closed because of elections, they weren't serving. And why wasn't it closed for those guys? The old woman gave no explanations: out, or she'd call the cops. The people went away, grumbling.

"Of course I remember." Don Fermín laughed. "But I never imagined that you were going to end up being shot through by an arrow from the Muse, Don Cayo."

The shadow of the shacks around the square was already longer than the strips of sunlight when the red van appeared again, loaded with men now. Trifulcio looked toward the shack: a group of voters was watching the van with curiosity, the two policemen were also looking in that

163

direction. Let's go, the man who gave the orders hurried the men, who jumped to the ground. The voting would be over soon, pretty soon they'd be sealing up the ballot boxes.

"I know why you did it, you poor devil," Don Fermín said. "Not because she was getting money out of me, not because she was blackmailing me."

Trifulcio, Téllez and Urondo came out of the bar and placed themselves at the head of the men from the truck. There weren't more than fifteen and Trifulcio recognized them: men from the cotton gin, farmhands, the two houseboys. Sunday shoes, cotton pants, big straw hats. Their eyes were burning, they smelled of alcohol.

"What do you think of this fellow Cayo?" Colonel Espina said. "I thought that all he did was work night and day, and look what he got for himself. A beautiful female, right, Don Fermín?"

They advanced as a platoon across the square and the people in the shack began to elbow each other aside. The two guards came out to meet them.

"But because of the anonymous note she sent me telling me about your woman," Don Fermín said. "Not to get vengeance for me. To get vengeance for yourself, you poor devil."

"There's been cheating here," the man who gave the orders said. "We've come to protest."

"I was flabbergasted," Colonel Espina said. "I'll be damned, quiet old Cayo with a woman like that. Unbelievable, isn't it, Don Fermín?"

"We won't stand for any fraud," Téllez said. "Long live General Odría, long live Don Emilio Arévalo!"

"We're here to maintain order," said one of the policemen. "We've got nothing to do with the voting. Make your protests to the people at the tables."

"Hurray!" the men shouted. "Arévalo-Odría!"

"The funny thing is that I gave him advice," Colonel Espina said. "Don't work so hard, enjoy life a little. And look what he came up with, Don Fermín."

The people had come closer, mingling with them, and they looked at them, looked at the policemen, and laughed. And then, out of the door of the shack came a little man who looked at Trifulcio, startled: what

164

was that noise all about? He was wearing a jacket and tie, eyeglasses, and he had a sweaty little mustache.

"Break it up, break it up," he said with a tremulous voice. "The polls are closed, it's already six o'clock. Guards, make these people go away."

"You thought I was going to fire you because of what I found out about that business with your woman," Don Fermín said. "You thought that by doing that you'd have me by the neck. Even you wanted to blackmail me, you poor devil."

"They say there's been cheating, sir," one of the policemen said.

"They say they've come to protest, doctor," the other one said.

"And I asked him when are you going to bring your wife down from Chincha," Colonel Espina said. "Never, she can stay in Chincha, that's all. Look how Cayo the country boy has livened up, Don Fermín."

"It's true that they're trying to cheat," said a man who came out of the shack. "They're trying to steal the election from Don Emilio Arévalo."

"Hey, what's wrong with you." The little man had opened his eyes as wide as saucers. "Didn't you oversee the voting as a representative of the Arévalo ticket? What cheating are you talking about? We haven't even counted the ballots yet."

"Enough, enough," Don Fermín said. "Stop crying. Wasn't that how it was, isn't that what you were thinking, didn't you do it because of that?"

"We won't stand for it," said the man who gave the orders. "Let's go inside."

"After all, he has a right to have some fun," Colonel Espina said. "I hope the General doesn't look too badly on this business of taking a mistress so openly like that."

Trifulcio grabbed the little man by the lapels and gently pulled him away from the door. He saw him turn yellow, felt him trembling. He went into the shack behind Téllez, Urondo and the man who gave the orders. Inside a young man in overalls stood up and shouted, you can't come in here, police, police! Téllez gave him a shove and the young man fell to the ground shouting police, police! Trifulcio picked him up and sat him in a chair: calm down, take it easy, man. Téllez and Urondo picked up the ballot boxes and went outside. The little man looked

165

terrified at Trifulcio: it was a crime, they'd go to jail, and his voice gave way.

"Shut up, you were paid by Mendizábal," Téllez said.

"Shut up, unless you want us to do it for you," Urondo said.

"We're not going to stand for any fraud," the man who gave the orders said to the policemen. "We're taking the ballot boxes to the District Board of Elections."

"But I don't think he will, because nothing Cayo does ever seems bad to him," Colonel Espina said. "He says that the greatest service I did for the country was digging Cayo up out of the provinces and bringing him to work with me. He's got the General in his pocket, Don Fermín."

"Come on, all right," Don Fermín said. "Don't cry anymore, you poor devil."

In the van Trifulcio sat up front. Out of the window he saw the little man and the boy in overalls arguing with the police at the door of the shack. The people were looking at them, some pointing at the van, others laughing.

"All right, you weren't trying to blackmail me, you were trying to help me," Don Fermín said. "You'll do what I tell you, all right, you'll obey me. But that's enough, don't cry anymore."

"All that waiting just for this?" Trifulcio said. "There were only two guys there for Mr. Mendizábal. The others were just looking on, that's all."

"I don't despise you, I don't hate you," Don Fermín said. "It's all right, you respect me, you did it for me. So I wouldn't suffer, all right. You're not a poor devil, all right."

"Mendizábal was so sure of himself," Urondo said. "Since this is his territory, he thought he'd run away with the election. But he got stuck."

"It's all right, it's all right," Don Fermín repeated.

10

THE POLICE HAD PULLED THE SIGNS off the walls of San Marcos, had erased the letters that said up the strike and down with Odría. No students were to be seen on the campus. Policemen were clustered together across from the founders' chapel, two patrol cars parked on the corner of Azángaro, a troop of assault guards in the neighboring vacant lots. Santiago went along Colmena, the Plaza San Martín. On the Jirón de la Unión at every sixty feet a policeman appeared, impassive among the pedestrians, a submachine gun under his arm, a gas mask slung over his shoulder, a cluster of tear-gas grenades on his belt. The people coming out of office buildings, the idlers and the Don Juans looked at them with apathy or with curiosity but without fear. On the Plaza de Armas there were also patrol cars and in front of the Palace gates helmeted soldiers were seen along with the sentries in black-and-red uniforms. But on the other side of the bridge, in Rímac, there weren't even any traffic police. Boys with the faces of hoodlums, hoodlums with tubercular faces, were smoking under the musty lampposts on Francisco Pizarro, and Santiago went along between bars that spat out the staggering drunks and beggars, the ragged children and stray dogs of other times. The Hotel Mogollón was narrow and long like the unpaved alley where it was located. There was nobody in the booth that served as a desk, the narrow lobby and the stairway were dark. On the second floor, four golden lines marked the door of the room, which was too small for its frame. He gave three light taps as a password and pushed it open: Washington's face, a cot with a blanket, a bare pillow, two chairs, a small chamber pot.

"Downtown is crawling with police," Santiago said. "They expect another lightning demonstration tonight."

"A piece of bad news, they picked up Half-breed Martínez as he was coming out of Engineering," Washington said; he was emaciated and baggy-eyed, so serious that he looked like a different person. "His family went to Police Headquarters but they couldn't see him."

Cobwebs hung from the beams of the ceiling, the only bulb was high up and the light was dirty.

"Now the Apristas can't say they're the only ones who get it," Santiago said; he smiled, confused.

"We have to change our location," Washington said. "Even tonight's meeting is dangerous."

"Do you think he'll talk if they work him over?" They had him tied up and a short, stocky figure wound up and struck, the half-breed's face contracted in a grimace, his mouth howled.

"You never can tell." Washington shrugged his shoulders and lowered his eyes for an instant. "Besides, I don't trust this guy in the hotel. This afternoon he asked to see my papers again. Llaque's coming and I haven't been able to tell him about Martínez."

"The best thing would be to get together on a quick plan and get out of here." Santiago took out a cigarette and lighted it; he took several puffs and then removed the pack again and held it out to Washington. "Is the Federation still going to meet tonight?"

"What's left of the Federation. Twelve delegates are out of action," Washington said. "In principle, yes, at the Medical School."

"They'll pounce on us there in any case," Santiago said.

"Maybe not. The government must know that the strike will probably be over tonight and will let us meet," Washington said. "The independents have been scared and want to retreat. The Apristas seem to want to too."

"What are we going to do?" Santiago asked.

"That's what we've got to decide now," Washington said. "Look, news from Cuzco and Arequipa. Things there are even worse than here."

Santiago went over to the cot, picked up two letters. The first was from Cuzco, the thick, erect hand of a woman, the signature was a scrawl with rhombuses. The cell had made contact with the Apristas to discuss the sympathy strike, but the police were ahead of them, comrades, they occupied the university and the Federation had been dissolved; at least twenty comrades arrested. The student masses were rather apathetic, but the morale of the comrades who escaped the repression was still high in spite of the setbacks. Fraternally. The letter from Arequipa was typewritten, with a ribbon that was neither black nor blue, but violet, and it wasn't signed or addressed to anyone. We had the campaign going well in the various faculties and the situation seemed favorable in support of the strike at San Marcos when the police came into the university, eight of our people were among those arrested, comrades: hoping to be able to send you better news soon and wishing you every success.

"In Trujillo the motion was defeated," Washington said. "Our people were only able to get them to approve a message of moral support. Which means nothing."

"No university is backing San Marcos, no union is backing the street-car workers," Santiago said. "So there's nothing to do but call off the strike."

"In any case, quite a lot has been accomplished," Washington said. "And with the prisoners now, there's a good banner to start out under again any time we want."

There were three taps on the door, come in said Washington, and Héctor came in, perspiring, dressed in gray.

"I thought I was going to be late and I'm one of the first to get here." He sat on a chair, mopped his brow with a handkerchief. He took a deep breath and exhaled it as if it were smoke. "It was impossible to get hold of any streetcar worker. The police have occupied union headquarters. We went there with two Apristas. They've lost touch with the strike committee too."

"They grabbed the half-breed as he was coming out of Engineering School," Washington said.

Héctor stood looking at him, his handkerchief at his mouth.

"As long as they don't give him a beating and disfigure his . . ." His voice and forced smile dimmed and went out; he took another deep

169

breath, put his handkerchief away. He was quite serious now. "We shouldn't have met here tonight, then."

"Llaque's coming, there wasn't any way to warn him," Washington said. "Besides, the Federation is meeting in an hour and a half and we've just got time to put our plans together."

"What plans?" Héctor said. "The independents and the Apristas want to call off the strike and that's the most logical thing to do. Everything's falling apart, we have to save what's left of the student organizations."

Three taps, greetings comrades, the red tie and the bird voice. Llaque looked around with surprise.

"Didn't you say eight o'clock? What happened to the others?"

"Martínez was taken this morning," Washington said. "Do you think we ought to call off the meeting and get out of here?"

The small face didn't tighten, his eyes didn't show alarm. He must have been used to news like that, he thinks, living in hiding and in fear. He looked at his watch, he was silent for a moment, thinking.

"If they arrested him this morning, there's no danger," he said at last with an embarrassed half-smile. "They won't question him until tonight or maybe at dawn. We've got more than enough time, comrades."

"But it would be better if you left," Héctor said. "You're the one who's taking the greatest risk here."

"Keep it down, I could hear you from the stairs," Solórzano said from the doorway. "So they caught the half-breed. Our first casualty, damn it."

"Did you forget about the three knocks?" Washington asked.

"The door was open," Solórzano said. "And you were all hollering."

"It's going on eight-thirty," Llaque said. "What about the other comrades?"

"Jacobo had to go see the textile workers, Aída was going to the Catholic University with a delegate from the School of Education," Washington said. "They won't be long, let's get started."

Héctor and Washington sat on the cot, Santiago and Llaque in the chairs, Solórzano on the floor. We're waiting, Comrade Julián, Santiago heard and gave a start. You were always forgetting your pseudonym, Zavalita, forgetting you were recording secretary and were to give the minutes of the last meeting. He did it rapidly, without standing up, in a low voice.

"Let's go on to the reports," Washington said. "Please make them short and to the point."

"We'd better find out first what happened to them," Santiago said. "I'm going to make a phone call."

"There isn't any phone in the hotel," Washington said. "You'll have to find a drugstore and the coming and going wouldn't be wise. They're only a half hour late, they'll be along presently."

The reports, he thinks, the long monologues where it was hard to distinguish object from subject, facts from interpretations, and interpretations from clichés. But that night they had all been quick, terse and concrete. Solórzano: the Association of Agricultural Students had rejected the motion as being too political, why should San Marcos get involved in a streetcar workers' strike? Washington: the leaders at the Normal School said there's nothing to be done, if we put it to a vote, ninety percent will be against the strike, we can only give them our moral support. Héctor: contacts with the Strike Committee of the streetcar workers have been broken off since the police took over the union headquarters.

"Agriculture out of it, Engineering out of it, the Normal School out of it, and we don't know about the Catholic University," Washington said. "The universities of Cuzco and Arequipa occupied, and Trujillo backing out. That's the situation in brief. There's almost certain to be a proposal to lift the strike at the Federation tonight. We've got one hour in which to decide our position."

It seemed that there wasn't going to be any discussion, he thinks, that they all agreed. Héctor: the movement had helped to politicize the student body, now it would be best to withdraw before the Federation disappeared. Solórzano: lifting the strike, yes, but only in order to start immediately to prepare a new movement, one more powerful and better coordinated. Santiago: yes, and to initiate at once a campaign to free the arrested students. Washington: with the experience we've gained and the lessons of these days of struggle, the University Section of Cahuide had

171

had its baptism of fire, he too was in favor of lifting the strike so they could regroup their forces.

"I'd like to say something, comrades," Llaque said, his voice timid but not at all hesitant. "When the section agreed to support the streetcar workers' strike, we knew all that."

What did we know? That the unions were yellow dogs, because the real labor leaders were dead or in jail or in exile, that with the strike would come repression and there would be arrests and that the other universities would turn their backs on San Marcos. What didn't we know, what wasn't foreseen, comrades, what was it? His little hand was going up and down beside your face, Zavalita, his soft little voice was insisting, repeating, convincing. That the strike would be this successful and make the government take its mask off and show all its brutality in the clear light of day. That things were going badly? With three universities occupied, with at least fifty students and labor leaders arrested, things were going badly? With the lightning demonstrations on the Jirón de la Unión and the bourgeois press obliged to report the repression, badly? For the first time a movement of that breadth against Odría, comrades, a crack for the first time after so many years of monolithic dictatorship. Badly, badly? Wasn't it absurd to retreat at that moment? Wasn't it more correct to try to extend and radicalize the movement? Judging the situation not from a reformist but from a revolutionary point of view, comrades. He was silent and they looked at him and at each other, uncomfortable.

"If the Apristas and the independents have agreed to lift the strike, we can't do anything," Solórzano finally said.

"We can fight, comrades," Llaque said.

And the door opened, he thinks, and they came in. Aída walked very quickly to the center of the room, Jacobo stayed behind.

"It's about time," Washington said. "You had us worried."

"Jacobo locked me up and wouldn't let me go to the Catholic University." In a string of words, he thinks, as if she'd learned what she was going to say by heart. "He didn't go see the textile workers either, as the section assigned him to. I ask that he be expelled."

"Now I can understand why you carried her in your head all these years, Zavalita," Carlitos said.

172

She was standing between the two chairs, under the focus of the light, her fists clenched, her eyes wide, her breath heavy. They looked at her without moving, swallowing, Héctor was sweating. There was Aída's heavy breathing beside you, Zavalita, her shadow wavering on the floor. Your throat was dry and you were biting your lips, your heart beating fast.

"All right, come on, comrade," Washington said. "We were just . . ."

"Besides, he tried to commit suicide because I told him I didn't want to go with him anymore." Livid, he thinks, her eyes opened wide, spitting out the words as if they were burning her tongue. "I had to trick him into letting me come. I ask that he be expelled."

"And the ground opened up," Santiago said. "Not because she'd come out with all that, there, in front of everybody. But because a fight like that, Carlitos, a fight like that, with locked doors and threats of suicide and all that."

"Have you finished?" Washington finally said.

"Up till then it hadn't occurred to you that they were going to bed together." Carlitos laughed. "You thought they were looking into each other's eyes and holding hands and reciting poems by Mayakovsky and Nazim Himet, Zavalita."

Now they were all moving in place, Héctor was drying his face, Solórzano exploring the ceiling, why didn't he come forward and say something, what was he doing back there mute. Aída was still standing beside you, Zavalita, her hands no longer closed but open, a silver-plated ring with her initials on her little finger, her nails cut like a man's. Santiago raised his hand and Washington gave him the floor with a gesture.

"There's less than an hour left before the Federation meets and we haven't come to any agreement." Thinking in terror I'm going to lose my voice, he thinks. "Are we going to waste our time discussing personal problems now?"

He stopped speaking, lighted a cigarette, the match rolled on the floor, still burning, and he stepped on it. He saw the faces of the others beginning to recover from the surprise, becoming furious. Anxious, labored, Aída's breathing was still there.

173

"Of course we're not interested in personal affairs," Washington murmured. "But Aída has brought up something very serious."

A barbed silence, he thinks, a sudden heat that brutalized and smothered.

"I don't give a damn if two comrades have a fight, lock each other up, or commit suicide," Héctor said, his handkerchief against his mouth. "But I would like to know what happened with the textile workers, at the Catholic University. If the comrades who were supposed to have gone there didn't go, I'd like them to explain why."

"The comrade has just explained," the bird voice whispered. "Let the other comrade give his version and let's be done with it."

Eyes turning toward the door, Jacobo's slow steps, Jacobo's silhouette beside Aída's. His light blue suit wrinkled, his shirttails half out, his jacket unbuttoned and his tie loosened.

"What Aída said is true, I lost my nerve." Choking up on every word, he thinks, swaying like a drunk. "I was confused, it was weakness, it was the crisis. Maybe all these last days without any sleep, comrades. I accept any decision of the section, comrades."

"You didn't let Aída go to the Catholic University?" Solórzano asked. "Is it true that you didn't keep the appointment with the textile workers, that you tried to stop Aída from coming to the meeting?"

"I don't know what came over me, I don't know what came over me." His eyes intimidated, he thinks, tormented, and his look of a madman. "I ask everybody's forgiveness. I want to get through this crisis, help me through it, comrades. What the comrade said, what Aída said is true. I accept any decision, comrades."

He stopped speaking, withdrew toward the door and Santiago no longer saw him. Aída alone again, her hand purple from the tension. Solórzano's brow was wrinkled, he had stood up.

"I'm going to say frankly what I think." His face transformed with rage, he thinks, his voice disillusioned. "I voted in favor of this strike because Jacobo's arguments convinced me. He was the most enthusiastic, that's why we elected him to the Federation and the Strike Committee. I have to remember that while Comrade Jacobo was acting selfishly, they arrested Martínez. I think that we should punish a lapse like that in some way. The contacts with the textile workers, the Catholic Univer-

174

sity, at this time, well, why should I say what we all know. Something like this is intolerable, comrades."

"Of course it's serious, of course he's made a serious mistake," Héctor said. "But there's no time now, Solórzano. The Federation is meeting in half an hour."

"It's madness to keep on wasting time like this, comrades." The bird voice, perplexed, impatient, his little hand aloft. "We have to postpone this matter and get back to the subject under discussion."

"I move that discussion of this be put off until the next meeting," Santiago said.

"I don't want to offend anyone, but Jacobo shouldn't be present at this meeting," Washington said; he hesitated a second and added: "I don't think he can be trusted anymore."

"Put my motion to a vote," Santiago said. "Now you're the one who's making us waste time, Washington. Are you going to forget about the strike, the Federation, in order to spend the whole night arguing about Jacobo?"

"Time is passing," Llaque insisted, implored. "Keep that in mind, comrades."

"All right, we're going to vote," Washington said. "Do you have anything to add, Jacobo?"

The steps, the silhouette, he'd taken his hands out of his pockets and was wringing them. A few blond locks of hair covered his ears, his eyes weren't self-assured and sarcastic the way they'd been during debates, he thinks, his whole appearance showed defeat and humility.

"I thought the only thing there was for him was the section and the revolution," Santiago said. "And all of a sudden it was a lie, Carlitos. Flesh and blood too, like you and me."

"I can understand why you have your doubts, why you don't trust me anymore," he babbled. "I'm ready to make my self-criticism, I submit to any decision. Give me another opportunity to show you, in spite of everything, comrades."

"You'd better leave the room while we vote," Washington said.

Santiago didn't hear him open the door; he knew he'd gone out when the light wavered and the shadows on the wall moved. He stood up, took Aída's arm and showed her the chair. She sat down. Her hands on her

175

knees, he thinks, her dark lashes moist, her hair in disorder around her neck, and her ears as if she were cold. If only your hand had come up, he thinks, and lowered and touched that neck and fondled it and straightened out that hair and if your fingers had become entwined in that hair and pulled it slowly and let it go and pulled it: oh, Zavalita.

"Let's vote on Aída's petition first," Washington said. "Those in favor of expelling Jacobo from the section raise your hands."

"I made a previous motion," Santiago said. "My motion should be voted on first."

But Washington and Solórzano had already raised their hands. Everybody turned to look at Aída: her head was lowered, her hands motionless on her knees.

"You're not voting in favor of what you requested?" Solórzano said, almost shouting.

"I've changed my mind," Aída sobbed. "Comrade Llaque is right. We have to postpone discussion of this matter."

"This is incredible," the bird voice said. "What's going on, what is this?"

"Are you putting us on?" Solórzano said. "What's your game, Aída?"

"I've changed my mind," Aída whispered, without raising her head.

"God damn it," the bird voice said. "Where are we, what are we playing?"

"Let's put an end to this joke," Washington said. "Those in favor of postponing discussion of this."

Llaque, Héctor and Santiago raised their hands, and a few seconds later Aída did also. Héctor was laughing, Solórzano was holding his stomach as if he were going to throw up, what is all this, the bird voice repeated.

"Women really are something," Carlitos said. "Call girls, Communists, middle class, peasants, they all have something we haven't got. Maybe we'd be better off being fairies, Zavalita. Getting involved with something you know and not with those strange animals."

"Call Jacobo, then, the circus is over," Washington said. "Let's get back to serious business."

Santiago spun around: the open door, Jacobo's baffled face bursting into the room.

176

"There are three patrol cars by the door," he whispered. He'd grabbed Santiago's arm. "A lot of plainclothesmen, an officer."

"Close that door, God damn it," the bird voice said.

They'd all stood up at once. Jacobo had shut the door and was holding it with his body.

"Hold it shut," Washington said, looking at everyone, stumbling. "The papers, the letters. Hold the door, it hasn't got a lock."

Héctor, Solórzano and Llaque went to help Jacobo and Santiago, who were holding the door, and they all went through their pockets. Leaning over the night table, Washington was tearing up papers and putting them in a chamber pot. Aída was passing him the notebooks, the pieces of paper that the others were handing her, she was going back and forth on tiptoe from the door to the bed. The pot was already on fire. Outside not a sound was to be heard; they all had their ears tight against the door. Llaque left them, put out the light, and in the darkness Santiago heard Solórzano's voice: couldn't it have been a false alarm? The small flame in the pot was rising and falling, at regular intervals Santiago saw Washington's face appear as he blew on it. Someone coughed and the bird voice called for silence, and a couple of them began to cough at the same time.

"Too much smoke," Héctor whispered. "We have to open that window."

A silhouette drew away from the door and reached toward the skylight, but the hand could only reach the edge. Washington took him by the waist, lifted him up, and when the skylight opened a gush of fresh air came into the room. The flame had gone out, and now Aída was handing the pot to Jacobo, who, lifted up again by Washington, was putting the pot out through the skylight. Washington turned on the light: tight faces, sunken eyes, dry mouths. With gestures Llaque signaled them to leave the door, sit down. His face was withered, his teeth could be seen, he had aged in an instant.

"There's still a lot of smoke," Llaque said. "Everybody light up."

"False alarm," Solórzano murmured. "You can't hear anything."

Santiago and Héctor passed out cigarettes, even Aída, who didn't smoke, lighted one. Washington had placed himself by the door and was peeking through the keyhole.

"Don't you know you always have to bring your textbooks?" Llaque said; his little hand was waving hysterically. "We meet to talk about university problems. We're not political, we're not involved in politics. Cahuide doesn't exist, the section doesn't exist. You don't know anything about anything."

"They're coming up," Washington said and drew back from the door. A murmur was heard, silence, a murmur again, and two soft raps on the door.

"There are some people here to see you, sir," a raspy voice said. "It's urgent, they say."

Aída and Jacobo were together, he thinks, he had his hand on her shoulder. Washington took a step toward the door, but it opened first and a shooting star cut him off: a figure stumbling, reeling, other figures leaping, shouting, revolvers pointing at them, someone cursing, someone panting.

"What do you want?" Washington said. "Why did you come in like . . . ?"

"Anyone with weapons throw them on the floor," a short man wearing a hat and a blue tie said. "Put your hands up. Search them."

"We're students," Washington said. "We're . . ."

But a policeman pushed him and he was quiet. They frisked them from head to toe, made them file out with their hands up. On the street there were two policemen with submachine guns and a group of onlookers. They split them up, they shoved Santiago into a patrol car with Héctor and Solórzano. It was crowded on the seat, it smelled of armpits, the one driving was talking into a small microphone. The car started up: the Stone Bridge, Tacna, Wilson, Avenida España. It stopped at the gates of Police Headquarters, a plainclothesman whispered to the sentries and they were ordered out. A corridor with small open doors, desks, police and men in civilian clothes, in shirtsleeves, a stairway, another corridor that seemed to have a tile floor, a door that opened, go in, it was closed and the small sound of the key. A small room that looked like a notary's waiting room, with one small bench against the wall. They were silent, looking at the cracked walls, the shiny floor, the fluorescent light.

"Ten o'clock," Santiago said. "The Federation must be meeting."

"If all the other delegates aren't here too," Héctor said.

Would the news come out tomorrow, would his old man find out about it in the newspapers? You imagined the sleepless night at home, Zavalita, your mama's wailing, the hurly-burly and running to the phone and the visitors and Teté's gossiping in the neighborhood, Sparky's comments. Yes, the house was like a loony bin that night, son, Ambrosio says. And Carlitos: you must have felt like a Lenin. And all of a sudden a half-breed wound up and gave a kick: most of all afraid, Carlitos. He took out his cigarettes, just enough for the three of them. They smoked without talking, drawing in and blowing out the smoke at the same time. They'd crushed out the butts when they heard the little noise of the key.

"Which one of you is Santiago Zavala?" a new face said from the door. Santiago stood up. "All right, you can sit down."

The face sank into the shadows, the little noise again.

"It means your name's on file," Héctor whispered.

"It means they're going to let you out first," Solórzano whispered. "Get over to the Federation. They have to raise hell. For the sake of Llaque and Washington, they're the ones who'll be the most fucked up."

"Are you crazy?" Santiago asked. "Why should they let me go first?"

"Because of your family," Solórzano said with a little laugh. "They have to protest, raise hell."

"My family won't lift a finger," Santiago said. "More likely, when they find out I'm mixed up in this . . ."

"You're not mixed up in anything," Héctor said. "Don't forget that."

"Maybe with this roundup now the other universities will do something," Solórzano said.

They'd sat down on the bench, were talking, looking at the wall opposite or the ceiling. Héctor stood up, began to walk back and forth, he said that his legs had gone to sleep. Solórzano turned up his coat collar and put his hands in his pockets: chilly, isn't it?

"Do you think they brought Aída here too?" Santiago asked.

"They probably took her to Chorrillos, to the women's jail," Solórzano said. "Brand new, with individual cells."

"It was foolish wasting time on that lovers' quarrel," Héctor said. "It's enough to make you laugh."

"Enough to make you cry," said Solórzano. "Enough to send them off to make soap operas, get a job in Mexican movies. I'll lock you up, I'll kill myself, they should kick you out of the section, no, they shouldn't. Enough to pull down their pants and give those bourgeois brats a good spanking, God damn it."

"I thought they were getting along fine with each other," Héctor said. "Did you know that they were having fights?"

"I didn't know anything," Santiago said. "I haven't seen much of them lately."

"My old lady has a tantrum and the strike and the Party can go to hell, I'm going to commit suicide," Solórzano said. "Why don't they make soap operas? Shit."

"Comrades have their little affairs of the heart too." Héctor smiled.

"They probably made Martínez talk," Santiago said. "They probably beat him and . . ."

"Try to hide the fact that you're afraid," Solórzano said. "It's worse if you can't."

"You're probably the one who's afraid," Santiago said.

"Of course I am," Solórzano said. "But I don't show it by turning pale."

"Because if you did, it couldn't be noticed," Santiago said.

"The advantages of being a half-breed." Solórzano laughed. "Don't get hot under the collar, man."

Héctor sat down; he had one cigarette and they smoked it among the three of them, one puff apiece.

"How did they know my name?" Santiago asked. "Why did that guy come by?"

"Since you come from a good family, they're going to fix some kidneys in wine for you so that you'll feel at home," Solórzano said, yawning. "Well, I'm getting tired."

He squatted down against the wall and closed his eyes. His husky body, his ash-colored skin, his broad nose, he thinks, his straight hair, and it was the first time he'd been arrested.

"Will they put us in with the common criminals?" Santiago asked.

"I hope not," Héctor said. "I don't feel like being raped by hoodlums. Look how the comrade's sleeping. He's got the right idea, let's get comfortable and see if we can get a little rest."

They leaned their heads against the wall, closed their eyes. A moment later Santiago heard steps and looked at the door; Héctor had also sat up. The little noise, the face from the last time.

"Come with me, Zavala. Yes, just you."

The short man led him out and as he left the room he saw Solórzano's eyes, which were opening, reddened. A corridor full of doors, steps, a hallway with tiles that went up and down, a guard with a rifle in front of a window. The fellow was walking beside him with his hands in his pockets; metal signs that he was unable to read. In here, he heard, and he was alone. A large room, almost in darkness: a desk with a small lamp without a shade, bare walls, a photograph of Odría wrapped in the presidential sash like a baby in a diaper. He drew back, looked at his watch, twelve-thirty, he went forward and, his legs weak, an urge to urinate. A moment later the door opened, Santiago Zavala? a faceless voice asked. Yes: here's the one, sir. Steps, voices, the profile of Don Fermín crossing the cone of light from the lamp, his arms opening up, his face against my face, he thinks.

"Are you all right, Skinny? Have they done anything to you, Skinny?"

"Nothing, papa. I don't know why they brought me here, I haven't done anything, papa."

Don Fermín looked into his eyes, embraced him again, let him go once more, half smiled and turned toward the desk where the other person had already sat down.

"There you are, Don Fermín." You could only see his face, Carlitos, a listless, servile voice. "There's your son and heir, safe and sound."

"This young man never gets tired of giving me headaches." The poor man was trying to be natural and he was theatrical, even comical, Carlitos. "I envy you, not having any children, Don Cayo."

"When a person starts getting old," yes, Carlitos, Cayo Bermúdez in person, "he'd like to have someone to represent him in the world when he's no longer here."

Don Fermín let out an uncomfortable laugh, sat down on a corner of the desk, and Cayo Bermúdez stood up: that's who it was, there he was. A dry, parchmentlike, insipid face. Didn't Don Fermín want to sit down? No, Don Cayo, he was fine.

181

"Look at the mess you've got yourself in, young fellow." In a friendly way, Carlitos, as if he was sorry. "Wasting your time on politics instead of using it to study."

"I'm not in politics," Santiago said. "I was with some friends, we weren't doing anything."

But Bermúdez had leaned over to offer a cigarette to Don Fermín, who immediately, with an artificial smile, took an Inca, the one who could smoke only Chesterfields and hated dark tobacco, Carlitos, and put it in his mouth. He puffed on it avidly and coughed, happy to be doing something that covered up his confusion, Carlitos, the terrible inconvenience. Bermúdez was looking at the swirls of smoke, bored, and suddenly his eyes found Santiago:

"It's all right for a young man to be a rebel, impulsive." As if he was mouthing nonsense at a social gathering, Carlitos, as if he gave a damn about what he was saying. "But conspiring with Communists is a different matter. Don't you know that Communism is outlawed? Imagine what would happen if the Internal Security Law was applied to you."

"The Internal Security Law doesn't apply to snotnoses who don't know what they're doing, Don Cayo." With restrained fury, Carlitos, without raising his voice, holding back his urge to call him a swine, a servant.

"Please, Don Fermín." As if scandalized, Carlitos, as if his jokes weren't understood. "Not to snotnoses and least of all the son of a friend of the government like yourself."

"Santiago's a difficult boy, I know that full well." Smiling and turning serious, Carlitos, changing his tone with every word. "But don't exaggerate, Don Cayo. My son doesn't conspire, least of all with Communists."

"Let him tell us about it himself, Don Fermín." Friendly, obsequious, Carlitos. "What he was doing in that little hotel in Rímac, what the section is, what Cahuide is. Let him explain all those little names."

He blew out a puff of smoke, mournfully contemplated the swirls.

"In this country Communists don't even exist, Don Cayo." Finding it hard to speak with his coughing and his anger, Carlitos, stepping on his cigarette with rage.

"There aren't many, but they're a nuisance." As if I'd left, Carlitos, or hadn't even been there. "They put out a little mimeographed newspa-

182

per, *Cahuide*. Terrible things about the United States, the President, me. I have a complete collection and I'll show it to you sometime."

"I don't have anything to do with that," Santiago said. "I don't know a single Communist at San Marcos."

"We let them play at revolution, at whatever they want, just so long as they don't go too far." As if everything he was saying bored him, Carlitos. "But a political strike, supporting the streetcar workers, whatever San Marcos has to do with streetcar workers, that's too much."

"The strike isn't political," Santiago said. "The Federation called it. All the students . . ."

"This young man is a delegate from his class, a delegate to the Federation, a delegate on the Strike Committee." Not listening to me or looking at me, Carlitos, smiling at my old man as if he was telling him a joke. "And a member of Cahuide, that's the name of the Communist organization, for two years. Two of those arrested with him have thick files, they're known terrorists. There wasn't anything else we could do, Don Fermín."

"My son can't be kept under arrest, he's no criminal." Unable to hold back any longer, Carlitos, pounding on the desk, raising his voice. "I'm a friend of the government, and not just since yesterday, since the very beginning, and they owe me a lot of favors. I'm going to talk to the President right now."

"Don Fermín, please." As if wounded, Carlitos, as if betrayed by his best friend. "I called you so we could settle this thing between ourselves, I know better than anyone that you're a good friend of the government. I wanted to let you know what this young man was up to, that's all. Of course he's not under arrest. You can take him home right now, Don Fermín."

"Thank you very much, Don Cayo." Confused again, Carlitos, wiping his mouth with his handkerchief, trying to smile. "Don't worry about Santiago, I'll take charge of setting him on the right path. Now, if you don't mind, I'd like to leave. You can imagine the state his mother is in."

"Of course, go and reassure the lady." Distressed, Carlitos, trying to vindicate himself, ingratiate himself. "Oh, and naturally, the young man's name won't appear anywhere. There's no file on him. I assure you that there won't be any trace of this incident."

183

"Yes, that would have hurt the boy later on." Smiling, nodding, Carlitos, trying to show him that he'd already made up with him. "Thank you, Don Cayo."

They left. Don Fermín went ahead and the small, narrow figure of Bermúdez, his striped gray suit, his short, quick little steps. He didn't return the guards' salutes, the greetings of the plainclothesmen. The courtyard, the front of the Headquarters building, the gates, fresh air, the avenue. The car was at the bottom of the steps. Ambrosio took off his cap, opened the door, smiled at Santiago, good evening, young sir. Bermúdez nodded and disappeared into the main door. Don Fermín got into the car: home, quickly, Ambrosio. They left and the car headed toward Wilson, turned toward Arequipa, picking up speed at each corner, and all that air coming in the window, Zavalita, so he could breathe, so he didn't have to think.

"That son of a bitch is going to pay for this." The annoyance on his face, he thinks, the fatigue in his eyes that were looking straight ahead. "That shitty half-breed isn't going to humiliate me like this. I'll teach him his place."

"The first time I ever heard him curse, Carlitos," Santiago said. "Insult somebody like that."

"He's going to pay for it." His brow eaten with wrinkles, he thinks, a cold rage. "I'm going to teach him how to treat his betters."

"I'm sorry I put you through such a bad time, papa, I swear that . . ." And his face spinning around quickly, he thinks, and the slap that shut your mouth, Zavalita.

"The first and only time he ever hit me," Santiago says. "Do you remember, Ambrosio?"

"You're going to answer to me too, snotnose." His voice changed into a grunt, he thinks. "Don't you know that if you want to plot you've got to be on the ball? That only an imbecile would plot on the telephone from his house? That the police might be listening in? The telephone was tapped, you dummy."

"They'd recorded at least ten conversations of mine with the people from Cahuide, Carlitos," Santiago said. "Bermúdez had had him listen to them. He felt humiliated, that's what pained him most."

When they got to the Colegio Raimondi there was a detour; Ambrosio

184

turned toward Arenales, and they didn't speak until the corner of Javier Prado.

"Besides, it wasn't because of you." His voice depressed, worried, he thinks, hoarse. "He was keeping track of me. He took advantage of this occasion to let me know without saying it to my face."

"I don't think I ever felt as bitter, until that time in the whorehouse," Santiago said. "Because they'd been arrested on my account, because of the business between Jacobo and Aída, because I'd been released and not them, because the old man was in such a state."

Avenida Arequipa again, almost deserted, headlights and quick palm trees, gardens and darkened houses.

"So you're a Communist, just as I predicted, you didn't go to San Marcos to study but to play politics." His bitter little tone, he thinks, harsh, mocking. "Letting yourself be taken in by drifters and malcontents."

"I passed my exams, papa. I've always gotten good marks, papa."

"What the hell do I care if you're a Communist, an Aprista, an anarchist, or an existentialist?" Furious again, he thinks, slapping his knee, not looking at me. "If you're a bomb-thrower or a murderer? But only after you've reached the age of twenty-one. Until then you're going to study and only study. Obey, only obey."

He thinks: there. Didn't it occur to you that you were going to make your mother a nervous wreck? He thinks no. That you were going to get your father in a mess? No, Zavalita, it didn't occur to you. The Avenida Angamos, Diagonal, Quebrada, Ambrosio hunched over the wheel: you didn't think, it didn't occur to you. Because you were quite comfortable, everything taken care of, right? Daddy fed you, daddy gave you clothes to wear and paid for your schooling and gave you money, and you playing at Communism, and you plotting against people who were giving your daddy work, not that, God damn it. Not the slap, papa, he thinks, that's what hurt me. The Avenida 28 de Julio, its trees, the Avenida Larco, the little worm, the snake, the knives.

"When you make some money and support yourself, when you don't depend on your daddy's pockets anymore, then it'll be all right." Softly, he thinks, savagely. "Communist, anarchist, bombs, whatever you want. In the meantime you study and obey."

185

He thinks: which I didn't forgive you for, papa. The garage in the house, the lighted windows, Teté's profile in one of them, here comes Superbrain, mama!

"And was that when you broke with Cahuide and your buddies?" Carlitos asked.

"You go in, Skinny, I've got to get this mess fixed up." Sorry now, he thinks, trying to make friends with me. "And take a bath. God knows how many lice you brought back from Police Headquarters."

"And with Law School and with my family and with Miraflores, Carlitos."

The garden, mama, kisses, her face with tears, couldn't he see what had happened to him for being so crazy? even the cook and the maid were there, Teté's excited little shouts: the return of the prodigal son, Carlitos, if I'd been in for a day instead of a few hours, they would have welcomed me with a brass band. Sparky flew down the stairs: you gave us quite a turn, man. They sat him down in the living room and surrounded him, Señora Zoila rumpled his hair and kissed his brow. Sparky and Teté were dying with curiosity: in the penitentiary, at Headquarters, had he seen thieves, murderers? The old man had tried to call the Palace, but the President was sleeping, but he called Headquarters and gave them hell, Superbrain. Some fried eggs, Señora Zoila said to the cook, a glass of chocolate milk, and if that lemon tart is left. He hadn't done anything, mama, it had been a mistake, mama.

"He's glad he was arrested, he feels like a hero," Teté said. "Now there'll be no holding him."

"Your picture's going to come out in *El Comercio*," Sparky said. "With your number and a hoodlum face."

"What's it like, what did they do to you in jail?" Teté asked.

"They undress you, put a striped uniform on you and shackle your feet," Santiago said. "The dungeons are crawling with rats and there aren't any lights."

"Hush up, you fibber," Teté said. "Tell us, tell us what it was like."

"So you see now, you crazy boy, you see what's come of wanting to go to San Marcos so much?" Señora Zoila said. "Will you promise me that next year you'll transfer to the Catholic University? That you won't ever get involved in politics again?"

186

He promised you mama, never mama. It was two o'clock when they went to bed. Santiago got undressed, put on his pajamas, turned out the lamp. His body felt dull, hot.

"Didn't you ever look up the Cahuide people again?" Carlitos asked.

He pulled the sheet up to his neck, but sleep fled and fatigue beat on his back. The window was open and a few stars could be seen.

"Llaque was in jail for two years, Washington was exiled to Bolivia," Santiago said. "The others were released two weeks later."

A restless feeling like a thief prowling in the darkness, he thinks, remorse, jealousy, shame. I hate you papa, I hate you Jacobo, I hate you Aída. He felt a terrible urge to smoke and he didn't have any cigarettes.

"They must have thought you got scared," Carlitos said. "That you betrayed them, Zavalita."

Aída's face, Jacobo's and Washington's and Solórzano's and Héctor's and Aída's again. He thinks: a desire to be small, to be born again, to smoke. But if he went to ask Sparky he'd have to talk to him.

"I was scared, in a way, Carlitos," Santiago said. "I did betray them, in a way."

He sat up on the bed, dug in the pockets of his jacket, got up and went through all the suits in the closet. Without putting on his bathrobe or slippers, he went down to the first landing and into Sparky's room. The pack and the matches were on the night table and Sparky was sleeping face down on the sheets. He went back to his room. Sitting beside the window, anxiously, deliciously, he smoked, flicking ashes into the garden. A while later he heard the car stop at the door. He saw Don Fermín come in, saw Ambrosio on his way to his small room in back. Now he must have been opening his study, now turning on the light. He felt for his slippers and bathrobe and went out of his room. From the stairs he saw that the light in the study was on. He went down, stopped beside the glass door: sitting in one of the green easy chairs, the glass of whiskey in his hand, with his late-night eyes, the gray hairs on his temples. He only had the floor lamp turned on, as on nights when he stayed home and read the newspapers, he thinks. He knocked on the door and Don Fermín came over and opened it.

"I'd like to talk to you for a minute, papa."

"Come in, you're going to catch cold out there." No longer angry,

Zavalita, happy to see you. "It's very damp, Skinny."

He took his arm, led him in, went back to the easy chair, Santiago sat down across from him.

"Have you all been up till now?" As if he'd already forgiven you, Zavalita, or had never quarreled with you. "Sparky has a good excuse not to go to the office tomorrow."

"We went to bed a while back, papa. I couldn't get to sleep."

"Couldn't get to sleep because of so many emotions." Looking at you tenderly, Zavalita. "Well, that's not so bad. Now you have to tell me everything in all its details. Did they really treat you well?"

"Yes, papa, they didn't even interrogate me."

"Well, the scare wasn't so bad, then." Even with a touch of pride, Zavalita. "What did you want to talk to me about, Skinny?"

"I've been thinking about what you said and you're right, papa." Feeling your mouth go dry all of a sudden, Zavalita. "I want to leave home and look for a job. Something that would let me keep on with my studies, papa."

Don Fermín didn't joke, didn't laugh. He raised his glass, took a drink, wiped his mouth.

"You're angry with your father because he slapped you." Leaning over to put a hand on your knee, Zavalita, looking at you as if telling you let's forget about it, let's make up. "As old as you are, a hunted revolutionary and all that."

He straightened up, took out his pack of Chesterfields, his lighter.

"I'm not mad at you, papa. But I can't go on living one way and thinking another. Please try to understand me, papa."

"You can't go on living how?" A bit wounded, Zavalita, suddenly distressed, tired. "What is there here that goes against your way of thinking, Skinny?"

"I don't want to depend on handouts." Feeling your hands trembling, your voice, Zavalita. "I don't want anything I do to bounce back on you. I want to be dependent on myself, papa."

"You don't want to be dependent on a capitalist." Smiling in an afflicted way, Zavalita, pained but without any rancor. "You don't want to live with your father because he gets government contracts? Is that why?"

188

"Don't get angry, papa. Don't think I'm trying to . . . papa."

"You're grown up now, I can trust you now, isn't that so?" Stretching out a hand toward your face, Zavalita, patting your cheek. "I'm going to explain to you why I got so mad. There's something that was on the point of being wrapped up just now. Military men, senators, a lot of influential people. The phone was tapped because of me, not because of you. Something must have leaked out, that peasant Bermúdez took advantage of you so he could let me know that he suspected something, that he knew. Now we have to stop everything, start all over again. So you see, your father isn't one of Odría's lackeys, far from it. We're going to get him out, we're going to call for elections. You can keep the secret, can't you? I wouldn't have told this to Sparky, you can see that I'm treating you like a grown man, Skinny."

"General Espina's conspiracy?" Carlitos asked. "Your father was involved too? It never came out."

"So you thought you could take off and your father could go to the devil." Telling you with his eyes it's all over, let's not say anything more, I love you. "You can see that my relationship with Odría is precarious, you can see that you haven't got any reason to have scruples."

"That's not why, papa. I'm not even sure whether politics interest me or not, whether I'm a Communist or not. It's so I can be able to decide better what I'm going to do, what I want to be."

"I was thinking in the car just now." Giving you time to collect your thoughts, Zavalita, still smiling. "Would you like me to send you abroad for a while? Mexico, for example. Take your exams and in January you can go study in Mexico for a year or two. We'll find some way to convince your mother. What do you say, Skinny?"

"I don't know, papa, it hadn't occurred to me." Thinking that he was trying to buy you off, Zavalita, that he'd just made that up in order to buy time. "I'll have to think about it, papa."

"You've got plenty of time until January." Standing up, Zavalita, patting your face again. "You'll see things better from there, you'll see that the world isn't the little world of San Marcos. Agreed, Skinny? And now let's go to bed, it's already four o'clock."

He finished his drink, turned out the light, they went upstairs together. By his bedroom Don Fermín leaned over to kiss him: you had to trust

189

your father, Skinny, no matter who you were, no matter what you did, you were the one he loved best, Skinny. He went into his room and collapsed onto the bed. He lay looking at the piece of sky in the window until it dawned. When there was enough light, he got up and went over to the closet. The wire was where he'd hidden it the last time.

"It had been a long, long time since I'd stolen from myself, Carlitos," Santiago said.

Fat, snouty, his tail curled, the pig was between the pictures of Sparky and Teté, beside his prep school pennant. When he finished getting the bills out, the milkman had already come by, the bread man, and Ambrosio was cleaning the car in the garage.

"How long after that did you come to work on *La Crónica?*" Carlitos asked.

"Two weeks later, Ambrosio," Santiago says.

TWO

1

I'M BETTER OFF THAN AT SEÑORA ZOILA'S, Amalia thought, than at the laboratory, one week when she wasn't dreaming about Trinidad. Why did she feel so content in the little house in San Miguel? It was smaller than Señora Zoila's, also two floors, elegant, and the garden, how well taken care of, it really was. The gardener came once a week and watered the lawn and pruned the geraniums, the laurels and the vine that climbed up the front like an army of spiders. In the entrance there was a built-in mirror, a small table with long legs and a Chinese vase on it, the rug in the small living room was emerald green, the chairs amber-colored and there were cushions on the floor. Amalia liked the bar: the bottles with their colored labels, the little porcelain animals, the boxes with cellophane-wrapped cigars. And the pictures too: the veiled woman looking out on the Acho bullring, the cocks fighting in the Coliseo. The dining room table was very strange, half round, half square, and the chairs with their high backs looked like confessionals. There were all kinds of things in the sideboard: platters, silverware, stacks of tablecloths, tea sets, glasses that were large and small and short and long and wineglasses. On the tables in the corners the vases always had fresh flowers—Amalia change the roses, Carlota buy gladioli today, Amalia glads today—it smelled so nice, and the pantry looked as if it had just been painted white. And the funny cans, thousands of them with their red tops and their Donald Ducks, Supermen and Mickey Mice. All kinds of things in the

193

pantry: crackers, raisins, potato chips, slippery jellies, cases of beer, whiskey, mineral water. In the refrigerator, enormous, there was an abundance of vegetables and bottles of milk. The kitchen had black and white tiles and opened onto a courtyard with clotheslines. That was where the rooms of Amalia, Carlota and Símula were, their small bath and toilet, their shower and their washbasin.

∞

A needle pierced his brain, a hammer was beating on his temples. He opened his eyes and squashed the button on the alarm clock: the torture was over. He lay motionless, looking at the phosphorescent sphere. A quarter after seven already. He picked up the telephone that was connected to the entrance, ordered his car for eight o'clock. He went to the bathroom, spent twenty minutes showering, shaving and getting dressed. The bad feeling in his head grew with the cold water, the toothpaste added a sweetish taste to the bitterness in his mouth. Was he going to vomit? He closed his eyes and it was as if he saw small blue flames consuming his organs, the blood circulating thickly under his skin. He felt his muscles garroted, his ears buzzing. He opened his eyes: more sleep. He went down to the dining room, put aside the boiled egg and the toast, drank the cup of black coffee with revulsion. He dropped two Alka-Seltzers into a half-glass of water, and as soon as he swallowed the bubbling liquid, he belched. In the study he smoked two cigarettes while he packed his briefcase. He went out and at the door the policemen on duty lifted their hands to the visors of their caps. It was a clear morning, the sun brightened the roofs of Chaclacayo, the gardens, and the bushes along the riverbank looked very green. He smoked as he waited for Ambrosio to get the car out of the garage.

∞

Santiago paid for the two hot meat tarts and the Coca-Cola and went out and the Jirón Carabaya was aglow. The windows on the Lima–San Miguel trolley reproduced the advertising signs and the sky was also reddish, as if Lima had changed into the real hell. He thinks: the shitpile turning into the shitty real one. The sidewalks were boiling with well-groomed ants, pedestrians invaded the streets and went along among the cars, the worst thing is to get caught downtown just as the offices are letting out Señora Zoila said every time she came back from shopping, worn out and grumbling, and Santiago felt the tickling in his stomach: one week already. He went into the old doorway; a spacious entranceway, heavy rolls of newsprint up against the soot-stained walls. It smelled of ink, old age, it was a hospitable smell. At the gate a doorman dressed in blue came over to him: Mr. Vallejo? The second floor, in back, where it says Editorial Offices. He went up uneasily, the broad stairway that creaked as if gnawed by rats and moths since time immemorial. A broom had probably never swept there. What had been the use of having Señora Lucía go to the trouble of pressing his suit, wasting a sol to have his shoes shined. That must be the editorial office: the doors were open, there wasn't anybody there. He stopped: with voracious, virgin eyes, he explored the empty office, the typewriters, the wicker wastebaskets, the desks, the photographs hanging on the walls. They work at night and sleep by day, he thought, a rather bohemian profession, rather romantic. He raised his hand and knocked discreetly.

⑨

The stairway from the living room to the second floor had a red carpet held down by gold staples and on the wall there were little Indians playing the *quena,* driving herds of llamas. The bathroom gleamed with tiles, the washbasin and the tub were pink, in the mirror Amalia could see her whole body. But the prettiest of all was the mistress's bedroom, during the first days she would use any excuse to go up there and she never got tired of looking at it. The rug was sea blue, the same as the drapes by the balcony, but what attracted her most was the bed, so broad, so low, with its crocodile legs and its black spread with that yellow animal that breathed fire. And why so many mirrors? It had been hard for her to get used to that multiplication of Amalias, to see herself repeated like that, cast like that from the mirror on the dressing table to the one on the screen and from the one on the closet (so many dresses, blouses, slacks, turbans, shoes) to that useless mirror hanging from the ceiling, where the dragon appeared as if in a cage. There was only one picture and her face burned the first time she saw it. Señora Zoila would never have hung a naked woman clutching her breasts with such brazenness in her bedroom, showing everything with such impudence. But here everything was daring, beginning with the wild spending. Why did they buy so much at the food stores? Because the lady gives a lot of parties, Carlota told her, the master's friends were important people, they had to be well taken care of. The mistress was like a multimillionaire, she didn't worry about money. Amalia had been ashamed when she saw the bills Símula brought. She was robbing her blind in the daily budget and she as if nothing was wrong, you spent all that? all right, and she would take the change without bothering to count it.

⑨

While the car was going along the central highway, he was reading papers, underlining sentences, making notes in the margin. The sun disappeared when they got to Vitarte, the gray atmosphere grew cooler as they approached Lima. It was eight-thirty-five when the car stopped at the Plaza Italia and Ambrosio got out and ran to open the door for him: Ludovico should be at the Club Cajamarca at four-thirty, Ambrosio. He went into the Ministry, the desks were empty, there wasn't anyone where the secretaries worked either. But Dr. Alcibíades was already at his desk, going over the newspapers with a red pencil in his hand. He stood up, good morning, Don Cayo, and the latter handed him a handful of papers: these telegrams right away, doctor. He pointed to the secretaries' desks, didn't those ladies know they were supposed to be there at eight-thirty, and Dr. Alcibíades looked at the clock on the wall: it was just eight-thirty, Don Cayo. He was already going off. He went into his office, took off his jacket, loosened his tie. The correspondence was on the blotter: police reports on the left, telegrams and communiqués in the center, letters and applications on the right. He moved the waste-basket over with his foot, began with the reports. He read, took notes, separated, tore up. He was finishing looking through the correspondence when the telephone rang: General Espina, Don Cayo, are you in? Yes, yes, he was in, doctor, put him on.

⑨

The man with white hair gave him a friendly smile and offered him a chair: so, young Zavala, of course Clodomiro had spoken to him. In his

196

eyes there was the gleam of an accomplice, in his hands something cheery and unctuous, his desk was immaculately clean. Yes, Clodomiro and he had been great friends ever since their schooldays; on the other hand his dad, Fermín, right? he'd never known him, he was quite a bit younger than us, and he smiled again: so, you had problems at home? Yes, Clodomiro had told him. Well, that's part of the times, young people want to be independent.

"That's why I have to get a job," Santiago said. "My Uncle Clodomiro thought that maybe you . . ."

"You're in luck." Mr. Vallejo nodded. "It so happens we've been looking for some extra help in the local news section."

"I haven't got much experience, but I'll do everything possible to learn fast," Santiago said. "I thought that if I got a job on *La Crónica,* maybe I could still go to Law School."

"Since I've been here I haven't seen many newspapermen who've gone on with their studies," Mr. Vallejo said. "I have to warn you about something, in case you didn't know. Journalism is the worst-paying profession there is. The one that leads to the most bitterness too."

"I always had a liking for it, sir," Santiago said. "I always thought that it was the one that had the closest contact with life."

"Fine, fine." Mr. Vallejo ran his hand over his snowy head, nodded with benevolent eyes. "I know you haven't worked on a newspaper before, we'll see how it turns out. Now I'd like to get an idea of your qualifications." He became very serious, put on a somewhat affected voice: "A fire at the Casa Wiese. Two dead, five million soles in damages, the firemen worked all night to put the fire out. The police are investigating to find out whether it was an accident or a criminal act. Just a couple of typewritten pages. There are plenty of machines in the editorial room, take any one of them."

Santiago nodded. He stood up, went into the editorial room and when he sat down at the first desk his hands began to sweat. It was good there wasn't anybody there. The Remington in front of him looked like a small coffin, Carlitos. That's exactly what it was, Zavalita.

Next to the mistress's bedroom was the study: three small easy chairs, a lamp, a bookcase. That's where the master would shut himself up on his visits to the little house in San Miguel, and if he was with somebody, there wasn't to be any noise, even Señora Hortensia would go down to the living room, turn off the radio and if there was a telephone call, she wouldn't talk. What a bad temper the master must have had if they put on such an act, Amalia was surprised the first time. Why did the mistress have three servants if the master only came from time to time? Black Símula was fat, gray-haired, quiet, and she made a bad impression on her. On the other hand, she made friends right away with her daughter Carlota, tall and skinny, without breasts, kinky hair, very pleasant. She doesn't have three because she needs them, Carlota told her, but so she can have something to spend the money the master gives her on. Was he very rich? Carlota widened her big eyes: very rich, he was in the government, he was a minister. That's why when Don Cayo came to spend the night, two policemen would appear on the corner, and the chauffeur and the other man in the car would spend the whole night waiting for him by the door. How could such a young and pretty woman go with a man who only reached to her ear when she wore high heels? He was old enough to be her father and he was ugly and he didn't even dress well. Do you think the mistress is in love with him, Carlota? How could she be in love with him, she's more likely in love with his money. He must have had a lot in order to set her up in a house like that and to have bought her all those clothes and jewels and shoes. How come, being so pretty, she hadn't been able to get him to marry her? But Señora Hortensia didn't seem to care very much about marriage, she was happy the way she was. She never seemed anxious to have the master come. Of course, when he did appear, she killed herself looking after him, and when the master called to say I'm coming to have dinner with a few friends, she spent the whole day giving instructions to Símula, watching to see that Amalia and Carlota left the house spotless. But the master would leave and she wouldn't mention him again, she never called him on the phone and she seemed so happy, so unworried, so involved with her girl friends that Amalia thought she doesn't even think about him. The master wasn't at all like Don Fermín who you could see just by looking at him had breeding and money. Don Cayo was very small, his

198

face was leathery, his hair yellowish like shredded tobacco, sunken eyes that looked coldly and from a distance, wrinkles on his neck, an almost lipless mouth and teeth stained from smoking, because he always had a cigarette in his hand. He was so skinny that the front part of his suit almost touched the back. When Símula couldn't hear them, she and Carlota had a great time making fun of him: imagine him naked, what a little skeleton, such little arms, legs. He rarely ever changed suits, his neckties were poorly tied, and his nails were dirty. He never said hello or good-bye, when they greeted him he replied with a grunt and didn't look. He always seemed busy, worried, in a hurry, he lighted his cigarettes with the butt of the one he was going to put out and when he spoke on the telephone he only said yes, no, tomorrow, all right, and when the mistress joked with him, he barely wrinkled his cheeks and that was his laugh. Could he be married, what kind of life did he live outside? Amalia imagined him living with an old, very religious woman who was always dressed in mourning.

9

"Hello, hello?" General Espina's voice repeated. "Hello, Alcibíades?"

"Yes?" he said softly. "Uplander?"

"Cayo? Well, at last." Espina's voice was harshly jovial. "I've been calling you since the day before yesterday and there wasn't any way to reach you. Not at the Ministry, not at home. I hope you're not trying to avoid me, Cayo."

"You've been trying to call me?" He had a pencil in his right hand, sketching a circle. "The first I heard of it, Uplander."

"Ten times, Cayo. What do I mean, ten times? fifteen at least."

"I'll check on it and find out why they didn't give me the message." A second circle, parallel to the other one. "Tell me what it is, Uplander, I'm at your service."

A pause, an uncomfortable cough, Espina's spaced breathing:

"What's the meaning of that plainclothesman in front of my house, Cayo?" He was covering up his bad mood by speaking slowly, but it made it worse. "Is it for protection or to keep an eye on me or just what the hell is it?"

"As an ex-minister you rate at least a doorman paid by the government, Uplander." He finished the third circle, paused, changed his tone. "I don't know anything about it, friend. They've probably forgotten that you don't need protection anymore. If that fellow bothers you, I'll see that he's removed."

"He doesn't bother me, he surprises me," Espina said dryly. "Tell me straight, Cayo. Does that fellow there mean that the government doesn't trust me anymore?"

"Don't talk nonsense, Uplander. If the government doesn't trust you, who could they trust, then?"

"That's just it, that's just it." Espina's voice was slow, stumbled, was slow again. "Why shouldn't I be surprised, Cayo. You probably think I'm too old not to recognize a plainclothesman when I see one."

"Don't get all upset over foolishness." The fifth circle: smaller than the others, with a small dent in it. "Do you think we'd put a plainclothesman on you? It must be some Don Juan making time with your maid."

"Well, he'd better disappear from here, because I'm in a bad mood, you know well enough." Angry now, breathing heavily. "I might get worked up and put a bullet in him. I wanted to warn you just in case."

"Don't waste bullets on a buzzard." He fixed the circle, made it bigger, rounded it, now it was the same size as the others. "I'm going to check on it today. Lozano was probably trying to butter me up by putting an agent on you to look after your house. I'll have him removed, Uplander."

"All right, I wasn't serious about shooting him." Calmer now, trying to joke. "But you can understand how this thing has made me mad, Cayo."

"You're a mistrustful and ungrateful Uplander," he said. "What more could you ask but someone to guard your house with so many sneak thieves on the loose. All right, forget about the whole thing. How's your family? Why don't we have lunch one of these days?"

"Whenever you say, I've got all the time in the world now." A little short, hesitant, as if ashamed of the peevishness he found in his own voice. "You're the one who probably doesn't have much time, right? Since I left the Ministry you haven't called me even once. And it's going on three months."

"You're right, Uplander, but you know what it's like here." Eight circles: five in one row, three underneath; he started the ninth one, carefully. "I've been about to call you several times. Next week, come what may. Take care, Uplander."

He hung up before Espina finished saying good-bye, looked at the nine circles for a moment, tore up the sheet of paper and threw the pieces into the wastebasket.

(9

"It took me an hour to do it," Santiago said. "I rewrote the two pages four or five times, I corrected the punctuation by hand in front of Vallejo."

Mr. Vallejo was reading attentively, the pencil poised over the sheet of paper, he was nodding, he marked a small cross, he moved his lips a little, another cross, fine fine, simple and correct language, he calmed him with a merciful look, that means a lot already. Just that . . .

"If you hadn't passed the test you would have gone back to the fold and now you'd be a model Mirafloran." Carlitos laughed. "Your name would be in the society columns like your brother's."

"I was a little nervous, sir," Santiago said. "Shall I do it over again?"

"Becerrita put me through the test," Carlitos said. "There was an opening on the police beat. I'll never forget."

"Don't worry, it's not too bad." Mr. Vallejo shook his white head, looked at him with his friendly pale eyes. "Just that you'll have to go on learning the trade if you're going to work with us."

"A nut goes into a whorehouse on Huatica in a drunken rage and knifes four girls, the madam and two fairies," Becerrita grunted. "One of the chippies dies. Two pages in fifteen minutes."

"Thank you very much, Mr. Vallejo," Santiago said. "You don't know how grateful I am."

"I had the feeling he was pissing on me," Carlitos said. "Oh, Becerrita."

"It's simply a question of placing the facts according to their importance and also to economize your words." Mr. Vallejo had numbered a few sentences and given the pages back to him. "You have to start with the dead people, young man."

201

"We all said bad things about Becerrita, we all hated him," Santiago said. "And now all we do is talk about him, we all love him and we'd like to bring him back to life. It's absurd."

"What's most eye-catching, what attracts people's attention," Mr. Vallejo added. "That makes the reader become concerned about the news. Maybe because we all have to die someday."

"He was the most authentic thing in Lima journalism," Carlitos said. "Human filth elevated to its maximum power, a perfect model. Who wouldn't remember him with affection, Zavalita?"

"And I put the deaths at the end, that was stupid of me," Santiago said.

"Do you know what those three lines are?" Mr. Vallejo looked at him roguishly. "What the Americans, the sharpest newspapermen in the world, you should know, call the lead."

"He gave you the full lesson," Carlitos said. "On the other hand, Becerrita barked at me you write with your feet, you're being kept on only because I'm tired of giving tests."

"All the important facts summed up in the first three lines, in the lead," Mr. Vallejo said affectionately. "Or: two dead and five million soles damage is the cost so far of the fire that destroyed a large part of the Casa Wiese, one of the main buildings of downtown Lima, last night; firemen had the flames under control after eight hours of dangerous work. Do you see?"

"Try writing poetry after you've set those formulas in your head," Carlitos said. "A person has to be crazy to work on a newspaper if he has any liking for literature, Zavalita."

"Then you can color up the story," Mr. Vallejo said. "The origins of the fire, the anguish of the workers, the statements of witnesses, et cetera."

"I never had any more after my sister made a fool of me," Santiago said. "I was happy to join *La Crónica*, Carlitos."

(9)

How different, on the other hand, Señora Hortensia. He so ugly and she so pretty, he so serious and she so merry. She wasn't haughty like Señora Zoila, who seemed to be speaking from a throne, even when she raised

202

her voice she didn't make her feel like an inferior. She spoke to her without any pose, as if she were speaking to Miss Queta. And she really did such wild things. Such a lack of shame in certain things. My only vices are drinking and pills, but Amalia thought your only vice is cleanliness. If she saw a little dust on the rug, Amalia, the dust mop! an ashtray with butts, as if she'd seen a rat, Carlota, this filth! She bathed when she got up and when she went to bed, and, worst of all, she also wanted them to spend their lives in water. The day after Amalia came to the little house in San Miguel, when she was bringing up her breakfast in bed, the mistress looked her up and down: did you bathe yet? No, ma'am, Amalia said with surprise, and then she showed the signs of disgust of a little girl, run and get in the shower, she had to bathe every day here. And half an hour later, when Amalia, her teeth chattering, was under the spray of water, the bathroom door opened and the mistress appeared in her robe, a cake of soap in her hand. Amalia felt her body burning, turned off the faucet, didn't dare reach for her clothes, stayed with her head down, frowning. Are you embarrassed by me? the mistress laughed. No, she stammered, and the mistress laughed again: you were taking a shower without any soap, just as I imagined; here, soap yourself up. And while Amalia was doing that—the soap slipped out of her hands three times, she rubbed so hard that her skin burned—the mistress remained there, tapping her toe, enjoying her embarrassment, now your little ears, now your little feet, giving her commands in a merry way, looking at her as bold as life. All right, that's how she had to bathe and scrub herself every day and she opened the door to leave, but she took the time to give Amalia such a look: you've got nothing to be ashamed of, even though you're skinny, you're not too bad. She left and outside another loud laugh.

Would Señora Zoila have done something like that? She felt nauseous, her face on fire. Button your uniform up all the way, don't wear such short skirts. Later, while they were cleaning the living room, Amalia told Carlota about it and she rolled her eyes: that's the way the mistress was, she wasn't embarrassed by anything, she came in to see her showering too, to see if she was using plenty of soap. But not just that, she made her put powder under her armpits too, so she wouldn't sweat. Every morning, half asleep, stretching, the mistress's good morning was did

203

you take a bath? did you use the deodorant? And just as she was intimate about things like that, she didn't care if they saw her either. One morning Amalia saw her bed empty and heard water running in the bathroom: should she leave her breakfast on the night table, ma'am? No, bring it in to me here. She went in and the mistress was in the tub, her head resting on a pillow, her eyes closed. The room was full of steam, everything was warm and Amalia stopped in the doorway, looking with curiosity, with uncertainty at the white body under the water. The mistress opened her eyes: I'm really hungry, bring it here. Slowly she sat up in the tub and reached out her hands for the tray. In the foggy atmosphere, Amalia saw her breasts appear, covered with small drops of water, the dark nipples. She didn't know where to look or what to do, and the mistress (with cheery eyes she began to drink her juice, butter her toast) suddenly saw her standing petrified by the tub. What was she doing there with her mouth open? and with a mocking voice don't you like what you see? Ma'am, I, Amalia murmured, drawing back, and the mistress a loud laugh: go ahead, you can pick up the tray later. Would Señora Zoila have allowed her to come in while she was bathing? How different she was, how shameless, how pleasant. The first Sunday in the little house in San Miguel, in order to make a good impression she asked her, can I go to mass for a while? The mistress gave one of her laughs: go ahead, but watch out that the priest doesn't rape you, little church mouse. She never goes to mass, Carlota told her afterward, we don't go anymore either. That was why there wasn't a single Sacred Heart of Jesus in the little house in San Miguel, a single Saint Rose of Lima. She too stopped going to mass after a little while.

❧

There was a knock on the door, he said come in and Dr. Alcibíades came in.

"I haven't got much time, doctor," he said, pointing to the pile of newspaper clippings Alcibíades was carrying. "Anything important?"

"The news from Buenos Aires, Don Cayo. It appeared in all of them."

He reached out his hand, thumbed through the clippings. Alcibíades had marked the headlines with red ink—"Anti-Peruvian incident in Buenos Aires," *La Prensa* said; "Apristas stone Peruvian Embassy in

Argentina," said *La Crónica;* "Peruvian flag torn and insulted by Apristas," *El Comercio* said, and he'd marked the end of the story with arrows.

"They all published the cable from Ansa," he yawned.

"United Press, Associated Press and the other agencies took the news out of their dispatches as we asked them to," Dr. Alcibíades said. "Now they're going to protest because Ansa got a scoop. Ansa wasn't given any instructions, because as you . . ."

"It's all right," he said. "Get me, what's the name of that fellow at Ansa? Tallio, isn't it? Have him come over immediately."

"Yes, Don Cayo," Dr. Alcibíades said. "Mr. Lozano's waiting outside now."

"Have him come in and don't let anyone interrupt us," he said. "When the Minister gets in, tell him I'll be in his office at three o'clock. I'll sign the correspondence later. That's all, doctor."

Alcibíades left and he opened the first drawer of the desk. He took out a small bottle and looked at it for a moment with displeasure. He took out a pill, wet it with his saliva and swallowed it.

(9)

"How long have you been a newspaperman, sir?" Santiago asked.

"About thirty years, just imagine." Mr. Vallejo's eyes wandered off in the depths of time, a slight tremor shook his hand. "I began by carrying stories from the editorial room to the presses. Well, I've got no complaints. It's an ungrateful profession, but it also gives a little satisfaction."

"The greatest satisfaction they gave him was by making him resign," Carlitos said. "I was always surprised that a guy like Vallejo was a newspaperman. He was so gentle, so innocent, so proper. It wasn't possible, he had to end up in a bad way."

"You'll start officially on the first." Mr. Vallejo looked at the Esso calendar on the wall. "Next Tuesday, that is. If you want to get into the swing of things, you can take a look into the editorial room at night before then."

"You mean that to be a newspaperman the first condition is not to know what the lead is?" Santiago asked.

205

"No, to be a swine, or at least to know how to act like one." Carlitos nodded jovially. "I don't have to make an effort anymore. You still do a little bit, Zavalita."

"Five hundred soles a month isn't very much," Mr. Vallejo said. "While you're catching on. You'll get more later on."

When he left *La Crónica* he passed a man at the entrance who had a millimetric little mustache and an iridescent tie, Hernández the headline writer, he thinks, but on the Plaza San Martín he'd already forgotten about the interview with Vallejo: could he have been looking for him, left a note, be waiting for him? No, when he went into the boardinghouse, Señora Lucía only said good evening to him. He went down the dark hallway to call his Uncle Clodomiro.

"It worked out fine, uncle, I start on the first. Mr. Vallejo was very nice."

"Well, I'm glad, Skinny," Uncle Clodomiro said. "I can see that you're happy."

"Very happy, uncle. Now I can pay back what you loaned me."

"There's no hurry." Uncle Clodomiro paused. "You ought to call your parents, don't you think? They won't ask you to come back home if you don't want to, I already told you that. But you can't leave them the way they are, with no news."

"I'll call them soon, uncle. I'd rather wait a few more days. You've already told them I'm fine, that there's no need to worry."

"You always talk about your father and never about your mother," Carlitos said. "Didn't she go into a fit over your running away?"

"She probably cried her eyes out, I suppose, but she didn't come looking for me either," Santiago said. "She wasn't going to lose the excuse to see herself as a martyr."

"You mean you still hate her," Carlitos said. "I thought you were all over that."

"I thought so too," Santiago said. "But you can see, all of a sudden I come out with something and it turns out that I'm not."

2

WHAT A DIFFERENT LIFE Señora Hortensia led. Such disorder, such habits. She would get up very late. Amalia would bring up her breakfast at ten o'clock, along with all the newspapers and magazines she could find at the stand on the corner, but after having her juice, her coffee and her toast, the mistress would stay in bed, reading or relaxing, and she never came downstairs before twelve. After Símula went over the accounts with her, the mistress would fix her little drink, her peanuts or potato chips, put on some records, and start her telephone calls. For no reason, just because, just like the ones between Missy Teté and her girl friends: did you see that the Chilean girl is going to work at the Embassy Club, Quetita? in *Última Hora* they said that Lula was twenty pounds overweight, Quetita, they accused China of fooling around with a bongo player, Quetita. She called Miss Queta most of all, told her dirty jokes, would jabber about everybody, Miss Queta probably told her stories and jabbered too. And what a mouth. During the first days at the little house in San Miguel she thought she was dreaming, was Polla really going to marry that faggot, Quetita? that dummy of a Paqueta was going bald, Quetita: the foulest words and laughing as if they were nothing. Sometimes the cursing would reach the kitchen and Símula would close the door. At first it shocked Amalia, later on she would die laughing and run to the pantry, what she was gossiping about to Miss Queta or Miss Carmincha or Miss Lucy or Señora Ivonne. When she sat down to lunch

207

the mistress had already had two or three drinks and was flushed, her eyes glowing with deviltry, almost always in a good mood: are you still a virgin, black girl? and Carlota stupefied, her big mouth open, not knowing what to answer; do you have a lover, Amalia? what a thing to think, ma'am, and the mistress laughing: if you don't have one, you probably have two, Amalia.

①

What was it that rubbed him the wrong way about him? His greasy face, his little pig eyes, his fawning eyes? Was it his smell of a plainclothesman, an informer, a brothel, armpits, gonorrhea? No, it wasn't that. What was it, then? Lozano had sat down in one of the leather chairs and was meticulously putting papers and notebooks in order on the small desk. He picked up a pencil, his cigarettes, and sat down in another chair.

"How's Ludovico getting along?" Lozano smiled, leaning over. "Are you satisfied with him, Don Cayo?"

"I haven't got much time, Lozano." It was his voice. "Be as brief as possible, please."

"Of course, Don Cayo." The voice of an old whore, or a retired cuckold. "Where do you want to start, Don Cayo?"

"Construction workers." He lighted a cigarette, watched the chubby hands riffling eagerly through the papers. "The election results."

"Espinoza's ticket elected by a wide margin, no incidents," Lozano said with an enormous smile. "Senator Parra was present at the installation of the new union. They gave him a big hand, Don Cayo."

"How many votes did the redtails' ticket get?"

"Twenty-four as against a little over two hundred." Lozano's hand made a gesture of disdain, his mouth tightened with disgust. "Agh, nothing."

"I hope you didn't lock up all of Espinoza's opponents."

"Only twelve of them, Don Cayo. Well-known redtails and Apristas. They'd been campaigning for Bravo's ticket. I don't think they're dangerous people."

"Let them out after a few days," he said. "First the redtails, then the Apristas. We have to build up that rivalry."

208

"Yes, Don Cayo," Lozano said; and a few seconds later, proud: "You've probably seen the papers. That the elections were held very peacefully, that the nonpolitical ticket was elected democratically."

⑨

He'd never worked full time with them, sir. Only spells at a time, when Don Cayo went on a trip and loaned him to Mr. Lozano. What kind of chores, sir? Well, a little of everything. The first had to do with the shantytowns. This is Ludovico, Mr. Lozano had said, this is Ambrosio, that's how they met. They shook hands, Mr. Lozano explained everything to them, then they went out to have a drink at a bar on the Avenida Bolivia. Would there be trouble? No, Ludovico thought it would be easy. Ambrosio was new here, right? He was on loan, he was a chauffeur.

"Mr. Bermúdez' chauffeur?" Ludovico had said, dumbstruck. "Let me give you a hug, let me congratulate you."

They hit it off, sir, Ludovico had made Ambrosio laugh telling him things about Hipólito, the other one in the trio, the one who turned out to be a degenerate. Now Ludovico was Don Cayo's chauffeur and Hipólito his helper. At nightfall they got into the van, Ambrosio drove and they parked a long way off from the shantytown because it was a mudhole. They continued on by shank's mare, swishing flies, getting stuck in the mud, and asking around they found the guy's house. A fat, Chinese-looking woman opened the door and looked at them with mistrust: could they talk to Mr. Calancha? He'd come out of the dark: fat, shoeless, in his undershirt.

"Are you the headman of this settlement?" Ludovico had asked.

"There's no room for anyone else." The fellow had looked at them with pity, sir. "We're full up."

"We have to talk to you about something urgent," Ambrosio said. "Why don't we take a walk while we talk?"

The guy had stood looking at them without answering and finally come in, they could talk right here. No, sir, it had to be in private. Fine, anything you say. They walked in the wind, Ambrosio and Ludovico on either side of Calancha.

"You're getting into deep water and we came to warn you," Ludovico said. "For your own good."

"I don't understand what you're talking about," the guy said in a weak voice.

Ludovico took out some oval cigarettes, offered him one, lighted it for him.

"Why are you going around telling people not to go to the rally on the Plaza de Armas on October twenty-seventh, mister?" Ambrosio asked.

"Even going around saying bad things about General Odría," Ludovico said. "What's the meaning of that?"

"Who told you lies like that?" As if he'd been pinched, sir, and then and there he sweetened up. "Are you from the police? Glad to make your acquaintance."

"If we were we wouldn't be treating you so nice," Ludovico said.

"Who could ever have said that I'd say anything against the government, worse yet against the President," Calancha protested. "Why, this very settlement is called October 27 in his honor."

"Then why did you advise people against going to the rally, mister?" Ambrosio said.

"Everything comes out in this little life of ours," Ludovico said. "The police are beginning to think that you're a subversive."

"Nothing of the kind, that's a lie." A good actor, sir. "Let me explain it all to you."

"That's fine, people with brains get to understand each other by talking," Ludovico said.

He'd told them a teary tale, sir. A lot of them were fresh down from the hills and didn't even speak Spanish, they'd settled on that piece of land without doing any harm to anyone, when Odría's revolution came they'd named it October 27 so they wouldn't send the cops down on them, they were thankful to Odría because he hadn't kicked them out of there. These people weren't like them—soft-soaping us, sir—or like him, but poor people with no education, they'd elected him President of the Association because he could read and he was from the coast.

"What's that got to do with it?" Ludovico had asked. "Are you trying to make us feel sorry? It won't work, Calancha."

210

"If we get involved in politics now, the ones who come after Odría will send the cops down on us and kick us out of here," Calancha explained. "You see?"

"That business of coming after Odría smells subversive to me," Ludovico said. "Doesn't it to you, Ambrosio?"

The fellow gave a start and the butt fell out of his mouth. He bent down to pick it up and Ambrosio leave it there, here, have a fresh one.

"I don't want that to happen, as far as I'm concerned I hope he stays forever," kissing his fingers, sir. "But Odría might die and an enemy of his might come to power and say those people from October 27 used to go to his rallies. And they'd send the cops down on us, sir."

"Forget about the future and think about what's good for you," Ludovico said. "Get your people all ready for the twenty-seventh of October."

He patted him on the shoulder, took his arm like a friend: this has been a nice talk, Calancha. Yes, sir, of course, sir.

"The buses will pick them up at six o'clock," Ludovico said. "I want everyone there, old people, women, children. The buses will bring them back. Then you can organize a blowout if you want. There'll be free drinks. All set, Calancha?"

Of course, of course he was, and Ludovico gave him twenty soles to pay for the bother of having got his digestion all upset, Calancha. Then he knocked himself out thanking them, sir.

12

Miss Queta almost always came after lunch, she was the most intimate, pretty too but nowhere near as pretty as Señora Hortensia. Slacks, low-cut, tight-fitting blouses, colored turbans. Sometimes the mistress and Miss Queta would go out in Miss Queta's little white car and come back at night. When they stayed home, they spent the afternoon talking on the telephone and it was always the same bits of gossip and teasing. The whole house would become infected with the carryings-on of the mistress and Miss Queta, their laughter reached into the kitchen and Amalia and Carlota ran to the pantry to listen to the jokes they were pulling. They would speak with a handkerchief over their mouths, get too close to the telephone, change their voices. If a man answered: you're a nice boy and

211

I like you, I'm in love with you, but you won't even look at me, do you want to come to my house tonight? I'm a friend of your wife's. If a woman: your husband's cheating on you with your sister, your husband's crazy about me but don't get worried, I'm not going to take him away from you because he has a lot of boils on his back. Your husband's going to do you dirty at five o'clock in Los Claveles, you know who with. At first, hearing them left something of a bad taste in Amalia's mouth, later on she would die with laughter. All the mistress's girl friends are in show business, Carlota told her, they work in radio, in nightclubs. They were all good-looking, Miss Lucy, fresh, Miss Carmincha, very high heels, the one they called China was one of the Bim-Bam-Booms. And another day, lowering her voice, want me to tell you a secret? The mistress used to be a singer too, Carlota had found an album in her bedroom where her picture appeared, all elegant and showing everything. Amalia searched through the night table, the closet, the dressing table, but she couldn't find the album. But it must have been true, what else could the mistress have been but a singer, she even had a beautiful voice. They heard her sing while she bathed, when she was in a good mood they would ask her, ma'am, could we have "Caminito" or "Noche de Amor" or "Rosas Rojas para Ti" and she would give them what they wanted. At the small parties she never had to be begged when they asked her to sing. She would run and put on a record, take a glass or a doll from the shelf as a microphone, and stand in the center of the room and sing, the guests would applaud her madly. You can see now, can't you, that she used to be a singer, Carlota whispered to Amalia.

2

"Textiles," he said. "Yesterday the discussion of the list of demands was broken off. Last night the employers went to tell the Ministry of Labor that there was a threat of a strike, that the whole thing was politically motivated."

"I'm sorry, Don Cayo, that's not the way it is," Lozano said. "You know, textiles, always an Aprista hotbed. That's why a good cleanup had been made there. The union can be trusted completely. Pereira, the secretary general, you know him, has always cooperated."

"Talk to Pereira today," he interrupted him. "Tell him that the threat of a strike is going to remain just that, a threat, we can't take a strike right now. They have to accept the mediation of the Ministry."

"Everything is all explained here, Don Cayo, permit me." Lozano leaned over, quickly drew out a sheet from the pile of papers on the desk. "It's a threat, that's all. A political ploy, not to scare the employers, but to let the union recover some prestige with its membership. There's been a lot of resistance against the present leadership, this is going to make the workers come back to . . ."

"The raise proposed by the Ministry is fair," he said. "Pereira should convince his people, discussion of that list of demands has to stop. It's creating a tense situation there, and tensions favor agitation."

"Pereira thinks that if the Labor Ministry would only accept point number two on the list, he could . . ."

"Explain to Pereira that he's being paid to obey, not to think," he said. "He was put in there to facilitate things, not to complicate them with his thinking. The Ministry has got some concessions from the employers, now the union has to accept the mediation. Tell Pereira that the thing has got to be settled in forty-eight hours."

"Yes, Don Cayo," Lozano said. "Absolutely, Don Cayo."

19

But two days later Mr. Lozano was in a rage, sir: that damned fool Calancha hadn't gone to the committee meeting and hasn't shown his face, it was only three days until the twenty-seventh and if the shanty-towns didn't go in a body, the Plaza de Armas wouldn't be filled. Calan-cha's the man, they had to teach him how to give in, offer him up to five hundred soles. You see, he'd tricked them, sir, turning out to be a hypocritical sly bugger. They got into the van, got to his house and didn't knock on the door. Ludovico rammed the piece of tin down with a blow of his hand: inside there was a lighted candle, Calancha and the Chinese-looking woman were eating, and around them something like ten children crying.

"Come on out, mister," Ambrosio said. "We have to have a talk."

The Chinese-looking woman had picked up a stick and Ludovico began to laugh. Calancha cursed her, grabbed the stick away from her, you have to excuse her, an awful play-actor, sir, she was worked up

213

because they'd come in without knocking. He went out with them and that night he only had his pants on and reeked of alcohol. As soon as they were away from the house, Ludovico gave him a mild slap on the face, and Ambrosio another, neither very hard, to lower his morale. What a fuss he made, sir: he threw himself to the ground, don't kill me, there must have been some misunderstanding.

"You seven-milked son of a bitch," Ludovico said. "I'll give you a misunderstanding."

"Why didn't you do what you promised, mister?" Ambrosio asked.

"Why didn't you go to the committee meeting when Hipólito went to arrange for the buses?" Ludovico asked.

"Look at my face, look at it. Isn't it yellow?" Calancha was weeping. "Every once in a while I get an attack that lays me low, I was sick in bed. I'll go to the meeting tomorrow. It'll all be set up."

"If the people from here don't go to the rally, it'll be your fault," Ambrosio said.

"And you'll be arrested," Ludovico said. "And what they do to political prisoners, oh, mama."

He gave them his word, swore by his mother, and Ludovico hit him again and Ambrosio again, a little harder this time.

"You're probably saying that it's foolishness, but those slaps are for your own good," Ludovico said. "Can't you see that we don't want to see you arrested, Calancha?"

"This is your last chance, man," Ambrosio had said.

His word, on his mother's name, he swore to us, sir, don't hit me anymore.

"If all the mountain people go to the square and the thing comes off well, there'll be three hundred soles for you, Calancha," Ludovico said. "Choose between three hundred soles or being arrested, you can decide which'll be better for you."

"That's too much, I don't want any money." Such a tricky fellow, sir. "I'll do it for General Odría and no other reason."

They left him like that, swearing and promising. Could a simpleton like that have a word to keep, Ambrosio? He did, sir: the next day Hipólito went to bring them the banners and Calancha had met him in front of the whole committee, and Hipólito saw that he was giving the word to his people and he cooperated as nice as you could ask.

9

The mistress was taller than Amalia, shorter than Miss Queta, dark black hair, skin as if she'd never been in the sun, green eyes, a red mouth that she was always biting with her even little teeth in a flirty way. How old could she have been? Over thirty Carlota said, Amalia thought twenty-five. From the waist up her body was so-so, but the bottom part what curves. Shoulders thrown back a little, breasts standing out, the waist of a little girl. But her hips were heart-warming, broad broad, and they closed in as they went down, and her legs slowly thinned out, thin ankles and feet like Missy Teté's. Little hands too, long fingernails, always painted the same color as her lips. When she was wearing a blouse and slacks everything stood out, the tops of her elegant dresses left her shoulders, half her back and half her breasts out in the air. She would sit down, cross her legs, her skirt would run up above her knees and from the pantry, as excited as chickens, Carlota and Amalia would comment on how the guests' eyes followed the mistress's legs and neckline. Gray-haired, fat old men, they thought of all kinds of tricks, lifting their whiskey glasses from the floor, leaning over to flick the ashes off their cigarettes, to get their eyes close and take a look. She didn't get annoyed, she would even provoke them by sitting like that. The master isn't jealous, is he? Amalia said to Carlota, anybody else would have become furious if they became that intimate with his lady. And Carlota, why should he be jealous of her? all she is is his mistress. It was so strange, the master may have been old and ugly but he didn't seem to have a stupid hair on his head, and yet he was so calm when the guests, a little high now, began to take liberties with the mistress and fool around. For example, they'd be dancing and kiss her on the neck or stroke her back and the way they held her tight. The mistress would give her little laugh, give a playful slap to the bold one, playfully pushing him into a chair, or keep on dancing with him as if nothing was going on, letting him go too far. Don Cayo never danced. Sitting in a chair, glass in hand, he would chat with the guests, or would look with his washed-out face at the mistress's coquetry and flirting. A red-faced gentleman shouted one

215

day you've got to lend me your siren for a weekend at Paracas, will you, Don Cayo? and the master she's yours, General, and the mistress all set, take me to Paracas, I'm yours. Carlota and Amalia were dying with laughter listening to the jokes and watching the horsing around, but Símula wouldn't let them spy for very long, she would come into the pantry and close the door, or the mistress would appear, eyes glowing, cheeks flushed, and send them off to bed. From her bed Amalia could hear the music, the laughter, the squeals, the sound of glasses, and would huddle under the covers, awake, restless, laughing to herself. The next morning she and Carlota had to do triple work. Piles of cigarette butts and bottles, furniture pushed against the walls, broken glasses. They would clean, pick up, rearrange so that when the mistress came down she wouldn't start with oh, what a mess, such filth. The master would sleep over when there was a party. He would leave very early, Amalia saw him, yellow and baggy-eyed, cross the garden quickly, wake up the two men who'd spent the night in the car waiting for him, he must have paid them a lot to spend the night like that, and as soon as the car left the policemen on the corner left too. On those days the mistress would get up very late. Símula would have a platter of oysters with onion sauce and lots of chili prepared and a glass of cold beer. She would appear in her bathrobe, her eyes swollen and red, would have lunch and go back to bed, and in the afternoon she would ring for Amalia to bring her up some mineral water, some Alka-Seltzers.

i9

"Olave," he said, blowing out a puff of smoke. "Did the people you sent to Chiclayo come back?"

"This morning, Don Cayo." Lozano nodded. "All taken care of. Here's the Governor's report, here's a copy of the police report. The three leaders are in jail in Chiclayo."

"Apristas?" He let out another puff of smoke and saw that Lozano was holding back a sneeze.

"Only a certain Lanza, an old Aprista leader. The other two are young, no previous record."

"Have them brought to Lima and get them to confess their sins, mortal and venial. A strike like that on Olave isn't organized just like that. It took time to prepare it, and professionals. Has work on the ranch begun again?"

"This morning, Don Cayo," Lozano said. "The Governor told me on the telephone. We've left a small detachment at Olave for a few days, even though the Governor assures us . . ."

"San Marcos." Lozano closed his mouth and his hands sped to the table, picked up three, four sheets of paper and handed them to him. He put them on the arm of the chair without looking at them.

"Nothing this week, Don Cayo. Small groups meet, the Apristas more disorganized than ever, the redtails a little more active. Oh yes, we've identified a new Trotskyite group. Meetings, conversations, nothing. Next week there are going to be elections at the Medical School. The Aprista ticket might win."

"Other universities." He blew out the smoke and this time Lozano sneezed.

"The same thing, Don Cayo, meetings of small groups, fights among them, nothing. Oh yes, our source of information at the University of Trujillo is finally working. Here it is, memorandum number three. We've got two elements there that . . ."

"Only memos?" he asked. "Aren't there any fliers, handouts, mimeographed papers?"

"Of course, Don Cayo." Lozano picked up his briefcase, opened it, took out a folder with an air of triumph. "Fliers, handouts, even the typewritten communiqués of the Federated Centers. Everything, Don Cayo."

"The President's trip," he said. "Did you talk to Cajamarca?"

"All the preparations have already begun," Lozano said. "I'll leave on Monday and Wednesday morning I'll give you a detailed report, so that on Thursday you can go and take a look at the security arrangements. If that's all right with you, Don Cayo."

"I've decided that your people will travel to Cajamarca by land. They'll leave Thursday, by bus, so they'll get there on Friday. We don't want the airplane crashing with no time to send replacements."

"The way the roads are in the mountains, I don't know but that the bus is more dangerous than the plane," Lozano joked, but he didn't smile and Lozano became serious at once. "A very good idea, Don Cayo."

217

"Leave all these papers with me." He stood up and Lozano imitated him immediately. "I'll give them back to you tomorrow."

"I won't take any more of your time, then, Don Cayo." Lozano followed him to his desk, his enormous briefcase under his arm.

"Just a minute, Lozano." He lighted another cigarette, dragged on it, closing his eyes a little. Lozano was facing him, waiting, smiling. "Don't squeeze any more money out of old Ivonne."

"Beg pardon, Don Cayo?" He saw him blink, become confused, turn pale.

"I don't care if you get a few soles out of Lima's naughty girls," he said in a friendly way, smiling, "but leave Ivonne alone, and if she ever has a problem, help her out. She's a good person, understand?"

The fat face had become covered with sweat, the little pig eyes were anxiously trying to smile. He opened the door for him, patted him on the shoulder, see you tomorrow, Lozano, and went back to his desk. He picked up the phone: connect me with Senator Landa, doctor. He picked up the papers that Lozano had left, put them in his briefcase. A moment later the telephone rang.

"Hello, Don Cayo?" Landa's jovial voice. "I was about to call you just now."

"So you see, senator, there is such a thing as thought transmission," he said. "I've got some good news for you."

"I know, I know, Don Cayo." Oh so happy, you son of a bitch. "I know, work began again at Olave this morning. You don't know how grateful I am to you for taking an interest in the matter."

"We've arrested the ringleaders," he said. "Those fellows won't be creating any problems for quite some time."

"If the harvest had been delayed it would have been a catastrophe for the whole district," Senator Landa said. "How's your free time, Don Cayo? Have you got anything on for tonight?"

"Come have dinner with me in San Miguel," he said. "Your admirers are always asking about you."

"I'd be delighted, how does around nine o'clock suit you?" Landa's little laugh. "Fine, Don Cayo. See you later, then."

He hung up and dialed a number. Two, three rings, only with the fourth a sleepy voice: yes, hello?

218

"I've invited Landa for dinner tonight," he said. "Call Queta too. And tell Ivonne they won't be squeezing any more money out of her. Go back to sleep."

9

Early in the morning of the twenty-seventh he'd gone with Hipólito and Ludovico to get the buses and trucks, I'm worried Ludovico said but Hipólito there won't be any problem. From a distance they saw the people from the shantytown all gathered together, waiting, so many that you couldn't see the shacks, sir. They were burning garbage, ashes and buzzards flying. The committee came to meet them. Calancha had greeted them all milk and honey, what did I tell you? He shook hands, introduced them to the others, they took off their hats, embraced. They had hung pictures of Odría from the roofs and on the doors, and they all had their banners. LONG LIVE THE REVOLUTION OF RESTORATION, LONG LIVE ODRÍA, THE SETTLEMENTS FOR ODRÍA, HEALTH, EDUCATION, WORK. The people looked at them and the children grabbed them by the legs.

"They're not going to the Plaza de Armas with those funeral faces," Ludovico had said.

"They'll cheer up when the time comes," Calancha had said, very shifty, sir.

They put them in the buses and trucks, there were all kinds, but a predominance of women and mountain people, they had to make several trips. The square was almost full with spontaneous arrivals and people from other shantytowns and from the ranches. A sea of heads could be seen from the cathedral, the signs and pictures floating about them. They took the shantytown people to where Mr. Lozano had said. There were ladies and gentlemen in the windows of the Municipal Building, the shops, the Club de la Unión, Don Fermín had most likely been there, right, sir? and suddenly Ambrosio look, one of those on that balcony was Mr. Bermúdez. Those fairy fishes have got each other by the tail, Hipólito laughed pointing at the fountain, and Ludovico you ought to know, queenie: they always teased Hipólito like that and he never got mad, sir. They began to stir up the people, make them shout and blow horns. They laughed, moved their heads, liven it up Ludovico said, Hipólito was

219

running around like a mouse from one group to another more happiness, more noise. The bands arrived, they were playing waltzes and *marineras*, finally the balcony of the Palace opened and the President came out along with a lot of gentlemen and military men and the people began to get happy. Then, when Odría talked about the revolution, Peru, they got all worked up. They shouted on their own, when the speech was over there was lots of applause. Did I keep my word or didn't I? Calancha had asked them at sunset in the shantytown. They gave him his three hundred soles and it was his turn because they had to have some drinks together. Drinks and cigarettes had been handed out, there were a lot of drunks wandering about. They had some piscos with Calancha and then Ludovico and Ambrosio went off, leaving Hipólito in the shantytown.

"Mr. Bermúdez must be happy, eh, Ambrosio?"

"He couldn't help but be, Ludovico."

"Couldn't you fix it so I could work with you in the car instead of Hinostroza?"

"Taking care of Don Cayo is the worst job in the world, Ludovico. Hinostroza's half crazy from all the bad nights."

"But it's five hundred soles more, Ambrosio. And besides, they might put my name on the list. And besides, we'd be together, Ambrosio."

So Ambrosio had spoken to Don Cayo, sir, so that he'd take Ludovico on in place of Hinostroza, and Don Cayo had laughed: now even you've got people to recommend, black boy.

3

IT WAS THE DAY AFTER A PARTY that Amalia got her great surprise.
She had heard the master come down the stairs, had gone into the living
room, had looked out through the Venetian blinds and seen the car leave
and the cops on the corner go away. Then she went up to the second
floor, gave a little knock on the door, could she pick up the polisher,
ma'am? and she opened the door and tiptoed in. There it was, beside the
dressing table. The dim light from the window illuminated the crocodile
legs, the screen, the closet, everything else was in the shadows and a
warm vapor floated about. She didn't look at the bed while she went
toward the dressing table, except when she turned around, pulling the
polisher. She froze: there was Miss Queta too. Part of the sheets and
blanket had slipped onto the rug, Miss Queta was asleep, turned toward
her, one hand on her thigh, the other hanging down, and she was naked,
naked. Now she also saw, over Miss Queta's dark back, a white shoulder,
a white arm, the jet black hair of the mistress, who was sleeping on the
other side, covered by the sheets. She went on her way, the floor seemed
covered with thorns, but before leaving, an invincible curiosity made her
look: a light shadow, a dark shadow, the two so quiet, but something
strange and sort of dangerous was coming from the bed and she saw the
dragon coming apart in the ceiling mirror. She heard one of them murmur something in her sleep and was frightened. She closed the door,
breathing fast. On the stairs she began to laugh, she reached the kitchen

221

covering her mouth suffocating with laughter. Carlota, Carlota, Miss
Queta's up there in bed with the mistress, and she lowered her voice and
looked into the courtyard, the two of them without anything on, the two
of them bare naked. Bah, Miss Queta always slept over, and suddenly
Carlota stopped yawning and lowered her voice too, the two of them
without anything on, the two of them bare naked? All morning while
they were cleaning the rooms, changing the water in the vases and
shaking out the rug, they nudged each other, the master had slept on the
couch in the study? dying with laughter, under the bed? and all of a
sudden the eyes of one filled with tears and the other slapped her on the
back, what could have happened, what could they have been doing the
way they were? Carlota's big eyes looked like horseflies, Amalia was
biting her hand to hold back her laughter. That was how Símula found
them when she came back from the market, what was wrong with them,
nothing, on the radio they'd heard a very funny joke. The mistress and
Miss Queta came down at noon, they had some oysters and chili, drank
cold beer. Miss Queta had put on one of the mistress's robes, which was
much too small for her. They didn't make any telephone calls, they
listened to records and chatted, Miss Queta left at nightfall.

9

Mr. Tallio was there, Don Cayo, should he send him in? Yes, doctor. A
moment later the door opened: he recognized his blond curly hair, his
beardless, ruddy face, his elastic walk. Opera singer, he thought, spa-
ghetti-bender, eunuch.

"Delighted to see you, Mr. Bermúdez." He came in with his hand
outstretched and smiling, let's see how long your happiness lasts. "I hope
you remember me, last year I had . . ."

"Of course, we talked right here, didn't we?" He guided him to the
chair that Lozano had been sitting in, sat down opposite him. "Would
you like a cigarette?"

He accepted, hastened to take out his lighter, bowing.

"I've been meaning to come and see you one of these days, Mr.
Bermúdez." He was restless, moving in the chair as if he had worms. "So
it was as if . . ."

"Your thought had been transmitted to me," he said. He smiled and

222

saw that Tallio was nodding and opening his mouth, but he didn't give him time to speak: he handed him the pile of clippings. An exaggerated gesture of surprise, he thumbed through them very seriously, nodded. So, fine, read them, make me believe that you're reading them, you damned guinea.

"Oh yes, I saw that, trouble in Buenos Aires, right?" he finally said, no longer restless, not moving around. "Is there some communiqué from the government about this? We'll send it right out, naturally."

"All the newspapers published the Ansa dispatch, you were way ahead of the other agencies," he said. "You scooped them."

He smiled and saw that Tallio was smiling, not with happiness any-more, only because of good manners, eunuch, his cheeks rosier than ever, I'll make a present of you to Robertito.

"We thought it was best not to send that news to the papers," he said. "It's terrible for the Apristas to stone the embassy of their own country. Why print that here?"

"Well, the truth is that I was surprised that only the Ansa cable was published." He shrugged his shoulders, raised his index finger. "We included it in our bulletins because I hadn't received any indication about it. The news came through the Information Service, Mr. Bermúdez. I hope there wasn't any mistake."

"All the agencies suppressed it except Ansa," he said, saddened. "In spite of the cordial relations we have with you, Mr. Tallio."

"The item came through here with all the others, Mr. Bermúdez." Red-faced now, really surprised now, without any poses now. "I didn't get any instructions, any note. I wish you'd call Dr. Alcibíades, I'd like to get this cleared up right now."

"The Information Service doesn't classify good or bad." He put out his cigarette, calmly lighted another. "It only acknowledges receipt of the bulletins sent to it, Mr. Tallio."

"But if Dr. Alcibíades had only asked me, I would have suppressed the item, I've always done that." Anxious now, impatient, perplexed. "Ansa hasn't got the slightest interest in spreading things that place the government in an uncomfortable position. But we're not fortune tellers, Mr. Bermúdez."

"We don't give any instructions," he said, interested in the patterns

223

the smoke was making, the white dots on Tallio's necktie. "We only suggest in a friendly way, and very rarely, that news items displeasing to the country not be published."

"Yes, of course, of course I know that, Mr. Bermúdez." Now I've got him just right for you, Robertito. "I've always followed Dr. Alcibíades' suggestions to the letter. But this time there wasn't any indication, no suggestion. I beg of you . . ."

"The government hasn't wanted to set up an official censorship system so as not to hurt the agencies, for just that reason," he said.

"If you don't call Dr. Alcibíades this will never be cleared up, Mr. Bermúdez." Your jar of vaseline and forward, Robertito. "Have him explain to you, have him explain to me. Please, sir. I don't understand any of this, Mr. Bermúdez."

9

"Let me order," Carlitos said, and to the waiter: "Two German beers, the kind that comes in cans."

He had leaned against the wall that was papered with covers from *The New Yorker*. The reflector was lighting up his curly hair, his wide eyes, his face darkened by a two-day beard, his reddish nose, of a rummy, he thinks, a person with a cold.

"Is that beer expensive?" Santiago asked. "I'm a little tight on cash."

"I'm treating, I just got an advance out of those bastards," Carlitos said. "By coming here tonight with me, your reputation as a proper little boy is dead, Zavalita."

The covers were brilliant, humorous, multicolored. Most of the tables were empty, but on the other side of the grill work that divided the two parts of the place there were murmurs; at the bar a man in shirtsleeves was drinking a beer. Someone hidden in the darkness was playing the piano.

"I've left whole pay checks behind me here," Carlitos said. "I feel at home in this den."

"It's my first time at the Negro-Negro," Santiago said. "A lot of artists and writers come here, don't they?"

"Shipwrecked artists and writers," Carlitos said. "When I was a young squirt I used to come in here like a religious old biddy into church. From that corner I used to spy, listen in, when I recognized a writer my heart would swell up. I wanted to be close to the geniuses, I wanted to be infected by them."

"I knew you were a writer too," Santiago said. "That you've published poetry."

"I was going to be a writer, I was going to publish poetry," Carlitos said. "Then I joined *La Crónica* and switched vocations."

"Do you like journalism better than literature?" Santiago asked.

"I like drinking best." Carlitos laughed. "Journalism isn't a vocation, it's a frustration, you'll find out soon enough."

He shrugged, sketches and caricatures and titles in English where his head had been, and there was the grimace that twisted his face, Zavalita, his clenched fists. He touched his arm: didn't he feel well? Carlitos straightened up, leaned his head against the wall.

"Probably my ulcer again." Now he had a crow-man on one shoulder and a skyscraper on the other. "Probably the lack of alcohol. Because even though I may seem drunk, I haven't had anything all day."

The only one you have left and in the hospital with the d.t.'s, Zavalita. You'd go see him tomorrow without fail, Carlitos, you'd take him a book.

"I'd come in here and feel I was in Paris," Carlitos said. "I thought, I'll get to Paris someday, and boom, a genius, as if by magic. But I never got there, Zavalita, and here I am with stomach cramps of a pregnant woman. What were you going to be when you were cast away on *La Crónica?*"

"A lawyer," Santiago said. "No, a revolutionary, I mean a Communist."

"Communist and journalist rhyme at least, but poet and journalist, on the other hand," Carlitos said, and, starting to laugh: "A Communist? They fired me from a job for being a Communist. If it hadn't been for that I wouldn't have got on the paper and I'd probably be writing poetry."

"Do you know what the d.t.'s are?" Santiago asks. "When you don't want to know something, nobody will ever get ahead of you, Ambrosio."

"What in hell would I be doing being a Communist," Carlitos said. "That's the funniest part of it, the truth is I never did find out why they

225

fired me. But they screwed me, and here I am, a drunk with ulcers. Cheers, proper little boy, cheers, Zavalita."

Ω

Miss Queta was the mistress's best friend, the one who came the most to the little house in San Miguel, the one who never missed parties. Tall, long-legged, red hair, dyed, Carlota used to say, cinnamon-colored skin, a body that attracted more attention than Señora Hortensia's, her clothes too, and her way of talking and her antics when she was drinking. She was the liveliest one at the parties, a daredevil for dancing, she really did put herself at the service of the guests, she never stopped provoking them. She would sneak up behind them, muss their hair, pull their ears, sit them down on her knees, a bold one. But she was the one who livened up the night with her madness. The first time she saw Amalia she stood looking at her with a very strange smile, and she examined her and looked at her and was thinking and Amalia what's the matter with her, what's wrong with me. So you're the famous Amalia, I've finally met you. Famous for what, ma'am? The one who steals hearts, who destroys men, Miss Queta was laughing, Amalia the passion flower. Crazy but so nice. When she wasn't playing tricks on the phone with the mistress, she was telling jokes. She would come in with a perverse joy in her eyes, I've got a thousand new stories, kid, and from the kitchen Amalia would hear her carrying on, gossiping, making fun of everybody. She also played tricks on Carlota and Amalia which left them mute and with their faces burning. But she was very good, whenever she sent them to the Chinaman's to buy something she would give them one or two soles. On one day off she had Amalia get into her little white car and she drove her to the streetcar stop.

Ω

"Alcibíades telephoned your office in person asking that that piece of news not be sent to the newspapers." He sighed, barely smiling. "I wouldn't have bothered you if I hadn't already looked into it, Mr. Tallio."

"But it can't be." His ruddy face devastated by his upset, his tongue

226

suddenly thick. "My office, Mr. Bermúdez? But my secretary gives me all the . . . Dr. Alcibíades in person? I don't understand how . . ."

"They didn't give you the message?" he helped him, without sarcasm. "Well, I imagine something like that. Alcibíades spoke to one of the editors, I think."

"One of the editors?" Not a trace of the smiling aplomb, the exuberance of before. "But it can't be, Mr. Bermúdez. I'm all mixed up, I'm terribly sorry. Do you know which editor, sir? I've only got two, and well, all I can say is that I can assure you it won't happen again."

"I was surprised because we've always had good relations with Ansa," he said. "National Radio and the Information Service buy your complete bulletins. That costs the government money, as you well know."

"Of course, Mr. Bermúdez." So get mad now and sing your aria, opera singer. "Can I use your phone? I'm going to find out right now who got Dr. Alcibíades' message. This is going to be cleared up right now, Mr. Bermúdez."

"Sit down, don't worry about it." He smiled at him and offered him a cigarette, lighted it for him. "We have enemies everywhere, there must be someone who doesn't like us in your office. You can investigate later, Mr. Tallio."

"But those two editors are a couple of boys who . . ." Grieved, with a tragicomic expression. "Well, I'm going to clear this up today. I'm going to ask that in the future Dr. Alcibíades always communicate with me personally."

"Yes, that would be the best thing," he said; he reflected, observing as if by chance the clippings that were dancing in Tallio's hands. "The sad part is that it's created a bit of a problem for me. The President, the Minister are going to ask me why we buy bulletins from an agency that gives us headaches. And since I'm the one responsible for the contract with Ansa, you can imagine."

"That's precisely why I'm bothered, Mr. Bermúdez." And that's so true, you probably wish you were miles away from here. "The person who spoke to the doctor will be fired today, sir."

"Because things like this are bad for the government," he said, as if thinking aloud and with melancholy. "Enemies take advantage when a

227

piece of news like that appears in the press that way. They already give us enough problems. It isn't right for friends to give us problems too, don't you think?"

"It won't happen again, Mr. Bermúdez." He had taken out a pale blue handkerchief, was drying his hands furiously. "Of that you can be sure. You can be sure of that, Mr. Bermúdez."

❿

"I admire the dregs of humanity." Carlitos doubled over again as if he'd been punched in the stomach. "The police beat has corrupted me, as you can see."

"Don't have any more to drink," Santiago said. "We'd better go."

But Carlitos had sat up straight again and was smiling.

"With the second beer the jabs disappear and I feel great, you still don't know me. This is the first time we've had a drink together, isn't it?" Yes, Carlitos, he thinks, it was the first time. "You're so serious, Zavalita, you finish work and you take off. You never come to have a drink with us castaways. Are you afraid we'll corrupt you?"

"I can just get by on my salary," Santiago said. "If I went to brothels with you people, I wouldn't be able to pay my rent."

"Do you live by yourself?" Carlitos asked. "I thought you were a good family boy. Haven't you got any relatives? And how old are you? You're just a kid, aren't you?"

"A lot of questions all at the same time," Santiago said. "I have a family, yes, but I live alone. Listen, how can you people get drunk and go to whorehouses with the money you make? I can't understand it."

"A professional secret," Carlitos said. "The art of living in debt, dodging creditors. And why don't you go to whorehouses, have you got a woman?"

"Are you going to ask me if I jerk off too?" Santiago said.

"If you haven't got one and you don't go to whorehouses, I imagine you must jerk off," Carlitos said. "Unless you're a fag."

He doubled over again and when he straightened up his face was all twisted. He leaned his curly head against the magazine covers, kept his eyes closed for a moment, then dug into his pockets, took out something that he put to his nose and breathed in deeply. He stayed with his head

228

back like that, his mouth half open, with an expression of peaceful drunkenness. He opened his eyes, looked mockingly at Santiago.

"To put the daggers in my belly to sleep. Don't look surprised, I'm not proselytizing."

"Are you trying to surprise me?" Santiago asked. "You're wasting your time. A drunk, an addict, I knew it all the time, everybody on the paper told me. I don't pass judgment on people over things like that."

Carlitos smiled affectionately at him and offered him a cigarette.

"I had a bad impression of you because I'd heard you'd been hired on somebody's recommendation and because you didn't hang around with us. But I was wrong. I like you, Zavalita."

He was speaking slowly and on his face there was a growing ease and his gestures were becoming more and more ceremonious and slow.

"I sniffed coke once, but it made me sick." It was a lie, Carlitos. "I vomited and my stomach got all upset."

"You still haven't turned bitter and you've already been on *La Crónica* for three months, right?" Carlitos was saying with absorption, as if he were praying.

"Three months and a half," Santiago said. "I just finished the trial period. They gave me a contract on Monday."

"I feel sorry for you," Carlitos said. "Now you've got your whole life ahead of you as a newspaperman. Listen, come closer so nobody can hear. I'm going to tell you a big secret. Poetry is the greatest thing there is, Zavalita."

9

That time Miss Queta arrived at the little house in San Miguel at noon. She blew in like a storm, as she passed she pinched Amalia's cheek when she opened the door for her and Amalia thought high as a kite. Señora Hortensia appeared at the top of the stairs and Miss Queta threw her a kiss: I've come to rest awhile, girl, old Ivonne's been looking for me and I'm dead from lack of sleep. How popular you've become, the mistress laughed, come on up, girl. They went into the bedroom and a while later a shout from the mistress, bring us some cold beer. Amalia went up with the tray and from the door she saw Miss Queta collapsed on the bed with just her slip on. Her dress and shoes and stockings were on the floor, and she was singing, laughing and talking to herself. It was as if the mistress had been infected by Miss Queta, because even though she hadn't had anything to drink in the morning, she too was laughing, singing and joking with Miss Queta from the stool by the dressing table. Miss Queta pounded the pillow, did gymnastics, her red hair covering her face, in the mirrors her long legs looked like those of an enormous centipede. She saw the tray and sat down, oh, she was so thirsty, she drank half her glass in one swallow, oh, how delicious. And suddenly she grabbed Amalia by the wrist, come here come here, looking at her with such deviltry, don't leave me. Amalia looked at the mistress, but she was looking at Miss Queta roguishly, as if thinking what are you going to do, and then she laughed too. Listen, you find good ones, girl, and Miss Queta pretended to threaten the mistress, you've been cheating on me with this one, haven't you? and the mistress let out one of her laughs: yes, I've been cheating on you with her. But you don't know who this little innocent has been cheating on you with, Miss Queta was laughing. Amalia's ears began to buzz, Miss Queta shook her arm and began to sing, an eye for an eye, girl, a tooth for a tooth, and she looked at Amalia and as a joke or seriously? tell me Amalia, in the morning after the master leaves do you come to console this girl? Amalia didn't know whether to be annoyed or to laugh. Sometimes yes, then she stammered and she must have said something funny. Oh, you devil, Miss Queta exploded, looking at the mistress and the mistress, dying with laughter, I'll loan her to you, but take good care of her for me, and Miss Queta gave Amalia a push and made her sit on the bed. It was good that the mistress got up, ran over and, laughing, struggled with Miss Queta until she let her go: go on, get out of here, Amalia, this nut is going to corrupt you. Amalia left the room, pursued by the laughter of both of them, and went down the stairs laughing, but her legs were trembling and when she went into the kitchen she was serious and furious. Símula was scrubbing the washbasin, humming: what's the matter. And Amalia: nothing, they're drunk and they were trying to embarrass me.

9

"It's a shame this had to happen just now when the contract with Ansa is about to run out." Through the waves of smoke he was looking for

Tallio's eyes. "You can imagine how hard it's going to be for me to convince the Minister that we should renew it."

"I'll talk to him, I'll explain it to him." There they were: clear, disconsolate, alarmed. "I was just about to talk to you about renewing the contract. And now, with this absurd mixup. I'll explain everything to the Minister, Mr. Bermúdez."

"It would be better not to deal with him until he gets over his anger." He smiled and got up suddenly. "In any case, I'll try to straighten things out."

The color came back to the milky face, hope, loquacity, he walked beside him to the door, almost dancing.

"The editor who talked to Dr. Alcibíades is out of the agency as of today." He smiled, sweetening his voice, sparkling. "You know that the renewal of the contract means life or death for Ansa. I don't know how to thank you, Mr. Bermúdez."

"It ends next week, doesn't it? Well, make arrangements with Alcibíades. I'll try to get the Minister's signature as soon as possible."

He reached a hand toward the doorknob but didn't open it. Tallio hesitated, he'd begun to blush again. He was waiting, without taking his eyes off him, for him to get up his courage and say something.

"Regarding the contract, Mr. Bermúdez." You seem to be swallowing the shit, you eunuch. "Under the same conditions as last year. I'm referring to, I mean . . ."

"My services?" he said, and saw the uneasiness, the discomfort, Tallio's difficult smile; he scratched his chin and added modestly: "This time it's not going to cost you ten, it's going to cost you twenty percent, friend Tallio."

He saw him open his mouth a little, wrinkle and unwrinkle his forehead in a second; he saw that he'd stopped smiling and was nodding with his look suddenly far off.

"A check made out to cash drawn on a New York bank; bring it to me personally next Monday." You were making calculations, Caruso. "You know that the paper work in the Ministry takes a while. Let's see if we can get it through in a couple of weeks."

He opened the door, but when Tallio made a gesture of anguish, he closed it. He waited, smiling.

231

"Very good, it will be wonderful if it can be done in a couple of weeks, Mr. Bermúdez." His voice had grown hoarse, he was sad. "As far as, that is, don't you think that twenty percent is a little steep?"

"Steep?" He opened his eyes a little as if he didn't understand, but he recovered immediately, with a friendly gesture. "Let's say no more. Forget about the whole thing. Now you have to excuse me, I have a lot of things to do."

He opened the door, the chatter of typewriters, Alcibíades' silhouette in the background, at his desk.

"No problem at all, everything's agreed on," Tallio blurted, waving his arms in desperation. "No problem at all, Mr. Bermúdez. Monday at ten o'clock, is that all right?"

"Fine," he said, almost pushing him. "Until Monday, then."

He closed the door and immediately stopped smiling. He went to the desk, sat down, took the little vial from the right drawer, filled his mouth with saliva before he put the pill on the tip of his tongue. He swallowed, kept his eyes closed for a moment, his hands flattening out the blotter. A moment later Alcibíades came in.

"The Italian's all upset, Don Cayo. I hope that editor was there at the agency at eleven o'clock. I told him that was when I called."

"He's going to fire him in any case," he said. "It's not right for a fellow who signs manifestoes to work at a news agency. Did you give my message to the Minister?"

"He expects you at three, Don Cayo," Dr. Alcibíades said.

"All right, tell Major Paredes I'm coming by to see him, doctor. I'll be there in about twenty minutes."

ᴐ

"I came to La Crónica without any enthusiasm, just because I had to make some money," Santiago said. "But now I think that out of all the possible jobs, it may be the least bad of the lot."

"Three and a half months and you haven't been disillusioned?" Carlitos asked. "That's enough to put you in a cage and show you off at the circus, Zavalita."

No, you hadn't been disillusioned, Zavalita: the new Ambassador from Brazil Dr. Hernando de Magalhães presented his credentials this morning, I am optimistic about the future of tourism in the country the Director of Tourism declared last night at a press conference, the Entre Nous Society celebrated another anniversary with a well-attended and select reception. But you liked that garbage, Zavalita, you sat down at your typewriter and you were happy. No more of that careful detail with which you wrote short articles, he thinks, that fierce conviction with which you corrected, tore up and rewrote the pages before you took them to Arispe.

"How long did it take you to become disillusioned with journalism?" Santiago asked.

Those little articles and pygmy boxes that you'd look for anxiously the next morning in the copy of *La Crónica* you bought at the newsstand next to the boardinghouse in Barranco. That you would show with pride to Señora Lucía: I wrote that, ma'am.

"A week after I came to *La Crónica*," Carlitos said. "At the agency I wasn't in journalism, I was more of a typist. I had a schedule that went straight through without any breaks, by two o'clock I was off and I could spend my afternoons reading and my nights writing. If they hadn't fired me, literature wouldn't have lost a great poet, Zavalita."

You were due at five, but you got to the editorial room much earlier, and from three-thirty on you were already watching the clock in the boardinghouse, impatient to go get on the streetcar, would they give you an outside assignment today? a reporting job? an interview? to arrive and sit down at your desk waiting for Arispe to call you: put this information into ten lines, Zavalita. Never again such enthusiasm, he thinks, the desire to do things, I'll get myself a scoop and they'll congratulate me, never again such plans, they'll move me up. What went wrong, he thinks. He thinks: when, why.

"I never knew why, one morning that fag queen came into the agency and told me you've been sabotaging the service, you Communist," and Carlitos laughed in slow motion. "Are you serious?"

"Quite serious, God damn you," Tallio said. "Do you know how much your sabotage is going to cost me?"

"It's going to cost you your mother's name if you curse me or raise your voice to me again," Carlitos said, happy all over. "I didn't even get any severance pay. And then and there I came to *La Crónica* and then and there I found the tomb of poetry, Zavalita."

"Why didn't you quit journalism?" Santiago asked. "You could have found a different kind of job."

"You get in and you can't get out, it's quicksand," Carlitos said, as if going away or falling asleep. "You keep on sinking, sinking. You hate it, you can't free yourself. You hate it and suddenly you're ready for anything just to get a scoop. Staying up all night, getting into incredible places. It's an addiction, Zavalita."

"I've had it up to here, but they're not going to put a lid on me, you know why?" Santiago says. "Because I'm going to finish my law degree one way or another, Ambrosio."

"I didn't pick the police beat, it so happened that Arispe couldn't stand me on local news anymore or Maldonado on cables either," Carlitos was saying, far, far away. "Only Becerrita could stand to have me working for him. The police beat, the worst of the worst. Just what I like. The dregs, my element, Zavalita."

Then he was silent and sat motionless and smiling, looking into space. When Santiago called the waiter, he woke up and paid the check. They went out and Santiago had to hold his arm because he was bumping into tables and walls. The arcade was empty, a pale blue strip of sky was creeping in over the rooftops of the Plaza San Martín.

"It's strange that Norwin didn't come by," Carlitos was reciting in a kind of quiet tenderness. "One of the best of the castaways, a magnificent part of the dregs. I'll introduce you to him someday, Zavalita."

He was staggering, leaning against one of the columns of the arcade, his face dirty with a growth of beard, his nose igneous, his eyes tragically happy. Tomorrow without fail, Carlitos.

4

SHE WAS COMING BACK from the drugstore with two rolls of toilet paper when she came face to face with Ambrosio at the service entrance. Don't look so serious, he said, I haven't come to see you. And she: why should you be coming to see me, there's nothing between us. Didn't you see the car? Ambrosio asked, Don Fermín's up there with Don Cayo. Don Fermín, Don Cayo? Amalia asked. Yes, why was she surprised. She didn't know why, but she was surprised, they were so different, she tried to imagine Don Fermín at one of the parties and it seemed impossible.

"It would be better if he didn't see you," Ambrosio said. "He might tell him that you were thrown out of his house or that you ran out on the laboratory, and Señora Hortensia might fire you too."

"What you don't want is for Don Cayo to find out that you brought me here," Amalia said.

"Well, that too," Ambrosio said. "But not because of me, because of you. I already told you that Don Cayo has hated me ever since I left him to go work for Don Fermín. If he found out that you know me, you'd be all through."

"My, what a good person you've become," she said. "The way you worry about me now."

They'd been chatting by the service entrance and Amalia kept looking to see if Símula or Carlota was coming. Hadn't Ambrosio told her that Don Fermín and Don Cayo didn't see each other the way they used to?

235

Yes, ever since Señor Cayo had young Santiago arrested they weren't friends anymore; but they had business together and that's probably why Don Fermín is in San Miguel now. Was Amalia happy here? Yes, very happy, she had less work than before and the mistress was very good. Then you owe me a favor, Ambrosio said, but she cut off his joking: I already paid you a long time back, don't you ever forget it. And she changed the subject, how was everybody in Miraflores? Señora Zoila very good, young Sparky had a girl friend who'd been a runner-up for Miss Peru, Missy Teté a young lady now, and young Santiago hadn't been back to the house since he ran away. You couldn't mention his name in front of Señora Zoila because she'd start crying. And all of a sudden: San Miguel's been good for you, you've turned into a good-looking girl. Amalia didn't laugh, she looked at him with all the fury she could muster.

"Sunday's your day off, isn't it?" he said. "I'll wait for you there at the streetcar stop, at two o'clock. Will you come?"

"Not in your wildest dream," Amalia said. "Is there something between us that we should go out together?"

She heard a sound in the kitchen and went into the house without saying good-bye to Ambrosio. She went to the pantry to spy: there was Don Fermín, saying good-bye to Don Cayo. Tall, gray-haired, so elegant in gray, and she remembered all at once all the things that had happened since she'd seen him last, Trinidad, the alley in Mirones, the Maternity Hospital, and she felt the tears coming on. She went to the bathroom to wash her face. Now she was furious with Ambrosio, furious with herself for having stopped to talk to him as if there was anything between them, for not having told him did you think that just because you told me they needed a maid I'd forgotten, that I'd forgiven you? I hope you drop dead, she thought.

2

He tightened his tie, put on his jacket, took his briefcase and left the office. He passed by the secretaries with an absent-minded face. The car was parked by the door, the Ministry of War, Ambrosio. It took them fifteen minutes to cross the downtown area. He got out before Ambrosio

236

could open the door for him, wait for me here. Soldiers who saluted, a hallway, stairs, an officer who smiled. In the waiting room of the Intelligence Service a captain with a little mustache was expecting him: the Major is in his office, Mr. Bermúdez, go right in. Paredes got up when he saw him come in. On the desk there were three telephones, a small flag, a green blotter; on the walls maps, city plans, a photograph of Odría and a calendar.

"Espina called me to complain," Major Paredes said. "If you don't get rid of that man at the door I'll take a shot at him. He was furious."

"I already ordered the plainclothesman withdrawn," he said, loosening his tie. "At least he knows he's being watched now."

"I'll say again that it's a waste of time," Major Paredes said. "Before he was let go he was promoted. Why should he start plotting?"

"Because it hurts his pride not being Minister," he said. "No, he wouldn't plot on his own, he's too dumb for that. But they can use him. Anybody can get his finger into the Uplander's mouth."

Major Paredes shrugged his shoulders, made a skeptical gesture. He opened a cupboard, took out an envelope and handed it to him. He thumbed distractedly through the papers, the photographs.

"All his movements, all his telephone conversations," Major Paredes said. "Nothing suspicious. He's spending his time consoling himself through his fly, you can see. Besides the mistress in Breña, he's taken on another one, in Santa Beatriz."

He laughed, muttered something, and he could see them for an instant: fat, fleshy, their teats hanging down, advancing one after the other with a perverse joy in their eyes. He put the papers and photographs back into the envelope and laid it on the desk.

"The two mistresses, the dice games at the Military Club, one or two drinking bouts a week, that's his life," Major Paredes said. "The Uplander is a used-up man, believe me."

"But with a lot of friends in the army, lots of officers who owe him favors," he said. "I've got the nose of a hound dog. Stay with me, give me a little more time."

"All right, if you insist so much, I'll have them watch him for a few days more," Major Paredes said. "But I know it's a waste of time."

237

"Even though he's retired and dumb, a general is a general," he said. "I mean he's more dangerous than all the Apristas and redtails put together."

9

Hipólito was a brute, yessir, but he had his feelings too, Ludovico and Ambrosio had found out that time in Porvenir. They still had some time and they were going to get a drink when Hipólito appeared and took each one by the arm: he was inviting them to a snort. They'd gone to the dive on the Avenida Bolivia, Hipólito ordered three short ones, took out his oval cigarettes and lighted the match with a trembling hand. You could see he was nervous, sir, he was laughing listlessly, running his tongue over his mouth like a thirsty animal, looking behind, and the depths of his eyes were dancing. Ludovico and Ambrosio looked at each other as if to say what ails this guy.

"You seem to be carrying some problem around, Hipólito," Ambrosio said.

"Did you catch the clap in some whorehouse, brother?" Ludovico asked.

He shook his head no, drained his glass, asked the Chinaman for another round. What was wrong, then, Hipólito? He looked at them, blew smoke in their faces, he'd finally decided to let the cat out of the bag, sir: he was bothered by that whoopty-do in Porvenir. Ambrosio and Ludovico laughed. There was nothing to it, Hipólito, the crazy old women would start running with the first whistle, it was the easiest work in the world, brother. Hipólito drained the second glass and his eyes popped out. He wasn't afraid, he knew what the word meant, but he'd never felt it, he'd been a boxer.

"Fuck off, you're not going to start telling us about your fights again?" Ludovico said.

"It's something personal," Hipólito said sorrowfully.

It was Ludovico's turn to pay for another round, and the Chinaman, who'd seen that they were going along at full speed, left the bottle on the bar. Last night he couldn't sleep because of that whoopty-do, you can imagine what it was like. Ambrosio and Ludovico looked at each other as if to say has he gone crazy? Talk to us straight out, Hipólito, that's

238

why they were friends. He coughed, he was just about to but he changed his mind, sir, his voice got stuck in the end but he loosened it up: a family affair, something personal. And without further ado, he poured out a mournful story, sir. His mother made mats and had her stand in the Parada market, he'd grown up in Porvenir, lived there, if you could call that living. He'd washed and polished cars, run errands, unloaded trucks at the market, picking up pennies where best he could, sometimes sticking his hand in where he shouldn't have.

"What do they call people from Porvenir?" Ludovico interrupted him. "People from Lima are called Limans, people from Bajo el Puente are Bajopontines, what about people from Porvenir?"

"You don't give a shit about what I'm saying," Hipólito had said furiously.

"By no means, brother." Ludovico patted him on the back. "That question just came to me all of a sudden. I'm sorry, go ahead."

That even though it had been some years since he'd been back there, here inside, and he touched his chest, sir, Porvenir was still home to him: besides, that's where he'd started boxing. That a lot of the old women in Parada knew him, that some of them were going to recognize him, maybe.

"Oh, now I get it," Ludovico said. "There's no reason for you to get upset, who's going to recognize you after so many years? Besides, they won't even see your face, the lighting in Porvenir is awful, the punks keep throwing stones at the street lights and breaking them. There's nothing to worry about, Hipólito."

He'd stood there thinking, licking his lips like a cat. The Chinaman brought salt and a lemon, Ludovico salted the tip of his tongue and squeezed half of the lemon into his mouth, drained his glass and exclaimed that the drink had gone up in quality. He'd started talking about something else, but Hipólito silent, looking at the floor, the bar, thinking.

"No," he'd said suddenly. "I'm not bothered by somebody recognizing me. I'm bothered by the whole idea of the whoopty-do."

"But why, man?" Ludovico said. "Isn't it better to put a scare into old women than students, for example? All they do is holler and jump, Hipólito. Noise can't hurt anyone."

"What if I have to swat one of the ones who fed me when I was a kid?"

239

Hipólito had said, pounding on the table, all worked up, sir.

Ambrosio and Ludovico as if saying here comes the crybaby stuff again. But man, brother, if they fed you then they're good people, religious, law-abiding women, do you think they'd get mixed up in political fights? But Hipólito. He wouldn't be convinced, he was shaking his head as if you can't convince me.

"I'm doing this today, but I don't like it," he said finally.

"Do you think anybody likes it?" Ludovico asked.

"I do," said Ambrosio, laughing. "It's like a rest for me, an adventure."

"That's because you only come along once in a while," Ludovico said. "You've got a great life as the big boss's chauffeur and this is just a game for you. Wait till you get your head split open by a stone, the way it happened to me once."

"Then let's hear you tell us that you still like it," Hipólito had said.

Lucky for him nothing ever happened to him, sir.

19

How dared he? On her days off when she didn't go to see her aunt in Limoncillo or Señora Rosario in Mirones, she would go out with Anduvia and María, two maids in the neighborhood. Because he'd helped her get that job, did he think she'd forgotten? They'd take walks, go to the movies, one Sunday they'd gone to the Coliseo to see the folk dancing. Just because you chatted with him did he think you'd forgiven him already? Sometimes she went out with Carlota, but not too often, because Símula wanted her to have her home before dark. You shouldn't have treated him so well, dummy. When they left, Símula would drive them crazy with her instructions, and when they got back with her questions. She was really going to stand him up on Sunday, coming here all the way from Miraflores in vain, oh, she was going to get one up on him. Poor Carlota, Símula wouldn't let her stick so much as her nose out onto the street, she worked hard to frighten her about men. All week long she was thinking he's going to be waiting for you, sometimes it sent her into a rage that made her tremble, sometimes into laughter. But he probably wouldn't come, she'd told him not in your wildest dream and he'd say to himself why should I go. On Saturday she pressed the shiny blue dress

240

that Señora Hortensia had given her, where are you going tomorrow? Carlota asked her, to her aunt's. She looked in the mirror and insulted herself: you're already thinking about going, dummy. No, she wouldn't go. That Sunday, for the first time, she put on the high-heeled shoes she'd just bought and the bracelet she'd won in a raffle. Before leaving she put a little lipstick on.

She cleared the table quickly, ate practically no lunch, went up to the mistress's room to look at herself in the full-length mirror. She went straight to the Bertoloto Hotel, passed it, and on Costanera she felt fury and a tingling in her body: there he was at the streetcar stop, waving. She thought go back, she thought you won't speak to him. He had a brown suit, white shirt and red tie on and was wearing a handkerchief in his jacket pocket.

"I was praying you wouldn't stand me up," Ambrosio said. "I'm glad you came."

"I came to get the streetcar," she said, indignant, turning away from him. "I'm going to my aunt's."

"Fine," Ambrosio said. "Let's ride downtown together."

○

"I was forgetting one detail," Major Paredes said. "Espina's been seeing a lot of your friend Zavala."

"That doesn't mean anything," he said. "They've been friends for years. Espina got his laboratory the concession to supply the army commissaries."

"There are a few things about that big shot that I don't like," Major Paredes said. "I keep an eye on him from time to time. He's had meetings with Apristas."

"Thanks to those important Apristas he learns lots of things and thanks to him I learn about them," he said. "Zavala's no problem. You're wasting your time on him."

"I've never been convinced of the loyalty of that big shot," Major Paredes said. "He's with the government in order to do business. Strictly a matter of convenience."

"We're all with the government out of convenience; the important thing is for it to be convenient for people like Zavala to be with the

241

government." He smiled. "Can we take a look at the Cajamarca business?"

Major Paredes nodded. He picked up one of the three telephones and gave an order. He was thoughtful for a moment.

"At first I thought you were only posing as a cynic," he said then. "Now I'm convinced you really are. You don't believe in anything or anybody, Cayo."

"I'm not paid to believe, I'm paid to do my job." He smiled again. "And I'm doing a good job, right?"

"If you're only in this out of convenience, how come you haven't accepted other offers a thousand times better than what the President has offered you?" Major Paredes laughed. "You see, you are a cynic, but not as much as you'd like to think you are."

He stopped smiling and looked at Major Paredes wistfully.

"Maybe because your uncle gave me an opportunity that no one else gave me," he said, shrugging his shoulders. "Maybe because I haven't found anyone who can serve your uncle in this job the way I can. Or maybe because I like the work, I don't know."

"The President is concerned about your health and so am I," Major Paredes said. "In three years you've aged ten. How's your ulcer?"

"Healed over," he said. "I don't have to drink milk anymore, thank God."

He reached for his cigarettes on the desk, lighted one and had a coughing attack.

"How many do you smoke a day?" Major Paredes asked.

"Two or three packs," he said. "But dark tobacco, not that crap you smoke."

"I don't know what's going to do you in first." Major Paredes laughed. "Tobacco, the ulcer, amphetamines, the Apristas, or some resentful army officer like the Uplander. Or your harem."

He gave a touch of a smile. There was a knock on the door, the captain with the little mustache came in with a file folder: the photostats were ready, Major. Paredes spread the map out on the desk: red and blue marks at certain intersections, a thick black line that zigzagged along many streets and came to an end in a square. They leaned over the map for some time. Danger points, Major Paredes was saying, troop concen-

242

trations, the route of the movement, the bridge to be inaugurated. He was taking notes in a small book, smoking, asking questions in his monotonous voice. They went back to their chairs.

"Tomorrow I'm traveling to Cajamarca with Captain Ríos to take a last look at the security precautions," Major Paredes said. "There's no problem on our side, security will function like clockwork. What about your people?"

"I'm not worried about security," he said. "I'm worried about something else."

"His reception?" Major Paredes asked. "Do you think they'll do something unpleasant?"

"The senator and the deputies have promised to fill the square," he said. "But promises like that, you know. This afternoon I'm going to meet with the reception committee. I had them come to Lima."

"Those uplanders would be ungrateful shits not to receive him with open arms," Major Paredes said. "He's building them a road, a bridge. Who ever remembered there even was a Cajamarca before that?"

"Cajamarca's always been an Aprista hotbed," he said. "We've done some cleaning up, but something unforeseen could happen."

"The President thinks the trip will be a success," Major Paredes said. "He says you've assured him there'll be forty thousand people at the rally and no trouble."

"There will be, and there won't be any trouble," he said. "But those are the things that are aging me. Not the ulcers or the tobacco."

い

They'd paid the Chinaman, gone out, and when they got to the courtyard the meeting had already begun, sir. Mr. Lozano looked angrily at them and pointed to the clock. There were some fifty there, all dressed in civilian clothes, some were laughing like idiots and what a stink. This one on the regular list, this one a hired hand like me, the other one from the list, Ludovico was pointing them out, and a police major was talking, potbellied, half-stuttering, who kept repeating "so that." So that there were assault guards on the outskirts, so th-th-that there were patrol cars too, so that the c-c-cavalry was hidden in some garages and c-c-corrals. Ludovico and Ambrosio looked at each other as if to say c-c-comical,

243

sir, but Hipólito kept a funeral face. And then Mr. Lozano came forward, all very quiet to listen to him.

"But the idea is that the police won't have to intervene," he'd said. "It's something Mr. Bermúdez has asked about especially. And there isn't to be any shooting either."

"He's bringing in the big boss because you're here," Ludovico had said to Ambrosio. "So you'll go back and tell him."

"So that that's why they didn't issue pistols, just c-c-clubs and other h-h-hand weapons."

A sound of stomachs, throats, feet had arisen, they were all protesting but without opening their mouths, sir. Quiet, the Major said, but the one who settled things in an intelligent way was Mr. Lozano.

"You're a first-class bunch and you don't need bullets to break up a handful of crazy women. If things get rough the assault guards will go into action." Very smart, he made a joke: "Anybody who's afraid raise your hand." Nobody. And he: "Fine, because otherwise you'd have to give your drinks back." Laughter. And he: "Carry on with your instructions, Major."

"So th-th-that understood, and before you get your weapons take a good look at each other's f-f-faces so that you won't be hitting each other by m-m-mistake."

They had laughed, out of politeness, not because his joke was funny, and where the weapons were they had to sign a receipt. They gave them clubs, brass knuckles and bicycle chains. They returned to the courtyard, mingled with each other, some were already so bashed they could barely speak. Ambrosio got them into conversation, where they were from, if they'd been chosen by lot. No, sir, they were all volunteers. Happy to get a few extra soles, but some were scared at what might happen to them. They were smoking, fooling around, pretending to hit each other with the clubs. That's the way they were until around six o'clock when the Major came to tell them that the bus is here. On the square in Porvenir half of them stayed with Ludovico and Ambrosio, in the center, by the swings. Hipólito had taken the others over near the movie theater. Broken down into groups of three, four, they'd gone into the amusement park. Ambrosio and Ludovico looked at the flying seats, wild for lifting up women's skirts, right? No, sir, you couldn't see a thing, there wasn't enough light. The others were buying Italian ices, mashed yams, a couple of them had brought their flasks and were taking their drinks beside the Ferris wheel. It smells as if Lozano had been given a bum steer, Ludovico had said. They'd been there a half hour already and not a sign of anything.

9

On the streetcar they sat together and Ambrosio paid her fare. She was so furious for having come that she didn't even look at him. Why are you so mad, Ambrosio was saying. Her face close to the window, Amalia was looking at the Avenida Brasil, the cars, the Beverly theater. Women have good hearts and bad memories, Ambrosio was saying, but you're just the opposite, Amalia. That day when they'd met on the street and he told her I know of a place in San Miguel where they were looking for a maid, hadn't they had a nice chat? She the Police Hospital, the Magdalena Vieja oval. And the other day at the service entrance, hadn't they had a nice chat? The Salesian School, the Plaza Bolognesi. Was there another man in your life now, Amalia? And at that moment two women got on, sat down opposite them, they looked like bad sorts and they began to look at Ambrosio fresh as you like. What was wrong with their going out together once like good friends? Laughing at him, looks and flirting, and suddenly, without realizing it, her mouth said right out, looking at the two women, not at him: all right, where shall we go? Ambrosio looked at her with surprise, scratched his head and laughed: what a woman. They went to Rímac, because Ambrosio had to see a friend. They found him in a little restaurant on the Calle Chiclayo, eating chicken and rice.

"Let me introduce you to my girl friend, Ludovico," Ambrosio said.

"That's not so," Amalia said. "We're just friends."

"Sit down," Ludovico said. "Have a beer with me."

"Ludovico and I worked together for Don Cayo, Amalia," Ambrosio said. "I drove the car and he took care of him. Rough nights, right, Ludovico?"

There were only men in the restaurant, some of them looked awful, and Amalia felt uncomfortable. What are you doing here, she thought, why are you so stupid. They were watching her out of the corner of their

245

eyes but they weren't saying anything. They were probably afraid of the two big men with her, because Ludovico was as tall and as strong as Ambrosio. Except so ugly, his face pockmarked and gaps in his teeth. The two of them were talking between themselves, asking about friends, and she was bored. But suddenly Ludovico pounded on the table: that's it, they were going to the Acho bullring, he'd get them in. He got them in, not through the public entrance but through an alley, and the policemen greeted Ludovico like an old friend. They sat down in the Shade, high up, but since there weren't many people, when the second bull came out they went down to the fourth row. There were three bullfighters, but the star was Santa Cruz, it was odd to see a black man dressed as a bullfighter. You're rooting for him because he's your blood brother, Ludovico teased Ambrosio, and he, without being annoyed, yes and besides he's got guts. He did: he spun around, knelt down, turned his back on the bull. She'd only seen bullfights in the movies and she closed her eyes, she shrieked when the bull knocked down an apprentice, the picadors are savages she said, but with Santa Cruz's last bull she waved her handkerchief too, like Ambrosio, and asked them to give him an ear. She was happy leaving Acho, at least she'd seen something new. It was so silly wasting her day off helping Señora Rosario hang clothes, listening to her aunt complain about her boarders, or walking all over with Anduvia and María with noplace to go. They had some dark chicha at the entrance to Acho and Ludovico said good-bye. They walked toward the Paseo de Aguas.

"Did you like the bullfight?" Ambrosio asked.

"Yes," Amalia said. "But it's awfully cruel for the animals, isn't it?"

"If you liked it, we can come back another time," Ambrosio said.

She was going to answer him not in your wildest dream but she had second thoughts and closed her mouth and thought stupid girl. It occurred to her that it had been more than three years, almost four, since she'd gone out with Ambrosio, and suddenly she felt sad. What do you want to do now? Ambrosio asked. Go to her aunt's in Limoncillo. What could he have been doing all those years? You can go another time, Ambrosio said, let's go to the movies instead. They went to one in Rímac, to see a pirate picture, and in the darkness she felt her eyes filling with

246

tears. Were you remembering when you used to go to the movies with Trinidad, stupid girl? When you used to live in Mirones and you spent days, months without doing anything, not talking, not even thinking? No, she was remembering from before that, the Sundays they saw each other in Surquillo, and the nights they got together secretly in the little room next to the garage and what happened. She felt rage again, if he touches me I'll scratch his eyes out, I'll kill him. But Ambrosio didn't even try, and when they went out he invited her to have a snack. They walked along to the Plaza de Armas, talking about everything except before. Only when they were waiting for the streetcar did he take her arm: I'm not what you think I am, Amalia. And you're not what you think you are either, Queta said, you're what you do, that poor Amalia makes me feel sorry. Let me go or I'll scream, Amalia said, and Ambrosio let go of her. But they weren't fighting, Amalia, I'm only asking you to forget what happened. It's been such a long time, Amalia. The streetcar came, they rode to San Miguel in silence. They got off at the stop by the Canonesas School and it had grown dark. You had another man, the textile worker, Ambrosio said, I haven't had another woman. And a while later, getting to the corner of the house, with a resentful voice: you've made me suffer a lot, Amalia. She didn't answer him, she started to run. At the door of the house, she turned to look: he'd stayed on the corner, half hidden in the shadows of the little branchless trees. She went into the house, making an effort not to let herself be sentimental, furious at feeling sentimental.

9

"What about that lodge of officers in Cuzco?" he asked.

"As soon as the lists are presented to congress, Colonel Idiáquez is going to get his promotion," Major Paredes said. "As a general he won't be able to stay on in Cuzco, and without him the ring will break up. They haven't done anything yet; they meet, they talk."

"It isn't enough just getting Idiáquez out of there," he said. "What about the commandant, and the little captains? I don't understand why they haven't been broken up yet. The Minister of War assured me that the transfers would start this week."

247

"I've spoken to him ten times, showed him the reports ten times," Major Paredes said. "Since it's a question of officers with prestige, he wants to drag his feet."

"The President has got to intervene, then," he said. "After his trip to Cajamarca, the first order of business is breaking up that little ring. Are they being watched closely?"

"You can imagine," Major Paredes said. "I even know what they have for dinner."

"When we least expect it somebody is going to lay a million soles on the table in front of them and we'll have a revolution on our hands," he said. "They've got to be broken up and sent to faraway garrisons as soon as possible."

"Idiáquez owes the government a lot of favors," Major Paredes said. "The President is always getting tremendously disappointed by people. It's going to hurt him when he finds out that Idiáquez is stirring up officers against him."

"It would hurt him more if he found out they'd risen in revolt," he said; he stood up, took some papers out of his briefcase and handed them to Major Paredes. "Take a look at these and see if you've got any files on the people there."

Paredes accompanied him to the door, held him back by the arm when he was about to leave.

"And that news from Argentina this morning, how did it get by you?"

"It didn't get by me," he said. "Apristas stoning a Peruvian embassy is a good piece of news. I talked to the President and he agreed that it should be printed."

"Well, yes," Major Paredes said. "The officers here who read it were indignant."

"You see how I think of everything?" he said. "See you tomorrow."

◊

But in a little while Hipólito had come over to them, his face very sad, sir: there they were, with their signs and everything. They'd come in by one of the corners of the square, and the men approached like curious bystanders. Four of them were carrying a sign with red letters, behind came a small group, the ringleaders Ludovico had said, who made the others holler, and the others were half a block long. The people from the amusement park had also come close to look at them. They were shouting, especially those in front, and it couldn't be understood, and there were old women, young women, children, but no men, just as Mr. Lozano said, Hipólito had said. A lot of braids, a lot of full skirts, a lot of hats. These people believe in the procession, Ludovico had said: there were three who were holding their hands as if they were praying, sir. Some two hundred or three hundred or four hundred and they finally all came into the square.

"Bread and butter, you see?" Ludovico had said.

"Stale bread and rancid butter, maybe," said Hipólito.

"We get in the middle of them and divide them up," Ludovico had said. "We'll keep the head and you can have the tail."

"I hope the lash of the tail is softer than the butt of the head," Hipólito said, trying to make a joke, sir, but it didn't come off. He pulled up his collar and went to round up his group. The women went around the square and they had followed them, from behind and separately. When they were by the Ferris wheel, Hipólito had appeared again: I've got second thoughts, I want to leave. I like you a lot but I like myself more, Ludovico had said. I'm warning you I'll screw you, you faggot. That slap in the face had lifted his morale, sir: he gave a furious look, shot off. They'd got their people together, had stirred them up with words and had sneaked into the demonstration. The women were gathered together by the Ferris wheel, the ones with the sign were facing the others. All of a sudden one of the leaders climbed up onto a platform and began to make a speech. More people had crowded together, they were jammed in there, the music from the wheel had stopped, but you couldn't hear what she was talking about. The men had been working in, clapping, the stupid women are making way for us, Ludovico said, and on the other side Hipólito's people were sneaking in too. They were clapping, embracing, good fine bravo, some of the women were looking at them funny but others come in come in, shook hands with them, we're not alone. Ambrosio and Ludovico had looked at each other as if saying let's not get separated in this mess, buddy. They'd already cut them in two, they were jammed into them just like a wedge, right in the middle. They'd taken out their taunts, their whistling, Hipólito his megaphone, down with the troublemaker! long live General Odría! down with the enemies of the people! the truncheons, the whips, long live Odría! A terrible mess, sir. Troublemakers, the woman on the platform was howling, but the noise swallowed up her voice and around Ambrosio the women were shrieking and shoving. Get out of here, Ludovico was telling them, you've been tricked, go back home, and at that moment a hand had suddenly grabbed him and it felt like she was pulling off a strip of my neck, Ludovico had told Ambrosio afterwards, sir. That's when the clubs and chains had come into play, the whacks and punches, and that's when a million women had begun to bellow and kick. Ambrosio and Ludovico were together, one would slip and the other would help him up, one would fall and the other would lift him. The hens had turned into fighting cocks, Ludovico had said, dumb old Hipólito was right. Because they really did defend themselves, sir. They'd knock them down and they'd stay on the ground there, like dead, but from the ground they grabbed them by the feet and pulled them down. They kept on kicking, jumping, curses rang out like shotgun blasts. There are only a few of us, one of them had said, bring in the assault guards, but Ludovico, God damn it, no! They rushed them again and made them fall back, the fence around the wheel fell down and a pile of crazy women too. Some of them dragged themselves off and now instead of long live Odría the men were shouting fuckyourmothers, whores, at them, and finally the head of the column had been broken up into small groups and it was easy to chase them. From two, from three they would pick one and beat up on her, then another and beat up on her, and Ambrosio and Ludovico even joked about their sweaty faces. That was when the shot rang out, sir, goddamnyourfuckinghide the one who fired, Ludovico had said. It wasn't there, but in back. The tail had been all together and wiggling, sir. They went to help and broke it up. Somebody named Soldevilla had shot, ten of them had me cornered, they were going to scratch my eyes out, he hadn't killed anybody, he'd shot into the air. But Ludovico got worked up all the same: who the fuck gave you a revolver? And Soldevilla: this weapon doesn't belong to the platoon, it belongs to me. You've fucked yourself up just the same, Ludovico had said, I'm making a report and you've lost your bonus. The amusement park was deserted, the fellows who ran the Ferris wheel, the whip, the rocket were trembling in their huts, the same as the gypsy women in their tents. They took count and one of them was missing, sir. They'd found him asleep beside a damned woman who was crying. Several of them got mad, what have you done, you whore, and they landed on her. His name was Iglesias, he was from Ayacucho, his mouth was busted, he got up like a sleepwalker, what, what. O.K., Ludovico had said to the ones who were beating up on the woman, it's all over. They had taken the bus by the bar and nobody was talking, dead tired. When they got out they'd begun to smoke, look at each other's faces, it hurts me here, my wife will never believe that I got this scratch as an accident at work. Fine, very good, Mr. Lozano had said, you did your job, now go fix yourselves up. That was the kind of job it was, more or less, sir.

5

ALL WEEK LONG AMALIA WAS PENSIVE, absent-minded. What are you thinking about, Carlota had said, and Símula a person who laughs to herself is thinking about what she's done wrong, and Señora Hortensia where are you, come back down to earth. She wasn't furious with him anymore, she wasn't angry with herself for having gone out with him anymore. You hate him and he gets the better of you again, why are you so crazy. One night she dreamed that on Sunday, when she was going out, she would run into him at the streetcar stop, waiting for her. But that Sunday Carlota and Símula had a christening to go to and her day off was Saturday. Where would she go? She went to see Gertrudis, she hadn't seen her for months. She got to the laboratory when they were coming out and Gertrudis took her home to have lunch. Ungrateful wretch, such a long time, Gertrudis said, she'd gone to Mirones any number of times and Señora Rosario didn't know the address where you were working, tell me how things are going for you. She was about to tell her that she'd seen Ambrosio again but she thought better of it, she'd cursed him out so much before. They made a date for the next Sunday. She went back to San Miguel while it was still light and went to lie down on her bed. After all he did to you you're still thinking about him, stupid. At night she dreamed about Trinidad. He was insulting her and at the end he warned her, livid: I'm waiting for you when you die. On Sunday Símula and Carlota left early and the mistress a while later with Miss

Queta. She washed the silverware, sat in the living room, turned on the radio. It was all horse races and soccer and she was starting to get bored when there was a knock on the kitchen door. Yes, it was him.

"Your mistress isn't home?" With his cap and his blue chauffeur's uniform.

"Are you afraid of the mistress too?" Amalia asked, serious.

"Don Fermín sent me out on some errands and I took a little time off to see you for a while," he said, smiling at her, as if he hadn't heard. "I left the car around the corner. I hope Señora Hortensia doesn't recognize it."

"Or too much time will pass and you'll be more afraid of Don Fermín," Amalia said.

The smile vanished from his face, he made a listless gesture and stood looking at her, not knowing what to do. He pushed his cap back and made an effort to smile: he was taking a chance on getting bawled out for coming to see you and look how you receive me, Amalia. What happened happened, Amalia, it's all erased now. She should act as if they'd just met, Amalia.

"Do you think you're going to do the same thing to me again?" Amalia was heard to say, trembling. "You're wrong."

He didn't give her time to draw back, he'd already grabbed her by the wrist and was looking into her eyes, blinking. He didn't try to embrace her, he didn't even get close. He held her for a moment, put on a strange expression, and let her go.

"In spite of the textile worker, in spite of the fact I haven't seen you for years, as far as I'm concerned you've never stopped being my woman," Ambrosio said huskily and Amalia felt her heart stop. She thought he was going to cry, I'm going to cry. "For your information, I still love you the way I used to."

He stood looking at her again and she drew back and closed the door. She saw him hesitate for a moment; then he straightened his cap and left. She went back into the living room and caught sight of him turning the corner. Sitting beside the radio, she rubbed her wrist, amazed that she didn't feel angry. Could it be true, did he still love her? No, it was a lie. Could he have fallen in love with her all over again maybe, that day they ran into each other on the street? There wasn't a sound outside, the curtains were drawn, a green sunbeam was coming in from the garden. But his voice seemed sincere, she thought, tuning in to one station after another. No soap operas, everything was horse races and soccer.

9

"Go get some lunch," he said to Ambrosio when the car stopped in the Plaza San Martín. "Be back in an hour and a half."

He went into the bar of the Hotel Bolívar and sat near the door. He ordered a gin and two packs of Incas. At the next table three men were talking and in a mutilated way he managed to hear the jokes they were telling. He'd smoked one cigarette and his glass was half empty when he saw him through the window crossing Colmena.

"I'm sorry I kept you waiting," Don Fermín said. "I was in a game and Landa, you know the senator, when he gets his hands on the dice he never lets go of them. Landa's quite happy, the strike at Olave's been settled."

"Did you come from the Club Nacional?" he asked. "Your oligarch friends aren't plotting any conspiracy, are they?"

"Not yet." Don Fermín smiled and, pointing to the glass, told the waiter the same. "What's that cough, have you got a cold?"

"Cigarettes," he said, clearing his throat again. "How are things going with you? Is that bad boy of yours still giving you headaches?"

"Sparky?" Don Fermín picked up a handful of peanuts. "No, he's straightened out and is behaving himself at the office. The one who has me worried now is the second one."

"Does he like to go on sprees too?" he asked.

"He wants to go to that can of worms called San Marcos instead of the Catholic University." Don Fermín savored his drink, made a gesture of annoyance. "He's taken to saying bad things about priests, military men, everything, just to get his mother and me angry."

"All boys have got a bit of the rebel in them," he said. "I think I even did."

"I can't understand it, Don Cayo," Don Fermín said, serious now. "He used to be so proper, he always got the best grades, he was even religious. And now he doesn't believe in anything, follows his whims. All

254

I need is for him to turn out a Communist, an anarchist, something like that."

"Then he'd start giving me headaches." He smiled. "But look, if I had a son I think I'd rather send him to San Marcos. There's a lot undesirable about it, but it's more of a university, don't you think?"

"It isn't just because they play politics at San Marcos," Don Fermín said with a distracted air. "It's lost standing too, it isn't what it used to be. Now it's a nest of half-breeds. What kind of connections can Skinny make there?"

He looked at him without saying anything and watched him blink and lower his eyes, confused.

"Not that I've got anything against people of mixed blood." You caught it, you son of a bitch. "Quite the contrary, I've always been very democratic. But what I want is for Santiago to have the future he deserves. And in this country it's all a question of connections, you know that."

They finished their drinks, ordered a second round. Only Don Fermín was pecking at the peanuts, olives, potato chips. He was drinking and smoking.

"I see there's a new bid, another stretch of the Pan-American Highway," he said. "Is your company going to take part in it too?"

"We've got all we can handle for now with the Pacasmayo road," Don Fermín said. "Sometimes you can bite off more than you can chew. The lab takes a lot of my time, especially now that we've begun to replace the old equipment. I want Sparky to learn and relieve me of some of the work before I expand the construction company."

They talked vaguely about the flu epidemic, the stones the Apristas had thrown at the Peruvian Embassy in Buenos Aires, the threat of a textile strike, would long or short skirts be the style, until the glasses were empty.

○

"Inocencia remembered that it was your favorite dish and she's made you a shrimp stew." Uncle Clodomiro winked at him. "The poor old woman doesn't cook as well as she used to. I planned to take you out

255

to dinner, but I let her have her way so as not to hurt her feelings."

Uncle Clodomiro poured him a glass of vermouth. His small apartment in Santa Beatriz, so neat, so clean, old Inocencia so good, Zavalita. She'd raised the two of them, she used the familiar form with them, once she'd pulled your old man's ear in front of you: it's been too long since you came to see your brother, Fermín. Uncle Clodomiro took a sip and wiped his lips. So neat, always with a vest, his collar and cuffs heavily starched, his lively little eyes, his small, elusive figure, his nervous hands. He thinks: did he know, can he know? Months, years you hadn't gone to see him, Zavalita. You had to go, I have to go.

"Do you remember how many years older Uncle Clodomiro was than papa, Ambrosio?" Santiago asks.

"You don't ask old people their age." Uncle Clodomiro laughed. "Five years, Skinny. Fermín's fifty-two, so, if you figure it out, I'll be turning sixty pretty soon."

"And yet he looks older," Santiago said. "You've kept yourself young, uncle."

"Well, it's nice of you to call me young." Uncle Clodomiro smiled. "Maybe because I never got married. Did you finally go see your parents?"

"Not yet, uncle," Santiago said. "But I will, I promise you I will."

"It's been a long time, Skinny, too long," Uncle Clodomiro admonished him with his fresh, clean eyes. "How many months has it been? Four, five?"

"They'll raise an awful fuss over me, mama will start shouting for me to come back." He thinks: six already. "I'm not going to go back, uncle, they have to understand that."

"Months without seeing your parents, your brother and sister, living in the same city." Uncle Clodomiro shook his head in disbelief. "If you were my son, I would have gone looking for you, I would have whacked you a couple of times and brought you home the next day."

But he hadn't gone looking for you, Zavalita, or whacked you, or made you come back. Why, papa?

"I don't want to give you advice, you're a grown man now, but you haven't been behaving right, Skinny. Wanting to live by yourself is crazy enough, but after all. Refusing to see your parents, that's wrong, Skinny.

You've got Zoila all beside herself. And every time that Fermín comes to ask me how is he, what's he doing, he looks more depressed to me."

"If he came to look for me it wouldn't get him anywhere," Santiago said. "He can take me home by force a hundred times and I'll run away again a hundred times."

"He doesn't understand, I don't understand," Uncle Clodomiro said. "Did you get annoyed because he got you out of Police Headquarters? Did you want him to leave you locked up with the other madmen? Hasn't he always given you what you wanted? Hasn't he spoiled you more than he has Teté, more than Sparky? Be frank with me, Skinny. What have you got against Fermín?"

"It's hard to explain, uncle. Right now it's better for me not to go to the house. After a little time passes I'll go, I promise."

"Stop your nonsense and go on over," Uncle Clodomiro said. "Neither Zoila nor Fermín is against your staying on at *La Crónica*. The only thing that worries them is that you're going to drop your studies because you're working. They don't want you to spend the rest of your life as just another wage earner like me."

He smiled without bitterness and filled the glasses again. The stew was just about ready, Inocencia's worn-out voice, and Uncle Clodomiro shook his head compassionately, the poor old woman can barely see anymore, Skinny.

⑨

How fresh, how shameless, Gertrudis Lama said, looking you up again after what he did to you? horrible. And Amalia horrible. But that's the way he was, ever since the first he'd been like that. And Gertrudis: what do you mean, what had he been like? He took his time, he made things into a mystery. He looked for excuses to get into the pantry, the rooms, the courtyard when Amalia was there. At first he wouldn't say anything to her with his mouth, but he spoke with his eyes, and she was frightened that Señora Zoila or the children would catch on and notice the looks. It was a long time before he got up the courage to say things to her, and Gertrudis what things? you're nice and young, you've got a springtime face, and she frightened because that had been her first job. But in spite of that, she soon calmed down. He may have been fresh, but he was

257

smart, or a coward, rather: he was more afraid of the folks than I was, Gertrudis. He wouldn't even let himself be caught by the other servants, he'd be teasing her and the cook or the other maid would appear and he'd take off. But when they were alone he'd go from mouth to hand flirting, and Gertrudis laughing what about you? Amalia would slap him, once a good one. I can take everything from you, you hit me and it tastes like a kiss, those lies he tells, Gertrudis. He contrived to get the same day off as she, found out where she lived, and one day Amalia saw him going back and forth in front of her aunt's house in Surquillo, and you inside spying on him happily Gertrudis laughed. No, annoyed. He made a good impression on the cook and the other girl, they would say so tall, so strong, when he's dressed in blue they get the shivers and dirty things like that. But not her, Gertrudis, for Amalia he was just like anybody else. If it wasn't because of his looks then how did he get you, Gertrudis said. Probably because of the presents he used to hide in her bed. The first time he came and put a little package in her apron she gave it back without opening it, but afterwards—stupid, wasn't it, Gertrudis?—she accepted them, and at night she would think I wonder what he's left for me today. He would put them under the blanket, God knows when he got in there, a bracelet, handkerchiefs, so that you were already his girl friend, Gertrudis said. Not yet. One day when her aunt wasn't home in Surquillo and he appeared, she—stupid, wasn't I?—went out. They chatted in the street, had some ices together, and the next week, on her day off, they went to the movies. Was it there? Gertrudis asked. Yes, she'd let him hug her, kiss her. From then on he probably thought he had the right or something, they'd be alone and he'd try to take advantage, Amalia had to run away. He slept beside the garage, his room was bigger than the maids', its own bathroom and everything, and one night and Gertrudis what, what. The folks had gone out, Missy Teté and young Santiago were probably already asleep, young Sparky had gone back to the Naval School in his uniform—what, what—and she, what a fool I was, had listened to him, the fool had gone to his room. Naturally, he took advantage, and Gertrudis so that there, dying with laughter. He made her cry, Gertrudis, feel all kinds of fear, all kinds of pain. But that very night Amalia had begun to be disappointed, that very night he humiliated her, and Gertrudis hahaha, hahaha, and Amalia don't be silly, not because of that, don't be dirty, you make me feel ashamed. What were you disappointed in, then? Gertrudis asked. They had the light out, lying on the bed, he consoling her, telling her those lies, he'd never thought he'd find me a virgin, kissing her, and then they heard talking by the door, they'd come home. There Gertrudis, because of that Gertrudis. How was it possible that she had got in that position, how? What, when. His hands were wet with sweat, hide, hide, and he pushed her, get under the bed, don't move, almost crying he was so afraid, a big man like him, Gertrudis, shut up and suddenly he covered her mouth furiously, as if I was going to shout or something, Gertrudis. Only when they heard them crossing the garden and going into the house did he let her go, only then did he fake it, for you, so they wouldn't catch you, bawl you out, fire you. And that they had to be very careful, Señora Zoila was so strict. How strange she'd felt the next day, Gertrudis, with an urge to laugh, feeling sorry, happy, and so ashamed when she went to wash the bloodstains off the sheets in secret, oh I don't know why I'm telling you these things, Gertrudis. And Gertrudis: because you've already forgotten about Trinidad, girl, because now you're dying for that Ambrosio again, Amalia.

9

"I was with the gringos this morning," Don Fermín finally said. "They're worse than Saint Thomas. They've been given every security but they insist on talking to you, Don Cayo."

"It is a question of several millions, after all," he said benevolently. "Their impatience makes sense."

"I'll never understand gringos, don't they seem like little children to you?" Don Fermín said with the same casual, almost indifferent tone. "Half-savages besides. They put their feet on the desk, take off their jackets wherever they are. And the ones I'm talking about aren't no-bodies, important people, I imagine. Sometimes I feel like giving them one of Carreño's books on etiquette."

He was looking out the window at Colmena where the streetcars were coming and going, listening to the endless jokes of the men at the next table.

"The whole thing's all set," he said suddenly. "Last night I had dinner

259

with the Minister of Development. The winning bid should appear in the *Official Journal* on Monday or Tuesday. Tell your friends they've won the contract, they can sleep in peace."

"My partners, not my friends," Don Fermín protested, smiling. "Could you be the friend of gringos? We don't have much in common with those boors, Don Cayo."

He didn't say anything. Smoking, he waited for Don Fermín to reach his hand out to the little dish of peanuts, lift his glass of gin to his mouth, drink, wipe his lips with his napkin and look into his eyes.

"Is it true that you don't want those shares?" He watched him avert his eyes, suddenly interested in the empty chair opposite him. "They insist I convince you, Don Cayo. And really, I can't see why you won't accept them."

"Because I don't know anything about business," he said. "I've already told you that during my twenty years in business I never made a good deal."

"Shares made out to the bearer, the safest, most discreet thing in the world." Don Fermín was smiling at him in a friendly way. "Which can be sold at twice their value in a short time, if you don't want to keep them. I hope you don't think it improper for you to accept those shares."

"It's been a long time since I've known what was proper or improper." He smiled. "Only whether it suits me or not."

"Shares that won't cost the state a cent, just those gringo boors." Don Fermín smiled. "You're doing them a favor, and it's logical for them to reimburse you. Those shares mean a lot more than a hundred thousand soles in cash, Don Cayo."

"I'm a modest man, the hundred thousand soles is plenty for me." He smiled again, an attack of coughing made him stop speaking for a moment. "Let them give them to the Minister of Development, he's a businessman. I only take what I can handle and count. My father was a moneylender, Don Fermín, and he used to say that. I've inherited it from him."

"Well, to each his own," Don Fermín said, shrugging his shoulders. "I'll take care of the deposit, the check will be ready today."

They were silent for a moment until the waiter came over to pick up the glasses and brought the menu. Don Fermín ordered a consommé and corvina, and he a steak with salad. While the waiter was setting the table, he was listening, sparingly, to Don Fermín, who was talking about a way to lose weight and still eat that had appeared in that month's *Selecciones del Reader's Digest.*

⑲

"They never invited you to the house," Santiago said. "They've always treated you as if they were better than you."

"Well, thanks to your running away we see each other more now." Uncle Clodomiro smiled. "Even if it's only for their own interest, they do come to see me all the time to get news of you. Not just Fermín, Zoilita too. It was about time that absurd distance between us came to an end."

"Where did that distance come from, uncle?" Santiago asked. "We almost never saw you."

"Zoilita's foolishness," as if he were saying charms, he thinks, Zoilita's charming manias. "Her delusions of grandeur, Skinny. I know she's a great woman, every inch a lady, naturally. But she was always stand-offish with our family because we were paupers and didn't have any family tree. She infected Fermín with it."

"And you can forgive them for that," Santiago said. "Papa spends his life insulting you and you let him."

"Your father has a horror of mediocrity." Uncle Clodomiro laughed. "He probably thinks that if we saw a lot of each other he'd become infected by me. He's always been ambitious, ever since he was a boy. He always wanted to be somebody. Well, he got to be and you can't reproach anyone for that. You should be proud instead. Because Fermín got what he has with hard work. Zoilita's family may have helped him afterward, but when they were married he already had a fine position. While your uncle was rotting away buried alive in provincial branches of the Banco de Crédito."

"You always talk about yourself as being mediocre, but underneath it all I don't think you really believe it," Santiago said. "And I don't believe it either. You may not have any money, but you live a contented life."

"Contentment isn't happiness," Uncle Clodomiro said. "That horror

261

your father has for what my life has been used to seem unjust to me, but I can understand it now. Because sometimes I start thinking and I can't find one single important memory. Office, home, home, office. Foolish little things, routines, that's all. Well, let's not get sad."

Old Inocencia came into the small living room: dinner was on the table, they could come in. Her slippers, her shawl, the apron that was too big for her small, rachitic body, her weary voice. There was a plate of stew steaming at his place, but at his uncle's there was only coffee and a sandwich.

"That's all I can eat at night," Uncle Clodomiro said. "Go ahead and start in before it gets cold."

From time to time Inocencia would come in and to Santiago how is it, is it good? She took his face in her hand, how big you'd gotten, what a fine young man you were, and when she left Uncle Clodomiro would wink: poor Inocencia, so warm to you, to everybody, poor old woman.

"I wonder why my Uncle Clodomiro never got married," Santiago says.

"Tonight you're letting all your questions out," Uncle Clodomiro said without rancor. "Well, I made the mistake of spending fifteen years in the provinces, thinking that in that way I'd get ahead faster in the bank. In those small towns I couldn't find a suitable girl."

"Don't be scandalized, what if he was?" Santiago says. "It happens in the best of families, Ambrosio."

"And when I got to Lima the shoe was on the other foot, the girls didn't think I was suitable." Uncle Clodomiro laughed. "After the bank gave me the boot, I had to start all over again at the Ministry with a miserable salary. So I stayed a bachelor. But don't think I haven't had my share of fun, nephew."

"Wait a minute, child, don't get up yet," Inocencia shouted from inside. "There's still dessert to come."

"She can barely see or hear anymore and the poor thing works all day," Uncle Clodomiro whispered. "Several times I tried to take on another girl so she could get some rest. Absolutely not, she went into a terrible fit, saying I wanted to get rid of her. She's as stubborn as a mule. She'll go straight to heaven, Skinny."

262

You're crazy, Amalia said, I haven't forgiven him and I'm not going to, she hated him. Did they fight a lot? Gertrudis asked. Not much and always because he was such a coward, if he hadn't been they would have gotten along famously. They'd see each other on their days off, go to the movies, go walking, at night she'd cross the garden in her bare feet and spend an hour with Ambrosio, two hours. All very fine, not even the other maids suspected anything. And Gertrudis: when did you realize he had another woman? The morning she saw him cleaning the car and talking to young Sparky. Amalia was looking at him out of the corner of her eye while she was putting the clothes into the washer, and suddenly she saw that he was confused and she heard what he was saying to young Sparky: me, son? What a thing to say, he could like that one? he wouldn't take her as a gift, son. Pointing to me, Gertrudis, knowing that I was listening. Amalia felt like dropping the clothes, running over and scratching him. That night she went to his room only to tell him I heard you, who do you think you are, thinking that Ambrosio would ask to be forgiven. But he didn't, Gertrudis, he didn't, nothing of the sort: go on, beat it, get out of here. She'd been confused in the darkness, Gertrudis. She wasn't going to go, why do you treat me like this, what have I done, until he got up from the bed and closed the door. Furious, Gertrudis, full of hate. Amalia had begun to cry, do you think I didn't hear what you said to the boy about me? and now why are you kicking me out, why are you treating me like this. The boy's getting suspicious, he shook her by the shoulders, with such fury, don't ever set foot in my room again, with such desperation, Gertrudis: never again, understand? get out of here. Furious, frightened, crazy, he was shaking her against the wall. It's not because of the master and the mistress, don't look for excuses, Amalia was trying to say, you've found someone else, but he dragged her to the door, pushed her out and closed it: never again, understand. And still you've forgiven him, and you still love him, Gertrudis said, and Amalia are you crazy? She hated him. Who was the other woman? She didn't know, she'd never seen her. Shamed, humiliated, she ran to her room crying so hard that the cook woke up and came in to her, Amalia had to pretend that it was her period, it always hurts me a lot. And since then never again? Never again. Naturally, he'd tried to make friends, let me explain, let's still go together, but only seeing each other outside. Hypocrite, coward, liar, damn him, Amalia's voice rose and he flew off in fright. At least he didn't leave you pregnant, Gertrudis said. And Amalia: I didn't speak to him again until later, much later. They would pass in the house and he good morning and she would turn her head away, hello Amalia and she as if a fly had passed. Maybe it wasn't an excuse, Gertrudis said, maybe he was afraid they'd catch you and fire you both, maybe he didn't have any other woman. And Amalia: do you think so? The proof that after years he saw you on the street and helped you get a job, Gertrudis said, if not, why had he looked her up, invited her out. Maybe he'd always loved her, maybe while you were with Trinidad he was pining for you, thinking about you, maybe he really was sorry for what he'd done to you. Do you think so? Amalia said, do you think so?

(2)

"You're losing a lot of money because of that attitude," Don Fermín said. "It's absurd for you to be satisfied with a paltry amount, absurd for you to keep your capital tied up in a bank."

"You still insist on my getting into the world of business." He smiled. "No, Don Fermín, I learned my lesson before. Never again."

"For every twenty or fifty thousand soles that you get, there are people getting triple the amount," Don Fermín said. "And it's not fair, because you're the one who decides things. As to the other part, when are you going to make up your mind to invest something? I've already proposed four or five things that anybody would have jumped at."

He was listening to him with a courteous smile on his lips, but his eyes were bored. The steak had been on the table for a few minutes already and he hadn't touched it.

"I explained it to you already." He picked up the knife and fork, sat looking at them. "When this government comes to an end, I'll be the one stuck with the broken dishes."

"All the more reason to secure your future," Don Fermín said.

"Everybody will jump on me and the first ones will be the people in the government," he said, looking at the meat, the salad, depressed. "As if by slinging mud at me they'll be keeping themselves clean. I'd have to be an idiot to invest a single penny in this country."

"My, you're pessimistic today, Don Cayo." Don Fermín pushed aside his consommé, the waiter brought his corvina. "Someone would think that Odría is about to fall from one moment to the next."

"Not yet," he said. "But there's no such thing as a government that lasts forever, you know that. Besides, I'm not ambitious. When all this comes to an end, I'll go live quietly outside the country, to die in peace."

He looked at his watch, tried to get through a few pieces of meat. He was chewing without pleasure, sipping mineral water, and finally he called the waiter to take the plate away.

"I've got an appointment with the Minister at three and it's two-fifteen already. Didn't we have another little matter to discuss, Don Fermín?"

Don Fermín ordered coffee for both of them, lighted a cigarette. He took an envelope out of his pocket and laid it on the table.

"I've prepared a memorandum for you so you can study the facts at your leisure, Don Cayo. A land claim in the Bagua region. They're young, dynamic engineers who aren't afraid of hard work. They want to bring in cattle, you'll see. The application has been stuck at the Ministry of Agriculture for six months."

"Did you write down the number of the application?" He put the envelope into his briefcase without looking at it.

"And the date when the whole procedure started and all the departments it's been through," Don Fermín said. "This time I haven't got any interest in the deal. They're people I want to help. Friends."

"I can't promise you anything without looking into it," he said. "Besides, I'm not too popular at the Ministry of Agriculture. In any case, I'll let you know."

"Naturally, these fellows will accept your conditions," Don Fermín said. "It's all right for me to do them a favor out of friendship, but not for you to be bothered for nothing by people you don't know."

"Naturally," he said without smiling. "I'm only bothered for nothing by the government."

They drank their coffee in silence. When the waiter brought the check they both took out their wallets, but Don Fermín paid. They went out onto the Plaza San Martín together.

"I imagine you're very busy with the President's trip to Cajamarca," Don Fermín said.

"Yes, a little. I'll call you when this matter goes through," he said, shaking hands. "There's my car. I'll see you later, Don Fermín."

He got into the car, ordered the Ministry, hurry. Ambrosio drove around the Plaza San Martín, went toward the Parque Universitario, down Abancay. He was looking through the envelope Don Fermín had given him, and sometimes his eyes would turn away and fasten on the back of Ambrosio's neck: the cocksucker didn't want his son to mix with half-breeds, he probably didn't want him to be infected with bad manners. That's probably why he invited people like Arévalo or Landa to his house, even the gringos he called boors, everybody but him. He laughed, took a pill out of his pocket and filled his mouth with saliva: he probably didn't want his wife and children infected with bad manners.

9

"You've been asking me questions all night and now it's my turn," Uncle Clodomiro said. "How are things going for you at *La Crónica?*"

"I'm learning to measure my stories now," Santiago said. "At first they were either too long or too short. I'm already used to working at night and sleeping by day too."

"That's something else that terrifies Fermín," Uncle Clodomiro said. "He thinks you're going to get sick with a schedule like that. And that you won't go to the university. Are you really attending classes?"

"No, that's a lie," Santiago said. "Since I left home I haven't been back to the university. Don't tell papa, uncle."

Uncle Clodomiro stopped rocking, his small hands moved around in alarm, his eyes were startled.

"Don't ask me why, I couldn't explain that either," Santiago said. "Sometimes I think it's because I don't want to run into the fellows that were left behind at Police Headquarters when papa got me out. Other times I realize that it's not that. I don't like the law, it all seems stupid to me, I don't believe in it, uncle. Why should I get a degree?"

266

"Fermín is right, I've done you a great disservice," Uncle Clodomiro said, downcast. "Now that you've got some money in your pockets you don't want to study."

"Didn't your friend Vallejo ever tell you what we get paid?" Santiago laughed. "No, uncle, I've got practically no money in my pockets. I've got the time, I could attend classes. But it's stronger than me, just the thought of walking into the university makes me sick to my stomach."

"Don't you realize that you can spend the rest of your life as just another little wage earner?" Uncle Clodomiro said, concerned. "A boy like you, Skinny, so bright, such a good student."

"I'm not bright and I'm not a good student, don't repeat what papa says, uncle," Santiago said. "The truth is that I'm mixed up. I know what I don't want to be, but not what I'd like to be. And I don't want to be a lawyer or rich or important, uncle. At the age of fifty I don't want to be what papa is, what papa's friends are. Can't you see that, uncle?"

"What I can see is that you've got a screw loose," Uncle Clodomiro said, with his desolate face. "I'm sorry I ever called Vallejo, Skinny. I feel responsible for the whole thing."

"If I hadn't gone to work at *La Crónica* I would have got some other job," Santiago said. "It would have come out all the same."

Would it have, Zavalita? No, it probably would have been different, probably poor Uncle Clodomiro was partly responsible. It was ten o'clock, he had to go. He got up.

"Wait, I've got to ask you something that Zoilita keeps asking me," Uncle Clodomiro said. "Every time she sees me she puts me through a terrible grilling. Who washes your clothes, who sews your buttons on?"

"The lady at the boardinghouse takes very good care of me," Santiago said. "She shouldn't worry."

"What about your days off?" Uncle Clodomiro asked. "Who do you see, where do you go? Do you go out with girls? That's something else that Zoilita loses sleep over. Whether or not you're having an affair with one of those girls, things like that."

"I'm not having an affair with anyone, get her to calm down." Santiago laughed. "Tell her I'm fine, I'm behaving myself. I'll go see them soon, I really will."

They went into the kitchen and found Inocencia asleep in her rocker.

267

Uncle Clodomiro scolded her and the two of them helped her to her room as she nodded sleepily. At the street door Uncle Clodomiro gave Santiago an embrace. Would he come to dinner next Monday? Yes, uncle. He took a taxi on the Avenida Arequipa and on the Plaza San Martín he looked for Norwin among the tables of the Zela Bar. He still hadn't arrived and after waiting for a moment he went to meet him on the Jirón de la Unión. He was at the door of *La Prensa* talking to another editor from *Última Hora*.

"What happened?" Santiago asked. "Didn't we have a date for ten o'clock at the Zela?"

"This is the most bastardly profession there is, make your mind up about that, Zavalita," Norwin said. "They took away all my writers and I had to fill the page myself. There's a revolution, some kind of dumb business. Let me introduce you to Castelano, a colleague."

"A revolution?" Santiago asked. "Here?"

"An abortive coup, something like that," Castelano said. "It seems that Espina was at the head of it, that general who was Minister of Public Order."

"There isn't any official communiqué and those bastards took my people away so they could go out and dig up some details," Norwin said. "Well, let's forget about it, let's go have a few drinks."

"Wait, I want to know," Santiago said. "Walk me to *La Crónica.*"

"They'll put you to work and you'll lose your night off," Norwin said. "Let's go have a drink and we'll stop by there around two o'clock and pick up Carlitos."

"But how did it happen?" Santiago asked. "What's the news?"

"There's no news, only rumors," Castelano said. "They started arresting people this afternoon. They say it was in Cuzco and Tumbes. The cabinet's meeting at the Palace."

"All reporters have been called in just for the fun of fucking them up," Norwin said. "They won't be able to publish anything in any case except the official communiqué and they know it."

"Instead of going to the Zela why don't we go to old Ivonne's?" Castelano asked.

"Who said that General Espina was mixed up in it?" Santiago asked.

"O.K., Ivonne's, and we can call Carlitos from there to join us,"

Norwin said. "There at the cathouse you'll find out more details of the plot than at *La Crónica,* Zavalita. And what the hell difference does it make to you? Do you give a damn about politics?"

"I was just curious," Santiago said. "Besides, I've only got about forty soles, Ivonne's is too expensive."

"That should be the least of your worries, working for *La Crónica.*" Castelano laughed. "As a colleague of Becerrita's, your credit there is unlimited."

6

AMBROSIO DIDN'T SHOW UP in San Miguel during the week that followed, but a week later Amalia found him waiting for her at the Chinaman's shop on the corner. He had sneaked away, for just a little while, to see you, Amalia. They didn't fight, they had a nice talk. They made a date for Sunday. My, you've changed, he told her as he was leaving, how nice you've become.

Could she really have got that much better? Carlota told her you've got everything a man should like, the mistress teased her along those lines too, the policemen on the block were all smiles, the master's chauffeurs all looks, even the gardener, the clerk at the food store, and the snotnose of a newsboy kept flirting with her: maybe it was true. In the house she went to look at herself in the mistress's mirrors with a roguish glow in her eyes: yes, it was true. She'd put on weight, she dressed better and that she owed to the mistress, so good she was. She gave her everything she didn't wear anymore, but not as if saying take this off my hands, but with affection. This dress doesn't fit me anymore, try it on, and the mistress would come, it has to be raised here, taken in a little here, these fringes don't look good on you. She was always telling her to clean your fingernails, comb your hair, wash your apron, a woman who doesn't take care of herself has had it. Not the way you'd talk to a servant, Amalia thought, she gives me advice as if I was her equal. The mistress had her get her hair cut in a boy's bob, once, when she had pimples, she put on one of her creams herself and in a week her face all nice and clean, another time she had a toothache and she took her to a dentist in Magdalena herself, had her fixed up, and didn't take it out of her pay. When had Señora Zoila ever treated her like that, worried about her like that? There wasn't anybody like Señora Hortensia. What was most important for her was for everything to be clean, for women to be pretty, and for men to be good-looking. It was the first thing she wanted to know about someone, was so-and-so pretty, what was he like? And one thing for sure, she never forgave anyone for being ugly. The way she made fun of Miss Maclovia because of her rabbit teeth, of Mr. Gumucio because of his belly, of the one they called Paqueta because of her artificial eyelashes and fingernails and breasts, and of Señora Ivonne because she was old. How she and Miss Queta made fun of Señora Ivonne! Dyeing her hair so much that she was going bald, how her false teeth fell out at lunch once, how the shots she took were making her more wrinkled instead of younger. They talked so much about her that Amalia was curious and one day Carlota told her there she is, she's the one who came with Miss Queta. She went out to get a look at her. They were having drinks in the living room. Señora Ivonne wasn't that old or that ugly, it wasn't fair. And such elegance, such jewels, everything sparkling all over her. When she left, the mistress came into the kitchen: forget that the old woman had been here. She threatened them with her finger, laughing: if Cayo finds out that she was here, I'll kill all three of you.

9

From the doorway he saw Dr. Arbeláez' small, shrunken face, his bony, rosy cheeks, his glasses low on his nose.

"I'm sorry I'm late, doctor." Your desk is too big for you, you poor devil. "I had a business lunch, please excuse me."

"You're right on time, Don Cayo." Dr. Arbeláez smiled at him without feeling. "Please sit down."

"I got your memo yesterday, but I couldn't come any sooner." He dragged over a chair, put his briefcase on his knees. "The President's trip to Cajamarca has been taking up all my time for the past few days."

Behind the glasses the myopic and hostile eyes of Dr. Arbeláez agreed.

"That's another matter I'd like us to talk about, Don Cayo." He

271

tightened his mouth, didn't conceal his annoyance. "The day before yesterday I asked Lozano for information on the preparations and he told me that you had given instructions that it wasn't to be given to anybody."

"Poor Lozano," he said pityingly. "You probably gave him a lecture, I imagine."

"No, no lecture," Dr. Arbeláez said. "I was so surprised that it didn't even cross my mind."

"Poor Lozano is useful but not very bright." He smiled. "The security preparations are still being studied, doctor, it isn't worth taking up your time with them. I'll let you know about everything as soon as we've completed the details."

He lighted a cigarette. Dr. Arbeláez handed him an ashtray. He was looking at him seriously, his arms folded, between a desk calendar and the photograph of a gray-haired woman and three smiling younger people.

"Did you have time to take a look at the memo, Don Cayo?"

"Of course, doctor. I read it very carefully."

"Then you probably agree with me," Dr. Arbeláez said dryly.

"I'm sorry to say I don't," he said. He coughed, excused himself and took another drag. "The security funds are sacred. I can't allow all those millions to be taken away from me. Believe me, I'm terribly sorry."

Dr. Arbeláez stood up quickly. He took a few steps in front of the desk, his glasses dancing in his hands.

"I expected that, of course." His voice was neither impatient nor furious, but he had grown noticeably pale. "However, the memo is clear, Don Cayo. We have to replace all those patrol cars that are falling apart from old age, we have to start work on the police stations in Tacna and Moquegua because they're going to collapse any day now. A thousand things are held up and prefects and subprefects are driving me crazy with their phone calls and telegrams. Where do you want me to get the millions I need? I'm not a magician, Don Cayo, I can't work miracles."

He nodded, very serious. Dr. Arbeláez was passing his glasses back and forth from one hand to the other, standing in front of him.

"Isn't there any way of using other parts of the budget?" he said. "The Minister of the Treasury . . ."

272

"He refuses to give us one penny more, and you know that quite well."
Dr. Arbeláez raised his voice. "At every cabinet meeting he says that the
expenses of the Ministry of Public Order are exorbitant, and that you
were monopolizing half of our outlay for . . ."

"I'm not monopolizing anything, doctor." He smiled. "Security demands money, what else do you want. I can't do my job if they cut my
security funds by a single penny. I'm terribly sorry, doctor."

9

There were other kinds of little jobs too, sir, but they did them, not
Ambrosio. That night we went out, Mr. Lozano said, tell Hipólito, and
Ludovico in the official car, sir? No, in the old Ford. They told him
afterward, sir, and that's how Ambrosio found out: follow guys, make
a note of who goes into a house, get arrested Apristas to confess what
they knew, that's where Hipólito got the way Ambrosio had told him
about, sir, or maybe Ludovico invented it all. When it got dark Ludovico
went to Mr. Lozano's house, got the Ford, picked up Hipólito, they went
to a crime movie at the Rialto, and at nine-thirty they were waiting for
Mr. Lozano on the Avenida España. And on the first Monday of every
month they went with Mr. Lozano to collect the monthly payoff, sir, they
say that's what he said. Naturally, he came out wearing dark glasses and
he huddled down in the back seat. He gave them cigarettes, cracked jokes
with them, what a good mood he gets into when he works for him,
Hipólito commented later, and Ludovico you'll say so when he has us
working for him. The monthly payment, the dough he got out of all the
whorehouses and shack-up joints in Lima, pretty slick, right, sir? They
started on the Chosica road, the little house hidden behind the restaurant
where chickens were for sale. You get out, Mr. Lozano said to Ludovico,
if not, Pereda will hold me up for an hour with his tales, and to Hipólito
let's take a little drive in the meantime. He was doing it on the sly, sir,
he probably thought that Don Cayo didn't know anything, later on when
Ludovico went to work with Ambrosio he told Don Cayo in order to get
in good with him and it turned out that Don Cayo knew all about it. The
Ford started up, Ludovico waited for it to disappear and pushed open
the gate. There were a lot of cars lined up, all of them with only their
parking lights on, and, bumping into fenders and bumpers trying to see

273

the faces of the couples, he got to the door where the sign was. Because what was there that Don Cayo didn't know about, sir? A waiter came out and recognized him, wait a minute, and Pereda came right away, what's this, where's Mr. Lozano? He's outside, but he's in a big hurry, Ludovico said, that's why he didn't come in. I've got to talk to him, Pereda said, it's very important. By going along with Mr. Lozano to collect the monthly payments, Ludovico and Hipólito got to know night-walking Lima, here we're kings of whoredom they said, you can imagine how they took advantage of it, sir. They walked to the gate, waited for the Ford, Ludovico got behind the wheel again and Pereda got in back: get going, Mr. Lozano said, we can't stay here. But the real wild one had been Hipólito, sir, Ludovico was mainly ambitious: he wanted to move up, that is have them put him on the regular list someday. Ludovico drove down the highway and at times would look at Hipólito and Hipólito would look back at him as if to say Pereda's such an ass-kisser, the stories he was telling him. Hurry up, I haven't got much time, Mr. Lozano said, what's so important. Why did they let him put the squeeze on them, sir? So-and-so who came by here this week, sir, what's-his-name, he brought a certain lady, and Mr. Lozano I know quite well that you know everybody in Peru, what's so important? Because couldn't he see that shack-up joints and whorehouses got permission at Headquarters, sir? Pereda changed the tone of his voice and Ludovico and Hipólito looked at each other, now the wailing would start. The engineer had been loaded down with expenses, Mr. Lozano, payments, bills, they didn't have any cash this month. So either they got it up or he'd take away their permission or fine them: they didn't have any other way out, sir. Mr. Lozano grunted and Pereda was like jelly: but the engineer hadn't forgotten his promise, Mr. Lozano, he'd left this postdated check, that didn't matter, did it, Mr. Lozano? And Ludovico and Hipólito as if saying here comes the bawling out. It matters to me, because I don't take checks, Mr. Lozano said, the engineer's got twenty-four hours to settle up because he's going to be closed down; we're going to drop Pereda off, Ludovico. And Ludovico and Hipólito said that he even got his cut from the renewal of whores' ID cards, sir. All the way back Pereda was explaining, making excuses, and Mr. Lozano not a word. Twenty-four hours, Pereda, not a minute more, he said when they got back. And afterwards:

a tightwad like that gets my balls all swollen. And Ludovico and Hipólito as if saying to each other Pereda's killed our night, he got him all worked up on us. That's why Don Cayo would say that if Lozano ever leaves the police force he'll become a pimp, sir: that's his real vocation.

9

On Saturday the telephone rang twice in the morning, the mistress went over to answer and there was nobody on the line. They're playing tricks on me, the mistress said, but in the afternoon it rang again, Amalia hello, hello? and she finally recognized Ambrosio's frightened voice. So you're the one who's been calling, she said to him laughing, nobody's here, go ahead and talk. He couldn't go out with her that Sunday or the following one either, he had to take Don Fermín to Ancón. It doesn't make any difference, Amalia said, some other day. But it did make a difference, Saturday night she couldn't get to sleep thinking. Could the business about Ancón be true? On Sunday she went out with María and Anduvia. They went walking in the Parque de la Reserva, bought some ice cream and sat on the grass chatting until some soldiers came over and they had to leave. Mightn't it have been because he had a date with someone else? They went to the movies at the Azul; they were in a good mood and, feeling safe, there being three of them, they let two fellows pay their admission. Mightn't it be that at that moment he was in some other movie theater with? But halfway through the picture they tried to take advantage and the girls ran out of the Azul with the guys behind shouting give us our money back, you swindlers! luckily they found a cop who chased them off. Mightn't it be that he'd gotten tired of what she was always reminding him about, how badly he'd behaved? All week Amalia, María and Anduvia talked about the men, and one by one they got scared, they're going to come, they've found out where we live, they're going to kill you, they're going to, with attacks of laughter until Amalia began to shake and ran home. But at night she would still think the same thing: mightn't it be that he wouldn't come to see her anymore? The next Sunday she went to visit Señora Rosario in Mirones. Celeste had run off with a guy and after three days had come back alone, with a long face. He whipped her until he drew blood, Señora Rosario said, and if the guy knocked her up I'll kill her. Amalia stayed until it was dark, feeling more

275

depressed than ever in the alley. She noticed the puddles of putrid water, the clouds of flies, the skinny dogs, and she was surprised to think that she'd wanted to spend the rest of her life in the alley when her little son and Trinidad had died. That night she woke up before dawn: what do you care if he doesn't come anymore, stupid, so much the better for you. But she was crying.

19

"In that case I'll be obliged to go to the President, Don Cayo." Dr. Arbeláez put his glasses on, silver links gleaming on the stiff cuffs of his shirt. "I've tried to maintain good relations with you, I've never asked for an accounting from you, I've let the Department of Security bypass me completely in a thousand different things. But you mustn't forget that I'm the Minister and you're under my orders."

He nodded, his eyes riveted to his shoes. He coughed, his handkerchief against his mouth. He raised his face, as if resigning himself to something that saddened him.

"You'd be wasting your time bothering the President," he said almost timidly. "I took the liberty of explaining the matter to him. Naturally I wouldn't have dared deny your request without the backing of the President."

He saw him clench his fists, remain absolutely motionless, looking at him with a detailed and devastating hatred.

"So you've already spoken to the President." His jaw was trembling, his lips, his voice. "You no doubt presented things from your point of view. Naturally."

"I'm going to speak frankly to you, doctor," he said, with no ill humor, no interest. "I am Director of Security for two reasons. First, because the General asked me. Second, because he accepted my conditions: to have at my disposal all the moneys necessary and not to have to report on my work to anyone except him personally. You have to excuse me for putting it so bluntly, but that's how things stand."

He looked at Arbeláez, waiting. His head was too big for his body, his myopic little eyes raked him over slowly, millimetrically. He saw him smile, making an effort that disfigured his mouth.

"I have no doubts about your work, I know that it's been outstanding,

276

Don Cayo." He was speaking in an artificial and panting way, his mouth was smiling, his eyes scorching him without cease. "But there are problems to be resolved and you have to help me. The security budget is exorbitant."

"Because our expenses are exorbitant," he said. "Let me show you, doctor."

"Nor do I doubt that you make use of your allotment with the greatest responsibility," Dr. Arbeláez said. "It's simply . . ."

"The cost of having loyal leaders in the unions, the network of information in working-class centers, universities and the administration." He recited that as he took a folder from his briefcase and put it on the desk. "The cost of rallies, the cost of finding out about the activities of the enemies of the government here and abroad."

Dr. Arbeláez had not looked at the folder; he was listening to him, fondling a cuff link, his little eyes still slowly hating him.

"The cost of placating malcontents, jealous people, the ambitious people who rise up every day within the government itself," he recited. "Tranquillity isn't just a matter of billy clubs, doctor, it has to do with money too. You're frowning and you have every right to. I take care of all these dirty things, you don't even have to know about them. Take a look at the papers there and tell me later if you think you can economize without jeopardizing security."

9

"But do you know why Don Cayo puts up with Mr. Lozano and his smart tricks with the shack-up joints and whorehouses, sir?" Ambrosio asked.

No sooner said than done, Mr. Lozano had lost his good humor: everybody in this country tries to be a sharpy, it was the third time Pereda'd come up with that story of a check. Ludovico and Hipólito, silent, looked at each other out of the corner of their eyes: God damn it, as if he'd been born yesterday. It wasn't enough for them to get rich by exploiting people's hot drives, they were trying to exploit him too. They weren't going to get away with it, the law would be enforced with them and then see where the shack-up joints would end up. They were already at the Claveles development, they had arrived.

277

"Get out, Ludovico," Mr. Lozano said. "Bring Gimpy out here to me."

"Because thanks to his contacts with the shack-up joints and whore-houses, Mr. Lozano knows all about people's lives and miracles," Ambrosio said. "That's what that pair said at least."

Ludovico was running toward the wall. There wasn't any line: the cars kept going around the block until one came out, then they would park in front of the gate, a signal with the lights, they'd open up for them and they would drive in. Everything was dark inside; the shadows of cars going into the garages, rays of light under the doors, the shapes of waiters bringing beer.

"Hello, Ludovico," Gimpy Melequías said. "How about a beer?"

"No time, brother," Ludovico said. "The man's waiting out there."

"Well, I don't know exactly what they found out, sir," Ambrosio said. "What woman was cheating on her husband and who with, what husband on his wife and who with. I imagine it was something like that."

Melequías limped to the wall and took down his jacket, grabbed Ludovico by the arm: be my cane so I can move faster, brother. All the way to the Pan-American Highway he didn't stop talking, the way he always did, and always about the same thing: his fifteen years on the force. And not just as a simple auxiliary, Ludovico, on the list, and about the hoodlums who'd fucked up his leg with their knives that time.

"And that information was very useful to Don Cayo, don't you think, sir?" Ambrosio said. "Knowing intimate things like that about people, he had them right in the palm of his hand, don't you think?"

"You ought to thank those hoodlums, Melequías," Ludovico said. "Thanks to them you've got this soft little job right here where you must be lining your pockets."

"Don't you believe it, Ludovico." They watched the cars humming by on the Pan-American Highway, no sign of the Ford. "I miss the force. A sacrifice, yes, but that was living. You know, brother, you've got a home here whenever you want. Free room, free service, even free drinks for you, Ludovico. Look, there comes the car."

"That pair thought that Mr. Lozano worked his blackmail with the information he got from the shack-up joints," Ambrosio said. "That he

278

got his cuts too so that people could avoid a scandal. A good man for that kind of business, right, sir?"

"I hope you haven't come to me with any sad tales, Gimpy," Mr. Lozano said. "Because I'm in a bad mood."

"What an idea," Gimpy Melequías said. "Here's your envelope with best regards from the boss, Mr. Lozano."

"What do you know, that's more like it." And Ludovico and Hipólito as if saying he's got him completely tamed. "What about that other matter, Gimpy, did the subject show up here?"

"He showed up on Wednesday," Gimpy said. "In the same car as last time, Mr. Lozano."

"Fine, Gimpy," Mr. Lozano said. "Well done, Gimpy."

"Do I think it was bad?" Ambrosio asked. "Well, sir, on the one hand of course it was, right? But police affairs, political affairs are never very clean. Working with Don Cayo you get to find that out, sir."

"But there was an accident, Mr. Lozano." Ludovico and Hipólito: he's caught him again. "No, I didn't forget how to work the machine, the guy you sent did a perfect job of setting it up. I turned it on myself."

"Where are the tapes, then?" Mr. Lozano asked. "Where are the pictures?"

"The dogs ate them, sir." Hipólito and Ludovico didn't look at each other, they twisted their mouths, hunched over. "They ate half of the tape, they tore up the pictures. The package was on top of the refrigerator, Mr. Lozano, and the animals . . .".

"Enough, Gimpy, enough," Mr. Lozano grunted. "You're not an imbecile, you're something else, words can't describe what you are, Gimpy. The dogs? The dogs ate them up?"

"Great big dogs, sir," Gimpy Melequías said. "The boss got them, hungry dogs, they eat anything they come across, they'd even eat a person if he didn't watch out. But the subject is sure to come back and . . ."

"Go see a doctor," Mr. Lozano said. "There must be some kind of treatment, injections, something, there must be some cure for such stupidity. Dogs, Jesus Christ, the dogs ate them. So long, Gimpy. Get going,

279

don't blame yourself and beat it now. To the Meiggs Extension, Ludovico."

"And besides, it wasn't just Mr. Lozano who took advantage," Ambrosio said. "Didn't Don Cayo too, in a different way? That pair said that on the force everybody on the list took bribes in some way, from the highest down to the lowest. That's why Ludovico's great dream was to become a regular. You mustn't think that everybody's as honest and decent as you are, sir."

"You get out this time, Hipólito," Mr. Lozano said. "Let them start getting to know you, since they won't be seeing Ludovico's face for quite a while."

"What do you mean by that, Mr. Lozano?" Ludovico asked.

"Don't play dumb, you know damned well why," Mr. Lozano said. "Because you're going to go to work for Mr. Bermúdez, just the way you wanted to, right?"

9

In the middle of the next week, Amalia was cleaning the mantel when the bell rang. She went to open the door and Don Fermín's face. Her knees shook, she was barely able to stammer good morning.

"Is Don Cayo in?" He didn't answer her greeting, he came into the living room almost without looking at her. "Please tell him that Zavala is here."

He didn't recognize you, she guessed, half frightened, half resentful, and at that moment the mistress appeared on the stairs: come in, Fermín, sit down, Cayo was on his way, he'd just called, could she give him a drink? Amalia closed the door, slipped into the pantry and spied. Don Fermín was looking at his watch, his eyes were impatient and his face worried, the mistress served him a glass of whiskey. What had happened to Cayo, he was always so punctual I don't think you like my company, you're so restless, the mistress said, I'm going to get angry. They treated each other with such familiarity, Amalia was startled. She went out the service entrance, crossed the garden, and Ambrosio had gone off a little way from the house. He greeted her with a terrified face: did he see you, did he talk to you?

"He didn't even recognize me," Amalia said. "Have I changed that much?"

"That's good, that's good." Ambrosio took a deep breath as if life was coming back to him; he was shaking his head, still upset, and looking at the house.

"Always secrets, always afraid," Amalia said. "I may have changed, but you're still the same."

But she said it with a smile so that he could see she wasn't mad at him, that she was teasing, and she thought how happy you are to see him, stupid. Now Ambrosio was laughing too and with his hands he made her understand what we were saved from, Amalia. He got a little closer to her and all of a sudden he took her hand: could they go out that Sunday, could they meet at the streetcar stop at two o'clock? All right, then, Sunday.

"So Don Fermín and Don Cayo have got to be friends again," Amalia said. "So Don Fermín will be coming around now. One of these days he's going to recognize me."

"Just the opposite, they're real enemies now," Ambrosio said. "Don Cayo is ruining Don Fermín's business because he's the friend of some general who tried to start a revolution."

He was telling her that when they saw Don Cayo's black car turning the corner, there he is, run, and Amalia went into the house. Carlota was waiting for her in the kitchen, her big eyes crazy with curiosity: did she know that man's chauffeur, what were they talking about, what did he say to you, he was a good-looking fellow, wasn't he? She was telling her some lies and then the mistress called her: take this tray up to the study, Amalia. She went up with the glasses and ashtrays that were dancing about, trembling, thinking that fool Ambrosio has infected me with his fear, what'll I say if he recognizes me. But he didn't recognize her: Don Fermín's eyes looked at her for a second without seeing her and turned away. He was sitting and tapping his foot, impatient. She put the tray on the desk and left. They were closeted for half an hour. They were arguing, you could hear their voices in the kitchen, loud, and the mistress came and closed the pantry door so they couldn't hear. When from the kitchen she saw Don Fermín's car leaving, she went up to get the tray.

281

The mistress and the master were talking in the living room. Such shouting, the mistress was saying, and the master: the rat was trying to get away when he thought the ship was sinking, now he's paying for it and he doesn't like it. What right did he have to call Don Fermín a rat? he was more respectable and a nicer person than he was, Amalia thought. He must have been jealous of him, and Carlota tell me, who was it, what were they talking about?

19

"I too have this job because the President asked me," Dr. Arbeláez said, softening his voice, and he thought good, let's make peace. "I'm trying to do something positive and . . ."

"Everything positive done in this ministry is done by you, doctor," he said forcefully. "I take care of the negative side. No, I'm not joking, it's true. I assure you that I'm doing you a great service, relieving you of everything that has to do with everyday police work."

"I didn't mean to offend you, Don Cayo," Dr. Arbeláez' chin wasn't trembling anymore.

"I'm not offended, doctor," he said. "I would have liked to have made those cuts in the security budget. I simply can't. You'll see that for yourself."

Dr. Arbeláez picked up the folder and handed it to him.

"Take it, you don't have to give me any proof, I believe you without it." He tried to smile, scarcely parting his lips. "We'll find some way to fix up those patrol cars and start the repairs in Tacna and Moquegua."

They shook hands, but Dr. Arbeláez didn't get up to see him to the door. He went directly to his office and Dr. Alcibíades went in behind him.

"The Major and Lozano have just left, Don Cayo." He handed him an envelope. "Bad news from Mexico, it seems."

Two typewritten pages, corrected by hand, notes in the margin in nervous writing. Dr. Alcibíades lighted his cigarette while he read, slowly.

"So the plot is taking shape." He loosened his tie, folded the papers and put them back in the envelope. "Did this seem so urgent to the Major and Lozano?"

282

"There were meetings of Apristas in Trujillo and Chiclayo, and Lozano and the Major think they have something to do with the news that the exile group is getting ready to leave Mexico," Dr. Alcibíades said. "They've gone to talk to Major Paredes."

"I hope those birds come back to the country so we can lay our hands on them," he said, yawning. "But they won't. This is the tenth or eleventh time, doctor, don't forget that. Tell the Major and Lozano that we'll get together tomorrow. There's no rush."

"The people from Cajamarca called to confirm the meeting at five o'clock, Don Cayo."

"Yes, fine." He took an envelope out of his briefcase and gave it to him. "Will you find out how this matter is going? It's a land claim in Bagua. Do it personally, doctor."

"First thing tomorrow, Don Cayo." Dr. Alcibíades thumbed through the memo, nodding. "Yes, how many signatures are missing, what reports there are, I'll find out. Fine, Don Cayo."

"Any moment now we'll get the news that the money for the plot has disappeared." He smiled, looking in the envelope from the Major and Lozano. "Any moment now the leaders will be accusing each other of being traitors and thieves. Sometimes you get bored with the same things always happening, don't you?"

Dr. Alcibíades nodded and smiled politely.

ø

"Why do I think you're so honest and decent?" Ambrosio asked. "Please, don't ask me hard questions like that, sir."

"Are they really going to assign me to take care of Mr. Bermúdez, Mr. Lozano?" Ludovico asked.

"You're bursting with happiness," Mr. Lozano said. "You worked it all out quite well with Ambrosio, didn't you?"

"I don't want you to think I don't want to work with you, Mr. Lozano," Ludovico said. "The fact is that the black fellow and I have gotten to be good friends and he's always telling me why don't you put in for a transfer and me no, I'm happy working with Mr. Lozano. Maybe Ambrosio made the request on his own, sir."

"All right." Mr. Lozano began to laugh. "It's a step up for you and

283

I think it's only right that you should want to better yourself."

"Well, starting with the way you talk to people," Ambrosio said. "You don't start off insulting people as soon as they turn their backs the way Don Cayo does. You don't put anyone down, you say good things about people, you're polite."

"I put in a good word with Bermúdez about you," Mr. Lozano said. "You do your job, you've got guts, everything the black fellow said about you was true. You won't be mad at me. You know, all I had to do was say you were no good and Bermúdez would have taken my advice. So you owe this promotion to me as much as to your black friend."

"Of course, Mr. Lozano," Ludovico said. "I don't know how to thank you, sir. I don't know how to make it up to you, I mean it."

"I do," Mr. Lozano said. "By behaving yourself, Ludovico."

"You just say the word and there I am, at your orders for whatever you want, Mr. Lozano."

"Keeping your tongue tucked away in your pocket too," said Mr. Lozano. "You never went out with me in the Ford, you don't know what a monthly payoff is. You can make it up to me that way, understand?"

"I swear you didn't have to tell me that, Mr. Lozano," Ludovico said. "I swear it wasn't necessary. What do you think I am?"

"You know that it's up to me if you want to get on the regular list someday," Mr. Lozano said. "Or if you never want to get on it, Ludovico."

"And the way you treat people too," Ambrosio said. "So elegant, always saying nice things to them, intelligent things. I can hear when you're talking to someone, sir."

"Here come Hipólito and Half-breed Cigüeña," Ludovico said.

They got into the Ford and Ludovico was so happy with the news of his transfer that I started driving the wrong way, he told Ambrosio later. Half-breed Cigüeña was repeating his usual tales.

"The plumbing broke down and it cost a lot of money, Mr. Lozano. Besides, we're getting fewer and fewer customers every day. People in Lima just aren't screwing anymore and we're going broke."

"Well, if business is that bad, then you won't mind if I shut you down tomorrow," Mr. Lozano said.

"You think they're lies I'm making up so I won't have to give you the payoff, Mr. Lozano," Half-breed Cigüeña protested. "But they're not, here it is, you know that it's something sacred with me. I'm only telling you my troubles as a friend, Mr. Lozano, so you'll know what they are."

"And the way you treat me too," Ambrosio said. "The way you listen to me, the way you ask me questions, the way we talk together. The trust you have in me. My whole life has changed ever since I came to work for you, sir."

7

ON SUNDAY, AMALIA TOOK AN HOUR to get herself ready and even Símula, always so dry, teased her Lord of mercy, such preparations to go out. Ambrosio was already at the streetcar stop when she got there and he squeezed her hand so hard that Amalia gave a little cry. He was laughing, happy, blue suit, a shirt as white as his teeth, a small tie with red and white dots: you always made him jumpy, Amalia, now too, he'd been wondering whether or not you were going to stand me up. The streetcar was half empty when it arrived and, before she sat down, Ambrosio took out his handkerchief and dusted off the seat. The window seat for the queen, he said, bowing deeply. Such a good mood, how he'd changed, and she told him: how different you get when you're not afraid they're going to catch me with you. And he was happy because he was thinking of other times, Amalia. The conductor was looking at them, amused, with the tickets in his hand, and Ambrosio sent him on his way asking him anything else we can do for you? You scared him, Amalia said, and he yes, this time nobody was going to come between them, no conductor and no textile worker. He looked seriously into her eyes: did I behave bad, did I go off with another woman? Misbehaving was when you left your woman for another one, Amalia, we fought because you didn't understand what I was asking of you. If she hadn't been so flighty, so stuck-up, they could have kept on seeing each other on the outside and he tried to put his arm around her shoulder, but Amalia took it away: let me go, you behaved bad, and there was laughter. The streetcar had filled up. They were silent for a while and then he changed the subject: they'd stop by and see Ludovico for a minute, Ambrosio had to talk to him, then they'd be alone and do whatever Amalia wanted to do. She told him that Don Cayo and Don Fermín were raising their voices in the study and that the master said afterward that Don Fermín was a rat. He's more likely the rat, Ambrosio said, after being such good friends now he's trying to make him go under in his business deals. Downtown they took a bus to Rímac and walked a couple of blocks. It was here, Amalia, on the Calle Chiclayo. She followed him to the end of a hallway, saw him take out a key.

"Do you think I'm crazy?" she said, taking his arm. "Your friend isn't here. The place is empty."

"Ludovico will be along later," Ambrosio said. "We'll talk while we wait for him."

"Let's walk while we talk," Amalia said. "I'm not going in there."

They argued in the muddy flagstone courtyard, watched by children who stopped running around, until Ambrosio opened the door and made her go in, with a shove, laughing. Everything was dark for Amalia for a few seconds until Ambrosio turned on the light.

9

He left the office at a quarter to five and Ludovico was already in the car, sitting next to Ambrosio. To the Paseo Colón, the Cajamarca Club. He was quiet and kept his eyes lowered during the ride, more sleep, more sleep. Ludovico accompanied him to the door of the club: should he go in, Don Cayo? No, wait here. He began to go up the stairs when he saw the tall figure appear on the landing, Senator Heredia's gray head, and he smiled: maybe Mrs. Heredia was here. They've all arrived, he shook hands with the senator, a miracle of punctuality among Peruvians. He should come in, the meeting would be in the reception room. Lights on, mirrors with gilt frames on the ancient walls, photographs of mustachioed old dodderers, men clustered together who stopped murmuring when they saw them come in: no, there weren't any women. The deputies came over, they introduced him to the others: names and surnames, hands, how do you do, good evening, he thought Mrs. Heredia and

287

Hortensia, Queta, Maclovia? he heard at your orders, delighted, and he glimpsed buttoned vests, hard collars, stiff handkerchiefs sticking out of jacket pockets, ruddy cheeks, and waiters in white jackets who served drinks, hors d'oeuvres. He accepted a glass of orangeade and thought so distinguished, so white, those well-cared-for hands, those manners of a woman used to giving orders, and he thought Queta so dark, so coarse, so vulgar, so used to serving.

"If you want, we can get started right away, Don Cayo," Senator Heredia said.

"Yes, senator," she and Queta, yes, "whenever you want."

The waiters arranged the chairs, the men sat down holding their pisco sours, there must have been twenty of them, he and Senator Heredia sat facing them. Well, here they were all together to talk informally about the President's visit to Cajamarca, the senator said, that city which everyone present loved so much and he thought: she could be her maid. Yes, she was her maid, a triple reason for rejoicing by the people of Cajamarca the senator was saying, not here but in the ranch house she probably had in Cajamarca, because of the honor that his visit to our region means the senator was saying, a ranch house full of old furniture and long hallways and bedrooms with thick vicuña rugs which she probably lazed about on while her husband attended to his senatorial duties in the capital, and because he is going to inaugurate a new bridge and the first stretch of the highway the senator was saying, a house full of pictures and servants, but her favorite maid was probably Quetita, her Quetita. Senator Heredia stood up: above all, an occasion for the people of Cajamarca to show their gratitude to the President for these public works which are so important for the department and the country. A movement of chairs, hands, as if they were going to applaud, but the senator was already speaking again, Quetita the one who probably served her breakfast in bed and listened to her confidences and kept her secrets: that's why this Reception Committee has been named, consisting of, and he noticed out of the corner of his eye that when they heard their names those mentioned smiled or blushed. The object of this meeting is to coordinate the program put together by the government itself for the presidential visit, and the senator turned to look at him: Cajamarca was a hospitable and a thankful place, Don Cayo, Odría would receive a welcome worthy of his accomplishments at the head of the nation's high destiny. He didn't get up; the glimmer of a smile, he thanked the distinguished Senator Heredia, the parliamentary delegation from Cajamarca for their selfless efforts to make the visit a success, in the back of the room behind some fluttering sheer curtains the two shadows dropped down beside each other in heat on a feather mattress that received them noiselessly, the members of the Reception Committee for having had the goodness to come to Lima to exchange ideas, and immediately muffled bold laughter broke out and the shadows clung together and rolled and were one single form on the white sheets under the curtains: he too was convinced that the visit would be a success, gentlemen.

"Excuse me for interrupting," Deputy Saravia said. "I just want to let you know that Cajamarca is going to turn its house inside out to receive General Odría."

He smiled, nodded, sure that it would be that way, but there was one detail about which he wanted to get the opinion of those present, Engineer Saravia: the rally on the Plaza de Armas, where the President would speak. Because the ideal thing would be, he coughed, softened his voice, for the rally to come off in such a way, he searched for words, that the President would not feel disappointed. The rally would be an unprecedented success, Don Cayo, the senator interrupted him, and there were confirmatory murmurs and nodding of heads, and behind the curtains it was all muffled sounds, rubbing and soft panting, an agitation of sheets and hands and mouths and skins that sought each other out and came together.

(9)

Mr. Santiago, the taps on the door came again, Mr. Santiago and he opened his eyes, ran a heavy hand across his face and went to open the door, dulled by sleep: Señora Lucía.

"Did I wake you up? I'm sorry, but did you hear the radio, hear what's happening?" She was stumbling over her words, her face excited, her eyes alarmed. "A general strike in Arequipa, they say that Odría may name a military cabinet. What's going to happen, Mr. Santiago?"

"Nothing, Señora Lucía," Santiago said. "The strike will last a couple of days and will end and the gentlemen of the Coalition will come back to Lima and everything will go on the same. Don't worry about it."

"But some people were killed, there were some wounded." Her little eyes sparkled as if they had counted the dead, seen the wounded. "At the Arequipa theater. The Coalition was holding a rally and the Odriists got in and there was a fight and the police threw bombs. It came out in *La Prensa,* Mr. Santiago. Dead, wounded. Is there going to be a revolution, Mr. Santiago?"

"No, ma'am," Santiago said. "Besides, why should you be afraid? If there's a revolution nothing's going to happen to you."

"But I don't want the Apristas to come back," Señora Lucía said, frightened. "Do you think they're going to throw Odría out?"

"The Coalition has nothing to do with the Apristas." Santiago laughed. "They're four millionaires who used to be friends of Odría and have had a falling out with him now. It's a fight among first cousins. And really, what does it matter to you whether the Apristas come back or not?"

"They're atheists, Communists," Señora Lucía said. "Aren't they?"

"No, ma'am, they're neither atheists nor Communists," Santiago said. "They're more right-wing than you are and they hate the Communists more than you do. But don't worry, they're not coming back and Odría still has some time left."

"You and your jokes all the time, Mr. Santiago," Señora Lucía said. "Excuse me for waking you up, I thought that as a newspaperman you'd have more news. Lunch will be ready in a little while."

Señora Lucía closed the door and he took a long stretch. While he was taking a shower he laughed to himself: silent nocturnal figures were coming through the windows of the old house in Barranco, Señora Lucía woke up howling, the Apristas! out of her mind, stiff with fright, she hugged her mewing cat and watched the invaders opening closets, trunks and dressers and taking away her dusty rags, her holey blankets, her moth-eaten clothes: the Apristas, the atheists, the Communists! They were coming back to steal the possessions of proper people like Señora Lucía, he thinks. He thinks: poor Señora Lucía, if you'd only known that according to my mother you weren't a proper person either. He was finishing dressing when Señora Lucía returned: lunch was ready. That pea soup and that lonely potato, a shipwrecked sailor in a plate of green water, he thinks, those stale vegetables with slices of shoe sole that Señora Lucía called beef stew. Clock Radio was turned on, Señora Lucía was listening with her forefinger to her lips: all activity in Arequipa was at a standstill, there had been a demonstration on the Plaza de Armas and the leaders of the Coalition had once more called for the resignation of the Minister of Government, Mr. Cayo Bermúdez, whom they held responsible for the serious incidents of the night before at the Municipal Theater, the government had called for calm and warned that it would not tolerate any disorders. Did he see, did he see, Mr. Santiago?

"You're probably right, Odría probably is going to fall," Santiago said. "Radio stations didn't use to dare broadcast news like that."

"What if the Coalition comes to power instead of Odría, will things be better?" Señora Lucía asked.

"They'll be the same or worse, ma'am," Santiago said. "But without military men and without Cayo Bermúdez maybe it wouldn't be so noticeable."

"You're always joking," Señora Lucía said. "You don't even take politics seriously."

"And when the old man was in the Coalition?" Santiago asks. "Didn't you get involved? Didn't you help out at the demonstrations the Coalition organized against Odría?"

"Not when I worked for Don Cayo and not when I worked for your papa," Ambrosio says. "I never got involved in politics, son."

"I have to go now," Santiago said. "I'll see you later, ma'am."

He went into the street and only then did he discover the sun, a cold winter sun that had rejuvenated the geraniums in the tiny garden. A car was parked across from the boardinghouse and Santiago passed by it without looking, but he vaguely noticed that the car started up and was going along beside him. He turned around and looked: hi, Skinny. Sparky was smiling at him from behind the wheel, on his face the expression of a child who has just been into mischief and doesn't know whether he'll be celebrated or scolded. He opened the car door, got in, and now Sparky was enthusiastically patting him on the back, God damn it you see I found you, and he was laughing with nervous joy, I did by God.

"How in hell did you find the boardinghouse?" Santiago asked.

"Lots of headwork, Superbrain." Sparky tapped his forehead, gave a big laugh, but he couldn't hide his emotion, he thinks, his confusion. "It took me a long time, but I finally found you, Skinny."

Dressed in beige, a cream-colored shirt, a pale green tie, and he looked tanned, strong and healthy, and you remembered that you hadn't changed your shirt for three days, Zavalita, that you hadn't shined your shoes for a month, and that your suit certainly must have been wrinkled and stained, Zavalita.

"Shall I tell you how I found you, Superbrain? I stationed myself in front of *La Crónica* for nights on end. The folks thought I was on a spree and there I was waiting to follow you. Twice I got you mixed up with somebody else who got out of the taxi before you. But yesterday I caught you and saw you go into the house. I must say I was a little worried, Superbrain."

"Did you think I was going to throw stones at you?" Santiago asked.

"Not stones, but I did think you'd go half crazy," and he blushed. "Since you're such a nut and no one can figure you out, what the hell. I'm glad you behaved like a good guy, Superbrain."

19

The room was large and dirty, cracked and stained walls, an unmade bed, a man's clothing hanging from hooks nailed to the wall. Amalia saw a screen, a pack of Incas on the night table, a cracked washbasin, a small mirror, it smelled of urine and from being closed up, and she realized that she was crying. Why had he brought her here? she was muttering, and always lies, so low that she could scarcely hear it herself, saying let's go see my friend, he wanted to trick her, take advantage, give her a kick in the pants like last time. Ambrosio had sat down on the unmade bed, and, through her big tears, Amalia saw him shaking his head, you don't understand me. What was she crying about? he was speaking lovingly, was it because I pushed you? looking at her with a contrite and mournful expression, you were making a scandal out there with your stubbornness about not coming in, Amalia, the whole neighborhood would have come asking what's going on, what would Ludovico have said later. He had lighted one of the cigarettes on the night table and slowly he began to observe her, her feet, her knees, he went unhurriedly up her body and

292

when he reached her eyes he smiled at her and she felt hot and ashamed: what a stupid girl you are. She made her face look as annoyed as she could. Ludovico would be there any minute, Amalia, he'd come and they'd leave, am I doing anything to you? and she you better watch out if you do. Come here, Amalia, sit down, let's talk awhile. She wasn't going to sit down, open the door, she wanted to leave. And he: did you start crying when the textile worker took you to his place? Her face grew bitter and Amalia thought he's jealous, he's furious, and she felt her anger leaving her. He wasn't like you, she said looking at the floor, and he wasn't ashamed of me, thinking he's going to stand up and hit you, he wouldn't have thrown me out because he was afraid of losing his job, thinking come on stand up, come on hit me, I came first with him, thinking stupid girl, you're hoping he'll kiss you. He twisted his mouth, his eyes were popping, he dropped the butt on the floor and squashed it. Amalia had her pride, you're not going to trick me twice, and he looked at her anxiously: if that guy hadn't died I swear to you I would have killed him, Amalia. Now he really was going to dare, now he was. Yes, he jumped up, and anyone else who got in his way too, and she saw him approach decisively, his voice a little hoarse: because you're my woman, that's what you're going to be. She didn't move, she let him take her by the shoulders and then she pushed him with all her might and saw him stumble and laugh, Amalia, Amalia, and try to grab her again. That's what they were doing, running around, pushing each other, pulling each other, when the door opened and Ludovico's face, looking very downcast.

(9)

He put out his cigarette, lighted another, crossed his legs, those listening leaned their heads forward so as not to lose a single word, and he listening to his own tired voice: the twenty-sixth had been declared a holiday, instructions had been given to the principals of private and public schools to bring their students to the square, that would guarantee a good turnout, and Mrs. Heredia would be watching the rally from a balcony of the City Hall, so tall, so serious, so white, so elegant, and in the meantime, he would already be at the ranch house convincing the maid: a thousand, two thousand, three thousand soles, Quetita? But of course, he smiled and with a glance saw that they were all smiling, it wasn't a question of the President's talking to schoolchildren, and the maid would say fine, three thousand, wait here and she'd hide him behind a screen. He had also calculated that civil servants would attend, but that wouldn't mean many people, and he there, motionless, hidden in the dark, would wait, looking at the vicuña rugs and the pictures and the broad bed with a canopy and curtains. He coughed, uncrossed his legs: the propaganda had been organized, besides. News items in the local press and on the radio, cars and vans with loudspeakers would go through the city passing out handbills and that would attract more people and he would count the minutes, the seconds, and feel his bones dissolving and icy drops running down his back and finally: there she would be, there she would come. But, and he leaned over and faced the men crowded together with charm and humility, since Cajamarca was an agricultural center it was hoped that the main body of those at the rally would come from the countryside, and that depended on you gentlemen. He would see her there, tall, white, elegant, serious, she would come in and sail across the vicuña rug and he would hear I'm so tired and she would call for her Quetita. Permit me, Don Cayo, Senator Heredia said, Don Remigio Saldívar, President of the Reception Committee and one of the most representative figures of those involved in agriculture in Cajamarca, has something to say about the rally, and he saw a heavy-set man, tan as an ant, strangled by a jowly neck, stand up in the second row. And there Quetita would come and she would tell her I'm tired, I want to go to bed, help me and Quetita would help her, would slowly undress her and he would watch, feel every pore in his body grow warm, millions of tiny craters on his skin begin to erupt. You'll have to excuse me, all of you and especially you, Mr. Bermúdez, Don Remigio Saldívar cleared his throat, he was a man of action, not speeches, that is, I can't speak as well as Fleafoot Heredia and the senator gave a chuckle and there was an outburst of laughter. He opened his mouth, wrinkled his face, and there she would be, white, naked, serious, elegant, motionless, while Quetita would delicately take off her stockings, kneeling at her feet, and with laughter they all celebrated Don Remigio Saldívar's oratorical prowess concerning his lack of oratory, and he heard come to the point Remigio, that's Cajamarca Don Remigio: she would roll them in slow motion and he would see the maid's hands, so large, so dark, so rough, lowering, lowering them over the legs that were so white, so white, and Don Remigio Saldívar assumed a hieratic expression: getting down to the matter at hand he wanted to tell them that he shouldn't worry, Mr. Bermúdez, they had thought about it, discussed it and taken all the necessary measures. Now she would have lain down on the bed and he would discern her lying white and perfect behind the curtains, and he would hear her you get undressed too Queta, come here Quetita. There wasn't even any need for the schoolchildren or the civil servants, there'd be so many people they wouldn't fit in the square, Mr. Bermúdez: it would be better for them to stick to their books and their jobs. Quetita would get undressed and she quick, quick, and her shoes would fall noiselessly on the vicuña rug. Don Remigio Saldívar made an energetic gesture: we'll supply the people for the rally, not the government, the people of Cajamarca wanted the President to have a good impression of our region. Now Quetita would run, fly, her long arms would pull and separate the curtains and her big burned body would silently descend onto the sheets: keep that in mind, Mr. Bermúdez. He had changed his merry tone and his rustic mannerisms for a grave, proud voice and solemn gestures and they were all listening: the agricultural community had collaborated magnificently in the preparations, and the business and professional men too, keep that in mind. And he would come out from behind the screen and get closer, his body would be like a torch, he would go up to the curtains, he would look and his heart would be in agony: keep in mind that we'll have forty thousand men in the square, if not more. There they would be under his eyes, embracing, smelling each other, perspiring on each other, getting all knotted together and Don Remigio Saldívar paused to take out a cigarette and look for matches, but Deputy Azpilcueta lighted it for him: it wasn't a problem of people, far from it, Mr. Bermúdez, but transportation, as he'd already explained to Fleafoot Heredia, laughter, and he automatically opened his mouth and wrinkled his brow. They couldn't come up with the number of trucks they needed to bring the people from the ranches and then back again, and Don Remigio Saldívar let out a mouthful of smoke that whitened his face: we've found twenty-odd buses and trucks, but they'd need a lot more. He leaned forward in his chair: you don't have to worry about that part, Mr. Saldívar, they could count on all facilities. The dark hands and the white ones, the thick-lipped mouth and the thin-lipped one, the rough, inflated nipples and the small, crystalline, soft ones, the tanned thighs and the transparent ones with blue veins, the dark straight hair and the golden curls: the military commandant would furnish them with all the trucks they needed, Mr. Saldívar, and he wonderful, Mr. Bermúdez, that's what we were going to ask for, if they had transportation they'd fill up the square as no one had ever seen in the history of Cajamarca. And he: you can all count on that, Mr. Saldívar. But there was also another matter he wanted to talk to them about.

19

"You took me by such surprise I didn't have time to get all worked up," Santiago said.

"The old man's in hiding," Sparky said, getting serious. "Popeye's father took him to his ranch. I came to let you know."

"In hiding?" Santiago asked. "Because of the trouble in Arequipa?"

"That bastard Bermúdez has had the house watched for a month," Sparky said. "Plainclothesmen follow the old man night and day. Popeye had to sneak him out in his car. Well, I imagine it won't occur to them to look for him on Arévalo's ranch. He wanted you to know about it, in case anything happened."

"Uncle Clodomiro told me that the old man had joined the Coalition, that he'd broken with Bermúdez," Santiago said. "But I didn't know that things were that serious."

"You've already seen what happened in Arequipa," Sparky said. "The Arequipans are standing firm. A general strike until Bermúdez resigns. They're going to get him out, God damn it. Just imagine, the old man was all set to go to that rally. Arévalo talked him out of it at the last minute."

"But I don't understand," Santiago said. "Did Popeye's father break with Odría too? Isn't he still the Odríist leader in the senate?"

"Officially, yes," Sparky said. "But underneath he's fed up with those shitheads too. He's behaved very well with the old man. Better than you, Superbrain. With all the trouble the old man's been going through this time, you still didn't go to see him."

"Was he sick?" Santiago asked. "Uncle Clodomiro didn't . . ."

"Not sick, but with a noose around his neck," Sparky said. "Didn't you know that after the little trick you played on him by running away that something worse fell on him? That son of a bitch Bermúdez thought he was mixed up in Espina's plot and set out to fuck him."

"Oh yes, that," Santiago said. "Uncle Clodomiro told me that he'd taken away the concession the laboratory had in the armed forces post exchanges."

"That was nothing, the worst part was that business with the construction company," Sparky said. "They haven't given us another nickel, they stopped all pay orders and we have to keep on paying off the letters of credit. And they've demanded that the work continue at the same pace and threaten us with a suit for breach of contract. A war to the death against the old man, to sink him. But the old man is a fighter and he won't give in, that's what's so great about him. He joined the Coalition and . . ."

"I'm glad the old man has turned against the government," Santiago said. "I'm glad that you're not an Odríist anymore too."

"You mean you're glad we're heading into ruin." Sparky smiled.

"Tell me about mama, about Teté," Santiago said. "Uncle Clodomiro says she's going with Popeye, is that true?"

"The one who's happy about your running away is Uncle Clodomiro." Sparky laughed. "With the excuse of bringing news from you, he pops by the house three times a week. Yes, she's going with Freckle Face, they don't keep such a tight rein on her anymore, they even let her go out to dinner with him on Saturdays. They'll end up getting married, I imagine."

"Mama must be happy," Santiago said. "She's been planning that match ever since Teté was born."

"All right, now you tell me," Sparky said, trying to appear jovial, but blushing. "When are you going to stop this foolishness, when are you coming back to live at home?"

"I'm never going back to live at home, Sparky," Santiago said. "We'd better change the subject."

"And why aren't you ever going to come back to live at home?" pretending to be surprised, Zavalita, trying to make you believe he didn't believe. "What have the folks done to you to make you not want to live with them? Stop playing the nut, man."

"Let's not get into a fight," Santiago said. "Do me a favor instead. Take me to Chorrillos, I've got to pick up a colleague, we're going on an assignment together."

"I didn't come to pick a fight with you, but nobody can figure you out," Sparky said. "You pick up and move overnight without anyone's having done anything to you, you don't show your face again, you fight with everybody in the family just because you feel like it. How in hell do you think anyone could ever figure you out, damn it?"

"Don't figure me out, just take me to Chorrillos, I'm late," Santiago said. "You've got time, haven't you?"

"O.K.," Sparky said. "O.K., Superbrain, I'll take you."

He started up the motor and turned on the radio. They were giving news about the strike in Arequipa.

❦

"Excuse me, I didn't want to bother you, but I have to pick up my clothes, I'm leaving on a trip right away." And Ludovico's face and voice were as bitter as if it were a trip to the grave. "Hello, Amalia."

Without looking at her, as if she were something Ludovico had seen in his room all his life, Amalia felt terribly ashamed. Ludovico had knelt down by the bed and was dragging out a suitcase. He began to put the clothes hanging from the hooks on the wall into the valise. He wasn't even surprised to see you, stupid girl, he knew you were there, Ambrosio had probably borrowed the room in order to, it was a lie that they had to see each other, Ludovico had just happened to come by. Ambrosio seemed uncomfortable. He had sat down on the bed and was smoking while he watched Ludovico arrange his shirts and socks in the suitcase.

"They take you here, they send you there," Ludovico was grumbling to himself. "What kind of a life is this?"

"Where are you going?" Ambrosio asked.

"Arequipa," Ludovico muttered. "The Coalition people are going to have a demonstration against the government there and it looks like there's going to be trouble. With those mountaineers you never know, things start off as a demonstration and end up as a revolution."

298

He threw an undershirt against the suitcase and sighed, depressed. Ambrosio looked at Amalia and winked, but she looked away.

"You're laughing, boy, because you're sitting pretty," Ludovico said. "You've already been through it and you don't even want to remember those of us who are still on the force. I'd like to see you in my skin, Ambrosio."

"Don't take it like that, brother," Ambrosio said.

"They should call you on your day off, the plane leaves at five." He turned to look at Ambrosio and Amalia with anguish. "You don't even know for how long or what's going to happen there."

"Nothing's going to happen and you'll get to know Arequipa," Ambrosio said. "Think of it as a pleasure trip, Ludovico. Are you going with Hipólito?"

"Yes," Ludovico said, closing the suitcase. "Oh, man, how nice it used to be when we were working for Don Cayo, as long as I live I'll be sorry I was transferred."

"But it's your own fault." Ambrosio laughed. "Didn't you use to be complaining you didn't have time for anything? Didn't you and Hipólito ask to be transferred?"

"Well, make yourselves at home," Ludovico said, and Amalia didn't know where to look. "Keep the key. When you leave you can drop it off with Doña Carmen at the entrance."

He gave a sad wave from the door and left. Amalia felt the rage rising all over her body, and Ambrosio, who had stood up and was coming over, stopped short when he saw the expression on her face.

"He knew I was here, he wasn't surprised to see me." Her eyes threatened him, her hands. "It was a lie that you were waiting for him, you borrowed the room in order to . . ."

"He wasn't surprised because I told him you were my woman," Ambrosio said. "Can't I come here with my woman when I feel like it?"

"I'm not now, never was and never will be," Amalia shouted. "You fooled me about your friend, you borrowed the . . ."

"Ludovico's like a brother to me, this is like home to me," Ambrosio said. "Don't be silly, I can do whatever I want here."

"He must think I haven't got any shame, he didn't even shake hands or look at me. He must think that . . ."

299

"He probably didn't shake hands because he knows I'm jealous," Ambrosio said. "He probably didn't look at you so as not to get me mad. Don't be silly, Amalia."

9

A waiter appeared with a glass of water and he had to stop speaking for a few seconds. He took a drink, coughed: the government wanted to let it be known that it was pleased with everyone in Cajamarca, most especially the gentlemen on the Reception Committee, for their efforts to make the visit an event, and he was able to make a decision and see a chain of sudden substitutions under the curtains: but all of that would call for expenses and it wouldn't be logical, besides the loss of time, the concern that the President's trip should call for them to spend some money too. The silence became accentuated and he could hear the listeners' suspended breathing, catch the curiosity, the suspicion in their eyes, fixed on him: she and Hortensia, she and Maclovia, she and Carmincha, she and China. He coughed again, frowned slightly: so he had instructions from the Ministry to put a sum of money at the disposal of the Committee to lessen their expenses and the figure of Don Remigio Saldívar suddenly dominated the room, she and Hortensia: just a moment, Mr. Bermúdez. Skins that got all mixed up between themselves and among the sheets and curtains, dark hair that became tangled and disentangled and in his mouth he felt a mass of warm saliva as thick as semen. When the Committee had been set up, the Prefect had indicated that he would put in for some help for the expenses of the reception, and Don Remigio Saldívar made a majestic and haughty gesture, and at that time we rejected the offer categorically. Murmurs of approval, a provincial and challenging pride in their faces and he opened his mouth and squinted: but bringing people from the countryside was going to cost them money, Mr. Saldívar, it was fine for them to pay for the banquet, the receptions, but not the other expenses and he heard the sounds of offense, recriminatory movements, and Don Remigio Saldívar had opened his arms arrogantly: they wouldn't accept a cent, that was all there was to it. They were going to honor the President out of their own pockets, they'd decided unanimously, there would be more than enough with the funds they'd collected, Cajamarca didn't need any help to pay

300

homage to Odría, that's all. He stood up, nodding, and the silhouettes vanished as if made of smoke: he wouldn't insist, he didn't want to offend them, he thanked them in the name of the President for that noble display, that generosity. But he still couldn't leave because the waiters had rushed into the room with snacks and drinks. He mingled with the people, had an orangeade, joked and frowned. So you can get to know the people from Cajamarca, Mr. Bermúdez, and Don Remigio Saldívar brought him over to a gray-haired man with an enormous nose: Dr. Lanusa, he had ordered fifteen thousand pennants with money from his own pocket, besides making a donation to the Committee funds the same as the others, Mr. Bermúdez. And don't think he made that gesture just so the highway would happen to pass in front of his ranch, Deputy Azpilcueta laughed. They celebrated the remark, even Dr. Lanusa laughed, oh, those Cajamarcan tongues. There's no denying that you people do things on a grand scale, he was heard to say himself. And you'd better keep your liver in good shape, Mr. Bermúdez, he spotted the twinkling eyes of Deputy Mendieta behind a glass of beer, you'll see how they'll take care of you. He looked at his watch, so late already? he was sorry but he had to go. Faces, hands, good-bye, glad to have met you. Senator Heredia and Deputy Mendieta accompanied him to the stairs, there a small, heavy-bearded dark man was waiting with respectful eyes. Engineer Lama, Don Cayo, and he thought a job, a recommendation, a business deal? a member of the Reception Committee and the leading agronomist in the district, Mr. Bermúdez. How do you do, what can I do for you. A nephew, he would have to pardon him for bringing it up at a time like this, his mother was half crazy and had insisted so much that. He calmed him down by smiling, took a notebook out of his pocket, what had the young man done? They'd sent him to the University of Trujillo with great sacrifice, sir, he must have got bad counseling there, must have fallen in with bad elements, he was never involved in politics before. Fine, Engineer, he'd take care of it personally, what was the young man's name, was he being held in Trujillo or in Lima? He went down the steps and the lights on the Paseo Colón had already gone on. Ambrosio and Ludovico were chatting and smoking by the door. They threw away their cigarettes when they saw him: to San Miguel.

"Take the first turn to the right," Santiago said, pointing. "That yellow house, the old one. That's right, here."

He rang the bell, stuck in his head and saw Carlitos at the top of the stairs in his pajama bottoms with a towel over his shoulder: I'll be right down, Zavalita. He went back to the car.

"If you're in a hurry, leave me here, Sparky. We can take a taxi to Callao. *La Crónica* pays for our transportation."

"I'll drive you," Sparky said. "I suppose we'll see each other again now, right? Teté wants to see you too. I suppose I can bring her, or would you be mad at Teté too?"

"Of course not," Santiago said. "I'm not mad at anyone, not even at the folks. I'm going to go by and see them soon. I just want them to get used to the idea that I'm going to keep on living by myself."

"They're never going to get used to it and you know that very well," Sparky said. "You're making their life bitter. Don't keep on with this silly scheme of yours, Superbrain."

But he stopped talking because Carlitos was there, looking at the car in a puzzled way, Sparky's face. Santiago opened the door for him: get in, get in, I want to introduce you to my brother, he's going to take us. Up front, Sparky said, there was plenty of room for the three of them. He started up, following the trolley tracks, and for a while no one spoke. Sparky offered them cigarettes and Carlitos was looking at us out of the corner of his eye, he thinks, and exploring the nickel-plated dashboard, the brand-new seat covers, Sparky's elegance.

"You didn't even notice that the car is new," Sparky said.

"That's right," Santiago said. "Did the old man sell the Buick?"

"No, this is mine." Sparky blew on his fingernails. "I'm buying it on time. I haven't even had it a month. What are you going to do in Callao?"

"Interview the Director of Customs," Santiago said. "Carlitos and I are writing a series on smuggling."

"Oh, that's interesting," Sparky said; and after a moment: "Do you know that ever since you started working we've been getting *La Crónica* delivered every day? But we never know what you write? Why don't you sign your articles? That way you'd get to be known."

There were Carlitos' mocking and startled eyes, Zavalita, there was the uncomfortable feeling you had. Sparky went through Barranco, Miraflores, turned down the Avenida Pardo and took the Coastal Highway. They were talking with long, uncomfortable pauses, only Santiago and Sparky, Carlitos was watching them out of the corner of his eye, with an intrigued and ironical expression.

"It must be very interesting being a newspaperman," Sparky said. "I could never be one, I can't even write a letter. But you're in your element, Santiago."

Periquito was waiting for them by the door of the custom house with his cameras on his shoulder and the newspaper's van a little way off.

"I'll come by and pick you up one of these days at the same time," Sparky said. "With Teté, O.K.?"

"Fine," Santiago said. "Thanks for the ride, Sparky."

Sparky was indecisive for a moment, his mouth half open, but he didn't say anything and limited himself to a wave. They watched the car go off through the puddles in the cobblestones.

"Is he really your brother?" Carlitos was shaking his head in disbelief. "Your family must be stinking rich, right?"

"According to Sparky they're on the verge of bankruptcy," Santiago said.

"I'd like to be on the verge of a bankruptcy like that," Carlitos said.

"I've been waiting half an hour, you lazy bums," Periquito said. "Did you hear the news? A military cabinet, because of the trouble in Arequipa. The Arequipans got Bermúdez out. This is the end of Odría."

"Don't be so happy," Carlitos said. "The end of Odría and the beginning of what?"

303

8

THE FOLLOWING SUNDAY Ambrosio met her at two o'clock, they went
to a matinee, had something to eat near the Plaza de Armas and took
a long walk. It's going to be today, Amalia thought, it's going to happen
today. He let her look sometimes and she realized that he too was
thinking it's going to be today. There's a good restaurant on Francisco
Pizarro, Ambrosio said when it got dark. It had both Peruvian and
Chinese food; they ate and drank so much they could barely walk.
There's a dance hall near here, Ambrosio said, let's look in. It was a
circus tent set up behind the railroad. The orchestra was on a platform
and they'd laid mats on the ground so that people could dance without
stepping in the mud. Ambrosio kept going out and coming back with
beer in paper cups. There were a lot of people, the couples were bouncing
where they were because there wasn't much room; sometimes a fight
would start but it would never end because two big fellows would separate the men and carry them out bodily. I'm getting drunk, Amalia was
thinking. With the growing heat she was feeling better, freer, and suddenly she herself pulled Ambrosio onto the dance floor. They mingled
with the couples, embracing, and the music never ended. Ambrosio was
holding her tightly, Ambrosio shoved away a drunk who had brushed
against her, Ambrosio kissed her on the throat: it was as if it were all
taking place very far away, Amalia was bursting with laughter. Then the
floor began to spin and she hung onto Ambrosio to stop from falling: I

304

don't feel well. She heard him laugh, felt him dragging her, and suddenly the street. The cold on her face half woke her up. She was walking, holding his arm, she felt his hand on her waist, she was saying now I know why you had me drink. She was happy, she didn't care, where were they going? the sidewalk seemed to be sinking, even if you don't tell me I know where. She recognized Ludovico's little room half in a dream. She was embracing Ambrosio, joining her body to Ambrosio's, looking for Ambrosio's mouth with her mouth, saying I hate you, Ambrosio, you didn't behave right with me, and it was as if she were a different Amalia the one who was doing those things. She let herself be undressed, laid down on the bed, and was thinking what are you crying about, stupid girl. Then a pair of strong arms encircled her, a weight that crushed her, a suffocation that strangled her. She felt that she was neither laughing nor crying and saw Trinidad's face passing by in the distance. Suddenly she was being shaken. She opened her eyes: the light in the little room was on, hurry up, Ambrosio was saying, buttoning up his shirt. What time was it? Four in the morning. Her head was heavy, her body ached, what would the mistress say. Ambrosio was handing her her blouse, her stockings, her shoes, and she got dressed in a rush, without looking into his eyes. The street was deserted, now the breeze made her feel bad. She leaned against Ambrosio and he embraced her. Your aunt wasn't feeling well and you had to stay with her, she thought, or you didn't feel well and your aunt wouldn't let you leave. Ambrosio was stroking her head from time to time, but they weren't speaking. The bus arrived when a weak light was breaking over the rooftops; they got out at the Plaza San Martín and it was daytime, newsboys with papers under their arms were running under the archways. Ambrosio accompanied her to the streetcar stop. This time wouldn't be like the other time, Ambrosio, would he behave right this time? You're my woman, Ambrosio said, I love you. She stayed in his embrace until the streetcar came. She waved to him from the window and she kept on looking at him, watching him grow smaller as the streetcar left him behind.

19

The car went down the Paseo Colón, around the Plaza Bolognesi, turned into Brasil. The traffic and the lights delayed him half an hour until

Magdalena; then, when they left the avenue, they went rapidly through lonely and poorly lighted streets and in a few minutes were in San Miguel: more sleep, going to bed early tonight. When they saw the car the policemen on the corner saluted. He went into the house and the girl was setting the table. From the stairs he glanced at the living room, the dining room: they'd changed the flowers in the vases, the silverware and the glasses on the table were sparkling, everything was neat and clean. He took off his jacket, went into the bedroom without knocking. Hortensia was at the dressing table putting on makeup.

"Queta didn't want to come when she found out that the guest was going to be Landa." Her face was smiling at him from the mirrors; he threw his jacket onto the bed, aiming at the dragon's head: the jacket covered it. "The poor girl hears the name Landa and she begins to yawn. She has to spy on all kinds of old-timers for you, you ought to invite some good young blood for her once in a while."

"Have them give the chauffeurs something to eat," he said, loosening his tie. "I'm going to take a bath. Would you get me a glass of water?"

He went into the bathroom, turned on the hot water, got undressed without closing the door. He watched the bathtub fill up, the room get thick with steam. He heard Hortensia giving orders, saw her come in with a glass of water. He took a pill.

"Do you want a drink?" she asked from the door.

"After I bathe. Please lay out some clean clothes for me."

He sank into the tub and stretched out, only his head out of the water, absolutely motionless, until the water began to turn cold. He soaped himself, rinsed himself under the shower with cold water, combed his hair, and walked into the bedroom naked. On the dragon's back there was a clean shirt, underwear, socks. He got dressed slowly, taking puffs on a cigarette that was burning in the ashtray. Then, from the study, he called Lozano, the Palace, Chaclacayo. When he went down to the living room, Queta had arrived. She was wearing a very low-cut black dress and had put her hair in a bun, which made her look older. The two women were sitting with whiskeys in their hands and had put some records on.

⑨

When Ludovico replaced Hinostroza, things had gone a little better, why? because Hinostroza was a bore and Ludovico was a regular fellow.

The worst part of being Don Cayo's chauffeur wasn't doing those extra little jobs for Mr. Lozano or not having a regular schedule or never knowing what day there'd be a trip, but the bad nights, sir. The nights when they had to take him to San Miguel and wait for him sometimes until the next morning. Regular saddle sores, sir, all that staying awake. Now you're going to find out what being bored is all about, Ambrosio had told Ludovico the day he started, and he, looking at the small house: so this is where Mr. Bermúdez has his little love nest, so this is where he dips in. It was better because there was conversation with Ludovico, while Hinostroza, on the other hand, would hunch down in the car like a mummy and sleep. With Ludovico they would sit on the garden wall, from there Ludovico could keep an eye on the whole street just in case. They would watch Don Cayo go in, hear the voices inside, Ludovico would entertain Ambrosio by guessing what was going on: they're probably having their drinks, when the upstairs lights went on, Ludovico would say the orgy's starting. Sometimes the cops on the corner would come over and the four of them would smoke and chat. At one time one of the policemen was a singer from Ancash. A beautiful voice, sir. "Muñequita Linda" was his best, what are you waiting for, you're in the wrong profession, they'd tell him. Around midnight the boredom would set in, desperation, because time didn't pass fast enough. Only Ludovico kept on talking. A terrible dirty mind, he was always telling dirty stories about Hipólito, he was really the big dirty one, sir. Don Cayo must be there already having a ball, he'd point to the balcony and suck in his mouth, I close my eyes and I can see this, that and the other thing, and so on until, begging your pardon, sir, the four of them would end up with a fierce urge to go to a whorehouse. He would go crazy talking about the mistress: this morning when I came alone to bring Don Cayo, I saw her, boy, something to look at, boy, a kind of thin little pink bathrobe you could see right through, with a pair of Chinese slippers, her eyes were sparkling. She takes one look at you and you fall over dead, another and you feel like Lazarus, a third one kills you again, and the fourth one brings you back to life: a funny fellow, sir, a good person. The mistress was Señora Hortensia, sir, naturally.

9

At the door she ran into Carlota, who was going out to buy bread: what happened to you, where were you, what did you do. She'd slept over at her aunt's in Limoncillo, the poor thing was sick, did the mistress get mad? They walked to the bakery together: she hadn't even noticed, she'd stayed up all night listening to the news from Arequipa. Amalia felt her soul return to her body. Don't you know that there's a revolution in Arequipa? Carlota was saying, all excited, the mistress was so nervous she'd infected their nerves and she and Símula had stayed in the pantry until two o'clock listening to the radio too. But what was going on in Arequipa, crazy girl. Strikes, troubles, people killed, now they were asking for the master to be thrown out of the government. Don Cayo? Yes, and the mistress couldn't find him anywhere, she'd spent the night cursing and calling Miss Queta. Buy double to have something on hand, the Chinaman at the bakery told them, if the revolution gets here tomorrow I'm not going to open up. They went out whispering, what was going to happen, why did they want to throw the master out, Carlota? The mistress in her rage last night said it was because he was too easygoing, and suddenly she grabbed Amalia by the arm and looked into her eyes: I don't believe that business about your aunt, you were with a man, I can see it on your face. What man, silly, her aunt had got sick, Amalia was looking at Carlota very seriously and inside she felt a tickling and a happy little heat. They went into the house and Símula was listening to the radio in the living room with an anxious face. Amalia went to her room, took a quick shower, she hoped she wouldn't ask her any questions, and when she went up to the bedroom with the breakfast, from the stairs she heard the ticking and the voice of the announcer on Clock Radio. The mistress was sitting up in bed smoking and didn't answer her good morning. The government had had a lot of patience with the people who were sowing unrest and subversion in Arequipa, the radio was saying, workers should return to work, students to their studies, and she saw the eyes of the mistress which were looking at her as if they'd just discovered her: what about the newspapers, fool? Run out and get them. Yes, right now, she ran out of the room, happy, she hadn't even noticed. She asked Símula for money and went to the newsstand on the corner. Something very serious must have happened, the mistress was so pale.

308

When she saw her come in, she jumped out of bed, snatched the papers and started looking through them. In the kitchen she asked Símula do you think the revolution is going to win, that they're going to get Odría out? Símula shrugged her shoulders: the one they were going to get out of the Ministry was the master, they all hate him. In a little while they heard the mistress coming down and she and Carlota ran into the pantry: hello, hello, Queta? The newspapers didn't say anything new, I haven't closed my eyes all night, and they saw her furiously throw *La Prensa* onto the floor: these sons of bitches are also calling for Cayo to resign, years flattering him and now they turn on him too, Quetita. She was shouting, cursing, Amalia and Carlota looked at each other. No, Quetita, he hadn't come by or called, the poor thing must have been very busy with that mess, he'd probably gone to Arequipa. Oh, if they'd only shoot them and make them stop their foolishness once and for all, Quetita.

19

"Old Ivonne is going around giving hell to the government and even to you," Hortensia said.

"Be careful about saying anything to her, she'd kill me if she knew I was spreading gossip about her," Queta said. "I don't want that harpy for an enemy."

He passed in front of them on his way to the bar. He poured himself straight whiskey with two cubes of ice and sat down. The maids, in uniform now, were fluttering around the table. Had they given the chauffeurs something to eat? They answered yes. The bath had made him drowsy, he was looking at Hortensia and Queta through a light mist, he barely heard their whispers and laughter. Well, what was the old woman going around saying.

"It's the first time I've ever heard her saying something bad about you in public," Queta said. "Up till now she was always pure honey when she mentioned your name."

"She was telling Robertito that the money Lozano gets out of her is split with you," Hortensia said. "Just imagine, telling that to the number one gossip in Lima."

"That if they kept on bleeding her like that, she's going to retire to live an honest life." Queta laughed.

309

He frowned and opened his mouth: oh, if they were only deaf-mutes, if women could only use sign language to communicate. Queta leaned over to reach the pretzel sticks, her neckline dropped and her breasts were exposed.

"Listen, don't tempt him." Hortensia gave her a slap. "Save that for when the old buzzard gets here."

"Not even that would wake Landa up." Queta returned the slap. "He's ready to retire to live an honest life too."

They laughed and he listened to them as he drank. Always the same jokes, had he heard the latest? the same topics of conversation, Ivonne and Robertito were lovers! now Landa would arrive and in the morning he'd have the feeling of having gone through a night just like other nights. Hortensia got up to change the records, Queta to fill up the glasses again, life was such a monotonous gummed label. They had time for still another whiskey before they heard a car stop at the door.

<p>②

Thanks to Ludovico's crazy ideas the wait was less boring for them, sir. Her mouth, her lips, her starry teeth, she smelled like roses, a body to make a person rise up out of his grave: he seemed to be wild about the mistress, sir. But whenever he was in front of her he didn't dare look at her for fear of Don Cayo. And did the same thing happen to him? No, Ambrosio listened to the things Ludovico said and laughed, that was all, he didn't say anything about the mistress, he didn't think she was so much of a gift from heaven either, he was only thinking about day coming so he could get some sleep. The other woman, sir? Whether Miss Queta didn't seem to be such a hot thing to him either? Not her either, sir. Well, she may have been pretty, but what urge did Ambrosio have to think about women with that killing pace of work, all his head could dream about was the day off he could spend lying in bed, recovering from those bad nights. Ludovico was different, from the moment he went to work for Don Cayo he got all important, now he really would get on the list, boy, and then he'd fuck everybody who'd fucked him because he was just a temporary. The great aim in his life, sir. On those nights, if he wasn't talking about the mistress, he was talking about that: he'd have a fixed salary, a badge, vacations, they'd respect him everywhere and

310

everybody might even want to propose some little deal with him. No, Ambrosio had never wanted to make a career out of the police, sir, he was too bothered by it, all the boredom of waiting. They'd chat and smoke, around one o'clock in the morning or two they'd be dead tired, freezing to death in winter, when it began to dawn they'd wet their faces at the spigot in the garden and watch the maids going out to buy bread, the first cars, the strong smell of the grass would get into their noses and they'd feel some relief because Don Cayo wouldn't be long in coming out. When will my luck change, when will I have a normal life, Ambrosio thought. And thanks to you it had changed and now he finally had one, sir.

9

The mistress spent the morning in her robe, one cigarette after another, listening to the news. She didn't want any lunch, she only had a cup of strong coffee and left in a taxi. A little while later Carlota and Símula went out. Amalia lay down on her bed with her clothes on. She felt a great fatigue, her eyelids were heavy, and when she awoke it was nighttime. She sat up and, sitting there, tried to remember what she had dreamed: about him, but she couldn't remember what, only that while she was dreaming she wanted it to last, don't stop now. Oh you liked the dream, stupid girl. She was washing her face when the bathroom door opened all of a sudden: Amalia, Amalia, there was a revolution. Carlota's eyes were popping out, what was going on, what had they seen. Police with rifles and machine guns, Amalia, soldiers everywhere. Amalia combed her hair, put on her apron and Carlota was leaping about, but where, what. At the Parque Universitario, Amalia, Carlota and Símula were getting off the bus when they saw the demonstration. Boys, girls, signs, FREEDOM, FREEDOM, A-RE-QUI-PA, A-RE-QUI-PA, BERMÚDEZ MUST GO, and they'd just stood there looking like a pair of fools. Hundreds, thousands, and all of a sudden the police appeared, the water cannon, trucks, jeeps, and Colmena was all full of tear gas, streams of water, running, shouting, stones being thrown, and then the cavalry. And they were there, Amalia, they were right in the middle of it not knowing what to do. They'd huddled against a doorway, hugging each other, praying, the gas was making them sneeze and cry, people ran by

311

shouting down with Odría and they'd seen them beating students and stones being thrown at the police. What was going to happen, what was going to happen. They went to listen to the radio and Símula's eyes were bloodshot and she was crossing herself: what they'd escaped, merciful heavens. The radio didn't say anything, they changed stations and advertisements, music, quiz shows, telephone-call programs.

Around eleven o'clock the mistress got out of Miss Queta's little white car, which left immediately. She came in, very calm, what were they doing up, it was late. And Símula: they were listening to the radio but it didn't say anything about the revolution, ma'am. What revolution or nonsense like that, Amalia realized that she was a little high, everything had all been taken care of. But they'd seen it, ma'am, Carlota said, the demonstration and the police and everything, and the mistress foolish women, nothing to be frightened about. She'd spoken to the master on the telephone, he was going to teach those Arequipans a lesson and tomorrow everything would probably be calm again. She was hungry and Símula cooked her a steak: the master didn't lose his calm over anything, the mistress was saying, I'm not going to worry about him like that again. As soon as the table was cleared, Amalia went to bed. There she was, she'd started everything all over again, stupid girl, you've made up with him. She felt a soft languor, a warm little weakness. How would they get along now, would they fight every so often? she wouldn't go to his friend's room anymore, he should rent a room and they could spend their Sundays there. You'd have it all nicely fixed up, stupid girl. If only she could talk to Carlota and tell her. No, she had to hold back her urge until she saw Gertrudis again.

9

Landa arrived with his eyes aglow, very talkative and smelling of alcohol, but as soon as he came in he put on a mournful face: he could only stay for a short while, what a shame. He leaned over to kiss Hortensia's hand, asked Queta for a little kiss on the cheek, fairying his voice, and he dropped into the chair between the two of them, declaiming: a thorn between two roses, Don Cayo. There he was, balding, dressed in an impeccably cut gray suit that hid his bulges, with a garnet tie, flirting with Hortensia and Queta and he thought the assurance, the ease that comes with money.

"The Development Commission is meeting at nine in the morning, Don Cayo, imagine what an hour," Landa said with a tragicomic grimace. "And I have to get eight hours' sleep on doctor's orders. What a pity."

"All tales, senator," Queta said, handing him a whiskey. "The truth is that your wife has got you by the neck."

Senator Landa drank to the two delights that surround me and to you too, Don Cayo. He drank, smacked his lips and started to laugh.

"I'm a free man, I can't even stand the chains of matrimony," he exclaimed. "My child, I love you very much, but I want to keep my freedom to go on a spree, which is really what's most important. And she understood. Thirty years married and she's never asked me for an explanation. Not a single jealous scene, Don Cayo."

"And you've taken advantage of that freedom to suit yourself," Hortensia said. "Tell us about your latest conquest, senator."

"Instead I'm going to tell you some jokes against the government I just heard at the club," Landa said. "Get closer so Don Cayo won't hear us."

He enjoyed himself with deep laughter that mingled with Queta's and Hortensia's, and he celebrated the jokes too, his mouth half open and his cheeks wrinkled. Well, if the illustrious senator had to leave soon, they'd better have dinner right away. Hortensia went into the pantry, followed by Queta. To your health, Don Cayo, yours, senator.

"That Queta's getting nicer every day," Landa said. "And Hortensia, well, there's no need even to say a word, Don Cayo."

"I'm very grateful for the Commission's decision," he said. "I gave Zavala the news at noon. Without you those gringos wouldn't have won the bid."

"I'm the one who has to give thanks here because of the Olave matter," Landa said, making a gesture that meant forget it. "Friends are meant to help each other, that's what friendship's all about."

And he saw the senator become distracted, his look turn toward Queta, who was swaying along as she came in: no talking business or politics here, it was against the law. She sat down beside Landa and he saw the sudden blink, the blush on Landa's cheeks as he leaned over and put his lips on Queta's throat for an instant. He wouldn't leave, he was going to stay, he'd make up a lie, get drunk and only at three or four in the morning would he take Queta home: he moved his thumbs without hesitating and her eyes popped like two grapes. You excited him, he stayed and it's your fault I didn't get any sleep today either: pay up. Go into the dining room, Hortensia said, and he still managed to bury the igneous bar between Queta's thighs and hear the crackle of the singed flesh: pay up. All during dinner, Landa dominated the conversation with an expansion that grew with every glass of wine: gossip, jokes, tales, flirting. Queta and Hortensia asked him questions, answered him, celebrated what he said, and he smiled. When they got up, Landa was talking in a rambling and excited way, he wanted Queta and Hortensia to take a puff on his Havana cigar, he was going to stay. But all of a sudden he looked at his watch and the joy vanished from his face: twelve-thirty, with pain in his soul he had to leave. He kissed Hortensia's hand and tried to kiss Queta on the mouth, but she turned her face and offered him her cheek. He accompanied Landa to the outside door.

9

SOMEONE WAS SHAKING HER, he's waiting for you, she opened her eyes, the chauffeur of the man who was here the other day, Carlota's mocking face: he was waiting for you there on the corner. She got dressed in a hurry, had she gone out with him on Sunday? combed her hair, was that why she hadn't come home to sleep? and she listened to Carlota's questions in a daze. She took the bread basket, went out, and Ambrosio was on the corner: hadn't anything happened there? He took her by the arm, he didn't want them to be seen, made her walk very fast, he was worried about you, Amalia. She stopped, looked at him, and what was supposed to have happened, what was he so worried about? but he made her keep on walking: don't you know that Don Cayo isn't a minister anymore? You're dreaming, Amalia said, everything had been arranged, last night the mistress but Ambrosio no, no, last night they'd dismissed Don Cayo and all the civilian ministers and there was a military cabinet. Didn't the mistress know anything? No, she probably didn't know yet, she was probably sleeping, the poor thing went to bed thinking that everything was being arranged. She took Ambrosio by the arm: and what would happen to the master now? He didn't know what would happen to him, but enough had happened to him already, hadn't it, by not being minister anymore. Amalia went into the bakery alone, thinking he was afraid because, came because, he loves you. When she came out she took his arm, and how did he get to San Miguel, what had he said to Don Fermín?

315

Don Fermín was hiding out, he was afraid he'd be arrested, the police had been watching his house, he was in the country. And Ambrosio happy, Amalia, while he was hiding out they'd be able to see more of each other. He backed her up against a garage, they couldn't be seen from the house there, got close to her and hugged her. Amalia stood on tiptoes to get close to his ear: were you afraid something had happened to me? Yes, she heard him laughing, now she would get high and mighty with him. And Amalia: it would be better now than the other time, wouldn't it? they wouldn't fight anymore, would they? And Ambrosio: no, not now. He accompanied her to the corner, when he said good-bye he suggested that if the girls had seen them, she should invent some lie, he'd come on an errand, you scarcely know me.

◊

He waited for Landa's car to start up and he came back into the house. Hortensia had taken her shoes off and was humming a tune, leaning against the bar; thank God the old buzzard left, Queta said from the chair. He sat down, picked up his glass of whiskey again and drank, slowly, looking at Hortensia, who was now dancing in place. He took the last swallow, looked at his watch and stood up. He had to go too. He went up to the bedroom and on the stairs he sensed that Hortensia had stopped singing and was coming up behind him. Queta laughed. Couldn't he stay, Hortensia followed him up and he felt her hand on his arm, her wheedling voice, drunk now, I've only seen you once this week. For house money, he said, laying some bills on the dressing table: he couldn't, he had things to do starting early in the morning. He turned around, Hortensia's almost liquid eyes, her loving and idiotic expression, and he ran his hand along her cheek, smiling at her: he was all tied up because of the President's trip, maybe he could come by tomorrow. He took his briefcase and went down the stairs, with Hortensia clinging to his arm, listening to her purr like an excited cat, feeling her unsteady, almost stumbling. Lying on the large sofa, Queta was swinging her half-filled glass in the air, and he saw her eyes turn to look mockingly at them. Hortensia let go of him, ran over clumsily, threw herself onto the sofa.

"He wants to move out, Quetita," her voice syrupy and comical, her

316

pouting theatrical. "He doesn't love me anymore."

"What do you care." Queta leaned over onto the chair, opened her arms, embraced Hortensia. "Let him go, girl, I'll console you."

He heard Hortensia's challenging laugh, saw her cling tightly to Queta and thought: always the same thing. Laughing, playing, giving in to the game, the two of them were embracing, soldered together on the couch so that their bodies overflowed, and he saw their lips pecking at each other, separating and coming together in the midst of laughter, their feet intertwined. He watched them from the bottom step, smoking, a benevolent half-smile on his lips, feeling a sudden indecision in his eyes, a burst of rage in his chest. Suddenly, with a gesture of defeat, he dropped into the chair and let go of the briefcase, which slid to the floor.

"That business about eight hours of sleep, the Development Commission is a lie," he thought, barely aware that he was also saying it. "He's probably gambling at the club right now. He wanted to stay but his vice was stronger."

They were tickling each other, with exaggerated little shouts, whispering secrets, and their quivering, hand-play and impudence was bringing them to the edge of the sofa. They never did fall off: they would advance and retreat, pushing each other, holding each other, laughing all the while. He didn't take his eyes off them, his face frowning, his eyes half closed but alert. His mouth felt very dry.

"The only vice I don't understand," he thought aloud. "The only one that's stupid in a man with Landa's money. Gambling, to get more, to lose what he has? Nobody's ever satisfied, there's always too much or too little of everything."

"Look at him, he's talking to himself." Hortensia lifted her face from Queta's throat and pointed at him. "He's gone crazy. He's decided not to leave, look at him."

"Get me a drink," he said, resigned. "You two are going to be the ruination of me."

Smiling, muttering something, Hortensia went to the bar, stumbling, and he sought Queta's eyes and indicated the pantry: close that door, the maids were probably awake. Hortensia brought him his glass of whiskey and sat on his lap. While he drank, holding the liquid in his mouth, savoring it with his eyes closed, he felt her bare arm around his neck, her hand as it mussed his hair, and heard her incoherent, tender voice: little Cayo Shithead, little Cayo Shithead. The fire in his throat was bearable, even pleasant. He sighed, pushed Hortensia away, got up and went up the stairs without looking at them. A ghost that suddenly took on substance and jumped on a person from behind and knocked him down: that's what probably had happened to Landa, to all of them. He went into the bedroom and didn't turn on the light. He felt his way over to the chair by the dressing table, heard his own grumpy little laugh. He took off his tie, jacket, and sat down. Mrs. Heredia was downstairs, she was on her way up. Rigid, motionless, he waited for her to come up.

⑨

"Are you worried about the time?" Santiago asks. "Don't worry about it. A friend gave me an infallible prescription against anguish, Ambrosio."

"We'd better stay here," Sparky said. "It's a drunken brawl out there. If we get out somebody will say something to Teté and there'll be a scuffle."

"Bring the car over closer, then," Teté said. "I want to watch them dance."

Sparky brought the car over to the curb and from inside they could see the shoulders and faces of the couples who were dancing in El Nacional; they could hear the drums, the maracas, the trumpet and the M.C. announcing the best tropical orchestra in Lima. When the music stopped, they heard the sea behind them, and if they turned around, over the wall of the Malecón they could make out the white foam, the breaking of the waves. There were several cars parked in front of the restaurants and bars on Herradura beach. The night was cool and starry.

"I just love our getting together in secret," Teté said, laughing. "I feel that we're doing something forbidden. Don't you people?"

"Sometimes the old man takes a spin by here at night," Sparky said. "It would be funny if he caught the three of us here."

"He'd kill us if he knew we were seeing you," Teté said.

"He'd burst out crying with emotion on seeing the prodigal son," Sparky said.

"You people don't believe me, but I'm going to show up in person at

318

the house any time now," Santiago said. "Without letting them know. Next week probably."

"I'm going to believe you, naturally, you've been telling us the same story for months." And Teté's face lighted up. "I've got it, it just occurred to me. Let's go home right now, you can make up with mama and papa tonight."

"Not now, another time," Santiago said. "Besides, I don't want to go with you, I want to go alone, so there'll be less melodrama."

"You're never coming home and I'll tell you why," Sparky said. "You're waiting for the old man to go to your boardinghouse to ask you to forgive him for something or other and to beg you to come back."

"You didn't even come when that damned Bermúdez was after him, you didn't even call him on his birthday," Teté said. "You're awful, Superbrain."

"You're crazy if you think the old man is going to cry over you," Sparky said. "You ran away out of sheer craziness and the folks have got every right to be resentful. The one who has to ask to be forgiven is you, dummy."

"Are we always going to keep on talking about the same thing?" Santiago asked. "Please change the subject. When are you going to marry Popeye, Teté?"

"What's wrong with you, you idiot," Teté said. "I'm not even going with him. He's just a friend."

"Milk of magnesia and a screw every week, Zavalita," Carlitos said. "With your stomach clean and your deal up to date, there's no anguish that can stand up to it. An infallible prescription, Zavalita."

9

In the house Carlota came to meet her, astounded: the master wasn't a minister anymore, the radio was saying, they'd replaced him with a military man. Oh yes? Amalia pretended, putting the loaves in the breadbox, what about the mistress? She was very mad, Símula had just brought the papers up to her and she cursed so you could hear it down here. Amalia brought her the pot of coffee, the orange juice and the toast, and from the stairs she heard the tick-tock of Clock Radio. The mistress was half dressed, the newspapers strewn all over the unmade bed, instead of

319

answering her good morning she said only black coffee, in a rage. She handed her the cup, the mistress took a sip and put the cup back on the tray. Amalia followed her from the closet to the bathroom to the dressing table, so that she could drink her coffee while she dressed, saw her hand all trembling, the line of her eyebrows twisted, and she was trembling too, listening to her: those ingrates, if it hadn't been for the master they would have got Odría and those thieves into a trap a long time ago. Now she wanted to see what those bastards would do without him, the lipstick fell out of her hands, she spilled her coffee twice, they wouldn't last a month without him. She left the room without finishing putting on her makeup, called a taxi, and while she was waiting she bit her lip and all of a sudden a curse. As soon as she left, Símula turned on the radio, they listened to it all day. They were talking about the military cabinet, giving the biographies of the new ministers, but they didn't mention the master's name on any station. At nightfall National Radio said that the Arequipa strike was over, tomorrow the schools, the university and the shops would open and Amalia remembered Ambrosio's friend: he'd gone there, maybe he'd been killed. Símula and Carlota were talking about the news and she was listening to them, her mind wandering sometimes, thinking about Ambrosio: he was afraid because of, he came because of, he. Maybe now that he's not in the government anymore he'll come to live here, Carlota was saying, and Símula that would be awful for us, and Amalia thought: if he was, would there be anything bad about Ambrosio's renting the little room for the two of them? Yes, it would be taking advantage of misfortune. The mistress came home late with Miss Queta and Miss Lucy. They sat in the living room and while Símula was preparing dinner, Amalia listened to the ladies consoling the mistress: they'd dismissed him to get the strike over with, but he'd still run things from his home, he was the strong man, Odría owed everything to him. But he hasn't even called me, the mistress was saying, walking back and forth, and they he was probably tied up with meetings, discussions, he'd call soon, he'd probably come by that very night. They drank their little whiskeys and when they sat down at the table they were laughing and telling jokes. Miss Lucy left around midnight.

Hortensia got there first, noiselessly: he saw her silhouette on the threshold, hesitant, like a flame, and he saw her feel around in the dark and
light the floor lamp. The black coverlet rose up in the mirror opposite,
the curly tail of the dragon gave life to the mirror on the dressing table
and he heard Hortensia start to say something and her voice got tangled
up. Better, better. She was coming toward him trying to keep her balance
and with her face wild with an idiotic expression that was erased when
she entered the shadows of the corner where he was. He cut her off with
a voice that sounded difficult and anxious: what about the madwoman,
had the madwoman gone yet? Instead of continuing toward him, Hortensia's silhouette changed course and zigzagged toward the bed, where she
collapsed softly. There the light half exposed her, he saw her hand, which
rose up and pointed to the door, and he looked: Queta had also sneaked
in. Her long, full figure, her reddish hair, her aggressive stance. And he
heard Hortensia: he didn't want anything to do with her, he was calling
you, Quetita, he was throwing her away and only asks about you. If only
they couldn't speak, he thought, and he gripped the shears decisively, a
single, silent cut, snip, and he saw the two tongues fall to the floor. They
were by his feet, two flat, red little animals that were staining the rug in
their death throes. In his dark refuge he laughed and Queta, who stayed
in the dark as if waiting for a command, laughed too: she didn't want
to have anything to do with little Cayo Shithead, girl, didn't he want to
leave, wasn't he going to take off ? Let him go, then, they didn't need him
and he with infinite anguish thought: she's not drunk, not her. She was
talking like a third-rate actress who's also starting to lose her memory
and is reciting slowly, afraid of forgetting her lines. Come in, Mrs.
Heredia, he murmured, feeling an invincible deception, an anger that
affected his voice. He saw her move, advance, pretending insecurity, and
he heard Hortensia did you hear him, do you know that woman, Quetita?
Queta had sat down beside Hortensia, neither of them was looking
toward his corner and he sighed. They didn't need him, girl, let him go
to that woman: why did he pretend, why did he talk, snip. He didn't
move his face, only his eyes turned from the bed to the mirror on the
closet to the one on the wall to the bed and his body felt hard and all

his nerves were alert as if the pillows in the easy chair might suddenly sprout nails. They had already begun to undress each other and caress each other at the same time, but their movements were too vehement to be sincere, their embraces too quick or slow or tight, and the fury with which their mouths attacked was too sudden and I'll kill them if, he would kill them if. But they didn't laugh: they'd lain down, entwined, still half undressed, silent at last, kissing each other, their bodies rubbing with a hesitant slowness. He felt his fury diminishing, his hands wet with sweat, the bitter presence of the saliva in his mouth. Now they were quiet, caught in the mirror of the dressing table, a hand on the catch of the bra, fingers stretching out under a slip, a knee nestled between two thighs. He was waiting, tense, his elbows fastened to the arms of the chair. They weren't laughing, yes, they'd forgotten about him, they weren't looking into his corner and he swallowed his saliva. They seemed to be waking up, suddenly there seemed to be more of them, and his eyes went rapidly from one mirror to another and to the bed so as not to lose any of the diligent, loose, skillful little figures that were undoing a shoulder strap, rolling down a stocking, slipping off a pair of panties, and helping each other and pulled and didn't speak. The items were dropping onto the rug and a wave of impatience and heat reached his corner. They were naked now and he saw Queta kneeling down, letting herself fall softly over Hortensia until she covered her almost completely with her large, dark body, but leaping from the ceiling to the bedspread to the closet he could still make her out, fragmented under the solid shadow lying over her: a piece of white buttock, a white breast, a very white foot, heels, and her black hair in the midst of Queta's rumpled reddish hair as the latter began to rock. He heard them breathe, pant, and he caught the soft creaking of the springs, saw Hortensia's legs break free from Queta's and rise up and alight on top of them, he saw the growing glow of skins and now he could also smell. Only waists and buttocks were moving, in a deep and circular movement, while the upper part of their bodies remained glued together and motionless. He had his nostrils wide open and even then he lacked air; he closed and opened his eyes, breathed hard through his mouth and he seemed to smell flowing blood, pus, decomposing meat, and he heard a noise and looked. Queta was now on her back and Hortensia could be seen, tiny and white, curled up, her head leaning over with lips half open and moist between the dark virile legs that were opening up. He saw her mouth disappear, her closed eyes barely showing over the underbrush of black fuzz and his hands unbuttoned his shirt, pulled off his undershirt, dropped his pants, and pulled furiously on the belt. He went toward the bed with the belt in the air, not thinking, not seeing, his eyes fixed on the darkness of the background, but he was only able to strike one blow: heads that rose up, hands that took hold of the belt, pulled and dragged him down. He heard a curse, heard his own laughter. He tried to separate the two bodies that were rebelling against him and he felt himself pushed, squashed, sweaty, in a blind and suffocating whirlwind, and he could hear the beating of his heart. An instant later he felt the pinprick in his temples and a kind of blow in the emptiness. He was motionless for a moment, breathing deeply, and then he separated himself from them, leaning his body away, with a distaste that he could feel growing cancerously. He remained lying down, his eyes closed, wrapped in a confused drowsiness, feeling darkly that they were rocking and panting again. He finally got up, nauseous, and, without looking behind, went into the bathroom: more sleep.

❡

"And when are you getting married, Sparky?" Santiago asked.

The waiter came over to the car, placed the tray on the window. Sparky poured Teté's Coca-Cola, their beers.

"I'd like to get married soon, but it's hard right now because of work," he said. "Bermúdez left us practically bankrupt. Things are only just now getting back into shape and I can't leave the old man alone. It's been years since I've been working without a vacation. I'd like to do some traveling. I'm going to make up for it on my honeymoon, I'm going to visit at least five different countries."

"You'll be so busy on your honeymoon that you won't have time to see anything," Santiago said.

"Stop your dirty talk in front of the squirt," Sparky said.

"Tell me what the famous Cary is like, Teté," Santiago said.

"She's not chicha and she's not lemonade either," Teté said, laughing. "She's a colorless girl from Punta who never opens her mouth."

"She's a great girl, we get along very well," Sparky said. "One of these days I'll introduce you, Superbrain. I would have brought her along one of these times, but, I don't know, can't you see all the problems you make for us with your foolishness?"

"Does she know that I don't live at home?" Santiago asked. "What have you told her?"

"That you're half nutty," Sparky said. "That you had a fight with the old man and moved out. I haven't even told her that Teté and I see you in secret, because all of a sudden she might come out with it at home."

"You're always asking us what we're doing but you never tell us anything about yourself," Teté said. "That's not fair."

"He likes to play it mysterious, but it won't work with me, Super-brain," Sparky said. "If you don't tell me what you're doing, who gives a damn. I just won't ask you anything."

"But I'm dying with curiosity," Teté said. "Come on, Superbrain, tell me something."

"If the only thing you do is go from your boardinghouse to the newspaper and from the newspaper to your boardinghouse, when do you go to San Marcos?" Sparky said. "You've been telling us a lot of tales. That's a lie about your attending the university."

"Have you got a girl friend?" Teté asked. "You can't make me believe you don't go out with girls."

"Just in order to prove that he's different from everyone else, he'll end up marrying a black, Chinese, or Indian girl." Sparky laughed. "You'll see, Teté."

"Tell us at least about the boyfriends you have, come on," Teté said. "Are they still all Communists?"

"He's gone from Communists to drunks." Sparky laughed. "He's got a friend in Chorrillos who looks like he was just let out of the Frontón jail. The face of an outlaw and a breath that makes you seasick."

"If you don't like newspaper work, I don't know what you're waiting for to make up with papa and come to work for him," Teté said.

"I like business even less than I do newspaper work," Santiago said. "That's fine for Sparky."

"If you're not going to be a lawyer and don't want to go into business, you're never going to have any money," Teté said.

"The problem is that I don't want money," Santiago said. "What for,

324

anyway? Sparky and you are going to be millionaires; you'll give me something when I need it."

"You're on tonight," Sparky said. "Might a person know what you've got against people who want to make money?"

"Nothing, it's just that I don't want to make money," Santiago said.

"Well, there's nothing easier in the world than that," Sparky said.

"Before you two get into a fight, let's have some chicken," Teté said. "I'm dying of hunger."

9

The next morning she woke up before Símula. It was only six on the kitchen clock, but the sky was already light and it wasn't cold. She swept her room and made the bed quite calmly, as always, she tested the water in the shower with her foot for some time and finally got in little by little; she soaped herself, smiling, remembering the mistress: footsies, breasties, behindy. She came out and Símula, who was making breakfast, told her to go wake Carlota. They had breakfast and at seven-thirty she went out to buy the papers. The boy at the newsstand was teasing her and instead of answering his bad manners in kind, she joked with him for a while. She felt in a good mood, there were only three days left until Sunday. They wanted to be awakened early too, Símula said, take their breakfast up right away. Only on the stairs did she see the picture in the newspaper. She knocked on the door several times, the mistress's sleepy voice yes? and she walked in talking: there was a picture of the master in *La Prensa*, ma'am. In the semidarkness one of the two forms on the bed sat up, lighted the lamp on the night table. The mistress threw her hair back and while she was placing the tray on the chair and moving it over to the bed, the mistress was looking at the newspaper. Should she open the curtain, ma'am? but she didn't answer: she was blinking, her eyes fastened to the newspaper. Finally, without moving her head, she stretched out her hand and shook Miss Queta.

"What do you want," the sheets complained. "Let me sleep, it's midnight."

"He left, Queta." She was shaking her furiously, looking at the newspaper with surprise. "He took off, he went away."

Miss Queta got up, rubbed her swollen eyes with both hands, leaned

325

over to look, and Amalia, as always, felt ashamed at seeing them so close together like that with nothing on.

"To Brazil," the mistress was repeating with a horrified voice. "Without coming by, without calling. He took off without saying a word to me, Queta."

Amalia was filling the cups, trying to read, but she only saw the mistress's black hair, Miss Queta's red hair, he'd gone away, what was going to happen.

"Well, he probably had to leave in a hurry," Miss Queta was saying, covering her breasts with the sheet. "Now he'll send you a ticket. He certainly must have left some note for you."

The mistress had fallen to pieces and Amalia watched how her mouth was trembling, the hand that clutched the newspaper was crumpling it: that bastard, Queta, without phoning, without leaving her a cent, and she sobbed. Amalia turned half around and left the room: don't act like that, girl, she heard while she flew down the stairs to tell Carlota and Símula.

9

He wiped his mouth, carefully cleaned his body, rubbed his head with a towel soaked in cologne. He dressed very slowly, his mind a blank and a thin buzzing in his ears. He went back to the bedroom and they had covered themselves with the sheets. In the shadows he could make out the hair in disarray, the rouge and mascara stains on the sated faces, the drowsy restfulness in their eyes. Queta had curled up to go to sleep already, but Hortensia was looking at him.

"Aren't you going to stay?" Her voice was indifferent and opaque.

"There's no room," he said from the door, and he smiled at her before leaving. "I'll come by tomorrow maybe."

He hurried down the stairs, picked up the briefcase on the rug, went out onto the street. Sitting on the garden wall, Ludovico and Ambrosio were chatting with the policemen from the corner. When they saw him they stopped talking and got to their feet.

"Good evening," he murmured, giving a couple of ten-sol notes to the policemen. "Get something to protect yourselves against the chill."

He scarcely glimpsed their smiles, heard their thanks, and got into the car: to Chaclacayo. He rested his head on the back of the seat, pulled up his jacket collar, told them to close the front windows. He listened, motionless, to the sound of Ambrosio and Ludovico's conversation, and from time to time he would open his eyes and recognize streets, squares, the dark highway: everything was buzzing in his head, monotonously. Two flashlights fell on the car when it stopped. He heard commands and good evenings, made out the silhouettes of the guards who were opening the main door. What time tomorrow, Don Cayo? Ambrosio asked. Nine o'clock. The voices of Ambrosio and Ludovico were lost behind him, and from the entrance to the house he could make out figures pulling the garage doors open. He sat at the desk for a few minutes trying to jot down in his notebook the business of the following day. In the dining room he poured himself a glass of ice water and went up to the bedroom with heavy steps, feeling the glass trembling in his hand. The sleeping pills were on the bathroom shelf, beside the electric razor. He took two, with a long swallow of water. In the dark he wound the clock and set the alarm for eight-thirty. He pulled the sheets up to his chin. The maid had forgotten to draw the curtains and the sky was a black square dotted with tiny bright spots. The pills took between ten and fifteen minutes to put him to sleep. He had lain down at three-forty and the phosphorescent hands of the alarm clock said a quarter to four. Five more minutes of wakefulness.

THREE

1

HE GOT TO THE NEWSPAPER OFFICE a little before five o'clock and was taking his jacket off when the telephone in the back of the room rang. He saw Arispe pick up the receiver, move his mouth, take a look at the empty desks and look at him: Zavalita, please. He crossed the room, stopped in front of the table piled high with cigarette butts, scraps of paper, photographs and rolls of galley proofs.

"The dummies on the police beat don't get here until seven o'clock," Arispe said. "You go, get the facts and give them to Becerrita later on."

"General Garzón 311," Santiago read on the paper. "In Jesús María, right?"

"Get on down there, I'll get word to Periquito and Darío," Arispe said. "We must have some pictures of her in the morgue."

"The Muse knifed?" Periquito asked in the van while he was loading his camera. "That's quite a story."

"She used to sing on Radio el Sol some years back," Darío the driver said. "Who killed her?"

"A crime of passion, it would seem," Santiago said. "I never heard of her."

"I took pictures of her when she was elected Carnival Queen, quite a woman," Periquito said. "Are you on the police beat now, Zavalita?"

"I was the only one in the office when Arispe got the news," Santiago said. "It'll teach me a lesson not to get in on time anymore."

331

The building was next to a drugstore, there were two patrol cars and people gathered in the street, there comes *La Crónica,* a boy shouted. They had to show their press cards to a policeman and Periquito took pictures of the front, the stairs, the first landing. An open door, he thinks, cigarette smoke.

"You're new to me," a jowly fat man dressed in blue said, examining his card. "What happened to Becerrita?"

"He wasn't at the paper when they called us." And Santiago smelled the strange odor, sweaty human flesh, he thinks, rotten fruit. "You don't know me because I work in a different section, Inspector."

Periquito's bulb flashed, the man with the jowls blinked and moved aside. Through the people who were whispering, Santiago could see a piece of wall with light blue paper, dirty tiles, a black coverlet. Excuse me, two men drew apart, his eyes went up, went down, and very quickly went up, the figure that was so white, he thinks, not pausing at the clotted blood, the red-black lips of the twisted wounds, the tangle of hair that covered her face, the mat of black fuzz bunched between her legs. He didn't move, he didn't say anything. Periquito's rainbows were flashing right and left, could he take a picture of the face, Inspector? a hand drew the tangles aside and a waxen, intact face appeared with shadows under the curved lashes. Thank you, Inspector, Periquito said, crouching beside the bed now, and the gush of white light burst forth again. Ten years dreaming about her, Zavalita, if Anita knew she'd think you'd fallen in love with the Muse and would be jealous.

"I can see that our reporter friend is new," the jowly man said. "Don't faint on us, young fellow, we've got enough trouble already with this lady here."

The faces veiled by smoke relaxed into smiles, Santiago made an effort and also smiled. When he touched his ballpoint, he discovered that his hand was sweating; he took out his notebook, his eyes took another look: splotches, breasts that overflowed, nipples that were scaly and somber like moles. The smell poured into his nose and made him nauseous.

"They even opened up her navel." Periquito was changing his bulbs with one hand, biting his tongue. "What a sadist."

"They opened up something else on her too," the man with the jowls said soberly. "Come closer, Periquito; you too, young fellow, do you want to see something awful?"

"A hole in the hole," an affected voice said and Santiago heard tenuous little laughs and unintelligible comments. He took his eyes away from the bed, took a step toward the man in blue.

"Could you give me some information, Inspector?"

"Introductions first," the one with the jowls said cordially and gave him a soft hand. "Adalmiro Peralta, Chief of the Homicide Division, and this is my adjutant, First Officer Ludovico Pantoja. Don't leave him out either."

You tried to revive your smile, keep it on your face while you were taking notes, Zavalita, while you watched the hysterical scratching of the pen as it ran over the paper, slipping along with no direction.

"One favor for another, Becerrita will explain." While you listened to Inspector Peralta's laughing and confidential voice. "We get you the scoop and you people give us a few plugs, which we can always use."

Laughter again, Periquito's flashes, the smell, the smoke all over: there, Zavalita. Santiago nodded, the notebook folded over, tight against his chest, scribbling lines now, dots, watching letters take shape like hieroglyphics.

"We got the tip from an old woman who lives alone in the next apartment," the Inspector said. "She heard shouting, came out and found the door open. They had to take her to Emergency, her nerves were all shot. You can imagine the fright she must have got when she found this."

"Eight stab wounds," First Officer Ludovico Pantoja said. "Counted by the medical examiner, young man."

"She was probably doped up," Inspector Peralta said. "From the smell and the way her eyes were, it looks that way. She was almost always on dope lately. She had a file this fat at the division. The autopsy will give us the final word."

"She was mixed up in some drug affair a year ago," Officer Ludovico Pantoja said. "They arrested her along with a woman who was a well-known addict. She'd fallen pretty low."

"Could I get a picture of the knife, Inspector?" Periquito asked.

333

"The lab men took it away," Inspector Peralta said. "An ordinary kind, a six-inch blade. Yes, lots of fingerprints."

"He hasn't been caught, but we'll grab him," Officer Ludovico Pantoja said. "He left traces all over the place, he didn't even take the weapon with him, he did it in broad daylight. He wasn't a professional, not by a long shot."

"We haven't been able to identify him because this lady here didn't have a lover, she had a whole lot of them," Inspector Peralta said. "Anybody could make it with her lately. She'd been going downhill, poor devil."

"All you have to do is look at the place she died in." Officer Pantoja pointed around the room with pity. "After having lived it up so much."

"She was Carnival Queen the year I joined *La Crónica,*" Periquito said. "Nineteen forty-four. Fourteen years ago, how about that."

"Life is like a swing, it goes up and down." Inspector Peralta smiled. "Put that in your little story, young fellow."

"I remembered her as being prettier," Periquito said. "Actually, she wasn't very much."

"The years go by, Periquito," Inspector Peralta said. "And besides, getting stabbed hasn't helped her looks any."

"Shall I take a picture of you, Zavalita?" Periquito asked. "Becerrita always has one taken beside the corpse, for his private collection. He must have a thousand or more by now."

"I know Becerrita's collection," Inspector Peralta said. "Enough to give the shivers even to a guy like me who's seen all there is to see."

"When I get back to the paper I'll have Mr. Becerra call you, Inspector," Santiago said. "I won't bother you anymore now. Thank you very much for the information."

"Tell him to come by the office around eleven o'clock," Inspector Peralta said. "Nice meeting you, young man."

They went out and on the landing Periquito stopped to take a picture of the door of the neighbor woman who had discovered the body. The onlookers were still on the sidewalk, peeking at the stairs over the shoulder of the policeman guarding the door, and Darío was in the van smoking: why hadn't they let him in, he would have liked to see it. They got in, drove off, a moment later they passed the van from *Última Hora.*

"You fucked them out of the scoop," Darío said. "There goes Norwin."

"Why, of course, man." Periquito cracked his knuckles and nudged Santiago. "She was Cayo Bermúdez' mistress. I saw her going into a Chinese restaurant on the Calle Capón with him once. Of course, man."

"I didn't see the newspapers and I don't know what you're talking about," Ambrosio says. "I must have been in Pucallpa when it happened, son."

"Cayo Bermúdez' mistress?" Darío said. "Then it really is a story."

"You felt like a Sherlock Holmes, digging into that foul story," Carlitos said. "And look what it cost you."

"You were his chauffeur and you didn't know that he had a mistress?" Santiago asks.

"I didn't know and I never saw her," Ambrosio says. "It's the first I ever heard of it, son."

An anxious excitation had replaced the dizziness of the first moment, a crude excitement as the van crossed the downtown area and you were trying to decipher the scribbling in your notebook and reconstruct the conversation with Inspector Peralta, Zavalita. He leaped out and strode up the stairs at *La Crónica*. The lights in the editorial office were on, the desks occupied, but he didn't stop to chat with anyone. Did you win the lottery? Carlitos asked him, and he a big story, Carlitos. He sat down at the typewriter and for an hour didn't take his eyes off the paper, writing, correcting and smoking ceaselessly. Then, chatting with Carlitos, he waited, impatient and proud of yourself, Zavalita, for Becerrita to arrive. And finally you saw him come in, dumpy, he thinks, adipose, ill-humored, aged Becerrita, with hat left over from other days, his ex-boxer's face, his ridiculous little mustache and his fingers stained with nicotine. What a disappointment, Zavalita. He didn't answer your hello, he practically didn't read the three pages, he listened without any expression of interest to the story Santiago was telling him. What was one crime more or less for Becerrita who got up in the morning, lived and went to bed in the midst of murders, Zavalita, robberies, embezzlements, fires, holdups, who had lived for a quarter of a century off stories of junkies, thieves, whores, cheating wives. But the disappointment didn't last long, Zavalita. He thinks: he never got enthusiastic about anything, but he knew his trade. He thinks: maybe he liked it. He took off his turn-of-the-century hat, his jacket, rolled up his sleeves which he had fastened at the elbows with a bookkeeper's armbands, he thinks, and loosened the necktie that was as threadbare and dirty as his suit and shoes, and weary and vinegary he went through the office indifferent to the nods, stolidly and slowly and straight to Arispe's desk. Santiago went over to Carlitos' corner to listen. Becerrita gave a little rap with his knuckles on the typewriter and Arispe raised his head: what could he do for him, my good sir?

"The centerfold all for me." His voice harsh and sickly, he thinks, weak, mocking. "And Periquito at my disposal for at least three or four days."

"Do you also want a house on the beach with a piano, my good sir?" Arispe asked.

"And some reinforcements, Zavalita, for example, because two people in my section are on vacation," Becerrita said dryly. "If you want us to do a thorough job on this, you'll have to put a writer on it night and day."

Arispe chewed his red pencil thoughtfully, thumbing through the pages; then his eyes wandered about the room, searching. You screwed yourself, Carlitos said, get out of it under any pretext. But you didn't use any, Zavalita, you went happily over to Arispe's desk, happily over to the jaws of the wolf. Excitement, emotion, blood: already fucked up for some time, Zavalita.

"Do you want to transfer to the police beat for a few days?" Arispe said. "Becerrita has asked for you."

"Do people have a choice now?" Becerrita muttered acidly. "When I started out on *La Crónica* nobody asked me what I thought. Go cover the police stations, we're setting up a police section and you're going to be in charge of it. They've kept me on it for twenty-five years and they still haven't asked me whether I like it or not."

"One day your bad mood's going to boil up in here, my good sir," Arispe touched his heart with his red pencil, "and it'll explode like a balloon. Besides, if they took you off the police page you'd die of sorrow, Becerrita. You're the top ace of the gory page in all Peru."

"I don't know what good it does me, because every week I'm in debt

336

up to here," Becerrita grunted, immodestly. "I'd rather not get so much praise and have my salary raised."

"Twenty years eating free off the most expensive whores, getting drunk free in the best brothels, and you're still complaining, my good sir?" Arispe said. "What effect do you think it has on those of us who have to pay out of our own pockets every time we have to get ourselves a drink or a fuck?"

The clicking of the machines had stopped, smiling faces followed the dialogue between Arispe and Becerrita from the desks, and the latter had begun to smile in a hybrid way, releasing little spasms of that hoarse and unpleasant laugh that would change into a thunder of hiccuping, belching and invectives when he was drunk, he thinks.

"I'm old now," he finally said. "I don't swill anymore, I don't like women anymore."

"You changed your tastes in your old age," Arispe said, and he looked at Santiago. "Watch out, now I can see why Becerrita asked for you for his section."

"My, the chief editors are in a good mood," Becerrita grunted. "What about that other matter? Will you give me the centerfold and Periquito?"

"You've got them, but take good care of them for me," Arispe said. "I want you to get people shook up and raise circulation for me. Icing on the cake, my good sir."

Becerrita nodded, turned halfway around, the typewriters began to clack again and, followed by Santiago, he went to his desk. It was in the rear, he saw everyone's back from there, he thinks, it was one of his constant themes. He would come in drunk and plant himself in the middle of the room, open his jacket, his fists on his chubby hips, they always send me to the asshole of the universe! The reporters hunched down in their seats, sank their noses into their machines, not even Arispe dared look at him, he thinks, while Becerrita, with slow, infuriated eyes, looked over the busy reporters, they looked down on his page and they looked down on him, didn't they? the concentrating copy editors, was that why they'd hemmed him in in the asshole of the office? Hernández the busy headline writer, so he could look at the asses of the local-news gentlemen, the asses of the foreign-news gentlemen? pacing back and forth like a restless general before a battle, so he'd get the gentlemen reporters' farts full in his chops? and raising his tortured laughter to the ceiling from time to time. But once when Arispe had suggested that he move his desk, he became indignant, he thinks: I'll have to be dead before they can haul me out of my corner, God damn it. His desk was low and a bit rickety, like him, he thinks, greasy like the shiny suit he usually wore decorated with food stains. He'd sat down, lighted a crumpled cigarette, Santiago was waiting on his feet, excited that he'd asked for you, Zavalita, already excited by the articles you'd write: going to the slaughterhouse like someone on his way to a party, Carlitos.

"All right, she's been given to us and we've got to move." Becerrita picked up the phone, dialed a number, spoke with his sour mouth close to the piece, his chubby hand with blackish fingernails were doodling on a writing pad.

"You were always looking for strong emotions," Carlitos said. "Somehow you seemed to get them."

"Yes, Porvenir, get over there right now with Periquito." Becerrita hung up the phone, fastened his rheumy little eyes on Santiago. "That woman used to sing there some time ago. The woman who runs it knows me. Get information, pictures. Her girl friends, her boyfriends, addresses, the kind of life she led. Have Periquito take some pictures of the place."

Santiago put on his jacket as he went down the stairs. Becerrita had called Darío and the van, parked in front of the door, was blocking traffic; the drivers blew their horns. A moment later Periquito appeared, furious.

"I'd warned Arispe that I wouldn't work for that slave driver anymore and now he gives me to Becerrita for a week." He was loading his camera, complaining. "He's going to grind us into dust, Zavalita."

"He may have the mood of a dog, but he fights like a lion for his reporters," Darío said. "If it wasn't for him old drunken Carlitos would have been fired long ago. Don't put Becerrita down."

"I'm going to quit the newspaper business, I've had enough," Periquito said. "I'm going to get into commercial photography. One week with Becerrita is worse than a dose of the clap."

The van went up Colmena to the Parque Universitario, down Azán-

338

garo, passed the whitish stone base of the Palace of Justice, turned into the rainy sunset of República, and when, on the right, in the middle of the shadowy park, the Cabaña appeared with its lighted windows and sparkling sign in front, Periquito began to laugh, calm all of a sudden: he didn't even want to look at that dive, Zavalita, his liver was still one big ulcer from the drunk he'd been on last Sunday.

"With a single item on his page he can sink any go-go girl, close any brothel, ruin the reputation of any nightclub," Darío said. "Becerrita is a god in Lima's bohemian world. And no page editor treats his people the way he does. He takes them to whorehouses, buys them drinks, gets women for them. I don't know how you can complain about him, Periquito."

"All right," Periquito admitted. "Keep a stiff upper lip in a storm. If we have to work with him, instead of getting bitter, let's try to exploit his weak point."

The brothels, the stinking dives, the promiscuous little bars with vomit and sawdust, the fauna of three o'clock in the morning. He thinks: his weak point. That's where he became human, he thinks, that's where he made himself liked. Darío put the brakes on: a faceless mass was moving along the sidewalks in the shadows of 28 de Julio, over the gloomy silhouettes the small, rancid light of the lamps of Porvenir languished. It was misty, the night was very damp. The door of the Montmartre was closed.

"Let's knock, Paqueta must be inside," Periquito said. "This dive opens late, the nightclubs pour out into here."

They knocked on the glass of the door—a piano player in the pink light of the window, he thinks, his teeth as white as the keys of his piano, two dancers with plumes on their behinds and their heads—steps were heard, a skinny boy in a white vest and a small bow tie who looked at them with concern: from *La Crónica*, right? Come in, madame was expecting them. A bar covered with bottles, a ceiling with platinum stars, a tiny dance floor with an upright microphone, empty tables and chairs. A small disguised door behind the bar opened, good evening said Periquito and there was Paqueta, Zavalita: her eyes with long false lashes and round halos of eyeshadow, her scarlet cheeks, her protuberant buttocks smothering in the tight slacks, her tiny tightrope-walker steps.

"Did Mr. Becerra talk to you?" Santiago asked. "It's about the murder in Jesús María."

"He promised to keep me completely out of it, he swore to me and I hope he keeps his word." Her spongy hand, her mechanical smile, her honeyed voice with a touch of alarm and hatred. "If there's any scandal, it's the place that will suffer, understand?"

"We only want a little information," Santiago said. "Who she was, what she did."

"I barely knew her, I don't know much of anything." The stiff lashes that fluttered evasively, Zavalita, the thick red lips that closed up like mimosa leaves. "She stopped singing here six months ago. Farther back than that, eight months ago. She'd just about lost her voice, I hired her because I felt sorry for her, she'd sing three or four numbers and leave. Before that she was at the Laguna."

She stopped speaking when the first rainbow burst and she remained looking, her mouth open: Periquito was peacefully taking pictures of the bar, the dance floor, the microphone.

"What are those pictures for?" she grumbled, pointing. "Becerrita swore to me that my name wouldn't be mentioned."

"Just to show one of the places where she sang, your name won't be mentioned," Santiago said. "I'd like to know something about the Muse's private life. Some story, anything."

"I don't know much of anything," Paqueta murmured, following Periquito with her eyes. "Outside of what everybody knows. That she was pretty famous a long time ago, that she sang at the Embassy Club, that later on she was the girl friend of you know who. But I imagine they won't say anything about that."

"Why not, ma'am?" Periquito laughed. "Odría isn't President anymore, Manuel Prado is, and *La Crónica* belongs to the Prados. We can say whatever we want to."

"And I thought we would be able to and I mentioned it in the first story, Carlitos." Santiago laughed. "Former mistress of Cayo Bermúdez stabbed to death."

"I think you're being a little dumb, Zavalita," Becerrita grunted, looking over the pages ill-humoredly. "Well, let's see what the big boss thinks."

340

"Nightclub star stabbed to death would have more impact," Arispe said. "And besides, they're orders from above, my good sir."

"Was she or wasn't she the mistress of that son of a bitch?" Becerrita asked. "And if she was and the son of a bitch isn't in the government and isn't even in the country, why can't we say it?"

"Because it suits the balls of the headman not to say it, my good sir," Arispe said.

"All right, that argument always wins me over," Becerrita said. "Change the whole story, Zavalita. Wherever you say former mistress of Cayo Bermúdez put former nightclub queen."

"And then Bermúdez abandoned her and left the country, during Odría's last days." Paqueta snorted: another bulb had just flashed. "You probably remember, during that trouble with the Coalition in Arequipa. She went back to singing, but she wasn't the same as before. Not her looks and not her voice. She drank a lot, once she tried to kill herself. She couldn't get work. The poor girl had a hard time of it."

"All the time you were with him you never knew him to have a woman?" Santiago asks. "He must have been queer, then."

"What kind of life did she lead?" Paqueta asked. "A bad life, I already told you. She drank, she couldn't hold onto boyfriends, always needing money. I hired her because I felt sorry for her, and I didn't keep her long, only a couple of months, maybe not even that long. The customers were bored. Her songs were out of style. She tried to get up to date, but she just couldn't get the new music."

"I didn't know him to have any mistresses, but he did have some women," Ambrosio says. "Whores, that is, son."

"And what was that drug trouble all about, ma'am," Santiago said.

"Drugs?" Paqueta said, stupefied. "What drugs?"

"He would go to whorehouses, I took him a lot of times," Ambrosio says. "To that one you remembered from way back. Ivonne's, that one. Lots of times."

"But you were involved too, ma'am, you were arrested with her," Santiago said. "And, thanks to Mr. Becerra, nothing came out in the papers, don't you remember?"

A quick tremor animated her fleshy face, the inflexible lashes vibrated with indignation, but then a challenging, reminiscent smile softened

Paqueta's expression. She closed her eyes as if to look inside and locate that lost episode among her memories: oh yes, oh that.

"And Ludovico, the fellow I told you about, the one who got me into a jam by sending me to Pucallpa, the one who took my place as Don Cayo's chauffeur, he used to take him to whorehouses all the time," Ambrosio says. "No, son, he wasn't any fairy."

"There weren't any drugs or anything like that involved, it was a mistake, it was cleared up right there," Paqueta said. "The police arrested a person who used to come here from time to time, he was pushing cocaine, it seems, and they called her and me as witnesses. We didn't know anything and they let us go."

"Who was the Muse going with when she was working here?" Santiago asked.

"Who was her lover?" Her overlapping and uneven teeth, Zavalita, her gossipy eyes. "She didn't have just one, she had a lot of them."

"Even if you don't give me their names," Santiago said, "at least tell me what kind of guys they were."

"She had her adventures, but I don't know the details, she wasn't my girl friend," Paqueta said. "I only know what everybody else does, that she'd fallen into a bad life and that's all."

"Do you know if she has any family here?" Santiago asked. "Or some girl friend who might be able to give us more information?"

"I don't think she had any family," Paqueta said. "She said she was Peruvian, but some people thought she was a foreigner. They said she got her Peruvian passport through you know who, when he was her lover."

"Mr. Becerra would like some photographs of the Muse when she was singing here," Santiago said.

"I'll give them to you, but please don't get me mixed up in this, don't mention my name," Paqueta said. "I'll help you under that condition. Becerrita promised me."

"And we'll keep his promise, ma'am," Santiago said. "Don't you know anyone who could give us more information on her? That's the last question and we'll leave you alone."

"When she stopped singing here I didn't see her again." Paqueta sighed, suddenly took on the mysterious air of an informer. "But you

342

heard things about her. That she'd gone into one of those houses. I'm not sure. I only know that she lived with a woman who was a hustler, who worked at the Frenchwoman's place."

"The Muse with one of the women from Ivonne's?" Santiago asked.

"You can name the Frenchwoman." Paqueta laughed, and her soft voice had become growly with hatred. "Use her name, so the police will bring her in for questioning. That old woman knows a lot of things."

"What was the name of the girl friend she lived with?" Santiago asked.

"Queta?" Ambrosio says, and a few seconds later, stupefied: "Queta, son?"

"If you say I gave the information they'll ruin me, the Frenchwoman is the worst enemy you could have." Paqueta softened her voice. "I don't know her real name. Queta's the name she went by."

"Didn't you ever see her?" Santiago asks. "Didn't you ever hear Bermúdez mention her?"

"They were living together and people said a lot of things about them," Paqueta whispered, winking. "That they were more than just girl friends. It was probably all gossip, of course."

"I never heard of her, I never saw her," Ambrosio says. "Don Cayo wasn't going to talk to me about his chippies, I was just his chauffeur, son."

They went out into the mist, dampness and darkness of Porvenir; Darío was nodding, leaning over the steering wheel of the van. When he started up the motor a dog barked mournfully from the sidewalk.

"She'd forgotten about the coke, that she'd been arrested with the Muse." Periquito laughed. "Some nerve, eh?"

"She's glad she got killed, you can see that she hated her," Santiago said. "Did you catch it all, Periquito? That she was a drunk, that she'd lost her voice, that she was a dyke?"

"But you got some good information from her," Periquito said. "You can't complain."

"This is all garbage," Becerrita said. "You've got to keep on digging until you hit the pus."

Those had been agitated and difficult days, Zavalita, you felt interested, restless, he thinks: alive again. Coming and going without rest: getting in and out of the van, going in and out of nightclubs, radio stations, boardinghouses, brothels, an incessant back and forth among the musty night-walking fauna of the city.

"The name Muse doesn't come off too well, we have to rechristen her," Becerrita said. "On the Track of the Nighttime Butterfly!"

You wrote long articles, short pieces, boxes, captions for the photographs with a growing excitement, Zavalita. Becerrita would read over the pages with sour eyes, scratching out, adding words with trembling red letters, and he would write the headlines: New Revelations in Dissipated Life of Nighttime Butterfly Murdered in Jesús María. Was Muse a Woman with a Terrible Past? *La Crónica* Reporters Uncover New Facts in Crime That Has All Lima Shocked, From Show Business Start to Bloody End of One-Time Night-Life Queen, Stabbed Nighttime Butterfly Had Fallen to Lowest Level of Immorality Manager of Nightclub Where Muse Sang Her Last Songs Declares, Did Nighttime Butterfly Lose Voice Because of Drugs?

"We've left *Última Hora* way behind," Arispe said. "Keep laying it on, Becerrita."

"More swill for the dogs, Zavalita," Carlitos said. "Those are the orders from the big boss."

"You're doing a good job, Zavalita," Becerrita said. "In twenty years you'll be a passable police reporter."

"Piling up shit with a great deal of enthusiasm, a small pile today, a little more tomorrow, a fair amount day after tomorrow," Santiago said. "Until there was a whole mountain of shit. And now to eat it, down to the last crumb. That's what happened to me, Carlitos."

"Are we through now, Mr. Becerra?" Periquito asked. "Can I go get some sleep?"

"We haven't even started," Becerrita said. "Let's go see Madama to find out if that muff business is true."

Robertito had come out to meet them, welcome to this house which is yours, how was life treating him, Mr. Becerra, but Becerrita took away his joy at once: they'd come on business, could they go into the parlor? Come in, Mr. Becerra, all of you.

"Bring the boys some beer," Becerrita said. "And bring me Madama. It's urgent."

Robertito shook his chestnut curls, nodded with an unfriendly chuckle, left with the leap of a ballet dancer. Periquito dropped into an easy chair with his legs stretched out, it was nice here, so elegant, and Santiago sat down beside him. The carpeted parlor, he thinks, the indirect lighting, the three paintings on the wall. In the first one a young man with blond hair and a mask was chasing along a tangled path after a very white girl with a wasp waist who was running on tiptoes; in the second one he had caught her and embracing they were sinking into a cascade of willows; in the third one the girl was lying on the grass, her bosom exposed, the young man was tenderly kissing her round shoulders and her expression was half alarmed and half languid. They were on the shore of a lake or a river and in the distance there was a group of long-necked swans.

"You're the most rotten younger generation in history," Becerrita said with satisfaction. "What else interests you besides drinking and whoring?"

His mouth was twisted in an almost smiling grimace, he was scratching his little mustache with his mustard-colored fingers, he'd pushed back his hat and was pacing up and down with one hand in his pocket, like the villain in a Mexican movie, he thinks. Robertito came in with a tray.

"The lady will be right along, Mr. Becerra." He bowed. "She asked me if you'd like some whiskey."

"I can't. My ulcer," Becerrita grunted. "Every time I take a drink I shit blood the next day."

Robertito went out and there was Ivonne, Zavalita. Her long and heavily powdered nose, he thinks, her dress with crepe and noisy spangles. Mature, experienced, smiling, she kissed Becerrita on the cheek, extended a courtly hand to Periquito and Santiago. She looked at the tray, hadn't Robertito served them? she gave a reproachful look, leaned over and filled the glasses expertly, halfway and without much foam, brought them to them. She sat down on the edge of the chair, stretched out her neck, crossed her legs, the skin was gathered into little folds under her eyes.

"Don't look at me with that face full of surprise," Becerrita said. "You know why we're here, Madama."

"I can't believe that you don't want anything to drink." Her foreign

345

accent, Zavalita, her affected gestures, her ease of a well-to-do matriarch. "You're an old-time drunk, Becerrita."

"I used to be, until my ulcer made mincemeat of my stomach," Becerrita said. "Now all I can drink is milk. From a cow."

"Still the same." Ivonne turned to Santiago and Periquito. "This old man and I are like a brother and a sister, for centuries now."

"A little incestuous at one point." Becerrita laughed, and opening up with the same intimate tone, "Make believe I'm a priest and you're making your confession. How long did you have the Muse here?"

"The Muse, here?" Ivonne smiled. "You make a funny priest, Becerrita."

"Now you don't trust me." Becerrita sat on the arm of Ivonne's chair. "Now you're lying to me."

"You're crazy, Father." Ivonne smiled and slapped Becerrita on the knee. "If she'd worked here I would have told you."

She took a handkerchief from her sleeve, wiped her eyes, stopped smiling. She knew her, of course, sometimes she'd come here when she was the girl friend of, well, Becerrita knew who. He'd brought her several times to have some fun, so she could spy from that little window that looked out into the bar. But as far as Ivonne knew she'd never worked in any house. She laughed again, elegantly. The little wrinkles around her eyes, on her neck, he thinks, her hatred: the poor thing worked off the street, like a bitch.

"It's easy to see that you had a lot of love for her, Madama," Becerrita grunted.

"When she was Bermúdez' mistress she looked down on everybody." Ivonne sighed. "She wouldn't even let me come to her house. That's why nobody helped her when she lost everything. And it was her own fault that she lost it. Drink and drugs."

"You're delighted she was knocked off." Becerrita smiled. "Nice feelings, Madama."

"When I read the papers I felt bad, crimes like that always make me feel bad," Ivonne said. "Especially the pictures, seeing the way she was living. If you want to say that she worked here I'd be delighted. Good publicity for the place."

"You feel so very confident, Madama," Becerrita said with a faded smile. "You must have found a protector as good as Cayo Bermúdez."

"Gossip. Bermúdez never had anything to do with this house," Ivonne said. "He was a customer like anyone else."

"Let's get back onto the pot, we're crapping on the ground," Becerrita said. "She didn't work here, O.K. Call the girl she lived with. She can give us some information and I'll leave you alone."

"The girl she lived with?" Her whole expression changed, Carlitos, she lost control completely, she got livid. "One of my girls living with her?"

"Oh, the police haven't found out yet." Becerrita scratched his little mustache and ran his tongue over his lips avidly. "But they're going to find out sooner or later and they'll come to question you and a certain Queta. You'd better be ready, Madama."

"With Queta?" Her whole world had collapsed, Carlitos. "What are you saying, Becerrita?"

"They change their names every day and people always get them mixed up, which one is she?" Becerrita murmured. "Don't worry, we're not the police. Call her. All we want is a quiet, confidential chat."

"Who told you that Queta was living with her?" Ivonne babbled: she was making an effort to recover her smile, her naturalness.

"I do trust you, Madama, I am your friend," Becerrita whispered with an open tone. "Paqueta told us."

"The worst kind of a whore's daughter who ever bore a whore." At first a wiggy old dame with the airs of a great lady, Carlitos, then a frightened old lady, and, when she heard Paqueta's name, a panther. "The kind that grew up gargling on her mother's menstrual blood."

"I do enjoy that mouth of yours, Madama." Becerrita put his arm around her shoulder, happy. "We'll avenge you, in tomorrow's article we'll say that the Montmartre is the joint with the worst reputation in Lima."

"Can't you see that she'll be ruined?" Ivonne said, grasping Becerrita's knee, squeezing it. "Can't you see that the police will bring her in for questioning?"

"Did she see something?" Becerrita asked, lowering his voice. "Does she know something?"

"Of course not, she just doesn't want to get into any trouble," Ivonne said. "You'll get her all messed up. Why would you want to do a bad thing like that?"

"I don't want anything to happen to her, just for her to tell me a few intimate details about the Muse," Becerrita said. "We won't say that they lived together, we won't use her name. Do you trust my word or not?"

"Of course not," Ivonne said. "You're another bastard just like Paqueta."

"That's the way I like you, Madama." Becerrita looked at Santiago and Periquito with a furtive smile. "The way you really are."

"Queta's a good girl, Becerrita," Ivonne said in a faint voice. "Don't torpedo her. It could be bad for you, besides. She's got a lot of good friends, I warn you."

"Just call her and cut out the dramatics." Becerrita smiled. "I swear to you that nothing's going to happen to her."

"Do you think she feels like coming to work after what happened to her friend?" Ivonne asked.

"All right, get hold of her and set up a date for me with her," Becerrita said. "I just want a few facts. If she doesn't want to talk to me, I'll print her name on the front page and she'll have to talk to the detectives."

"Do you swear that if I can arrange for you to see Queta you won't mention her at all?" Ivonne asked.

Becerrita nodded. His face was slowly filling up with satisfaction, his little eyes were gleaming. He stood up, went over to the table, with a determined gesture he picked up Santiago's glass and emptied it in a swallow. A rim of foam whitened his mouth.

"I swear to you, Madama, get hold of her and call me," he said solemnly. "You've got my number."

"Do you think she's going to call you, Mr. Becerra?" Periquito asked in the van. "I'll bet she tells that Queta that the people from *La Crónica* know that you were living with the Muse, get lost."

"But which one is Queta?" Arispe asked. "We must know her, Becerrita."

"She must be one of the exclusive ones who work at home," Becerrita said. "Maybe we do know her, but under a different name."

"That woman's worth her weight in gold, my good sir," Arispe said.

"You've got to find her, even if you have to turn over every stone in Lima."

"Didn't I tell you that Madama would call me?" Becerrita looked at them without vanity, mockingly. "Tonight at seven. Let me have the whole centerfold, boss."

"Come in, come in," Robertito said. "Yes, in the parlor. Have a seat."

In that way, with the light of dusk coming through the single window, the small parlor had lost its mystery and enchantment. The worn upholstery of the furniture, he thinks, the faded wallpaper, the cigarette burns and rips in the carpet. The girl in the paintings had no features, the swans were misshapen.

"Hello, Becerrita." Ivonne didn't kiss him, didn't shake hands. "I promised Queta that you're going to do what you promised. Why did you bring these people with you?"

"Have Robertito bring us some beers," Becerrita said without getting up out of his chair, without looking at the woman who'd come in with Ivonne. "I'll pay for these, Madama."

"Tall, beautiful legs, a mulatto girl with reddish hair," Santiago said. "I'd never seen her at Ivonne's, Carlitos."

"Sit down," Becerrita said with the air of the master of the house. "Aren't you people going to have something to drink?"

Robertito filled the glasses with beer, his hands trembled as he handed them to Becerrita, Periquito and Santiago, his lashes blinked rapidly, his look was frightened. He almost ran out, closing the door behind him. Queta sat down on a sofa, serious, not frightened, he thinks, and Ivonne's eyes were burning.

"Yes, you're one of the exclusive ones, because you're not seen much around here," Becerrita said, taking a sip of beer. "Do you only work outside, with special customers?"

"It's no business of yours where I work," Queta said. "And who gave you permission to use the familiar form with me?"

"Take it easy, don't carry on so," Ivonne said. "He's someone we can trust and that's all. He's only going to ask you a few questions."

"You couldn't be my client even if you wanted to, be happy with that," Queta said. "You'll never have enough money to pay what I charge."

"I'm not a client anymore, I've retired," Becerrita said with a mocking

349

smile and wiped his mustache. "How long did you live with the Muse in Jesús María?"

"I didn't live with her, that's one of that bitch's lies," Queta shouted, but Ivonne took her arm and she lowered her voice. "You're not going to get me mixed up in this. I warn you that . . . ."

"We're not cops, we're reporters," Becerrita said with a friendly expression. "It's not about you, it's about the Muse. You tell us what you know about her and we'll go away and forget all about you. There's no reason to get mad, Queta."

"Why the threats, then?" Queta shouted. "Why did you come and tell this lady you'd tell the police? Do you think I've got anything to hide?"

"If you haven't got anything to hide, there's no reason to be afraid of the police," Becerrita said and took another sip of beer. "I've come here as a friend, to have a little chat. There's no reason to get mad."

"He's a man of his word, he'll do what he says, Queta," Ivonne said. "He won't use your name. Answer his questions."

"All right, ma'am, I know," Queta said. "What are the questions?"

"This is a conversation among friends," Becerrita said. "I'm a man of my word, Queta. How long did you live with the Muse?"

"I didn't live with her." She was making an effort to control herself, Carlitos, she was trying not to look at Becerrita, when her eyes met his her voice fell apart. "We were friends, sometimes I slept over at her place. She moved to Jesús María, it must have been a little over a year ago."

"Did he mount an attack and break her?" Carlitos asked. "That's Becerrita's method. Break down the patient's nerves so they let everything out. It's the method of a detective, not a reporter."

Santiago and Periquito hadn't touched their beer: they were following the conversation from the edge of their seats, silent. He'd broken her, Zavalita, now she was answering everything. Her voice was rising and falling, he thinks, Ivonne was patting her arm, giving her courage. The poor thing was in bad shape, very bad shape, especially when she lost her job at the Montmartre, especially because Paqueta had been so bitchy with her. She'd thrown her out knowing that she'd starve to death, the poor thing. She'd had her affairs, but she couldn't get a lover anymore, someone who would give her something every month and pay her rent.

And all of a sudden she began to cry, Carlitos, not because of Becerrita's questions, but over the Muse. Or maybe loyalty did still exist, at least among a few whores, Zavalita.

"The poor thing must have been completely ruined then." Becerrita grew sad, his hand on his mustache, his sparkling eyes focused on Queta. "From drinking, from snuffing coke, I mean."

"Are you going to put that in too?" Queta sobbed. "On top of the horrors they're printing about her every day, that too?"

"That she was in bad shape, that she was half a whore, that she drank and screwed around, everything the newspapers have said," Becerrita sighed. "We're the only ones who have stressed her good side. That she was a famous singer, that she was elected Queen of the Nightclubs, that she was one of the most beautiful women in Lima."

"Instead of digging into her life so much, you ought to be worrying about who killed her, who had her killed," Queta sobbed and covered her face with her hands. "They don't talk about them, they don't dare."

At that moment, Zavalita? He thinks: yes, there. Ivonne's petrified face, he thinks, the suspicion and upset in her eyes, Becerrita's fingers immobilized on his mustache, Periquito's elbow on your hip, Zavalita, alerting you. The four had remained silent, looking at Queta, who was sobbing strongly. He thinks: Becerrita's little eyes perforating the red hair, all aflame.

"I'm not afraid, I print anything, the paper can take anything," Becerrita finally whispered softly. "If you dare, I dare. Who was it? Who do you think it was?"

"If you're dumb enough to get mixed up in something, that's your lookout." Ivonne's frightened face, Carlitos, her terror, the shout she gave. "If those dumb things you're thinking about, if that dumb thing you've invented . . ."

"You don't understand, Madama." The small, almost weepy voice of Becerrita, Carlitos. "She doesn't want the death of her friend to stay just like that, nowhere. If Queta dares, I dare. Who do you think it was, Queta?"

"They're not dumb things, you know I'm not making it up, ma'am," Queta sobbed, and she lifted her head and let it out, Carlitos: "You know that Cayo Shithead's strong-arm man killed her."

351

All pores sweating, he thinks, all bones creaking. Not missing the smallest gesture, not a syllable, not moving, not breathing, and at the entrance to his stomach the little worm growing, the snake, the knives, just like that time, he thinks, worse than that time. Oh, Zavalita.

"Are you going to cry now?" Ambrosio asks. "Don't have anything more to drink, son."

"If you want me to, I'll publish it, if you want, I'll tell it just the way it is, if you don't want me to, I won't put anything in," Becerrita said. "Is Cayo Shithead Cayo Bermúdez? Are you sure he ordered her killed? That bastard's living a long way off from Peru, Queta."

There was the face deformed by weeping, Zavalita, the eyes swollen and red, the mouth twisted with anguish, there were the head and hands denying: not Bermúdez.

"What killer?" Becerrita insisted. "Did you see him, were you there?"

"Queta was in Huacachina," Ivonne interrupted, threatening him with her forefinger. "With a senator, if you want to know who with."

"I hadn't seen Hortensia for three days," Queta sobbed. "I found out about it in the papers. But I know, I'm not lying."

"Where did the strong-arm man come from?" Becerrita repeated, his little eyes fastened on Queta, pacifying Ivonne with an impatient hand. "I won't publish anything, Madama, only what Queta wants me to say. If she doesn't dare, naturally, I won't either."

"Hortensia knew lots of things about a certain moneybags, she was starving to death, she just wanted to get away from here," Queta sobbed. "It wasn't out of meanness, it was just to get away and start all over again, where nobody knew her. She was already half dead when she was killed. From the awful way that swine Bermúdez behaved, from the awful way everybody behaved when they saw her down."

"She was getting money out of him and the guy had her killed so she wouldn't blackmail him anymore," Becerrita recited softly. "Who is the guy who hired the killer?"

"He didn't hire him, he must have talked to him," Queta said, looking into Becerrita's eyes. "He must have talked to him and convinced him. He had him under his power, he was like his slave. He could do whatever he wanted with him."

352

"I dare, I'll print it," Becerrita repeated, in a low voice. "What the hell, I believe you, Queta."

"Gold Ball had her killed," Queta said. "The killer was his pratboy. His name is Ambrosio."

"Gold Ball?" He leaped to his feet, Carlitos, blinking, he looked at Periquito, at me, he regretted it and looked at Queta, at the floor, and repeated, like an idiot: "Gold Ball? Gold Ball?"

"Fermín Zavala, you can see that she's crazy," Ivonne exploded, standing up too, shouting. "Isn't that a stupid thing, Becerrita? Even if it was true, it would be a stupid thing. Don't pay any attention to her, she's making it all up."

"Hortensia was getting money out of him, was threatening him with his wife, with telling the story about his chauffeur all over town," Queta roared. "It's not a lie, instead of buying her a ticket to Mexico, he had her killed by his pratboy. Are you going to tell it, are you going to print it?"

"We're not going to sprinkle everybody with shit." And he collapsed in his chair, Carlitos, without looking at me, snorting, suddenly he put on his hat so his hands would have something to do. "What proof have you got, where'd you pick up such a thing? It doesn't hold water. I don't like to be kidded, Queta."

"I told her it was foolishness, I told her a hundred times," Ivonne said. "She hasn't got any proof, she was in Huacachina, she doesn't know anything. And even if she did, who's going to listen, who's going to believe it. Fermín Zavala, with all his millions. You explain it to her, Becerrita. Tell her what can happen if she keeps on repeating that story."

"You're spattering yourself with shit, Queta, and you're spattering all of us too," he grunted, Carlitos, making faces, fixing his hat. "Do you want me to print that so they'll lock us all up in the booby hatch, Queta?"

"Incredible for him," Carlitos said. "All that filth was good for something. At least we found out that Becerrita is human too, that he can behave properly."

"You had something to do, didn't you?" Becerrita grunted, looking at his watch, his voice anxiously natural. "On your way, Zavalita."

353

"You damned coward," Queta said softly. "I knew you were only saying it, I knew you wouldn't dare."

"At least you were able to get on your feet and get out of there without bursting out into tears," Carlitos said. "The only thing that bothered me was that the whores knew about it and you couldn't go back to that brothel. After all, it's the best one in town, Zavalita."

"You mean at least I ran into you," Santiago said. "I don't know what I would have done that night without you, Carlitos."

Yes, it had been a piece of luck running into him, a piece of luck going to the Plaza San Martín and not to the boardinghouse in Barranco, a piece of luck not going home to cry with his mouth against his pillow in the loneliness of his little room, feeling that the world had ended and thinking about killing yourself or killing your poor old man, Zavalita. He'd got up, said so long, left the room, bumped into Robertito in the hall, walked to the Plaza Dos de Mayo without finding a taxi. You were breathing in the cold air with your mouth open, Zavalita, you felt your heart beating and sometimes you ran. You'd taken a group taxi, got out at Colmena, walked confusedly under the Portal, and suddenly there was Carlitos' broken-down figure standing by a table in the Zela Bar, his hand calling you. Had they come back from Ivonne's already, Zavalita, had that girl Queta shown up? What about Periquito and Becerrita? But when he got to Santiago he changed his tone: what was wrong, Zavalita.

"I feel sick." You'd taken his arm, Zavalita. "Awful sick, old man."

There was Carlitos looking at you with concern, hesitant, there was the pat he gave you on the shoulder: they'd better go have a drink, Zavalita. He let himself be dragged along, like a sleepwalker he went down the stairs of the Negro-Negro, crossed the floor blindly and stumbling in the half-empty shadows of the place, their usual table was empty, two German beers Carlitos said to the waiter and leaned against the *New Yorker* covers.

"We always end up shipwrecked here, Zavalita." His curly head, he thinks, the friendship in his eyes, his unshaven face, his yellow skin. "This den has got us hypnotized."

"If I'd gone to the boardinghouse I would have gone crazy, Carlitos," Santiago said.

"I thought it was a drunkard's moaning, but now I can see it wasn't,"

Carlitos said. "Everybody ends up having a fight with Becerrita. Did he get drunk and throw you the hell out of the whorehouse? Don't pay any attention to him, man."

There were the bright covers, sardonic and multicolored, the sound of conversation among invisible people. The waiter brought the beers, they drank in unison. Carlitos looked at him over his glass, offered him a cigarette and lighted it for him.

"This is where we had our first masochistic dialogue, Zavalita," he said. "This is where we confessed that we were failures as a poet and as a Communist. Now we're just a pair of newspapermen. This is where we became friends, Zavalita."

"I've got to tell you something because it's burning a hole in me, Carlitos," Santiago said.

"If it'll make you feel better, O.K.," Carlitos said. "But think it over. Sometimes I start telling secrets when I have a crisis and afterwards I'm sorry and I hate the people who know my weak points. I don't want you to hate me tomorrow, Zavalita."

But Santiago had started to cry again. Bending over the table, he was muffling his sobs by holding his handkerchief tight against his mouth, and he felt Carlitos' hand on his shoulder: take it easy, man.

"Well, it had to be that." Softly, he thinks, timidly, compassionate. "Did Becerrita get drunk and bring out that business about your father in front of the whole brothel?"

Not the moment when you found out, Zavalita, but there. He thinks: the moment I found out that everybody in Lima knew he was a fairy except me. Everybody on the paper, Zavalita, except you. The piano player had started to play, a woman's little laugh in the darkness occasionally, the acid taste of the beer, the waiter came with his light to take away the bottles and bring some new ones. You were talking and tearing your handkerchief, Zavalita, drying your mouth and your eyes. He thinks: the world wasn't going to end, you weren't going to go crazy, you weren't going to kill yourself.

"You know people's tongues, whores' tongues." Leaning forward and back in his chair, he thinks, startled, he was surprised too. "She brought out that story to take Becerrita down a peg, to shut his mouth because of the bad time he'd put her through."

"They were talking about him as if they were old chums," Santiago said. "And me there, Carlitos."

"The worst fucking part about it isn't that story about the murder, that's got to be a lie, Zavalita." He was stammering too, he thinks, he was contradicting himself too. "But that you found out about the other thing there and from that mouth. I thought you already knew, Zavalita."

"Gold Ball, his pratboy, his chauffeur," Santiago said. "As if they'd known him all his life. He in the midst of all that filth, Carlitos. And me there."

It couldn't be and you were smoking, Zavalita, it had to be a lie and you were taking a drink and getting worked up, and you were losing your voice and you kept on repeating it couldn't be. And Carlitos, his face dissolved in smoke, in front of the indifferent covers: it seemed terrible to you but it wasn't, Zavalita, there were more terrible things. You'd get used to it, you wouldn't give a damn and he ordered more beer.

"I'm going to get you drunk," he said, making a face. "Your body will be in such fucked-up shape that you won't be able to think about anything else. A few more drinks and you won't be able to think about anything else. A few more drinks and you'll see that it's not worth getting so bitter about, Zavalita."

But he was the one who got drunk, he thinks, like you now. Carlitos got up, disappeared into the shadows, the woman's small laugh that died out and reappeared and the monotonous piano: I wanted to get you drunk and the one who got drunk is me, Ambrosio. There was Carlitos again, he'd pissed away a quart of beer, Zavalita, what a waste of money, eh?

"And why did you want to get me drunk?" Ambrosio laughs. "I never get drunk, son."

"Everybody on the newspaper knew about it," Santiago said. "When I'm not there, do they talk about Gold Ball's boy, the fairy's son?"

"You talk as if the problem was yours and not his," Carlitos said. "Don't be dumb, Zavalita."

"I never heard anything, at school, in the neighborhood, at the university," Santiago said. "If it was true, I would have heard something, suspected something. Never, Carlitos."

"It could be one of those bits of gossip that float around in this

356

country," Carlitos said. "The kind that change into truth because they've lasted so long. Don't think about it anymore."

"Or maybe I didn't want to know," Santiago said. "I didn't want to be aware of it, Carlitos."

"I'm not consoling you, there's no reason to, you're out of it," Carlitos said, belching. "He's the one who should be consoled. If it's a lie, because they've stuck him with it, and if it's true, because his life must have been pretty well fucked up. Put it out of your mind."

"But that other business can't be true, Carlitos," Santiago said. "That other business must be a damned lie. It can't be true, Carlitos."

"That whore must hate him for some reason, she made that tale up to get back at him for something," Carlitos said. "Some bedroom intrigue, some piece of blackmail to get money out of him, maybe. I don't know how you can warn him. Especially since it's been years since you've seen him, hasn't it?"

"Me warn him? Do you think I èver want to see his face again after this?" Santiago said. "I'd die of shame, Carlitos."

"Nobody dies of shame." Carlitos smiled and belched again. "You'll know what to do in the end. In any case, the story will stay buried one way or another."

"You know Becerrita," Santiago said. "It isn't buried. You know what he's going to do."

"Consult with Arispe and Arispe with the owners, of course I know," Carlitos said. "Do you think Becerrita is dumb, that Arispe is dumb? Upper-crust people never appear on the police page. Were you worried about that, the scandal? You're still bourgeois, Zavalita."

He belched and started to laugh and kept on talking, wandering more and more: tonight you're a man, Zavalita, or you never will be. Yes, it had been a piece of luck: watching him get drunk, he thinks, listening to him belch, ramble on, having to drag him out of the Negro-Negro, hold him up in the Portal while a boy went for a cab. A piece of luck having had to take him to Chorrillos, bringing him up the ancient staircase of his house hanging on your shoulder, and undressing him and putting him to bed, Zavalita. Knowing that he wasn't drunk, he thinks, that he was pretending in order to distract you and keep you busy, so that you'd think about him and not about yourself. He thinks: I'll bring

357

you a book, I'll go by tomorrow. In spite of the bad taste in his mouth, the fog in his brain and the breakdown of his body, he'd felt better the next morning. Aching and at the same time stronger, he thinks, his muscles swollen from the uncomfortable easy chair where he'd slept with his clothes on, more peaceful, changed by the nightmare, older. There was the small shower crammed between the washbasin and the toilet in Carlitos' room, the cold water that made you shiver and finally woke you up. He got dressed slowly. Carlitos was still asleep on his belly, his head hanging off the bed, in his shorts and with his socks on. There was the street and the sunlight that the morning mist was unable to hide, only maim, there was the small café on the corner and the group of streetcar conductors with blue caps talking about soccer at the counter. He ordered coffee, asked what time it was, ten o'clock, he was probably in the office already, you didn't feel nervous or sentimental, Zavalita. In order to get to the telephone he had to go under the counter, through a corridor with sacks and crates, while he was dialing the number he watched a column of ants climbing up a beam. His hands suddenly grew moist as he recognized Sparky's voice: yes, hello?

"Hello, Sparky." Tickling all over his body there, the feeling that the ground was going soft. "Yes, it's me, Santiago."

"The coast isn't clear." Sparky's whispering and almost inaudible voice there, his tone of an accomplice. "Call me later, the old man's here."

"I want to talk to him," Santiago said. "Yes, to the old man. Put him on, it's urgent."

The long stupefied or baffled or amazed silence there, the remote clacking of a typewriter, and Sparky's unhinged little cough as he was probably swallowing the telephone with his eyes and not knowing what to say, what to do, and there his theatrical yell: hey, it's Skinny, it's Superbrain, and the typewriter stopped at once. Where've you been keeping yourself, Skinny, when did you rise up from the dead, Superbrain, what are you waiting for to come to the house? Yes papa, Skinny papa, he wanted to talk to you papa. Voices that rose over Sparky's and drowned it out and the rush of heat on your face there, Zavalita.

"Hello, hello, Skinny?" The identical voice from years past there, breaking, Zavalita, filled with anguish, joy, his confused voice which was shouting: "Son? Skinny? Are you there?"

"Hello, papa." There at the end of the hallway, behind the counter, the conductors were laughing and next to you a row of bottles of Pasteurina and the ants disappearing among tins of crackers. "Yes, I'm here, papa. How's mama, how's everybody, papa?"

"Angry with you, Skinny, waiting for you every day, Skinny." The terribly hopeful voice, Zavalita, disturbed, stumbling. "What about you, are you all right? Where are you calling from, Skinny?"

"From Chorrillos, papa." Thinking a lie, he wasn't, he thinks, calumny, he couldn't be. "I have to talk to you about something, papa. If you're not too busy now, could I see you this morning?"

"Yes, right away, I'll come right over." And suddenly alarmed, anxious. "Nothing's happened to you, has it, Skinny? You're not in any trouble, are you?"

"No, papa, no trouble. If you want, I'll meet you outside the Regatas Club. I'm not far away."

"Right away, Skinny. A half hour at the most. I'm leaving right now. Here's Sparky, Skinny."

The imaginable sounds of chairs, doors, and the typewriter again there, and in the distance horns, car engines.

"The old man got twenty years younger in one second," Sparky said euphorically. "He went out of here as if the devil was after him. And I was the one who didn't know how to hide it, man. What's the matter, are you in some kind of trouble?"

"No, nothing," Santiago said. "It's been a long time now. I'm going to make up with him."

"It's about time, it's about time," Sparky repeated, happy, still not believing. "Wait, I'm going to call mama. Don't go home until I tell her. So she doesn't have an attack when she sees you."

"I'm not going home now, Sparky." His voice began to protest there, but man you can't. "Sunday, tell her I'll come for lunch on Sunday."

"O.K., Sunday, Teté and I will prepare her," Sparky said. "O.K., you crazy kid. I'll tell her to make you a shrimp stew."

"Do you remember the last time we saw each other?" Santiago says.

"It must have been ten years ago, in front of the Regatas Club."

He left the café, went down the avenue to the Malecón, and instead of taking the stairway that went down to the Regatas Club, he kept on going slowly along the sidewalk, distracted, he thinks, surprised by what you'd just done. Down below he saw the two small empty beaches of the club. It was high tide, the sea had eaten up the sand, the small waves were breaking against the sea walls, a few tongues of foam were licking the terrace, deserted now, where there were so many umbrellas and bathers in summer. How many years had it been since you'd gone swimming at the Regatas, Zavalita? Before you went to San Marcos, five or six years which already seemed like a hundred to you by then. He thinks: a thousand by now.

"Of course I remember, son," Ambrosio says. "The day you made up with your papa."

Were they building a swimming pool? On the basketball court, two men in blue coveralls were shooting at the basket; the tank where the rowers practiced seemed to be dry, was Sparky still rowing at that time? You were already a stranger to your family, Zavalita, you no longer knew what your brother and sister were like, what they were doing, how and in what way they had changed. He got to the club entrance, sat down on the stone bench where the chain was attached, the gatekeeper's box was also empty. He could see Agua Dulce from there, the beach without tents, the stands closed, the mist that hid the cliffs of Barranco and Miraflores. On the rocky little beach that separated Agua Dulce from the Regatas Club—peasants from proper people mama would say, he thinks—there were some beached boats, one of them with its hull filled with holes. It was cold, the wind was ruffling his hair and he felt a salty taste on his lips. He took a few steps along the beach, sat down on a boat, lighted a cigarette: if I hadn't left home, I never would have found out, papa. The gulls were circling above, they would alight for a moment on the rocks and take off, the ducks were diving and sometimes they would dive and sometimes emerge with an almost invisible fish wriggling in their bills. The lead-green color of the sea, he thinks, the earth-colored foam of the waves that were breaking on the rocks, sometimes he could make out a shiny colony of jellyfish, strands of algae, I never should have gone to San Marcos papa. You weren't crying, Zavalita, your legs weren't trembling, he would come and you would behave like a man, you wouldn't run and throw yourself into his arms, tell me it's a lie papa, tell me it isn't true papa. The car appeared in the distance, zigzagging to avoid the potholes of Agua Dulce, raising dust, and it stopped and he went to meet it. Do I have to pretend, not let anything be noticed about me, should I not cry? No, he thinks, rather, was he driving, would he see his face? Yes, there was Ambrosio's big smile in the window, there his voice, Master Santiago how are you, and there the old man's figure. So many more gray hairs, he thinks, so many wrinkles and he'd gotten so thin, his broken voice there: Skinny. He didn't say anything else, he thinks, he'd opened his arms, he held him tightly against himself for a long time, there his mouth on your cheek, Zavalita, the smell of cologne, there your broken voice, hello papa, how are you papa: lies, calumnies, nothing was true.

"You don't know how happy the master was," Ambrosio says. "You can't imagine what it meant to him that the two of you should have finally made up."

"You must be frozen to death waiting here on such a nasty day." His hand on your shoulder, Zavalita, he was speaking very slowly so that his feelings wouldn't show, he was pushing you toward the Regatas Club. "Come on, let's go in, you've got to have something hot to drink."

They crossed the basketball court, walking slowly and in silence, they went into the club building through a side door. There was no one in the dining room, the tables weren't set. Don Fermín clapped a couple of times and soon a waiter appeared, hurrying, buttoning his jacket. They ordered coffee.

"A little while later you stopped working at the house, right?" Santiago says.

"I don't know why I still keep up my membership here, I never stop by." He was saying one thing with his mouth, he thinks, and with his eyes how are you, how have you been, I've been waiting every day, every month, every year, Skinny. "I don't think your brother and sister come anymore either. One of these days I'm going to sell my share. They're worth thirty thousand soles now. It only cost me three thousand."

"I can't remember too well," Ambrosio says. "Yes, I think it was a little while later."

"You're thin and you've got dark circles under your eyes, your mother's going to have a fright when she sees you." He was trying to scold you and he couldn't, Zavalita, his smile was emotional and sad. "Night work isn't good for you. It isn't good for you to live alone either, Skinny."

"Actually, I've put on weight, papa. You're the one who's lost a lot."

"I was getting to think that you weren't ever going to call, you've made me so happy, Skinny." It would have been enough for him to open his eyes a little more, Carlitos. "No matter what it was about. What's up with you?"

"Nothing with me, papa." To have closed his hands all of a sudden, Carlitos, or changed his face in a second. "There's a matter that, I don't know, it might make things complicated for you all of a sudden, I don't know. I wanted to warn you."

The waiter brought the coffee; Don Fermín offered Santiago a cigarette; through the windows they could see the two men in coveralls passing, shooting at the basket, and Don Fermín waited, his expression, his lack of interest.

"I don't know whether you've seen the papers, papa, that crime." But no, nothing, Carlitos, he was looking at me, examining my clothes, my body, was he going to pretend like that, Carlitos? "That singer who was killed in Jesús María, the one who had been Cayo Bermúdez' mistress in Odría's time."

"Oh, yes." Don Fermín made a vague gesture, he had the same affectionate look, only curious, as before. "The Muse, that one."

"At *La Crónica* they're investigating everything they can about her life." Everything was a story then, Zavalita, you see, I was right, Carlitos said, there wasn't any reason for you to get so bitter. "They're digging into the very bottom of that story."

"You're trembling, you didn't even put a sweater on with this cold." Almost bored with my story, Carlitos, intent only on my face, reproaching me with his eyes for living alone, for not having called before. "Well, that's not strange, *La Crónica* is a little sensationalist as papers go. But what about this business?"

"Last night an anonymous note arrived at the paper, papa." Was he going to put on that whole act, loving you so much, Zavalita? "Saying that the one who killed that woman used to be a killer for Cayo Ber-

362

múdez, someone who is so-and-so's chauffeur now, and your name was there, papa. They could have sent the same note to the police, and all of a sudden . . ." Yes, he thinks, precisely because he loved you so much. "Well, I wanted to warn you, papa."

"Ambrosio? Are you talking about him?" His surprised little smile there, Zavalita, his little smile that was so natural, so sure of himself, as if he'd just become interested, as if he'd just understood something. "Ambrosio a killer for Bermúdez?"

"I don't mean that anyone will believe that anonymous note, papa," Santiago said. "I just wanted to warn you."

"That poor nigger a killer?" His frank laugh there, Zavalita, merry, that kind of relief on his face there, and his eyes that said I'm glad it was foolishness like that, I'm glad it had nothing to do with you, Skinny. "The poor fellow couldn't kill a fly even if he wanted to. Bermúdez turned him over to me because he wanted a driver who also belonged to the police."

"I wanted you to know, papa," Santiago said. "If the reporters and the police start investigating they might bother you at home."

"Very well done, Skinny." He was nodding, Zavalita, smiling, sipping his coffee. "There's someone who likes to test my endurance. It isn't the first time, it won't be the last. People are like that. If the poor black man only knew that people think he's capable of such a thing."

He laughed again, took the last sip of coffee, wiped his mouth: if you only knew the number of stinking anonymous notes your father has got in his lifetime, Skinny. He looked tenderly at Santiago and leaned over to grasp his arm.

"But there's something I don't like at all, Skinny. Do they make you work on stuff like that at *La Crónica*? Do you have to cover crimes?"

"No, papa, I don't have anything to do with that. I'm on the local news section."

"But night work isn't good for you, if you get any thinner you'll get sick in the lungs. That's enough of journalism, Skinny. Let's try to find something that suits you better. Some kind of daytime work."

"Work at *La Crónica* is practically nothing, papa, a few hours a day. Less than at any other job. And I have a day free to go to the university."

"Are you attending classes, are you really attending classes?

363

Clodomiro tells me you are, that you pass your exams, but I never know whether to believe him or not. Is it true, Skinny?"

"Of course, papa." Without blushing, without hesitating, I probably got that from you, papa. "I can show you my grades. I'm in the third year of Law School already. I'm going to get my degree, you'll see."

"You still don't want to turn back?" Don Fermín asked slowly.

"It's going to be different now, Sunday I'm coming to have lunch at the house, papa. Ask Sparky, I told him to tell mama. I'm going to come see you all very soon, I promise you."

There the shadow that clouded his eyes, Zavalita. He sat up straight in his chair, let go of Santiago's arm and tried to smile, but his face was still downcast, his mouth sorrowful.

"I'm not demanding anything, but think about it at least and don't say no until you hear me out," he murmured. "Stay on at *La Crónica* if you like it so much. You'll have a key to the house, we'll fix up the room next to the study for you. You'll be completely independent there, just as much as you are now. But in that way your mother will rest more easily."

"Your mother is suffering, your mother is crying, your mother is praying," Santiago said. "But she got over it the first day, Carlitos, I know her. He's the one who counts the days, he's the one who can't get used to it."

"You've already proven that you can live alone and support yourself," Don Fermín went on. "Now it's time to come back home, Skinny."

"Give me a little more time, papa. I'll go to the house every week, I've already told Sparky, ask him. I promise you, papa."

"You're not only thin, but you haven't got anything to wear besides, you must be short of money. Why are you so proud, Santiago? What's your father for, if not to help you?"

"I don't need any money, papa. What I make is plenty for me."

"You earn fifteen hundred soles and you're starving to death." Lowering his eyes, Zavalita, ashamed that you knew that he knew. "I'm not scolding you, Skinny. But I don't understand why you don't want me to help you, I don't understand."

"If I needed money I'd have asked you, papa. But I've got enough, I'm not a big spender. The boardinghouse is quite cheap. I'm not in money trouble, I swear I'm not."

"You don't have to be ashamed that your father's a capitalist anymore." Don Fermín smiled listlessly. "That swine Bermúdez brought us to the brink of bankruptcy. He canceled our subsidies, several contracts, sent auditors to go over our books with a fine-toothed comb, and ruined us with taxes. And now under Prado the government has become a terrible Mafia. The contracts that we got back when Bermúdez left are being taken away from us again to give to Pradists. At this stage I'm ready to become a Communist like you."

"And you still want to give me money." Santiago tried to joke. "Before you know it, I'll be the one who's helping you out, papa."

"Everybody complained about Odría because he was stealing," Don Fermín said. "There's just as much or even more stealing now and everybody's happy."

"Now they steal but still observe certain niceties, papa. The people don't notice it so much."

"And how can you work for a newspaper that belongs to the Prados?" He was humbling himself, Carlitos, if I'd asked him beg me on your knees to come back and I'll come back, he would have knelt down. "Aren't they bigger capitalists than your father? Can you be an unimportant little employee of theirs and not come to work for me in some little businesses that are collapsing?"

"We were having a nice chat and all of a sudden you've got angry, papa." He was humbling himself, but he was right, Zavalita, Carlitos said. "Maybe we'd better not talk about this anymore."

"I'm not angry, Skinny." Getting frightened, Zavalita, thinking he won't come on Sunday, he won't call me, more years will pass and I won't see him. "I'm just sad that you still despise your father, that's all."

"Don't say that, papa, you know it isn't true, papa."

"All right, let's not argue, I'm not angry." He was calling the waiter, taking out his wallet, trying to hide his disappointment, smiling again. "We can expect you on Sunday, then. Your mother's going to be so happy."

They went back through the basketball courts and the players were no longer there. The mist had dissipated and they could see the cliffs, distant and gray, and the roofs of the houses along the Malecón. They stopped a few feet away from the car, Ambrosio got out to open the door.

365

"I don't understand you, Skinny." Without looking at you, Zavalita, head down, as if talking to the damp ground or the mossy stones. "I thought you'd left home because of your ideas, because you were a Communist and wanted to live like a poor man, to fight for the poor. But for this, Skinny? To have a mediocre little job, a mediocre future?"

"Please, papa. Let's not argue about it, I beg you, papa."

"I'm talking to you like this because I love you, Skinny." His eyes wide, he thinks, his voice breaking. "You can go a long way, you can get to be somebody, do great things. Why are you throwing your life away like this, Santiago?"

"I live close by here, papa." Santiago kissed him, moved away from him. "I'll see you Sunday, I'll come by around noontime."

He went off toward the small beach with long strides, turned on the court toward the Malecón, when he began to go up the hill he heard the car start: he saw it going off toward Agua Dulce, bouncing on the potholes, disappearing in the dust. He'd never adjusted, Zavalita. He thinks: if you were alive, you'd still be inventing reasons to get me to come home, papa.

"You see, you've read the paper, not a word about that Queta," Carlitos said. "And besides that, you made up with your father and you're going to make up with your mother. What a reception you're going to get on Sunday, Zavalita."

With laughter, jokes and weeping, he thinks. It hadn't been so hard, the ice had broken a moment after the door opened and he heard Teté's shout there he is now, mami! They'd just watered the garden, he thinks, the grass was damp, the basin dry. Ingrate, my son, my love, your mother's arms around you there, Zavalita. She was hugging you, sobbing, kissing you, the old man and Sparky and Teté were smiling, the maids were fluttering about, how long is this craziness going to last, son, aren't you ashamed for putting your mother through this torture, son? But he wasn't there: they hadn't been lies, papa.

"I could see how uncomfortable Becerrita felt when you came into the editorial room," Carlitos said. "He saw you and almost swallowed his butt. Incredible."

"There's nothing new, except for the stupid things that whore said, we'd better forget about them," Becerrita grunted, shuffling through some papers in desperation. "Write a page of filler, Zavalita. The investigation goes on, new clues being followed. Anything, one page."

"He's human, that's the wild thing about all this, Zavalita," Carlitos said. "To have discovered Becerrita's heart."

You're thin, you've got dark rings under your eyes, they'd gone into the living room, who does your laundry, he'd sat down between Señora Zoila and Teté, was the food at the boardinghouse good? yes mama, and in the old man's eyes nothing uncomfortable, were you attending classes? no complicity or upset in his voice. He was smiling, joking, hopeful and happy, he was probably thinking he's going to come back, everything's going to work out, and Teté tell us the truth, tricker, I can't believe you haven't got a girl friend. It was the truth, Teté.

"Did you know that Ambrosio left?" Sparky asked. "He took off all of a sudden just like that."

"Periquito avoids you, Arispe sucks his teeth when he talks to you, Hernández looks mockingly at you?" Carlitos asked. "That's probably what you wanted, you masochist. They've got too many problems of their own to waste their time feeling sorry for you. And besides, feeling sorry for you for what? For what, God damn it?"

"He went back to his hometown, he says he wants to buy a car and be a taxi driver." Don Fermín smiled. "Poor nigger. I hope it works out for him."

"That's just what you'd like." Carlitos laughed. "To have the whole paper talking about you, gossiping about you, giving you a hard time. But either they don't know or they were so surprised that they haven't opened their mouths. They screwed you, Zavalita."

"Now papa's started to do his own driving, he doesn't want to hire another chauffeur." Teté laughed. "If you could see him driving you'd collapse. Ten miles an hour and stopping at every corner."

"All of them so cordial with you, all of them making you feel bad with their smiles and friendliness?" Carlitos asked. "That must be what you wanted. Actually, they don't know anything at all or they don't give a shit, Zavalita."

"That's not true, I can get to the office from here faster than Sparky." Don Fermín laughed. "Besides, I'm saving money and I've discovered that I like to drive. My second childhood. My, that stew looks good."

367

Delicious, mama, of course he wanted some more, should she peel the shrimps for you? yes, mama. An actor, Zavalita, a Machiavelli, a cynic? Yes he would bring his clothes for the girls to wash, mama. One who could turn into so many different people that it was impossible to know which one was really he? Yes he would come for lunch every Sunday, mama. Another victim or victim-maker fighting tooth and nail to devour and not be devoured, another Peruvian bourgeois? Yes he would phone every day to tell how he was and if he needed anything, mama. Good at home with his children, immoral in business, an opportunist in politics, just like all the others? Yes he would get his law degree, mama. Impotent with his wife, insatiable with his mistresses, dropping his pants in front of his chauffeur? No he wouldn't stay up late at night, yes he would dress warmly, no he wouldn't smoke, yes he would take care of himself, mama. Putting vaseline on himself, panting and drooling like a woman in labor underneath him?

"Yes, I taught Master Sparky how to drive," Ambrosio says. "Behind your father's back, of course."

"I never heard Becerrita or Periquito say a word to the others," Carlitos said. "Maybe when I wasn't there, they know that we're friends. Maybe they talked about it for a few days, a few weeks. Then they all got used to it, forgot about it. Wasn't that how it was with the Muse, isn't that how it is with everything in this country, Zavalita?"

Years that get mixed up, Zavalita, mediocrity by day and monotony by night, beer, brothels. Stories, articles: enough paper to wipe yourself with for the rest of your life, he thinks. Conversations in the Negro-Negro, Sundays with shrimp stew, IOUs at the canteen at *La Crónica,* a handful of books to remember. Drunken sprees without conviction, Zavalita, screwing without conviction, journalism without conviction. Debts at the end of the month, a purgation, slow, inexorable immersion in the invisible filth. She'd been the only thing different, he thinks. She made you suffer, Zavalita, lose sleep, cry. He thinks: your worms shook me up a little, Muse, they made me live a little. Carlitos moved the back of his hand, raised only his thumb and sucked in; his head thrown back there, half his face lighted by the reflector, half his face sunken in something secret and profound.

"China's going to bed with a musician from the Embassy Club." His wandering glassy eyes there. "I have a right to have my problems too, Zavalita."

"All right, I can see that we'll be here until dawn," Santiago said. "I'll have to put you to bed."

"You're good and a failure like me, you've got what you have to have," Carlitos said syllable by syllable. "But you're lacking something. Don't you say that you want to live? Fall in love with a whore and you'll see."

He'd leaned his head over a little and with a thick, uncertain and slow voice, had begun to recite. He would repeat a single line of poetry, be silent, go back to it, sometimes laughing almost noiselessly. It was already close to three o'clock when Norwin and Rojas came into the Negro-Negro and Carlitos had been rambling on for some time.

"The championship race is over, we withdraw," Norwin said. "We're leaving the field free to you and Becerrita, Zavalita."

"Not another single word about the newspaper or I'm leaving," Rojas said. "It's three o'clock in the morning, Norwin. Forget about *Última Hora,* forget about the Muse, or I'm leaving."

"Shitty sensationalist," Carlitos said. "You look like a newspaperman, Norwin."

"I'm not on the police beat anymore," Santiago said. "This week I'm going back to local news."

"We've buried the Muse, we leave the field open for Becerrita," Norwin said. "It's all over, there's nothing left in it. Make up your mind to that, Zavalita, they're not going to find anything out. It's not news anymore."

"Instead of exploiting the baser instincts of the Peruvian people, buy me a beer," Carlitos said. "Shitty sensationalist."

"I know that Becerrita is going to keep on beating it to death," Norwin said. "Not us anymore. There's nothing left in it, make up your mind to that. You've got to recognize that up to here we've been in a tie getting the scoop, Zavalita."

"He's a mulatto with straightened hair and muscles like this," Carlitos said. "He plays the bongo drums."

"The detectives have already buried the whole thing, I'll pass the information on to you," Norwin said. "Pantoja confessed it to me this afternoon. We're digging around in the same place, we have to wait for

369

something to turn up. They're getting bored already, they're not going to discover anything more. Tell that to Becerrita."

Couldn't they discover anything more or didn't they want to? he thinks. He thinks: didn't they know or did they kill you twice, Muse? Had there been conversations in low voices, posh salons, coming and going, mysterious doors that opened and closed, Zavalita? Had there been visits, whispering, confidences, orders?

"I went to see him tonight at the Embassy Club," Carlitos said. "Are you looking for a fight? No, buddy, I came to have a talk. You tell me how China acts with you, then I'll tell you my side, and we can compare notes. We got to be friends."

Had it been the sloppiness, Lima and its moping ways, the stupidity of the detectives, Zavalita? He thinks: that no one demanded anything, insisted, that no one made a move on your behalf. Forget about it or did they really forget you, he thinks, bury the matter, or did they really bury it on their own? Did the same people kill you again, Muse, or did all Peru kill you this second time?

"Ah, I see why you're acting that way," Norwin said. "You had another fight with China, Carlitos."

They went to the Negro-Negro two or three times a week while the newspaper was still at the old location on the Calle Pando. When *La Crónica* moved into its new building on the Avenida Tacna they would meet in little cafés and bars on Colmena. The Jaialai, he thinks, the Hawaii, the América. The first days of the month Norwin, Rojas, Milton would appear in those dank caves and they would go to brothels. Sometimes they would find Becerrita, surrounded by two or three reporters, drinking and talking all buddy-buddy with the pimps and fairies and he always picked up the check. Getting up at noon, having lunch at the boardinghouse, an interview, a piece of information, sitting down at his desk and writing, going down to the canteen, back to the typewriter, leaving, going back to the boardinghouse at dawn, getting undressed watching the day grow over the ocean. And the Sunday lunches were getting confused, the little meals at the Rinconcito Cajamarquino celebrating Carlitos' birthday, Norwin's, or Hernández', and the weekly get-togethers with his father, mother, Sparky and Teté.

2

"MORE COFFEE, Cayo?" Major Paredes asked. "You too, General?"

"You got an O.K. out of me, but you still haven't convinced me. I still think it's stupid talking to him." General Llerena threw the telegrams onto the desk. "Why not send him a message ordering him to Lima? Or if not, what Paredes proposed yesterday. Bring him out of Tumbes by land, put him on a plane in Talara and bring him here."

"Chamorro may be a traitor, but he's not an imbecile, General," he said. "If you send him a telegram, he'll make it across the border. If the police show up at his house, he'll greet them with bullets. And we don't know what the reaction of his officers will be."

"I can answer for the officers in Tumbes," General Llerena said, raising his voice. "Colonel Quijano has kept us posted from the beginning and he can assume command. You don't negotiate with plotters, least of all when the plot has been crushed. This is all nonsense, Bermúdez."

"Chamorro is very popular with the officer corps, General," Major Paredes said. "I suggested that the four leaders all be arrested at the same time. But since three of them have already started to back down, I think Cayo's idea is the best."

"He owes everything to the President, he owes everything to me." General Llerena pounded on the arm of his chair. "I might have expected a thing like this from somebody else, but not from him. Chamorro has got to pay me for this."

371

"It's not a question of you, General," he admonished him in a friendly way. "The President wants this settled without any trouble. Let me do it my way, I assure you it's the best way."

"Chiclayo on the phone, General," a head with a military cap said from the door. "Yes, all three phones are connected, General."

"Major Paredes?" shouted a voice muffled by buzzing and acoustical vibrations. "Camino speaking, Major. I haven't been able to get in touch with Mr. Bermúdez to let him know. We've already picked up Senator Landa here. Yes, on his ranch. Protesting, yes. He wants to call the Palace. We've followed the instructions to the letter, Major."

"Very good, Camino," he said. "Yes, it's me. Is the senator there? Put him on, I want to speak to him."

"He's in the next room, Don Cayo." The buzzing grew louder, the voice seemed to disappear and come to life again. "Incommunicado, as you indicated. I'll have him brought right away, Don Cayo."

"Hello, hello?" He recognized Landa's voice, tried to picture his face and couldn't. "Hello, hello?"

"I'm terribly sorry about all the trouble we've been causing you, senator," he said in a friendly way. "We had to locate you."

"What's the meaning of all this?" Landa's angry voice exploded. "Why was I taken from my house by soldiers? What happened to parliamentary immunity? Who ordered this outrage, Bermúdez?"

"I wanted to let you know that General Espina is under arrest," he said calmly. "And the General insists on tying you in with some very sticky business. Yes, Espina, General Espina. He insists that you're involved in a plot against the government. We need you in Lima to clear this all up, senator."

"Me, in a plot against the government?" There was no hesitation in Landa's voice, only the same ringing fury. "But I belong to the government, I am the government. What kind of nonsense is this, Bermúdez, what are you up to?"

"I'm not up to anything, it's General Espina." He begged his pardon. "He's got proof, he says. That's why we need you here, senator. We'll have a talk tomorrow and I hope everything will all be cleared up."

"Have them get me a plane to Lima at once," the senator roared. "I'll rent a plane, I'll pay for it. This is absolutely absurd, Bermúdez."

"Very well, senator," he said. "Put Camino on, I'll give him instructions."

"I've been treated like a criminal by your police," the senator shouted. "In spite of my position as a member of parliament, in spite of my friendship with the President. You're responsible for all this, Bermúdez."

"Keep Landa there overnight for me, Camino," he said. "Send him to me tomorrow. No, no special plane. On the regular Faucett flight, yes. That's all, Camino."

" 'I'll rent a plane, I'll pay for it,' " Major Paredes said, hanging up the phone. "It'll do that big shot good spending a night in the cooler."

"One of Landa's daughters was chosen Miss Peru last year, wasn't she?" he said, and he could see her, hazy against the curtain of shadows by the window, taking off her fur coat, her shoes. "Cristina or something like that, wasn't it? She looked like a pretty girl from her pictures."

"Your methods still don't convince me," General Llerena said, looking ill-humoredly at the rug. "Things are settled better and quicker with a heavy hand, Bermúdez."

"There's a call from Police Headquarters for Mr. Bermúdez, General," a lieutenant said, sticking his head in. "A Mr. Lozano."

"The subject has just left his house, Don Cayo," Lozano said. "Yes, a patrol car is tailing him. In the direction of Chaclacayo, yes."

"Fine," he said. "Call Chaclacayo and tell them that Zavala's on his way. Have them let him in to wait for me. Don't let him leave until I get there. See you later, Lozano."

"The big fish is going to your house?" General Llerena asked. "What does that mean, Bermúdez?"

"It means he's realized that the plot's all washed up, General," he said.

"Is everything going to be settled so easily for Zavala?" Major Paredes muttered. "He and Landa are the brains behind this, they pushed the Uplander into this adventure."

"General Chamorro on the phone, General," a captain said from the door. "Yes, all three phones are connected to Tumbes, General."

"Cayo Bermúdez speaking, General." Out of the corner of his eye he saw General Llerena's face, drawn from lack of sleep, and Paredes' anxiety as he bit his lip. "I'm sorry to wake you up at this hour, but it's a very urgent matter."

373

"This is General Chamorro, at your service." An energetic voice that showed no age, sure of itself. "Tell me, how can I be of help, Mr. Bermúdez."

"General Espina was arrested tonight, General," he said. "The garrisons at Arequipa, Iquitos and Cajamarca have reaffirmed their loyalty to the government. All the civilians involved in the plot, from Senator Landa down to Fermín Zavala, are under arrest. I'm going to read you some telegrams, General."

"A plot?" General Chamorro whispered in the midst of various noises. "Against the government, you say?"

"A plot that was crushed before it could get started," he said. "The President is prepared to forget all about it. General Espina will leave the country, the officers involved won't be touched if they act reasonably. We know that you promised to back General Espina, but the President is prepared to forget about it, General."

"I only answer for my actions to my superiors, to the Minister of War or to the Chief of the General Staff," Chamorro's voice said haughtily, then, after a long pause with electric belches, "Who do you think you are? I don't give any explanations to some civilian flunky."

"Hello, Alberto?" General Llerena coughed, spoke more strongly. "The Minister of War is speaking, not your comrade in arms. I just want to confirm what you've just heard. I also want you to know that you can thank the President for this chance. I'd proposed bringing you up before a court-martial on the charge of high treason."

"I take full responsibility for my actions," Chamorro's voice replied indignantly, but something had begun to give way in it, something that showed through had begun to give way in it, something that showed through its drive. "It's not true that I've been involved in any act of treason. I'll answer for it before any court you want. I've always answered, you know that very well."

"The President knows that you're an outstanding officer, that's why he'd rather not think of you as being connected with this headstrong adventure," he said. "Yes, Bermúdez speaking. The President respects you and thinks of you as a patriot. He doesn't want to take any action against you, General."

"I'm a man of honor and I won't permit my good name to be sullied,"

General Chamorro affirmed vigorously. "This is an intrigue that was put together behind my back. I won't permit it. I have nothing to say to you, put General Llerena back on."

"All the leaders of the army have attested to your loyalty to the government, General," he said. "All that's needed is for you to do it yourself. The President expects it of you, General Chamorro."

"I won't allow myself to be slandered, I won't let my honor be put in doubt," Chamorro's voice repeated with vehemence. "This is some cowardly and swinish intrigue against me. I order you to put General Llerena on."

"Reaffirm unbreakable loyalty constitutional government and chief of state in mission national patriotic restoration. Signed, General Pedro Solano, Commander in Chief, First Military District," he read. "Commander in Chief Fourth District and officers confirm support sympathy patriotic regime national restoration. Stop. Will obey constitution laws. Signed, General Antonio Quispe Bulnes. Reaffirm support patriotic regime. Stop. Reaffirm decision fulfill sacred duties fatherland constitution laws. Signed, General Manuel Obando Coloma, Commander in Chief, Second District."

"Did you hear, Alberto?" General Llerena roared. "Did you hear, or do you want me to read you the messages again?"

"The President is waiting for your telegram, General Chamorro," he said. "He asked me to tell you personally."

"Unless you want to commit the madness of rebelling all by yourself," General Llerena roared. "And in that case I can give you my word that all I will need is a couple of hours to show you that the army is completely loyal to the government, in spite of what Espina may have made you believe. If you don't send the telegram before dawn, I'll consider you in revolt."

"The President has confidence in you, General Chamorro," he said.

"I don't have to remind you that you're in command of a frontier garrison," General Llerena said. "I don't have to tell you about the responsibility that will fall on you if you provoke a civil war at the very gateway to Ecuador."

"You can consult Generals Quispe, Obando and Solano by radio," he said. "The President is waiting for you to act with the same patriotism

375

they showed. That's all we wanted to tell you. Good night, General Chamorro."

"Chamorro's head is a can of worms right now," General Llerena murmured, running his handkerchief over his sweating face. "He's capable of doing something foolish."

"At this moment he's insulting the mothers of Espina, Solano, Quispe and Obando," Major Paredes said. "He could escape into Ecuador, but I don't think he'll want to ruin his career like that."

"He'll send out the telegram before dawn," he said. "He's an intelligent man."

"If he has an attack of lunacy and goes into revolt, he can hold out for several days," General Llerena said dully. "I've got him surrounded by troops, but I don't have much faith in the air force. When the question of bombing his headquarters came up, the Minister said that a lot of pilots wouldn't like the idea."

"None of that will be necessary, the plot has died without pain or glory," he said. "All told, a couple of sleepless nights, General. I'm going to Chaclacayo now to sew up the last stitch. Then I'll go to the Palace. If anything new comes up, I'll be at home."

"There's a call from the Palace for Mr. Bermúdez, General," a lieutenant said without coming in. "The white phone, General."

"Major Tijero speaking, Don Cayo." In the frame of the window a blue iridescence was breaking out in back of the mournful mass: the fur wrap slid down to her feet, which were pink. "A message has just arrived from Tumbes. It's in code, it's being deciphered. But we've already got the gist of it. Not bad, right, Don Cayo?"

"I'm very glad to hear that, Tijero," he said without any show of joy, and he caught a glimpse of Paredes' and Llerena's stupefied faces. "He didn't take a half hour to think it over. That's what you call a man of action. Good-bye, Tijero, I'll be over there inside of a couple of hours."

"We'd better get to the Palace right away, General," Major Paredes said. "This is the final stage."

"I'm sorry, Don Cayo," Ludovico said. "We weren't expecting you. Wake up, Hipólito."

"What's the matter, God damn it, what are you shoving me for?" Hipólito stammered. "Oh, I'm sorry, Don Cayo, I fell asleep."

376

"Chaclacayo," he said. "I want to get there in twenty minutes."

"The living room lights are on, you've got a visitor, Don Cayo," Ludovico said. "Look who's there in the car, Hipólito. It's Ambrosio."

"I'm sorry to have kept you waiting, Don Fermín," he said, smiling, watching the purple face, the eyes devastated by defeat and the long vigil, putting out his hand. "I'll have some coffee brought, I hope Anatolia's awake."

"Dark, strong and no sugar," Don Fermín said. "Thank you, Don Cayo."

"Two black coffees, Anatolia," he said. "Bring them to us in the living room and you can go back to bed."

"I tried to see the President and I couldn't, that's why I came here," Don Fermín said mechanically. "Something serious, Don Cayo. Yes, a plot."

"Another one?" He pushed the ashtray over to Don Fermín, sat down beside him on the sofa. "It's gotten so a week doesn't go by without something being uncovered."

"Military men at the center of it, several garrisons involved," Don Fermín recited with displeasure. "And people you'd least expect at the head of it."

"Have you got a match?" He leaned toward Don Fermín's lighter, took a long drag, blew out a cloud of smoke and coughed. "Well, here comes the coffee. Leave it here, Anatolia. Yes, please close the door."

"Uplander Espina." Don Fermín took a sip with a look of annoyance, stirred the coffee slowly. "He's got the support of Arequipa, Cajamarca, Iquitos and Tumbes. Espina is leaving for Arequipa this morning. The coup might come tonight. They wanted my support and it seemed prudent not to disappoint them, to give evasive answers, attend a few meetings. Because of my friendship with Espina most of all."

"I know what good friends you are," he said, tasting the coffee. "It was thanks to the Uplander that we first met, remember?"

"It seemed mad at first," Don Fermín said, staring at his cup of coffee. "Then not so mad. A lot of people in the government, a lot of politicians. The American Embassy knew about it. They suggested that elections be held six months after the new regime took office."

"A disloyal fellow, the Uplander," he said, nodding. "It pains me because we're old friends too. I owe my job to him, as you know."

"He thought he was Odría's right-hand man and just like that they took the Ministry away from him," Don Fermín said with a tired gesture. "He never got over it."

"He had things mixed up, he began working toward it in the Ministry, naming his people to prefectures, demanding that his friends get the key positions in the army," he said. "Too many political ambitions, Don Fermín."

"My news hasn't surprised you in the least, naturally," Don Fermín said with sudden boredom, and he thought he knows how to behave, he has class, he has experience.

"The officers owe a lot to the President and, naturally, they've kept us informed," he said. "Even about the conversations between you, Espina and Senator Landa."

"Espina wanted to use my name in order to convince some people who were hanging back," Don Fermín said with an apathetic and fleeting little smile. "But only the military men knew the plans in detail. They kept Landa and me in the dark. I only got adequate information yesterday."

"Everything will be all cleared up, then," he said. "Half of the plotters were friends of the government, all of the garrisons involved have given their support to the President. Espina is under arrest. All that remains is to clarify the position of a few civilians. Yours is beginning to be clear, Don Fermín."

"Did you also know that I'd be waiting for you here?" Don Fermín asked without sarcasm, a glow of sweat appearing on his brow.

"It's my job, I get paid to know whatever is of interest to the government," he admitted. "It's not easy, actually, it's getting harder and harder. Plots by university students are child's play. When generals start plotting, then it's more serious. And all the more so if they're plotting with members of the Club Nacional."

"Well, the cards are on the table," Don Fermín said. He paused briefly and looked at him. "I'd prefer to know right out what I can expect, Don Cayo."

"I'll speak to you in all frankness," he said, nodding. "We don't want any uproar. It would be bad for the government, it's not good for people

378

to know that there are splits. We're prepared not to take any reprisals. Provided that the other side observes the same discretion."

"Espina is proud and won't make any act of contrition," Don Fermín stated thoughtfully. "I can imagine how he feels after he found out that his comrades deceived him."

"He won't make any act of contrition, but instead of playing the martyr he'll prefer going abroad with a nice salary paid in dollars," he said, shrugging his shoulders. "He'll keep on plotting there to keep up his morale and get the bad taste out of his mouth. But he knows he hasn't got a ghost of a chance anymore."

"Everything is set for the military men, then," Don Fermín said. "What about the civilians?"

"It all depends on which civilians," he said. "It would be better for us to forget about little Dr. Ferro and the rest of the social climbers. They don't exist."

"And yet they do exist," Don Fermín sighed. "What's going to happen to them?"

"A short time in the shadows and they'll be sent abroad little by little," he said. "It's a waste of time thinking about them. The only civilians who matter are you and Landa, for obvious reasons."

"For obvious reasons," Don Fermín repeated slowly. "You mean?"

"You've both served the government from the very first and you've got connections and influence in sectors that we have to treat with kid gloves," he said. "I hope the President shows the same consideration to you that he has to Espina. That's my personal opinion. But the final word is up to the President, Don Fermín."

"Are you going to propose a trip abroad for me too?" Don Fermín asked.

"Since things have been settled so fast and, we might say, so well, I'm going to advise the President to leave you people alone," he said. "Outside of asking you to abandon all political activity, of course."

"I'm not the brains behind this plot, you know that," Don Fermín said. "I had my doubts from the beginning. They presented it to me all set up, they didn't consult me."

"Espina claims that you and Landa put up a lot of money for the coup," he said.

379

"I don't invest money in businesses that are shaky and you know that too," Don Fermín said. "I gave money and I was the first one to move heaven and earth to convince people to support Odría in 1948, because I had faith in him. I don't imagine the President has forgotten that."

"The President is an uplander," he said. "Mountain people have very good memories."

"If I'd really started plotting, things wouldn't have gone so badly for Espina, if Landa and I had been the authors of all this, there wouldn't have been four garrisons involved, there would have been ten." Don Fermín spoke without arrogance, without haste, with a tranquil security, and he thought as if everything he's saying is unnecessary, as if it was my obligation to have known that from the start. "With ten million soles behind it, no coup d'état in Peru can possibly fail, Don Cayo."

"I'm going to the Palace now to talk to the President," he said. "I'll do everything possible to make him understand and to have this settled in the best way, in your case at least. That's all I can offer you for now, Don Fermín."

"Will I be arrested?" Don Fermín asked.

"Of course not. The worst thing is that you might be asked to leave the country for a while," he said. "But I don't think that will be necessary."

"Will they take any reprisals against me?" Don Fermín asked. "Economic, I mean. You know that a large part of my business depends on the state."

"I'll do what I can to avoid it," he said. "The President doesn't hold grudges, and I hope that after a while he'll accept a reconciliation with you. That's all I can tell you, Don Fermín."

"I suppose that the things we had pending, you and I, will have to be forgotten," Don Fermín said.

"Buried, absolutely," he stated. "You can see I'm being sincere with you. First of all, I'm part of the government, Don Fermín." He paused, lowered his voice a little, and used a less impersonal, more intimate tone. "I know that you've been going through a bad time. No, I'm not talking about this business. About your son, the one who left home."

"What's happened to Santiago?" Don Fermín's face turned toward him quickly. "Are you still persecuting the boy?"

380

"We had him watched for a few days, but that's all over," he reassured him. "It seems that bad experience has disillusioned him about politics. He hasn't gone back to his old friends and I understand he leads a very proper life."

"You know more about Santiago than I do, I haven't seen him for months," Don Fermín murmured, standing up. "Well, I'm very tired and I'll leave you now. Good-bye, Don Cayo."

"To the Palace, Ludovico," he said. "That lazy lout Hipólito has fallen asleep again. Leave him alone, don't wake him up."

"Here we are," Ludovico said, laughing. "You're the one who fell asleep this time. You were snoring all the way over, Don Cayo."

"Good morning, you finally got here," Major Tijero said. "The President has retired to get some rest. But Major Paredes and Dr. Arbeláez are waiting for you inside, Don Cayo."

"He asked not to be awakened unless it's something very urgent," Major Paredes said.

"There's nothing urgent, I'll come back to see him later," he said. "Yes, I'll leave with you people. Good morning, doctor."

"I have to congratulate you, Don Cayo," Dr. Arbeláez said sarcastically. "No noise, not a drop of blood spilled, and no one to help or advise you. A complete success, Don Cayo."

"I was going to suggest we have lunch together so I can fill you in on all the details," he said. "Right up until the last minute we didn't know how it would go. Things came to a head last night and I didn't have time to bring you up to date."

"I'm not free at noontime, but thanks anyway," Dr. Arbeláez said. "I don't need to be brought up to date. The President filled me in about everything, Don Cayo."

"Under certain circumstances there's no other way except to go outside of channels, doctor," he murmured. "Last night it was more important to act than to get in touch with you."

"Of course," Dr. Arbeláez said. "This time the President has accepted my resignation and, believe me, I'm quite happy. We won't have any more arguments. The President's going to reshuffle the cabinet; not now, on the National Holiday. But in any case, he has his mind made up."

"I'll ask the President to reconsider his decision and not let you leave," he said. "Even though you may not think so, I like working under you, doctor."

"Under me?" Dr. Arbeláez let out a loud laugh. "Well. See you later, Don Cayo. Good-bye, Major."

"Let's go get something to eat, Cayo," Major Paredes said. "Yes, come in my car. Tell your chauffeur to follow us to the Military Club. Camino called to say that the Faucett flight will arrive here at eleven-thirty. Are you going to meet Landa?"

"I have to," he said. "If I don't die first from lack of sleep. That's three hours from now, right?"

"How did your chat with the big fish go?" Major Paredes asked.

"Zavala's a good gambler, he knows how to lose," he said. "Landa worries me more. He's richer and therefore he's prouder. We'll see."

"The fact is the whole thing was quite serious." Paredes yawned. "If it hadn't been for Colonel Quijano we would have had a good scare."

"The government owes its life to him, or almost," he nodded. "We have to get congress to promote him as soon as possible."

"Two orange juices and two strong coffees," Major Paredes said. "And quick, because we're falling asleep."

"What's worrying you?" he asked. "Let's have it."

"Zavala," Major Paredes said. "Your deals with him. He must have you by these things here, I imagine."

"Nobody's got me by anything yet," he said, stretching. "He's tried a thousand times, of course. He wanted to make me his partner, scrounge some shares of stock for me, a million different things. But it didn't work."

"That's not what I mean," Major Paredes said. "The President . . ."

"He knows everything, with all the warts and hairs," he said. "There's this here and that there, but no one can prove that those contracts were awarded because of me. My commissions were so much, always in cash. I've got my account overseas and it's so much. Should I resign, leave the country? No. What shall I do, then? Screw Zavala. Fine, I obey your orders."

"Screwing him ought to be the easiest thing in the world." Paredes smiled. "You can get him through his vice."

"Not that way," he said, and smiled at Paredes, yawning again. "That's the only way I won't."

"I know, you've told me before." Paredes smiled. "Vices are the only things you respect in people."

"His fortune is a sand castle," he said. "His lab gets by by supplying the armed forces. The orders are stopped. His construction company depends on highways and school buildings. All finished, he won't get another delivery. The Treasury Ministry will go over his books and he'll have to pay the taxes he dodged and the penalties. We won't be able to sink him completely, but we can hurt him some."

"I don't think so, those shitheads always find some way of coming out ahead," Paredes said.

"Are the cabinet shifts for certain?" he asked. "Arbeláez has to be kept on at the Ministry. He's a grouch, but a person can work with him."

"A change of ministers on the National Holiday is normal, it won't attract any attention," Paredes said. "Besides, poor Arbeláez is right. The problem would be the same with anyone else. Nobody will accept being a figurehead."

"I couldn't risk his knowing about this, with all his business connections with Landa," he said.

"I know, I'm not criticizing you," Paredes said. "That's precisely why, in order to avoid things like that, you've got to accept the Ministry. You can't turn it down now. Llerena has insisted on your replacing Arbeláez. It's been uncomfortable for the other ministers too, having one fake Minister of Public Order and one real one."

"I'm invisible as it is now and no one can scuttle my work," he said. "The Minister is exposed and vulnerable. The enemies of the government would rub their hands if they saw me minister."

"Those enemies don't count for much anymore, not after this failure," Paredes said. "They won't be lifting up their heads for a long time to come."

"When we're alone, we should be more frank," he said, laughing. "The strength of the government was based on the support of the groups that count. And that's all changed. None of them, the Club Nacional, the army, or the gringos, like us anymore. They're divided among themselves, but if they were to unite against us, we'd have to start packing our bags. If your uncle doesn't act fast, things are going to go from bad to worse."

"What more do they want him to do?" Paredes asked. "Hasn't he cleaned up the Apristas and the Communists? Hasn't he given the army things it never had before? Hasn't he put the big shots from the Club Nacional in ministries and embassies, hasn't he let them make all the decisions at the Treasury? Hasn't he let the gringos have their way in everything? What more do those bastards want?"

"They don't want him to change his policies, they'll do the same thing when they take power," he said. "They want him out. They called him in to exterminate the cockroaches in the house. Now that he's done that, they want him to give them back their house, which, after all, does belong to them, doesn't it?"

"No," Paredes said. "The President has won the people over. He's built them hospitals, schools, he gave them the Workers' Security Law. If he amends the constitution and runs for reelection, he'll win cleanly. All you have to do is look at the demonstrations of support every time he takes a trip."

"I've been organizing them for years." He yawned. "Give me the money and I can organize the same demonstrations for you. No, the only popular thing here is APRA. If they're offered a little something, the Apristas would be willing to come to terms with the government."

"Are you out of your mind?" Paredes asked.

"APRA's changed, it's more anti-Communist than you are, and the United States has lifted its veto of it," he said. "With the APRA masses, the machinery of the state and the sectors of the wealthy classes loyal to him, Odría could get himself reelected."

"You're out of your mind," Paredes said. "Odría and APRA together? Please, Cayo."

"The Aprista leaders are old and they come cheap," he said. "They'd accept anything in exchange for legal status and a few crumbs."

"The armed forces would never accept any agreement with APRA," Paredes said.

"Because the right wing educated them that way, making them think it was the enemy," he said. "But they can be reeducated and made to

384

see that APRA has changed. The Apristas will give the military all the guarantees they want."

"Instead of going to meet Landa at the airport, you should go see a psychiatrist," Paredes said. "These last few days without sleep haven't been good for you, Cayo."

"Well, then, some fat cat will take over the presidency in 1956," he said, yawning. "And you and I will go and have a nice rest from all this hustle-bustle. And, as far as I'm concerned, it's not such a bad idea. I don't know why we're talking about this. Political matters don't concern us. Your uncle's got his advisers. You and I have got our own business. By the way, what time is it?"

"You've got plenty of time," Paredes said. "I'm going to go get some sleep. I'm done in with all the tension of the past two days. And tonight, if my body's up to it, I'm going to unwind with a bender. You don't feel like one, do you?"

"No, Don Cayo, he's been asleep all the way from Chaclacayo, just the way you see him," Ludovico said, pointing to Hipólito. "You'll have to excuse me for driving so slow, but the fact is I'm falling asleep sitting up and I don't want to have an accident. We'll make the airport by eleven, don't worry."

"The plane will be here within ten minutes, Don Cayo," Lozano said with a hoarse, thin voice. "I brought two patrol cars and a few men. Since he's coming in on a commercial flight, I didn't know what the circumstances . . ."

"Landa's not under arrest," he said. "I'll meet him alone and take him to his house. I don't want the senator to see this display of police, take your men away. Is everything else in order?"

"All the arrests were made without incident," Lozano said, rubbing his unshaven face, yawning. "The only thing was a bit of trouble in Arequipa. Dr. Velarde, that big Aprista. Someone got word to him and he got away. He's probably trying to get to Bolivia. The border's been notified."

"Fine, you can go, Lozano," he said. "Look at Ludovico and Hipólito. Snoring again."

"The pair of them have put in for a transfer, Don Cayo," Lozano said. "You tell me why."

385

"I'm not surprised, they've already had enough bad nights to last anyone a long time." He smiled. "It's all right, get me another pair, a pair who don't like to sleep so much. So long, Lozano."

"Wouldn't you like to come into the office and sit down, Mr. Bermúdez?" a lieutenant asked him, saluting.

"No, thank you, Lieutenant, I'd rather get a little air," he said. "Besides, there's the plane now. Wake up those two instead and have them bring the car up. I'm going on ahead. . . . This way, senator, my car's over here. Please get in. San Isidro, Ludovico, Senator Landa's house."

"I'm glad we're going to my house and not to jail," Senator Landa muttered without looking at him. "I hope I'll be able to change my clothes and take a bath at least."

"Yes," he said. "I'm sorry about all this bother. There was no other way out, senator."

"As if they were attacking a fort, carrying machine guns and sirens blaring," Landa whispered, his mouth close to the window. "My wife almost had a stroke when they showed up at Olave. Did you give them orders to have me stay up all night sitting on a chair too, Bermúdez, in spite of my sixty years?"

"It's that big house, the one with the garden, isn't it, sir?" Ludovico asked.

"After you, senator," he said, pointing to the broad, leafy garden, and for an instant he caught a glimpse of them: white, naked, flitting among the laurels, laughing, her white, quick heels on the damp lawn. "Go ahead, go ahead, senator."

"Papa, papi!" the girl shouted, opening her arms, and he saw her porcelain face, her large, startled eyes, her short chestnut hair. "I just talked to mami on the telephone and she's frightened to death. What happened, papi, what happened?"

"Good morning," he murmured and quickly undressed her and pushed her toward the sheets where the female forms received her avidly.

"I'll tell you about it later, dear." Landa freed himself from his daughter and turned to him. "Come in, Bermúdez. Call Chiclayo and calm your mother down, Cristina, tell her I'm all right. Don't let anyone disturb us. Have a seat, Bermúdez."

"I'm going to speak to you in all sincerity, senator," he said. "If you

386

do the same, neither of us will waste any time."

"Your recommendation is too much," Landa said. "I never lie."

"General Espina has been arrested, all the officers who promised to help him have made peace with the government," he said. "We don't want this to go any farther, senator. Getting down to concrete matters, I'm here to propose that you reaffirm your loyalty to the government and stay on in your post as parliamentary leader. In a word, let's forget about everything that's happened."

"First I have to know what it is that's happened," Landa said. He had his hands on his knees, absolutely motionless.

"You're tired and I'm tired," he murmured. "Can't we stop wasting time, senator?"

"First of all I have to know what I'm being accused of," Landa repeated dryly.

"Of having served as the link between Espina and the commanders of the garrisons involved," he said with a resigned expression. "Of having collected money and put your own money into the venture. Of having brought together, in this house and at Olave, the twenty or so civilian plotters who are now under arrest. We've got signed declarations, tapes, all the proof you could ask for. But it's no longer a question of that, we don't want any explanations. The President is ready to forget all of this."

"It's a question of not having an enemy in the senate who knows the government inside out," Landa murmured, looking him straight in the eye.

"It's a question of not breaking up the parliamentary majority," he said. "Besides, the government needs your prestige, your name and your influence. All you have to do is say yes, senator, and nothing will ever have happened."

"What if I refuse to keep on collaborating?" Landa murmured in an almost inaudible voice.

"You'd have to leave the country," he said with an annoyed look. "I don't have to remind you either that you've got a lot of business interests that are tied in with the state, senator."

"First the insult, then the blackmail," Landa said. "I recognize your methods, Bermúdez."

"You're an experienced politician and a good judge, you're quite

387

aware of what's best for you," he said calmly. "Let's not waste our time, senator."

"What's to become of the people under arrest?" Landa murmured. "Not the military men, who have evidently settled their affairs quite well. The others."

"The government has shown you special consideration because we owe you for your services," he said. "Ferro and the others owe the government for what they are. Each one's background will be studied and appropriate measures will be taken."

"What kind of measures?" the senator asked. "Those people trusted in me as I trusted in those generals."

"Preventive measures, we don't want to be cruel with anyone," he said. "They'll stay in jail for a while, some of them will be exiled. As you can see, nothing very serious. It will all depend on your attitude, of course."

"There's something else." The senator hesitated slightly. "I mean . . ."

"Zavala?" he asked and saw Landa blink several times. "He hasn't been arrested and if you agree to cooperate he won't be bothered either. I had a chat with him this morning and he's anxious to make peace with the government. He must be home now. Talk to him, senator."

"I can't give you an answer now," Landa said after a few seconds. "Give me a few hours to think it over."

"All the time you need," he said, getting up. "I'll call you tonight, or tomorrow, if you prefer."

"Will your watchdogs leave me alone until then?" Landa asked, opening the door to the garden.

"You're not under arrest, not even under surveillance. You can come and go as you please, talk to anyone you want to. Good-bye, senator." He went out and crossed the garden, feeling them around him, elastic and fragrant, coming and going and coming back again in the flower bed, quick and moist under the shrubs. "Ludovico, Hipólito, wake up. Police Headquarters, quick. I want a tap on Landa's line, Lozano."

"Don't worry, Don Cayo," Lozano said, bringing over a chair for him. "I've got a patrol car and three policemen there. His telephone's been tapped for two weeks now."

"Get me a glass of water, please," he said. "I have to take a pill."

"The Prefect has prepared this résumé of the situation in Lima," Lozano said. "No, there's no news of Velarde. He must have got across the border. The only one out of forty-six, Don Cayo. All the others were arrested and without incident."

"We have to keep them incommunicado, both here and in the provinces," he said. "The calls are going to start coming in from their godfathers at any moment. Ministers, deputies."

"They've already started, Don Cayo," Lozano said. "Senator Arévalo just called. He wanted to see Dr. Ferro. I told him no one could see him without your authorization."

"Yes, turn them over to me." He yawned. "Ferro's got a whole bunch of people grouped together and they're going to move heaven and earth to get him out."

"His wife showed up here this morning," Lozano said. "All up in arms. Threatening us with the President, ministers. A very pretty lady, Don Cayo."

"I didn't even know that Ferro was married," he said. "Pretty, you say? That's probably why he's kept her hidden."

"You look all done in, Don Cayo," Lozano said. "Why don't you go get some rest? I don't think anything important will come up today."

"Do you remember three years ago, when there were rumors of an uprising in Juliaca?" he said. "We went for four nights without sleep, just as if nothing was happening. I'm getting old, Lozano."

"Can I ask you a question?" And Lozano's efficient and serviceable face softened. "It's about the rumors that are going around. That there'll be cabinet changes, that you'll be promoted to Public Order. I don't have to tell you how well that news has been received by the force, Don Cayo."

"I don't think it would suit the President to have me as Minister," he said. "I'm going to try to dissuade him. But if he insists, what else can I do but accept?"

"It would be great." Lozano smiled. "You've seen how little coordination there's been here sometimes because the ministers haven't had any experience. With General Espina, Dr. Arbeláez. With you it would be something else again, Don Cayo."

"Well, I'm going out to San Miguel to get a little rest," he said.

389

"Would you please call Alcibíades and tell him? I'm only to be awakened if it's something very urgent."

"I'm sorry, I fell asleep again," Ludovico babbled, shaking Hipólito. "San Miguel? Yes, sir, Don Cayo."

"You two go get some sleep and come by for me here at seven o'clock tonight," he said. "The mistress is in the bath? Yes, fix me something to eat, Símula. Hello there, girl. I'm going to get a little sleep. I've been off it for twenty-four hours."

"Your face looks horrible." Hortensia laughed. "Did you behave yourself last night?"

"I cheated on you with the Minister of War," he murmured, hearing a tenacious and secret buzzing in his ears, counting the uneven beats of his heart. "Have them bring me something to eat right away, I'm falling asleep on my feet."

"Let me fix the bed for you." Hortensia shook the sheets, drew the curtains, and he felt as if he were sliding down a rocky crag and in the distance he could see hulks moving in the darkness; he kept on sliding, sinking, and suddenly he felt he was being attacked, brutally being pulled out of that dark, dense refuge. "I've been hollering at you for five minutes, Cayo. From Headquarters, they say it's urgent."

"Senator Landa went into the Argentine Embassy a half hour ago, Don Cayo." He felt needles in his eyes, Lozano's voice was cruelly hammering in his ears. "He got in through a service door. The agents didn't know it led into the Embassy. I'm terribly sorry, Don Cayo."

"He wants a scandal, he wants to avenge his humiliation." He was slowly recovering the feeling of his senses, his members, but his voice seemed like somebody else's. "Keep your people there, Lozano. If he comes out, arrest him and take him to Headquarters. If Zavala leaves his house, arrest him too. Hello, Alcibíades? Get Dr. Lora as soon as possible, I have to see him right away. Tell him I'll be at his office in half an hour."

"Dr. Ferro's wife is waiting for you, Don Cayo," Dr. Alcibíades said. "I told her you weren't coming in, but she refuses to leave."

"Get rid of her and get hold of Dr. Lora right away," he said. "Símula, run tell the policemen on the corner that I need the patrol car right away."

"What's the matter, what's all the rush about?" Hortensia asked, picking up the pajamas he had just thrown on the floor.

"Problems," he said, putting on his socks. "How long have I been asleep?"

"An hour, more or less," Hortensia said. "You must be starved to death. Shall I have them warm up lunch?"

"I haven't got time," he said. "Yes, the Ministry of Foreign Relations, sergeant, and full speed. Don't stop for the lights, man, I'm in a big hurry. The Minister's waiting for me, I had them tell him I'm on my way."

"The Minister's in a meeting, I don't think he can see you." The young man with glasses, dressed in gray, was examining him from head to toe with mistrust. "Who shall I say is calling?"

"Cayo Bermúdez," he said, and he saw the young man jump to his feet and disappear behind a gleaming door. "I'm sorry to come bursting into your office like this, Dr. Lora, but it's very important, it concerns Landa."

"Landa?" The short, bald little man put out his hand, smiling. "Don't tell me that . . ."

"Yes, he's been in the Argentine Embassy for an hour," he said. "Probably asking for asylum. He wants to make a lot of noise and create problems for us."

"Well, the best thing would be to give him safe conduct immediately," Dr. Lora said. "For the fleeing enemy, a bridge of silver, Don Cayo."

"By no means," he said. "Talk to the Ambassador, doctor. Make it quite clear to him that he's not being sought, assure him that Landa can leave the country with his passport whenever he wants to."

"I can only give my word if that promise will be kept, Don Cayo," Dr. Lora said, smiling awkwardly. "You can imagine the position the government would be in if . . ."

"It will be kept," he said rapidly, and he saw that Dr. Lora was observing him, doubting. Finally he stopped smiling, sighed and pressed a button.

"The Ambassador just happens to be on the line." The young man in gray crossed the office with a small smooth-faced smile, made a kind of genuflection. "Such a coincidence, Mr. Secretary."

391

"Well, now we know that he's asked for asylum," Dr. Lora said. "Yes, while I'm talking to the Ambassador, you can use the phone in the outer office, Don Cayo."

"Can I use your phone a moment? I'd like to speak in private, please," he said, and he saw the young man in gray blush quickly, saw him nod with offended eyes and leave. "It's possible that Landa will leave the Embassy at any moment, Lozano. Don't bother him. Keep me informed of his movements. I'll be in my office, yes."

"Just as you say, Don Cayo." The young man was walking back and forth in the hall, lean, tall, gray. "Not Zavala either if he leaves his house? Fine, Don Cayo."

"He has, indeed, asked for asylum," Dr. Lora said. "The Ambassador was surprised. Landa, one of the parliamentary leaders, he couldn't believe it. He's agreed to the promise that he won't be arrested and that he can leave the country whenever he wants to."

"You've taken a great load off my mind, doctor," he said. "Now I'm going to try to put an end to this business. Thank you very much, doctor."

"Even though it may not be the time for it, I want to be the first to congratulate you," Dr. Lora said, smiling. "I was pleased to hear that you'll be joining the cabinet on the National Holiday, Don Cayo."

"Just rumors," he said. "Nothing's been decided yet. The President hasn't spoken to me yet, and I don't know whether or not I'll accept."

"Everything's been decided and we're all very pleased," Dr. Lora said, taking his arm. "You have to make a sacrifice and accept. The President trusts you, and with good reason. Good-bye, Don Cayo."

"Good-bye, sir," the young man in gray said with a bow.

"Good-bye," he said, and giving a violent tug with his own hands he castrated him and threw the gelatinous mass to Hortensia: eat it. "To the Ministry of Government, sergeant. Have the secretaries left yet? What's wrong, doctor, you're livid."

"France-Presse, Associated Press, United Press, they're all carrying the story, Don Cayo, look at the cables," Dr. Alcibíades said. "They're talking about dozens of arrests. Where'd they get it, Don Cayo?"

"The dateline is Bolivia, it's Velarde, that little lawyer," he said. "It could have been Landa too. When did the agencies start getting those dispatches?"

"Only about half an hour ago," Dr. Alcibíades said. "The correspondents have already started calling us. They'll be coming by here any minute now. No, the cables still haven't been sent to the radio stations."

"It'll be impossible to keep this all secret now, there has to be an official communiqué," he said. "Call the agencies and tell them not to distribute those cables, to wait for the communiqué. Get me Lozano and Paredes on the phone, please."

"Yes, Don Cayo," Lozano said. "Senator Landa just went into his house."

"Don't let him leave there," he said. "Are you sure he didn't speak to any foreign reporters on the phone? Yes, I'll be at the Palace, call me there."

"Major Paredes on the other phone, Don Cayo," Dr. Alcibíades said.

"You were a little too fast, the binge tonight will have to wait," he said. "Did you see the dispatches? Yes, I know where from. Velarde, an Arequipan who got away. They don't give any names, only Espina's."

"We just read them with General Llerena and we're going to the Palace," Major Paredes said. "This is serious. The President wanted to avoid this matter's getting out at all cost."

"A communiqué denying everything has to be issued," he said. "It's still not too late if a deal can be made with Espina and Landa. What's new with the Uplander?"

"He's stubborn. General Pinto has spoken to him twice," Paredes said. "If the President agrees, General Llerena will talk to him too. Well, I'll see you at the Palace, then."

"Are you leaving now, Don Cayo?" Dr. Alcibíades asked. "I forgot something. Dr. Ferro's wife. She was here all afternoon. She said she'd be back and she'd sit here all night if she had to."

"If she comes back, have the guards throw her out," he said. "And don't budge from here, doctor."

"Haven't you got your car?" Dr. Alcibíades asked. "Do you want to take mine?"

393

"I don't know how to drive. I'll take a taxi," he said. "Yes, fellow, to the Palace."

"Come in, Don Cayo," Major Tijero said. "General Llerena, Dr. Arbeláez and Major Paredes are waiting for you."

"I just spoke to General Pinto, his conversation with Espina has been rather positive," Major Paredes said. "The President's with the Foreign Minister."

"The foreign radio stations are talking about an unsuccessful plot," General Llerena said. "You see, Bermúdez, all the complications with those devils in order to keep the thing secret and it wasn't any good at all."

"If General Pinto can make a deal with Espina, the news will automatically be denied," Major Paredes said. "The whole problem now is Landa."

"You're a friend of the senator's, Dr. Arbeláez," he said. "Landa trusts you."

"I just talked to him on the phone," Dr. Arbeláez said. "He's a proud man and he refused to listen to me. Nothing can be done with him, Don Cayo."

"He's being given a way out and he won't accept it?" General Llerena said. "Then we've got to arrest him before he causes a scandal."

"I promised that it wouldn't happen and I'm going to keep that promise," he said. "You worry about Espina, General, and leave Landa to me."

"You're wanted on the phone, Don Cayo," Major Tijero said. "Yes, this way."

"The subject spoke with Dr. Arbeláez a moment ago," Lozano said. "Something that's going to surprise you, Don Cayo. Yes, let me play back the tape for you."

"I can't do anything at the moment, but hold on," Dr. Arbeláez said. "If you make one of the conditions for reconciliation with the President the firing of that jackal Bermúdez, I'm sure he'll agree."

"Don't let anyone into Landa's house except Zavala, Lozano," he said. "Were you sleeping, Don Fermín? I'm sorry to wake you, but it's urgent. Landa doesn't want to come to an understanding with us and he's making things difficult. We've got to convince the senator to keep his mouth shut. Can you figure out what I'm asking you to do, Don Fermín?"

"Of course I can," Don Fermín said.

"Rumors have started to spread abroad and we don't want them to get any bigger," he said. "We've reached an agreement with Espina, all we have to do is make the senator see the light. You can help us, Don Fermín."

"Landa can afford the luxury of being bold," Don Fermín said. "His money doesn't depend on the government."

"But yours does," he said. "So you see, the matter is urgent and I have to talk to you this way. Is it enough for me to promise that all your contracts with the state will be respected?"

"What guarantee do I have that the promise will be kept?" Don Fermín asked.

"At this moment only my word," he said. "I can't give you any other guarantee right now."

"All right, I accept your word," Don Fermín said. "I'll go talk to Landa. If your cops will let me leave my house."

"General Pinto's just arrived, Don Cayo," Major Tijero said.

"Espina seems to be quite reasonable, Cayo," Paredes said. "But the price is high. I doubt that the President will accept."

"Ambassador to Spain," General Pinto said. "He says that because of his status as a general and a former minister the post of military attaché in London would be a step down."

"Is that all he wants?" General Llerena said. "Ambassador to Spain, no less."

"The post is vacant and who better than Espina to fill it?" he said. "He'll do an excellent job. I'm sure Dr. Lora will agree."

"A beautiful reward for having tried to plunge the nation into blood and fire," General Llerena said.

"What better denial of the news that's going around than to announce tomorrow Espina's appointment as Ambassador to Spain?" he said.

"If you'll permit me, I'm of the same mind, General," General Pinto said. "Espina has put that condition on it and he won't accept any other.

The alternative would be to put him on trial and send him into exile. And any disciplinary measures against him would have a negative effect on a great many officers."

"Even though we don't always agree, Don Cayo, this time I'm with you," Dr. Arbeláez said. "This is how I see the problem: if it's been decided not to take any sanctions and to look for reconciliation, the best thing is to give General Espina a mission in line with his rank."

"The Espina matter is settled, in any case," Paredes said. "What about Landa? If his mouth isn't shut, the whole thing will have been to no avail."

"Is he going to be rewarded with an ambassadorship too?" General Llerena asked.

"I don't think he's interested," Dr. Arbeláez said. "He's already been ambassador any number of times."

"I don't see how we can publish a denial of the dispatches, if Landa's going to deny the denial tomorrow," Paredes said.

"Yes, Major, I'd like to use the telephone, in private," he said. "Hello, Lozano? Take the bug off the senator's phone. I'm going to talk to him and this conversation mustn't be taped."

"Senator Landa's not home, this is his daughter," the girl's nervous voice said, and he quickly tied her, with reckless, tight knots that made her wrists, her feet swell. "Who's calling?"

"Put him on immediately, young lady, I'm calling from the Palace, it's very urgent." Hortensia had the strap ready, so did Queta, so did he. "I want to let you know that Espina has been named Ambassador to Spain, senator. I hope this will clear away your doubts and change your attitude. We still consider you a friend."

"You don't keep a friend under arrest," Landa said. "Why is my house surrounded? Why don't they let me leave? What about Lora's promises to the Ambassador? Doesn't the Foreign Minister keep his word?"

"Rumors about what happened are floating around and we want to deny them," he said. "I imagine that Zavala is there with you and that he's already explained how everything depends on you. Tell me your conditions, senator."

"Unconditional freedom for all of my friends," Landa said. "A formal promise that they won't be bothered or discharged from the positions they hold."

"Under the conditions that those who aren't members join the Restoration Party," he said. "You see, we don't want an apparent reconciliation, we want a real one. You're one of the leaders of the government party, let your friends join up and be part of it. Do you agree?"

"Who will agree that as soon as I take a step toward reestablishing my relations with the government all this won't be used to hurt me politically?" Landa asked. "That they won't try to blackmail me again?"

"On the National Holiday the leadership of both chambers will be changed," he said. "I'm offering you the presidency of the senate. What more proof do you want that there won't be any reprisals?"

"I'm not interested in the presidency of the senate," Landa said, and he took a breath. All rancor had left the senator's voice. "I have to think about it, in any case."

"I can promise the President's backing for your candidacy," he said. "I give you my word that the majority will elect you."

"All right, get rid of the cops guarding my house," Landa said. "What do you want me to do?"

"Come to the Palace immediately, the parliamentary leaders are meeting with the President and you're the only one missing," he said. "Naturally, you'll be received with the same friendship as always, senator."

"Yes, the members of parliament are arriving, Don Cayo," Major Tijero said.

"Take this paper to the President, Major," he said. "Senator Landa will attend the meeting. Yes, himself. It's all fixed up, thank God, yes."

"Is it true?" Paredes asked, blinking. "Is he coming here?"

"As the government supporter that he is, as the leader of the majority that he is," he murmured. "Yes, he ought to be arriving any moment now. In order to save time, the communiqué should be drawn up. There wasn't any such plot, quote the telegrams of support from the army chiefs. You're the person most indicated to issue the communiqué, doctor."

"It will be my great pleasure to do so," Dr. Arbeláez said. "But since

397

you're practically my successor, you should start getting some practice in writing communiqués, Don Cayo."

"We've been running back and forth from one place to another, Don Cayo," Ludovico said. "From San Miguel to the Plaza Italia, from the Plaza Italia to here."

"You must be dead, Don Cayo," Hipólito said. "We at least got a few hours' sleep this afternoon."

"It's my turn now," he said. "Actually, I've earned a little sleep. Let's stop by the Ministry and then to Chaclacayo."

"Good evening, Don Cayo," Dr. Alcibíades said. "Mrs. Ferro here doesn't want to . . ."

"Did you give the communiqué to the radio stations and the press?" he asked.

"I've been waiting since eight o'clock in the morning and it's nine o'clock at night," the woman said. "You have to see me even if it's only for ten minutes, Mr. Bermúdez."

"I explained to Mrs. Ferro that you were very busy," Dr. Alcibíades said. "But she didn't . . ."

"All right, ten minutes, madam," he said. "Would you come into my office for a moment, doctor?"

"She's been sitting in the hall for almost four hours," Dr. Alcibíades said. "Neither threats nor promises did any good, Don Cayo, there was no way out."

"I told you to have the cops get her out," he said.

"I was going to, but since the communiqué announcing the nomination of General Espina arrived, I thought the situation had changed," Dr. Alcibíades said. "That Dr. Ferro would most likely be set free."

"Yes, it has changed, and Ferro will have to be turned loose too," he said. "Did you send out the communiqué?"

"To all newspapers, news agencies and radio stations," Dr. Alcibíades said. "National Radio has already broadcast it. Shall I tell the lady that her husband is going to be released and send her on her way?"

"I'll give her the good news myself," he said. "Well, now at last the whole affair is finished. You must be done in, doctor."

"To tell the truth, I am, Don Cayo," Dr. Alcibíades said. "It's been almost three days since I've had any sleep."

"Those of us who look after security are the only ones who do any real work in this government," he said.

"Did Senator Landa really attend the meeting of legislators at the Palace?" Dr. Alcibíades asked.

"He was at the Palace for five hours and tomorrow a picture will come out showing him greeting the President," he said. "It was a lot of work, but we pulled it off in the end. Have that lady come in and go get some sleep, doctor."

"I want to know what's happening to my husband," the woman said resolutely, and he thought she's not here to beg or weep, she's here to fight. "Why did you have him arrested, Mr. Bermúdez?"

"If looks could kill, I'd be a corpse right now." He smiled. "Calm yourself, madam. Sit down. I didn't know that my friend Ferro was married. Even less that he had married so well."

"Answer me, why did you have him arrested?" the woman repeated vehemently and he thought what's going on? "Why haven't they let me see him?"

"I'm going to surprise you but, with the greatest respect, I'm going to ask you something." A revolver in her purse? does she know something I don't know? "How is it that a woman like you can be married to Ferro, ma'am?"

"Have a care, Mr. Bermúdez, don't get the wrong impression of me." The woman raised her voice: she probably wasn't used to it, it must have been the first time. "I won't allow you to be disrespectful to me, or to say bad things about my husband."

"I'm not saying bad things about him, I'm saying good things about you," he said and thought she must have been forced to come here, she's disgusted because she came, they sent her. "I'm sorry, I didn't mean to offend you."

"Why is he in jail, when are you going to let him go?" the woman repeated. "Tell me what's going to happen to my husband."

"Only policemen and clerks come into this office," he said. "Women only rarely, and never one like you. That's why I'm so overcome by your visit, ma'am."

"Are you still teasing me?" the woman murmured, trembling. "Don't be so overbearing, don't abuse me, Mr. Bermúdez."

399

"All right, madam, your husband can tell you himself why he was arrested." What did she want, after all, what didn't she dare say? "Don't worry about him. He's being treated with all due consideration, he doesn't need anything. Well, he does need you, and that we can't provide, unfortunately."

"That's enough of vulgarities, you're talking to a lady," the woman said, and he she's made up her mind, now she's going to say it, do it. "Try to behave like a gentleman."

"I'm not a gentleman and you didn't have to come here to give me a lesson in manners, you came for something else," he murmured. "You know only too well why your husband was arrested. Tell me once and for all what you've come here for."

"I've come to propose a deal to you," the woman babbled. "My husband has got to get out of the country tomorrow. I want to know what the conditions are."

"That's more like it." He nodded. "My conditions to let Ferrito go? How much money, that is."

"I've brought the tickets so you could see them," she said, leaning forward. "The plane to New York, tomorrow at ten. You have to let him out tonight. I know you don't take checks. This is all I could put together."

"Not bad, ma'am." You're killing me with a slow fire, sticking pins in my eyes, skinning me with your nails: he undressed her, tied her, hunched over and asked for the whip. "And besides, in dollars. How much is there here? A thousand, two thousand?"

"I haven't got any more in cash, we haven't got any more," the woman said. "We can sign a paper, whatever you say."

"Tell me frankly what's going on and that way we can come to an understanding," he said. "I've known Ferrito for years, madam. You're not doing this because of the Espina affair. Speak to me frankly. What's the problem?"

"He has to leave Peru, he has to be on that plane tomorrow and you know why," the woman said quickly. "He's between the sword and the wall and you know it. It's not a favor, Mr. Bermúdez, it's a business deal. What are the conditions, what else do we have to do?"

"You didn't buy those tickets in case the revolution failed, and it's not a tourist trip," he said. "I can see that he's mixed up in something much worse. It's not smuggling either, that was fixed up, I helped him put the lid on it. I'm beginning to understand, madam."

"They took advantage of his good faith, he lent his name and now everything is falling down on his head," the woman said. "It's hard for me to do this, Mr. Bermúdez. He has to leave the country, you know that only too well."

"The housing project in Sur Chico," he said. "Of course, ma'am, now I see it. Now I see why Ferro started plotting with Espina. Did Espina offer to get him off the hook if he helped him?"

"The accusations have already been filed, the miserable people who got him into this have got out," the woman said with a broken voice. "It's millions of soles, Mr. Bermúdez."

"I knew about it, ma'am, but I didn't know that the collapse was so close." He nodded. "The Argentinians who were his partners took off? And Ferrito was going to go too, leaving the hundreds of guys who bought those houses that don't exist hanging in the air. Millions of soles, naturally. Now I know why he got involved in the plot, now I know why you're here."

"He can't take the responsibility for everything, they tricked him too," the woman said, and he thought she's going to cry. "If he's not on that plane . . ."

"He'll be behind bars for a long time, and not as a plotter but as a swindler." He was sorry, shaking his head. "And all the money he got out of it will be rotting away abroad."

"He didn't get a nickel out of it." The woman raised her voice. "They took advantage of his good faith. This whole business has ruined him."

"Now I understand why you had the nerve to come here," he repeated softly. "A lady like you coming to see me, lowering yourself like that. So you won't be here when the scandal breaks, so you won't see your name in the crime news."

"Not because of me, because of my children," the woman roared; but she took a deep breath and lowered her voice. "This is all I've been able to put together. Accept this as an advance, then. We'll sign a paper, whatever you say."

"Keep those dollars for your trip, Ferrito and you will need them more

401

than I do," he said very slowly, and he saw the woman become motionless, and saw her eyes, her teeth. "Besides, you're worth a lot more than all that money. All right, it's a deal. Don't shout, don't cry, tell me yes or no. We'll spend a little time together, we'll go get Ferro out, tomorrow you'll catch the plane."

"How dare you, you swine," and he looked at her nose, her hands, her shoulders, and he thought she doesn't shout, doesn't cry, doesn't act surprised, doesn't leave. "You miserable half-breed, you coward."

"I'm not a gentleman, that's the price, you knew that too," he murmured. "I can guarantee you the most absolute discretion, of course. It's not a conquest, it's a business deal, think of it that way. And make up your mind right now, the ten minutes are up, madam."

"Chaclacayo?" Ludovico asked. "Very well, Don Cayo, San Miguel."

"Yes, I'm going to stay here," he said. "Go get some sleep, come pick me up at seven o'clock. This way, madam. You'll freeze to death in the garden. Come in for a while, whenever you want to leave I'll call a taxi and take you home."

"Good evening, sir, excuse the way I look, I was getting ready for bed," Carlota said. "The mistress isn't home, she went out early with Miss Queta."

"Bring some ice and go to bed, Carlota," he said. "Come in, don't stand there in the doorway, sit down, I'll fix you a drink. Water or soda? Straight, then, just like me."

"What does this mean?" the woman finally managed to say, rigid. "Where have you brought me?"

"You don't like the house?" He smiled. "Well, you must be used to more elegant places."

"Who's that woman you asked about?" the woman whispered, holding her breath.

"My mistress, her name is Hortensia," he said. "One cube or two? Cheers, madam. Well, now, you didn't want a drink and you downed the whole thing. So I'll fix you another."

"I already knew, they already told me, you're the lowest, dirtiest person who ever lived," the woman said in a half-whisper. "What do you want? To humiliate me? Is that why you brought me here?"

"Just so we can have a few drinks and a little chat," he said. "Hor-

402

tensia isn't a vulgar half-breed like me. She's not refined and proper like you, but she's presentable enough."

"Go on, what else," the woman said. "How much more? Go on."

"This disgusts you most of all because it has to do with me," he said. "If I'd been someone like you, maybe you wouldn't be so repelled, right?"

"Yes." The woman's teeth stopped chattering for a second, her lips stopped trembling. "But a proper man wouldn't do a swinish thing like this."

"It isn't the idea of going to bed with someone else that makes you sick, it's the idea of going to bed with a half-breed," he said, drinking. "Wait, I'll get you a refill."

"What are you waiting for? That's enough, where have you got the bed you collect your blackmail in?" the woman said. "Do you think that if I keep on drinking I'm going to feel less disgusted?"

"Here comes Hortensia," he said. "Don't get up, it's not necessary. Hello, girl. Let me introduce you to the nameless lady. This is Hortensia, ma'am. A little high, but you can see, presentable enough."

"A little? The truth is I can barely stand." Hortensia laughed. "Charmed, nameless lady, pleased to meet you. Have you been here long?"

"We just got here," he said. "Sit down, I'll fix you a drink."

"Don't think I'm asking out of jealousy, nameless lady, just out of curiosity." Hortensia laughed. "I'm never jealous of pretty women. Whew, I'm done in. Do you want a cigarette?"

"Here, to get you back on your feet," he said, handing her the glass. "Where were you?"

"At Lucy's party," Hortensia said. "I made Queta take me home because they were already out of their minds. That nut of a Lucy did a complete strip-tease, I swear to you. Cheers, nameless lady."

"When friend Ferro finds out he's going to give Lucy a beating," he said, smiling. "Lucy is one of Hortensia's girl friends, ma'am, the mistress of a fellow named Ferro."

"What do you mean he'll kill her, just the opposite," Hortensia said with a loud laugh, turning toward the woman. "He loves for Lucy to do crazy things, he's depraved. Don't you remember, boy, that day Ferrito made Lucy dance all naked here on the dining room table? Say, you can really drain a glass, nameless lady. Give your guest another drink, tight-wad."

"A pleasant fellow, friend Ferro," he said. "Tireless when it comes to having a wild time."

"Especially when women are involved," Hortensia said. "He wasn't at the party, Lucy was furious and said that if he didn't come by twelve o'clock she'd call his home and cause a scandal. This is getting boring, let's put some music on."

"I have to be going," the woman blurted without getting up, without looking at either of them. "Would you please call me a taxi?"

"Alone in a taxi at this hour?" Hortensia said. "Aren't you afraid? The drivers are all a bunch of crooks."

"First I have to make a call," he said. "Hello, Lozano? I want you to let Ferro go at seven o'clock in the morning for me. Yes, see to it personally. Seven o'clock sharp. That's all, Lozano, good night."

"Ferro, Ferrito?" Hortensia asked. "Is Ferrito in jail?"

"Call a taxi for the nameless lady and keep your mouth shut, Hortensia," he said. "Don't worry about the driver, ma'am. I'll have the policeman on the corner go along with you. Consider the debt paid."

3

HAD THE MISTRESS loved Don Cayo? Not very much. She hadn't cried over him, but instead, because he'd gone off and left her flat: bum, dog. It's your own fault, Miss Queta said, she'd told her time and time again, at least get him to buy you a car, a house in your name at least. But during those first weeks there was scarcely any change in life in San Miguel; the pantry and the refrigerator were as chock full as ever, Símula continued to keep her tricky accounts for the mistress, at the end of the month they got their full pay. That Sunday, as soon as they met in the Bertoloto, they began to talk about the mistress. What would become of her now, Amalia said, who would help her. And he: she was a sharp one, she'd get herself another moneybags before the cock crowed three times. Don't talk about her that way, Amalia said, I don't like it. They went to see a picture from Argentina and Ambrosio came out talking Argentine slang and putting on the accent; nut, Amalia laughed, and all of a sudden Trinidad's face appeared. They were in the little room on the Calle Chiclayo, getting undressed, when a woman in her forties with artificial eyelashes came looking for Ludovico. Her expression became sad when Ambrosio told her he'd gone to Arequipa and hadn't come back. The woman left and Amalia made fun of her lashes and Ambrosio said he likes wild old women. And by the way, what could have happened to Ludovico? He hoped nothing had gone bad for him, the poor guy didn't feel like going at all. They had a snack downtown and walked until it got dark. Sitting on a bench on the Paseo de la República, they chatted, watching the cars go by. There was a breeze, Amalia cuddled against him and Ambrosio put his arm around her: would you like to have your own little house and me for your husband, Amalia? She looked at him with surprise. Pretty soon the day would come when they could get married and have children, Amalia, he was putting money away for that. Could it be true? Would they have a home, children? It seemed so far away, so difficult, and lying on her back in her bed, Amalia tried to picture herself living with him, cooking his meals and washing his clothes. She couldn't. But why not, silly? Weren't a lot of people getting married every day, why not you to him?

It must have been a month since the master had left when the mistress came into the house like a cyclone one day: all set, Quetita, starting at the fat man's next week, she would start rehearsing today. She had to take care of her figure, exercises, Turkish baths. Was she really going to sing in a nightclub, ma'am. Of course, just like before. She'd been famous once, Amalia, I gave up my career for that bum, now she was going to pick it up again. Come, let me show you, she took her by the arm, they ran upstairs, and in the study she took out an album of clippings, what she had wanted to see so much at last, Amalia thought, look, look. She was showing them to her, proud: in a long gown, in a bathing suit, with upswept hair, on a stage, as Queen, throwing kisses. And listen to what the newspapers said, Amalia: she was beautiful, she had a tropical voice, she was having success after success. The house became a shambles, all the mistress talked about was rehearsing and she went on a diet, some grapefruit juice and a small steak at noon, a salad with no dressing at night, I'm starving to death but what difference does it make, close the windows, the doors, if I catch cold before my opening I'll die, she was going to quit smoking, cigarettes were poison to singers. One day Amalia heard her complaining to Miss Queta: not even enough to pay the rent, the fat man was a tightwad. After all, Quetita, the main thing was the chance, she'd get her public back and make some demands. She would leave for the fat man's around nine o'clock, in slacks and wearing a turban, carrying a small valise, and return at dawn, with heavy makeup on. Her main worry was weight more than cleanliness now. She went through the newspapers with a magnifying glass, listen to what they're saying about me, Amalia! and she'd get angry if they said something good about someone else: that bitch paid them, she bought them.

After a while the little parties started up again. Amalia recognized a few elegant old boys who used to come during the master's time among the guests, but most of the people were different now: younger, not as well dressed, without cars but so gay, such neckties, such bright colors, theater people Carlota buzzed. The mistress could have died she was having such a good time, a native party tonight, Amalia! She told Símula to make chicken and chili or duck and rice, some marinated fish or potato salad as an appetizer and she sent out to the store for beer. She no longer locked the pantry door, she no longer sent them off to bed. Amalia watched the high jinks, the crazy goings-on, the mistress went from the arms of one to those of another, the same as her girl friends, she let herself be kissed, and she was the one who got the most drunk. But in spite of all that, the time she caught a man coming out of the bathroom the day after a party, Amalia felt ashamed and even a little angry. Ambrosio was right, she was a sharp one. In one month she'd caught another one, a month later still another. A sharp one, yes, but very good to her and on her days off Ambrosio asked her what's the mistress up to, she lied to him very sad since the master went away, so he wouldn't get a bad idea of her.

Which one do you think she'll pick? Carlota sputtered. It was true, the mistress had plenty to choose from: every day there was a flood of phone calls, sometimes flowers were delivered with little cards which the mistress would read to Miss Queta over the phone. She picked one who used to come during the master's time, one who Amalia had thought was involved with Miss Queta. What a shame, an old man, Carlota said. But a rich one, tall and well built. With his ruddy face and his white hair it didn't seem right to call him Mr. Urioste but grandpa, papa instead, Carlota laughed. Very fine manners, but when he drank, things would get the better of him and his eyes would pop out and he'd throw himself all over the women. He slept over once, twice, three times, and from then on he often woke up in the morning at the little house in San Miguel and he would leave around nine in his big brick-red car. The old-timer dropped you for me, the mistress would say with a laugh, and Miss Queta laughing: squeeze it out of him, girl. They had a good time making fun of the poor man. Can he still make it with you, girl? No, but it's better like that because that way I'm not cheating as much on you, Quetita. There was no doubt about it, she was going with him strictly for financial reasons. Mr. Urioste didn't inspire dislike and fear like Don Cayo, respect, rather, and even affection when he would come down the stairs with his fat cheeks aglow and his eyes tired, and he'd put a few soles into Amalia's apron pocket. He was more generous than Don Cayo, more proper. So that when he stopped coming after a few months, Amalia, thinking, thought he was right, just because he was an old man, should he let himself be deceived? He found out about the Pichón business, he had an attack of jealousy and took off, the mistress told Miss Queta, he'll be back soon, tame as a lamb, but he never did come back.

Is the mistress still so sad? Ambrosio asked her one Sunday. Amalia told him the truth: she'd gotten over it, she'd got herself a lover, had a fight with him, and now she was sleeping with different men. She thought he would say you see, didn't I tell you? and maybe order her not to work there anymore. But he only shrugged his shoulders: she was earning her three squares, leave her alone. She felt like answering and what if I did the same thing, would you care? but she held back. They saw each other every Sunday, they went to Ludovico's room, sometimes they would run into him and he would invite them out for a snack or some beers. Had he been in an accident? Amalia asked him the first day she saw him all bandaged up. The Arequipans gave me an accident, he laughed, it's nothing now, I was worse before. He seems happy, Amalia commented to Ambrosio, and he: because thanks to that beating they put him on the regular list, Amalia, he was making more money on the police force now and he was somebody important.

Since the mistress scarcely stayed home anymore, life was more relaxed than ever. In the afternoon, with Carlota and Símula, she would sit down to listen to soap operas, records. One morning, as she was taking breakfast up to the mistress, she ran into a face in the hall that left her breathless. Carlota, she came down on the run, all excited, Carlota, a young one, a real good-looker, and when she saw him I just melted away, she said, Carlota. The mistress and the man came down late, Amalia and Carlota looked at him, stupefied, without breathing, he had a look that made your stomach jump. The mistress seemed hypnotized too. All languid, all loving, all vanity and flirting, she touched him on the mouth with her fork, she played the little girl, she mussed his hair, she whispered in his ear, sweet love, honeybunch, lover. Amalia didn't recognize her, so soft, and those looks, and that tiny voice.

Mr. Lucas was so young that even the mistress looked old beside him, so good-looking that Amalia felt warm all over when he looked at her. Dark, with very white teeth, big eyes, a walk as if he owned the world. It wasn't for financial reasons with him, Amalia told Ambrosio, Mr. Lucas didn't have a cent. He was a Spaniard, he sang at the same place as the mistress. We met and we fell in love, the mistress confessed to Amalia, lowering her eyes. She was in love with him, she still loves him. Sometimes the master and the mistress, playing around, would sing a duet and Amalia and Carlota they should get married, have children, the mistress looked so happy.

But Mr. Lucas came to live in San Miguel and showed his claws. He almost never left the house before dark and he spent his time lying on the sofa calling for drinks, coffee. He didn't like any of the food, he had something bad to say about everything, and the mistress quarreled with Símula. He asked for strange dishes, what in Christ's hell is gazpacho, Amalia heard Símula grunt, it was the first time she'd ever heard her curse. The good impression of the first day was fading and even Carlota began to detest him. Besides being capricious, he was fresh. He took a free hand with the mistress's money, he'd send out for something and say ask Hortensia for the money, she's my bank. Besides that, he held parties every week, he loved them. One night Amalia saw him kissing Miss Queta on the mouth. How could she do that, being such a good friend of the mistress, what would the mistress have done if she'd caught him? Nothing, she would have forgiven him. She was madly in love, she took everything from him, one little loving word from him and her bad mood would disappear, she'd be rejuvenated. And he took advantage of it. Collectors came with bills for things Mr. Lucas had bought and the mistress paid or she told them some tale and to come back another time. That was when Amalia realized for the first time that the mistress was having money troubles. But Mr. Lucas didn't, every day he'd order more things. He went about all elegant, multicolored ties, made-to-order suits, suede shoes. Life is short, love, he would laugh, you have to live it, love, and he would open his arms. You're a baby, love, she would say. How can it be, Amalia thought, Mr. Lucas has turned her into a little silk pussycat. She watched her go over to the master, all full of affection, kneel at his feet, lay her head on his knees, and she couldn't believe it. She heard her say pay some attention to me, sweet, begging him so sweetly, for some love for your old lady who loves you so much, and she couldn't believe it, couldn't believe it.

During the six months Mr. Lucas was in San Miguel, the comforts slowly disappeared. The pantry emptied out, the refrigerator was left with nothing but milk and the day's vegetables, the deliveries from the liquor store stopped. The whiskey passed into history and now they drank pisco and ginger ale at the parties and had snacks instead of preparing native dishes. Amalia told Ambrosio about it and he smiled: a little pimp, that Lucas. The mistress took over the accounts for the first time, Amalia laughed inside watching Símula's face when she was asked for change. And one fine day Símula announced that she and Carlota were leaving. To Huacho, ma'am, they were going to open up a little food store. But the night before they left, seeing Amalia so sad, Carlota consoled her: it's a lie, they weren't going to Huacho, we'll still see each other. Símula had found a place downtown, she was going to be the cook and Carlota the maid. You ought to come too, Amalita, my mama says this house is going under. Would she go? No, the mistress was so good. She stayed and let herself be convinced instead that if she did the cooking she'd make fifty soles more. From then on the master and the mistress almost never ate at home, let's eat out instead, love. Since I can't cook, he couldn't stomach my meals, Amalia told Ambrosio, well done. But the work was tripled: tidying up, shaking out, making beds, washing dishes, sweeping, cooking. The little house wasn't as well ordered and bright anymore. Amalia could tell by the mistress's eyes how she suffered if a week went by without washing down the courtyard, three or four days without dusting the living room. She'd let the gardener go and the geraniums withered and the lawn dried up. Ever since Mr. Lucas had been living at the house, Miss Queta hadn't slept over again, but she still came by, sometimes with that foreign woman, Señora Ivonne, who made jokes about the mistress and Mr. Lucas: how are the lovebirds, the sweethearts. One day, when the master had gone out, Amalia heard Miss

Queta arguing with the mistress: he's ruining you, he's a sponge, you've got to drop him. She ran to the pantry; the mistress was listening to her, hunched in the easy chair, and suddenly she lifted up her face and she was crying. She knew all that, Quetita, and Amalia thought she was going to cry too, but what could she do, Quetita, she loved him, it was the first time in her life she'd ever really been in love. Amalia left the pantry, went to her room and locked the door. There was Trinidad's face, when he got sick, when they arrested him, when he died. She'd never leave, she'd stay with the mistress always.

The house was going under, yes, and Mr. Lucas was feeding on those ruins like a buzzard on a garbage pile. The broken glasses and vases weren't being replaced, but he would show up in a new suit. The mistress told sad tales to the bill collectors from the store and the laundry, but on his birthday he appeared with a ring and at Christmas time Santa Claus brought him a watch. He was never sad or angry: they've opened a new restaurant in Magdalena, shall we go, love? He would get up late and settle down in the living room to read the newspaper. Amalia would watch him, a good-looking boy, smiling, in his wine-colored dressing gown, his feet on the sofa, humming, and she hated him: she would spit in his breakfast, put hairs in his soup, in her dreams she would have him sliced up by the wheels of a train.

One morning, on the way back from the store, she ran into the mistress and Miss Queta, who were coming out in slacks, carrying small bags. They were going to the Turkish bath, they wouldn't be back for lunch, she should buy a beer for the master. They left and in a little while Amalia heard steps; he was already awake, he probably wanted his breakfast. She went upstairs and Mr. Lucas, in jacket and tie, was hurriedly packing his clothes in a suitcase. He was taking a trip to the provinces, Amalia, he was going to sing in theaters, he'd be back the next Monday, and he spoke as if he was already traveling, singing. Give this note to Hortensia, Amalia, and now call me a taxi. Amalia looked at him open-mouthed. Finally she left the room without saying anything. She got a taxi, brought the master's suitcase down, good-bye Amalia, see you Monday. She went into the house and sat down in the living room, upset. If only Doña Símula and Carlota could have been here when she gave the mistress the note. She couldn't do anything all morning, only watch

411

the clock and think. It was five o'clock when Miss Queta's little car stopped by the door. Her face close to the drapes, she watched them approach, all fresh, all young, as if they hadn't lost pounds but years at the Turkish bath, and she opened the door and her legs began to quiver. Come in, girl, the mistress said, have some coffee, and they came in and threw their bags onto the sofa. What was wrong, Amalia. The master had gone on a trip, ma'am, and her heart was beating hard, he'd left a note upstairs. She didn't change color, she didn't move. She looked at her very quietly, very seriously, finally her mouth trembled a little. On a trip? Lucas on a trip? and before Amalia could answer anything, she took half a turn and went upstairs, followed by Miss Queta. Amalia tried to listen. She hadn't started to cry or she was crying very low. She heard a noise, a rummaging, Miss Queta's voice: Amalia! The closet was wide open, the mistress was sitting on the bed. Didn't he say he was coming back, Amalia? Miss Queta pierced her with her eyes. Yes, miss, and she didn't dare look at the mistress, he was coming back Monday and she realized she was stammering. He wanted to run off with some girl, Miss Queta said, he felt himself tied down by your jealousy, girl, he'd be back on Monday asking you to forgive him. Please, Queta, the mistress said, stop playing the fool. A thousand times better that he took off, Miss Queta shouted, you've freed yourself from a vampire, and the mistress calmed her with her hand: the bureau, Quetita, she didn't dare look. She sobbed, covered her face, and Miss Queta had already run over and was opening drawers, rummaging through them, tossing letters, bottles and keys onto the floor, did you see if he took the little red box, Amalia? and Amalia was picking up, on her hands and knees, oh Lord, oh missy, didn't you see that he took the mistress's jewels? No, indeed, they'd call the police, he wasn't going to rob you, girl, they'd have him arrested, he'd give them back. The mistress was sobbing loudly and Miss Queta sent Amalia to make a cup of good, hot coffee. When she came back with the tray, trembling, Miss Queta was talking on the phone: you know people, Señora Ivonne, have them look for him, have them catch him. The mistress stayed in her room all afternoon talking to Miss Queta, and at nightfall Señora Ivonne arrived. The next day two fellows from the police appeared and one of them was Ludovico. He pretended not to know Amalia. They both asked questions and more questions about Mr. Lucas and finally they calmed the mistress down: she'd get her jewels back, it was only a matter of a few days.

They were sad days. Things had been going badly before, but from then on everything got worse, Amalia would think later. The mistress was in bed, pale, her hair disheveled, and all she had to eat were a few bowls of soup. On the third day Miss Queta left. Do you want me to bring my mattress up to your room, ma'am? No, Amalia, you go ahead and sleep in your own room. But Amalia stayed on the living room sofa, wrapped in her blanket. In the darkness, her face felt damp. She hated Trinidad, Ambrosio, all of them. She would nod and wake up, she was sorry, she was afraid, and one of those times she saw a light in the hall. She went up, put her ear to the door, she didn't hear anything and she opened it. The mistress was stretched out on the bed, uncovered, her eyes open: had she been calling her, ma'am? She went over, saw the fallen glass, the mistress's eyes showing white. She ran shouting into the street. She'd killed herself, and she rang the bell next door, she'd killed herself, and she kicked on the door. A man in his bathrobe came, a woman was slapping the mistress's face, they pressed on her stomach, they wanted her to vomit, they telephoned. It was almost daybreak when the ambulance arrived.

The mistress spent a week in the Loayza Hospital. The day she went to visit her, Amalia found her with Miss Queta, Miss Lucy and Señora Ivonne. Pale and thin, but more resigned. Here's my savior, the mistress joked. How can I tell her there isn't even anything to eat? she thought. Luckily, the mistress remembered: give her something for her expenses, Quetita. That Sunday she went to meet Ambrosio at the car stop and brought him to the house. He already knew that the mistress had tried to kill herself, Amalia. And how did he know? Because Don Fermín was paying the hospital bill. Don Fermín? Yes, she'd called him and he, gentleman that he is, seeing her in that situation had felt sorry for her and was helping her. Amalia fixed him something to eat and then they listened to the radio. They went to bed in the mistress's room and Amalia had a laughing attack she couldn't stop. So that's what the mirrors were for, so that's what, the mistress was a regular she-devil, and Ambrosio had to shake her by the shoulders and scold her, annoyed by her laughter. He hadn't spoken about the little house or getting married again, but

413

they got along well, he and she, they never fought. They always did the same thing: the streetcar, Ludovico's little room, the movies, one of those dances sometimes. One Sunday Ambrosio got into a fight in a native restaurant in Barrios Altos because some drunks came in shouting Long Live APRA! and he Down with It! Elections were coming up and there were rallies on the Plaza San Martín. The downtown area was full of posters, cars with loudspeakers. Vote for Prado, you know him! they said on the radio, fliers, they sang Lavalle is the man Peru wants! with waltz music, photos, and Amalia was taken by the polka Forward with Belaúnde! The Apristas had come back, pictures of Haya de la Torre came out in the newspapers and she remembered Trinidad. Did she love Ambrosio? Yes, but with him it wasn't the way it was with Trinidad, with him there wasn't that suffering, that joy, that heat the way there was with Trinidad. Why do you want Lavalle to win? she asked him, and he because Don Fermín was for him. With Ambrosio everything was peaceful, we're just two friends who also go to bed together crossed her mind once. Months passed without her visiting Señora Rosario, months without seeing Gertrudis Lama or her aunt. During the week she kept storing up everything that happened in her head and on Sunday she would tell Ambrosio, but he was so reserved that sometimes she would get furious. How's Missy Teté? fine, and Señora Zoila? fine, had young Santiago come back home? no, did they miss him much? yes, especially Don Fermín. What else, what else? Nothing else. Sometimes teasing, she would scare him: I'm going to pay a visit to Señora Zoila, I'm going to tell Señora Hortensia about us. He would start frothing at the mouth: if you go, you'll be sorry, if you tell her, we'll never see each other again. Why all the hiding, all the mystery, all the shame? He was strange, he was crazy, he had his ways. Would you feel the same sorrow you did for Trinidad if Ambrosio died? Gertrudis asked her once. No, she'd cry over him, but it wouldn't be like the end of the world, Gertrudis. It must be because we haven't lived together, she thought. Maybe if she'd washed his clothes and cooked for him and taken care of him when he was sick it would have been different.

Señora Hortensia came back to San Miguel all skin and bones. Her clothes were floppy on her, her face was sucked in, her eyes didn't shine the way they had before. Didn't the police get her jewels back, ma'am?

The mistress laughed listlessly, they'd never find them, and her eyes watered. Lucas was sharper than the police. She still loved him, poor thing. The truth was she hadn't had many left, Amalia, she'd been selling them because of him, for him. How foolish men were, he didn't have to steal them from her, Amalia, all he had to do was ask me for them. The mistress had changed. Bad things came to her one after the other and she indifferent, serious, quiet. Prado won, ma'am, APRA turned on Lavalle and voted for Prado and Prado won, that's what the radio said. But the mistress wasn't listening to her: I lost my job, Amalia, the fat man didn't renew my contract. She said it without fury, as if it were the most normal thing in the world. And a few days later, to Miss Queta, my debts are going to swamp me. She didn't seem scared or concerned. Amalia no longer knew what story to make up when Mr. Poncio came to collect the rent: she's not home, she went out, tomorrow, Monday. Before, Mr. Poncio had been nothing but flirtation and charm; now he was a hyena: he would get red, cough, swallow. So she's not home, eh? He gave Amalia a shove and barked Señora Hortensia, enough tricks! From the top of the stairs the mistress looked at him as if he were a little cockroach: what right do you have to shout like that, tell Paredes I'll pay him another time. You haven't been paying and Colonel Paredes is on my back, Mr. Poncio barked, we're going to get you out of here legally. I'll leave when I damned well please, the mistress said without shouting and he, barking, we'll give you until Monday or we'll take steps. Amalia went upstairs afterward thinking she'd be furious. But she wasn't, she was calm, looking at the ceiling with gelatinous eyes. In Cayo's time, Paredes refused to take any rent, Amalia, and now, what a difference. She was speaking with a terrible languor, as if she were far away or falling asleep. They'd have to move, there was no other way out, Amalia. Those were agitated days. The mistress would leave early, come home late, I looked at a hundred houses and all too expensive, she would call one man, and another, ask them for a note, a loan, and hang up the telephone and twist her mouth: thankless ingrates. On moving day, Mr. Poncio came by and shut himself up with the mistress in the little room that had been Don Cayo's. Finally the mistress came down and told the truckers to bring the living room and bar furniture back into the house.

The lack of that furniture wasn't even noticed in the apartment in

Magdalena Vieja, it was smaller than the little house in San Miguel. There were even too many things, and the mistress sold the desk, the easy chairs, the mirrors and the sideboard. The apartment was on the second floor of a green building, it had a dining room, bedroom, bath, kitchen, small patio, and a maid's room with its little bath. It was new, and once fixed up, it was quite pretty.

The first Sunday she met Ambrosio on the Avenida Brasil at the Military Hospital stop, they had a fight. Poor mistress, Amalia told him, the trouble she'd been through, they took away her furniture, Mr. Poncio's rudeness, and Ambrosio said I'm glad. What? Yes, she was a bitch. What? She sponged off people, she spent her time asking Don Fermín for money and he'd already helped her so much, she had no consideration. Drop her, Amalia, look for another house. I'll drop you first, Amalia said. They argued for about an hour and only half made up. All right, they wouldn't talk about her anymore, Amalia, it wasn't worth our fighting because of that crazy woman.

With the loans and from what she sold, the mistress wasn't doing too badly while she looked for work. She finally got a job at a place in Barranco, La Laguna. Once more she began to talk about giving up smoking and she awoke in the morning with her makeup still on. She never mentioned Mr. Lucas, only Miss Queta came to see her. She wasn't the same as before. She didn't crack jokes, she didn't have the wit, the grace, that careless, happy way she had before. Now she thought about money a lot. Quiñoncito is crazy about you, girl, and she didn't even want to look at him, Quetita, he didn't have a dime. Then, after a while, she began to go out with men, but she never let them in, she kept them waiting at the door or in the street while she got ready. She was ashamed to have them see how she was living now, Amalia thought. She would get up and fix herself her pisco and ginger ale. She listened to the radio, read the newspaper, phoned Miss Queta, and drank two, three. She didn't look as pretty, as elegant as before.

That was how days and weeks went by. When the mistress stopped singing at La Laguna, Amalia only found out about it two days later. The mistress stayed home a Monday and a Tuesday, wasn't she going to sing that night either, ma'am? She wasn't going back to La Laguna anymore, Amalia, they were exploiting her, she'd look for a better job. But on the days that followed she didn't seem too anxious to find another job. She'd stay in bed, the curtains drawn, listening to the radio in the shadows. She'd get up wearily and fix herself a pisco and ginger ale and when Amalia went into the bedroom she would see her, motionless, her gaze lost in the smoke, her voice weak and her gestures tired. Around seven o'clock she would start making up her face and fixing her nails, combing her hair, and around eight o'clock Miss Queta would pick her up in her little car. She would return at dawn, all done in, quite drunk, so tired out that sometimes she would wake Amalia up to help her undress. See how thin she's getting, Amalia said to Miss Queta, tell her to eat more, she's going to get sick. Miss Queta would tell her, but she didn't pay any attention to her. She kept taking her clothes to a seamstress on the Avenida Brasil to have them taken in. Every day she gave Amalia the money for the day and paid her wages punctually, where was she getting money from? No man had spent the night in the Magdalena apartment yet. She probably did her things elsewhere. When the mistress started to work at the Montmartre, she no longer talked about giving up smoking or worried about drafts. Now she didn't even give a hoot about singing. The way she put on her makeup was so dreary. And keeping the house neat and clean didn't interest her, she who used to get hysterical if she ran her finger across a table and found dust. And she didn't notice if the ashtrays were full of butts and hadn't asked her in the morning anymore did you take a shower, did you put on deodorant? The apartment looked a mess, but Amalia didn't have time for everything. Besides, cleaning was more work now. The mistress has infected me with her laziness, she told Ambrosio. It's funny seeing the mistress like this, so sloppy, Miss Queta, could it be that she hasn't gotten over Mr. Lucas? Yes, Miss Queta said, and also because drinking and tranquilizers keep her half dopey.

One day there was a knock on the door. Amalia opened it and there was Don Fermín. He didn't recognize her that time either: Hortensia's expecting me. How old he'd gotten since the last time, all those gray hairs, those sunken eyes. The mistress sent her out for cigarettes, and on Sunday, when Amalia asked what Don Fermín had been doing there, he made an expression of disgust: to bring her money, that damned woman had made a patsy out of him. What did the mistress ever do to you for you to hate her so much? Nothing to Ambrosio, but she was bleeding

Don Fermín, taking advantage of his goodness, anyone else would have told her to go to hell. Amalia became furious: what are you sticking your nose in for, what business is it of yours? Look for a different job, he insisted, can't you see that she's starving to death? leave her.

Sometimes the mistress would disappear for two or three days, and when she came back I was on a trip, Amalia. Paracas, Cuzco, Chimbote. From the window Amalia would spot her getting into men's cars with her suitcase. Some of them she knew by voice, on the telephone, and she tried to guess what they were like, how old they were. Early one morning she heard voices, she went to spy and saw the mistress in the living room with a man, laughing and drinking. Then she heard a door close and thought they've gone into the bedroom. But no, the man had left and the mistress, when she went to ask her if she wanted any lunch, was lying on the bed with her clothes on, a strange look in her eyes. She kept on looking at her with a silent little laugh and Amalia didn't she feel good? Nothing, all quiet, as if all of her body had died except her eyes, which were wandering, looking. She ran to the telephone and waited, trembling, for Miss Queta's voice: she killed herself again, she's on the bed there, she can't hear, she can't speak, and Miss Queta shouted shut up, don't be frightened, listen to me. Strong coffee, don't call the doctor, she'd be right over. Take this so you'll feel better, ma'am, Amalia whimpered, Miss Queta's on her way over. Nothing, mute, deaf, staring, so she lifted up her head and brought the cup to her lips. She drank obediently, two small streams trickling down her neck. That's the way, ma'am, all of it, and she stroked her head and kissed her hands. But when Miss Queta arrived, instead of feeling sorry she began to curse. She sent her out to buy some rubbing alcohol, made the mistress drink more coffee, she and Amalia together undressed her, rubbed her forehead and temples. While Miss Queta was scolding her, you fool, you nut, she didn't know what she was doing, the mistress was coming around. She smiled, what was all the fuss about, she moved, and Miss Queta was fed up, I'm not your nursemaid, you're going to get in a jam, if you want to kill yourself, do it right out and not little by little. That night the mistress didn't go to the Montmartre, but she was all better when she got up the next day.

One morning, it was after the trouble, Amalia was coming back from the store and saw a patrol car parked by the door of the building. A policeman and a plainclothesman were arguing with the mistress on the sidewalk. Just let me make a phone call, the mistress was saying, but they took her arms, put her in the car and left. She stood on the sidewalk, so frightened she didn't feel like going in. She called Miss Queta but she wasn't home; she called all afternoon and she didn't answer. They'd probably taken her to the police station too, they'd probably come and take her in too. The maids and neighbors came by to find out what happened, where they'd taken her. That night she couldn't shut her eyes: they're coming, they're going to take you away. The next day Miss Queta appeared and put on a terrible look when Amalia told her about it. She ran to the telephone: do something, Señora Ivonne, they can't keep her in jail, it was all Paqueta's fault, upset, frightened, Miss Queta too. She gave Amalia ten soles: they'd got the mistress mixed up in something ugly, the police or reporters would probably come, go to your family for a few days. Her eyes were full of tears and she heard her murmur poor Hortensia. Where would she go, where was she going. She went to her aunt's, who ran a boardinghouse in Chacra Colorada now. The mistress went on a trip, auntie, she gave me some time off. Her aunt grumbled at her for having disappeared for so long, and was looking at her. Finally she took her face and examined her eyes: you're lying, she fired you because she found out you're pregnant. She denied it, she wasn't, she protested, who could she be pregnant from. But what if her aunt was right, if that was why she wasn't bleeding? She forgot about the mistress, the police, what was she going to tell Ambrosio, what would he say. On Sunday she went to the stop by the Military Hospital, mumbling a prayer. She began to tell him about the business with her mistress, but he already knew. She was already back home, Amalia, Don Fermín had talked to some friends and they let her out. And why had they arrested the mistress? She probably did something dirty, something bad, and he changed the subject: Ludovico had loaned him his room for the whole night. They didn't see Ludovico much anymore, Ambrosio told her that it seemed he was going to get married and was talking about buying a house in the Villacampa development, Ludovico has come up in the world, hasn't he, Amalia? They went to a little restaurant in Rímac and he asked her why aren't you eating. She wasn't hungry, she'd had a big lunch. Why wasn't she talking? She was thinking about the mistress,

419

tomorrow I'll go see her early. As soon as they went into the little room she got up the nerve to say: my aunt says I'm pregnant. He sat down on the bed with a thump. What's this shit about your aunt thinks, he shook her by an arm, was she or wasn't she? Yes, she thought she was, and she began to cry. Instead of consoling her, Ambrosio started to look at her as if she had leprosy and might infect him. It couldn't be, he repeated, it can't be and his voice stumbled. She ran out of the room. Ambrosio caught up with her on the street. Calm down, don't cry, stupefied, he went with her to the car stop and he said I wasn't expecting it, don't think I'm mad, you just left me without anything to say. On the Avenida Brasil he said good-bye to her until Sunday. Amalia thought: he won't be coming anymore.

Señora Hortensia wasn't furious: hello, Amalia. She hugged her happily, I thought you'd been scared off and wouldn't come back. How could she think such a thing, ma'am. I know, the mistress said, you're a good friend, Amalia, a real friend. They'd tried to get her involved in something she hadn't done, people were like that, that shitty Paqueta was like that, they were all like that. The days, the weeks went back to what they always were, each day a little worse because of the money troubles. One day a man in uniform knocked at the door. Who did he want to see? But the mistress went out to receive him, hello, Richard, and Amalia recognized him. He was the same one who had come into the house early that other morning, except that now he was wearing a pilot's cap and a blue jacket with gold buttons. Mr. Richard was a pilot for Panagra, his whole life was spent traveling, gray sideburns, a blond lock on his forehead, chubby, freckle-faced, a Spanish mixed with English that made you laugh. Amalia thought he was nice. He was the first one to come into the apartment, the first one to sleep over. He would arrive in Lima on Thursday, come from the airport in his blue uniform, take a bath, rest awhile, and they would go out, coming back at dawn, making a lot of noise and sleeping until noon. Sometimes Mr. Richard would spend two days in Lima. He liked to get into the kitchen, put on one of Amalia's aprons and cook. She and the mistress, laughing, watched him fry eggs, cook spaghetti, pizzas. He was a jokester, merry, and the mistress got along well with him. Why didn't she marry Mr. Richard, ma'am? he's

420

so nice. Señora Hortensia laughed: he was married and had four children, Amalia.

Two months must have passed and once Mr. Richard arrived on Wednesday instead of Thursday. The mistress was shut up in the dark with her drink on the night table. Mr. Richard was frightened and called Amalia. Don't carry on so, she reassured him, it wasn't anything, it would go away, it was her medicine. But Mr. Richard was speaking English, red-faced from the surprise, and he gave the mistress some slaps that scratched her skin and the mistress looking at them as if they weren't there. Mr. Richard went into the living room, came back, made a phone call, and finally he went out and brought back a doctor, who gave the mistress a shot. When the doctor left, Mr. Richard went into the kitchen and he looked like a shrimp: red all over, furious, he began to speak in Spanish and switched into English. Sir, what's the matter, why was he shouting, why are you insulting me. He was waving his hands around and Amalia thought he's going to hit me, he's gone crazy. And at that moment the mistress appeared: what right have you got to raise your voice, what right have you got to shout at Amalia. She began to argue with him for having called the doctor, she shouted at him and he at her, and in the living room they kept on shouting, you shitty gringo, you shitty meddler, noise, a slap, and Amalia half-crazy picked up the frying pan and went in thinking he's going to kill the pair of us. Mr. Richard had left and the mistress was insulting him from the door. Then she couldn't hold back, she managed to lift up her apron, but it was no use, all the vomit fell on the floor. When she heard the retching, the mistress came running. Go to the bathroom, don't be frightened, everything's all right. Amalia rinsed out her mouth, went back to the living room with a wet cloth and a mop, and while she was cleaning she could hear the mistress laughing. There was no reason to get frightened, silly, she'd been meaning to get rid of that idiot for a long time and Amalia dying with shame. But all of a sudden the mistress was silent. Wait a minute, she got one of those little smiles she used to have in the old days, you sly little devil, come here, come here. She felt herself blushing, you're not pregnant, are you? getting dizzy, no, ma'am, what a thing to think. But the mistress took her by the arm: you little ninny, of course you are. Not annoyed, but surprised, laughing. No, ma'am, how could she be, and she felt her knees shaking. She began to cry, oh, ma'am. You sly little devil, the mistress said lovingly. She brought her a glass of water, made her sit down, who would have thought it. Yes, she was, ma'am, all this time, she'd felt so bad: thirsty, nauseous, that feeling that her stomach was flying off somewhere. She was weeping loudly and the mistress was consoling her, why didn't you tell me, silly, there wasn't anything wrong with it, I'd have taken you to a doctor, you wouldn't have worked so hard. She kept on crying and all of a sudden: because of him, ma'am, he said she'll throw you out. Don't you know me, silly, Señora Hortensia smiled, did you think I'd throw you out? And Amalia: that chauffeur, that Ambrosio you know, the one who brought you messages to San Miguel. He didn't want anyone to know, he's got his ways. She was weeping loudly and telling her, ma'am, he acted badly once before and now he was worse. Since he found out about the child he's got very strange, he didn't want to talk about it, Amalia would tell him she had vomiting attacks and he'd change the subject, Amalia it's moving now and he I can't spend time with you today I've got things to do. Now she only saw him for a short time on Sundays, just his duty, and the mistress was opening her eyes wide. Ambrosio? yes, he hadn't taken her to the little room again, Fermín Zavala's chauffeur? yes, he'd buy her something to eat and be on his way, you've been seeing him for years? and she was looking at her and shaking her head and saying who would have thought it. He was crazy, a maniac, his secrets all the time, ma'am, he was ashamed of her and now like the other time he was going to drop her. The mistress began to laugh and was shaking her head, who would have thought it. And then, serious now, do you love him, Amalia? Yes, he was her husband, if he knew now that I told you everything he'd leave her, ma'am, he might even kill me. She was crying and the mistress brought her another glass of water and hugged her: he's not going to find out that you told me, he wasn't going to leave her. They kept on talking and the mistress was calming her down, he'd never know, silly. Had she been to a doctor? No, you're such a fool, Amalia. How many months has it been? Four, ma'am. The next day she herself took her to a doctor who examined her and said her pregnancy was fine. That night Miss Queta came by and the mistress in front of Amalia, this woman is pregnant,

422

what do you think of that. Oh yes? Miss Queta said as if not surprised. And if you only knew who by, the mistress laughed, but when she saw Amalia's face she put a finger to her mouth: she couldn't tell, girl, it was a secret.

What was going to happen now? Nothing, she wasn't going to fire her. The mistress had taken her to the doctor and wanted her to take care of herself, don't do any bending, don't do any waxing, don't pick that up. The mistress was good, and she felt so relieved at having told someone. But what if Ambrosio found out? What difference does it make, since he's going to leave you in any case, stupid girl. But he didn't leave her, he showed up every Sunday. They talked, had something to eat, and Amalia thought everything we'd talked about sounds so false, so insincere. Because they talked about everything except that. They hadn't gone back to the little room, they went walking or to the movies and at night he would take her to the Military Hospital stop. She could see he was worried, his look would be lost for moments, and she was thinking but why are you acting like that, had she asked him to marry her, maybe, or for money? One Sunday, coming out of the movies, she heard his curt voice: how do you feel, Amalia? All right, she said and looked at the ground, was he asking that because of the child? When he's born you won't be able to keep on working, she heard him say. And why not, Amalia said, what do you think I'm going to do, how am I going to live. And Ambrosio: I'll have to take over. He didn't say anything else until they said good-bye. I'll take over? she thought darkly, rubbing her belly, him? Did he mean living together, the little house?

The fifth, the sixth month. She felt very heavy now, she had to pause in her work to catch her breath, in her cooking until the hot flashes passed. And one day the mistress said we're moving. Where to, ma'am? To Jesús María, this apartment is too expensive. Some men came to look at the furniture and discuss prices, they came back with a small truck and took the chairs, the dining room table, the rug, the phonograph, the refrigerator, the range. Amalia felt a tightening in her chest the next day when she saw the three suitcases and the ten bundles that contained all of her mistress's belongings. Why does it hurt you when she doesn't care, don't be stupid. But it did hurt, she was. Doesn't it make you sad to be left with almost nothing, ma'am? No, Amalia, do you know why? Be-

423

cause in a little while she was going to get out of this country. I'll take you abroad with me if you want, Amalia, and she laughed. What was going on with her? Where did that good mood come from all of a sudden, those plans, the mistress's urge to do things? Amalia grew cold when she saw the little apartment on General Garzón. Not that it was so small, but so old, so ugly! The combination living–dining room was tiny, the same as the bedroom, the kitchen and the bathroom looked like something out of a doll's house. In the maid's room, so narrow, there was only room for the cot. There was barely any furniture and it was so beat up. Did Miss Queta use to live here, ma'am? Yes, and Amalia couldn't believe it, with the little white car she had and the elegant way she dressed, she'd thought Miss Queta had lived much better. And where had Miss Queta gone now? To an apartment in Pueblo Libre, Amalia.

After they moved to Jesús María, the mistress's spirits and habits got better. She got up early, she ate better, she spent a good part of the day out, she talked. And she talked about her trip: Mexico, she was going to Mexico, Amalia, and she was never coming back. Miss Queta would come to see her and from the suffocating kitchen Amalia would hear them talking night and day about the same thing: she was going away, she was going to take a trip. It was true, Amalia thought, she's going to leave, and she was sorry. Because of you I'm getting in a funny way, she said, touching her belly, I cry over everything, everything makes me sad, how silly you've made me get. And when was she taking her trip, ma'am? Soon, Amalia. But Miss Queta didn't take her very seriously, Amalia heard her: stop daydreaming, Hortensia, don't think everything's going to work out so easily, you're getting in deep. Something strange was going on, but what, what was it. She asked Miss Queta and she told her women are idiots, Amalia: he's sending for her because he needs money, and that idiot of a Hortensia is going to bring it to him, and when he gets the money in his hands, he's going to drop her again. Mr. Lucas, Miss Queta? Of course, who else. Amalia thought she was going to faint. She was going to him? He'd left her, he'd robbed her, and to him? But she couldn't spend much time thinking about the mistress or anything else, she felt too sick. The first time she hadn't felt that fatigue, that heaviness, so big: sleepy morning and afternoon and back from the store she had to lie down. She'd brought a stool into the kitchen and she

424

cooked sitting down. How fat you've got, she thought.

It was summer, Ambrosio had to take the Zavalas to Ancón and Amalia only saw him on an occasional Sunday. Mightn't that business about Ancón have been a lie, an excuse to get away from her slowly? Because he was acting strange again. Amalia would go to meet him on the Avenida Arenales with a thousand things to tell him, and he'd throw cold water on it. So the mistress wanted to go to Mexico, eh, go back to that pimp? good, so the new place was fit for a midget? well. You're not listening to me, yes, I am, what are you thinking about, nothing. I don't care, Amalia thought, I don't love him anymore. Her aunt had told her when your mistress leaves you come here, Señora Rosario had told her if you're out on the street you've got a home here and Gertrudis the same. If you're sorry about what you offered me, it's best you forget about it and put a different face on, she told him one day, I haven't asked you for anything. And he, surprised, what did I offer you? Living together, she said. And he: oh, that, don't worry, Amalia. How could she have got friendly, got together with him again? One time she counted all the words Ambrosio said that Sunday and they didn't reach a hundred. Was he waiting for her to have the child to leave her? No, Amalia would leave him first. She'd look for work in another house, never see him again, how sweet her revenge would be when he came crying and asking for forgiveness: out, I don't need you, beat it.

She kept on getting fatter and the mistress talked about her trip all the time, but when was she going to take it? She didn't know exactly when, but soon, Amalia. One night she heard her shouting in an argument with Miss Queta. She ached so much that she didn't get up to spy: I've suffered too much, everybody had kicked her, I've got no reason to think about anybody. You're going to get yourself messed up, Miss Queta told her, you're only going to get the real kick now, you nut. One morning, on the way back from the market, she saw a car at the door: it was Ambrosio. She went over thinking what's he come to tell me, but he greeted her by putting a finger to his lips: shh, don't go in, go away. Don Fermín was upstairs with the mistress. She went to sit in the little square on the corner: he'd never change, he'd be a coward all his life. She hated him, he disgusted her, Trinidad was a thousand times better. When she saw the car leave, she went into the house and the mistress was like a wild animal. She was cursing, smoking, pushing the chairs around, and when she saw Amalia, what are you standing there for looking at me like an idiot, get in the kitchen. She went to shut herself up in her room, resentful. You've never insulted me, she thought. She fell asleep. When she went out into the living room, the mistress wasn't there. She returned at nightfall, sorry that she had shouted at her. She was a bundle of nerves, Amalia, some son of a bitch had sent her into a rage. Just go to bed, don't worry about supper.

That week she felt worse. The mistress spent the day out or in her room talking to herself, in a terrible mood. Thursday morning she was leaning over to pick up a towel when she felt as if her bones were breaking and she fell to the floor. She tried to get up and she couldn't. She dragged herself over to the phone: it's time, it's time, Miss Queta, and the mistress wasn't there, the pains, the wet legs, I'm dying. A thousand years later the mistress and Miss Queta came into the apartment and she saw them as if in a dream. They almost carried her down the stairs, put her in the little car and took her to the Maternity Hospital: don't be frightened, he wasn't going to be born yet, they'd come to see her, they'd be back, keep calm, Amalia. The pains were coming closer together, there was a smell of turpentine that made her nauseous. She tried to pray and she couldn't, she was going to die. They'd put her on a cart and an old woman with a hairy neck was undressing her and scolding her. She thought about Trinidad while she felt as if her muscles were tearing and a knife was sinking into her between her waist and her shoulders.

When she woke up her body felt like an open wound, as if coals were smoking in her stomach. She didn't have the strength to shout, she thought I'm dead. Warm balls closed off her throat and she couldn't vomit. Little by little she began to make out the ward full of beds, the faces of the women, the high, dirty ceiling. You've been out for three days, her neighbor on the right said, and the one on the left: they fed you with tubes. It was a miracle you were saved, a nurse said, and your little girl too. The doctor who came to see her: be careful not to have any more children, I can only work a miracle with a patient once. Then a very nice nun brought her a bundle that was moving: tiny, hairy, she had her eyes closed. She no longer felt thirsty, any pain, and she sat up in bed to let it nurse. She felt a tickling on her nipple and began to laugh like a crazy woman. Haven't you got any family? the one on the left asked her, and the one on the right: you're lucky they saved you, the ones without any family are sent off to the common boneyard. Hadn't anyone come to see her? No. A very white lady with dark hair and big eyes hadn't come? No. A young lady, tall, good figure, with red hair either? No, nobody. But why, how. Hadn't they called to ask about her either? Is that the way they had acted, had they dumped her there without coming back, without asking? But she didn't get angry or feel sorry. The tickling was going all up and down her body and the little bundle kept on eagerly, she wanted more. Hadn't those women come? and she was dying with laughter: what are you sucking so hard for since no more's coming out, silly.

On the sixth day the doctor said you're in good shape, I'm going to discharge you. Take care of yourself, the operation has left you very weak, rest at least for a month. And no more children, you know that already. She got up and had a dizzy spell. She'd grown thin, yellow, with sunken eyes. She said good-bye to her neighbors and to the nun, step by step slowly to the street, and at the door a policeman called a taxi for her. Her aunt's mouth trembled when she saw her appear in Chacra Colorada with the baby girl in her arms. They embraced, wept together. Had the mistress acted so bad as not to call up and ask or go see you? Yes, that's how it was, and she, so stupid, had always helped her and hadn't wanted to walk out on her. And the fellow didn't appear either? He either, auntie. When you're feeling better, we'll go to the police, her aunt said, they'll make him recognize the child and give you money. The house had three bedrooms, her aunt slept in one and her boarders in the others, there were four of them. An old couple who spent the day listening to the radio and cooking on a portable stove that filled the house with smoke; he'd been a postal employee and had just retired. The others were two men from Ayacucho, one an ice cream man in D'Onofrio and the other a tailor. They didn't eat at the boardinghouse, they spent their time singing songs in Quechua at night. The aunt put a cot in her room and Amalia slept with her. She almost didn't get out of bed for a week, nauseous every time she stood up. She wasn't bored. She played with Amalita, looked at her, whispered in her ear: they would go collect her pay from that ungrateful woman and tell her I'm not working for you

427

anymore, if that other lowlife put in his appearance one day, so long, we don't need you. I can probably get you a job in a store some friends of mine have in Breña, her aunt said.

After a week she got her strength back and her aunt loaned her the bus fare: get the very last cent out of her, Amalia. She'll see me and be sorry, she thought, she'll ask me to stay. Don't be so dumb the next time. She got to General Garzón with the child in her arms and at the door of the building she ran into Rita, the lame maid from the first floor. She smiled at her and thought what's wrong with me, what's wrong with this one: hello, Rita. She looked at her with her mouth open, as if ready to run away. Have I changed so much that you don't recognize me? Amalia laughed, I'm the one from the second floor, it was Amalia. Did they let you go? Rita asked, had they caught you? The police, caught me? If they see me with you, won't they take me in? Rita said, frightened, wouldn't they grab her too? Because that's all she needed, they'd already hollered at her, asked her about her life and other miracles, and the same thing with the one across the way, and the one on the third floor, and the one on the fourth floor, in a nasty way, where is she, where did she go, where was she hiding, why did that Amalia disappear. In a nasty way, cursing, threatening, confess or we'll take you in. As if we knew something, Rita said. She took a step toward Amalia and lowered her voice: where did they find you, what did they tell you, had Amalia confessed to them who killed her? But Amalia had leaned against the wall and was babbling take her, take her. Rita took Amalita, what's wrong, what did you have, what did they do to you. She brought her into the kitchen on the first floor. Good that the folks aren't home, sit down, have a glass of water. Killed? Amalia repeated, and Rita with Amalita in her arms, don't shout like that, don't shake like that, Señora Hortensia killed? Rita went to look out the window, she'd locked the door, finally she gave back the child, be quiet, the whole neighborhood will hear you. But where have you been, how come you didn't know, it was in all the papers, all those pictures of your mistress, didn't they talk about it at the Maternity Hospital, hadn't she been listening to the radio? And Amalia feeling as if her teeth were chattering, a touch of fever, Rita, some tea, anything, Rita made her a cup of coffee. What more can you ask but that you got away, she said, the police, reporters, they came and knocked on the door

428

and asked questions, they went away and others came, they all wanted to know where you were, she must know something because she left, she must have done something because she went into hiding, it's good they didn't find you, Amalia. She was drinking the coffee in small sips, she said yes, thanks a lot Rita and was rocking Amalita who was crying. She'd leave, she'd hide, yes, she'd never come back, and Rita: if they catch you they'll treat you worse than they did us, God knows what they'd do to her. Amalia got up, thanks again, and left. She thought she was going to faint, but when she got to the corner the nausea had passed, and she was walking fast, holding Amalita tight against her breast so that her crying wouldn't be heard. A taxi and it didn't stop, another, and she kept on trotting, they were police, that one was, that one was going to grab her when he passed, and finally one stopped. Her aunt grumbled when she asked for money for the cab fare. You could have come back by bus, she wasn't a millionaire. She went to shut herself up in the bedroom. She was so cold that she covered herself with her aunt's blankets and only at dusk did she stop pretending to sleep and answer questions: no, the mistress wasn't there, auntie, she'd gone on a trip. Yes, of course she'd go back to collect; of course she wouldn't let herself be robbed, auntie. And she thought: I've got to telephone. She opened her aunt's purse, took out a sol and went to the store on the corner. She hadn't forgotten the number, she remembered it very well. But the voice of a girl she didn't know answered: no, no Miss Queta lived there. She called again and a man: she wasn't there, they didn't know her, they'd just moved in, maybe she was the former tenant. She leaned against a tree to get her breath back. She felt so frightened, she thought the world had gone mad. That's why she hadn't come to the Maternity Hospital, that's the murder they were talking about on the radio and she was the one they were looking for. They'd arrest her, ask her questions, beat her, kill her the way they did Trinidad.

She spent a few days without leaving the house, helping her aunt clean. She didn't open her mouth, she thought they killed her, she was dead. Her heart stopped whenever someone was at the door. On the third day she went with her aunt to the parish to christen Amalita and when the priest asked what name she answered: Amalia Hortensia. Her nights were a blank, hugging Amalita, feeling empty, guilty, forgive me for

429

having said bad things about you, how could she have known, ma'am, thinking I wonder what became of Miss Queta. But on the fourth day she recovered: you're making too much of it, why so afraid, stupid girl. She'd go to the police, she'd been in the Maternity Hospital, check on it, they'd see that it was true and they'd leave her alone. No: they'd insult her, they wouldn't believe her. At sundown her aunt sent her out to buy sugar and when she was turning the corner a figure left the lamppost and stepped in front of her, Amalia gave a cry: I've been waiting for you for hours, Ambrosio said. She let herself fall against him, unable to speak. That was how she was, swallowing tears and mucus, her face on his chest, and Ambrosio was consoling her. People were looking, don't cry, he'd been looking for her for three weeks, what about his little son? Little daughter, she sobbed, yes, she was born healthy. Ambrosio took out his handkerchief, cleaned her face, made her sneeze, took her to a café. They sat down at a back table. He put his arm around her, let her cry as he patted her back. It's all right, it was all right, Amalia, that's enough. Was she crying about Señora Hortensia? Yes, and about the way she felt, so all alone, so frightened. The police are looking for me, as if she knew anything, Ambrosio. And because she thought he'd abandoned her. And how could he have gone to see her at the Maternity Hospital, silly, did he know maybe, was he going to guess maybe? He'd gone to wait for her on Arenales and you didn't come, when the news about the mistress came out in the papers I was looking for you like crazy, Amalia. He'd gone to the house where your aunt used to live, in Surquillo, and from there they sent me to Balconcillo, and from there to Chacra Colorada, but they only knew the street, not the number. He'd come, asked every-where, every day, thinking she's going to come out, I'm going to find her. It's good I finally did, Amalia. What about the police? Amalia asked. You're not going, he said. He'd asked Ludovico and he thought they'd keep you locked up at least a month, asking questions, checking things out. It's best if they didn't see her face, better if she left Lima for a while until we forget about her. And how would she leave, Amalia was pout-ing, where was she going to go. And he: with me, together. She looked into his eyes: yes, Amalia. He had evidently already made up his mind. He was looking at her very seriously, do you think I'm going to let them arrest you even for one day? his voice was very serious, they'd leave

430

tomorrow. What about your job? That was the least of their worries, he'd work on his own, they'd go away. She kept looking at him, trying to believe, but she couldn't. Living together? Tomorrow? In the jungle, Ambrosio said, and put his face close: for a while, they'd come back when they've forgotten about you. She felt everything tumbling down again: had Ludovico told him? But why were they looking for her, what had she done, what did she know? Ambrosio hugged her: nothing was going to happen, they'd leave tomorrow on the train, then they'd take a bus. Nobody would find her in the jungle. He huddled up against her, was he doing all that because he loved her, Ambrosio? Of course, silly, why do you think I don't? There was a relative of Ludovico's in the jungle, he'd go to work for him, he'd help them out. She was struck dumb with fright and surprise. Don't say anything to your aunt, she wouldn't say anything, nobody should know, nobody would know. It might be dangerous, she, yes, of course, yes. Did she know where the Desamparados station was? Yes, she did. He went with her to the corner, gave her money for the taxi, leave under any pretext, and she would come very quietly. All night long, her eyes open, she listened to her aunt's breathing and the tired snoring that came from the old couple's room. I'm going back to the mistress's to collect, she told her aunt the next day. She took a taxi and when she got to Desamparados, Ambrosio scarcely looked at Amalita Hortensia. Was that her? Yes. He had her go into the station, sit and wait on a bench among mountain people with bundles. He'd brought two large suitcases and I not even a handkerchief, Amalia thought. She didn't feel happy about leaving, living with him; she felt strange.

4

"IT'S ABOUT TIME, Ambrosio," Ludovico said. "It's bad enough for a person to get himself all fucked up without having his friends turn their backs on him."

"Do you think I wouldn't have come to see you sooner?" Ambrosio said. "I only found out this morning, Ludovico, because I ran into Hipólito on the street."

"That son of a bitch told you?" Ludovico asked. "But he most likely didn't tell you everything."

"What's with Ludovico, what's happened?" Ambrosio asked. "He went to Arequipa a month ago and not a peep out of him."

"He's all bandaged up from head to toe at the Police Hospital," Hipólito said. "The Arequipans gave him a beating."

It was still early in the morning when the man who gave the orders kicked on the door of the shed and shouted let's be on our way. The stars were still out, the cotton gin wasn't working yet, it was chilly. Trifulcio stretched his arms on his cot, shouted I'm coming and mentally cursed the mother of the man who gave the orders. He'd slept in his clothes, all he had to put on were his sweater, his coat and his shoes. He went out to the spigot to wet his face, but the wind made him change his mind and he only rinsed out his mouth. He smoothed his curly hair, cleaned the sleep out of his eyes with his fingers. He went back to the shed and Téllez, Urondo and Martínez the foreman were already up, complaining

432

about the early hour. The lights were on in the ranch house and the van was by the door. The kitchen maids gave them some mugs of coffee which they drank surrounded by growling dogs. Don Emilio came out to see them off in slippers and bathrobe: well, boys, behave yourselves there. Don't worry, Don Emilio, they would behave themselves, senator. Get in, said the man who gave the orders. Téllez sat in front, and in back Trifulcio, Urondo and Martínez the foreman. You wanted the window seat but I got in the other side and beat you to it, Urondo, Trifulcio thought. He didn't feel well, his body ached. All set? Arequipa, said the man who gave the orders and they started out.

"Dislocations, contusions, body water," Ludovico said. "When the doctor comes by he gives me a regular lesson in medicine, Ambrosio. These past days have been motherfuckers for me."

"Just last Sunday Amalia and I were talking about how you didn't feel much like going to Arequipa," Ambrosio said.

"I can sleep now at least," Ludovico said. "During the first days, even my fingernails ached, Ambrosio."

"But you're covered, think of it that way," Ambrosio said. "You were beaten up on duty and they have to reward you."

"Just who are those Coalition people?" Téllez asked.

"I was on duty and I wasn't on duty," Ludovico said. "They sent us and they didn't send us. You don't know how whorey the whole thing turned out, Ambrosio."

"Just be happy to know that they're a bunch of shitheads." The man who gave the orders laughed. "And that we're going to fuck up their rally."

"I was only asking to find something we could talk about and make the trip a little livelier," Téllez said. "It's a big bore."

Yes, Trifulcio thought, a big bore. He tried to sleep, but the van was bouncing and his head kept hitting the roof and his shoulder the door. He had to ride all hunched over, hanging onto the backrest in front. He should have sat in the middle, by trying to fuck up Urondo he'd fucked himself up. Because Urondo, squeezed in between Trifulcio and Martínez the foreman, who cushioned him against the bumps, was snoring away. Trifulcio looked out the window: sand dunes, the black snake of a road getting lost in clouds of dust, the ocean and diving gulls. You're

433

getting old, he thought, one early-rising morning and your whole body starts to rust.

"A bunch of millionaires who used to lick Odría's boots and want to test his patience now," the man who gave the orders said. "That's the Coalition."

"Then why does Odría let them hold rallies against him?" Téllez asked. "He's softened up a lot. In the old days, you make a fuss and it's the lockup and a good beating. Why not now?"

"Odría held out his hand to them and they crawled all the way up to the elbow," the man who gave the orders said. "But that's as far as they got. They're going to be taught a lesson in Arequipa."

Lazy bum, Trifulcio thought, looking at Téllez' shaved neck. What did he know about politics, what did he care about politics? He was asking questions just to ass-kiss. He took out a cigarette and in order to light it he had to lean on Urondo. He opened his eyes in surprise, what, are we there already? How could they be there, they'd just gone through Chala, Urondo.

"It's the kind of story where I don't know where to begin, it was all lies," Ludovico said. "It all came out backwards. Everybody tricked us. Even Don Cayo was tricked."

"You can say that again," Ambrosio said. "If anybody caught it with that business in Arequipa, it was him. He lost his ministry and he had to leave Peru."

"Your boss must be happy over what's happened, right?" Ludovico said.

"Naturally. Don Fermín more than anyone else," Ambrosio said. "He didn't want to screw Odría as much as he did Don Cayo. He had to hide out for a few days, he thought they were going to arrest him."

The van entered Camaná around seven o'clock. It was beginning to get dark and there weren't many people on the streets. The man who gave the orders drove them directly to a restaurant. They got out, stretched. Trifulcio felt cramps and chills. The man who gave the orders took the menu, ordered beer and said I'm going to do some checking. What's the matter with you, Trifulcio thought, none of the others here is as tired as you are. Téllez, Urondo and Martínez the foreman were eating and cracking jokes. He wasn't hungry, only thirsty. He drank

434

down a glass of beer without taking a breath and thought of Tomasa and Chincha. Are we going to spend the night here? Téllez asked, and Urondo wondered if there was a whorehouse in Camaná. There must be, Martínez the foreman said, one thing there's no shortage of anywhere are whorehouses and churches. Finally they asked him what's wrong, Trifulcio. Nothing, I've got a touch of a cold. What you've got is you're getting old, Urondo said. Trifulcio laughed but he hated him inside. While they were having dessert the man who gave the orders came back, in a bad mood: what kind of a mess was that, who could understand that mix-up.

"No mess at all," the Subprefect said. "Secretary Bermúdez explained it to me quite clearly on the telephone."

"A truck will be coming through with Senator Arévalo's people, Subprefect," Cayo Bermúdez said. "Take care of them, please give them anything they may need."

"But Mr. Lozano only asked Don Emilio for four or five," the man who gave the orders said. "What truck is he talking about? Has the Minister gone crazy?"

"Five people to break up a demonstration?" the Subprefect asked. "Somebody's crazy, but not Mr. Bermúdez. He told me a truck, twenty or thirty people. I set up beds for forty just in case."

"I tried to talk to Don Emilio, but he's not at the ranch anymore, he left for Lima," the man who gave the orders said. "And with Mr. Lozano, but he's not at Headquarters. God damn it."

"Don't worry, the five of us are enough and more than enough." Téllez laughed. "Have a beer, sir."

"Can't you get some reinforcements?" asked the man who gave the orders.

"No hope," the Subprefect said. "The people of Camaná are a lazy bunch. The whole Restoration Party here is me."

"Well, let's see how we can get out of this mess," the man who gave the orders said. "No whorehouses, no drinking. Get some sleep. We've got to be fresh for tomorrow."

The Subprefect had set up lodgings for them at the police station and as soon as they got there Trifulcio flopped down on his cot and wrapped himself up in his blanket. Quiet and covered up, he felt better. Téllez,

435

Urondo and Martínez the foreman had sneaked in a bottle and were passing it from bed to bed, chatting. He was listening to them: if they'd asked for a whole truckload the thing must be rough, Urondo was saying. Bah, Senator Arévalo told them an easy job, boys, and he hasn't tricked us yet, Martínez the foreman said. Besides, if something went wrong, that's what they had cops for, said Téllez. Sixty, sixty-five? Trifulcio was thinking, I wonder how old I am now.

"It started going bad for me the minute we got on the plane here," Ludovico said. "It was so rough that I got sick and puked all over Hipólito. I was a mess when I got to Arequipa. It took a few drinks of pisco to get me back in shape."

"When the newspapers wrote about what went on in the theater, that people were killed, good Lord, I thought," Ambrosio said. "But your name wasn't on the list of victims."

"They sent us to the slaughter knowing all about it," Ludovico said. "When I hear the word theater, I begin to feel the punches. And the feeling of being strangled, Ambrosio, that terrible feeling of being strangled."

"They were able to raise a row like that," Ambrosio said, "because the whole city rose up against the government, right, Ludovico?"

"Yes," Senator Landa said. "Grenades were thrown in the theater and people were killed. Bermúdez is all washed up, Fermín."

"If Lozano wanted a truck, why did he tell Don Emilio four or five are enough," the man who gave the orders cursed for the tenth time. "And where are Lozano and Don Emilio, why is it impossible to get anyone on the phone?"

They'd left Camaná while it was still dark, without any breakfast, and the man who gave the orders did nothing but grumble. You spent all night trying to phone and you're dying from lack of sleep, Trifulcio thought. He hadn't been able to sleep either. It got colder as the van climbed up into the mountains. Trifulcio nodded at times and listened to Téllez, Urondo and Martínez the foreman as they passed cigarettes around. You've grown old, he thought, you're going to die one of these days. They arrived in Arequipa at ten o'clock. The man who gave the orders took them to a house where there was a sign with red letters: Restoration Party. The door was closed. Knocking, ringing the bell, nobody opened. On the narrow street people were going into shops, the sun didn't warm anything, newsboys were hawking papers. The air was very clean, the sky looked very high. Finally a boy in bare feet came to open up, yawning. Why were party headquarters closed, the man who gave the orders scolded him, it was ten o'clock already. The boy looked at him with surprise: they were always closed, they only opened them on Thursday nights when Dr. Lama and the other gentlemen came. Why did they call Arequipa the white city, when none of the houses were white? Trifulcio was thinking. They went in. Desks with no papers on them, old chairs, pictures of Odría, posters, Long Live the Revolution of Restoration, Health, Education, Work, Odría Is the Nation. The man who gave the orders ran to the telephone: what happened, where were the people, why wasn't there anyone to meet us. Téllez, Urondo and Martínez the foreman were hungry: could they go out and get some breakfast, sir? Be back in ten minutes, the man who gave the orders said. He gave them ten soles and they left in the van. They found a café with small tables and white cloths, they ordered coffee and sandwiches. Look, Urondo said, Everybody to the Municipal Theater Tonight, All with the Coalition, they'd done their little publicity job. Will I get mountain sickness? Trifulcio wondered. He was breathing and it was as if the air wasn't entering his body.

"Arequipa's nice, clean," Ludovico said. "Women on the street who aren't too bad. Apple-cheeked, of course."

"What did Hipólito do to you?" Ambrosio asked. "He didn't say anything to me. Just it was bad for us, brother, and he took off."

"He feels guilty because he acted like a fairy," Ludovico said. "What a coward of a guy, Ambrosio."

"And to think I might have been there, Ludovico," Ambrosio said. "It was lucky Don Fermín didn't go."

"Do you know who we found as the big boss at the post in Arequipa?" Ludovico asked. "Molina."

"Chink Molina?" Ambrosio asked. "Wasn't he in Chiclayo?"

"Do you remember the way he used to put on with those of us who weren't on the regular list?" Ludovico said. "He's a different person now. He received us as if we were old buddies."

"Welcome, colleagues, come in," Molina said. "Did the others stay on the square flirting with the girls of Arequipa?"

"What others?" Hipólito said. "Only Ludovico and I have come."

"What do you mean what others," Molina said. "The twenty-five others Mr. Lozano promised me."

"Oh yes, I heard him say that people were probably coming from Puno and Cuzco," Ludovico said. "Haven't they got here?"

"I just spoke to Cuzco, and Cabrejitos didn't say anything about it," Molina said. "I don't understand. Besides, there's not much time. The Coalition rally is at seven o'clock."

"The tricks, the lies, Ambrosio," Ludovico said. "The confusion, the fairying around."

"I see now, it's an ambush," Don Fermín said. "Bermúdez has been waiting for the Coalition to grow and now he wants to pounce on them. But why did he pick Arequipa, Don Emilio?"

"Because it would be good for publicity," Don Emilio Arévalo said. "Odría's revolution had its start in Arequipa, Fermín."

"He wants to show the country that Arequipa is an Odría town," Senator Landa said. "The people of Arequipa stop the Coalition from holding a rally. The opposition looks ridiculous and the Restoration Party has a clear path in the '56 elections."

"He's going to send twenty-five plainclothes cops from Lima," Don Emilio Arévalo said. "And he's asked me for a truckload of peasants who are good in a fight."

"He's prepared his bomb with great care," Senator Landa said. "But this time it won't be like Espina's time. This time the bomb is going to blow up in his face."

"Molina tried to talk to Mr. Lozano and he'd disappeared," Ludovico said. "And Don Cayo too. His secretary answered, he's not here, not here."

"Send you reinforcements, Chink?" Cabrejitos said. "You must be dreaming. Nobody told me anything and even if I wanted to, I couldn't. My people are up to their necks in work."

"Chink Molina was tearing his hair," Ludovico said.

"It's good Senator Arévalo is sending us help," Molina said. "Fifty, I think, and tough. With them, you and the people on the force we'll do what we can."

438

"I'd like to try some of those stuffed chilis they have in Arequipa, Ludovico," Hipólito said. "Since we're here."

After breakfast, disobeying orders, they took a little walk through the city: narrow streets, a cold little sun, houses with grillwork and big entranceways, shining cobblestones, priests, churches. The gates to the Plaza de Armas looked like the walls of a fortress. Trifulcio was taking in air with his mouth open and Téllez was pointing at the walls: the Coalition people have sure done a lot of publicity work. They sat down on a bench in the square across from the gray façade of the cathedral, and a car passed with loudspeakers: Everybody to the Municipal Theater at Seven O'Clock, Everybody Come Hear the Opposition Leaders. Out of the car windows they were throwing fliers that the people picked up, looked at and threw away. The altitude, Trifulcio was thinking. They'd told him: your heart like a drum and you have trouble breathing. He felt as if he'd been running or fighting: pulse fast, temples throbbing, veins hard. Or maybe old age, Trifulcio thought. They couldn't remember the way back and they had to ask. Restoration Party? people asked, is that something to eat? Some party Odría has, Martínez the foreman laughed, people don't even know where it is. They got there and the man who gave the orders bawled them out: did they think they'd come here as tourists? There were two guys with him. One short with glasses and a small necktie, and the other half-breed-looking and hefty, in shirtsleeves, and the short one was arguing with the man who gave the orders: they'd promised him fifty and he'd sent five. They weren't going to make a fool of him like that.

"Call Lima, Dr. Lama, try to locate Don Emilio, or Lozano, or Mr. Bermúdez," said the man who gave the orders. "I tried all night and I couldn't. I don't know, I understand it even less than you do. Mr. Lozano told Don Emilio five and here we are, doctor. Let them explain who's right and who's wrong."

"It's not that we don't have people, but that we need specialists, people with experience," Dr. Lama said. "And besides, I'm protesting on principle. They lied to me."

"What difference does it make if they haven't sent more, doctor?" the hefty half-breed said. "Let's go to the market, we can round up three hundred and they'll tear the theater apart just the same."

439

"Can you count on the people from the market?" the man who gave the orders asked. "I don't have much faith in you, Ruperto."

"Absolutely," Ruperto said. "I've had experience. We'll draft the whole market and we'll fall on the Municipal Theater like a landslide."

"Let's go see Molina," Dr. Lama said. "His people must have come."

"And at Headquarters we met Senator Arévalo's famous bruisers," Ludovico said. "The fifty turned out to be five."

"Somebody is pulling somebody's leg here," Molina said. "This isn't possible, Prefect."

"I've been trying to talk to the Minister to get instructions," the Prefect said. "But it seems that his secretary won't let me through. He's not in, he left, he still hasn't arrived. Alcibíades, that fag."

"This isn't a misunderstanding, it's sabotage," Dr. Lama said. "Are these your reinforcements, Molina? Two instead of twenty-five? Oh no, this is too much."

"Alcibíades is my man," Don Emilio Arévalo said. "But the key is Lozano. He's rather understanding and he hates Bermúdez. His palm, of course, will have to be crossed."

"Five poor devils and, to top it off, one of them an old man with mountain sickness," Ludovico said. "Do you think those five and us are going to break up a rally? Not even if we were all Superman, Prefect, sir."

"He'll get what he wants," Don Fermín said. "I'll talk to Lozano."

"We'll have to use your people, Molina," the Prefect said. "It wasn't part of the plan, Mr. Bermúdez didn't want people from here involved. But there's no other way out."

"Not you, Fermín," Senator Arévalo said. "You belong to the Coalition, officially an enemy of the government. I'm part of the government, Lozano trusts me more. I'll take care of him."

"How many of your people can we count on, Molina?" Dr. Lama asked.

"Around twenty, counting officers and men," Molina said. "But they're on the regular list and they won't do it. They'll want a guarantee against risks, extra pay."

"Promise them whatever they want, we've got to break up this rally any way we can," Dr. Lama said. "I made a promise and I'm going to keep it, Molina."

"The truth is we're all worrying for no good reason at all," the Prefect said. "They won't even fill up the theater. Nobody here knows the Coalition big shots."

"We know from experience that only curiosity-seekers will be going and that curiosity-seekers start running at the first sign of trouble," Dr. Lama said. "But it's a matter of principle. They've deceived us, Prefect."

"I'm going to keep on trying to get in touch with the Minister," the Prefect said. "Maybe Mr. Bermúdez changed his mind and we have to let them hold the rally."

"Could you give a pill or something to one of my men?" the man who gave the orders asked. "The black fellow, doctor. He's about to pass out from altitude sickness."

"But if you didn't have the people, why did you go into the theater?" Ambrosio said. "It was crazy with so few, Ludovico."

"Because they told us a tall story and we swallowed it," Ludovico said. "We believed it so much that we went off to eat some of the stuffed chilis that Hipólito wanted."

"Tiabaya, that's where they make the best ones," Molina said. "Wash them down with some good corn wine and come back around four to take them to the Restoration Party. That's the assembly point."

"The reason?" Don Emilio Arévalo asked. "You know only too well, Lozano. To bring down Bermúdez, naturally."

"More likely to give the Coalition a helping hand, senator," Lozano said. "This time I can't help you. I can't do a thing like that to Don Cayo, you understand. He's the Minister, my direct superior."

"Of course you can, Lozano," Don Emilio Arévalo said. "You and I can. Everything depends on the two of us. The people don't get to Arequipa, and Bermúdez' plan goes up in smoke."

"What about afterwards, senator?" Lozano asked. "Don Cayo won't ask you for an explanation. But he will me. I'm his subordinate."

"You think I'm working for the Coalition and that's where you're wrong, Lozano," Don Emilio Arévalo said. "No, I'm working for the government. I'm a government man, an enemy of the Coalition. The government has problems because certain branches have gone rotten, and the worst one is Bermúdez. Do you understand me, Lozano? It's a question of serving the President, not the Coalition."

"Does the President know about it?" Lozano asked. "In that case, everything is different, senator."

"Officially, the President can't know about it," Don Emilio Arévalo said. "That's what we, the friends of the President, are here for, Lozano."

The corn wine made me worse, Trifulcio thought. His blood had stopped, ready to boil over. But he faked, stretching out his hand toward his enormous glass and smiling at Téllez, Urondo, Ruperto and Martínez the foreman: cheers. They were already a little high. The hefty half-breed was putting on a show of culture, in the house next door Bolívar had slept, the best corn wine in the world came from Yanahuara, and he laughed with satisfaction: in Lima they didn't have things like that, did they? They'd explained to him that they came from Ica, but he didn't understand. Trifulcio thought: if I'd taken two pills instead of one, the mountain sickness wouldn't have come back. He was looking at the sooty walls, the women going back and forth between the stove and the table with the platters of chilis, and he took his pulse. It hadn't stopped, his blood was still circulating, but very slowly. And it was boiling, that it was, there were the hot waves beating against his chest. If night would only come, if the work at the theater were only over, getting back to Ica right away. Isn't it time to go to the market? Martínez the foreman asked. Ruperto looked at his watch: there was still time, it wasn't four yet. Through the open doors of the bar Trifulcio could see the small square, the benches and the trees, children spinning tops, the white walls of the little church. It wasn't the altitude, it was old age. A car with loudspeakers passed. Everybody to the Municipal Theater, Everybody with the Coalition, and Ruperto let out a fuck you: they'll find out. Quiet, Arequipa boy, Téllez said, hold it for after. How's your mountain sickness, grandpa? Ruperto asked. Much better, grandson, Trifulcio smiled. And he hated him.

"All set, senator, except that I've taken my precautions," Lozano said. "They'll go, but fewer of them, and the rest will arrive too late. I'm counting on you in case . . ."

"You can count on me for everything, Lozano," Don Emilio Arévalo said. "And besides, you can count on the thanks of the Coalition. Those gentlemen will think it's a service to them. Let them think so, so much the better for you."

"You still can't reach Arequipa?" Cayo Bermúdez asked. "This is too much, doctor."

"I didn't like the famous chilis at all," Hipólito said. "I'm burning all over, Ludovico."

"I've only been able to convince ten," Molina said. "The others odd man out, they won't even think about going in there in civilian clothes, not for all the bonuses we give them. What do you think, Prefect?"

"Ten plus Lima's two and the senator's five make seventeen," the Prefect said. "If it's true that Lama can enlist the market people it might work out. Seventeen guys with balls can turn the place inside out, of course. I think so, Molina."

"I may be stupid, but not as stupid as those gentlemen think, senator," Lozano said. "I never accept checks."

"Hello, Arequipa?" Cayo Bermúdez said. "Molina? What's going on, Molina, where the hell have you been?"

"They're not so stupid either," Don Emilio Arévalo said. "It's made out to cash, Lozano."

"But the one who's been calling all day is me, Don Cayo," Molina said. "And the Prefect too, and Dr. Lama. The one who wasn't anywhere to be found was you, Don Cayo."

"Is anything wrong in Arequipa, Don Cayo?" Dr. Alcibíades asked.

"Not just one but a thousand things wrong," Molina said. "We won't have enough people, Don Cayo. I don't know if we can pull the thing off with so few."

"Didn't Lozano's people get there?" Cayo Bermúdez asked. "Didn't Arévalo's truck arrive? What are you talking about, Molina?"

"We've got ten from the force, but even then, seventeen isn't very many, Don Cayo," Molina said. "Confidentially, I don't trust Dr. Lama too much. He promised five hundred, a thousand. But he inflates things, you know."

"Only two from Lima, only five from Ica?" Cayo Bermúdez said. "This can be rough for you, Molina. Where are the rest of the people?"

"They didn't come, Don Cayo," Molina said. "I'm the one who's asking where they are, why all those they told us were coming didn't get here."

"And nice and naïve, after the chilis we took a walk through the square," Ludovico said. "Nice and naïve, looking around the Municipal Theater to get the lay of the land."

"My opinion is that in spite of the mix-ups it can be brought off, Don Cayo," the Prefect said. "The Coalition doesn't exist here. They've put out a lot of publicity, but they won't even fill the theater. A hundred curiosity-seekers or so at most. But how is it possible that you thought all the people had arrived, Don Cayo?"

"Somebody's got his hand in this, there'll be time to clear that up later," Cayo Bermúdez said. "Is Lama there?"

"Hello, Mr. Secretary?" Dr. Lama said. "I want to protest in the most energetic way. You promised us eighty men and you send seven. We've promised the President to turn the Coalition rally into a great popular demonstration in favor of the government and they're sabotaging us. But let me tell you, we're not turning back."

"Quit making speeches, Lama," Cayo Bermúdez said. "I've got to know one thing and be absolutely frank. Can you reinforce Molina's people with some twenty or thirty men? It doesn't matter how much it costs. Twenty or thirty good men. Can you?"

"And fifty or more too," Dr. Lama said. "The number is no problem, Mr. Secretary. We can get more than enough people. The thing is that you offered us people who were experienced in this kind of thing."

"All right, get about thirty more to go into the Municipal Theater with Molina's people," Cayo Bermúdez said. "How's the counterdemonstration coming?"

"The people from the Restoration Party are spread out through the slums making propaganda," Dr. Lama said. "We'll spill them out at the doors of the Municipal Theater. And we've organized another rally at the market for five o'clock. We'll have thousands of people together. The Coalition will die here, Mr. Secretary."

"Fine, Molina, we'll go ahead with things," Cayo Bermúdez said. "I know Lama exaggerates, but there's nothing we can do but trust him. Yes, I'll talk to the Commandant about doubling his forces downtown, just in case."

A strange illness, Trifulcio thought, it comes and goes. He felt that he was dying, coming back to life, dying again. Ruperto was challenging him with his glass in the air. Cheers, Trifulcio smiled and drank. Urondo,

Téllez and Martínez the foreman were humming out of tune and the bar had filled up. Ruperto looked at his watch: it was time to go now, the vans would already be at the market. But Martínez the foreman said one for the road. He asked for a pitcher of corn wine and they drank it standing up. Let's start right here, Ruperto said, and he jumped up on a chair: men of Arequipa, brothers, listen to me for a minute. Trifulcio leaned against the wall and closed his eyes: was he going to die here? Little by little everything stopped spinning, his blood began to run again. Everybody to the Municipal Theater to show these Limans what Arequipans are like, Ruperto roared, staggering. The people kept on eating, drinking, and here and there someone laughed. To your health, gentlemen, and to Odría, Ruperto said, lifting a glass, we'll see you at the doors of the Municipal Theater. Téllez, Urondo and Martínez the foreman took Ruperto out onto the street embracing him; they had to get going, Arequipan, it was getting late. Trifulcio came out clenching his teeth and his fists. He wasn't moving, he was boiling. They stopped a taxi, to the market.

"Naïve on two counts," Ludovico said. "We thought there were more Restorationists in Arequipa, and we didn't know the Coalition had hired so many thugs."

"The newspapers said it started because the police went into the theater," Ambrosio said. "Because they started shooting and throwing grenades."

"It's a good thing they did come in, it's a good thing they did throw grenades," Lucovico said. "Otherwise I'd still be there. I may be all fucked up, but at least I'm alive, Ambrosio."

"Yes, go take a look in the market, Molina," Cayo Bermúdez said. "And call me right back."

"I just went by the Municipal Theater, Don Cayo," the Prefect said. "Still empty. The assault guards are already stationed around it."

The taxi dropped them on a corner by the market and Ruperto see? there were his people already. The two vans with loudspeakers parked in the midst of the booths were making a hellish noise. Music was coming from one, a ringing voice from the other, and Trifulcio had to hang onto Urondo. What was the matter, black boy, did he still have mountain sickness? No, Trifulcio murmured, it went away. Some men were handing out fliers, others calling the people with bullhorns, the group around the vans was growing little by little. But most of the men and women went on buying and selling at the booths with vegetables, fruit and clothing. You're a big success, Trifulcio, Martínez the foreman said, all they do is stare at you. And Téllez: the advantages of being ugly, Trifulcio. Ruperto climbed up onto a van, embraced two guys who were there, and grabbed the microphone. Come closer, come closer, Arequipans, listen. Urondo, Téllez, Martínez the foreman mingled with the vendor women, the buyers, the beggars, and urged them: come closer, come on, listen. About five hours left until the theater bit was over, Trifulcio was thinking, and eight hours more of night, and they probably wouldn't leave until noon: he wouldn't be able to stand so much of it. Night was falling, it was getting colder, in among the stands of merchandise there were tables lighted with candles where people were eating. His legs were shaking, his back was soaked, fire in his temples. He dropped down onto a crate and felt his chest: it was throbbing. The woman selling cotton cloth looked at him from the counter and let out a laugh: you're the first one I've ever seen, only in the movies till now. It's true, Trifulcio thought, there aren't any colored people in Arequipa. Are you sick? the woman asked, do you want a glass of water? Yes, thanks. He wasn't sick, it was the altitude. The water made him feel better and he went to help the others. Get ready to show those people, Ruperto was roaring, his fist in the air, and a lot of people were listening to him now. They were blocking the street and Téllez, Urondo, Martínez the foreman and the guys in the trucks were going back and forth applauding and stirring up the bystanders. To the Municipal Theater, let's show those people, and Ruperto was pounding his chest. He's drunk, Trifulcio thought, avidly sucking in air.

"What made them think there were so many Odríists in Arequipa?" Ambrosio asked.

"The counterdemonstration of the Restoration Party at the market," Ludovico said. "We went to see and everything was all heated up."

"What did I tell you, Molina?" Dr. Lama pointed to the crowd. "Too bad Bermúdez can't see this."

"Talk to them and get it over with, Dr. Lama," Molina said. "I've got to take my people away soon to give them instructions."

"Yes, I'll say a few words to them," Dr. Lama said. "Open a way to the vans for me."

"The plan was to make a fish-cake sandwich out of the Coalition people?" Ambrosio asked.

"We were to go into the theater and start a row in there," Ludovico said. "And when they came out, they'd run smack into the counter-demonstration. It was a good idea, but it didn't work out."

Crushed against the people who were listening, laughing and applauding, Trifulcio closed his mouth. He wasn't dying, it didn't seem that his bones were going to crack with the cold, he didn't feel as if his heart was going to stop anymore. And the jabbing in his temples had stopped. He was listening to Ruperto howling and he saw the people pushing toward the van where they were handing out drinks and free gifts. In the half-light he recognized the faces of Téllez, Urondo and Martínez the foreman, scattered among the audience, and he imagined them applauding, stirring things up. He wasn't doing anything, he was breathing slowly, taking his pulse, he thought if I don't move I can get through it. And at that moment there was movement, jostling, the sea of heads began waving up and down, a group of men approached the van and those on top helped them up onto the platform. Three cheers for the Secretary General of the Restoration Party! Ruperto shouted and Trifulcio recognized him: the one who had given him the medicine for mountain sickness, the doctor. Quiet, Dr. Lama was going to speak to them, Ruperto howled. The man who gave the orders had got up onto the truck too.

"With all of these, everything's set," Ludovico said.

"There are enough people, yes," Molina said. "Don't get them too drunk, just enough."

"We're going to have a few police in the theater, Don Cayo," the Prefect said. "In uniform and armed, yes. I told the Coalition. No, they weren't against it. It's a usual precaution, Don Cayo."

"How many people did Lama get together at the market?" Cayo Bermúdez asked. "Tell me what you counted with your own eyes, Molina."

"I can't make an estimate, but quite a few," Molina said. "A thousand people, maybe. Things look good. The ones who are going to go in are already at party headquarters. I'm talking to you from there, Don Cayo."

It was getting dark fast and Trifulcio couldn't see Dr. Lama's face any longer, only hear him. It wasn't Ruperto, he knew how to speak. Hard to understand and elegant, in favor of Odría and the people, against the Coalition. Good, but not as good as Senator Arévalo, Trifulcio thought. Téllez grabbed him by the arm: we were leaving, black boy. They elbowed their way through, on the corner there was a van and inside Urondo, Martínez the foreman, the man who gave the orders and two from Lima, talking about stuffed chilis. How was the mountain sickness, Trifulcio? Better now. The truck went down some dark streets, stopped in front of the Restoration Party. The lights on, the rooms full of people, and the throbbing, the cold, the suffocation again. The man who gave the orders and Chink Molina were making introductions: take a good look at each other's faces, you're the ones who are going into the hot spot. They'd brought them drinks, cigarettes and sandwiches. The two men from Lima were tight, the ones from Arequipa dead drunk. Don't move, take deep breaths, get through it.

"We divided up into teams of two," Ludovico said. "They split Hipólito and me up."

"Ludovico Pantoja with the black man," Molina said. "Trifulcio, isn't it?"

"For a partner they gave me the guy who was all crumpled up with mountain sickness," Ludovico said. "One of the ones who was killed in the theater. You can see how close I came to it, Ambrosio."

"There are twenty-two of you, eleven pairs," Molina said. "Get to know one another, don't get confused."

"They killed three and sent fourteen of us to the hospital," Ludovico said. "And that coward Hipólito without a scratch, tell me if you think that's fair."

"I want to be sure you've understood me," Molina said. "Let's see, you there, repeat what you're supposed to do."

The one who was going to be his partner passed him the bottle and Trifulcio took a drink: little worms running through his body, and heat. Trifulcio put out his hand: pleased to meet you, his being from Lima, didn't the altitude affect him? Not at all, Ludovico said, and they smiled. You, Molina said, and a man stood up: me to the orchestra seats, left rear, with this fellow here. And Molina: what about you? Another one stood up: to the balcony, in the center, with that fellow. They all stood up to answer, but when it was Trifulcio's turn, he remained seated: the orchestra, by the stage, with this gentleman. I thought niggers had to sit in the second balcony, Urondo said, and there was laughter.

"Just so you all know," Molina said. "Don't do anything until you hear the whistle and the voice giving the signal. That is, Long Live General Odría! Who's giving the signal?"

"I am," said the man who gave the orders. "I'll be in the first row of the balcony, right in the middle."

"But there's one thing I want to make clear, Inspector Molina," a sheepish voice said. "They've come prepared. Known hoodlums, Inspector. Argüelles, for example. An old hand with a knife, sir."

"They've also brought in some thugs from Lima," another voice said. "Fifteen of them at least, Inspector."

"Those police that Molina talked into it had no experience, their morale was low," Ludovico said. "I began to get the smell that if things got rough they'd take off."

"If anything goes wrong, that's why the assault guard will be there," Molina said. "Their orders are quite clear. So that you should stop thinking like a bunch of sissies."

"If you think it's because I'm scared, you're wrong, Inspector," the sheepish voice said. "I just wanted to make things clear."

"All right, you've made them clear for me," Molina said. "The gentleman here gives the signal and you people start the earthquake. Push people out into the street and the counterdemonstration will be there already. You'll join the people from the Restoration Party and after the rally at the square, back here again."

They gave out more drinks and cigarettes, and then newspapers in which to hide the chains, knives, clubs. Molina and the man who gave the orders reviewed them, keep them well hidden, button that coat, and when they got to Trifulcio, the man who gave the orders cheered him up: I can see you're feeling better, boy. Yes, Trifulcio said, I am, and he thought fuck your mother. Watch out for any wild shooting, Molina said. The taxis were waiting on the street. You and me here, Ludovico Pantoja said, and Trifulcio followed him. They got to the theater ahead of the others. There were people at the entrance handing out fliers, but the orchestra seats were almost empty. They sat in the third row and Trifulcio closed his eyes: now, yes, he was going to explode, the blood would spatter all over the theater. Don't you feel good? the man from Lima asked. And Trifulcio: no, I'm fine. The other pairs were arriving and taking their places. Some young people had begun to shout Free-dom, Free-dom. People kept on coming in and the orchestra seats were filling up.

"It's good we got here early," Trifulcio said. "I wouldn't have liked standing up all through it."

"Yes, Don Cayo, it's already started," the Prefect said. "They've more or less filled the theater. The counterdemonstration should be leaving the market."

The orchestra seats were filled, then the balcony, then the aisles, and now in front of the stage there were people crowded together fighting to break the barrier of men with red armbands who were acting as marshals. On the stage, twenty-odd chairs, a microphone, a Peruvian flag, large posters that said National Coalition, Freedom. When I don't move I feel better, Trifulcio thought. The people kept on chorusing Free-dom, and another group had started a different chant down at the orchestra: Le-gal-i-ty, Le-gal-i-ty. Applause was heard, cheers, and everybody was talking in shouts. Several people started coming on stage to take their seats. A salvo of applause greeted them and the shouts grew strong again.

"I don't understand what they mean by legality," Trifulcio said.

"For the parties that have been outlawed," Ludovico said. "Along with the millionaires, there are Apristas and Communists here too."

"I've been to a lot of rallies," Trifulcio said. "In 1950, in Ica, working for Senator Arévalo. But that was out in the open. This is the first one I've been to in a theater."

"There's Hipólito in back," Ludovico said. "He's my buddy. We've been working together for ten years."

"You're lucky you didn't get mountain sickness, it's a strange one," Trifulcio said. "Say, why are you shouting Freedom too?"

"You shout too," Ludovico said. "Do you want them to find out who you are?"

"My orders are to go up on stage and disconnect the microphone, not to shout," Trifulcio said. "The one who's giving the signal is my boss and he's probably looking at us. He's a hothead and bawls us out for everything."

"Don't be foolish, boy," Ludovico said. "Shout, man, applaud."

I can't believe I feel so well, Trifulcio thought. A short guy with a bow tie and glasses was making the audience shout Freedom and introducing the speakers. He said their names, pointed them out, and the people, more and more excited and noisy, applauded. There was competition between the Free-dom ones and the Le-gal-i-ty ones to see who could shout the louder. Trifulcio turned to look at the other pairs, but with so many people standing, a lot of them weren't visible anymore. The man who gave the orders, on the other hand, was there, surrounded by four more, listening and looking all around.

"There are fifteen just guarding the stage," Ludovico said. "And look how many more guys with armbands are scattered around the theater. Not counting the ones who'll come out of nowhere when things start up. I don't think we're going to be able to do it."

"Why won't we be able?" Trifulcio asked. "Didn't that fellow Molina make it all clear?"

"There'd have to be fifty of us and well trained," Ludovico said. "These Arequipans are a lily-livered lot, I've noticed. We won't be able to do it."

"We have to be able to do it." Trifulcio pointed to the balcony. "If not, there'll be no holding that one."

"The counterdemonstration must be getting here by now," Ludovico said. "Can you hear anything from outside?"

Trifulcio didn't answer, he was listening to the man in blue standing in front of the microphone: Odría was a dictator, the Internal Security Law was unconstitutional, the man in the street wanted freedom. And he was buttering up Arequipa: the rebel city, the martyr city, Odría's tyranny may have bloodied Arequipa in 1950, but he hadn't been able to kill its love for freedom.

"He speaks well, don't you think?" Trifulcio said. "The same with Senator Arévalo, even better than this fellow. He makes people cry. Have you ever heard him speak?"

"A fly couldn't fit in here and they're still coming in," Ludovico said. "I hope that dummy of a boss of yours forgets to give the signal."

"But this one is better than Dr. Lama," Trifulcio said. "Just as elegant, but not as hard to understand. You can get everything."

"What?" Cayo Bermúdez asked. "The counterdemonstration a complete failure, Molina?"

"Only two hundred people, Don Cayo," Molina said. "They gave them too much to drink. I warned Dr. Lama, but you know him. They'd get drunk, they wouldn't leave the market. Some two hundred at most. What shall we do, Don Cayo?"

"It's coming back," Trifulcio said. "Because of those bastards smoking. Another round of it, God damn it."

"He'd have to be crazy to give the signal," Ludovico said. "Where's Hipólito? Can you see where my buddy is?"

The tightness, the shouts, the cigarettes had turned the place into a kettle and the faces were glowing with sweat; some had taken off their jackets, loosened their ties, and the whole theater was shouting: Freedom, Le-gal-i-ty. In anguish, Trifulcio thought: again. He closed his eyes, hunched over, took a deep breath. He touched his chest: strong, again very strong. The man in blue had finished speaking, a chant was heard, the one in the bow tie was moving his arms like an orchestra conductor.

"All right, they've won," Cayo Bermúdez said. "Under these conditions, it's best to call the whole thing off, Molina."

"I'll try to, but I don't know if it will be possible, Don Cayo," Molina said. "The people are inside, I doubt that I can get the counterorder to them in time. I'll hang up now and call you back, Don Cayo."

Now a tall, fat man dressed in gray was speaking, and he must have been someone from Arequipa, because they all chanted his name, waved their hands at him. Quick, now, Trifulcio thought, he wasn't going to be able to make it, why didn't he do it all out right now? Hunched in his seat, his eyes half open, he was taking his pulse, one-two, one-two. The fat man was raising his arms, waving them, and his voice had grown hoarse.

"I really do feel bad now, yes, sir," Trifulcio said. "I need more air, sir."

"I hope he won't be that dumb, that he won't give the signal," Ludovico whispered. "And if he does give it, you and I don't move. We stay quiet, do you hear, black man?"

"Shut your mouth, you millionaire!" The voice of the man who gave the orders broke out up above. "Don't try to fool the people! Long live Odría!"

"Good, I was suffocating. And there's the whistle," Trifulcio said, standing up. "Long live General Odría!"

"Everybody was flabbergasted, even the one speaking," Ludovico said. "They were all looking up at the balcony."

Other shouts of Long live Odría broke out in different parts of the hall, and now the fat man was shrieking provokers, provokers, his face purple with rage, while exclamations, shoves and protests buried his voice and a storm of disorder turned the theater upside down. Everyone had stood up, in the back of the orchestra there was pushing and shoving, insults could be heard, and people were already fighting. Standing up, his chest going up and down, Trifulcio shouted Long live Odría! again. Someone in the row behind grabbed him by the shoulder: provoker! He got free with a jab of his elbow and looked at the man from Lima: now, let's go. But Ludovico Pantoja was hunched over like a mummy, looking at him with eyes bulging. Trifulcio grabbed him by the lapels, made him get up: move, man.

"What else could I do, they were all mixing it up," Ludovico said. "The black man took out his chain and drove toward the stage, shoving. I took out my pistol and followed him. With two other guys we managed to get to the first row. There the ones with the armbands were waiting for us."

Some of the people on stage were running for the exits, others looked at the marshals, who had formed a wall and were waiting, their clubs in the air, for the big black man and the other two who were advancing, waving their chains over their heads. Break them up, Urondo, Trifulcio shouted, break them up, Téllez. He cracked his chain like a bull drover cracking his whip, and the armband man closest to him let go of his club and fell to the floor clutching his face. Get up there, boy, Urondo shouted, and Téllez we'll hold them off, boy! Trifulcio saw them attacking the small group defending the stairs to the stage and, whirling his chain, he attacked too.

"I got separated from my partner and the others," Ludovico said. "There was a wall of thugs between them and me. They were fighting with about ten men and there were at least five surrounding me. I held them off with my pistol and kept shouting Hipólito, Hipólito. And then the end of the world came, brother."

The grenades fell from the balcony like a handful of brown stones, bounced with crisp sounds on the seats of the orchestra and the floor of the stage, and immediately spirals of smoke began to rise. In a few seconds the air turned white, hardened, and a thick, burning vapor was mixing in and blotting out the bodies. The shouting grew louder, the sound of rolling bodies, chairs breaking, coughs, and Trifulcio stopped fighting. He felt his arms go limp, the chain fell out of his hands, his legs doubled under and his eyes, in the midst of the burning clouds, managed to make out the figures on stage who were fleeing with handkerchiefs to their mouths, and the guys with the armbands who had come together and, covering their noses, were approaching him as if swimming. He couldn't get up, he pounded his chest with his fist, opened his mouth as wide as he could. He didn't feel the blows that started landing on him. Air, like a fish, Tomasa, he still managed to think.

"I was blinded," Ludovico said. "And the worst thing was the strangling, brother. I began shooting wildly. I didn't realize they were grenades, I thought I'd been shot from behind."

"Tear gas in a closed place, several dead, dozens wounded," Senator Landa said. "Could you ask for anything more, Fermín? Even though he's got nine lives, Bermúdez won't survive this one."

"I ran out of bullets one-two-three," Ludovico said. "I couldn't open my eyes. I felt my head splitting and I fell into a deep sleep. There were so many on top of me, Ambrosio."

"A few incidents, Don Cayo," the Prefect said. "It seems they broke up the rally, they did manage that. People are running out of the theater scared to death."

"The assault guards have started into the theater," Molina said.

454

"There was shooting inside. No, I still don't know if anyone's been killed, Don Cayo."

"I don't know how much time passed, but I opened my eyes and the smoke was still there," Ludovico said. "I felt worse than dead. Bleeding all over, Ambrosio. And that's when I saw that bastard Hipólito."

"He was kicking your partner too?" Ambrosio laughed. "I mean, he fooled them. He didn't turn out as dumb as we thought."

"Help me, help me," Ludovico shouted. "Nothing, as if he didn't know me. He kept on kicking the black man, and all of a sudden the others with him saw me and jumped on top of me. The kicking again, the beating. Then I passed out again, Ambrosio."

"Have the police clear the streets, Prefect," Cayo Bermúdez said. "Don't allow any demonstrations, arrest all the leaders of the Coalition. Have you got the casualty lists yet? Was anyone killed?"

"Like waking up and still seeing the dream," Ludovico said. "The theater was already almost empty. Everything broken, spattered with blood, my partner in a puddle of it. I can't even remember if the old man had any face left. And there were guys sprawled out coughing."

"Yes, a big demonstration on the Plaza de Armas, Don Cayo," Molina said. "The Prefect is with the Commandant now. I don't think it would be wise, Don Cayo. There are thousands of people."

"Have them break it up immediately, you idiot," Cayo Bermúdez said. "Can't you see that the thing is going to get bigger after what happened? Put me in touch with the Commandant. Clear the streets immediately, Molina."

"Then the guards came in and one of them gave me still another kick, seeing me like that," Ludovico said. "I'm a detective, I'm on the force. Finally I saw Chink Molina's face. They took me out a side door. Then I passed out again and I didn't come to until I was in the hospital. By then the whole city was on strike."

"Things are getting worse, Don Cayo," Molina said. "They've torn up the streets, there are barricades all over the downtown area. The assault guards can't break up a demonstration like that."

"The army has to intervene, Don Cayo," the Prefect said. "But General Alvarado says he'll only call out the troops if the Minister of War orders it."

"My roommate was one of the senator's men," Ludovico said. "A broken leg. He filled me in on what was going on in Arequipa and it shook me up. Boy, was he scared."

"It's all right," Cayo Bermúdez said. "I'm going to get General Llerena to give the order."

"I'm going to get out of here, the street's safer than the hospital," Téllez said. "I don't want to happen to me what happened to Martínez or the black fellow. I know someone named Urquiza. I'll ask him to hide me in his house."

"Nothing's going to happen, they won't come in here," Ludovico said. "Let them have their general strike. The army will open fire on them."

"But where is the army? It's nowhere to be seen," Téllez said. "If they get a notion to lynch us, they can walk right in here and make themselves at home. There isn't even a guard at the hospital."

"No one knows we're here," Ludovico said. "And even if they did know, they'd think we belonged to the Coalition and were victims."

"No, because they'd know we weren't from around here," Téllez said. "They'd know we were outsiders. Tonight I'm going to Urquiza's. I can walk in spite of this cast."

"He was half crazy with fright because two of his buddies had been killed in the theater," Ludovico said. "They're asking for the resignation of the Minister of Public Order, he was saying, they'll come in here and hang us from a lamppost. But what the hell is going on, God damn it?"

"A near revolution is going on," Molina said. "The people have taken over the streets, Don Cayo. We've even had to withdraw the traffic police so they won't be stoned. Why hasn't the order come for the army to intervene, Don Cayo?"

"What about them, sir?" Téllez asked. "What have they done with Martínez and the old man?"

"Don't worry, we've already buried them," Molina said. "You're Téllez, aren't you? Your boss has left money at headquarters so you can get back to Ica by bus as soon as you can walk."

"Why have they buried them here, sir?" Téllez asked. "Martínez has a wife and kids in Ica, Trifulcio has relatives in Chincha. Why didn't they send them there so their families could bury them? Why here, like dogs? Nobody's ever going to come and visit them, sir."

"Hipólito?" Molina asked. "He took his bus to Lima in spite of my orders. I asked him to stay and help and he took off. Yes, I know he didn't behave well in the theater, Ludovico. But I'm going to make a report to Lozano and screw him."

"Calm down, Molina," Cayo Bermúdez said. "Calmly now, with details, piece by piece. What, exactly, is the situation?"

"The situation is that the police are no longer able to restore order, Don Cayo," the Prefect said. "I'll say it once more. If the army doesn't intervene, anything could happen here."

"The situation?" General Llerena said. "Very simple, Paredes. Bermúdez' imbecility has put us between the sword and the wall. He messed things up and now he wants the army to fix it with a show of force."

"A show of force?" General Alvarado said. "No, sir, if I call out the troops there'll be more dead than in 1950. They've set up barricades, there are people with weapons and the whole city is on strike. I warn you that a lot of blood will flow."

"Cayo assures me that it won't, General," Major Paredes said. "Only twenty percent are observing the strike. The uproar was unleashed by a small group of agitators hired by the Coalition."

"A hundred percent are observing the strike, General," General Alvarado said. "The people are lord and master of the streets. They've formed a committee made up of lawyers, workers, doctors, students. The Prefect has been insisting that I call out the troops since last night, but I want the decision to come from you."

"What's your opinion, Alvarado?" General Llerena said. "In all frankness."

"As soon as they see the tanks, the rioters will go home, General Llerena," Cayo Bermúdez said. "It's madness to go on losing time like this. Every minute that passes makes the agitators stronger and the government loses prestige. Give the order at once."

"Quite sincerely, I don't think the army has any business getting its hands dirty for the sake of Mr. Bermúdez, General," General Alvarado said. "It's not a question of the President, the army, or the government here. The gentlemen from the Coalition have come to see me and they've given me assurances. They promise to calm the people down if Bermúdez resigns."

"You know the leaders of the Coalition quite well, General Llerena," Senator Arévalo said. "Bacacorzo, Zavala, López Landa. You can't think that those gentlemen are tied in with Apristas or Communists, can you?"

"They have the greatest respect for the army and especially for you, General Llerena," Senator Landa insisted. "All they want is for Bermúdez to resign. It's not the first time Bermúdez has put his foot in it, General, you know that. It's a good chance to rid the government of an individual who's doing everybody harm, General."

"Arequipa is indignant at what happened in the Municipal Theater," General Alvarado said. "It was a miscalculation on the part of Mr. Bermúdez, General. The leaders of the Coalition have channeled the indignation very well. They put all the blame on Bermúdez, not the government. If you want me to, I'll call out the troops. But think about it, General. If Bermúdez leaves the cabinet, this will be settled peacefully."

"We're losing in a few hours what it took us years to get, Paredes," Cayo Bermúdez said. "Llerena answers me with evasions, the other ministers won't show their faces to me. It's a question of a regular ambush against me. Have you talked to Llerena?"

"All right, keep the troops in their barracks, Alvarado," General Llerena said. "The army shouldn't get mixed up in this unless it's attacked."

"I think that's the most intelligent course of action," General Alvarado said. "Bacacorzo and López Landa of the Coalition have come back to see me, General. They suggest a military cabinet. Bermúdez could leave and the government wouldn't give the impression of having given in. It could be a solution, couldn't it, sir?"

"General Alvarado has behaved very well, Fermín," Senator Landa said.

"The country is tired of Bermúdez' abuses, General Llerena," Senator Arévalo said. "The business in Arequipa is just one sign of what could happen all over Peru if we don't get rid of that fellow. This is a chance for the army to win the sympathy of the country, General."

458

"The business in Arequipa doesn't surprise me in the least, Dr. Lora," Dr. Arbeláez said. "On the contrary, we've won the lottery. Bermúdez is already starting to smell like a corpse."

"Remove him from the cabinet?" Dr. Lora asked. "The President will never do that, Arbeláez, Bermúdez is his favorite spoiled little child. He'd prefer for the army to go at it blood and thunder in Arequipa."

"The President isn't too sharp, but he's not too stupid either," Dr. Arbeláez said. "We can explain it to him and he'll understand. The hatred against the government is concentrated on Bermúdez. Throw them that bone, and the dogs will calm down."

"If the army doesn't intervene, I can't remain in the city, Don Cayo," the Prefect said. "Headquarters is only protected by a couple of dozen guards."

"If you budge an inch out of Arequipa, you're fired," Bermúdez said. "Control your nerves. General Llerena will give the order any moment now."

"I'm penned in here, Don Cayo," Molina said. "We can hear the demonstration on the Plaza de Armas. They might attack the post. Why don't the troops come out, Don Cayo?"

"Look, Paredes, the army isn't going to muddy its boots saving Bermúdez' cabinet post," General Llerena said. "No, not in any way. One thing is sure, we have to put an end to this situation. The military leaders and a group of loyalist senators are going to propose the formation of a military cabinet to the President."

"It's the simplest way of liquidating Bermúdez without the government's appearing to have been defeated by the Arequipans," Dr. Arbeláez said. "Resignation of civilian ministers, a military cabinet, and the whole matter settled, General."

"What's going on?" Cayo Bermúdez asked. "I've been waiting four hours and the President won't see me. What does this mean, Paredes?"

"The army comes out perfectly clean with this solution, General Llerena," Senator Arévalo said. "And you earn an enormous political dividend. Those of us who respect you feel very happy, General."

"You can get into the Palace without his aides' stopping you," Cayo Bermúdez said. "Run over there, Paredes. Explain to the President that there's a high-level conspiracy, that at this moment everything depends on him. That he make Llerena understand things. I don't trust anyone anymore. Even Lozano and Alcibíades have sold me out."

"No arrests or anything crazy, Molina," Lozano said. "You stay right there at your post with your people, and no shooting unless it's a matter of life and death."

"I don't understand, Mr. Lozano," Molina said. "You tell me one thing and the Minister of Public Order tells me something else."

"Forget about Don Cayo's orders," Lozano said. "He's under quarantine and I don't think he's going to last much longer as Minister. What about the wounded?"

"The most serious ones are in the hospital, Mr. Lozano," Molina said. "About twenty of them."

"Did you bury those two guys of Arévalo's?" Lozano asked.

"With the greatest discretion, as Don Cayo ordered," Molina said. "Two others went back to Ica. There's only one left in the hospital. A man named Téllez."

"Get him out of Arequipa as soon as possible," Lozano said. "And the same goes for the two I sent you. Those people can't stay on there."

"Hipólito's already left, in spite of my orders," Molina said. "But Pantoja's in the hospital, very serious. He won't be able to be moved for some time, sir."

"Ah, I understand," Cayo Bermúdez said. "Well, under the present circumstances I understand quite well. It's a solution, yes, I agree. Where do I sign?"

"You don't look so sad, Cayo," Major Paredes said. "I'm awfully sorry, but I couldn't back you up. In political matters friendship has to be put to one side sometimes."

"Don't give me any explanations, I understand only too well," Cayo Bermúdez said. "Besides, I've wanted to get away for some time now, you know that. Yes, I'm leaving early tomorrow morning, by plane."

"I don't know how I'm going to feel as Minister of Public Order," Major Paredes said. "It's too bad you won't stay on to give me some advice, with all the experience you've had."

"I'm going to give you one good piece of advice." Cayo Bermúdez smiled. "Don't even trust your mother."

"Mistakes are costly in politics," Major Paredes said. "It's like war, Cayo."

"That's true," Cayo Bermúdez said. "I don't want anyone to know I'm leaving tomorrow. Please keep that secret for me."

"We've got a taxi that will take you to Camaná, there you can rest for a couple of days before going on to Ica, if you want," Molina said. "And it would be better if you didn't open your mouth about what happened to you in Arequipa."

"Fine," Téllez said. "I'll be glad to get out of here as soon as I can."

"What happens to me?" Ludovico asked. "When are they going to send me off?"

"As soon as you're able to stand," Molina said. "Don't worry, there's no reason to anymore. Don Cayo has left the government and the strike's going to be over."

"Don't be angry with me, Don Cayo," Dr. Alcibíades said. "The pressures were very strong. They didn't give me a chance to act any other way."

"Of course not, doctor," Cayo Bermúdez said. "I'm not angry with you. On the contrary, I'm impressed by the able way you handled it. Behave yourself with my successor, Major Paredes. He's going to name you Director of Security. He asked my opinion and I told him you had what it takes for the job."

"I'll always be here to serve you, Don Cayo," Dr. Alcibíades said. "Here's your ticket, your passport. Everything in order. And if I don't see you, have a good trip, Don Cayo."

"Come in, brother, I've got great news for you," Ludovico said. "Guess what, Ambrosio?"

"It wasn't to rob her, Ludovico," Ambrosio said. "No, it wasn't for that either. Don't ask me why I did it, brother, I won't tell you. Will you help me?"

"They put me on the regular list!" Ludovico said. "Run out and buy a bottle of something and sneak it in here, Ambrosio."

"No, he didn't order me to, he didn't even know," Ambrosio said. "Just be satisfied with the fact that I killed her. I thought it up all by myself, yes. He was going to give her the money to go to Mexico with,

461

he was going to let himself be bled for the rest of his life by that woman. Will you help me?"

"A third-class officer, Homicide Division," Ludovico said. "And do you know who came to give me the news, brother?"

"Yes, to do him a favor, to save him," Ambrosio said. "To show him my gratitude, yes. Now he wants me to go away. No, it isn't ingratitude, he isn't evil. It's because of his family. He doesn't want this to dirty them. He's a good person. Let your friend Ludovico advise you and I'll give him a token of my thanks, he says, you see? Will you help me?"

"Mr. Lozano in person, just imagine," Ludovico said. "All of a sudden he appeared in the room and I could have dropped dead, Ambrosio, you can imagine."

"He gives you ten thousand and I give you ten thousand out of my savings," Ambrosio said. "Yes, fine, I'll leave Lima and you'll never see my face again, Ludovico. Fine, I'll take Amalia too. We'll never set foot in this city again, brother, agreed."

"The salary is twenty-eight hundred, but Mr. Lozano is going to get them to recognize my seniority on the force," Ludovico said. "I'll even have my increments, Ambrosio."

"To Pucallpa?" Ambrosio asked. "But what can I do there, Ludovico?"

"I know that Hipólito behaved very badly with you," Mr. Lozano said. "We're going to give him a post where he can rot while he's still alive."

"And do you know where they're going to send him?" Ludovico laughed. "To Celendín!"

"But you mean they're going to put Hipólito on the regular list too?" Ambrosio said.

"What difference does it make, if he has to live in Celendín," Ludovico said. "Oh, brother, I feel so good. And I owe it to you too, Ambrosio. If I hadn't gone to work for Don Cayo, I'd still be a nothing. It's something I'm in debt to you for, brother."

"You're so happy because you're all healed, you can even move," Ambrosio said. "When are they letting you out?"

"There's no hurry, Ludovico," Mr. Lozano said. "You get well at your leisure, consider this time in the hospital as a vacation. You've got

462

nothing to complain about. You sleep all day, you get your meals in bed."

"The fact is, everything's not that rosy, sir," Ludovico said. "Don't you realize that while I'm here I'm not making any money?"

"You're going to draw your full salary all the time you're here," Mr. Lozano said. "You've earned it, Ludovico."

"We part-timers only get paid by the job, Mr. Lozano," Ludovico said. "You forget I'm not on the list."

"You are now," Mr. Lozano said. "Ludovico Pantoja, Third-Class Officer, Homicide Division. How does that sound to you?"

"I almost jumped out of bed and kissed his hand, Ambrosio," Ludovico said. "Really, did they really put me on the regular list, Mr. Lozano?"

"I spoke about you to the new Minister, and the Major recognizes your services," Mr. Lozano said. "We got your appointment through in twenty-four hours. I came to congratulate you."

"I'm sorry, sir," Ludovico said. "I'm ashamed, Mr. Lozano. But the news has got me so worked up, sir."

"Go ahead and cry, don't be ashamed," Mr. Lozano said. "I can see that you've got a warm feeling for the force and that's very good, Ludovico."

"You're right, we've got to celebrate, brother," Ambrosio said. "I'm going to go get a bottle. I hope the nurses don't catch me."

"Senator Arévalo must be all worked up, right, sir?" Ludovico said. "His people were the ones who got it the worst. They killed two of them and the other got it bad."

"You'd better forget about all that, Ludovico," Mr. Lozano said.

"How can I forget, sir?" Ludovico said. "Can't you see what they did to me? You remember a beating like that for the rest of your life."

"Well, if you don't forget, I don't know why I've gone to so much trouble for you," Mr. Lozano said. "You haven't understood a thing, Ludovico."

"You've got me all confused, sir," Ludovico said. "What is it I have to understand?"

"That you're an officer of investigations, on the same level as those who've come out of the School," Mr. Lozano said. "And an officer can't have done any work as a hired thug, Ludovico."

"Go back to work?" Don Emilio Arévalo said. "What you're going to do now is get well, Téllez. A few weeks with your family, with full pay. Only when you're completely recovered will you go back to work."

"That kind of work is done by the part-timers, the poor devils without any training," Mr. Lozano said. "You've never been a thug, you've always been on high-level operations. That's what your service record says. Or do you want me to erase all that and put you down as a nobody?"

"There's no reason for you to thank me, boy," Don Emilio Arévalo said. "People are good to me and I'm good to them, Téllez."

"Now I understand, Mr. Lozano," Ludovico said. "I'm sorry I didn't catch on. I was never a part-timer, I never went to Arequipa."

"Because somebody might complain, say he's got no right to be on the regular list," Mr. Lozano said. "So that, forget about all that, Ludovico."

"I've already forgotten, Don Emilio," Téllez said. "I never left Ica, I broke my leg riding a mule. You don't know how good I feel over what you've done for me, Don Emilio."

"Pucallpa for two reasons, Ambrosio," Ludovico said. "They've got the worst police post in all of Peru there. And second, because I've got a relative there who can give you a job. He's got a bus company. You see, I'm offering it to you on a silver platter, brother."

464

FOUR

1

"THE BIM-BAM-BOOMS?" Ambrosio says. "I never saw them. Why do you ask me that, son?"

He thinks: Ana, The Kitty, the Bim-Bam-Booms, the tiger love of Carlitos and China, the old man's death, the first gray hair: two, three, ten years, Zavalita. Had the bastards on *Última Hora* been the first to exploit The Kitty as news? No, it had been the ones on *La Prensa*. It was a new kind of bet and at first the horse players stuck to the daily double. But one Sunday a typesetter picked nine of the ten winning horses and won the hundred thousand soles of The Kitty. *La Prensa* interviewed him: he smiled in the center of his relatives, toasting around a table loaded with bottles, kneeling before the image of Our Lord of Miracles. The next week the prize for The Kitty was double and *Última Hora* had a picture on the front page of two Ica businessmen euphorically holding up the winning ticket, and the following week the four hundred thousand soles were won, all by himself, by a fisherman from Callao who had lost an eye in a barroom fight in his youth. The pot kept growing and among the newspapers the hunt for the winners started. Arispe picked Carlitos to cover the news of The Kitty and after three weeks *La Crónica* had lost all the scoops: Zavalita, you'll have to take over, Carlitos hasn't been able to get his foot on the ball. He thinks: if it hadn't been for The Kitty, there wouldn't have been any accident and you'd probably still be single, Zavalita. But he was happy with the assignment; there wasn't much to do and, thanks to that invertebrate kind of work, he was able to steal hours on end away from the newspaper. On Saturday nights he had to stand watch at the main office of the Jockey Club to check on how high the stakes were climbing, and early Monday morning it was already known whether the winner of The Kitty was one or many and what office had sold the prize-winning ticket. Then the hunt for the lucky person started. On Mondays and Thursdays the office was deluged with calls from meddlesome tipsters and he had to go back and forth in the van with Periquito checking out the rumors.

"Because of that woman over there with all the makeup on," Santiago says. "She looks like one of the Bim-Bam-Booms, the one named Ada Rosa."

With the pretext of tracking down presumptive winners of The Kitty, you could stay away from the newspaper, Zavalita, go to a movie, go to the Patio or the Bransa and have a coffee with people from other papers, or go with Carlitos to the rehearsals of the company of chorus girls that the impresario Pedrito Aguirre was putting together and in which China danced. He thinks: the Bim-Bam-Booms. Up till then he'd only been in love, he thinks, but from then on infected, intoxicated with China. For her sake he did publicity for the Bim-Bam-Booms, writing spontaneous artistico-patriotic articles that he slipped into the entertainment page: why did we have to content ourselves with those Cuban and Chilean chorus girls who were second-rate artists, when there were girls in Peru just as capable of stardom? For her sake he resolutely wallowed in the ridiculous: all they needed was a chance and the support of the public, it was a matter of national prestige, everybody to the opening of the Bim-Bam-Booms. With Norwin, with Solórzano, with Periquito they went to the Teatro Monumental to watch the rehearsals and there was China, Zavalita, her coltish body with its fierce behind, her striking roguish face, her wicked eyes, her husky voice. From the deserted orchestra seats in the midst of the dust and the fleas, they watched her arguing with Tabarín, the fairy choreographer, and they followed her in the whirlwind of figures on stage, dizzy from so much mambo, rumba, guaracha and subi: she's the best of the lot Carlitos, bravo Carlitos. When the Bim-Bam-Booms began appearing in theaters and cabarets, China's picture would appear at least once a week in the show column, with

468

captions that praised her to the skies. Sometimes, after the performance, Santiago would accompany Carlitos and China to have something to eat at El Parral, to have a drink at some dismal bar. During that time the couple had got along quite well, and one night in the Negro-Negro, Carlitos put his hand on Santiago's arm: we've already passed the acid test, Zavalita, three months without a storm, one of these days I'm going to marry her. And on another night, drunk: these have been happy months, Zavalita. But the fights started up again when the company of the Bim-Bam-Booms broke up and China began to dance at El Pingüino, a nightclub that Pedrito Aguirre had opened up downtown. At night, when they left *La Crónica,* Carlitos would drag Santiago through the arches of the Plaza San Martín, along Ocoña, to the dismally decorated sticky cave of El Pingüino. Pedrito Aguirre wouldn't charge them a minimum, sold them beer at cost and accepted IOUs. From the bar they would watch the seasoned pirates of Lima night life set out to board the chorus girls. They sent them notes by the waiters, had them sit at their tables. Sometimes, when they arrived, China would have left already and Pedrito Aguirre would give Carlitos a fraternal pat on the back: she hadn't felt well, she'd left with Ada Rosa, she'd got word that her mother was in the hospital. Other times they would find her at a candlelit table in the back listening to the laughter of some prince of bohemia, curled up in the shadows beside some elegant older man with graying sideburns, dancing tight in the arms of a young Apollo. And there was Carlitos' downcast face: her contract called for her to entertain the customers Zavalita, or in light of the circumstances let's go to a whorehouse Zavalita, or I only keep on seeing her out of masochism Zavalita. From that point on the love between Carlitos and China had gone back to the butchering rhythm of before, reconciliations and breaks, scandals and public fisticuffs. During the intermissions of her romance with Carlitos, China showed herself off in the company of millionaire lawyers, adolescents with good names and the look of ruffians, cirrhotic businessmen. She takes on all comers as long as they're family men, Becerrita would say poisonously, she doesn't have the calling of a whore but of an adulteress. But those adventures would only last a few days, China always ended up calling *La Crónica.* There the sarcastic smiles in the editorial room, the perfidious winks over the typewriters, while Carlitos, his sunken-eyed face kissing the phone, moved his lips with humility and hope. China kept him in total bankruptcy, he went about borrowing money everywhere and collectors even showed up at the newspaper with IOUs of his. At the Negro-Negro they cut off his credit, he thinks: he must have owed you at least a thousand soles, Zavalita. He thinks: twenty-three, twenty-four, twenty-five years. Memories that exploded like the bubbles Teté used to make with that gum of hers, ephemeral, like the stories about The Kitty, whose ink had been erased by time, Zavalita, useless, like the pages tossed into the wicker wastebaskets at night.

"What an entertainer, that one," Ambrosio says. "Her name is Margot and she's a hustler and famous for it. Every day she drops by La Catedral."

(9)

Queta was making the gringo drink beautifully: whiskey after whiskey for him and for her little glasses of vermouth (which was watered-down tea). I got you a gold mine, Robertito had told her, you've already got twelve tabs. Queta could only understand confused bits and pieces of the story the gringo was telling her along with laughter and mimicry. The robbery of a bank or store or train he'd witnessed in real life or in the movies or read about in a magazine and which, she didn't know why, brought on a thirsty hilarity. A smile on her face, one of her hands going around his freckled neck, Queta was thinking while they danced: twelve tabs, is that all? And at that moment Ivonne appeared behind the curtain of the bar, bubbling in her mascara and rouge. She winked at her and her silver-clawed hand called her. Queta put her mouth to the ear with blond fuzz on it: I'll be right back, love, wait for me, don't go off with anyone else. What, qué, did you say? he said, smiling, and Queta squeezed his arm affectionately: in a minute, I'll be right back in a minute. Ivonne was waiting for her in the hallway with a festive face: a very important one, Quetita.

"He's there in the parlor with Malvina." She was examining her hair, her makeup, her dress, her shoes. "He wants you there too."

"But I'm tied up," Queta said, pointing toward the bar. "That . . ."

"He saw you from the parlor, he liked you." Ivonne's eyes were twinkling. "You don't know how lucky you are."

"What about that one there, ma'am?" Queta insisted. "He's drinking a lot and . . ."

"With a golden glove, the way you would a king," Ivonne whispered avidly. "So he leaves here happy, happy with you. Wait, let me fix you up, your hair's become mussed."

Too bad, Queta thought while Ivonne's fingers were going through her hair. And then, while they went along the hall, a politician, a military man, a diplomat? The door of the parlor was open and when she went in she saw Malvina tossing her slip onto the floor. She closed the door but it opened immediately and Robertito came in with a tray; he slipped across the carpet all bent over, his smooth face folded up into a servile grimace, good evening. He put the tray on the small table, went out without straightening up, and then Queta heard him.

"You too, fine girl, you too. Aren't you hot?"

A voice devoid of emotion, dry, somewhat despotic and drunk.

"Such a rush, lovey," she said, searching for his eyes, but she couldn't see them. He was sitting in a chair that had no arms, under the three small pictures, partially hidden by the shadows of that corner of the room where the light from the elephant-tusk lamp didn't reach.

"One's not enough for him, he likes them by twos." Malvina laughed. "You're a hungry one, aren't you, lovey? You've got a way about you."

"Right now," he ordered, vehemently and yet glacially. "You too, right now. Aren't you dying from the heat?"

No, Queta thought, and with regret she thought of the gringo in the bar, longingly. While she was unbuttoning her skirt, she saw Malvina, already naked: a toasted and fleshy shape in a pose that she wanted to be provocative under the light of the lamp and talking to herself. She seemed a little tight and Queta thought: she's got fat. It doesn't suit her, her breasts were drooping, pretty soon the old woman would send her to take the Turkish baths at the Virrey.

"Hurry up, Quetita." Malvina patted her, laughing. "The one with the whims can't stand it anymore."

"The one without manners, you mean," Queta murmured, slowly rolling down her stockings. "Your friend didn't even say good evening."

But he didn't want to joke or talk. He was silent, rocking in the chair with a single obsessive and identical motion until Queta finished undress-

471

ing. Like Malvina, she had taken off her skirt, blouse and bra, but not her panties. She folded her clothing slowly and placed it on a chair.

"You're better off like that, much cooler," he said with his disagreeable little tone of cold, impatient boredom. "Come, the drinks are getting warm."

They went over to the chair together, and while Malvina dropped onto the man's knees with a forced little laugh, Queta could see his thin and bony face, his bored mouth, his tiny icy eyes. Fifty years old, she thought. Huddled against him, Malvina was purring comically: she was cold, warm me up, a little loving. An impotent man full of hate, Queta thought, a masturbator full of hate. He'd put an arm around Malvina, but his eyes, with their unmovable lack of desire, were running up and down her as she waited, standing by the small table. Finally she leaned over, picked up two glasses, and handed them to the man and Malvina. Then she picked up hers and drank, thinking a deputy, maybe a prefect.

"There's room for you too," he ordered, while he drank. "A knee for each one, so you won't fight."

She felt him pulling on her arm, and when she let herself go against them, she heard Malvina cry out, oh, you hit me on the bone, Quetita. Now they were tight together, the chair was rocking like a pendulum, and Queta felt disgust, his hand was sweating. It was skeletal, tiny, and while Malvina, already quite comfortable or doing a good job of faking, was laughing, joking and trying to kiss the man on the mouth, Queta felt the quick fingers, wet, sticky, tickling her breasts, her back, her stomach and her legs. She started to laugh and began to hate him. He was petting both of them with method and obstinacy, one hand on the body of each, but he wasn't even smiling, and he looked at them alternately, mute, with a remote and pensive expression.

"This rude gentleman isn't much fun," Queta said.

"Let's go to bed now," Malvina shrilled, laughing. "You're going to make us come down with pneumonia this way, lovey."

"I don't dare with both of you, that's too much chicken for me," he murmured, pushing them softly away from the chair. And he ordered: "First you've got to get a little merry. Dance something."

He's going to keep us like this all night, Queta thought, let him go to hell, back to the gringo for her. Malvina had gone off and, kneeling

472

against the wall, was plugging in the phonograph. Queta felt the cold, bony hand pulling her toward him again and she leaned over, put out her head, and separated her lips: sticky, incisive, a form that reeked of strong tobacco and alcohol passed over her teeth, gums, flattened her tongue and withdrew, leaving a mass of bitter saliva in her mouth. Then the hand moved her away from the chair rudely: let's see if you can dance better than you can kiss. Queta felt a rage coming over her, but her smile, instead of getting smaller, grew. Malvina came over to them, took Queta by the hand, dragged her to the rug. They danced a guaracha, twirling and singing, barely touching each other with the tips of their fingers. Then a bolero, soldered together. Who is he? Queta murmured in Malvina's ear. Who knows, Quetita, just one of those motherfuckers.

"Show a little more love," he whispered slowly, and his voice was different; it had warmed up and was almost human. "Put a little more heart into it."

Malvina gave out with her sharp and artificial laugh and began to say in a loud voice baby, mama, and to rub eagerly against Queta, who had taken her by the waist and was rocking her. The movement of the chair began again, faster now than before, uneven and with a stealthy sound of springs, and Queta thought that's it, now he'll come. She looked for Malvina's mouth and while they were kissing, she closed her eyes to keep her laugh in. And at that moment the shattering squeal of an automobile putting on its brakes drowned out the music. They let go of each other, Malvina covered her ears, said noisy drunks. But there was no collision, just the sound of a car door after the sharp and sibilant brakes, and finally the doorbell. It buzzed as if it had got stuck.

"It's nothing, what's the matter with you," he said with dull fury. "Keep on dancing."

But the record was over and Malvina went to change it. They embraced again, started dancing, and suddenly the door smashed against the wall as if it had been kicked open. Queta saw him: black, big, muscular, as shiny as the blue suit he was wearing, skin halfway between shoe polish and chocolate, tightly straightened hair. Hanging in the doorway, a big hand holding the knob, his eyes white and enormous, he looked at her. Not even when the man leaped out of the chair and crossed the rug in two strides did he stop looking at her.

473

"What the fuck are you doing here?" the man asked, standing in front of the Negro, his little fists clenched as if he were going to strike him. "Don't you ask permission to come into a room?"

"General Espina's outside, Don Cayo." He seemed to withdraw, he let go of the doorknob, he was looking at the man in a cowardly way, his words stumbled. "In his car. He wants you to come down, it's very urgent."

Malvina was quickly putting on her skirt, blouse, shoes, and Queta, while she was getting dressed, looked at the door again. Over the back of the little man she caught the black man's eyes for a second: frightened, dull.

"Tell him I'll be right down," the man murmured. "Don't you ever come into a room like that again, unless you want a bullet in you someday."

"I'm sorry, Don Cayo." The black man nodded, backing up. "I didn't think, they told me you were here. I'm sorry."

He disappeared in the hallway and the man closed the door. He turned to them and the light of the lamp illuminated him from head to toe. His face was cracked, there was a rancid and frustrated glow in his little eyes. He took some bills from his wallet and put them on a chair. He went over to them, straightening his tie.

"To console you for my leaving," he murmured in a coarse way. And he gave Queta a command: "I'm sending for you tomorrow. Around nine o'clock."

"I can't go out at that time," Queta said quickly, giving Malvina a look.

"You'll find out that you can," he said dryly. "Around nine o'clock, be ready."

"So, are you throwing me into the trash can, sweetie?" Malvina laughed, stretching over to look at the bills on the chair. "So, your name is Cayo. Cayo what?"

"Cayo Shithead," he said on his way to the door without turning around. He went out and slammed it shut.

9

"They just called you from home, Zavalita," Solórzano said when he saw him come into the office. "Something urgent. Yes, about your father, I think."

474

He ran to the first desk, dialed the number, long, stabbing rings, an unfamiliar upland voice: the master wasn't home, nobody was home. They'd changed butlers again and this one didn't know who you were, Zavalita.

"It's Santiago, the master's son," he repeated, raising his voice. "What's wrong with my father? Where is he?"

"Sick," the butler said. "He's in the hospital. Don't know which one, sir."

He borrowed ten soles from Solórzano and took a taxi. When he went into the American Hospital he saw Teté on the telephone at the desk: a boy who wasn't Sparky was holding her shoulders and only when he got close did he recognize Popeye. They saw him, Teté hung up.

"He's better now, he's better now." Her eyes were teary, her voice broken. "But we thought he was dying, Santiago."

"We called you an hour ago, Skinny," Popeye said. "At your boardinghouse, at *La Crónica*. I was going to go looking for you in my car."

"But it wasn't that time," Santiago says. "He died from the second attack, Ambrosio. A year and a half later."

It had been at teatime. Don Fermín had come home earlier than usual; he didn't feel well, he was afraid he was coming down with the flu. He'd had some hot tea, a drink of cognac, and was reading *Selecciones del Reader's Digest*, wrapped up in a blanket in the study, when Teté and Popeye, who were listening to records in the living room, heard the noise. Santiago closes his eyes: the heavy body face down on the carpet, the face immobilized in a grimace of pain or fear, the blanket and the magazine on the floor. The shouts that mama must have given, the confusion that must have reigned. They'd wrapped him in blankets, put him in Popeye's car, taken him to the hospital. In spite of the terrible thing you people did in moving him, he's resisted the infarction quite well, the doctor had said. He needed complete rest, but there was no cause for fear now. In the hallway outside the room was Señora Zoila, Uncle Clodomiro and Sparky were calming her. His mother gave him her cheek to kiss, but didn't say a word and looked at Santiago as if reproaching him for something.

475

"He's conscious now," Uncle Clodomiro said. "When the nurse comes out you can see him."

"Just for a moment," Sparky said. "The doctor doesn't want him to talk."

There was the large room with lime-green walls, the anteroom with flowered curtains, and he, Zavalita, in garnet-colored silk pajamas. The lamp on the night table lighted the bed with a dim church light. There the paleness of his face, his gray hair in disarray over his temples, the dew of animal terror in his eyes. But when Santiago leaned over to kiss him, he smiled: they'd finally found you, Skinny, he thought he wasn't going to see you.

"They let me in on the condition you don't talk, papa."

"The scare is over, thank God," Don Fermín whispered; his hand had slipped out from under the sheets, had grasped Santiago's arm. "Is everything all right, Skinny? The boardinghouse, your job?"

"All fine, papa," he said. "But please don't talk."

"I feel a knot here, son," Ambrosio says. "A man like him hadn't ought to die."

He stayed in the room for a long time, sitting on the edge of the bed, watching the thick, hairy hand that rested on his knee. Don Fermín had closed his eyes, he was breathing deeply. He didn't have a pillow, his head was resting on its side on the mattress and he could see his fluted neck and the gray specks of his beard. A short time later a nurse in white shoes came in and made a sign for him to leave. Señora Zoila, Uncle Clodomiro and Sparky were sitting in the anteroom; Teté and Popeye were standing and whispering by the door.

"Before it was politics, now it's the lab and the office," Uncle Clodomiro said. "He was working too hard, it was inevitable."

"He wants to be on top of everything, he doesn't pay any attention to me," Sparky said. "I'm tired of asking him to let me take charge of things, but there's no way. Now he'll be forced to take a rest."

"His nerves are shot." Señora Zoila looked at Santiago with rancor. "It isn't just the office, it's this young squirt too. He's dying to get news about you and keeps begging you more and more to come back home."

"Don't shout like a madwoman, mama," Teté said. "He can hear you."

476

"You won't let him live in peace with the fits of anger you give him," Señora Zoila sobbed. "You've made your father's life bitter, you young squirt."

The nurse came out of the room and, as she passed, whispered keep your voices down. Señora Zoila wiped her eyes with her handkerchief and Uncle Clodomiro leaned over her, regretful and solicitous. They were silent, looking at each other. Then Teté and Popeye began whispering again. How everyone had changed, Zavalita, how old Uncle Clodomiro had become. He smiled at him and his uncle returned a sad smile. He had become shrunken, wrinkled, his hair was almost all gone, only white tufts scattered about on his skull. Sparky was already a man; in his movements, his way of sitting down, in his voice, there was an adult assurance, an ease that seemed both physical and spiritual at the same time, and his look was calmly resolute. There he was, Zavalita: strong, tanned, gray suit, black shoes and socks, the clean white cuffs of his shirt, the dark green tie with a discreet clasp, the rectangle of the white handkerchief showing in the breast pocket of his jacket. And there was Teté, talking to Popeye in a low voice. They were holding hands, looking into each other's eyes. Her pink dress, he thinks, the broad loop that went around her neck and down to her waist. Her breasts were visible, the curve of her hips was becoming noticeable, her legs were long and lithe, her ankles thin, her hands white. You weren't like them anymore, Zavalita, you were a peasant now. He thinks: now I know why you got so furious as soon as you saw me, mama. He felt neither victorious nor happy, only impatient to leave. The nurse came over stealthily to tell them that visiting hours were over. Señora Zoila would sleep at the hospital, Sparky took Teté home. Popeye offered Uncle Clodomiro a ride, but he would take a group taxi, it dropped him off right in front of his house, it was too much trouble, thank you.

"Your uncle is always like that," Popeye said; they walked along slowly heading downtown in the new night. "He never wants to be driven home or picked up."

"He doesn't like to bother anyone or ask for any favors," Santiago said. "He's a very simple person."

"Yes, a very good person," Popeye said. "He's lived everywhere in Peru, hasn't he?"

477

There was Popeye, Zavalita: freckle-faced, red, his blond hair standing up straight, the same friendly, healthy look of before. But heavier, taller, more sure of his body and the world. His checkered shirt, he thinks, his flannel jacket with leather-trimmed lapels and elbows, his corduroy pants, his loafers.

"We had an awful scare with your old man." He was driving with one hand, turning the radio with the other. "It was lucky it didn't happen on the street."

"You're already talking like a member of the family," Santiago interrupted him, smiling. "I didn't know that you were going with Teté, Freckle Face."

"Hadn't she said anything to you?" Popeye exclaimed. "It's been going on for at least two months, Skinny. You're completely out of touch with things."

"I haven't been going to the house for a long time," Santiago said. "But I'm very happy for the both of you."

"Your sister's been giving me a hard time." Popeye laughed. "Ever since school, remember? But persistence pays off, as you can see."

They stopped at the Tambo, on the Avenida Arequipa, ordered two coffees, talked without getting out of the car. They resurrected memories held in common, reviewed their lives. He'd just got his architect's degree, he thinks, he'd started working for a big company, while he and some colleagues planned to set up their own firm. What about you, Skinny, how have things been going for you, what are your plans?

"I'm in good enough shape," Santiago said. "I haven't got any plans. Just to stay on at *La Crónica.*"

"When are you going to get your degree as a shyster?" Popeye asked with a cautious laugh. "You're made to order for that."

"I don't think I ever will," Santiago said. "I don't like the law."

"Just between you and me, that's made your father pretty depressed," Popeye said. "He goes around telling Teté and me, work on him so he finishes his degree. Yes, he tells me everything. I get on quite well with your old man, Skinny. We've gotten to be chums. He's an awfully nice person."

"I don't want to be a doctor of anything," Santiago joked. "Everybody in this country is doctor of something."

478

"And you've always wanted to be different from everybody." Popeye laughed. "Just like when you were a kid, Skinny. You haven't changed a bit."

They left the Tambo, but they sat chatting for a while on the Avenida Tacna across from the milky *La Crónica* building before Santiago got out. They had to get together more often, Skinny, especially now that we're practically brothers-in-law. Popeye had wanted to look him up a number of times, but you were invisible, brother. He'd pass the word to some of the people in the neighborhood who are always asking about you, Skinny, and they could have lunch together one of these days. Hadn't you seen anybody in our class, Skinny? He thinks: the class. The cubs who were lions and tigers now, Zavalita. Engineers, lawyers, managers. Some were probably married already, he thinks, they probably had mistresses already.

"I don't see many people because I lead the life of an owl, Freckle Face, because of the newspaper. I go to bed at dawn and get up when it's time to go to work."

"A real bohemian life, Skinny," Popeye said. "It must be wild, right? Especially for an intellectual like you."

"What are you laughing at," Ambrosio says. "I think what he said about your papa is true."

"It's not that," Santiago says. "I'm laughing at my intellectual face."

The next day he found Don Fermín sitting up in bed reading the newspapers. He was animated, breathing easily, his color had returned. He'd been in the hospital a week and he'd been to see him every day, but always in the company of other people. Relatives he hadn't seen for years and who looked him over with a kind of mistrust. The black sheep, the one who'd left home, the one who'd embittered Zoilita, the one who had a grubby little job on a newspaper? Impossible to remember the names of those uncles and aunts, Zavalita, the faces of those cousins; you'd probably passed them many times on the street without recognizing them. It was November and it was starting to get a little warmer when Señora Zoila and Sparky took Don Fermín to New York for a checkup. They returned ten days later and the family went to spend the summer in Ancón. You hadn't seen them for almost three months, Zavalita, but you spoke to the old man every week on the telephone. Toward the end

479

of March they returned to Miraflores and Don Fermín had recovered and had a tanned and healthy-looking face. The first Sunday he had lunch at the house again, he saw that Popeye was kissing Señora Zoila and Don Fermín. Teté had permission to go dancing with him on Saturdays at the grillroom of the Hotel Bolívar. On your birthday Teté and Sparky and Popeye had come to wake you up at the boardinghouse, and at home the whole family was waiting with packages. Two suits, Zavalita, shoes, cuff links, in a little envelope a check for a thousand soles that you spent in a whorehouse with Carlitos. What else was worthwhile remembering, Zavalita, what else except surviving?

ﾌ

"Drifting at first," Ambrosio says. "Then I was a driver and, you'll have to laugh, son, even half-owner of a funeral parlor."

The first weeks in Pucallpa had been bad for her. Not so much because of Ambrosio's disconsolate sadness as because of the nightmares. The white body, young and beautiful, as during the San Miguel days, would come out of the remote shadows, glimmering, and she, on her knees in her narrow little room in Jesús María, would begin to shake. It would float, grow, stop in the air surrounded by a golden halo and she could see the large purple wound in the mistress's neck and her accusing eyes: you killed me. She would wake up in terror, cling to Ambrosio's sleeping body, stay awake until dawn. At other times she was being chased by policemen in green uniforms and could hear their whistles, the noise of their big shoes: you killed her. They didn't catch her, all night long they stretched their hands out toward her as she drew back and sweated.

"Don't talk to me about the mistress anymore," Ambrosio had told her with the face of a whipped dog the day they arrived. "I forbid it."

Besides, right from the start she'd felt mistrust for that hot and deceptive town. They had lived first in a place overrun with spiders and cockroaches—the Hotel Pucallpa—near the half-finished square, and from the windows you could see the docks with their canoes, launches and barges rocking in the dirty water of the river. How ugly everything was, how poor everything was. Ambrosio had looked at Pucallpa with indifference, as if they were only there temporarily, and only one day when she complained about the suffocating heat had he made a vague

480

comment: the heat was like it was in Chincha, Amalia. They'd been at the hotel for a week. Then they'd rented a cabin with a straw roof near the hospital. There were a lot of funeral parlors in the area, even one that specialized in little white boxes for children and was called the Limbo Coffin Co.

"Poor sick people in the hospital," Amalia had said. "Seeing so many funeral parlors around, they must be thinking that they're going to die all the time."

"That's what they have most of there," Ambrosio says. "Churches and funeral parlors. You can get dizzy from all the religions they've got in Pucallpa, son."

The morgue was across from the hospital too, a few steps from the cabin. Amalia had felt a shudder the first day when she saw the gloomy concrete building with its crest of vultures on the roof. The cabin was large and in the back there was a lot covered with weeds. They could plant something there, the owner, Alandro Pozo, had told them the day they moved in, have a little garden. The floor of the four rooms was dirt and the walls were discolored. Wasn't there even a mattress? where were they going to sleep? Especially Amalita Hortensia, the bugs would bite her. Ambrosio had tapped his back pocket: they'd buy what they needed. That same afternoon they'd gone downtown and bought a cot, a mattress, a small crib, pots, plates, a portable stove, some small curtains, and Amalia, when she saw that Ambrosio was still picking things out, had become alarmed: that's enough, you'll use up all your money. But he, without answering, had kept on ordering things from the delighted salesman at Wong Supplies: this too, and that, the oilcloth.

"Where did you get so much money from?" Amalia had asked him that night.

"I'd been saving it up all those years," Ambrosio says. "To set myself up and go into business, son."

"Then you should be happy," Amalia had said. "But you're not. Leaving Lima bothers you."

"I won't have any more boss, I'll be my own boss now," Ambrosio had said. "Of course I'm happy, silly."

A lie, he only started being happy later on. During those first few weeks in Pucallpa he'd been very serious, almost never speaking, his face

481

extremely troubled. But in spite of that, he'd been very good to her and Amalita Hortensia from the very first. The day after they got there, he'd left the hotel and come back with a package. What was it? Clothes for the two Amalias. Her dress was much too big, but Ambrosio hadn't even smiled when he saw her disappear inside the flowered frock that poured off her shoulders and kissed her ankles. He'd gone to the Morales Transportation Co. as soon as he arrived in Pucallpa, but Don Hilario was in Tingo María and wouldn't be back until ten days later. What would they do in the meantime, Ambrosio? They'd look for a house and, until the day came when he would have to start sweating again, they'd have a little fun, Amalia. They hadn't had much fun, she because of her nightmares and he because he probably missed Lima, even though they'd tried, spending a wad of money. They'd gone to see the Shipibo Indians, they'd eaten tons of fried rice, deep-fried shrimp and fried won tons in the Chinese restaurants along the Calle Comercio, they'd taken a boat ride on the Ucayali, a trip to Yarinacocha, and on several nights had gone to the Cine Pucallpa. The movies were doddering with old age and sometimes Amalita Hortensia would unleash her wailing in the darkness and people would shout take her out. Give her to me, Ambrosio would say, and he would quiet her by giving her his finger to suck.

Little by little, Amalia had been getting used to things, little by little, Ambrosio's face was getting happier. They'd worked hard on the cabin. Ambrosio had bought paint and had whitewashed the front and the walls, and she'd scraped the filth off the floor. In the mornings they'd gone to the small market together to buy food and they learned to differentiate among the churches they passed: Baptist, Seventh-Day Adventist, Catholic, Evangelical, Pentecostal. They'd begun to talk to each other again: you were so strange, sometimes I thought a different Ambrosio had got into your skin, that the real one had stayed behind in Lima. Why, Amalia? Because of his sadness, his tense face and his eyes which would suddenly turn off and wander away like those of an animal. You were crazy, Amalia, the one who'd stayed behind in Lima was the false Ambrosio. He felt good here, happy with this sun, Amalia, the cloudy sky back there made him depressed. She hoped it was true, Ambrosio. At night, as they had seen the people who lived there do, they too went out to sit by the street and enjoy the coolness that came up from the river and to chat, lulled by the frogs and the crickets crouching in the grass. One morning Ambrosio had come in with an umbrella: there, so Amalia wouldn't complain about the sun anymore. So all she needed was to go out of the house with hair curlers to look like a jungle woman, Amalia. The nightmares had become farther apart, disappearing, and also the fear she felt every time she saw a policeman. The remedy had been to keep busy all the time, cooking, washing Ambrosio's clothes, taking care of Amalita Hortensia, while he tried to convert the vacant lot into a garden. Barefoot, starting early in the morning, Ambrosio had spent hours weeding, but the growth came back quickly and stronger than before. Across from their cabin was one painted blue and white with an orchard full of fruit trees. One morning Amalia had gone to ask some advice from the neighbor woman and Señora Lupe, the wife of a man who had a farm upriver and only put in an appearance on rare occasions, had received her with affection. Of course she would help her in anything she could. She'd been the first and best friend they had in Pucallpa, son. Doña Lupe had taught Ambrosio to clear and plant at the same time, sweet potatoes here, manioc here, potatoes here. She had given them some seeds and had taught Amalia how to cook the mixture of bananas fried with rice, manioc and fish that everybody in Pucallpa ate.

2

"WHAT DO YOU MEAN, you got married by accident, son?" Ambrosio laughs. "Do you mean you were forced into it?"

It had started on one of those white, stupid nights which, through a kind of miracle, had been transformed into a party of sorts. Norwin had called *La Crónica* saying that he was waiting for them in El Patio and, after work, Santiago and Carlitos had gone to meet him. Norwin wanted to go to a whorehouse, Carlitos to El Pingüino, they flipped for it and Carlitos won. Were they expecting a wake? The nightclub was dreary and there were few customers. Pedrito Aguirre sat down with them and bought them beers. When the second show was over, the last customers left and then, suddenly, unexpectedly, the girls in the show and the boys in the band and the bartenders all ended up together in a happy round of tables. They'd started off with jokes, toasts, anecdotes and teasing, and suddenly life seemed happy, lively, spontaneous and pleasant. They drank, sang, began to dance, and next to Santiago, China and Carlitos, silent and close together, were looking into each other's eyes as if they'd just discovered love. At three in the morning they were still there, drunk and loving one another, generous and talkative, and Santiago felt he was in love with Ada Rosa. There she was, Zavalita: short, fat-assed, dark. Her pigeon-toed feet, he thinks, her gold tooth, her bad breath, her cursing.

"A real accident," Santiago says. "An auto accident."

484

Norwin was the first to disappear, with a chorus girl in her forties who had a wild hairdo. China and Carlitos convinced Ada Rosa to go with them. They took a taxi to China's apartment in Santa Beatriz. Sitting beside the driver, Santiago had a distracted hand on Ada Rosa's knee. She was riding in back, dozing beside China and Carlitos, who were kissing furiously. At the apartment they drank all the beer in the refrigerator and listened to records and danced. When the light of day appeared in the window, China and Carlitos shut themselves up in the bedroom and Santiago and Ada Rosa were left alone in the living room. At El Pingüino they had kissed and here they caressed and she had sat on his knees, but now when he tried to take her clothes off, Ada Rosa reared up and began to shout and insult him. It was all right, Ada Rosa, no fighting, let's go to sleep. He put the cushions from the easy chair on the floor, dropped down and fell asleep. When he woke up, through bluish clouds he saw Ada Rosa curled up like a fetus on the sofa, sleeping with her clothes on. He stumbled to the bathroom, bothered by a bilious heaviness and the resentment of his bones, and he put his head under the cold water. He left the house: the sun wounded his eyes and brought tears to them. He had a cup of black coffee at a cheap café on Petit Thouars and then, with vague, fluctuating nausea, he took a group taxi to Miraflores and another to Barranco. It was noon on the Town Hall clock. Señora Lucía had left a note on his bed: call *La Crónica,* very urgent. Arispe was crazy if he thought you were going to call him, Zavalita. But just as he was about to get into bed, he thought that his curiosity would keep him awake and he went down to phone in his pajamas.

"Are you unhappy with your marriage?" Ambrosio asks.

"My, my," Arispe said. "A nice voice from beyond the grave, my good sir."

"I went to a party and I'm all hung over," Santiago said. "I haven't slept a wink."

"You can sleep on the trip," Arispe said. "Get on over here right away in a taxi. You're going to Trujillo with Periquito and Darío, Zavalita."

"Trujillo?" A trip, he thinks, a trip at last, even if it was only to Trujillo. "Can't I leave a little . . ."

"Actually, you've already left," Arispe said. "A sure piece of information, a million-and-a-half winner in The Kitty, Zavalita."

485

"All right, I'll grab a shower and be right over," Santiago said.

"You can phone the story in to me tonight," Arispe said. "Forget about the shower and get right over here, water is for pigs like Becerrita."

"No, I'm happy with it," Santiago says. "The only thing is that I really wasn't the one who made the decision. It was imposed on me, just like the job, like everything that's ever happened to me. Nothing was ever my doing, it was more like I was their doing."

He got dressed in a hurry, wet his head again, ran down the stairs. The taxi driver had to wake him up when they got to *La Crónica*. It was a sunny morning, there was a bit of heat that delightfully entered the pores and lulled muscles and will. Arispe had left the instructions and money for gasoline, meals and hotel. In spite of your not feeling well and your sleepiness, you felt happy with the idea of the trip, Zavalita. Periquito sat next to Darío and Santiago stretched out on the back seat and fell asleep almost immediately. He woke up as they were getting into Pasamayo. On the right there were dunes and steep yellow hills, on the left the blue, resplendent sea and the precipice that kept getting higher, in front the highway painfully climbing the bald flank of the mountains. He sat up and lighted a cigarette; Periquito was looking into the abyss with alarm.

"The Pasamayo curves have sobered you sissies up." Darío laughed.

"Slow down," Periquito said. "And since you haven't got eyes in the back of your head, it would be better if you didn't turn around to chat."

Darío was driving fast, but he was sure of himself. There were hardly any cars in Pasamayo, in Chancay they stopped for lunch at a truck stop by the side of the road. They started out again and Santiago, trying to sleep in spite of the jiggling, listened to them talking.

"This Trujillo business is most likely a lie," Periquito said. "There are shitheads who spend all their time giving false tips to newspapers."

"A million and a half soles for one single person," Darío said. "I didn't use to believe in The Kitty, but I'm going to start playing it."

"Change a million and a half into females and then talk to me about it," Periquito said.

Moribund villages, aggressive dogs that came out to meet the van with their teeth in the air, trucks parked beside the road, sporadic cane fields. They were passing milestone 48 when Santiago sat up and had another

486

smoke. It was a straight stretch, with sand flats on both sides. The truck hadn't taken them by surprise; they saw it glimmering in the distance at the top of a rise and they watched it coming closer, slow, heavy, corpulent, with its load of drums tied with ropes in the back. A dinosaur, Periquito said, at that instant Darío slammed on the brakes and turned the wheel, because at the very point where they were going to pass the truck, a hole ate away half the road. The wheels of the van fell into the sand, something crunched under the vehicle, straighten out! Periquito shouted and Darío tried and there we were, fucked up, he thinks. The wheels sank in, instead of climbing up the edge they skidded, and the van kept on going forward, tilting way over like a monster until, overcome by its own weight, it rolled like a ball. An accident in slow motion, Zavalita. He heard or gave a cry, a twisted, slanting world, a force that threw him violently forward, a darkness with stars. For an indefinite time everything was quiet, dark, painful and hot. He first tasted something bitter, and even though he'd opened his eyes, it took him a while to realize that he'd been thrown out of the vehicle and was stretched out on the ground and that the harsh taste was the sand that was getting into his mouth. He tried to stand up, dizziness blinded him and he fell back down again. Then he felt himself grabbed by the feet and hands, lifted, and there they were, in the background of a long, hazy dream, those strange and remote faces, that feeling of infinite and lucid peace. Would it be like that, Zavalita? Would it be that silence without any questions, that serenity without any doubts or remorse? Everything was weak, vague and alien, and he felt himself being placed on something soft that was moving. He was in a car, lying on the back seat, and he recognized the voices of Periquito and Darío and he saw a man dressed in brown.

"How do you feel, Zavalita?" Periquito's voice asked.

"Drunk," Santiago said. "My head aches."

"You were lucky," Periquito said. "The sand held the van back. Another turn and it would have squashed you."

"It's one of the few important things that ever happened to me, Ambrosio," Santiago says. "Besides, that was how I met the girl who's now my wife."

He was cold, nothing hurt, but he was still groggy. He heard talk and murmuring, the sound of the motor, other motors, and when he opened

487

his eyes they were putting him on a rolling stretcher. He saw the street and the sky that was starting to get dark, he read La Maison de Santé on the façade of the building they were going into. They took him up to a room on the second floor, Periquito and Darío helped undress him. When he was covered up to his chin by sheets and blankets, he thought I'm going to sleep for a thousand hours. Half asleep, he answered the questions of a man with glasses and a white apron.

"Tell Arispe not to print anything, Periquito." He barely recognized his voice. "My father mustn't know about this."

"A romantic meeting," Ambrosio says. "Did she win your love by healing you?"

"Sneaking me smokes is more like it," Santiago says.

Ø

"This is your night, Quetita," Malvina said. "You look positively royal."

"You're going to be picked up by a chauffeur." Robertito blinked. "Like a queen, Quetita."

"It's true, you've won the lottery," Malvina said.

"Me too and all of us," Ivonne said, taking leave of her with a malicious smile. "You know, with golden gloves, Quetita."

Earlier, when Quetita was getting ready, Ivonne had come to help her set her hair and oversee her dressing personally: she had even loaned her a necklace that matched her bracelet. Have I won the lottery? Queta was thinking, surprised at not being excited or happy or even curious. She went out and at the door of the house she gave a little start: the same daring and startled eyes from yesterday. But the black man looked at her directly for only a few seconds; he lowered his head, murmured good evening, hastened to open the door of the car, which was black, large and severe like a hearse. She got in without answering his good evening, and she saw another fellow there in front next to the chauffeur. Also tall, also strong, also dressed in blue.

"If you're cold and want me to close the window . . ." the Negro murmured, sitting behind the wheel now, and she saw the whites of his large eyes for an instant.

The car started up in the direction of the Plaza Dos de Mayo, turned down Alfonso Ugarte toward Bolognesi, went along the Avenida Brasil, and when they went under the lampposts, Queta noticed the greedy little animals still in the rear-view mirror, looking for her. The other man had started to smoke and didn't turn to look at her or even take a peek in the mirror during the whole drive. Near the Malecón now, they entered Magdalena Nueva along a side street, following the streetcar line toward San Miguel, and every time she looked at the mirror, Queta saw them: burning, fleeing.

"Have I got monkeys on my face?" she said, thinking this idiot is going to run into something. "For you to keep looking at me?"

The heads in front turned and went back into place, the black man's voice came out unbearably confused, him? sorry, was she talking to him? and Queta thought how afraid you are of Cayo Shithead. The car went this way and that down the small, dark, silent streets of San Miguel and finally came to a stop. She saw a garden, a small two-story house, a window with curtains that let the light filter through. The black man got out to open the door. He was there, his ash-colored hand on the door handle, head down and cowardly, trying to open his mouth. Is it here? Queta murmured. The little houses were identical, one after the other in the stingy light, behind the little trees lined up on the gloomy sidewalks. Two policemen were looking at the car from the corner and the fellow inside made a signal as if to tell them it's us. It wasn't a large house, it couldn't be his house, Queta thought: it must be the one he uses for his filthy stuff.

"I didn't mean to bother you," the black man babbled, with an oblique and humble voice. "I wasn't looking at you. But if you think I was, I'm terribly sorry."

"Don't be afraid, I won't mention it to Cayo Shithead." Queta laughed. "I just don't like fresh people."

She went through the garden that smelled of damp flowers, and when she rang the bell she heard voices, music from the other side of the door. The lights inside made her blink. She recognized the thin, small figure of the man, his devastated face, the boredom of his mouth and his lifeless eyes: come in, welcome. Thanks for sending the car for me, she said, and was silent: there was a woman there, looking at her with a curious smile, in front of a bar covered with bottles. Queta was motionless, her hands hanging alongside her body, disconcerted suddenly.

"This is the famous Queta." Cayo Shithead had closed the door, had sat down, and now he and the woman were observing her. "Come in, famous Queta. This is Hortensia, the mistress of the house."

"I thought they were all old, ugly and peasants," the woman shrilled liquidly and Queta managed to think in confusion, boy, is she drunk. "Or did you lie to me, Cayo?"

She gave another laugh, exaggerated and graceless, and the man, with a weak half-smile, pointed to the chair: sit down, she was going to get tired standing up. She came forward as if over ice or wax, afraid to slip, to fall, and sink into an even worse confusion, and she sat down on the edge of the chair, rigid. Again she heard the music that she had forgotten about or which had stopped; it was a tango by Gardel and the phonograph was there, mounted in a mahogany cabinet. She saw the woman get up weaving and saw her clumsy uncertain fingers manipulating a bottle and glasses at one end of the bar. She studied her tight iridescent silk dress, the whiteness of her shoulders and arms, her coal-black hair, the hand that sparkled, her profile, and, still perplexed, thought how much she looked like her, how much they looked alike. The woman came toward her with two glasses in her hands, walking as if she didn't have any bones, and Queta looked away.

"Cayo told me she was quite beautiful and I thought it was a tale." She was looking at her from the feet up and hesitating, looking at her from the top down with the glassily smiling eyes of a pampered cat, and when she leaned over to give her the glass, she smelled her belligerent, incisive perfume. "But it's true, the famous Queta is quite beautiful."

"Cheers, famous Queta," Cayo Shithead commanded without emotion. "Let's see if a drink will lift your spirits."

Mechanically, she raised the glass to her mouth, closed her eyes and drank. A spiral of heat, a tickling in her eyes, and she thought straight whiskey. But she took another long sip and took a cigarette from the pack the man offered her. He lit it for her and Queta discovered the woman sitting next to her now, smiling with familiarity. Making an effort, she also smiled.

"You look just like . . ." she got the courage to say and a thread of falseness invaded her, a sticky feeling of the ridiculous. "Just like a certain singer."

490

"What singer?" The woman encouraged her, smiling, looking at Cayo Shithead out of the corner of her eye, looking back at her again. "Like?"

"Yes," Queta said; she took another sip and breathed deeply. "Like the Muse, the one who used to sing at the Embassy Club. I saw her several times and . . ."

She stopped speaking because the woman was laughing. Her eyes were shining, glassy and fascinated.

"That Muse is an awful singer," Cayo Shithead commanded, nodding. "Don't you think so?"

"I don't think so," Queta said. "She sings nice, especially boleros."

"You see? Ha! Ha!" the woman broke out, pointing to Queta, making a face at Cayo Shithead. "You see how I'm wasting my time with you? See how you're ruining my career?"

It can't be, Queta thought, and that feeling of the ridiculous came over her again. It burned her face, she felt the urge to run, break things. She finished her glass in one swallow and felt flames in her throat and a touch of warmth in her stomach. Then a pleasant visceral warmth that gave her back a little of her self-control.

"I knew it was you, I recognized you," she said, trying to smile. "Just that . . ."

"Just that you've finished your drink," the woman said in a friendly way. She got up like a wave, weaving slowly, and looked at her happily, euphorically, gratefully. "I adore you for what you said. You see, Cayo, you see?"

While the woman stumbled over to the bar, Queta turned toward Cayo Shithead. He was drinking seriously, looking into the dining room, he seemed absorbed in intimate and grave meditations, far away from there, and she thought it's absurd, she thought I hate you. When the woman handed her the glass of whiskey, she leaned over and spoke to her in a low voice: could she tell her where the . . .? Yes, certainly, come along, I'll show you where. He didn't look at them. Queta went upstairs behind the woman, who was clutching the railing and feeling the steps with mistrust before putting her foot down, and it occurred to her she's going to insult me, now that the two of them were alone she was going to throw her out. And she thought: she's going to offer you money to leave. The Muse opened a door, showed her the inside without smiling now and

Queta murmured a quick thanks. But it wasn't the bathroom, it was the bedroom, one out of a movie or a dream: mirrors, a thick carpet, mirrors, a screen, a black bedcover with an embroidered yellow animal that was spitting fire, more mirrors.

"There, in the back," was said behind her, without hostility, in the woman's insecure, alcoholic voice. "That door."

She went into the bathroom, locked the door, breathed with anxiety. What was that all about, what kind of a game was that, what were those people thinking about? She looked in the bathroom mirror; her face, all made up, still had the look of perplexity, upset, surprise. She turned the water on to fake it, sat on the edge of the tub. Was the Muse his . . . ? He'd had her come to . . . ? Did the Muse know that? It occurred to her that they were spying on her through the keyhole and she went to the door, knelt down and looked through the small opening: a circle of rugs, shadows. Cayo Shithead, she had to get out of there, she wanted to get out of there, Shithead Muse. She felt rage, confusion, humiliation, laughter. She stayed inside a short while longer, tiptoeing on the white tiles, wrapped in the bluish light of the phosphorescent tube, trying to put her boiling head in order, but she only got more confused. She flushed the toilet, fixed her hair in front of the mirror, took a breath and opened the door. The woman had lain across the bed, and Queta felt for an instant that she was distracted, looking at the reclining figure motionless with such white skin, in contrast to the jet black shiny bedcover. But the woman had raised her eyes in her direction. She was looking at her slowly, inspecting her with a slow, prolonged relaxation, not smiling, not annoyed. An interested and at the same time thoughtful look, under the drunken mirror of her eyes.

"Might I know what I'm doing here?" she asked with drive, taking a few resolute steps toward the bed.

"Come on, all we need is for you to get mad." The Muse lost her seriousness, her sparkling eyes were looking at her in amusement.

"Not mad, I just don't understand." Queta felt herself reflected, projected on all sides, thrown upward, sent back, attacked by all those mirrors. "Tell me why they had me come here."

"Stop your nonsense and talk to me in the familiar form," the woman whispered; she moved a little on the bed, contracting and expanding her body like an earthworm, and Queta saw that she had taken off her shoes, and for a second, through her stockings, she saw her painted toenails. "You know my name, Hortensia. Come on, sit down here, stop your nonsense."

She was speaking to her without hatred or friendship, with her voice a little evasive and calm because of the alcohol, and she kept looking fixedly at her. As if appraising me, Queta thought, nauseous, as if . . . She hesitated a moment and sat on the edge of the bed, all the pores of her body alert. Hortensia was leaning her head on a hand, her posture was abandoned and soft.

"You know only too well why," she said, without anger, without bitterness, with a lascivious trace of mockery in her eyes that she was trying to hide and Queta thought what? Her eyes were large, green, with lashes that didn't look artificial and which shaded her eyelids; she had thick, moist lips, her throat was smooth and long and the veins could be sensed, thin and blue. She didn't know what to think, what to say, what? Hortensia fell back, laughed as if in spite of herself, covered her face with her arm, stretched with a kind of avidity and suddenly reached out a hand and took Queta by the wrist: you know only too well why. Like a customer, she thought, frightened and not moving, as if, looking at the white fingers with blood-red nails on her dull skin and now Hortensia was looking at her intensely, without hiding it now, challenging now.

"I'd better go," she heard herself say, stammering, quiet and astonished. "You'd rather I left, wouldn't you?"

"I'm going to tell you something." She was still holding her, she had got a little closer to her, her voice had grown thicker, and Queta felt her breath. "I was terrified that you'd be old, ugly, that you'd be dirty."

"Do you want me to leave?" Queta babbled stupidly, breathing with effort, remembering the mirrors. "Was I brought here for . . . ?"

"But you're not," Hortensia whispered and brought her face even closer and Queta saw the exasperated joy in her eyes, the movement of her mouth as it seemed to smoke. "You're pretty and young. You're nice and clean."

She put out the other hand and took Queta's other arm. She was looking at her boldly, mockingly, twisting her body a little to sit up,

murmuring you're going to have to teach me, letting herself fall backward, and looking at her from below, her eyes open, exultant, she was
smiling and raving use the intimate form with me right now, if they were
going to bed together she couldn't address her formally, could she?
without letting go of her, obliging her with soft pressure to lean over, to
let herself go against her. Teach you? Queta thought, me teach you?
giving in, feeling her confusion disappearing, laughing.

"Good," commanded a voice behind her that was beginning to come
out of its boredom. "You finally became friends."

9

He woke up ravenous; his head no longer ached, but he felt jabs in his
back and cramps. The room was small, cold and bare, with windows
opening on a passageway with columns along which nuns and nurses
passed. They brought him his breakfast and he ate voraciously.

"Please don't eat the dish," the nurse said. "I'll bring you another roll,
if you want."

"And more coffee too, if you can," Santiago said. "I haven't eaten a
bite since yesterday noon."

The nurse brought him another full breakfast and stayed in the room,
watching him eat. There she was, Zavalita, so dark, so neat, so young
in her white unwrinkled uniform, her white stockings, her short boy's
bob and her starched cap, standing by the bed with her trim legs and her
filiform model's body, smiling with her hungry teeth.

"So you're a newspaperman?" Her eyes were lively and impertinent
and she had a thin mocking voice. "How did you happen to turn over?"

"Ana," Santiago says. "Yes, very young. Five years younger than I."

"The bumps you got, even though nothing is broken, sometimes leave
a person a little foolish." The nurse laughed. "That's why they've kept
you under observation."

"Don't lower my morale like that," Santiago said. "Give me some
encouragement instead."

"Why does the idea of being a father bother you?" Ambrosio asks. "If
everybody in Peru had that idea, there wouldn't be any people left in the
country, son."

"So you work for *La Crónica*?" she repeated; she had one hand on the

494

door as if she were going to leave, but she'd been standing there for five minutes. "Journalism must be very interesting, isn't it?"

"Although I have to confess that when I found out I was going to be a father I got terrified too," Ambrosio says. "It takes you a while to get used to it, son."

"It is, but it's got its bad points, a person can crack his skull from one moment to the next," Santiago said. "You can do me a great favor. Could you send someone out to buy some cigarettes?"

"Patients aren't allowed to smoke," she said. "You'll have to bear with it while you're here. It's better that way, you'll get rid of all the poison."

"I'm dying for a smoke," Santiago said. "Don't be mean. Get me some. Even if it's just one."

"What does your wife think?" Ambrosio says. "Because she must certainly want to have children. Women like being mothers."

"What will you do for me in return?" she asked. "Will you print my picture in your newspaper?"

"I suppose so," Santiago says. "But Ana's a good person and does what I like."

"If the doctor finds out, he'll kill me," the nurse said with the look of an accomplice. "Smoke it on the sly and put the butt in the bedpan."

"Ugh, it's a Country," Santiago said, coughing. "Do you smoke this crap?"

"My, how choosy," she said, laughing. "I don't smoke. I went out and stole it for you so you could keep up your habit."

"The next time steal a Nacional Presidente and I give you my promise I'll print your picture on the society page," Santiago said.

"I stole it off Dr. Franco," she said, making a face. "God protect you from falling into his hands. He's the nastiest one here, and stupid besides. All he ever prescribes are suppositories."

"What did this poor Dr. Franco ever do to you?" Santiago asked. "Does he flirt with you?"

"What a thing to think, the old man hasn't got any wind left." Two dimples appeared on her cheeks and her laugh was quick and sharp, uncomplicated. "He must be over a hundred."

All morning they had him back and forth between one room and another, taking x-rays and giving tests; the hazy doctor from the night before put him through a questioning that was almost a police grilling. There was nothing broken, apparently, but he didn't like those shooting pains, young man, they'd see what the x-rays said. At noon Arispe came by and joked with him: he'd covered his ears and made a sign against the evil eye, Zavalita, he could imagine the curses he'd gotten. The editor sends his greetings, that you should stay in the hospital all the time you need, the newspaper would also pay for any extras just as long as you didn't order any banquets from the Hotel Bolívar. You really don't want your family notified, Zavalita? No, the old man would get a scare and it wasn't worth it, there was nothing wrong with him. In the afternoon Periquito and Darío came; they only had a few bruises and they were happy. They'd got two days off and that night they were going to a party together. A while later Solórzano, Milton and Norwin arrived, and when they'd all left, there appeared as if just rescued from a shipwreck, cadaverous and lovey-dovey, China and Carlitos.

"Look at your faces," Santiago said. "You must have kept that wild time of the other night going right up till now."

"We did," China said, yawning ostentatiously; she flopped onto the foot of the bed and took off her shoes. "I don't know what day it is or even what time it is."

"I haven't been to *La Crónica* for two days," Carlitos said, yellow, his nose red, his eyes jellylike and happy. "I called Arispe and invented an attack of ulcers and he told me about the accident. I didn't come earlier so I wouldn't run into anyone from the paper."

"Regards from Ada Rosa." China gave a loud laugh. "Hasn't she been to see you?"

"Don't talk to me about Ada Rosa," Santiago said. "The other night she turned into a panther."

But China interrupted him with her torrential, fluvial laugh: they already knew, she'd told them what happened herself. Ada Rosa was like that, she'd get someone all worked up and back down at the last minute, a tease, crazy. China laughed with contortions, clapping her hands like a seal. Her lips were painted in the shape of a heart, a very high baroque hairdo that gave her face a haughty aggressiveness, and everything about her seemed more excessive than ever that night: her gestures, her curves,

496